William McDonnell

Exeter Hall

A Theological Romance

William McDonnell

Exeter Hall
A Theological Romance

ISBN/EAN: 9783337008246

Printed in Europe, USA, Canada, Australia, Japan

Cover: Foto ©Andreas Hilbeck / pixelio.de

More available books at **www.hansebooks.com**

A Theological Romance.

"What is Truth?"

SEVENTH THOUSAND.

BOSTON:

WILLIAM WHITE AND COMPANY,

158 WASHINGTON STREET.

NEW YORK: THE AMERICAN NEWS COMPANY,

115, 117, 119 NASSAU STREET.

1873.

ADVERTISEMENT

TO SECOND EDITION.

On the publication of the first edition of EXETER HALL, the author had some grave misgivings as to the success of the work. Not that he was influenced, — considerable as his outlay had been, — by any pecuniary sentiment; for the book was written without the slightest reference to worldly gain or fame: but what he feared was, that, through the opposition of the churches and certain influential portions of the press, he should be prevented from obtaining a general and candid hearing. This opposition, and much of an acrimonious private character, he has encountered, and overcome through the support afforded him by a few independent journals, and the countenance of many fearless friends and readers. Hence the appearance of the present edition, and the existence of the lively hope, that another and yet another shall give further evidence of the liberal tendencies of the age, and the growing desire of the human family to free themselves from the degrading superstitions which have so long embarrassed the world, retarded the progress of true civilization, and set man at enmity with his neighbor.

THE AUTHOR.

LINDSAY, Ontario, Canada, November, 1870.

EXETER HALL.

CHAPTER I.

EXETER HALL.

EXETER HALL is a very large building situated near the Strand, one of the principal streets of London. It has accommodation for over four thousand persons, and it is the great Protestant forum and centre of attraction for all those who anxiously desire the spread of the Gospel, the dissemination of Christianity, and the evangelization of the world. It is also the head-quarters and grand rallying-point of those armies of prelates, preachers, professors, missionaries, and other devoted men who, from time to time, assert a renunciation of the world, its pomps and vanities; many of whom, taking their lives in their hand, as eager to suffer in the glorious cause, sever social and domestic ties, and leave home and country, to spread in distant lands and over the dark places of the earth "the unsearchable riches" among the millions yet destitute, of the degraded and perishing sons and daughters of Adam.

Exeter Hall has a fame. Since its erection, about 1831, no other place in the world has attracted such crowds of social renovators, moral philosophers, philanthropists, and Christians. Of late years, almost every great measure for the amelioration of the condition of the human family has here had its inception, its progress, and its triumph. Surrounded as it is by theatres, Shakespearean temples devoted to the drama, or, as many of the religious world assert, to profane, vicious, and ungodly purposes, Exeter Hall alone has the proud distinction of being the great theatre for the concentration of Protestant Christianity. From this great stand-point, the wisdom, intelligence, and power of whole nations have been brought to bear against usages, systems, and laws antagonistic to the pure faith; and a remedy suggested and provided for the moral and religious destitution of the world.

But not altogether are measures purely religious enacted in this great building. Secular schemes of practical benevolence, scarcely second in importance to any other, are here developed; social and national reforms are here patronized; music, science, philosophy, and literature are encouraged; and personal, national, and political wrongs feelingly depicted; and often some British Demosthenes will here make a stirring appeal before a thousand freemen in behalf of an oppressed people or down-trodden country; and then there is a shout for human rights, and in that shout, as is always the case, the voice of Exeter Hall is heard over all the earth.

But it is in the genial month of May that this great theatre displays its power, and exercises its wonted energies. Like the season, it seems invigorated; there is an infusion of new life for a fresh effort, and in that effort lie the germs which, having been generously moistened by national dew-drops of a peculiar kind, are sure to mature into a bountiful harvest. In May there is, as it were, a flowing of the nations of the world toward its great capital; and at that particular period the rush through the Strand to the immense Hall is wonderful, and its walls resound to the tramp of people of every clime and tongue. Delegates and representatives from almost every nation under heaven then assemble beneath its roof. The language of every capital in Europe is here spoken, and the utterances of far distant tribes here recognized. The once wild natives of Asia, Africa, America and the South Sea Islands here meet in friendly council, and are touched and softened by words of welcome in their native tongue. The children of the world meet and mingle, and lay down their offerings in a common cause, and —glorious result!—mythical ideas of origin and superiority are then forgotten, and *nationality*, the great idol of discord is, happily, for the time, hurled from its desecrated pedestal, and lies neglected or trampled in the dust.

The regular anniversary meetings of Exeter Hall are looked forward to with great interest by the religious world. Protestants of all denominations hail the approach of these periods with the most agreeable anticipation. A spirit of emulation is engendered; and each particular church or society makes a strong endeavor to win pious fame on the great platform where the representatives of so many creeds annually fraternize, and who on the occasion tacitly cease doctrinal bickerings, in order to exhibit to the skeptic and scoffer an exemplary assiduity in the common cause. For months before this stated period the most energetic efforts are made to accumulate a sum sufficient to correspond with the presumed wealth and influence of each respective denomination. In this connection what is called a "laudable rivalry" is encouraged, and graduated honors are in due time awarded on the credit side of the published accounts. There are some, alas! who in religious as well as in secular affairs, cling to the idea that the most money ought to have the most merit, and persons most liberal in endowments are generally awarded the highest place.

To obtain as large an amount as possible, the most thorough and ingenious methods, have been devised. Sunday-school children are lectured to importune for missionary pence, and to reserve their own petty accumulations of the most humble produce of the mint for the "missionary box;" and seldom indeed will either painted toy or tempting candy induce the juvenile collector to withdraw the little donation from its place of deposit. The money is looked upon as belonging to the treasury of the Lord; and if the infant Protestant mind should happen to tolerate a little superstition in this respect, no objection has yet been offered. A public recognition of such services by children is highly satisfactory to religious parents, and is naturally found to be a powerful stimulus to entice and actuate younger disciples.

Then, again, there are "Young Men's Associations," and therein persons are appointed to perambulate certain places and localities for help for the heathen—haunts and purlieus where it would not be always safe and never proper for respectable religious females to be seen.

Thus the dissipated and abandoned are often besought, and, strange to say, are often donors to this great fund. It may be that at stated periods many recklessly rushing to sin and shame feel a degree of satisfaction in being solicited, as if the solicitation and the gift were still proofs, though ever so weak, that the poor dissipated wanderer was not as yet disowned by society, or considered as hopelessly sunk among the outcast and degraded.

Matrons have also an allotted task. Mature members of wealthy mercantile companies, ancient annuitants, gray-headed state pensioners, and musty officials are sought and softened by importunate appeals which will take no denial; and, the flinty man, wrapped up in freezing dignity, is generally unfolded, even to prove to himself that, mummy-like as he may appear to others, "a heart still throbs within his leathern breast," and that its pulsations are yet human.

Stewards, deacons, lay-preachers, and ministers have a peculiar field of labor, and are often more successful with wealthy or well-to-do-widows, and comfortable spinsters of an uncertain age, than other persons. The pleading, however, of ministers with all classes has a drawing effect; but as their duties are too multifarious, their visits for such purposes are necessarily circumscribed. The potency of a minister's influence is more particularly in a general and pathetic appeal to a congregation,

or in private whispers at the bedside of the man who has walked the earth for the last time, and who, previous to settling his last account, is earnestly reminded of his final and most important duty of "honoring the Lord with his substance"—it would not be needed in the grave.

But by far the most invincible and successful collectors are the young and beautiful female members of the church. Such persons are classified as the "young lady collectors," and they prove themselves to be by all odds the most daring and triumphant. In this respect it has been asserted that one young lady is equal to thirteen and a half gentlemen; and pecuniary results have justly entitled the adolescent of the softer sex to this proportionate superiority. In collecting tours, the young ladies generally go in pairs, the more attractive and accomplished the better. As the duty is readily undertaken, every suitable place is visited with the most unflinching determination. Shopkeepers, office-clerks, young business-men, and men of fashion—the grave and the gay, the great and the humble, and all classes within reach that may with propriety be called on, are made to yield to solicitations which in nine cases out of ten are irresistible; and if figures are facts, the returns ever prove that young lady collectors are far in advance of all others in this particular line of pious usefulness. The rocky, sordid hearts that can not be softened by apostolic prayers or sighs seem to melt and bubble up beneath the missionary fervor of youth and beauty.

Thus it is, that by a peculiar and systematic organization almost every individual connected with a church or religious society, from the mere child to the man or woman with gray hairs, may be made an active agent for the collection of small sums for missionary or other religious purposes, and which sums in the aggregate annually swell to an immense amount; and thus it is that without ostentation or an apparent effort the greater portion of the annual princely revenue of the British and Foreign Bible Society is obtained from the people by a mild but determined enforcement of the "voluntary principle."

The orthodox Englishman is proud of Exeter Hall. In the rustic church or great cathedral he had heard of the wonderful success of the primitive apostles, and had been instructed in the mystic doctrines of Christianity, and told of its superiority over more ancient Pagan creeds. While the Bible had been held up as the great mirror of truth, he had been cautioned against various modern interpretations of the "unlearned," leading to false doctrine, heresy, and schism; and in the sanctuary, while often bewildered by contradictory tenets, or led into a maze of doubt and theological speculation by seeming contradictory texts, in Exeter Hall he seldom or never heard a conflicting opinion. In this place, the history, the contests, the persecution, and the triumphs of Christianity were mapped out before his mind in interesting recitals. There he had heard of the adventures of primitive Christians in their endeavors to propagate the "truth" in the midst of powerful and imperial heathenism; and had been told how august potentates became enraged at the pious innovation, and at the disrespect shown to the gods; how the great Roman empire thundered forth its denunciations in fierce and bloody persecutions under Nero, Domitian, Trajan, Marcus Aurelius, and others clothed with the imperial purple, down to the reputed conversion of Constantine. Here he had heard of the fierce contests between the rival bishops of the Eastern and Western, or Greek and Roman Churches, and of the final establishment of the "man of sin;" how God's so-called "vicegerent" in the fullness of his power crushed with unfeeling heart all who dared to dispute his spiritual dictation; how in the pride of his assumed and terrible preëminence, the simple minded, unoffending, and defenseless Waldenses and Albigenses were hunted like wild beasts from their humble homes, and mutilated and slaughtered by the bloody Montfort; how, more than a century later, the valleys of Piedmont were again deluged with the blood of these poor people by the brutal Oppede. It was in this place that his eyes were suffused with tears when in connection with the foregoing narrations, he first heard, amid the deep silence of a multitude, the solemn but beautiful verses of the great Milton:

"Avenge, O Lord! thy slaughtered saints whose
  bones
Lie scattered on the Alpine mountains cold,
Even them who kept thy faith so pure of old,
When all our fathers worshiped stocks and stones,
Forget not; in thy book record their groans
Who were thy sheep and in their ancient fold
Slain by the bloody Piedmontese that rolled
Mother with infant down the rocks. Their moans
The vales redoubled to the hills, and they
To Heaven. Their martyred blood and ashes sow
O'er all the Italian fields, where still doth sway
The tripled tyrant; that from these may grow
A hundred-fold, who having learned thy way
Early may fly the Babylonian woe."

Then when some fervid speaker, after having recited these verses, would close his remarks with an indignant denunciation of such cruelty, the pent-up feeling of the multitude would become liberated and significantly audible.

In Exeter Hall the Englishman had heard of the Inquisition; of its depths, its dungeons, its terrors, its cruelties, and its victims. Here, too, he had heard of the great massacre of St. Bartholomew, and had warnings, time after time, against the treachery and intrigue and cruelty of Papal Rome. Here he was told of the struggles of the Reformation, and of its heroes, princely and reverend, who stood out against the imperious mandates of the great ecclesiastical tyrant; and as fact after fact was adduced to prove that that great convulsion, the violent upheaving of an ancient despotism, was designed by Providence for the freedom of the human mind, he felt that Britain—his own loved land—had acted no secondary part in reducing and humbling the towering pretensions of so terrible an enemy.

Many other religious historical facts were there brought to his notice; and although the subsequent acts of many of the Protestant reformers were, alas! of a fearful and diabolical character, no mention was ever made of *that* iniquity, nor of the unholy secrets of that more modern inquisition—the Protestant Star Chamber. A blush of shame was spared, and the fraternal partiality of Exeter Hall very wisely and prudently threw the mantle of oblivion over all.

These tracings of a particular history, first permanently impressed on his memory in such a place, and under peculiar existing circumstances, associated with the warm applause awarded to strong and passionate assertions in favor of freedom of speech, liberty of conscience, liberty of the press, and of liberty itself, and all identifying his native country as the progenitor of such ideas, may well lead the impulsive Englishman to revere forever the name of Exeter Hall.

Thus it is that at the immense meetings of this distinguished forum, that monster organization, the British and Foreign Bible Society, the great evangelical giant of Christendom is again nourished and recuperated; and thus its prodigious arms are again strengthened and stretched out, overshadowing deserts, oceans islands, and continents, and only meeting to inclose within its vast embrace the whole unconverted world.

CHAPTER II.

THE wild March winds had passed away, having spent their fury over distant moor, bleak heath, and through trembling, naked trees. Broken, pendent branches, and piles of drifted, withered leaves in wall angles and hedge corners were remaining proofs of the rough season that had followed in the dreary track of ten thousand others of the same kind. The distant ocean was again calm, albeit that there might still remain on its grand surface terrible mementoes of some fearful struggle between the daring skill of impetuous man and the still more wild and impetuous waves, now again wearied and slumbering in the stillness of immensity. The earth, too, was calm and beautiful. The glorious day-dawn that was dreamingly stealing from out of the night-shadow looked like the timid virgin light of a new planetary creation. A sun-gleam tipped the distant tree-tops, now gently stirred by the first breath of a new morn; the lark in heaven and the song of the rushing stream on earth, were to the pausing and wondering wayfaring man like whispers from a long-lost paradise.

As it was, Hampstead never looked more like the original garden said to have been so pleasing and delightful to our great progenitor. Every cottage seemed imbedded in surroundings of quiet loveliness, as its outline became more fully developed in the new dawn; and every object, hill and vale, tower and tree, rock and river, was adorned in the soft, rosy light of the young day.

On a gentle slope, facing the great, dim metropolis beneath, stood Heath Cottage, an unobtrusive object in the picture. It was in the middle of a pleasant garden, around the walls of which were a number of fine old trees that, sentinel-like, had stood the blast of over a hundred winters. The house was a modern structure; there was nothing stylish in its architecture; it was a plainly built, comfortable English homestead, and sufficiently capacious for a family much larger than that which had occupied it for many years. There were shade trees and neat hedges by the roadside, and in front there were smiling flower-beds in which the crocus, hyacinth, and tulip were already conspicuous. Shrubs and plants and rose-trees were in profusion, and curious little winding walks, with trim boxwood borders, invited you pleasingly onward to a sun-dial, close to which there was a miniature fountain tossing up its little jet of spray to welcome the sunbeams, and moistening the moss-covered rock-work rising out of the graveled space before the door-steps.

Ascending these steps the entrance was besieged by flower pots of various shapes and sizes; some perched on rustic stands, and looking as if determined to pop in from the elevation through the side lights, and storm the chattering and defiant bird cages which flanked the sun-lit passage. Ambitious young vines were curiously peering through the intricate traceries around the bay windows at each side of the door, and pendent stems of ivy alternately tapped at the dormer panes that looked out from the steep roof.

As you entered Heath Cottage, the hall was ornamented, embellished, or incumbered with quaint and incongruous articles. Besides cages and canaries, there were pictures of London in the olden time, engravings of the flags and gods of all nations; the scene of an "Auto da fe;" of the massacre of St. Bartholomew; of a persecution of Jews by Christians, and of Quakers by Puritans; there were pieces of armor, war clubs from the Sandwich Islands, a boomerang from Australia, an idol from Japan, relics from the wreck of the Armada, and a few of the smaller instruments of torture from the British Star Chamber and Spanish Inquisition. Many of these strange things were suggestive of ideas not at all pleasing or honorable to humanity, nor creditable to the religious toleration of a former period; and here now were hung, as mere curiosities, some of those terrible aids to faith which could afford to the student positive illustrations of historic truth. There were also a few specimens of mechanical or engineering skill, such as the models of a ship, a bridge—the whole giving the place a museum-like appearance.

The first door to the right led to a neat, well-furnished parlor; not one of the stately freezing looking places where chairs and tables and mirrors and marble are muffled up in musty dignity, only to be exposed and made cheerful looking on great occasions. It was an apartment for home use, and not alone for the reception of occasional visitors. There was no pretense about the place; it was what it looked—a cottage parlor, and every thing in it was made subservient to the happiness of home. As a proof of this, many passing Heath Cottage might be seen treading with slower pace in order to hear the fine tones of the piano skillfully brought out; or oftener delayed to listen to soft voices mingled in some beautiful duo, and accompanied by that instrument. Indeed, many ardent lovers of music had been heard to remark that it was difficult at times to keep from loitering near the cottage, or to pass it by and leave so much harmony behind you. Opposite the parlor was a large apartment called the family room, from which you entered a small but well stocked library, connected with which was a little room that looked out on a patch of garden, and was well adapted for writing or quiet study.

Behind the dwelling, there was a small orchard and a summer-house covered with grape vines; and a space of greensward for play-ground, along which you passed to the sheds and stable. Taking it all in all, Heath Cottage was just such a place as a person with moderate means and limited desires might find to be a pleasant retreat from ambitious cares or the envy of the aspiring. Such it had been for many years to its proprietor, Martin Mannors, who now, on this fair, first morning of April, was looking down with beaming face from one of the dormer windows into the garden.

"What! Merry Pop, down before me? Oh! I see; you were determined to win, and I suppose you got up before day."

"Indeed I did not, Pa; I bet that I would be down before you on the first of April, and here I am, ready for the wager."

"Well, here it is," and out flew a pair of lavender gloves from the window, falling at the feet of Mary Mannors.

"Down, Flounce, down, sir!" but Flounce would not stay. Away he gamboled with the gloves in his mouth, over flower-beds and bushes, until met at a corner by a delicate looking boy, Mary's brother, who grasped Flounce by the neck and rescued the gloves.

"Pop," said Mr. Mannors, "Flounce knows this is the first of April, and wants to make an April fool of you."

"Pa, indeed you have pampered that saucy dog too much; but neither he nor you shall make a fool of me to-day," replied the excited girl, looking up at the window through her beautiful brown, shining curls.

"Oh! of course not. You're too wise, Pop, to be caught with chaff—not you." Mr. Mannors then, apparently surprised, looked for a moment at some object in front of the house, and hastily cried, "Look, Will, look, Mary! That surely is the identical April fool, if there ever was one, standing at the garden gate." Mary and her brother looked at once in that direction, but as the intervening trees prevented any object from being clearly seen, away Mary started, followed by her brother; there was a race for the gate, then there was a dead halt, then a pause of doubt, and then a shout of laughter from Mr. Mannors; for instead of there being but one April fool at the gate there were actually two.

"Well, Martin," pettishly observed Mrs. Mannors, who had by this time got to the window, "how silly! What an example of deception to show the children! What value can they place on your word? You should be the very last to deceive them with such an old wife's fable, or encourage them to think of such stupid nonsense."

"Nonsense, did you say, Emma? Well, if every fable that is taught for truth in this wise and sanctimonious age, and believed in by older children, were as harmless, there would be far more peace and good-will among men and women too—ay, far more happiness. But I must go down to the garden. You may tell them to try and be serious. I will bid them laugh and enjoy their cheerful impulses; I know which will make them most happy in the long run, at least in this world."

In another minute Martin Mannors stood close to the little fountain; his cheery voice rang through the garden like music, and again he laughed aloud at the ruse he had so successfully practiced. Mary and her brother had returned, and once more the laugh was general. Flounce, too, was springing about, giving repeated barks of approbation as if he knew all about it, and was delighted at the performance.

There was no doubt as to the heartfelt pleasure of the whole party, and he must have been a cynic indeed who could have looked upon the happy faces of that group and assert that the cause of so much pleasure was a sin.

Even Mrs. Mannors, who now witnessed their joyful meeting, and who had but just lectured her husband upon his indiscretion, felt the influence of their cheerful emotions; and, to appear consistent, she had to turn away quickly from the window to hide from father and children the smile that was then shining on her own face.

Martin Mannors, the proprietor of Heath Cottage, was just past the middle age of life, but healthy, hearty, and joyous. His actual years might number fifty-seven, yet at first view he looked scarcely beyond forty. He was of medium height, squarely built, vigorous, and active; he had a mild, gray eye, and a most benevolent expression of countenance. "Time had not thinned his flowing hair," neither had it as yet scarcely altered its color. A few white hairs, like intruders, might have been discovered screening themselves among his brown locks; but only a few, the scantiest number of the harbingers of the still far-off winter. He wore a manly beard, as nature intended; and if he had reached the summit of life's hill, he now trod the declining way as cheerfully and contentedly as he had made the ascent.

He was a person not easily disconcerted or annoyed about any thing. If an evil befell him, his philosophy came to the rescue, and he would say, "It might have been worse." Although comparatively indifferent about himself, he felt most acutely for the wants or afflictions of others; these, he would say, were the particular thorns that made his life most unhappy; and he always asserted that poverty in the abstract was the certain result of social injustice; and that crime, to a great extent, was the consequence. He was fortunate, however, in being placed beyond the contingencies of want; as the recipient of a liberal annuity, he was possessed of sufficient means to secure, for himself and those depending on him a great share of the good things of this life;

besides, he had a vested interest in Heath Cottage, and being a person careful and prudent in every expenditure, he was not at all likely to suffer from pecuniary difficulties. Having had the benefit of a good education, he was still more fortunate. He was a great reader, and devoured the contents of books on almost every ordinary subject with the greatest avidity. For him one side of a question was never sufficient; each proposition or idea was mentally handled and scrutinized, and viewed at every point before he came to a decision; and every assertion, or opinion, or theory, or doctrine, no matter how trivial or profound, how new or how old, how popular or condemned, had to undergo its ordeal of investigation in his mind before he either accepted or rejected it as truth or error. For truth he seemed willing to make any sacrifice; and the boldness of his statements relative to many of our most venerable and cherished ideas often startled the timid doubter, and many times engendered in the minds of some stiff-necked worshippers of traditionary or hereditary opinions a feeling of haughty scorn or of actual enmity.

Apart from more abstruse subjects he had a fine appreciation of music, painting, and poetry; in fact, he readily cultivated every thing most refined and intellectual in art or science, and his judgment in these matters was considered sound and conclusive. Such was Martin Mannors; kind, humane, and just; a man of comprehensive mind and boldness of thought; one who never sought to obtrude his opinions rudely, but who, singly and alone, was ever ready to defend them before a thousand opponents. Far and around he was known and respected; he was regarded by the poor and unfortunate as a true, sympathizing friend, and his name was a passport to the hearts of toiling men. But though he was idolized at home, and loved by many, being intellectually in advance, and a "skeptic" in theology, as a consequence, he too had maligners and enemies.

Mrs. Mannors was, in many respects, as unlike her husband as it was possible to imagine. She was comely in person and kind in disposition. She loved her husband and children and home; and she had the reputation of being generous to the deserving, and charitable to the poor, and was justly regarded as a very exemplary person in most things. But intellectually she fell far behind; it was a trouble for her to think. Ready-made ideas, particularly if the emanations of some reverend Spurgeon or popular Boanerges of the church militant, were by her readily adopted and held sacred. She had a religious mania; and the sanctuary was her gate to heaven, and the home of her strongest affections. Reason, she asserted, had particular and circumscribed limits, and *faith* was the great point upon which her fondest hopes centred and turned.

From her earlier years she had been trained to regard the world as a vale of tears, and to consider earthly things as of little consequence, and every moment of time spent on earth as scarcely sufficient to secure the promised enjoyments of a future state. Periodically, however, she was a busy bustling woman in ordinary affairs, but generally an enthusiast in religion; so much so, that she very often seemed to forget or neglect some of the duties of life, and to resign many of the pleasures of earth for the purpose of securing the inconceivable happiness of heaven.

To this end she became a strict Methodist; she joined the church, attended class-meetings; she would quote and lecture and pray in church and at home, in season and out of season, and found frequent opportunities to beseech some ungodly friend or acquaintance " to flee from the wrath to come." She was a collector of funds for churches, missionaries, Bibles, tracts, and tea-meetings; and next to herself she considered her husband as the "chief of sinners," and running blindly to his own destruction. She had cautioned and admonished him time after time, but, alas! so far without effect; he could not perceive his danger; on the contrary, he told her he was happy enough, he knew nothing of the sinfulness of sin, and often after she had discoursed to him in her most serious and tearful m od, he would laugh at the terrors which she had portrayed for his edification.

As a matter of duty she tried to impress on the minds of her children the value of religion and the worthlessness of the world. Besides leading them to the sanctuary, she had their memory crowded with catechetical questions and answers, and with a multitude of texts and pious verses. She had done her duty in this respect, and there was no interference on the part of her husband; but, alas! all her well meant efforts were undesignedly counteracted.

Mary Manners, now in her seventeenth year, was, like her father, naturally hopeful and joyous. She was of medium size, and had beautiful brown hair that hung in tresses around her graceful neck. Her eye was a clear mild blue, and her face singularly pleasing and attractive. Her education had not been neglected, and her mind was stored with a fair share of general knowledge. She had a fine voice, and could sing and play with the most exquisite taste and feeling. Her manner was quite unaffected; and now, as she was just budding into womanhood, her maidenly attractions were increased by a most affectionate and confiding disposition, and she looked and spoke and acted with an honest boldness that made her almost irresistible. She was an especial favorite with her father, and was like him in thought and disposition, and she considered him unequaled. Her brother William, her junior by about four years, was constitutionally delicate. He was a slight, frail boy, with a feminine cast of countenance. His face was handsome, yet without the force of expression, which made the contrast between him and his sister so great. In manner he was mild and affectionate, and was the idol of his mother, who evinced the greatest anxiety on account of his health. Altogether he was a tender plant, which required particular care.

Mary and he were almost inseparable. When he could not attend school, she was not only his companion but his preceptress; and under her tender tuition he often made greater progress than by the direction of the best master. His father was most indulgent; and when the spring days grew warm and fine, he and Mary and William, and always, Flounce would ramble for miles away over sunny hills and through green meadows; and, when tired, would sit by some clear stream to hear its murmurs as it wandered along on its way through shadow and sunshine. Ah me! these were pleasant rambles, pleasant to be remembered in long, long after years, and to be hung like some fair picture in the memory.

As for Mr. Manners, he had not for many years attended a place of worship. He had made a study of theology; and, having pierced its very depths, seemed to have discovered something unsightly and then to have rejected its principles forever. Mrs. Manners therefore felt it the greater necessity to be punctual herself, and a stronger adherent to the faith; but it was not always that she could secure the attendance of her children. Mary, as if by intuition, seemed able to comprehend the motive which too often actuated others. In her own quiet way she was a close observer, and she used to remark that a hundred attended church as a fashionable pastime for every one that went to pray. She, like her father, did not object to have her acts and motives fully understood. She did not care to be the slave of a popular mania, or to follow in the footsteps of a gayly dressed hypocritical multitude as a matter of policy; neither did she heed the censure of the self-righteous or the uncharitable insinuations of church-going adherents. When she bowed her head, it was from the impulse of the heart; and often when she had been obliged to conform to the prevailing mode of frivolous worship, reason gave its silent rebuke, and then she would wish to be with loved ones at home; or away, wandering through green lanes or on pleasant mossy banks, or by some gentle stream, clear and pure as her own thoughts.

On bright Sabbath mornings, if William pleaded indisposition, another ramble was sure to be the remedy; this was always suggested in preference to a drive—confinement in church being urged as injurious—and there surely could be no impropriety in stealing quietly away to the pure air on the hills. On such occasions it was useless for poor Mrs. Manners to oppose. She might and she did often murmur her disapprobation that the Sabbath services should be neglected; but her kind motherly feelings could relax religious discipline, and many times as she gave her reluctant consent, she would wistfully follow them with her eyes, as hand in hand they took their departure.

Mrs. Manners had, however, one great comfort in the religious companionship of an old and faithful maid servant named Hannah; a creature simple minded, guileless, and confiding. Hannah had read and re-read the Bible, and ventured to profess that she understood it; and although there were texts and passages in that book with regard to which she could form no intelligent or satisfactory conclusion, yet, with her mistress, she would boldly assert that the whole was plain and easily understood, and that the "wayfaring man, though a fool, need not err therein." She, too, had read with positive delight the *Pilgrim's Progress*. That similitude, and the story of the trials and temptations of poor Christian, had for her a special attraction. She generally kept this prized little volume within reach; it seemed to be her chief study, and were she asked to really choose between the Bible and John Bunyan's *Pilgrim*, in her heart of hearts she would choose the latter.

Hannah almost worshiped her mistress; she was her ideal of perfection. She wondered at her patience and long-suffering; she wondered at the faith that could still bear her up and lead her to hope for the conversion of her husband and the rescue of her dear children. As for Mr. Mannors, she considered him a fit subject for the united prayers of God's people. He was, however, to her a kind friend and master, and in all other things except his duty to God a fair and worthy example to men. But in his present state he was a "barren fig-tree," unregenerate, and under the curse of the law, as she believed that every worshiper of our benighted reason must be.

Maid and mistress were, however, toward each other what the Scripture says "iron is to iron." In fact it might be said that they had their own way in matters secular as well as religous. They alone consulted about or regulated household affairs, as well as planned religious tea-meetings or donation parties. They concerted plans respecting missions or Magdalenes, and to bring the "word" to her very hearth-stone, at the suggestion of Hannah Mrs. Mannors had decided that her house should be the head quarters for the next junior preacher appointed to the Hampstead circuit. This suggestion was looked upon as an interposition in answer to prayer; for, thought Mrs. Mannors, "as neither my prayers nor any thing I can say seem to have any effect upon my husband, perhaps the Lord might reach his heart through the lips of one of his chosen servants."

It therefore might be said that Mrs. Mannors was religiously afflicted. She morbidly fancied that the love of her children, the many comforts of home, the bright sunshine, the song of birds or the odor of flowers, were like snares ready to draw her aside from the narrow and thorny way in which she fancied a Christian should travel. Yet as a mortal she felt the "unholy attraction" of these things; and in the contest between her human feelings and her faith, she had often to bewail the coldness of her spiritual love, and the flighty, flickering light of her endurance. This condition was often aggravated by the following favorite texts: "He that loveth father or mother more than me is not worthy of me, and he that loveth son or daughter more than me is not worthy of me." Matt. 10 : 37. "If any man come to me and hate not his father and mother, and wife and children, and brothers and sisters, yea his own life also, he can not be my disciple." Luke 14 : 26. These texts and others of similar import were the cause of sore trials to Mrs. Mannors. There

was often and often, even when it was least expected, a sullen strife between the teachings of the word and the impulses of her nature, and it led her through much tribulation. But did not the saints glory in tribulations? Here was comfort. Alas! alas! how little did she yet know of afflictions. If "tribulation worketh patience," what comfort would it bring to her were she to lose her gentle, delicate son! Dreadful thought! Or her fair, joyous daughter? and oh—sorrow of sorrows—were she called upon to part forever with her dear husband, even though the spirit of God had stricken the scales from his eyes and changed his heart; even though he were snatched like a brand from the .burning, or raised forever from out of the "horrible pit and miry clay !" What would this avail her in that hour of dread tribulation, were she left to behold those dear eyes closed forever in death, and to know with terrible certainty that the pulsations of that tender, loving heart had forever ceased? Even now the very thought of these tribulations was fearful—nature had again its triumph—and as a woman, wife, and mother Mrs. Mannors buried her face in her hands and wept.

Fortified as she was with numerous comforting passages from the Bible, yet the thought of such possible affliction was almost overwhelming. In vain had she prayed for strength. The thought of such a calamity would recur again and again, leaving her greatly depressed ; and now, on this fair April morning her mind was thus clouded. Her husband had left her but a short time; she looked from her chamber upon the bright sky and pleasant earth, and father and daughter and son were still in the garden. Their laughter had ceased, and the traditionary April fool was again forgotten. They stood silently hand in hand in the soft fresh radiance of the spring morning, looking intently at some distant object. Save the hum of the bee, or the song of a bird, there was almost perfect stillness ; even Flounce with drooping head dozed quietly behind, as if spell-bound.

The view from the dormer window of Mrs. Mannor's apartment was very fine. London and its churches, its steeples, and its thousands of habitations were seen in the mazy distance, together with the dim outlines of the Surrey hills, and the silver Thames threading and glittering on its winding way to the ocean. Now, indeed, there was a change. A cloud or pall of smoke which had settled during the preceding night was completely spread over the vast city beneath, hiding the distant hills and burying the highest towers and steeples. Like Gomorrah, the whole city seemed to have been blotted out from the face of the earth ; but there was one object yet visible and attractive. The morning sun had just risen over the lost city, and had spread its beams far and wide over its murky shroud. The great gilt cross on the dome of St. Paul's alone towered up to the sunlight, flushing and glittering in the path of clear sky around it. As it thus appeared, it was a peculiar object of beauty to the little group of spectators in the garden ; but to Mrs. Mannors it was as a vision, working on her feelings of awe and veneration. The bright cross was then to her like some apostolic representation, or like another Abraham with outstretched arms silently pleading, "yet again," for the doomed city and its denounced inhabitants.

CHAPTER III.

IT is well known that the Rev. John Wesley, the celebrated founder of that popular system of religion called "Methodism," was a man of the most indomitable perseverance. No person could have been better fitted for the task which he had undertaken—the reform of the Established Church.

What Luther was to Catholicity, John Wesley was in a great measure to Protestantism; and the little offshoot which he unostentatiously planted in Britain has already spread its branches nearly over the whole earth.

He was eminently a man for the time. The potentates of the national church, surfeited in luxury and indulgence, were too much absorbed in courtly adulation, or too much engaged in political intrigue, to pay any great attention to the common pastors, and little indeed to the common people. The grandees of the Establishment had then, as they have now, their parliamentary authority for ecclesiastical usurpation, and for their landed and pecuniary rights independent of the clamors of the toiling multitude. The church was the pillar of state, and the state was the support of the church; and on these props rested, and perhaps still rests, the grand fabric of the British Constitution.

What cared the "Lords spiritual" for the murmurs of the dissatisfied populace? They, the regal parasites, never sympathized with the discontented. What cared the titled and wealthy dignitaries and beneficiaries of the English "church militant" for the bodies or souls of their mental flock? The claimants to apostolical succession seemed to satisfy their conscience by the rigid performance of one particular duty—the inculcation of the texts—"Fear God; honor the king;" "Obey them that have rule over you, and submit yourselves;" and if any further exercise was required it was concentrated in one grand effort—to take care of themselves.

John Wesley, though an humble and submissive minister of the Establishment, and one who always contended for its superiority, was a man of kindly feeling, possessing a deep sympathy for the large number of neglected people, members of the church; and he bewailed the spiritual destitution of the whole nation. His candid suggestions to his superiors were rejected with pompous and official disdain; and though he was grieved to take one step in advance of those whose duty it was to lead, yet he took that step, and did what he considered requisite to mature a good project, and with what success the Methodism of the present day can fully attest. He started almost alone, and with but one great object in view—the spiritual benefit of his fellowmen; and if it can be said that his efforts in this respect were misdirected, it must also be

said that no man was ever more truly honest and sincere. His self-denial was wonderful, and his labors were great; and were he to recount his struggles and trials, he might with an apostle have truly said: "In journeyings often, in perils of waters, in perils of robbers, in perils of mine own countrymen, in perils by the heathen, in perils in the city, in perils in the wilderness, in perils in the sea, in perils among false brethren; In weariness and painfulness, in watchings often, in hunger and thirst, in fastings often, in cold and nakedness." Such a spirit was destined to overcome all opposition, and his triumph was in a great measure complete.

Among other peculiarities, it was the habit of the Rev. Mr. Wesley to record in a journal every circumstance of any note that took place during the day; this he continued to do for many years. In his numerous journeyings by land and sea, he made entries respecting the state of his mind, and of his trials, temptations, conversations, correspondence, and reading. But there were other entries which were more particularly dwelt upon, such as strange mental impressions, premonitions, interpositions, or any event which might under the influence of enthusiasm, or in the light of his reputed credulity, be construed into a special act of Providence.

Nearly all through his journals many entries of this kind are recorded, and many indeed giving minute details entering deeply into the supernatural or spiritual. Some of these relations are strangely curious and interesting, and to this day "Wesley's Journals" occupy a prominent place in the library, or on the bookshelf of every studious Methodist.

Following the practice of their pious founder, it is common among members of the Wesleyan societies to keep similar journals. The preachers of the primitive body, for many years after the decease of Mr. Wesley, made it a point of duty to erect these spiritual memorials, and the duty was looked on by many as highly beneficial, and almost considered a special "means of grace;" and often in the declining years of life, the quiet perusal of these records would remind the aged Christian of the earlier trials which had beset him, and of the many spiritual triumphs that encouraged him on his way.

But if it is yet common to keep such journals, it is by no means general. Those who now continue it as a duty are not principally of "such as are called to minister in sacred things." The practice in this respect seems to have been reversed; formerly it was the preacher, now it is mostly the private member. In the struggling days of Methodism, the preachers were spiritual Sampsons, humble minded, energetic, and devoted men; but many of their successors at the present time are like an entirely new race; they feel the effects of their "connectional" influence; they have become more aspiring and lofty in thought, and are busy courting popularity and political influence, establishing "foreign missions," striving for an eminence in leading popular schemes, or planning how to obtain money to erect richly decorated and attractive churches, or to circumambulate the globe, in order that their teachings and religious discipline may take precedence of all others. It is now conceded that Methodist preachers are by far the most systematic and successful class of Protestant beggars in all Christendom.

Several of the leading preachers of that sect now choose to be known as "ministers" or "clergymen," and who, with the prefix of "Rev." or "Doctor" to their names, are to a certain extent as towering in pretension and as arrogant in authority as their more learned and aristocratic brethren of the national church—the real "successors of the apostles." There are, however, noble exceptions in the ranks of Methodism—men who do not assume a higher position in the church or in society than that held by their laborious predecessors, and who are still content to be recognized as "preachers," and indifferent as to whether they are called upon to deliver the "word of life" from the richly cushioned pulpit, towering up beneath the gilt and stuccoed ceiling of a fashionable marble edifice, or from behind the rude chair in the remote and humble cottage of the peasant.

It is yet correct to state that many private members, and it may be some preachers, still adhere to the old practice of Mr. Wesley, and profess to find the keeping of a daily record very beneficial, and an incentive to good works.

In this particular, Mrs. Mannors followed the example of the venerable founder of her church. The religious services of the Methodists are, in some respects, if not novel, at least very singular. Among these services, one of a peculiar nature is known as "class, meeting." A *class* is composed of five or six, or may be of a dozen, actual members of the society, in good standing. Every such class has its "leader"—a person who has been well tried and approved, and one of known experience in "holy things," appointed to meet these members at stated periods. At such meetings, each member is personally addressed by the leader, and is required to express in his own way the dealings of God with his soul, and to give a brief account of his or her religious experience since they last met. As each individual concludes, the leader gives a few appropriate words of admonition or encouragement, and generally recommends a greater attention to prayer, and a closer observance of some duty hitherto neglected.

The leader of the class of which Mrs. Mannors was a member strongly urged the duty of watchfulness; and, as a means of detection, advised that each member should if possible keep a journal, and daily make therein such entries respecting trials, temptations, and suggestions from the Evil One, as might be deemed applicable. Mrs. Mannors, therefore, kept a journal, and noted for her perusal every incident or matter which her feelings led her to think might affect her spiritual interest; and the entry made by her on the first day of April was as follows:

"April 1st.—This morning was again blest in believing. Oh! for more faith. Would that the faith of the saints were given to un-

believers! I still hope. God's arm is not shortened; his power is still great, even to the sending of signs and visions. This morning his glorious cross was visible to my mortal eyes. Satan would have it a delusion; but I will believe." Then followed these lines from one of Wesley's hymns:

"Lift up for all mankind to see,
The standard of their dying God,
And point them to the shameful tree,
The cross all stained with hallowed blood."

Although it was not unusual to see a vast cloud of smoke stretching over London, sufficient even at times almost to hide the tops of the highest steeples, yet it was an uncommon sight indeed to find the city so completely hidden as it appeared to be that morning—the lone cross the only distinct object. To the natural philosopher it was a beautiful sight; it was very much so to Mr. Mannors and his companions. There was no mystery to them about the matter; even William, if asked by his father, could have given an explanation of the appearance and the atmospheric cause. But to his mother it was something more. Her mind was strongly impressed that she had been permitted to behold a vision, and she felt certain that some revelation or promise was thereby intended for her special edification.

During a long period of the religious career of Mrs. Mannors, she had often had dreams and visions of a singular and impressive character. In seasons of active religious duty and continued prayer, she would go forth in dreams to Calvary, on which the cross and Saviour would be for her again erected; she would give a minute description of his person and tell of the benignant smile that he bestowed on her. Then again she would relate some curious interposition; and a circumstance that might pass entirely unnoticed at other times would at these particular periods be traced to the hand of a special providence. It appeared, therefore, that her mind was occasionally best by illusions; and during certain periodical religious excitements, she ate and drank, or walked about, or slept, in hourly expectation of being the chosen bearer of some supernatural burden.

When she entered the breakfast room that morning, her reason was evidently perplexed by the vivid feelings which then had the control. Mr. Mannors, who at once noticed the appearance of anxious excitement depicted on her face, and who always felt and manifested the most tender interest respecting her, laid his hand gently on her shoulder and said:

"My dear, I think you did wrong by following our example, and leaving your room so early."

Mr. Mannors was seated on a sofa, and her looks certainly betrayed the strong emotions which affected her at the moment; she tried to appear calm, but her anxiety was plainly visible. Mary and William sat close to her, and were impulsive echoes of what their father had just said.

"You know, Ma," said Mary, "that Pa, and I, and William agreed to be up very early this morning. Pa wagered that he would be in the garden first, and William and I agreed that whichever of us awoke soonest should call the other, so that we should get out before Pa; but I think Pa would have won only for the plan which William took."

"The way I did, Ma, I saw Robert last evening in the stable, and I knew that he intended to drive to Camden very early. I told him to call me as soon as he could see the dawn, so he did; then I called Mary; that was how she won the gloves. No doubt Pa wondered how we out-generaled him. Wasn't my plan a good one, Ma?"

This hurried account of how the wager was won was but so many cheerful words, spoken as much to attract the attention of Mrs. Mannors and amuse her, in order that the settled gravity of her looks might gradually brighten into the wished for parental smile of approval. To effect this with certainty, they went on without a pause to monopolize the conversation.

"See, Ma," said Mary, pulling out her gloves, "are not these pretty? This is my wager."

Then the story of the April fool was related; but while Mrs. Mannors seemed to listen, it was plain that her thoughts were preoccupied; she looked wistfully from one to the other, but said not a word.

"Are not these beautiful?" said William, presenting his mother with a bunch of fresh spring flowers. "See what a nice bouquet I have brought you!"

He began to arrange them in a small vase; and when done, he playfully held it toward his mother's face in order to have her catch the perfume.

The breakfast room of Heath Cottage looked that morning a pleasing picture in a happy home. The table neatly set; the white cloth, the shining cups, and the polished kettle. The chairs, sofa, and other articles in the room stood around as if they were enjoying themselves, and determined to exhibit to the best advantage their glistening outlines in the sunshine that flooded the whole apartment.

It did look like home. Mary's little straw hat lay on the sofa where she hurriedly tossed it as she rushed in, laughing, chased by her brother; and now as she stood before them she looked as beautiful inside of the house as the fair spring morning did outside. No three beings could have been apparently more happy—poor Mrs. Mannors alone being the shadow. Here she was surrounded with cheerfulness and worldly comforts, loved and waited on by those who would have been delighted to add to her happiness; but she was not happy; and as you looked at her now, seated demurely at the table, you would have every moment expected to hear her sigh out: "Alas, alas! all is vanity."

"O Ma!" said Mary, as if suddenly recollecting, "if you had only been in the garden you would have had a most magnificent view. You know the city is very often hidden by the immense volume of smoke that descends during the night. Well, this morning in particular, London was as completely lost to our sight as if it had been swallowed up in the ocean; and as you looked away, away, in the seeming boundless distance, you could see the sunbeams centre

on the dome of St. Paul's, and the great cross being the only object visible might be easily fancied a light-house far, far out at sea. We all declared that it was singularly attractive. I do wish, Ma, you had seen it."

"My dear child," said Mrs. Mannors, "why let your fancy interfere with an appearance that God probably called forth, and intended as a sign of his good-will and of his long-suffering and forbearance? I saw the hallowed object from the window; I, too, saw the sacred emblem of our religion, so much despised by the world, exalted on high in the blessed sunlight, and pointing to heaven while the world beneath seemed buried in iniquity. A revelation from God is not an impossibility even at the present day; his elect have proof of this. We have now the clear light of his sacred word, and if this fails—as, alas! it too often does—he may in his mercy and loving-kindness give us even again signs and tokens as he did of old. If our hearts continue to stray from him, he may use extraordinary means to wean us from the world. If we remain stiff-necked and stubborn, instead of the cross, held up as a token of his love, we may but witness the fierce lightning of his indignation. God's special providence may have produced a sign and a token this morning for us; let us not look on it as a trivial occurrence. How often are we warned in dreams and visions of the night. The cross which we but an hour since witnessed is the emblem of Christianity, and was no doubt, in my mind, a special token for us. By that blessed token, the Almighty has often with great condescension converted others; by that, a persecuting Paul, and the debased and heathen emperor Constantine, were brought to a saving knowledge of the truth. We have just had an evidence of divine interposition; then let us not neglect the great salvation."

As she spoke, any evidence of gloom that might have been previously traced on her countenance had now entirely disappeared. Her face brightened up, and was overspread with a sudden flush; but there was something inexpressible in her eye, something that would have been once mistaken as prophetic. She was again calm, and what she had expressed was spoken with great sincerity and affection. Her mind had been overcharged with strangely misshapen ideas, and, as the words fell from her lips, the mental burden seemed to become lighter and lighter.

"I will not dispute with you, my dear," said Mr. Mannors, "as to what the Scriptures state respecting the miraculous light St. Paul is said to have witnessed; you firmly believe in what you call the 'written word,' and would not allow a doubt concerning it to exist in your mind. Were I fully competent, it might perhaps be useless for me to try and affect your belief relative to that mid-day vision."

"Indeed, it would. I am as satisfied of the truth of what the New Testament relates as to the conversion of St. Paul as I am of the truth of my own existence. There is not a passage nor even a word recorded in that holy book, but has my full and entire belief; and to listen to any evidence against its inspired statements would be only soliciting and welcoming a temptation from the evil one. If we are to go on doubting according to the foolish suggestions of our blind reason, morality, religion, and faith would soon disappear, and leave the world in midnight darkness."

"The very strong assertions which you have just made," rejoined Mr. Mannors, "must forever debar you from investigation; and if you always adhere to the expressions you have used respecting Scriptural truth, you must ever remain bound to a belief that would now be terribly embarrassing to some of the most prominent teachers of the Christian faith. I need scarcely inform you that many eminent Commentators, who have made it the study of their lives to explain and reconcile conflicting texts, admit its impossibility, and confess themselves exceedingly perplexed with the numerous interpolations and contradictory passages which they have discovered in the Bible. There are, for instance, gross discrepancies in the inspired accounts of Paul's conversion ; and you are already aware that Luther, the great apostle of the Reformation, totally rejected as spurious the entire Revelation of St. John—the last *twenty-two* chapters of the New Testament.

"But I have no desire at present to give you instances of other doubts which have been raised against the credibility of the Scriptures. I would like to call your attention to historical facts in relation to the supposed conversion of Constantine.

"Are you satisfied that the legend about Constantine and the cross has any foundation in fact ? Do you believe the story of the sign which is said to have appeared to him in the heavens, bearing the motto, 'By this conquer' ? Do you really believe that this reputed miraculous vision was the cause of the heathen Emperor's conversion to Christianity ?"

"I have no reason, nor have I any right, to doubt it. The most eminent men of that period were satisfied of its truth ; and even to the present day many of the most learned and faithful of the church of God have, time after time, related the story for general belief. We should not undervalue the Bible because there are or may be different interpretations of it. The Scriptures warn us against 'perverse teachings ;' for we know that even ministers of religion have tried to twist the true meaning of the word to accommodate their own views. As for Luther's opinion of the Apocalypse, I care but little ; he was but an erring man, his acts were not always defensible. He was at times a skeptic, and would have been a persecutor."

"Well, I shall not contend with you now as to why religious doctors will differ so widely respecting what they assert in the press and pulpit to be so easily understood. You are inclined to accept as truth the relation about Constantine ; but if we allow our feelings or impressions to be the foundation of an opinion, we are very likely to be deceived. Long before that emperor circulated the account of the appearance which he said he had seen in the heavens, the heathen multitude were taught to believe that he was permitted to behold with mortal eyes the visible majesty

of their tutelar deity, and that whether waking or in visions—which were then quite common—he was blessed with the auspicious omens of a long and victorious reign.* These are historical words; and it is therefore plain that visions were not a novelty to Constantine whenever he found that they could be of personal or political service. The miraculous view of the cross had in reality but little effect upon himself. The common impression is, that he immediately became a reformed man—that is, a Christian ; but history relates that he lived for many years afterward, and alternately encouraged heathenism and Christianity, and that it was only during his last illness that he actually received Christian baptism. Constantine was a dissembler and a monster of cruelty. He drowned his unoffending wife Fausta in a bath of boiling water ; and the very year in which it is said he presided at the council of Nice, he beheaded his eldest son Crispus. He murdered the husbands of his sisters Constantia and Anastasia ; he murdered his father-in-law, and his nephew, a boy only twelve years old, and murdered others. Then, again, he caused the destruction of the Pagan priest, Sopater, who honestly refused the remorseless, royal murderer the last consolations of heathenism ; and then, because he was promised immediate forgiveness through Christ, he warmly espoused Christianity. Such, then, is the historical character given of the man whom Christians are taught to revere ; the man to whom it is said that Christianity owes its legal establishment. He was cruel and rapacious, a heathen one day and a Christian the next ; and his name at last became infamous as an unfeeling, dissimulating tyrant and heartless murderer.

So much, then, for the great convert and his vision. I was as much pleased with the appearance of the shining cross which was visible to us this morning as it was possible for me to have been. It was a beautiful sight, but beyond that it was nothing. You believe it was a vision, a special appearance for our edification ; no doubt that is your impression. But why are we not all impressed alike ? If God really intended to manifest himself to us by a sign, it is only reasonable to suppose that he would have made the evidence so satisfactory that there could remain no shadow of doubt as to its object. What is evidence to one may not be so to another. You can no more believe for me than you can breathe for me. Genuine belief is not a voluntary act ; it is the result of thought and patient investigation. If I, therefore, can not believe that the Almighty manifested himself to us this morning by a sign, your fancied vision is a failure as far as *I* am concerned."

The conversation now related took place during the time occupied at breakfast. Mr. Mannors expressed himself with unusual earnestness ; he spoke as if he felt that every word was truth, and that truth must be spoken, no matter what the consequence ; and were it not that he thought it might be painful to give his wife other similar proofs of the

* Gibbon's Roman Hist.

vile character of men imposed upon the credulous and simple as being the sanctified fathers of the church, he would have done so. Many instances of the treachery and deceit of such persons occurred to him, but he felt that he had said enough; he knew by experience that it was useless to confine Mrs. Mannors to fair argument. Her controversial method was naked assertion; and if she listened to an opponent, it was often as if in pity for his presumed ignorance and unbelief.

Mary and her brother were quiet listeners to what had been said; she did not wish to make any remark for or against the opinions or statements advanced. Mrs. Mannors had also listened, as it were, thoughtfully, and with unusual patience. She firmly believed in the honesty of her husband's convictions. She knew that he never dealt in rash assertions, or in unkind remarks. What he said she knew he believed, and if he acted in any other way he would be untrue to his own character. She would hear what he said, painful as it might be to listen; and while he reasoned with her, she would mentally pray for his enlightenment; she would ever hope and wait until the Lord's good time. She had great faith that if the inspired word could prevail with the heathen, and the ignorant and polluted, that her husband and her dear children, though unclean, debased, and condemned by original sin, would be yet brought to a saving knowledge of the truth. To her, in her fond affection, they were as superior beings, and she had an idea that the Lord would look upon them as such, and send conversion in answer to her prayers.

Breakfast and discussion having now ended, Mr. Mannors retired to the little apartment connected with the library. He sat musing at the open window. The morning was still fair and beautiful; the very air was fragrance, as its gentle breathings stole like the sunlight over his face. The outer world was very quiet; the hum of the distant busy commerce was now as soft as the hum of the busy bee in the garden. It was a time just fit for musing, a time when, if you are not careful, your thoughts are apt to mutiny, and, like sprites, to scatter the mind in fragments away into the dreamy twilight of oblivion.

But Mr. Mannors was thinking; he had ever food for thought, and his thoughts were ever vigorous. He dwelt upon the multitude of conflicting opinions that agitated mankind. Every country and people and creed has each its peculiar idea of truth, and all are struggling and contending for that absolute idea which is unattainable by man. Wonderful is the mystery of belief; the deeper the mystery the greater the faith. All religionists are great believers; and what a multitude of religions and diversity of creeds! The evidence which brings belief to one generates doubt in another. What is truth in England is error in Rome! Belief, therefore, is a mystery, and faith has made this very world the "bedlam of the universe."

In order to establish a religion, you must have attendant mysteries and visions. The ancient heathen priests wrought on the minds of their followers almost entirely by such agencies. The Egyptians, the Persians, the Jews, the Grecians, and Romans would have found their altars deserted were it not for this resource; and no kind of religious imposition has ever yet failed where visions and oracles have been well applied.

The Bible is a history of visions; and from such, prophets and apostles derived their mission and their inspiration. The advent of Christ was made known to the shepherds by a vision, and his life was a kaleidoscope of visions. The apostles had visions, and by this means St. Paul was converted. Then, besides a multitude of later ones, there was Constantine's visions of the gods, and his celebrated vision of the cross. There was Mohammed's vision of the angel Gabriel. Still later, there were Luther's visions, and Swedenborg's visions, and visions to the Mormon prophet, and to the Spiritualists, and to Latter-day Saints; and last of all, the vision this morning to—my wife.

He still mused, and the soft wind-whispers that stirred the young spring leaves flew in fragrant ecstasy from bud to bud. Mary's sweet song from the summer house reached his ear like the low murmur of distant melody, but which after awhile gradually swelled out to a sound like martial music, slow, plaintive, and funereal.

He looked, and a strange procession passed before him. A solemn company of men of antiquated appearance, attired in ancient looking costumes, and headed by a motley band of melancholy musicians, marched slowly onward. Each of the antiquated men carried a large inflated bundle on his shoulder, and when he arrived at a certain spot, which seemed to be a deep, dark gulf, dashed his bundle down with great force. There was a flash and an explosion, and then some grotesque monster or horrid vision would appear and disappear in a moment! He then saw two demure-looking men advancing toward him from opposite sides; as they drew nigher they spat at, and scowled upon each other: one he took to be the Pope, and the other the archbishop of Canterbury. They held with firm grip stout episcopal crosiers, and when they approached sufficiently near, they stared at him with an angry frown, and then together let fall their pastoral staffs heavily on his head. Mary had just stolen in and given her father a smart pat on the shoulder, and Martin Mannors lifted his head and—awoke.

CHAPTER IV.

IT is a prevailing opinion among certain of the worldly-minded that persons who are very religious must of necessity be also very ascetic; this is a mistake. It is quite possible that the devotee or religious enthusiast of the present day may be one who, above all others, is able and willing not only to enjoy the creature comforts within his reach, but also with many of the aforesaid comforts and delicacies to seek and secure secular distinctions for which crowds of common sinners are most clamorous.

The servants of the church were never yet debarred from reasonable enjoyments; and we find that their appreciation of things conducive to personal ease and comfort has not at all lessened. Many of the "successors of the apostles" can now innocently display their humble wealth in palatial residences, and can appear in public in gorgeous sackcloth as "lords" of the "spiritual" realm. The "pious" seem to understand the true meaning of pastoral self-denial; for presentations of gold and silver plate to those who minister in sacred things are quite common; and if genuine comfort is to be enjoyed on this side of the grave, priests of the altar, with, it may be presumed, the greatest purity of motive, strive to obtain it to the fullest extent.

In very old times, to be sure, before people ever thought of trying to reconcile religion with common sense, to be a devotee *then* was to be almost as entirely dead or indifferent to what concerned your body as if it did not belong to you, and was only carried about as a curse or temptation to be got rid of as soon as possible. And the recluses of that dark period had a gloomy belief that existence itself was a burden, from which to be early released was only to gain a readier passport to paradise.

Yes, indeed; popular piety in those morose ages led to strange misconceptions of man's duty here, and of his destiny in a future state. But no matter whether pious emotions arose from a contemplation of the virtues of Vishnu, or Siva, or from any of the ancient "Saviours," or from other gods or goddesses of the most remote antiquity, religion in every form has had its frantic votaries, its therapeutæ, its fakirs, its monks, its anchorites, its convulsionaries, and its many other wild unreasoning visionaries. Setting aside particular instances of the fanaticism of Egyptian or Indian gymnosophists, or of the priests of the Syrian goddess who flogged themselves in her honor, or of the priests of Isis who did the same, or of the priests of Bellona or Diana who covered themselves with wounds, or of the priests of Cybele who made themselves eunuchs, or of fakirs who went loaded with chains, or of savage devotees who, to propitiate some god, would as readily fling an infant into the Ganges or Nile as an Israelitish Jehu would destroy the child of an Ahab, how fearful, alas! is the lesson we have to learn respecting the vicious and inhuman impulses which men in all times have derived from the influence of what is called "religion." No other influence has ever been so terribly potent; it has robbed them of their reason, it has made them brutes, and guilty of acts and practices diabolical and most degrading to humanity.

But from the praises which have been lavished on the Christian scheme, from its protean creeds, and its millions of worshipers; from the submission of great minds to its inspiration; from its promises of "peace and goodwill;" from its reputed virtue, its great wealth or its vast popularity, who could have expected such terrible results to follow the establishment of a system which promised so much charity, so much benevolence, so much virtue, and so much peace? In the history of the world, the plodding progress of Christianity, the religion of warlike and desolated Europe, can be traced all over the earth in dread characters of blood and ruin.

Is it not, then, deplorable to discover that austerities and debasements and horrid cruelties did not cease upon the inculcation of doctrines which, like others more ancient, especially claimed a divine origin and authority. From its earliest days, the new faith was incumbered with delusions and absurdities of the most degrading character. There seemed to be no modification of extravagant practices like those of ancient heathen devotees, and intolerance was bid to reign in dread earnest. Multitudes of Christian hermits and monks abandoned the duties of life to rush idiotically into some monastery or wilderness, professing that the perfection of human nature was the annihilation of genial feeling or affection, and that the passions which kind nature had implanted should, if possible, be uprooted or destroyed. For this purpose, many of these fanatics went nearly naked, letting their hair and nails grow, dwelling in gloomy caves, or in such rocky recesses as would afford temporary shelter. It has been written that " the more rigid and heroic of the Christian anchorites dispensed with all clothing except a rag, or a few palm-leaves around the loins. Most of them abstained from the use of water for ablution, nor did they usually wash or change the garments they had once put on; and it is said that St. Anthony bequeathed to Athanasius a skin in which his sacred person had been wrapped for half a century."[*]

Among the most remarkable of these wretched fanatics is that of Paul, the hermit, who, it is recorded, lived for over ninety years in an Egyptian desert more like a beast than a human being. Gregory Nazianzen tells of such early fanatics in the following words: "There were some who loaded themselves with chains, in order to bear down their bodies; others who shut themselves up in cabins, and appeared to nobody; some continued twenty days and twenty nights without eating, often practicing the half the fast of our Lord. One individual is said to have abstained entirely from speaking, and another passed whole years in a church with extended hands, like an animated statue."

But it is said that the most astonishing account in ecclesiastical history of self-punishment is that recorded of an infatuated person called St. Symeon, a native of Syria. He lived thirty-six years on a pillar, erected on a mountain in that country. From this pillar it is said he never descended except to take possession of another, which he did four times. The last one which he occupied was loftier than the others, being sixty feet high, and but three feet broad; and the account states that on the last pillar he stood for several years, day and night, summer and winter, exposed to heat and cold, and to all the sudden changes of a severe climate. The breadth of the pillar was not sufficient to permit him to lie down; and it is said that he used to spend most of the day in meditation and

* See Dowling's History of Romanism, p. 88, Taylor's Ancient Christianity, pp. 436–461, etc., etc.

prayer, and in the afternoon until sunset harangue the crowds from all countries who flocked to hear him.

The superstitions abounding in the early ages of the Christian Church were most degrading, and overwhelmed the reason of all classes. According to Mosheim, there were fascinated biographers in the sixth century who used to "amuse their readers with gigantic fables and trifling romances. The examples they exhibit are those of certain delirious fanatics whom they call *saints*, men of corrupt and perverted judgment, who offered violence to reason and nature by the horrors of an extravagant austerity in their own conduct, and by the severity of those singular and inhuman rules which they prescribed to others. For by what means were these men sainted? By starving themselves with a frantic obstinacy, and bearing the useless hardships of hunger, thirst, and inclement seasons with steadfastness and perseverance; by running about the country like madmen, in tattered garments and sometimes half naked, or shutting themselves up in a narrow space where they continued motionless; by standing for a long time in certain postures with their eyes closed in the enthusiastic expectation of divine light—all this was saint-like and glorious; and the more that any ambitious fanatic departed from the dictates of reason and common sen e, and counterfeited the wild gestures and incoherent conduct of an idiot or a lunatic, the surer was his prospect of obtaining an eminent rank among the heroes and demigods of a corrupt and degenerate church."*

Then in the tenth century, scourging as a penance was the prevailing custom, and sinners of the highest rank cheerfully submitted themselves. Henry II. was flogged by the monks of Canterbury in 1207. Raymond, Count of Toulouse, was flogged with a rope around his neck at the door of St. Giles's church. The chaplains of Louis VIII., King of France, were flogged by order of the Pope's legate, and Henry IV. of France was treated the same way by a cardinal.

In the thirteenth century, men almost naked, with a rod in one hand and a crucifix in the other, flogged themselves in the public streets, and from that time flagellation became a common practice nearly all through Europe until the sixteenth century; and it was thought so commendable that Henry III., by the advice of his confessor, the Jesuit, Edmund Auger, placed himself at the head of the flagellators. Even to the present day, in parts of Italy and Spain, persons may still be found who practice this bodily chastisement; and now, in the middle of the nineteenth century, when we find ritualism on the increase, when we find a Protestant Ignatius in England, and nunneries, and other gloomy places of refuge for pious visionaries, in every part of Europe, as well as in Asia and America, one may well exclaim, that the race of silly saints or of wild fanatics is not yet quite extinct.

Protestant Christians, however, as a body, desire to claim an exemption from such acts of folly and barbarity, and assert that their belief does not require a denial of any proper or reasonable enjoyment. But Protestants, though perhaps not yet as guilty to the same extent as the faithful of Rome, can not assert that they are free from this charge. They never had the same opportunities; but when opportunity offered, they have been as intolerant, as bitter in persecution, and altogether as overbearing in spirit, as were the cruel dogmatists of any other form of religion. Protestants ought not to boast of their religious liberality, or freedom from religious folly. What has been the liberality of that monster of cupidity, the English Establishment? Already in Britain the black draped sorts of the High Church, yearning for heathen and Romish formalities, have done much in a quiet way to establish religious orders, and confessionals, and places of seclusion; and were it not for the strong common sense of the common people; were it not for the hatred of oppression and the proud love of freedom that exist in that little isle among nature's great legion of honor, there would be another Star Chamber, and another importation of relics and thumb-screws; and we should find crosses and pictures and holy water and holy candles, and other sanctified trumpery in many places of worship erected under the auspices and authority of that greedy insatiable mammoth.

Are Dissenters or Nonconformists free from the sin? Not at all. Cromwell's praying legions were a set of morose jangling fanatics; mouthing texts of vengeance, and whetting their swords to glut them with blood. To the elect of the Puritan cast, we are indebted for genuine specimens of ascetic folly, superstition, and intolerance; they recognized witchcraft in America, and gave weeping, pleading, and feeble old women to the flames in Boston; they hounded, persecuted, and destroyed unoffending Quakers; and established a rule of terror in the noted Blue laws of Connecticut.*

Although there are by far too many good Christians who, like Mrs. Mannors, still think that they should be ready and willing to resign the dearest earthly treasure—jewels of the heart—husband or wife or children, in the vain fancy that the sacrifice would be pleasing to God; yet the majority of pious people are getting more sensible—a sacrificial *theory* to this extent has the preference—and the godly seem determined to enjoy themselves. And now, if you had an opportunity, Asmodeus-like, to peep in through the little parlor window of the comfortable house of the Rev. James Baker, you would at once have a convincing proof that the straitest of formalists and the strictest of church-members can be, at certain times, as cosy and contented, and can enjoy the creature comforts as well as the most worldly-minded.

Looking, then, into this little parlor, we see a smiling set of faces around a cheerful tea-table. The carpeted apartment was very pleasant; the pretty landscapes which hung on the papered walls seemed to look their best; the bright tea-pot glistened, and its odorous fumes twirled around and around as if in ecstasy to reach the white ceiling. It was

.* See Mosheim, century vi. part 2, chapter iii.

*See Note A.

not exactly what might be called a small tea-party; it was more like a moderate female convention. There were eight ladies quietly sipping the fragrant decoction; most of them were of rather mature age, and they seemed to be engaged in the pleasant discussion of some subject which alternately produced very opposite feelings.

The lady who presided was Mrs. Baker, wife of the minister, and leader of the class in which Mrs. Mannors met for religious exercise. Mrs. Baker was a person evidently well fitted for the position assigned her in the church. Though her mental culture was imperfect, she was confident in manner, fluent in words, and well supplied with hymns and texts, which enabled her to give force and point to any religious remarks she might make. She led in conversation as readily as she did in prayer; and if she could use texts to a good purpose with her own sex, she could also occasionally give wings to a joke, and drive away any superfluous gloom that might follow her successive phrases of pious observation.

The ladies who were guests at Mrs. Baker's that afternoon were the members of her class who met at her house, by regular appointment, one evening in every week; and it often happened that after the performance of their religious duties most of them would be induced to remain for tea. Thus these periodical reunions were very social, pleasant, and profitable; and through the week this meeting was anticipated with much pleasure. The conversation which their little parties found most interesting generally related to the peculiar interests or concerns of their own society—something about new churches, new ministers, or new members; and anecdotes concerning the formation of choirs, or Sunday-schools, or tea meetings; but the subject most generally attractive was that about great public assemblages, in which Methodism was expected to appear in particular refulgence. Regular anniversaries were therefore talked of for months previous to their recurrence; and meetings of conference, or missionary meetings, or Bible society meetings became for a period not only a household theme, but one which for a time absorbed all others.

Mrs. Mannors being one of the most regular attendants at class was, of course, among those who remained at Mrs. Baker's little party; but as she labored under a peculiar spiritual depression—a frequent liability—she had the corresponding sympathy of her sisters. With the usual formal recital at class of the trials and temptations and impressions of the week that had just passed, she gave a glowing account of her supposed vision, and her inference as to its appearance being a providential token of spiritual succor to her and her house; and she claimed the prayers of all present on behalf of those so near and dear to her. The appeal had its intended effect; she had the tears of many, and the promise of the affectionate prayers of all; and for the time she felt how good it was to be there, and she grew more confident that, where two or three met together in her behalf, the expected blessing would be sure to follow.

Mrs. Mannors had another object in view;

she expressed a desire to entertain at her house the next junior preacher appointed to the circuit; she hoped that such a person in social intercourse with her husband might be able to counteract or eradicate the skeptical notions which he unfortunately entertained. As it was, he never attended any place of worship; and as she had failed to influence him, or give his thoughts the direction she desired, she trusted and hoped that the preacher, as a temporary member of the family, might be able to drop a word, time after time, which, with the supplication of God's people, might have a good effect.

"Sister Mannors," said Mrs. Baker, with great earnestness, "I approve of your plan; and it is most singular that it occurred to you at the present time. Strange, I never thought of telling you that Mr. Baker was notified by the district chairman that a young preacher would be sent to Hampstead at once, and that if he was found acceptable, the Conference might sanction his continuance." Mrs Mannors was delighted with the information and she immediately told her sisters in the faith that she looked upon this intelligence as the first-fruits of her prayers; and her confidence in the vision grew stronger than ever.

"When do you expect Mr. Baker home?" she asked eagerly. "Let me see, he left for the circuit on Wednesday; he expected to meet the new preacher at brother Moffatt's, and it is likely that he may be here to-morrow evening, or perhaps sooner."

"This is Friday," observed one of the sisters; "Mr. Baker has not been long from home."

"Indeed, I wish he was away less," replied Mrs. Baker. "I often envy most of you. When you are at home with your family—with children and friends—I am here mostly alone, and my poor man may be wandering over hill and dale, as the song says. Well, well, I sometimes think that this way of serving God is very hard."

"And so it is, sister," said a member of the class; "but you know it is a great privilege to be a helpmate to a servant of the Lord; I often wish that my John had a call. What an advantage to be the wife of a true minister!"

"I feel it to be so; but you must not forget how rebellious we are by nature, and how dissatisfied we are apt to become at times. When I am here alone thinking, I often wonder why so much money and labor should be required for the spread of the Gospel: why there should be so much running to and fro; why such crowds of preachers, and why so many voices to make known that which our presumption says ought to be as free as air; but these are unworthy thoughts. Who can understand the way of the Lord?

'How beauteous are their feet
Who stand on Zion's hill,
Who bring salvation on their tongues
And words of peace reveal.'

Oh! this reminds me of the great meeting we shall soon have in Exeter Hall."

"Exeter Hall?—to be sure," said another in delighted surprise; "yes, next month, you know, will bring the anniversary of the great Bible Society."

Half a dozen sisters now became most pleasingly excited, and concentrated a look of inquiry at Mrs. Baker. Mrs. Mannors forgot aught else at the moment, and exclaimed:

"Yes, that will be a great meeting, that will be a blessed time; eternity alone can tell of the good works of Exeter Hall!"

"Well," continued Mrs. Baker, "I have heard that our next meeting there is to be something wonderful," and she was now the object of a rapturous stare from all present. "The last time our district chairman was here, he told me that native missionaries, I think he said from a place called Tongataboo, were expected; and that a Chief from the Feejees, who but a few months ago was as wild as a Turk, is to appear in his curious dress and with his horrid weapons, and he is to talk to us in his native language."

"Won't that be interesting?" said a delighted sister; "how I wish they would make him perform one of his war dances; it would give one an idea of how savage they were by nature."

"Indeed, it would," replied several.

"You remember," said Mrs. Baker, "that last year we had a most interesting missionary meeting. I do like them meetings the best; I almost forget now all the strange things which we heard and saw. Don't you remember, sister Mannors, the ugly idols that the black man took out of a bag? What a lot of big and little ones there was! You remember the war-clubs, and the tomahawks, and the horrid scalps, and what the big Indian said about *fire water*, something worse than vitriol I suppose, and about drinking blood? I thought it very interesting. What a dreadful state these poor creatures must be in without the Gospel! We must all pray that the chariot wheels of the Lord may move faster.

'Lord over all, if thou hast made,
   Hast ransomed every soul of man,
Why is thy grace so long delayed?
Why unfulfilled the saving plan?
The bliss for Adam's race designed
   When will it reach to all mankind?'"

"Well, it is a mystery why saving grace is so long delayed, and poor sinners suffered to perish. Lord, hasten thy coming!"

Just as Mrs. Baker finished speaking, the rattle of wheels was heard at the door; she hurriedly went toward the window, and exclaimed, "As I live, here is Mr. Baker and the new preacher."

In a moment Mrs. Mannors and every sister in the room made a rush to the window. Sure enough, there was Mr. Baker, home before his expected time, and with him the person above all others in whom Mrs. Mannors for a special purpose felt most interested.

"Why, bless me, sister Baker," cried Mrs. Mannors, "but this *is* providential! Praise the Lord for all his mercies! Who would have thought it?" And as she quickly rubbed her hands in actual delight in response to the rushing thoughts of sure and certain victory, she again exclaimed, "This *is* providential!"

The sisters stood around as Mr. Baker entered; he did not come empty-handed. He carried two baskets, which he said contained presents from some of the brethren. The young man followed, and was introduced to the assembled sisters as "Brother Capel." Then, indeed, there was a shaking of hands. Mrs. Mannors was the very first to dash at the young preacher, and was so rejoiced that were she to have followed the strong impulse which almost controlled her, she would have saluted him with her lips; as it was, he had a narrow escape, and one might judge from his looks that he actually thought so. The other ladies followed in turn, and on the whole he was, no doubt, not a little surprised at the warmth of his reception and at the number of "mothers in Israel" who were present to meet him.

It was evident at once that his appearance told much in his favor. He was of middle height, his hair was nearly black and inclined to curl, his eye was dark, but without any vicious ray; his cheek was red, and its color was now much heightened by his peculiar reception. The expression of his face was mild and pleasing, and though his manner was somewhat diffident, he was sufficiently at ease, even before so many ladies, to reply with readiness to their inquiries.

Mr. Baker himself was no way surprised at the number present; he took it as a matter of course; he knew that the class met at his house on that day, and that Mrs. Baker's social afternoons were not few and far between. Indeed, as his wife had no children to take care of, he rather preferred that she should thus enjoy herself in his absence. Although a matter of pounds, shillings, and pence was of as much consequence to him as to most other householders, yet he lost nothing by the hospitality of his wife; none of her visitors ever hesitated to bring a parcel of something useful or necessary in domestic matters, and very often his table was in this way quietly and abundantly replenished, even with the addition of sundry delicacies so agreeable to the palate of ladies in general. He therefore felt as little discomposed as a man could be under the circumstances; he rather derived a kind of satisfaction from the knowledge that his wife could make herself the centre and attraction of her class. In the most bland and cordial manner he addressed a few words to each sister, answered some unimportant inquiries, and in a few minutes the ladies resumed their conversation, while Mr. Baker and his friend retired to partake of refreshment.

The Rev. James Baker had long been a preacher in the Methodist connection. He was now over sixty years of age, nearly thirty of which were spent as an itinerant. He was a thin, delicate-looking man; his iron-gray hair and sallow, beardless face, with such a hard, worn expression, might lead one to think that he was an invalid; but soon as he began to converse on a favorite topic—Methodism—he would, as it were, warm up, his eye would kindle with a peculiar light, and you could then perceive that he possessed great energy of character, and that sufficient physical power was not at all wanting. He was an active, untiring preacher, and went through the laborious duties of his circuit with punctuality and faithfulness. There was, in his opinion, nothing equal to Methodism; it was that alone which could meet the religious requirements of the age. He did not believe in the efficacy of any system which only required that a modern apostle should preach but on one day of the week and let the other days take care of themselves. Every one, he thought, who had a call to preach, should be at the work as long as he could get a sinner to stand before him. The Established Church he looked upon as a rapacious monster, burrowing out the vitality of the Gospel; and he always felt indignant when certain servile prominent Methodist ministers would obsequiously pander in public to its spiritual lordships, and assert that the National Church was "the strongest bulwark of our beloved Protestantism." It was, in his opinion, no better than downright popery.

He had a show of toleration for some of the minor sects; but he considered Presbyterianism as a creed, cold, formal, and lifeless; moral in its aspect, but deadening in its influence. Methodism was the all in all to him; he could dwell for hours on the virtues of "our founder," John Wesley, and he believed that no man since the days of St. Paul ever equaled the curate of Wroote. The Methodist body was, therefore, the "salt of the earth," and its ministers were destined to be the true apostles of the world. On doctrinal points, he was a resolute stickler for Arminian views; he had a leaning to controversy, in which he was expert; and it always gave him particular pleasure to harass an opponent into an admission of the scriptural views of the venerable Wesley.

Such was Mr. Baker as a preacher: he was unwearied in his work; and now, as that work was becoming too extended, the timely assistance of his younger brother in the ministry would be the means of supplying every call on the circuit. Of Mr. Capel he had heard the best accounts. He was recommended as one "holding fast the form of sound words," and who would be an example to believers "in word, in conversation, in charity, in spirit, in faith, in purity;" he therefore had no doubt but that there would be a great extension of their beloved Methodism; and that their efforts to "win souls" would be sure to prosper.

Mrs. Mannors could not now forget one of the main objects of her visit; and as soon as an opportunity offered, she made known her desire to Mr. Baker, and he admitted that success might follow the adoption of her plan; but he would not be too hopeful. It was, however, a peculiar failing of his—in common with most Christian ministers—that he could never exercise sufficient patience to contend or even reason with any person of skeptical views; he thought such opinions the best proof of the wickedness and presumption of the human heart, and that no man who was not both vile and stupid could for a moment resist the overwhelming evidences in favor of divine revelation. He therefore kept aloof from all such persons, doubtful alike of their honor or honesty; and during the period he had been in charge of his present circuit, he rarely visited Heath Cottage, and scarcely ever addressed Mr. Mannors beyond a few words of ordinary politeness. Upon consideration, however, he was pleased with what Mrs. Mannors

had suggested; for he had not as yet made arrangements as to where Mr. Capel should find a temporary home during his stay on the circuit.

The itinerant system of the Methodist requires that a preacher shall be regular in his ministrations, according to what is called a "plan;" and in the course of a month the greater part of the time is spent in traveling from place to place, preaching often two or three times a day. The remainder of the period may be spent officiating at or near home; and during that time, with younger preachers, they are required to attend to certain prescribed studies preparatory to ordination, which rite is not conferred until about the end of the fourth year from the time of their admission as itinerants; nor are they members of Conference until after that period.

"My dear sister," said Mr. Baker, "I see no difficulty in making the arrangement. Mr. Capel has left himself, as it were, in my hands, to locate him where I may; we will speak to him at once, and I have no doubt but that in the course of a few days, if your worthy husband should not object, you will find him dwelling beneath your roof."

"You should know, brother," replied Mrs. Mannors with a little warmth, "that I would not have made such a proposal if I anticipated any objection from my husband. To do him justice, he does his best in most respects to contribute to my happiness; he never interferes with any arrangement I choose to make; neither does he offer to limit what I may desire to give for the support of the Gospel. He is truly kind—I might almost say good, were it not for his unbelief—and I therefore long for his conversion."

"My opinion is, sister, that your husband has sense enough to know that you are right, and that he is wrong; were it not for this, he would oppose you. If he were honest in his convictions, he would resist; and his conduct toward you is but a plain proof of human depravity. While he, like many others, boastfully sneers at our faith, there are solemn moments when his conscience bids him beware."

"I know him to be sincere, brother Baker; no man was ever more true to his belief. In times past, I would not accuse him of a denial of the truth; I would not do so now; he speaks what he thinks; and he still asserts that scarcely one at the present day can be truly liberal or tolerant who remains bound to any of the principal sects of Christianity. I may profess what I like; he would not interfere with me if my happiness consisted in a worship of Juggernaut."

Notwithstanding this generous defense of her husband, Mr. Baker was not convinced. He would never believe that an undisguised skeptic could be a trustworthy person, or a good member of society. He had no more faith in their integrity than he had in the docility of a wild beast; nothing but the grace of God could subdue the heart; and a person who, like Martin Mannors, had, from a pious, patient wife, line upon line, and precept upon precept, and who could after all, in semblance or in reality, successfully resist the prayers of the people of the Lord and the promptings of the Divine Spirit was a person to be avoided. With such he desired to have neither intercourse nor communication. For this view had he not scriptural precepts?

"But though we or an angel from heaven preach any other gospel unto you than that which we have preached unto you, let him be accursed." "If there come any unto you, and bring not this doctrine, receive him not into your house, neither bid him God speed. For he that biddeth him God speed is a partaker of his evil deeds." A person, therefore, like the Rev. James Baker, who thoroughly worshiped the Bible, could not possibly resist the force of such texts. He was therein told to "beware of dogs," and like a true believer he acted accordingly.

When the offer of Mrs. Mannors was made known to Mr. Capel, he expressed himself quite satisfied; he was, he said, in the hand of Providence, ready to enter whatever door was opened for him. A few arrangements had yet to be made, and in the course of the following week he would possibly avail himself of her kind and generous proposal.

Here, indeed, was a consummation! Who but the Lord, thought good Mrs. Mannors, could have brought this thing to pass? She could now return with renewed hope, and—a thought struck her—would it not be well that before they departed that evening their closing prayer should be made to the throne of grace on behalf of her unconverted husband? The proposal was readily accepted; and after they had nearly all prayed in turn, the closing appeal was made by Mr. Baker, who, while kneeling erect, with closed eyes and extended arms, and head thrown back, thus concluded his petition:

"And now, O Lord! thou knowest how sinful and depraved we are by nature. Thou knowest that through the fall of Adam we, his descendants, are but filth and pollution in thy sight, truly hell-deserving, and only worthy of eternal banishment from thee. In thy sight we are so corrupt that without grace our best actions are but an abomination. But, blessed be thy name, thou hast provided a ransom for us, even in the death of the second Adam. For since by man came death, by man came also the resurrection of the dead; and now as there is blood upon the mercy-seat, wilt thou not be appeased? Wilt thou not again, O God! stretch forth thy hand and raise some dead Lazarus from the tomb? We plead for our afflicted sister; we plead before thee for the conversion of her unbelieving husband. O Lord! break his stony heart. Unloose the bands of unbelief, and set him free. Set his feet upon the Rock of Ages, and turn his face Zion-ward. For years thou hast borne with his rebellion, and hast not cut him off. For years with unrelenting heart he has denied thee access, and resisted the drawings of thy Spirit; and yet he is out of hell, out of that abyss where neither hope nor mercy ever comes. Then spare him, oh! spare him a little longer. Lengthen thou the day of grace. But if, O Lord! in regard to thy divine justice, thy Spirit has forever taken its flight; if now he stands like a condemned wretch awaiting the execution of thy sentence, and ready to be hurled over the precipice of destruction when thy sword falls, and when he is lost—forever lost—and writhing under thy merited vengeance with the eternal tortures of the damned, when neither sighs, nor tears, nor prayers, nor sacrifice can move thee again in his behalf, then, O God! pity, oh! pity our poor afflicted sister; support her while passing through the deep waters, but above all things enable her to approach the throne of grace, to be reconciled to thy decision, and to acknowledge the purity of that justice which overwhelmed thine enemy. Amen, amen."*

There was a dismal pause, a feeling of awe, a great silence. Mrs. Mannors's heavy sobbing alone fell upon the ears of those kneeling around her, like the tapping of a muffled drum in a solemn dead-march. But even then, if an angel could have lifted the vail of distance, and have exhibited to them the object of their prayerful solicitude, Martin Mannors might be seen with smiling face handing bread to a beggar at his gate. Mary and William could be found close by, and, like their father, following with pitying eye the feeble steps of the old mendicant as he moved slowly away. The setting sun might be seen as if lingering on a distant hill, while parting beams in fading glory were spread far around. Then if, during the pause, the angel could have touched the ears of those who had been praying, the mellow voice of Martin Mannors could be heard to exclaim as he looked upward into the sunlight, "How beautiful! how beautiful!"—and the poor wanderer's blessing would seem to brighten the sunbeam that now rested like an aureola upon the head of his benefactor.

CHAPTER V.

AFTER Mrs. Mannors and the other guests had departed, Mr. Baker and his wife and Mr. Capel sat around the parlor fire. There was a lull in the conversation, and each was looking in thoughtful silence at the few half-consumed coals that were losing their fierce glow of redness and getting every moment darker and darker. Mr. Baker appeared very reflective, as if some mental problem had to be solved, and that he was determined to succeed. The expression of his face changed very often and very suddenly. His lips would be compressed, and a rapid and peculiar contraction of the brow indicated a struggle of emotions which one might hope was rather unusual. He was now very absent, and apparently lost in a flurry of wild, conflicting ideas.

Mr. Capel looked at him, as if desirous of making some remark, but he noticed his abstraction at a glance; he therefore dallied a little longer with his own thoughts, and went hand in hand with memory a long, long distance.

* The charity exhibited in the above clerical prayer is fairly illustrated in an extract taken from an American paper, namely: Rev. Mr. ——, of Oberlin, Ohio, in a recent prayer made the following invocation: 'But how shall I pray for the President? O Lord! if thou canst manage him, without crushing him, spare him. Otherwise, crush him!'

But the silence was suddenly broken. " Be ye not unequally yoked together with unbelievers: for what fellowship hath righteousness with unrighteousness? and what communion hath light with darkness? and what concord hath Christ with Belial? or what part hath he that believeth with an infidel?" "Yes," said Mr. Baker, " that woman is deceived; she has been unequally yoked, yet she would now shield and even hope for a blasphemer that openly denies the Lord who bought him. I can not and will not forever sympathize with her; she still clings to a wretch that may yet drag her down with him to deserved perdition." The preacher spoke with his teeth almost clenched, and the nails of his fingers were buried in the soft palm of his tightly shut hand.

Mr. Capel gave another earnest look at his superintendent; and his eye turned immediately from the dark frown that met his view. The individual before him was almost completely changed from what he had been a short time previously. The seemingly courteous Christian was now a bitter, vindictive accuser, and the zeal of intolerance and persecution flashed in his eager eye. His last prayer, uttered so affectingly, had brought tears from almost every one present; but with him, to make such an appeal was a ministerial faculty. He could raise his supplicating voice and make others weep; and, strange to say, could at such moments even weep himself: yet his own heart would not be affected; while his face was bathed in tears, that very heart could be as cold and as hard as iron.

"She need not tell me," he continued, "of his honor or his honesty; he is a deceiver, base and black as the father of lies, and the poison of his vile tongue will yet bring many to eternal ruin. It is hard to pray for such an enemy. Would it not be better for the church of God that a visitation swift, sudden, and destructive should bury such an apostate in his own sin, and be another signal warning to the black brood of scoffers increasing around us? Would it not be better that some of the vile sneering herd should remain deceived and be swept away, rather than that they should remain to delude others with eternal misery?

" ' For this cause God shall send them a strong delusion that they should believe a lie. That they all might be damned who believed not the truth, but had pleasure in unrighteousness.' "

" Brother," continued Mr. Baker, "you have a curious mission before you. Your prayers must be divided between a believer and an unbeliever. You must become a practiced hand in dealing out spiritual sympathy to sister Mannors, while you have daily to confront the infidel blasphemies of her sneering husband. What do you think of that? She, poor simpleton! imagines that you may be able to influence a man who would deny the bread of life even to his own children—who would leave their minds a perfect blank as to religion. Reason with him, indeed! why, he is and has been all reason, and philosophy, and common sense ever since I knew him; yet these worldly-wise-isms only leave him more deluded, and a still more furious and determined

scoffer at the truth. You will find none more plausible; he thinks that by a show of liberality his sin can be overlooked; it might be, were it only to bring destruction on himself; but look at the pernicious influence of his teaching, for I have heard, alas! that some have even fallen away from grace, and have become confirmed backsliders through his vile but honeyed words. Talk of education and enlightenment and progress! would it not be better for the souls of men that gross ignorance of all other things should prevail, rather than that the world should be depraved with that scum of modern reasoning—Infidelity? Would it not be better that all secular knowledge, and science, and high sounding philosophy, should be completely lost to man, rather than that the knowledge of the true God should be forgotten in the vain rush after the flighty speculations of modern science? As soon as we are so weak and uncertain as to submit our glorious gospel light and our blessed faith to scientific investigation; as soon as we submit faith to reason, or allow our confidence in divine inspiration to waver in the least, so soon may we close the Bible forever, and let the enemy of souls have full sway."

Mr. Baker here stood up and commenced to pace the room. He had gradually evoked a feeling of Christian indignation. The very thought of presumptuous opposition to what he deemed the inspired word embittered his spirit to such an extent as to make him almost ready to consent that another fire should be kindled in Smithfield, rather than Protestant truth should suffer. Unknown even to himself, intolerance was here doing its work in the mind of one who claimed to have been regenerated; and James Baker, who had a strong belief that he was chosen and called to preach a "gospel of peace," might now be easily induced to plant a stake and kindle a faggot or buckle on a weapon—verily a sword of the spirit—and become at last, like a thousand others of his calling, a fierce persecutor.

" James," said Mrs. Baker quietly, " I fear that you allow the carnal feeling to govern your words sometimes. Would you become the avenger of the Lord? Would you ask assistance from Satan to put down unbelief? If God is willing that some should be deceived, or if he is willing to exercise patience and long-suffering with such as are puffed up in their own vain imaginations, shall man do less? We have been furnished with weapons for the enemies of the Gospel that the Evil One will never use—weapons that are sure to overcome. Have we not prayer and faith?"

" Very true, wife, very true. I admit that I am sometimes rash; but when I think of the labor I undergo for the spread of Bible truth; when I think of what is sacrificed in missions; when I think of the years which I and others have spent in the ministry, calling sinners to repentance, and then, may be, when we fancy our harvest is ready, in rushes some midnight plunderer and destroys our prospects. It is perhaps wrong to be too impatient in such matters; but who can justly tolerate crime? Yes, patience may be necessary; but who can submit to the presumption of gross, palpable error? I can not help believing that our present laws are far too lenient; the faith should be more rigidly upheld; there should be some determined stop put to the open dissemination of pagan error; there should be some stern, 'Thus far shalt thou go and no further.' Our nation can not surely prosper while wicked men are allowed to beguile others away from the truth. Reason and liberalism are now rampant all over the land, despoiling the pious efforts of centuries. They must be tramped out. To be plain, if coercion is necessary to enforce the laws of erring man, how much more requisite is it thus to enforce the mandates of a just and jealous God? Are we not liable to incur his divine wrath by our apathy, our forbearance, or our so-called toleration?"

"My dear brother," said Mr. Capel, "let the wicked man and the scoffer and the worshiper of the glory of this world remain in the fortress of their own strength. The Lord has promised to conquer all his adversaries, and he will do so in his own good time. Has he not said that 'kings shall fall down before him,' and that 'all nations shall serve him'? and have we not an abundance of precious promises in his word of how he is to overcome the world, and does he not bid us to be of 'good cheer'? Then, brother, let us wait; we have our allotted work to perform; let us be faithful, and God will not be forgetful of his waiting saints. The Lord still says, 'I have sworn by myself; the word is gone out of my mouth in righteousness and shall not return, that unto me every knee shall bow, every tongue shall swear.' With these blessed words, who can doubt? Let the heathen rage, and let the world scorn us as it may, what is erring presumptuous man before Omnipotence? He says, 'Ask of me, and I shall give thee the heathen for thine inheritance, and the uttermost parts of the earth for thy possession.' 'Thou shalt break them with a rod of iron; thou shalt dash them in pieces like a potter's vessel.' 'Evil doers shall be cut off; but those that wait upon the Lord shall inherit the earth.' These are assurances that should make us patient. I have no fear, brother; a good work will yet be accomplished, and truth must prevail."

Mr. Baker already felt that he had shown symptoms of indiscreet zeal before his co-worker. He now appeared more satisfied. He was again reassured, and his wonted confidence returned. He was much pleased with Mr. Capel's words and modest remarks, and, like him, he was again willing to trust in the Lord rather than in the arm of flesh.

"Brother," said he, "I have been in the vineyard of the Lord for a long time. I have often witnessed the closing scenes of life and the final triumph of many of the people of God. I have seen them, while languishing in their last moments, bear witness for the truth. Then, again, I have seen men once strong in the faith fall—oh! to what a depth—and pass away forever in the whirlwind of unbelief. How mysterious are the dealings of the Almighty! Why are millions still left in darkness to perish for lack of knowledge? Why is unbelief yet allowed to prevail? Why are not all saved? What a number of

enemies we have around us! What traitors we meet on all sides! And those we have most to dread profess to belong to the household of faith, to believe in the written word, yet bring it into contempt. Alas! how the infidel can laugh at Christianity. Crowds of believers, and crowds contending for forms and ceremonies and precedence. Rome anathematizing England, and England gloating over the degradation of Rome—one desiring to usurp over the other. The so-called Christian church is a mystery to many. Who are its members. Are the numerous sects which bitterly denounce each other deserving of that distinction? Are the emissaries of the Popish system of delusion and superstition to be acknowledged as such? Should the credulous slaves of its Greek sister be set down as members? What are we to call those who allow the rapacious apostles of our wealthy Church Establishment to rule over them? Shall we include as members all who cling to Presbyterian morality and its election and reprobation? How are we to designate the exclusionists of close communion and immersion? What are Unitarians, and Trinitarians, and Quakers, and Dunkers, and Universalists, and the fifty other sects to be called? Who are the real exponents of the true faith? There are sectaries of every degree, many of whom have in turn routed and persecuted each other, all claiming to be members of the true church, yet nearly all differing widely in what many of them deem essentials. We may talk as we like about unity of spirit. Some think there may be unity in diversity, and diversity in unity; but experience goes to prove disunity in contending bodies, and a leaven of bitter jealousy working through the whole. The Evangelical Alliance promised great things at Exeter Hall; but where is the fulfillment? And what is our own Methodism? it is not at the present day what it once was, the most scriptural of all systems. It is not, alas! what it ought to be. Look, brother, at our aspiring men, and at our connectional hankering and ambition. Our Conference is aiming for power and influence, and wishes to make its oft assumed authority felt and recognized outside of its own proper limits. I feel that Methodism is fast drifting down to worldliness, and that it will soon be another synonym for pomp and vanity. Its love for money is unspeakable."

"My dear," replied Mrs. Baker, "we all know that it is impossible for us to read the heart; God alone can do that. Aspiring men have no doubt entered among us, and have caused heart-burnings and divisions; but when we know that Satan himself will sometimes appear like an angel of light to gain his own ends, when we find pretended friends in our midst, our duty then is to be more faithful ourselves. Methodism is God's right hand in the salvation of men; it is a rock of strength: though it has enemies within and without, and though many on the side of Church and dissent would unite to-morrow for its downfall, let us not fear, but say—

' Come, glorious Lord, the rebels spurn;
Scatter thy foes, victorious King;

And Gath and Askelon shall mourn,'
And all the sons of God shall sing.'

"Well, let them rejoice when it happens.
No doubt Satan would rejoice over the downfall of our beloved Wesleyanism also. Yes,
wife, I know some of those spouting Protestants—rank dissenters, too—who profess to be
ready to join hands with us for the conversion
of wild Indians, or for a crusade against English or Romish Popery, and who, under the
pretense of Christian love, will meet and counsel and pray with us, and who yet would at the
same time give us a stab in the dark if a
chance offered. Yes, I know them; they will
fraternize with us on a public platform, they
will make great speeches about the poor
heathen, and about missions, and Bibles, and
tracts, and temperance, and all that, but,
bless you! they are merely acting—they hate
us. When religious teachers enter our pulpits and dissemble to such an extent, what
can we expect from Papists and unbelievers?
A worthy old brother once whispered to me,
when we were seated together on a missionary
platform, and after we had heard some fine
speeches and a great display of liberal sentiments from the reverend representatives of
various hostile denominations who took part
on the occasion, 'Brother,' said he, 'I thought
I knew these men, but I see every man has
a mask, and puts it on before he addresses the
people.' He had them that time."

Just then there was a rap at the door and a
note was handed in for Mr. Baker. He tore
it open at once, and after looking at it a moment read aloud:

"A meeting of the Hampstead Branch Bible
Society will be held, God willing, in the
Baptist Church on Tuesday evening next.
The chair will be taken precisely at half-past
seven o'clock. A full attendance is requested
in order to select delegates and to make other
preparatory arrangements in view of the
great anniversary meeting to be held next
month at Exeter Hall."

When Mr. Baker read this little epistle, he
closed his left eye and looked down thoughtfully at the floor, which he patted smartly at
the same time with his foot. After a few sec-
onds' cogitation, he spoke very slowly, as if to
himself: "In the Baptist Church, on Tuesday
evening next—very, very sharp practice—
very." The words fell from his lips as separate
and distinct as if there were no possible connection between them—as if he had been merely
practicing an elocutionary utterance.

"Now, brother," said Mr. Baker, recovering
himself, "here is a nice little plot, dexterously
managed and arranged, to keep us as a body
in the background; and I think we are also
indebted to the supineness and extra liberality
of some of our wise members for such a very
agreeable invitation. If this is not a happy
illustration of the sectarian jealousy which
we were just deploring, it is a very forcible
one, and not at all pleasant to my feelings. I
can see through it. They have made a rat's
paw of the Baptists to put the Methodists on
the shelf—that's it. I understand the manœu-
vre. I can see the Presbyterian finger in the
pie just as plainly as I can see that table. If
you want a plotter of the right kind, give me

one of your moral, smooth-faced Free-Church-
men, one who wears a continual smile, just as
attractive to some as the glitter of a serpent's
eye to a foolish bird. A first-class wire-puller
always smiles; he wears an appearance of
great candor, but he always keeps in the
background and will not show his hand if he
can help it. He holds the wires; for instance,
he pulls one for the Baptists, and another for
the Independents, and one for some other sect
or creature willing to fall in with the rest;
and this is what we find the Rev. Andrew
Campbell of the Free Church has just been
doing. He has burrowed pretty deep and
thinks to hide himself; but I will unearth him,
and that before he is aware of it."

And Mr. Baker rubbed his hands in eager
anticipation of a brush with his reverend an-
tagonist.

"Brother Capel," he continued, "here is a
plain case of jealousy and dissembling on the
part of a man who claims to be the pastor of a
most exemplary body of Presbyterians. Last
year, a minister of our Society was appointed
a delegate to represent our Branch Bible Society at Exeter Hall. There were murmurs
as usual from several of Mr. Campbell's people,
and from some others who are always grumbling at the Methodists, but he, worthy man!
appeared to be quite satisfied; indeed he said
he would not have selected any other person
were the choice left to himself. So far, so
good; but in the course of a few weeks, a rumor was heard in one place and in another
that the Methodists had succeeded in getting
the meeting held in their own church, and
that by force of numbers a Methodist delegate had been chosen to display his eloquence
on the platform at Exeter Hall. After a little
inquiry, I traced this report direct to the Reverend man himself; there was no chance for
his escape. And you may judge of my astonishment when he told me to my face at a committee meeting that it was every word true;
that he never denied having said so, and that
I and my adherents on all occasions tried to
monopolize certain positions before the public
to the exclusion of better men. When he told
me this, he looked no more shame-faced than a
parson who was pocketing tithes. With such
a man, it was useless to waste words. It
would be very unseemly to contend with him
before a committee. I withdrew as soon as I
conveniently could, and I have never met him
since."

"The feeling that Mr. Campbell has toward
us," said Mrs. Baker, "has influenced many
others with whom we were formerly on terms
of friendship. For instance, but a short way
from this house there are two maiden sisters
residing; they used to visit us very often, and
we frequently went together on missionary
tours and on tract collections. They were
never, to be sure, very warm toward us as a society, but they never made any unkind remarks; they are, however, members of Mr.
Campbell's congregation, and since the occurrence at the committee meeting they have
never entered our door, and if I happen to meet
them at a Dorcas meeting or at any other place,
they merely give me a formal bow. Why,
bless you! I never thought people could be so

uncharitable as we now find many of the Baptists and Presbyterians."

"And what is worse," urged Mr. Baker, "after the discreditable conduct of Campbell, I tried to keep the matter as quiet as possible. I did not wish to let it be known around that a number of professing Christians who had met in order to devise ways and means for the circulation of the Scriptures had, at such a meeting, a fierce altercation among themselves. I said as little as I could about it; but the following week out comes the *Evangelist*, the newspaper or organ of the Presbyterian body, with a communication denouncing the 'shabby tricks' (this was the expression) 'of a certain Methodist *preacher*, whom it did not name, and the hypocritical rabble that followed at his heels,' and then it went on retailing the current scandal about the appointment of a delegate. To this, I sent a contradictory reply, with certain explanations which I trusted would not be offensive; but back came my manuscript; they would not insert any thing I had written; and now to this day we have the greatest trouble to keep up appearances and prevent another outbreak more scandalous than the last. You know in the course of the year there are many occasions on which we have to meet. Protestants of all denominations, with the exception of the High Church party, profess to unite their efforts at Bible meetings and tract meetings, and for other objects of common interest; but lately I find it hard work to keep my temper among them, and were it not that scoffers might triumph I would enjoy far more peace of mind by staying at home, like our pious, prudent friend, the Rev. Andrew Campbell."

"Scenes like this you have described," said Mr. Capel, "I am sorry to say, have been witnessed in other places than this neighborhood. The very first year I was on a circuit we had a difficulty nearly in the same way with the New Connection Methodists; I hope never to witness the like again. What happened there was a scandal to the whole church for months afterward; I would be ashamed to mention even now all that occurred."

"You need not tell me, brother; I think I know it just as well as if it was written for me; but I tell you now that before you are much older, you are likely to be present at a scene which may altogether surpass any you have yet witnessed. We shall see whether this sleek, jealous, undermining calumniator can do as he pleases, even protected as he will be by the streaming walls of a Baptist Conventicle. He no doubt has had every Presbyterian and Baptist and Congregationalist within his reach warned to attend; but we can play the same game, and in a way that will open their eyes and make their lank faces a little longer. We are as numerous as they are altogether, and I think that between this and Tuesday, we can get a sufficient number of our friends to vote down any hostile resolution, and turn the tables on them. What do you say, brother? Don't you think we can succeed?"

Mr. Capel was very reluctant to give an opinion; the very idea of another scene was not relished by him. He did not wish to anti-cipate trouble; but it was plain to him that Mr. Baker was determined to enter a contest and to drag him into it also. How was he to escape from this? The thought of going to a public meeting called for the ostensible purpose of promoting the circulation of the word of God, and then and there to enter into all the arrangements for a display of sectional strife and unholy disunion, was painful; it was actually to descend from his position as a preacher of peace to fraternize with men who gave way to angry feelings. He was very much perplexed. In the short period of his ministerial career, he had had sufficient proof of the bitterness and animosity that existed between sects. It was to him astonishing how preachers and people loudly boasting of a religion of peace and love, preaching about the "unity of the spirit," quoting texts about the "bonds of peace," and almost forever talking and writing and preaching about humility and harmony and brotherly love, and spending time and money in the circulation of an inspired book which was said to be sufficient to enlighten all to the way of virtue, and to make "the wolf and the lamb feed together, and the lion eat straw like a bullock," and yet to find these very people who were always pitying and rebuking the heathen and the unbelieving and the ungodly, as willing and as ready on certain occasions to indulge hatred, engage in strife, and harbor malice as the veriest barbarian! He often wondered at the pompous and expensive display of physical force material by Christian nations and people, and of their readiness for battle and murder. He contrasted certain acts of so-called pious monarchs—the profuse shedding of human blood—with those of the rulers of even idolatrous people, and in nearly all cases he was forced to decide against the cruelty of Christian potentates, and to admit the many proofs of the superior spirit and humanity of imperial heathenism—the superiority of a Julian to a Constantine. But to think that the "people of God" should, by "anger and clamor and evil-speaking," degrade themselves even below those that knew not the Lord nor his word; to think that those who openly professed regeneration should by controversial brawls strengthen the position of the scoffer, was to him incomprehensible. He therefore did not wish to attend such a meeting; but how was he to escape?

"I will tell you what I think," said Mr. Capel, after some reflection. "I would far rather let these people have their own way than that we should follow in their footsteps and assist in perpetuating strife. Of what consequence is it to us whether a Methodist or a Baptist or an Independent is chosen as a delegate? The great cause of Christianity will not suffer, or be more benefited one way or other by the result. I therefore think that our wisest plan will be, to let things take their own course at the meeting, and no doubt a greater good will eventually result."

"See here, brother Capel," replied Mr. Baker, with assumed calmness, "such sentiments may do very well with persons who are real and true Christians; the course you advise might then be most proper toward such a class; but remember with whom we have to treat, men who are continually endeavoring to bring *our* church and *our* discipline into disrepute, who are madly jealous of *our* success, and who now try to lessen us in the estimation of the world.

"No; in this matter we must have our own way, we must fight them with their own weapons—ay, fight; the strongest will be sure to win;" and Mr. Baker quickly snapped his large bony fingers in defiance.

"Well, as for myself, brother Baker, I am but a stranger here yet, and I would not like to make my first appearance as a partisan. If, however, you think it right for me to attend, I will do so; but it will be rather to throw oil on the troubled waters, should any arise, than allow sectarian distrust and alienation to grow stronger. It may be after all, brother, that these people will give us no cause to complain."

"Indeed, I hope not. It would be a great satisfaction, a very agreeable disappointment, were I to discover that a better feeling existed; but I have little hope of that. I know them, and I know that the Calvinistic crowd will show their dark faces for a certainty. Yes, I am doubtful of Campbell, and, as you already know, not without cause. And, friend Capel, you must recollect that at the present day, when we find outsiders and the unconverted attracted toward a religious body as much on account of its reputed standing and influence and popularity—even by the size and grandeur of its churches—as by its intrinsic piety or merit, we must be on the look out, and, in a worldly sense, catch all we can. We must not allow our denominational interests to suffer through a sentimental diffidence, or a reluctance to enter the field as competitors. For a denominational prize, I will not shirk enrollment as a gladiator, not I; Greek to Greek, our church against all others. But, brother, we will talk this matter over tomorrow; it is now getting late, and after a word of prayer we will retire."

When Mr. Capel was left alone that night, a multitude of thoughts crowded upon him, and seemed to overturn each other in their struggle for precedence. He felt unnerved by an utter feeling of loneliness and despondency. He had but lately left his native country, Ireland, and was now for the first time among people comparatively unknown to him. His father had been dead for several years, and he had seen within the last fifteen months the remains of his brother and mother conveyed to the silent grave; he had now scarcely a relative living, and was here thrown among strangers to follow a line of life not altogether in accordance with his own feelings, but more out of a dutiful compliance with the earnest and affectionate desires of a pious mother. Previous to her death, he had traveled nearly a year on a circuit near the city of Cork, in Ireland; and he had recently been advised by certain friends to offer his services to the English Conference. He came highly recommended, and the district chairman being anxious to supply the wants of a few places on the out-

skirts of London sent Mr. Capel for a few months under the superintendence of Mr. Baker until the next meeting of Conference.

No wonder then that his thoughts came fast, and that, from what he had just heard, he was nearly bewildered with strange ideas about contending sects and inconsistent teachers; about the sordid and unholy motives which seemed to actuate preachers as well as people. He was surprised at the vehemence of Mr. Baker, with whom he had but lately become acquainted. He thought of the strange mission that was to be imposed on him by a residence at Heath Cottage, and he tried to fancy what kind of a person Martin Mannors could be, of whom Mr. Baker spoke so bitterly—of whose impure and dangerous sentiments he had heard so much. Already he began to feel a distaste for his mission, and a prejudice against a person whom he had never yet seen, and whom it was expected he might enlighten.

But his own heart told him that such a prejudice was unfair, unmanly, and unjust, and he tried to banish the feeling with all his might. He disliked controversy, particularly when called upon to combat opinions against divine revelation. He could not rely upon his own strength with a wily adversary. He never doubted scriptural truth; but even to him, as well as to others, there were things in the Bible hard to be understood, but which he believed would be made plain "in the great day of the Lord." He felt a deep sympathy for Mrs. Mannors; and in humble confidence would strive to remove the mountain of unbelief that overshadowed her dwelling. He would simply do his best to establish divine truth, and if he failed, God would not judge him for neglect. He would take up this cross; and if he succeeded, would he not bring happiness to one home, and would not his mother in heaven rejoice with the vast assembly of saints at the repentance of a sinner, and whose conversion he might after ward claim as a seal to his ministry?

The mild moon was shining through his window as he looked out, and her soft, sympathizing light brought back the most tender recollections. Memory presented its fairest pictures, and the dim scene in the distance was changed in imagination to his own still loved home. He heard his mother's evening hymn, and again he saw his little tired brother sit sleeping by her side. In imagination he stood once more upon the pleasant banks of the river Lee, and wandered away among the green meadows by its margin; he saw the well known tall trees, and their long shadows on its shining water. He looked again; but that home had faded with the past; the dear ones had fled, and the pure love of that mother's eye would be seen no more forever. In his dreams, that night he again heard the sweet sounds of the Bells of Shandon, and again he saw the waters of the pleasant river; but before he awoke, he was once more standing and weeping by his mother's grave, hand in hand with his tired brother, in the old churchyard of St. Finn Bar.

CHAPTER VI

THE church in which the Rev. Andrew Campbell officiated was situated on the high road between London and Hampstead, rather closer to the city. Indeed, speaking more correctly, it might be said to be within the suburbs which every year stretch out farther and farther. His pastoral charge, however, included a very extensive district and extended to the north as far as Hampstead. The church was therefore in a central situation, and was very convenient not only for the regular ministrations, but for the occasional transaction of other matters affecting the interests of the denomination to which it belonged. It was also a very suitable place for clerical reunions, and for small private meetings of such of the ministers, elders, and deacons of other religious bodies as understood each other, and who were prepared to fraternize and form a compact against the encroachments of a sectarian enemy. At these quiet conventions, a great many plans were matured, and when any important object was to be attained, a special meeting could be easily held at the shortest notice.

In old times, to be sure, before the establishment of Methodism, the Presbyterians in and about London formed a very strong body of Christians, who, with the additional force of other dissenters and non-conformists were often very successful in their attacks on the proud pretensions of the Episcopal Church. For many years, the united efforts of these bodies were mainly directed against the Establishment, which, like a leviathan, was confident of its own strength, and satisfied with its envied position as a national institution. But in the course of time, when Methodism raised its head and became a power on the earth, a "little horn which waxed exceeding great," those bodies discovered in it an insidious and dangerous intruder; one most likely to attract the common people, and, therefore, more to be feared than the old State Church which was fast losing ground in popular affection. The great policy of the Church Establishment seemed to be the acquisition of wealth and political power, and as long as that object was secured, it was not of so much importance as to the number of its adherents: wealth and power will always attract followers enough to secure for the grossest usurpation and tyranny a spurious popularity. As long as the church had the monarch and a majority of the nobility and great men of the nation, and as long as its status of superiority was legally acknowledged, the English hierarchy were quite indifferent as to the clamorings of disappointed and disaffected aspirants.

But Methodism was a power that made itself felt. From small beginnings, it gradually grew and gained strength; stooping to conquer, and leaving nothing undone to gain the multitude. At last it strode out like a pampered giant, lifting in its brawny arms first the poor and illiterate, then impulsive working men and traders, then the more intelligent and worldly wise—class above class—until finally, bearing its head aloft, it entered with stately step the palace of the people, and placed its representatives on the floor of the imperial parliament.

This was a power, then, to be dreaded. In little more than a century, from an insignificant sect it had gained such a footing in Britain as to leave nearly all other denominations completely in the shade. Churches that for centuries had stood the successive assaults of Popery and Prelacy now became more and more forsaken and desolate; and the once popular preachers of the metropolis had often to deliver their lengthy and somniferous expositions to bare walls and empty seats, while Wesley and Whitfield were followed from place to place, and could only accommodate increasing and excited multitudes by winning them to Christ under the great cathedral vault of heaven.

It was difficult, indeed, for ordinary human nature to stand this. It was not easy to feel indifferent, and see your household scattered; to see the children you had nurtured and trained from lisping infancy leave you in their sturdy manhood, and give to strangers the comfort and support to which you considered yourself entitled by the natural ties of spiritual consanguinity.

But, it might be said, what difference did it make, if the children about whom you were so anxious were now receiving an abundance of every thing necessary, and were plentifully supplied with bread of a better quality than that perhaps which you yourself had to offer; what difference did it make if you were desirous to start them in life with a certain amount of capital, and that another person came forward and generously granted them a sum greater than your limited means could insure—what was the difference?

This mode of reasoning might satisfy some, but if you were doubtful of the quantity of nutriment your children were getting; if you were dissatisfied as to the quality of bread, or had discovered by your own testing that it contained a subtle poison which would produce drivelling idiocy, or a desire for death; or if you believed that instead of their being the recipients of a liberal allowance, they were but meagrely fed, and while busy, laboring, handed to strangers the wages of their toil which you needed so much yourself; if you saw this, and could see your children pass you, and even disown you, would there not be a feeling of resentment against the obtruder?

It was from this stand-point that Methodism was judged by the older sects to which the people were once so much attached; and it required more grace and patience than had yet been bestowed to become reconciled to the rule of such specious pretenders.

Policy, however, demanded great caution in making an attack on a system which had already obtained such a hold on the popular mind; the approaches should be made with secrecy. It would not do to array powerful texts, and openly denounce its anti-scriptural teachings with regard to election and predestination and backsliding; it would not do to speak too rudely about its unlearned preachers and their noisy harangues, their pulpit shouting, or their wild, absurd, and maddening protracted meetings. Religion has at all times best succeeded when the feelings were enlisted in its favor; and if the Methodists were so eminently successful by such strategy, a reserve in denouncing their peculiar mode might be most prudent. In the course of time, the most excitable people would begin to reason, and reason would bring reflection, and reflection, even in such matters, might bring common sense. If a man becomes infatuated, it is not always the best way to set him right by force of ridicule; opportunities would arise when a blow could be struck without observation; there was even then a Methodist schism, several branches had been lopped off the parent tree, and the disinterested hand of apparent sympathy might be extended to these scions without evincing too great a desire to increase the rupture or advance secession.

Thus thought many of the principal men of the older sects; and they acted accordingly. There was the usual display of courtesy, pulpits were exchanged, there were union prayer meetings, and fraternization at public meetings; there was the mutual denunciation of Popery, and the tacit understanding against the High Church; and, therefore, while on the surface every thing looked calm and pleasant, there was in reality a working of deep designs, and a determination, when opportunity offered, of detracting and humiliating the rampant Methodism of the day.

On the evening before the meeting which Mr. Baker was notified to attend, there was a special reunion in Mr. Campbell's church of most of the principal ministers and official members of the Presbyterian, Baptist and Congregational churches, and of one or two minor sects. Besides the usual number of ministers, deacons, and elders, there were also some of the great ones present on the occasion. Dr. Theophilus Buster, moderator of the General Assembly, attended; so did the Rev. Caleb Howe, a distinguished preacher and administrator of the Baptists; there were also the Rev. Jonah Hall of the Independents, and some of the most shrewd and active members of other denominations.

Dr. Buster, the moderator, was sitting at the end of a large table near the vestry door, and three or four ministers sat close by, exclusively engaged on some subject of importance. There seemed to be a disagreement; for occasionally a fist would come down on the table with sufficient force to attract the attention of other persons dispersed in twos and threes in different parts of the church. The discussion at the table related to some plan which was to be submitted to all present that evening, and seemed to keep the reverend debaters somewhat restless; while the mutter of conversation around indicated a probable difference of opinion on the subject which then engaged attention.

An indifferent looker-on that evening would have readily discovered that even the select ministers there assembled were not of one mind; and that within the very precincts of Mr. Campbell's sanctuary all was not harmony. Faint whispers, those shadows of thought, after awhile gave way to loud words which followed faster and faster from the lips of excited men. Away from the rest, two deacons sat astride of a form, and facing each other; they had once been members of the Close Communion Church under the pastorate of the Rev. Caleb Howe; but recently, one of the deacons became more liberal, and allied himself to the Open Communionists. For this he was chided by his more steadfast and conservative brother; there was a lively controversy for a time, and a grand flourish of texts in attack and defense of their different views.

"I tell you what, John," said the steadfast deacon, "you left us because you had itching ears, and wanted to hear novelties. The Scriptures are plain and positive on the subject of my belief, and any who will not conform to the strict letter of the law have neither part nor lot in the matter. 'Come out from among them, and be ye separate,' is the command, and you know it, John, as well as I do."

"And why don't you keep separate?" replied the other. "The Regular Baptists show the same inconsistency that you do now. Here you are among unbelievers in one of your very essentials—ready to take counsel from them and advise with them upon church matters; and yet you believe that the majority present, because they differ in opinion with you, are outside of the pale, and unregenerate. Tut, man, if I didn't think these people fit to sit with me at the table of the Lord, I would keep clear of them altogether. I have read and re-read the tract of the great Robert Hall on your illiberal Close Communion; he was a true Baptist, and I well remember his words. He wrote, 'It is too much to expect an enlightened public will be eager to enroll themselves among the members of a sect which displays much of the intolerance of Popery.' These were the deliberate words of that saint; get over them if you can."

"Ay; but Robert Hall, the saint as you call him, wasn't gospel," said one of a few listeners who had gathered around the pair of deacons; "neither was he what I would wish a man to be who pretended to continue 'stead fast and immovable.'"

"There was no pretense about him, friend; you haven't a man among you, at any rate, that is his equal," replied another.

"I think," said a Presbyterian brother, siding with the defender of Mr. Hall, "I think that man was an honor to this age; and although I entirely differ from his opinion as to what Christian baptism ought to be, he was a man of free mind and made of the right kind of stuff. If a person finds himself in error, he ought not to be called inconsistent because he is willing to be set right, and then sticks to what he has proved to be truth."

"Eh, now, friend, but that's a strange view to take," said the steadfast man. "I doubt if ever any one who had the witness of the Spirit would be so ready to change his opinion at every hand's turn as to the meaning of the plain command of God. Robert Hall's belief as to how baptism ought to be administered was right enough; but when he advocated open communion with the supporters of infant sprinkling, he was wrong. We can't budge a peg from the true word; nay, man, we have no right to recognize people as worthy communicants who have not been properly baptized."

"Infant sprinkling! Well, do you mean to say," retorted the other, "that any Christian man who has not been thrust under water like a gaping duck has not received the proper baptismal rite? Do you mean to say to my face that I am not yet baptized; I, who was sprinkled by the great Doctor Chalmers himself even before I was a week old?"

"I mean, friend, that unless we are, according to Colossians the 2d and 12th, *buried* with him in baptism, we will be buried in the earth without it. A mere fillip of mist in the face may do for Methodists and such Papist-like folk, but will never do for men who wish to conform to the plain word—never, man."

"Ah, mon! but yee're delooded!" struck in an irritated North Briton, "ye wad twist an twist the scriptur to suit yoursel. Wha merit hae ye in a ploonge aboon a sprinkle? ye hae nae mickle. Why the poorest body o' a Methodist wad sniffle a' that."

A Congregationalist brother now came to the rescue of the church of John Knox, and insisted that the language used against infant baptism was not what might be expected from any person who knew any thing of divine grace. It ill became a set of sour, deluded divers at the present day to cast a reflection on the descendants of men who had shed their blood for the truth. It was a proof that the baptism of which they boasted so loudly was not sufficient to bestow that charity that 'thinketh no evil;' and as the brother grew warmer on the subject, his declamation became stronger.

At this stage of the discussion, there was quite an excitement, and it was apparent that any thing but a religious feeling, or even a desire to exhibit ordinary forbearance, was manifested by a large majority of those present. By this time, several of the ministers had approached, and stood here and there, outside the circle of heads that surrounded the original combatants; and while the deacons and their respective adherents still hotly contended, the ministers took sides, and from their winks, nods, and gestures of impatience, it might be only reasonable to infer that something more serious than an ordinary altercation would ensue unless a stop were put to the gross irregularity of a few hot-headed men. It would be a curious thing, indeed, to see the validity of a religious doctrine tested within the very walls of a church by a resort to physical force, or by a display of the barbarous science of the trained athletes so disgustingly detailed in *Bell's Life*. There would be a nice winding up of this little reunion of select saints, if it may be the moderator himself had to leave the sacred edifice with a bandage over his eye, or his arm in a sling. What an example for unbelievers! and what hosannas would be sung alike by High Church and Papist! What heart-breaking comments would be conspicuously printed in the Methodist *Watchman* of the ensuing week! It would never do. Baptists and Pedobaptists,

and all others engaged must at once give up the unseemly strife, and turn their attention to the common enemy.

An announcement was made that the moderator desired to make a few remarks on the present aspect of affairs, in relation to the position and prospects of the denominations represented by the persons present, and to devise means whereby a greater union could be established between themselves, in order to expose the errors and spiritual delinquencies of an aspiring sect, and to prove that its pretended zeal was not so much for the glory of God as for the honor and emolument, particularly of its clerical adherents.

An intimation to this effect was made in a hurried manner by one of the elders, who, while speaking, kept extending and closing his arms, and gently thrusting himself between some who still stood their ground, as if indifferent to any thing else but the merits of the particular mode of baptism which they had been advocating. By dint of patience, however, and by giving the wink of fellowship to one, and a confidential nudge to another, and by the gentle force of a few of the more sensible and discreet of the brethren, the principals were separated, and in a few minutes nearly all were found either seated or standing in front of the table occupied by the moderator and ministers; but although a truce was thus obtained, it could be easily perceived from the number of excited eyes, and from certain flushed faces, and by the lingering looks of defiance that passed from one to another, that the troubled waters had not yet fully subsided.

The Rev. Andrew Campbell, minister of St. Andrews Church, in which the present little assembly met, was a stout, low-sized man, evidently well fed. He had a florid face and reddish hair; he wore spectacles over a pair of very prominent eyes, and his countenance indicated no very marked intelligence. There was, as had been once observed, a kind of clerical sheepishness about his looks which his reputed learning could not qualify; but as he had been indoctrinated into the complexities of Calvinism at an early age, and had the training necessary to enable him as a Presbyterian teacher to explain passages of scripture in support of that belief, he was ever ready to combat antagonistic opinions, and was stubborn enough to retain his own views at any sacrifice, even against the many contradictory texts to be found in the Bible in support of opposite tenets.

Nearly in front of this favored pastor sat the Rev. Caleb Howe, the Baptist minister; he was a little taller and a great deal thinner than his clerical brother of St. Andrews; he, too, wore spectacles, but they were slightly shaded and it was no doubt uncharitably said, that they were worn as much to hide the "cast" in one of his eyes as to be of assistance to his vision. He was mild in appearance, and one would imagine of a constitution too delicate to administer a spiritual bath to another without injury to himself. Notwithstanding, however, the little rumpus that had just taken place, he seemed to be in no way disconcerted, but was now just as ready for other business as he would have been to defend his idea of the proper baptismal rite, were it necessary.

Then, there was the Rev. Jonah Hall, the Independent minister. He was known as one of the most popular preachers in London, rather humorous occasionally, and his pulpit jokes were retailed far and wide, while his church was generally filled with the most select and fashionable of congregations. He was a wiry, determined-looking man, alternately affected by pride and humility; but in defense of the faith, one upon whom you might rely, and one who was ever ready to back his opinions, either by words or blows, or in any other manner most convenient to an opponent.

The other ministers were unobtrusive looking persons, connected with small sects, yet men who felt that their spiritual authority was something to be recognized; and some of the elders and deacons were sufficiently belligerent in aspect to justify the conclusion, that in a moral combat, not to go any further, you might rely on them as being steadfast and uncompromising. One could, however, observe that most of the persons just referred to, particularly the ministers, tried to appear very mild and courteous, and such was their ordinary address, unless agitated by doctrinal disputes, which it seemed were too often prevalent, even among the reputed heralds of peace.

But the individual considered the most important personage present that evening was the Rev. Dr. Theophilus Buster, who, by special request, favored the brethren with his presence; and with a few exceptions all within the church paid him the greatest deference and attention. He was a very tall man, portly and pompous in appearance; he stood erect, and his height seemed to be increased by the manner in which his coarse bristly hair was brushed up from his low receding forehead. He certainly wished to be considered a person of no ordinary importance, and he used all the recognized airs to make that impression. He wore a suit of the deepest clerical black, cut and fitted in the most approved style; a neck-cloth of spotless white was wound around his stout neck in such a manner as if intended to splice his head to his body more securely; an exceedingly white pair of shirt-wrists peeped out below his coat sleeves, and though the severe look of his cold grey eye was not obscured by spectacles, yet there was pendant from his neck a rich gold-mounted eye-glass attached to a plain black ribbon; this ornament must have added much to his dignity; for when he gave one of his many formal bows, the little glistening glass would tip against the chain of his gold repeater, and make a tinkling sound, like that which in some places might be expected to announce the coming of some great high priest.

Then his clerical attitude was most perfect —perfect dignity. His head and shoulders were thrown back, and his thumbs inserted into the arm-holes of his smoothly fitting vest, giving to his soft open hand on each side, the appearance of a rudimentary wing, which might be supposed to indicate a preparation for his final flight from the pomps and vanities of this world to a more exalted sphere of labor.

He was dignified; not a smile cheered the sage serenity of his countenance. He was superbly demure, and in nearly every other respect fitted to make a profound impression on the ordinary race of believers. From his tact and finesse in the pulpit, he won the religious affections of his congregation—the ladies in particular were enraptured—and by such means his church became crowded with admiring worshipers, and his pews were let at exorbitant rates, the gross rental being annually a very large sum. He was also immensely popular with his more wealthy hearers; and by his courtesy and address toward his ministerial brethren, by his advocacy of sound Calvinistic views, and demand for a puritanical observance of the Sabbath, he won his way until he attained the important position as moderator of the General Assembly.

Dr. Buster's influence with the ladies of his flock partly arose from another cause; he was laboring under a painful difficulty, of a domestic nature. Thoroughly orthodox, he could never sanction any under his control to interpret Scripture so as to conflict with his ideas; and while he abhorred a schismatic, he seemed to exult in pronouncing a dreadful woe against any unfortunate who dared to doubt a single passage of the word of God. Strange to say, his own wife differed from him. Her mind had been cast in a different mould from his; she was highly intelligent, liberal in opinion, and benevolent, and could not be forced to believe contrary to her convictions. She was not sufficiently passive to be the wife of a minister; she would make no empty formal profession; and this independence of thought and action highly exasperated the doctor, and ultimately led to alienation, and systematic persecution. Of this, she was at last forced to complain; but the doctor won the sympathy of true believers. He made affecting private appeals to many of the chief men, and to some of the admiring women, who were spiritually fed by his hand. None would countenance the recreancy of his wife; he was looked upon as an afflicted man, whose efforts to establish truth should be applauded. None would believe that he was capable of harshness; and when he was thus sustained by nearly all, he became more positive and exacting, until it was at last rumored that a separation had taken place, that his domestic happiness was at an end, and that his wife had taken her departure, none knew whither.

He was now left the sole guardian and protector of his two children, a boy and a girl, both of tender years. He had placed them under the care of an old housekeeper who had lived for some time in his family, and subsequently under the management of a more active person, who was a member of his own church, a woman who would be sure to impress their minds with sound religious principles. No wonder then, deserted as he was, that the doctor had so many fair sympathizing friends. The ladies of his congregation looked upon him as one whose name might yet be handed down to posterity as an example of patience under affliction. Therefore, as an injured uncomplaining man in the cause of truth, his trials were almost a constant theme at tea-parties; and a great portion of the time, not taken up by missionary or church affairs, was spent by his spiritual sisters and daughters, in devising how to add a little comfort or sunshine to the dreary, wintry life of this suffering and exemplary Christian pastor.

There were some reputed wise ones, however, who were bold enough to assert that the chastened moderator was not altogether a true pattern of saintly perfection. There were many, who, like the Rev. Jonah Hall, for instance, thought he was but a specious pretender, a cold, unfeeling hypocrite, and that time would yet develop his true character. There were murmurs and mutterings here and there, that the doctor's public and private life were in sad contrast. What had become of his wife? Did he cast her from him, or was she now the hidden victim of his resentment? Was it possible that he knew nothing of her? Why did he keep his house like a prison, and his children with a stranger? There was something irreconcilable in his conduct; and, as these things were, time after time, mooted, the knowing ones grew daily more mysterious.

But the doctor stood fair with the members of his own church; such defaming reports grew out of sectarian jealousy—nothing else could be expected. The great Presbyterian body looked upon him with pride as the embodiment of learning and piety; and now, as he was about to address the few assembled in St. Andrew's Church, wrangling elders and deacons subsided, and all awaited in silence.

The reverend doctor, on rising with a kind of easy dignity to address the few around him, first drew from his pocket a white cambric handkerchief which he delicately applied to his lips, as if to remove any impediment to the flow of words which might be expected to follow. He then made a stately inclination and commenced:

"Rev. gentlemen and most esteemed friends, a concurrence of circumstances has rendered it imperative on me to solicit your attention for a short period this evening. I desire to state a few important facts, for the purpose of stimulating you to prompt action against encroachments of a peculiar nature. I wish not to excite an unchristian ebullition, or a mere effervescence of transient indignation. No, my friends, we must not be betrayed into any unseemly demonstration; we must proceed cautiously. Therefore, first, I desire calm deliberation, secondly, confidence and coöperation, and thirdly, strenuous and persevering effort."

He paused; the lengthened words uttered with such classical precision by the learned doctor seemed to have stepped out from his lips with measured pace, and to have ranged themselves about him like a body-guard of grenadiers.

No wonder that the Rev. Andrew Campbell should look upon this fountain of eloquence with a feeling of denominational pride. No wonder that elders and deacons, and simple pastors should stand almost amazed at the sound of language which they could scarcely comprehend; while others huddled closer to the speaker, as if they fully understood the deep meaning, at the close of the finished period.

The learned doctor continued for some minutes in the same strain. He again urged them to be active; and though he cautioned them to be as wise as serpents, he was forgetful of the context concerning harmlessness of doves. He made some very pointed and severe remarks about the illiterate and presumptuous preachers of the day; he alluded to one particular sect which he said was as overbearing in its ignorance as was the Church of St. Peter—the Romish—with all its scholastic attainments. An effort must be made to keep such men in their proper position. It was not for Presbyterians, who, through many trials, had once held in submission the Popery and Prelacy of a former period, to retire before such a religious rabble; something more than a formal protest was necessary; it would never do to leave the field to others.

By this time the doctor grew warm; the dignified placidity which at first seemed to hang like a silken vail over his face, was now drawn aside, and a countenance depicting fierce and vindictive passion was exposed to view; even his very admirers felt somewhat uneasy at the transition, and found relief when he took his seat and applied the white handkerchief to his heated brow.

There was a murmur of applause, but it was only a murmur. The brethren breathed more freely, and looked at each other as if they had but just escaped from some impending danger.

In a moment or two, the Rev. Mr. Howe stood up; he approved of what the Rev. moderator had suggested, and remarked that he was quite free to admit the services and pious determination of his Presbyterian brethren in times past, but they must not forget what others had done. No religious body of people were ever more ready to make a sacrifice for the truth than the Baptists, of whom he was an unworthy minister. He wished to speak plainly; he had no confidence in the pretensions of Methodists or their allies. He had been among them often, and had once hoped that people who could meet and pray together for the dissemination of the word, and for the downfall of Popery—not excepting that of the High Church—would find no reason to be on their guard against each other. The Methodists were full of monopolizing designs, he could not trust them; and he regretted that after all that had been said and done by the boasted Evangelical Alliance, sectarian jealousy still existed and was particularly manifested by the Wesleyans.

These remarks were agreeably received. The spirit of the meeting was, "Down with the Methodists!"

"I am glad that the Reverend gentleman has partly explained himself," said the Rev. Jonah Hall, of the Independents, "though I wish that while he is so liberal toward Presbyterians and Baptists, he would not be so forgetful of what Independents have done. I hope," said he humorously, "that he does not intend to leave my particular friends out in the cold, or to classify them with the blatant ranters of the day. The Independents could and would be independent of all others, if necessary; they had suffered in the cause, and would occupy no secondary position in the struggle for right. But, friends, we have not met here to discuss private opinions of superiority; we came here to try and counteract the mischievous designs of a common enemy, and this is the time and place to begin the work."

There were cries of "hear, hear," and the worthy men assembled felt as if they were about entering into the spirit of the thing.

"I tell you what," he continued, "no matter now about the trifling differences that may exist among ourselves, we must put a stop to the gallop of these Methodist cavaliers who are cantering about so confidently. It may be some time yet before they take the beggar's ride; but the swaddlers are on horse-back, and as they are the chief beggars of Christendom, the adage must come true, for they will surely, ride to the—well, of course, in this place, and in presence of so distinguished a divine—" and he accompanied this ironical expression with a bow to the moderator—"I won't say where. Anyway, we must put a five-barred gate in their way that they can't jump."

There was a burst of applause, some loud laughter, and fresh cries of, "hear him, hear him." The Rev. moderator about this time began to show symptoms of displeasure. Had they forgotten who he was? His dignity was hurt; for the speaker's irony was rather pointed. This was a case of ministerial jealousy, the general result of mixed assemblies.

"Now, my friends," continued Mr. Hall, "we have the ranters in a corner. They want to flourish again at Exeter Hall. Let us meet them to-morrow night on our own ground, and rout them. Let us now decide who shall be nominated to-morrow evening as our delegate at the coming anniversary; by so doing, we go there prepared to take the wind out of their sails."

"Yes, that's it," cried two or three, "let us go prepared for them, and have our man ready."

The Rev. moderator now suggested that such a course might be premature; the number then present was too insignificant to take a proceeding of that kind. They would meet many additional friends to-morrow evening who might wish to have a voice in the selection; and were they now to name a person for a delegate, it would be unpleasant to be obliged to lay him aside. It would be better to let the delegate be chosen at the regular meeting.

The Rev. Andrew Campbell concurred in this view. It would no doubt be more prudent to leave the selection to the meeting; while here, they could make other arrangements.

The Rev. Jonah Hall could not see the force of such objections to a nomination. What other arrangement could they make at present? He could not understand the motive for delay. "With all due deference to the superior judgment of the distinguished moderator," said he, in his former ironical strain, "there might be a few present who would approve of taking action at once. Let us choose some name to be presented at the meeting; none of our absent friends can object. We are now comparatively calm; we might not be so much so to-morrow evening."

"I propose," said an Open Communion brother, starting up, "that the Rev. Jonah Hall be the person nominated."

Cries of "no, no, yes, yes," were now heard. Several persons spoke out together, and some curious expressions were audible. The moderator and Mr. Campbell jumped up at the same moment, and almost with one voice rudely condemned the proposal.

Already, there was not only a division but a subdivision. The moderator, and Mr. Campbell, and Mr. Howe, the Regular Baptist minister, with a few others, were in favor of delay; while the Rev. Jonah Hall, and the members of his church, one or two other preachers, and nearly all of the Open Communionists were for proceeding at once; while still a few others from each party stood apparently indifferent, but ready to join the majority.

A considerable time was thus spent, as it were, in charging and counter-charging. The Rev. Jonah Hall and his supporters being most numerous, would not give way, but continued in angry altercation and bitter recriminations. The Rev. Mr. Campbell was denounced in his own church. He might, he was told, order them out if he liked; but if he tried to overrule them as he seemed willing to do at present, the motive would be only too plain. If he had a majority on his side sufficient to support the nomination of the moderator, all would be pleasant enough; but the moderator was not the man for them, and they would endeavor to prove it on the very first opportunity.

The discomfited minister of St. Andrew's had to hide his mortification the best way he could. The result of this select meeting was very unexpected. He had hoped that the merits of Dr. Buster would have been sufficient to decide in his favor; and although he expressed a desire to delay the nomination of any person for delegate, yet he would not have made the least objection had the doctor been chosen.

What an utter want of appreciation and respect was thus shown by the leader of an insignificant sect toward such a person as the moderator of the General Assembly! In a few minutes, the manifestations were fast becoming personal, and the spirit of sect was again in the ascendant. The moderator and his particular friends were in high dudgeon, and were preparing to leave the church; but the Rev. Jonah Hall and his party, desirous of showing their contempt of the whole proceeding, collected in a body, and as they hastened away together, the heavy bang of the great church door resounded through the whole building.

Half an hour after the departure of these great religious luminaries, the sexton of St. Andrew's extinguished the lesser lights in that church—what purpose had they served? and as he walked away, alone, along the dreary street, he met shivering women and hungry children; and he looked back at the stately proportions of the edifice, looming up in the misty night, and thought of the thousands of homeless wanderers who would be glad to find even temporary shelter within such walls. But there is no humanity in their marble bosoms; those splendid and costly religious monuments could not be desecrated to charity. They were not erected as a refuge for the wretched and forlorn; they were not intended for the mitigation of real suffering. If they do not open their spacious doors to shelter the living poor, they can, like the great Abbey of Westminster, receive and protect the withering remains of the wealthy dead.

CHAPTER VII.

IF the Rev. Dr. Buster had reason to feel aggrieved at the want of courtesy shown him in St. Andrew's church, and at the indignity to which he had been subjected by the minister of a petty sect of Independents, he felt in some degree compensated by the distinguished reception he met with at the house of his reverend friend, Mr. Campbell. When it was known that the doctor was to be the guest of the minister of St. Andrew's, the ladies of that congregation turned out in companies of five, or six, and, by their constant calls for several hours, fairly besieged the dwelling of their pastor, which was for the present to be the transient or rather temporary abode of one of the elect, whose Calvinistic virtues and domestic long-sufferings endeared him to so many.

It is almost needless to say, that the reverend doctor was always particularly pleased by such attentions. To be ministered unto by the soft hands of Christian sisters, and to be looked at with affection through their softer eyes, ought, in a measure, to enable any man to feel reconciled or indifferent to the unkindness or hostility of his unscrupulous opponents in the struggle for precedence or distinction. The reverend doctor was but a man in these matters, and was highly gratified at meeting with many of his fair friends; and to look at him, as he sat in the handsome parlor of Mr. Campbell, surrounded by so much sweet sympathy, one might be led to suppose that the doctor would be willing to suffer some slight misfortune every day, in order to be restored by such a delightful remedy.

To woman, in every relation of life, man is indebted for his noblest and most persevering efforts. Without the cheering word or stimulating smile of woman, many a vast project would have been forsaken, and many a conspicuous laurel never worn; and, although the orthodox of the present day might not, in all cases, be willing to select the women of the Bible as patterns of feminine goodness, or domestic virtue, or as models for the heroines of modern civilization, yet it is asserted that without her influence religion would decay or languish into the most trivial formality; that patriotism would become extinct, and that many of our most cherished notions would be forsaken.

In every age of the world, woman figures on the page of history as the handmaid of religion. No matter in what form it has appeared, how rude or how perfect has been its revelation, she has favored its progress and has assisted in its extension, either as priestess, sibyl, vestal, or nun. The Roman, as well as the Reformed Church is loud in her praise; and Protestant missionaries would have very little success without her coöperation. Among the distant, rude, half-starved tribes, the missionary's wife in the kitchen may be often far more persuasive than the missionary himself in the pulpit; and the shipwrecked mariner in his distress is often comforted by the prayer he learnt at his mother's knee, or by the possession of *her* Bible as the last endearing token of her memory.

All sects, therefore, readily acknowledge that by woman's pious industry churches are built, endowments made, missions established, Bibles printed, tracts circulated, Sunday-schools opened, and worldly comforts secured for ministers. In fact, by her zeal, nearly all the religious machinery of the age is lubricated and kept in operation. As her faith is unequaled, so her constancy is secure; and while doubting, reasoning, incredulous man is restlessly wandering in flighty speculation, woman's eye remains unalterably fixed on some bright particular star of hope, and it watches fondly and lovingly there forever.

It is well, then, that those devoted men who undertake the performance of so much ministerial drudgery can count on her assistance; and it is well that in seasons of personal trial, or spiritual adversity, sisters of the church, whether of Russia, Rome, England, or Utah, can be found ready to soothe the priesthood into forgetfulness of private wrongs, and encourage them to "press forward to the mark of their high calling."

This sweet influence had ever a most potent and peculiar effect on the Rev. Doctor Buster. No matter what private wrongs, what ministerial jealousy, what vile misrepresentations might disturb his Christian serenity, or cause him to feel for a moment the combative promptings of the old Adam still strong within him, when the fair members of his own denomination cared for him, and defended him, and prayed for him, what cause had he to fear? Why should he despond? Backed by such an angelic host, he could overpower every assailant, and triumph over every enemy.

The worthy doctor was, therefore, ever most gracious in his intercourse with Christian ladies; indeed, his preference for female society of any kind was a marked characteristic; but with sisters of the faith, he could for the time forget every thing of a personal nature; with them, even in the more formal interchange of spiritual courtesies, he appeared to realize perfect happiness. Thus it is that good men—the persecuted ministers of the Lord—are ever rewarded; thus, while the world affects to despise and frown upon humble servants of the cross, they are privileged to bask in the bright smiles of pious, devoted woman. What a sweet reward for personal sacrifice in the cause of religion, while the scoffer and the scornful may be but a prey to sullen discontent and uncertainty!

Next to the interest which the doctor's visit created, there was that caused by the meeting of the Branch Bible Society, to be held that evening. The doctor would be present on that occasion, and the ladies of Mr. Campbell's congregation were in a state of commotion: a number of fair collectors were marshaling their forces, and making out sums total; all were anxious to have a large amount placed to the credit of Presbyterian energy. Then there was to be a great preliminary tea-meeting, at which the doctor would ask the blessing; would not this be a treat? And then to hear him relate some missionary anecdote, or repay your own Sunday-school trials with one of his bland smiles; would not that be agreeable? It was altogether a time of great interest to the pious ladies crowded together, and one might be inclined to excuse the total neglect of sundry little household matters, when such affairs of religious importance had to be transacted; the Lord's business of course required their first attention.

However, while the soirée at which the doctor presided was comfortably crowded with the well-dressed ladies of St. Andrew's, and while the extensive tea-table at Mr. Campbell's was enlivened by innocent chit-chat, and by the smart witticisms and soft flattery of the moderator, the Rev. Jonah Hall was similarly engaged at a tea-meeting in his own house. There, also, many of the gay but sanctified sisters of Israel met to sip Bohea and discuss its price; and afterward to ascertain the amount of local collections for the circulation of the Great Book, and to make out certain lists of lady collectors for the ensuing year. Presbyterians, and Methodists, and others had of late succeeded in getting a choice of such officials almost to the exclusion of the Independents, and an attempt was to be made at the meeting that night to rectify this omission, as well as to teach Dr. Buster and other aspiring people a lesson of humility. Pastors are generally regarded with great interest by the female members of their congregations, and the Rev. Jonah Hall was not an exception. There was a certain dash about him which made his manner rather attractive to the younger women of his flock; and of course, in their opinion, he was every way superior to the pompous, pretentious moderator of the Presbyterian Assembly.

After these respective tea-meetings were over, it was expected that all concerned would wend their way to the Baptist church. The annual gathering of the friends of the Hampstead Branch Bible Society was always an occasion of great interest to worldlings as well as to worshipers; more particularly to pious dissenters. Indeed, taking it altogether, the society was a popular institution. To be an officer, to be one of its many vice-presidents, or to be able to contribute a fair amount to its funds was sure to pay, or to turn out a good investment. The meeting that evening would no doubt be very interesting; it would be like Exeter Hall on a small scale; there would be the local ministers of several denominations; there would be a few great ones, like Doctor Buster; and there would be anthems and anecdotes, and speeches, and thrilling extracts from missionary reports. And then how pleas-

ant it would be to see ministers and members of different sects meet as one body, act with one spirit, and be enlivened by the same Gospel vitality; it would be pleasant, indeed; would it not be a sight to abash the scoffer and infidel? There would be the place to prove how Christians could be "kindly affectionate one to another, in honor preferring each other." That would be the place to put unbelievers to shame, and to prove how worthless were the insinuations and predictions uttered against Christian fellowship. Yes, the harmony that should prevail among an assembly of believers would be an overwhelming evidence in favor of the "unity of spirit" and the "bonds of peace."

What wrecks of fancy are strewn upon the rocks of fact! Our once bright hopes are now but phantoms to the memory! Upon what moonbeams have our noblest structures been erected! How seldom are our most pleasing anticipations realized! how often, on the contrary, are the budding leaves of Hope suddenly withered and blown into our faces by some chilling blast of adversity! It is hard to see the creations of faith, that look so bright and beautiful in the distance, become dim and faded on nearer approach; but such is the experience of life, and the lesson is often and often taught us when perhaps we least expect its repetition.

While many of the good people who were then in social intercourse and enjoyment at the respective houses of the Rev. Mr. Campbell and the Rev. Jonah Hall, and while many other less demonstrative Christians were making preparations to attend the meeting that evening, the Rev. James Baker was at home with a few friends, making ready for the same occasion. He had only returned an hour or two previously, after having taken a long ride through various parts of his circuit, not for the purpose of filling his regular appointments, but he had been to places where he was sure to find some of the strongest friends of Methodism, and some of the stoutest and most bitter opponents of Calvinism. That his journey, for whatever purpose undertaken, had been successful, was apparent at a glance.

The preacher was in the best humor. It was quite plain that he felt like a man who held a trump card, that the game was secure, or that he could checkmate his opponent at the proper moment. The friends who were now his guests were men who could be relied on; their mental bias was unalterable. They were prominent local preachers and circuit stewards. They, too, had a confident look about them, which seemed to say, we're ready for a brush, for we know we can win. There was no mistaking their appearance as being church functionaries of some kind. They wore black coats of peculiar cut, and heavy whitish neckerchiefs; only one or two were dressed in a more worldly fashion.

Mrs. Baker also had company. A few of the members of her class had, as usual, remained after their religious duties were over, among whom was Mrs. Mannors. Altogether, there was a good number of persons present, mostly all of one mind, and lively in anticipation of an assured success. Tea had been provided for all, and the various topics pleasantly discussed at the table were on this occasion particularly interesting. After Mr. Baker and his friends had partaken of the good cheer, they retired, as if for a short rehearsal of the respective parts to be performed at the meeting. During their absence, the ladies continued sipping at their cups, and were engaged in the frivolous chat which among church-members becomes almost religious under the mild inspiration of Young Hyson.

Mrs. Mannors made some anxious inquiries about Mr. Capel. He had not yet returned from the circuit, but was expected every moment. She wished to let him know how pleased her husband felt that he consented to make her house his home for a season. She contented herself in the mean time, however, by edifying her sisters with the relation of a very strange dream she had had since her first meeting with the young preacher, and she was curious to know what would be his interpretation.

The church of the Rev. Caleb Howe, the regular Baptist minister, was a plainer edifice than St. Andrew's, but fully as large, and might possibly accommodate a greater number. Its pews were not so richly cushioned as the luxurious dens of the Presbyterian sanctuary, and, therefore, not so liable to be injured during demonstrations at religious anniversaries. The building was brilliantly lighted up; a spacious platform had been erected and covered with rich carpeting. There was a fine arm-chair for the president, and a small table at which the secretary could sit, with a sufficient number of chairs for the accommodation of the reverend gentlemen, and other speakers who were expected to address the meeting. It was yet early in the evening; only a few elderly persons had entered the pews, and several ladies of the congregation were completing sundry little arrangements necessary for the occasion.

There were two large arched doorways in front of the building. In a few minutes, there was a rush of persons through them, who, upon entering the church, hastily took possession of the front seats and pews, and of such other places as would afford the best views of the different speakers. The rush continued. In they came, disorderly enough; there was crushing and crowding for any spot nearest the platform, and with many persons there was as little propriety of manner as if they had been jostling each other at a circus. The respect usually shown for the house of the Lord now seemed to have been forgotten, and so punctual was the attendance on this particular evening, that in about half an hour from the time of the first rush, the church was completely filled in every part; even standing-room in any spot of the building could be found but with great difficulty. There was a perfect jam; and many of the more orderly church-goers wondered, no doubt, at the very unusual zeal or fervor exhibited by such a number of professed Christians.

There was not, however, the same hurry shown to occupy the platform; the chairs were yet vacant; and although there were a few elders and deacons present, they merely stood conversing in a quiet corner, as if awaiting orders. There were none of the rulers yet to be seen, unless the Rev. Mr. Howe, the pastor of the church, might be called one of that class. He was of course there to receive those who were about to honor his tabernacle; and lest there should be any show of impatience exhibited by the expectant crowd, he directed the choir to sing an anthem. The trained voices were soon heard; but before the anthem was ended, the Rev. Doctor Buster had been allotted the most conspicuous place on the carpeted elevation. He was followed or attended by the Rev. Mr. Campbell, and one or two others. The doctor had scarcely been seated before the Rev. Jonah Hall took up a position, and, immediately afterward, the Rev. James Baker, Mr. Capel, and the secretary, took their seats upon the platform. As each minister made his appearance, he made rather a formal bow to his clerical brethren, and a kind of partisan greeting could be heard here and there from people in the pews, though not sufficiently loud to attract any particular attention.

Other preachers had arrived; every thing was now ready. The different ministers and speakers were seated like enthroned saints before the assembly, and a deep silence prevailed, something of the same nature as the ominous stillness which it is said precedes for a short time an impending battle, while the combatants stand ranged before each other awaiting the dread command for the beginning of deadly strife.

The Rev. Mr. Howe, pastor of the church, stepped, at last, to the front of the secretary's table and gave out a hymn. He read it slowly, and then the choir, aided by a few of the ministers and by several voices in the body of the church, sung it through. Mr. Howe then called on the Rev. Andrew Campbell to offer up a prayer. That gentleman stood up, and having piously closed his eyes and lifted his hand, began a prayer which for genuine fervency could not be surpassed. He alluded to the gross darkness which once prevailed over the whole earth, and to the great and glorious effects of the Gospel in enlightening the human mind, and in dispelling the clouds of error and superstition which in times past had overshadowed the world. He spoke of the salutary influence of Christianity on the heart, and of its power in softening and humanizing men who were by nature and habit hardened in iniquity. Without the Gospel, what would the world be, how deplorable the condition of mankind; but what blessed results had followed in its footsteps. Now, the scoffer and unbeliever could witness its efficacy in bringing together men who were once aliens; in making men of every land and clime love each other with childlike simplicity, and in establishing a spirit of union and harmony among all who became subject to its divine influence. Yes, it was the proud boast of Christianity that it was peculiarly the religion of peace and love.

The reverend gentleman toiled for some time through the various repetitions of his prayer; he was felt to be tedious; but he, worthy man, was almost tearfully affected by the solemn sound of his own words, and no doubt many persons in the church followed him in his pious ejaculations. But there were two or three friends near him, who, although in the various attitudes of devotion most approved of by their respective sects, did not seem to heed his petition, but were intently watching the peculiar expression of his face. The Rev. James Baker knelt on one side of him, while the Rev. Jonah Hall stood in the opposite direction; and, although neither of the ministers could see the other, their steady gaze was fixed on the importuning pastor of St. Andrew's as if perfectly astonished by the liberality of his address, or at some personal singularity which seemed to engage their whole attention.

When the prayer was ended, another anthem was sung by the choir with good effect; and at the conclusion of this service, the secretary intimated that, as the president was unavoidably absent, it would be necessary to appoint a chairman, in order that the report might be read and the business of the evening forwarded.

He had scarcely finished these words before several persons started up, each as it determined upon naming a different gentleman for chairman. This was the cause of some confusion, as nobody could be distinctly heard. At last, during a momentary pause, the Rev. Mr. Baker rose, and moved that Thomas Bolster, Esq., take the chair.

Mr. Wesley Jacobs, a local preacher, seconded the motion.

Mr. John Thompson, a deacon of the Regular Baptists, said he regretted that such a motion had been made; it was a great breach of decorum to nominate any other than the vice-president; it was his place to take the chair in the absence of the president. He thought the motion of Mr. Baker was significant; it boded no good to the society. He would therefore move in amendment that the vice-president do take the chair.

The Rev. Doctor Buster said it was a very unusual thing indeed to exclude at a public meeting any officer from his proper place. The position of chairman was due this evening to the vice-president, and he would second the amendment.

There was then a great outcry on the platform. The Revs. Baker, Campbell, Dr. Buster, and others, all vociferating together, either for or against the amendment; while, at the same time, strong symptoms of excitement were manifest among the people.

Shouts of "Motion, motion, motion" were now heard around; and the secretary after some delay and much altercation declared the amendment carried, and called on Mr. Thomas Johnson, the vice-president, to take the chair.

A scene of great confusion now ensued; people in different parts of the church were using loud, angry words; and the wild and rapid gesticulations of many almost terrified the greater number of ladies present.

The vice-president then moved toward the chair, but it was pulled aside just as he was going to take his seat, and he would have fallen violently, were it not for the readiness and activity of the Rev. Mr. Hall in arresting his backward descent.

The Rev. Caleb Howe cried out, "Order, order, order!" and declared that such conduct was most disgraceful. He was going on to speak, but fresh cries of "Chair, chair, chair!" obliged him to retire without being further heard.

The vice-president at last became seated; but the Rev. Mr. Baker in an excited manner immediately cried out; "I protest against this decision. The chairman has not yet been fairly appointed; I move that—"

Here the uproar increased to such an extent that many left the pews and got upon the platform, which was now nearly crowded. Doctor Buster and the Rev. Jonah Hall stood face to face, as if boldly defying each other, and using gestures which might lead one every moment to expect that the argument between these brethren was not going to be entirely decided by mere noisy words.

The vice-president, in order the better to attract attention, now stood on the chair, and winding about his arms, loudly demanded to be heard even for a few moments. He must have had some courage to do this; for he was swayed about on his narrow standing place and one might expect every instant to see him fall over on the heads of the reverend combatants by whom he was surrounded.

"If you are Christians, I demand to be heard, I wish to say a few words. I will not detain you. Let me say only a—"

The Rev. Doctor Buster fairly staggered under the load of humanity that had just flopped into his arms. The poor vice-president was as much astonished at the suddenness of his own descent. There was no time for apology, and he as suddenly remounted the chair; and while the doctor was trying to recover his surprise and look calm, the vice-president again demanded the right to be heard for a few moments.

Appearances were now becoming more favorable for him. Voices from all sides were heard, and the words "Hear him, hear him!" came so fast and loud, that all seemed willing for a new issue by hearing somebody.

The vice-president then said, that it had been objected that he should occupy the chair at that meeting. Why such an objection was raised, he could not say. He did not wish to claim any right to dictate, but this he did know, that in any other place, or on any other occasion, or among the most worldly people, more respect would have been shown to any one occupying the position of vice-president of a society than had been shown to him by that assembly of Gospel ministers and professing Christians; even the well-known decency and decorum observed among open unbelievers should put them to shame. The usages of Exeter Hall were entirely different; such conduct would not be tolerated there for a moment. The professed object of the meeting that evening was to promote the circulation of the Holy Scriptures; but it was apparent that that was not the sole object of all present. If a sectarian battle had to be fought in that place, he would not be the umpire; neither would he be the standard-bearer for any party. He only saw an array of sect against sect, and not a union of well disposed men. He would now leave the chair, for he was pained to see Christianity so degraded by its professed friends.

"Then leave it at once," shouted some one at his elbow, after which there was cheering and hisses.

The Rev. Mr. Baker again called lustily for his nominee, Mr. Bolster. "I again demand that Mr. Bolster take the chair."

The noise was now much increased; there were hootings and cat calls from several parts; and the Rev. Mr. Howe once more tried to say something, but could not get a hearing.

The Rev. Jonah Hall here rushed to the front, raising and flourishing his shut fist; he wanted to know if British law would not protect them in their just rights; he wanted to know if—A concert of yells prevented another word from being heard, and after a continued struggle with the discordant crowd before him, he was forced to retire; but all the while made desperate efforts to raise his voice higher and higher.

The platform was now one scene of confusion. Doctor Buster still sat with an apparent stubborn indifference to what was going on; he cast occasional side glances at his Reverend brothers Hall, and Baker, and thought what a relief it would then be to him could he consistently throw aside, but for a few moments, his wearied, injured dignity, and give these irritating brethren a slight evidence of his physical power—even of his right arm and shut fist—or even the laying on of but one hand, that they long might remember. But this could not be; and the doctor still sat looking quietly at the side-lights—one would think the most patient of men—heroically indifferent to the squabbles of contending clergy and official members. Yes, there the doctor sat in exemplary forbearance, as the distinguished moderator of the General Assembly.

The Rev. Mr. Campbell was, however, very much agitated. He had for the last half hour made several attempts to speak; but as sure as he began, his words were drowned in groans, and hisses, and yells, innumerable; one could see his lips and jaws going, in a vain effort to make himself heard; yet, after having manfully faced the storm, making the best use of his most practical frowns, he had to retire in confusion from shouts of laughter. What made his case worse was, that by some means in the mêlée one of the glasses of his spectacles got knocked out; and as he violently waved and nodded his head about, the remaining glass gave his face a singular appearance as if he were trying to wink continually with but one glistening eye.

Again, cries and yells came from all parts of the church: "Chair, chair!" "Campbell!" "Bolster!" "Buster!" "Baker!" "Hall!" and then there was a waving of hats and handkerchiefs; and even many of the ladies now caught the excitement, and held up their hands, waving away violently whenever a favorite name was shouted.

It was now felt by nearly all present who could still think with any calmness within the circle of such a babel that to try and hold a meeting that night, and in that church, was, or would be, an utter impossibility. With the exception of Mr. Capel, and another young minister, every preacher, and deacon, and elder in the place was as excited and as ready for fight as his neighbor; and the continued shouting, and laughter, and confusion in the body of the church was almost deafening. The secretary had prudently bundled up his books and papers, and stepped down from the platform, anxious to push through the agitated mob that was still crushing and crowding. With some difficulty he was permitted to force his way to a side door, where he and a few others found egress from the building, and who were, no doubt, glad to reach the open air again.

At this stage of the proceedings, when nearly all were satisfied that it would be useless to try to transact any business, perhaps the only person then within the church who could say with any effect, "Peace, be still!" now advanced toward the secretary's table. There was no trace of either fear or excitement upon his countenance; he was perfectly calm, and his very appearance created such an interest in his favor that all seemed anxious to hear him speak. There was a lull in the storm, and in a few minutes the breathing of an infant might have been heard, so great was the sudden stillness.

Mr. Capel then stood before the people, and in a low, but audible voice, addressed them.

He said he was but a stranger, and he might say in a strange land. He had but lately left his own country to labor in their favored island, and in the vineyard of the Lord, among the followers of Knox, and Baxter, and Wesley. He did not come as the supporter of sectarianism. He did not want to know who was for a Paul, or for an Apollos, or for a Cephas; but who was for Christ. He appeared that night before them as his unworthy servant, to say that he was grieved at the great disunion manifested, and that it was plain to perceive that they seemed entirely forgetful of the great object for which they had ostensibly met. As it was, it would be now better to depart in peace, until some more gracious opportunity would bring them together. He felt pained to say one word by way of reproach, but he must speak plainly, and say, that God was dishonored among his own people, and in his own house. He would now ask all present to retire, and not by any further attempts at discord to bring the Gospel into contempt and give a triumph to unbelievers.

He spoke some time longer in the same strain; and his words had the desired effect with a number of persons. A great many immediately left the building; but the spirit of contention was not yet subdued, and the speaker no sooner took his seat than some one cried out:

"A speech from Doctor Buster!—Buster, wake up!"

The learned doctor felt indignant to be thus rudely called out to face a rabble; but he apparently suppressed every feeling of agitation by merely turning his elegant eye-glass in the direction from where the voice had proceeded.

Shouts were again renewed for "Buster!" "Baker!" "Campbell!" "Hall!" Numbers were leaving the church as fast as they could; nearly all the ministers had left, but there were many who remained jeering, shouting, and laughing, determined, as they said, "to see the fun out." The church had now a dim appearance; it was getting gloomy, as the gas had been turned off in many places; but there still lingered on the platform a set of reckless fellows, as if expecting something else to occur, and their expectations were soon gratified.

There was one of these, a strong partisan of Mr. Baker, who was an adept at mimicry, and who tried, as if on a stage, to give a burlesque representation of the air and manner of Doctor Buster, and to turn the moderator into ridicule. This conduct was not approved of by at least one stout man, who, with a heavy stick, struck the mock actor a violent blow, and was going to repeat the experiment, when in a moment there was a rush of excited persons, and the platform was at once converted into something like a prize ring. Two angry men were struggling for possession of the stick, and there was a swaying to and fro among a knot of men, pushing and kicking in all directions.

At this time, the noise could be heard some distance from the church; seats were knocked about, pew-doors pulled off, and books torn; and were it not for the timely arrival of a party of constables, the building itself might have been much injured. The sectarian revel was over; no good had been done, no delegate had been chosen, but the reverend chief actors in their jealousy had determined, each for his party, to support independently and more fully, with God's help, the noble cause of cheap Bibles at the next great anniversary in Exeter Hall.*

When Mr. Baker got home that night, he felt highly pleased, and in the best humor. With his open hand he gave his wife a hearty slap between the shoulders, and said: "I told you we would be ready for Campbell. Ha, ha! I wonder what the great Dr. Buster now thinks of us! He tries to make others believe that Methodist influence is waning. I fancy his notion is a little changed already. Let them send a delegate to Exeter Hall, and we will show ourselves there too, by way of no thanks. God will prosper us, in spite of all they can do. Won't poor Campbell pray for us after this? Ha, ha!"

Mrs. Baker, good woman, though not at all dissatisfied at the result of the meeting, was yet more guarded in her expressions; she saw that Mr. Capel was very silent; she knew that young preachers, like fresh converts, are for a time very ardent and fraternal, and she did not wish that any thing should be said to make him feel that her husband was too sectarian, or forgetful of his position as a Christian minister. Nevertheless, she was greatly pleased that the Presbyterian scheme was defeated, and her faith grew stronger and stronger in the God of Wesleyanism.

After Mr. Capel had retired to his room he

* See Note B.

felt like one that had been dreaming. He fancied that he still sat on the platform; he saw the people before him; he saw the glare of lights, and he again heard the wild confusion. Was it all a dream? He could hardly realize that he had been to a church where a public meeting was to have been held by serious Christian men, and that from the hatred of sects the work of the Lord had been entirely disregarded, in order to secure a sectarian triumph. Could he believe that such loud profession should, after all, be but as "a sounding brass or tinkling cymbal;" that men who loved their Bibles, and who prayed and wept for sinners, should exhibit such hatred toward each other? Was this the grand result of what the Gospel had done for them —was this Christianity? And if that Gospel had thus failed in controlling the impulses of the semi-civilized of Britain, what could it do among barbarians at Madagascar? He had often discovered hypocritical professors of religion, but he did not expect to witness such actual jealousy and hatred among a class, many of whom had made an open declaration of faith, and who had solemnly testified that they felt moved by the Spirit of God to go and preach the Gospel. Were these men mad or deluded? Why were there so many creeds, even among Protestants, bitterly anathematizing each other as teachers of error? If the Scriptures were truth, and if the truth was so plain, why so much contention—why such diversity of opinion? He then dwelt upon the historical havoc caused by Christianity, and the solemn question arose: What has the Bible done for mankind?

In times of great doubt or perplexity, Mr. Capel often resorted to the common practice of opening his Bible, and reading the first passage or text that met his eye. In doing this, he sometimes thought that he had found many comforting assurances. He now opened the "inspired book" in several places, but conflicting verses only caused greater depression.

"No man hath seen God at any time." John 1 : 18.
"For I have seen God face to face, and my life is preserved." Gen. 32 : 30.

"And God saw every thing that he had made, and behold it was very good." Gen. 1 : 31.
"And it repented the Lord that he had made man on the earth, and it grieved him at his heart." Gen. 6 : 6.
"For I am the Lord; I change not." Mal. 3 : 6.

"For God is not the author of confusion, but of peace." 1 Cor. 14 : 33.
"I make peace and create evil, I the Lord do all these things." Is. 45 : 7.
"Out of the mouth of the Most High proceedeth not evil and good." Lam. 3 : 18.

"For every one that asketh receiveth, and he that seeketh findeth, and to him that knocketh, it shall be opened." Matt. 7 : 8.
"Then shall they call upon me, but I will not answer; they shall seek me early, but they shall not find me." Prov. 1 : 28.

"Let no man say when he is tempted, I am tempted of God : for God can not be tempted with evil, neither tempteth he any man." Jas. 1 : 13.
"And it came to pass after these things that God did tempt Abraham." Gen. 22 : 1.

"If any of you lack wisdom, let him ask of God that giveth to all men liberally, and upbraideth not; and it shall be given him." Jas. 1 : 5.

"He hath blinded their eyes and hardened their heart, that they should not see with their eyes nor understand with their heart, and be converted, and I should heal them. John 12 : 40.

"Who will have all men to be saved, and to come unto the knowledge of the *truth.*" 1 Tim. 2 : 4.

"And for this cause God shall send them strong delusion that they should believe *a lie.*" 2 Thess. 2 : 11.

God delude men unto the belief of a lie! Could this be so? He paused a long time, and his finger still touched the passage he had just read. If the Lord is "abundant in goodness and truth," can he or will he ensnare a man to his own destruction? This was what he now thought; and the contradictory texts which had opened to him seemed to rise up— a horrible cloud of doubt, cold, bleak, and desolate. He was startled, and looked eagerly around as if hope and happiness had left him forever. Again he ventured to seek another text, and read :

"The Lord is merciful and gracious, slow to anger and plenteous in mercy." Ps. 103 : 8.
"His anger endureth but a moment." Ps. 30 : 5.
"The Lord is very pitiful and of tender mercy. Jas. 5 : 11.
"For his mercy endureth forever." 1 Chron. 16 : 34.

These were blessed reassuring words; and he opened the book again.

"I will not pity, nor spare, nor have mercy, but destroy." Jer. 13 : 14.
"If I whet my glittering sword, and mine hand take hold on judgment. I will render vengeance to mine enemies and reward them that hate me. I will make mine arrows drunk with blood, and my sword shall devour flesh; and that with the blood of the slain and of the captives from the beginning of revenges upon the enemy." Deut.
"Depart from me, ye cursed, into everlasting fire." Matt 25 : 41.

Again he relapsed into despondency! For the first time he began to think whether he could really love an omnipotent Being who was so implacable. He closed the Bible and put it aside, and then sat with his head reclined on the table until it was far in the night, thinking of the crimes, and battles, and brutalities; and of the butcheries, murders, blood, and obscenities, recorded as the authorized transactions of a benevolent Deity. He shuddered at the fearful record; it was revolting! Was there blasphemy on his lips when he muttered, "Good God! It is like the revelation of a fiend!"? Again he bent his head, and as the spectral shadows of his own thoughts closed around him, he became startled from his reverie of skepticism, to retire languidly to bed; and the clock struck more than one tedious hour before he could again visit the smiling friends and beautiful land of his dreams.

CHAPTER VIII.

DURING the forenoon of the day after the disturbance in the Baptist church, three priests were leisurely pacing up and down the inclosed yard connected with the Roman Catholic chapel at Moorfields. They were walking abreast, and only the middle clergyman wore his *soutane.* He was reading a morning paper for their edification, and occasionally they would laugh heartily at some ludicrous circumstance in the narration. Certain ungodly correspondents and news-mongers had supplied exciting accounts of the fracas at the Bible meeting, and the burlesque of the clerical actors thereat was made particularly extravagant. The priest who was reading the paper, Father Thomas McGlinn, was about fifty years of age, a stout, low-sized man, with dark hair. He had a very red face, and the top of his nose was remarkably florid; and when he laughed, he displayed a set of teeth which with ordinary care might be warranted to last him for another half-century. He was a ruddy, jovial, good-natured looking person; and he had to utter but one word to satisfy you of his pure Milesian extraction. His ready wit and humor were genuine, and would have at once obtained for him the standing of a "rale jolly Irish gintleman" even though appearing, like many of his predecessors, as a missionary from the Emerald Isle to the heretical and deluded Sassenach. His two companions were also natives of the same country, so justly reputed for its heroic men, and virtuous women.

"Well, begorra, Father Mick," said he, raising his fist and bringing it down on the paper with a whop, "fast day and all as it is, I'd like to drhink the fellow's health that upset the chairman; it was so nately done as a commencement. Oh! divil a better."

"Faith, I wouldn't mind to do the same myself," said Father Mick Daily, the priest on his right, "even if it should come to the ears of the bishop that the dose was a little extra."

"By my sowl," said Father Tom, "Buster, as they call him, musn't have felt very comfortable with such a *gorsoon* in his arms; 'twas an afficting sight. Didn't Campbell cut a pretty figure with his one glass eye? Well, bedad, but it was a beautiful row at any rate. What a blessing it was to see the pack of haythens pitching into each other; and if it wasn't for the cloth, I wouldn't want better fun than to be there myself. 'Tis a pity the ould joker of a moderator didn't lave the sign of the cross on some of them; but sure that sign isn't in his track, and never will be."

"And d'ye mind the Rev. Jonah," said Father Dennis Lynch, the other priest, "Jonah didn't lave them have their own way for nothing. There's a dhrop of the right blood in that fellow, if he had only the training. He stood up before the moderator in rale style. That same Jonah is a whale in himself, and wouldn't mind taking a hand in, if he had a good backer."

"Och! isn't Baker a beauty," said Father Tom; "swaddler and ranter and all as he is, he is able for them. He gave the Knox men a full baker's dozen on the occasion. How the divil did he escape a walloping at all at all? It's a wonder that Buster didn't moderate him with a *pax terum* betune the eyes."

"But, Father Tom, didn't you know that Capel?" asked Father Mick.

"To be sure he did," at once replied the Rev. Dennis Lynch; "he used to live near Blackpool, in Cork."

"Oh! no; you're wrong," said Father Tom, "Harry Capel's father lived on Patrick street; he was a saddler; but whin I knew him, he was in the police. He was a daycent creature enough to be among such a gang. Many a pot of Beamish and Crawford's porter we had together before I went to Maynooth."

"But, wasn't he a rale *paudreen?*" asked Father Lynch.

"Paudreen? Musha he was, and he wasn't," replied Father Tom. "Divil a much he cared what he was, at any rate. He's dead now, God rest his sowl! 'Twould be well for the ould sod if there was more like him."

"Well, isn't this Capel, who is mentioned in the paper, his son? and if he is, how the mischief did he get among the swaddlers?"

"Sure you know," replied Father Tom, "his ould mother was always among them, and never aisy whin she wasn't psalm-singing or street begging for them hungry thieves of preachers. Her husband, poor Tom Capel, left her have her own way with the children, as well as with every thing else. He didn't much care; in fact, it was said that he was one of those free-thinkers that are now so plenty, and he never asked whether she went to a Cathedral, or Conventicle, or to Quakers' meeting; she might go to a Synagogue for the matter of that. He used to say, by way of a joke, that if there was any difference they were all alike. She, of coorse, hoisted the children away with her. But, God help us! they're all dead now; Harry is the only one left."

"Well, isn't he a swaddling preacher, doesn't he rant along with the rest?—Of coorse he's promoted to the saddle-bags?"

"Well, I believe he is; but sure his mother wouldn't let him rest until he promised to go and do the work of the Lord, rambling about like a showman. I met him by chance the other day, and he tould me that they sent him out to Hampstead with ould Baker. Someway, I don't think he cares for that wandering kind of a life. He's honest in his error, anyway; there's a good deal of his father in him, and the Lord knows what he may be yet. But, Father Dinny," said the priest, lowering his voice to seriousness, "he is now like ourselves; he is just what circumstances have made him; exactly so. He has had no control over the circumstances of his birth, of his country, or of his religion; he is now what he was brought up to be, and in Turkey he might have been a Mussulman, or in India he might have been a Brahmin or a Parsee; and so might we."

"Very good, Father Tom, very good; if the bishop heard all that, I wonder what he'd think of one of his priests. He'd make you cry '*in a culpa*' during *secula seculorum.*"

"But a rishin, faith he might, Dinny; but many a time, in my own quiet way, I've made the bishop stagger a little himself, ay, just while you'd be looking about you. His mitre doesn't cover an inch more brain than he got from his mother, may be not so much; and if his father had been a Quaker, the bishop, in stead of wearing a mitre, might figure about with a broad brimmed hat and a drab coat, eh, Dinny?"

"Be me sowl," said Father Lynch, "you'll have to say the seven penitential psalms backward for this, and may be a few dozen extra *paters* and *aces* in the bargain. Och! what's the use in talking? Sure, we know your ways. But faith, Tom, we must be going, and

we'll expect to meet you at five. You know we can't have much of a dinner to-day—divil take these fasts—but any way, if we don't have any thing stronger we'll have a noggin of holy water and a rosary together. And, Father Tom, acushla, as I b'lieve you've got some dealings with the Ould Boy, after all is over, and if you're able to stand, I'll exorse se you."

"Faith you may, Dinny; but if I was to return the compliment, after the job was done, I might only hear the cackle of a goose instead of a yell from your frien I with the hoof an I horns." And here, with mock piety, Father Tom made the sign of the cross on his forehead with the thumb of his right hand.

A general laugh then took place; the two priests went their way, and Father Tom was left alone. For a few minutes he continued walking rather briskly around the consecrated building; he then paced more leisurely, and seemed in deep thought, as if bearing some mental burden which caused him anxiety; and he often paused, looking down intently at the hallowed ground upon which he stood.

The Irish Catholic population of the city of London is very large, and wherever the Irish people go, the priest is sure to follow. Between the Irish Catholic and his priest, there has ever existed, not merely warm friendship, but strong affection; the presence of a priest in an Irish neighborhood is almost indispensable, and, should he, as is asserted, venture on the occasional use of the blackthorn by way of argument, or as an incentive for the performance of duty, many consider it his privilege and submit; while with others less under control, it is a matter which can be soon forgotten. As a general rule, it is only regarded as a friendly mode of persuasion rather than an act of clerical tyranny.

Now, throughout the city of London there was not a priest, no matter what his degree, could rival Father Tom McGinn in the affections of the Irish Catholics; he was beloved even by children, who, it must be confessed, have a kind of instinctive dread of any person wearing a soutane; but his heart overflowed with good nature, and children forgot that he was a priest when they saw him smile. Then he boasted of "ould Ireland," and of his countrymen, and of Cork, his native city; and at certain times when he grew into a peculiarly soft mood, he would talk and sing about the "Bells of Shandon," and of the river Lee, and of Sundays-Well, until the remembrance of these fond things and places filled his good-natured eyes with big tears; and, priest as he was, he felt just as kindly disposed to his countrymen of all creeds as if they were members of his own church. Indeed, after all, he seldom judged of a man by his nation; nationality was an idea out of which he tried to grow: but on occasions when he used to recount the wrongs inflicted by Britain upon his church and country, then he asserted his nationality, and became almost vindictive.

For many years Father Tom officiated in Cork, under the friendly eye of Doctor Murphy, his Catholic bishop; but after the death of that prelate, he took a notion to remove to London; he was successful in obtaining a good parish, and among the priests as well as among the people of that city he became a great favorite. If, however, he had many of the virtues of his countrymen, he had also a few of their failings. Although he had been intimate for a long period with the late Father Mathew, and had expressed an approval of his temperance principles, yet, with regard to self-indulgence in one particular, he never had strength of mind sufficient to turn up his nose at a tumbler of hot whisky-punch, that is to say, after a certain hour toward evening. His adherence to the temperance pledge, if he ever took it, only lasted during the excitement of the time, and like a majority of his countrymen he relapsed into a usage almost canonical among the clergy.

He was, however, a little singular in this respect, he seemed to have his appetite under perfect control; for no human being could induce him to touch a drop of strong liquor until after the clock had struck three in the afternoon; he might then take an odd tumbler immediately before dinner, just to regulate his appetite, but when that meal was over, particularly if he had a few genial friends with him, he would resolutely confine his legs under the mahogany and drink and debate, and debate and drink, until every opponent was silenced, or until every man was reduced to a state of blissful oblivion. On such occasions, Father Tom became fiercely polemical, and was rewarded by the sobriquet of "Controversial Tom."

About the time that Father Tom had imbibed a dozen tumblers, his eyes would attain an unnatural brightness, and he used to say that he was then getting "into good tune;" after that, no matter how much more he swallowed, it seemed to have no other effect than that of increasing his thirst, and he could then be scarcely civil to any man in his company whom he thought could not stand the thirtieth tumbler.

To spend a night, then, with Father Tom was by many regarded as a privilege. After his reverence got in good tune, his peculiarity was then to become controversial; and from him there was no escape. He would badger away until he found an opponent—no matter whether priest, parson, or pope—and he would then argue from the fathers, and from an overwhelming array of texts and traditions, just as fiercely as if the very fate of his church depended upon the issue; and many of his brother priests, knowing his weakness, would not let the opportunity pass, for one or another was always ready to make an attack and assume the position of an opponent in order to draw him out and hear his defense. At such times, his whole theme would be his church and its supremacy, with an occasional dash at the apostasy of Britain; and then, if he even knew that it was the pope in state who disputed with him, he would still argue away, quite indifferent to his holiness or to the splendor of his triple crown.

No two persons could be more unlike than Father Tom in the forenoon and the same Father Tom in the evening. He was humorous and good-natured enough at all times;

but in the morning, when reason had full control, he would be more priest-like, more serious, and more thoughtful; in the evening, when he was less troubled with doubts and speculations, he was full of wit, and at the right stage, when fully primed, he would mount the controversial hobby, and ride away as if for dear life.

There was some secret influence, however, to work this change. Father Tom in morning conversation often expressed strange opinions regarding many of the rites and doctrines of his church, and even before priests he would say some very startling things; but they said they knew him, wasn't he "controversial Tom"? the very divil for argument, and what was the use in minding any thing he said? He was, they asserted, sound to the backbone, a stout defender of the faith. They had often heard his expositions after the fifteenth tumbler. That was the time to see what was in him. In vino veritas.

Yet Father Tom was not understood; for years he had been troubled with grave doubts concerning many points of his religious belief; and while he had to appear before his co-laborers as faithful and submissive to the dicta of his church, and to manifest the conventional contempt and hostility toward heretical teaching, yet he dreaded to subject the mysteries and doctrines of his religion to the ordeal of reason; it was an insatiable interrogator! He was often very much perplexed, and dreaded uncertainty. He loved the great old ecclesiastical structures of which Peter was the head. The ceremonies of the Romish faith were grand and attractive, and it cost him a severe struggle to entertain ideas which were not strictly orthodox. The very existence of doubt made him irritable at times, as if some rapacious intruder had stealthily entered his dwelling and would not depart. He tried to persuade himself into full belief; and thus it often was that in combating the views of an imaginary opponent, he was in reality trying to defeat himself, and get rid of his own doubts by force of argument with another.

After his clerical friends went away, Father Tom still continued pacing up and down; even the noise and street sounds of the great city did not seem to distract him for a moment. He had celebrated mass that morning, and was in a short time to enter the confessional. This was a duty he disliked very much, but he dare not murmur. He was still superstitiously circumspect in the performance of his various obligations as a priest, in the hope that his faithfulness in holy orders might yet dispel his doubts, and enable him more clearly to understand and appreciate the doctrines, mysteries, and imposing ceremonies of the "Mother Church." He was, in his uncertainty, still anxious to cling to the ancient faith, and to uphold its supremacy even while he trampled upon his reason; but he dreaded to investigate the authority for confession, and indulgences, and invocation, and, above all, the authority for transubstantiation; this was too great a strain on his faith. He was ready to admire the shapely exterior of the sepulchre, but recoiled at the idea of entering its gloom, to grope amid relics and rottenness. Between these things, poor Father Tom often had an uneasy mind, while many of the credulous faithful with whom he was in constant intercourse believed him to be the happiest of men, and felt proud of him as a champion of the church.

He was still moodily thinking; and as he stepped alone over the inclosed greensward, he began to dwell upon what he had said that morning before he administered the sacrament to the few devotees who were regular attendants. He thought again of the formal words he had used—wonderful, if true—and now, as he repeated them to himself, he stopped suddenly and frowned at their meaning, and at his own partial incredulity.

"*Ecce Agnus Dei*—Behold the Lamb of God—monstrous! This can not be; no matter what either pope, or council, or bishop may say to the contrary. The simple wafer which I held in my hand this morning was no more the Lamb of God than I am. Good God! to believe that I can swallow the great Creator as I would a pill! What an outrage on my reason! Yet how many believe this; how many of the learned and profound submit, where I doubt! Am I right, or am I on the great highway to perdition? Heaven direct me!" And Father Tom, in his mental agitation, still stood looking intently on the ground, as if he waited and longed to have the earth open and swallow him up forever. He then commenced to walk rapidly, and after a few minutes, he entered the church; and as he almost involuntarily bent before the high altar, he muttered to himself, "If this is truth, then woe unto me, for I am undone!"

Father Tom was very punctual that afternoon; he seemed, or tried to be, in good spirits, and when he entered the domicile of Father Dinny Lynch, he swept in among them like a warm glow of sunshine. A more jovial set of priests never sat at a table. Besides Father Tom, and Father Mick, and Father Dinny, there were two or three other old friends, not in orders; and, although it was fast-day with many of the faithful, the clergy seldom or never took the trouble to apply for a special license to eat meat; the privilege they might grant to another they could surely partake of themselves; and therefore the roast and boiled on Father Dinny's table appeared and disappeared in good time, after which digestion was assisted by a rousing glass of *scholteen*, prepared by the Rev. Mr. Lynch himself, after an old receipt by one of the ancient Irish Fathers.

"Well," said Father Tom, after some other matters had been discussed, and who now began to feel very comfortable and loquacious, "I wish I was on the ould sod once more; I'm get ing tired of the cockneys. You may talk as you like about Saxons and Celts, and about your big city—your modern Sodom—but give me the Island of Saints yet, where our church can count nearly fifty to one with any other. Sure, here we are like wheat among tares, cheek by jowl with Baptists, and Swaddlers, and Ranters, that are ready to tear each other to pieces for the love of God. The Virgin save us! Och! the Lord be with you, sweet Cork! betune you and me, I'd like to be back there now. *Ullagone*, sure it's not in this wilderness of brick and mortar that you'd have me spend my days. Wait, Dinny avick, if I don't show you a clean pair of heels it's no matter." And Father Tom began, in a kind of regretful mood, to hum the "Groves of Blarney," an air which always had for him a most inspiring effect.

"Tom," said one of the priests, "give us Father Prout's song; you can do it; you'll never forget 'Shandon Bells,' although they're hung in a Protestant steeple. Here's the way it goes—"

"Arrah, sure that's '*Sheela na guira*' you're trying to whistle, you *ommadhaun*! Micky, allannah, I can't easily forget them bells; I never can! I remember once, long ago, when I was singing a litany, the ould bells were chiming away, and every now and then I thought they sent back a longing response to our ancient service; and when I'd sing, 'Sancta Maria,' down came the rushing sound in reply, like a saintly voice from paradise—' *Ora pro nobis*.' Ah Micky! I often liked to hear them of a fine summer's evening; their sweet vibrations used to return to me like the hum of my poor mother's soft song, when she was putting me to sleep long ago. God be merciful to her! Amen. *Requiescat in pace!*" And Father Tom, almost in tears, devoutly made the sign of the cross on his forehead.

"Well," continued Father Tom, wiping his lips with his hand, and laying down the empty tumbler, "there's a smack of the rale bogwater about that, anyhow. Isn't that from Tom Wise? Faith, his distillery is only one of the few factories we have left to remind these foreigners of what we once were. They may talk of their fabrics, and of their cattle shows, and of their great exhibitions; but they can't bate *that*, divil a bit. The dirty Thames is as polluted as British royalty; they haven't the clear waters of the Lee to draw from." He said this as he was diligently mixing his seventh tumbler, and he gave a very meaning sigh, as he stirred the spoon in the smoking contents. "Micky, what are you doing? Don't be afeard of that; there's not a headache in a whole puncheon of it."

"Come, Father Tom, don't forget the song; just one verse, to begin with."

"Arrah, Mick, I can't forget the bells, but 'pon my sowl I forget the song; more shame on me! Let me see, it goes this way—

' With deep affection, and sweet recollection,
  I often think of those Shandon bells,
Whose song so wild would, in the days of childhood,
  Fling round my cradle their magic spells.
Oh—this I, I—'

Och, divil take it, asking Father Prout's pardon, I can't make it out. I'm afeard I'll soon forget my *pater noster*, and every thing else that's good, if I stay in this benighted country. But stop, I'll make a verse for you." He hummed for a moment or two, and then began,

"For Cork's own city, so fair and witty,
  I'll sing this ditty, though far away;
And still remember, to life's chill December,
  My native town, that's across the say.

My heart is swelling for Sundays-Well, in
 That beauteous quarter where you could see
The bells of Shandon, that wound so grand on
 The pleasant waters of the river Lee."

"Bravo, bravo! well done! illigant! sublime!" and then sundry heavy thumps made the glasses dance on the table. "Put that in print, Father Tom, and faith, your fortune is made."

This was not a labored impromptu with the priest. His voice was soft and musical; he sung slowly and with great feeling, and the words followed each other in an easy order of versification, adapted to the popular air..

"I'm no poet; however, I'm glad you're pleased. But, Dinny avick, if I was a jaynuine poet, I might make some verses that his holiness the pope might clap in the Index Prohibitorius."

"Sure, Father Tom, you wouldn't mount your Pegasus and canter away from the church? You wouldn't write any thing, no matter how inspired, that you'd be afraid to let your bishop see?"

"See? God help the see that he blinks at! *Thigum*, he can't see a hole through a ladder sometimes. I know it, and Micky, ould Wiseman's an ass; he is, by Gor!"

"O Tom, Father Tom, aisy, aisy, aisy!"

"He's an ass I say, and the prince of asses," and Father Tom repeated a verse of the song generally sung at Beauvais, France, during the Romish festival, in praise of the ass, on the 14th of January.

 "Ecce magnis auribus! Subjugalis filius;
 Asinus egregius. Asinorum dominus!"*

"See here; the whole of you are afraid of that ould thief, but I'm not, divil a bit. He's a half-Spaniard. What did they send him here for? to be one of our cardinal points? sure, he wouldn't let me take a quiet smoke the other night, he didn't want the smell of tobacco; yet he carries a gold snuff-box to stuff his own ould beak. I tould him in double quick time that I'd lave the palace and go to more humble quarters, somewhere else, and so I did, there now.—If they had him in Ireland, they'd choke him,"

It was useless now to make any attempt to control Father Tom. By this time, he had swallowed the twelfth tumbler; and if the Pope himself were to enter the room, he would face him with a pipe in his mouth and arms akimbo.

Father Tom, after a moment's oblivion, now gave a disdainful side-look around the table; he appeared to rise wonderfully in his own estimation; every doubt had almost vanished, and, champion-like, he felt itching for a brush with an opponent. Looking from under a frown at his friends, he began:

"You're a lot of interlopers! What do you benighted heretics know?" And he imagined for the moment that he was engaged in a regular set-to with some stiff Protestant, some sanctified *souper* of the Establishment.

I'm a priest. I'm none of your wolves in

 * See that broad, majestic ear,
 Born he is the poke to wear;
 All his fellows he surpasses,
 He's the very lord of asses!

sheep's clothing. I'm a priest of the rale ould church founded by Peter.—D'ye want proof? 'Upon this rock I will build my church, and I will give to thee the keys.' Yes, the keys, and divil a in you'll ever get unless *we* open the door. Put that in your pipe, and smoke it. What do the Scriptures say? 'Many shall come in my name.'—Yes, a lot of thieving, blind guides, with their texts, and their tracts, rummaging up and down the country, begging, and praying, and feasting, and gormandizing. Arrah, the divil sweep them, but it's a nice time of day with us whin we've got to stand aside and make way for your snub-nosed Busters, and Bakers, and Buntings! Wasn't that a nice sample they gave at the Bible meeting of their Christianity? Be gor! the public papers say that they went at it on the very platform, before the whole crowd of psalm-singers in ould Howe's conventicle, and sure they tumbled one fellow clear over, and knocked out Campbell's eye; pity they spoiled his squint! Och! God be with the place where, if they commenced such a row, we could aisily get a dozen or so of the boys to step in among them with a few blackthorns to feather free grace into them. Wouldn't there be ructions? Musha, blessed be the ould sod; after all the tithes, and extortion, and oppression of the gambling interlopers of parsons, they can't make much headway there. They may think that they soften some of the hungry craythers, once in awhile, whin they come with a bowl of soup in one hand and their dirty rag of a Bible in the other. The bowl is sure enough émptied, and the book, 'printed by His Majesty's special command,' is just as certain to be left at some huckster's stand on the Coal Quay, while Paddy has got more than the value of it in his pocket in the shape of tuppence' worth of tobacco.

"Then, Lord save us! at one of their next big missionary meetings, or may be at their great Exeter Hall, how they'll turn up their eyes, while some dandy parson, or thieving ould ranter delights a moping crowd with lying accounts of the wholesale conversion of deluded Papists.—Divil a bit but 'tis hard to have patience with such a gang. Well, faith, there's a few texts in store for them. 'Ye serpents, ye generation of vipers, how can ye escape the damnation of hell?' 'And through covetousness shall they with feigned words make merchandise of you, whose judgment now of a long time lingereth not, and their damnation slumbereth not.' 'Let them alone: they be blind leaders of the blind. And if the blind lead the blind, both shall fall into the ditch.'—'Woe unto you, Scribes and Pharisees, hypocrites! for ye compass sea and land to make one proselyte; and when he is made, ye make him twofold more the child of hell than yourselves.'—Faith, there would be more truth in that if it had been written 'ten-fold;' but sure that's enough for them, even out of their own book. We are tould to 'let them alone,' and that their 'damnation slumbereth not.' So you see, there's comfort in store for them anyhow. D'ye hear that, my friend?" said he, giving a self-sufficient wink at Father Mick. "'Aures habent et non audient.' They have ears to hear, but they will not hear. Be gor! it's a wonder they don't, for sure they're long enough."

Father Tom here drew another sigh, and began to compound another restorative; then in a minute or so he said, reflectively, "Yes, I'm a priest of the Holy Roman Catholic and Apostolic Church, and I think the divil a fear of me if I stay where I am; and now I defy any of you to say that its not the rale true ould Mother Church. What d'ye say to that?" said he, looking defiantly at Father Dinny Lynch, whom he now took for an opponent.

"Well," replied Father Dinny, assuming a controversial attitude, "I admit what you say, I don't deny but that yours is the rale *mother* church, for you know the faithful of Rome always pay more regard to the *mother* than they do to the *son*."

This answer rather staggered Father Tom; but after a short pause, he quietly closed his left eye and kept the other on his man, as much as to say, "Poor fool, I pity you,". Then quickly changing the point at issue, he said, "D'ye mane to deny the *rale presence?* d'ye mane to deny that blessed mystery of our church that has puzzled the whole of you for over a thousand years? You won't say a word to that; that's the belief that bothers your raison and philosophy; that's *our* prime mystery. You'll niver get transubstantiation through your thick skulls, divil a bit, *allannah!* What have you got to say against our confessional? Doesn't the Scriptures say, 'Confess your sins one to another'? D'ye mane to turn up your noses at purgatory? Faith, *avick*, I'm afeard you're in a fair way of going a little further down. Pshaw! What do you know about indulgences, or penance, or prayer to the blessed saints? Nothing. *Nabocklish*, you'll be glad to have the Hill of Howth tumble over and hide ye, some of these fine days. Where d'ye get your authority, let me ask you? You talk of your 'apostolical succession'—a set of fox-hunting, card-playing, tithe-grabbing, vagabond parsons! Succession indeed! Bad luck to the success you'll ever have. Lord help us! If St. Peter was to take a trip back again, and see such a batch of greedy wolves and hounds claiming to be his successors, wouldn't he roar? Wouldn't he burst his sides? wouldn't he split right open? Faith, he'd laugh at the idea until he'd shake himself into his very grave. Where d'ye get your authority? Tell me that."

"Out of the Bible, to be sure," said Father Dinny.

"Oh! of course, out of the Bible, the Bible is your Pandora's box. Sure, you'll get authority in the Bible for any thing. Every one of your forty or fifty different sects can quote authority out of that for their capers, until their contention gets as wild as a hurroo at Donnybrook. Out of the Bible the Baptist proves immersion, and another proves sprinkling. The Methodist proves '*free grace*,' and the Presbyterian '*election* and *reprobation;*' one to pray without ceasing, and another to wait till the Spirit moves. In the Bible you can get authority for love and for hatred; for peace and for war; for hope and despair; for

blessing an I for cursing; for revenge and forgiveness; for faith and for works; for liberty and slavery, and for almost every thing else; and sure the divil himself on a pinch could find an odd text or two for his own justification. Don't talk of the Bible and its authority; you're distracted yourselves about its rale maning; you're all pulling, and dragging, and hauling each other, scarcely any two of ye thinking alike. Expunge, according to order, and what would ye have left? Divil a bit. Sure Luther, that bastely apostate, began at the end of your Bible and wanted to sweep away the book of Revelation altogether because it foretold of his own downfall. Not a man of ye is certain as to what your Bible is; the blessed books which we accept as canonical, you timidly reject as apocryphal. Your own commentators say that certain chapters are doubtful, or even spurious; others, that whole books have been lost; one, that certain texts are interpolations, and another, that there are various wrong translations. You talk of your *four* Gospels! What do ye do with the other fifty or sixty which for all ye know have just as good a right to be included? Why, it is admitted that about one hundred and fifty thousand different readings of ancient manuscripts of the New Testament have been discovered, and yet none of your present writings are older than the sixth century? Now with these trifling facts staring ye in the face, can ye trust your Bible—your paper idol? How do ye know you're right?"

"Well, and how do *you* know?" said Father Dinny.

"How do *we* know, d'ye say? Faith, we know that according to our feeble reason it is impossible to regulate these matters, or to reconcile our Bible contradictions, or to tell what is what; but we take the interpretation of our church without a murmur; we submit to *its* authority. We know we're right because the church is founded on a rock, and can not err; and then we have our blessed traditions to make us more secure. We had them before there was a chapter of your New Testament put in writing. There's no danger of us; and if you don't retrace your steps, and stop your wandering, and hurry back to the ould faith, begorra, in coorse of time you'll find yourself in a warm corner where you can roast a herring across the palm of your hand, or light your pipe with the top of your finger. Hurry back, allannah, hurry back!"

Father Tom continued in this strain for some time longer; he had got rid of every doubt, and was once more fully persuaded that the Roman Church was the pillar and ground of truth. Between the spirits in his glass and its effects upon his imagination, he became at last violent in his declamation, and as unruly in his theology as St. Dominic himself. It was late that night before his proof texts were duly arrayed and his denunciations expended, and he would not consent to retire until all had made due submission.

No person who attended morning mass the next day at Moorfield's Chapel would for a moment imagine that the demure priest who officiated, and who bent and bowed with such graceful solemnity before the lighted altar, was the advocate for thirty tumblers, or the doubting controversialist—Father Tom Mc-Glinn.

CHAPTER IX.

HAMPSTEAD Cottage never looked more home-like and cheerful than it did on the bright April afternoon that Mr. Capel and Mrs. Baker drove up to the garden-gate of that pleasant dwelling. Although he had consented to make this house his temporary abode, yet he never had the curiosity to inquire whether it was a modern red brick building, bolt up to the street side, or a massive stone structure in the same position, with thick walls very little windows, and great dreary looking gables, having acute angles of the olden time; he never gave it a thought. He was but a wayfaring man, content to sojourn a few months in one place, and may be a year or more in another; and when he had formed an agreeable intimacy with a few persons, he was sent away to some distant circuit, never perhaps to meet them again. It was from this that a feeling of indifference had been engendered as to where he should reside; but when he saw the neat cottage surrounded by fine trees, and the trim garden, and the young buds, and the clear sun-lit sky, and heard the songs of a thousand birds, many of which seemed to flit with delight through the fragrant air, the scene was most agreeable, and one that his fancy would have readily created as a picture of home.

But if he never thought of the house, he had often thought of its proprietor. Mrs. Mannors had already evinced her kind disposition towards him, was in fact like a mother. She was also a sister in the church, and he well knew that he had her sympathies and her prayers; her husband, however, the master of Heath Cottage, was an entire stranger to him personally, and not only that, but according to report, an utter stranger to the truth of God, and even, it was said, an avowed enemy to the Christian faith. How could he meet this man, and be content to remain as his guest—as one of his family? Would he not, by accepting this offer of hospitality, be often, perhaps, obliged to submit and listen to unpleasant insinuations against religion, or to the open blasphemous attacks of an unbeliever? One who is firmly satisfied of the truth of the Bible is actually shocked at the bare idea of infidelity, and therefore presumes that a person who can persistently reject inspiration must be wilfully perverse, and should be avoided as far as possible. He is presumed to be a gloomy, dissatisfied cynic, devoid of tender sympathies, and of the kindlier feelings of our nature; a man whose word is but a snare, and whose honor but a lie, whose passions are under no proper control, leaving him sordid, heartless, and brutal. There was no denying the fact that the idea which he had formed concerning Mr. Mannors was not very flattering; he had been represented to him by Mr. Baker as a very dangerous person, whose principles and character could not meet the approval of either God or man.

Thus it is that too often an unwarrantable prepossession may raise a barrier between us and an estimable person, who, if better known, might exhibit genial and intellectual qualities of a high order, and with whom intercourse and intimacy might be a source of the greatest enjoyment, by engendering a friendship which would make life more happy, and even, after a final separation, leave a ray of light forever on the memory.

No wonder, then, that Mr. Capel was anxious to see the individual under whose roof he was for a time to find a home, at whose table he was to sit, and whose mind he was to try and impress with Gospel truth. Judging, however, from the surroundings of his habitation, the young preacher fancied that his host must be a lover of rural beauty. Every thing seemed to indicate the possession of the most exquisite taste and love of order. If such natural attractions gave a bent to his mind, it could not be in a very wrong direction; and it might be, after all, that the infamy which some were ready to attach to his name was but the result of an unfair prejudice which our present social enlightenment has not yet repudiated. Detraction could surely be no aid to religion. He would now, however, be soon able to judge for himself, and he would try to do so impartially.

Such were Mr. Capel's reflections while he looked from the vehicle at the gate-side into the pleasant garden. Neither he nor Mrs. Baker had yet been observed from the house and, as if by a tacit agreement, they sat still to listen to the warbling of birds from a number of cages by the hall door; they could see the young vines creeping through the trellis-work, and sunshine and shadow commingling around the ivied windows and meeting on the flower-stands; and then they heard the mellow sound of harmony from a piano and voices in the parlor. Mr. Mannors and his daughter were practising a favorite duet, and as the full swell or diminuendo reached the ear, Mr. Capel, who had a cultivated taste for music, almost fancied himself at one of the pearly gates of heaven instead of being near the entrance to the residence of a doomed unbeliever. He still listened; and while this pleasing fancy lingered, the door opened, and out rushed Mary from the house, as bright as an angel of the earth as ever met his eyes. Mrs. Mannors followed, and then came Mr. Mannors himself; while Hannah, from one of the dormer windows, shouted out the arrival of Mrs. Baker. Mrs. Mannors was the first to reach the gate, and she impulsively reached up both hands to Mr. Capel in a hearty shake; she almost neglected Mrs. Baker, in her eagerness to bestow her welcome upon the young preacher. Mr. Mannors waited for no introduction, but greeted him in the kindest manner, and Mr. Capel was actually surprised at the warmth of his reception. Mary Mannors, now blushing, hesitated to approach, and with becoming diffidence stood at a short distance holding her brother's hand, and waiting to be made acquainted with their visitor.

The young preacher's eyes wandered from Mary Mannors to her brother, then to Mrs. Mannors, and then to the courteous gentleman who had so kindly welcomed him, and who was now, without waiting for assistance, busily engaged removing the small trunk he had brought from Mr. Baker's. Mr. Capel was most agreeably surprised, and for a few moments watched Mr. Mannors intently. Is this, thought he, the person against whom I was warned? Is this the man whose dark countenance and vulpine aspect betrayed the unholy emotions which governed his mind? Is this he whom Mr. Baker has so long despised, and against whom he has hurled so many denunciatory texts? Surely it can not be! He found it impossible to believe that the gentleman with mild, cheerful face, who had just assisted Mrs. Baker to alight, who was now leading her to the house, and whose smile seemed so attractive to that fair girl and her delicate brother, was the Martin Mannors of his imagination—the gloomy skeptic, the monster of unbelief, the denounced infidel, who made his pious wife so miserable, and who wantonly treated divine revelation with so much contempt. Was this the man whom he had to try to warn, reprove, and reform? Well, considered Mr. Capel, if this is to be my mission here, I have a harder task before me than I imagined. There is nothing vicious lurking in his heart, there is nothing dark or designing in that generous countenance which throws such a halo of happiness all around. If the heart of man is by nature "deceitful above all things, and desperately wicked," were it not that it would involve the palpable contradiction of Holy Writ, I should say that Martin Mannors was an exception to the general rule, and as guileless as a child.

Had Mr. Capel entertained any doubt as to the friendliness of his reception at Heath Cottage, that doubt was now effectually dispelled by the genuine kindness already shown him, and by the great satisfaction manifested by all upon his arrival. In fact, had he been some poor prodigal who had long wandered away from his father's house, and had now returned, remorseful and repentant, he could not have found a truer welcome. Mrs. Mannors was fairly in ecstasies, she almost wept with joy; and never, since the death of his mother, had Mr. Capel met with any person who appeared to take such an interest in his welfare.

His kind hostess was indeed joyfully excited; accompanied by Mrs. Baker, she led him around the place. He was shown the garden, and the birds, and the curiosities in the hall; he was taken to different rooms, and then she led him to the comfortable apartment placed at his disposal, where, to his surprise, he found a number of theological works side by side, for his edification. There stood Baxter, Doddridge, Pascal, Paley, Wesley, and many others, besides memoirs and commentaries sufficient to afford him ample range for study; and he was still more surprised to learn that these works had been carefully read by Mr. Mannors himself. Upon opening several of them, he discovered numerous marginal notes in his writing, illustrative of close reading, and of the great interest taken in the contents by the reasoning skeptic.

After having tried to interest him with other matters, Mrs. Mannors did not forget to remind him of the task she wished him to undertake respecting her husband. She said she had no doubt whatever of his success, for her prayers in his behalf had been constant; and even her dreams led her to believe that God was waiting to be gracious, and would not be forgetful of his promise.

Were it asserted that Mr. Mannors was in a happier mood than usual that evening, it might not be strictly correct. He was peculiarly blessed with a very agreeable disposition; scarcely any thing seemed to affect his equanimity. Persons who had known him intimately for years seldom discovered any difference in his manner. He was always happy, always indifferent to the bauble honors which so much engrossed the pious as well as the profane; and those who felt gloomy or depressed before they had spoken to him of their troubles generally went away more hopeful. Whether Mr. Mannors had discovered something in the unassuming modest demeanor of Mr. Capel, or whether it was the superior glow of intelligence in the face of the young man that excited an unusual interest, it could not be denied but that the master of Heath Cottage was particularly happy that evening. He had found a new friend; and without waiting to ascertain what his peculiar views might be on this or that subject, he felt intuitively that the young preacher was a person of superior mind, and who, from the tenor of his remarks, was possessed of a liberality not permitted by strict theological training; he, no doubt, anticipated much pleasure in his society, especially as he was now for a time to be an inmate of Heath Cottage, and, as it were, a member of the family; but he had not the least idea that Mr. Capel's visit was so contrived by Mrs. Mannors as to make it a special mission for the benefit of himself, her erring husband.

For a young man, Mr. Capel was gifted with great power of discrimination; not judging Mr. Mannors, therefore, by his favorable appearance, but from the acute observations made by him on many subjects, he was astonished at his great intelligence, and at the vast powers of his mind. Though but a very short time in his society, he was inclined to think that he had never met his equal. No matter what any person might assert concerning the peculiar religious views of such a man, a mind like his was too fearless and comprehensive to reject any proposition without its due share of consideration. He already felt that with Mr. Mannors there would be no necessity of going round and round in order to ask a fair question and demand a fair answer; he found in him one who was quite willing that you should know his opinion on any proper subject, and ever ready to give the reasons which led him to a conclusion; that he was a person as willing to learn as to teach, and one before whom you might lay your opinions, in full confidence that he would deal justly, and give a true verdict according to the evidence.

The mission, therefore, which Mr. Capel had timidly undertaken was no longer dreaded;

it was now to be a source of pleasure instead of a reluctant effort; and the repugnance which he might have once felt in complying with the mutual desire of Mrs. Mannors and Mrs. Baker continued no longer.

The two persons who but a few hours before were utter strangers to each other were now seen arm in arm walking around the garden, and engaged in agreeable conversation. It was evident that an acquaintance had been already formed which would, in all probability, continue for a long time. It was pleasant to see them thus together as they wandered through the winding walks, or standing in friendly debate in the shadow of some huge evergreen. Both were lovers of nature, and occasionally paused to see the evening sunlight rush down in bright streams through the moss covered branches of venerable trees, and to hear the soft whispering of young leaves. It was cheerful to see this, and to hear the hearty, joyous laugh of Mr. Mannors as he related some anecdote which almost convulsed his friend with laughter, bringing tears to his eyes.

Mrs. Mannors was very much interested. She watched the progressive intercourse which was now gradually begetting that confidence most desirable between the young preacher and her husband. She hurriedly left Mrs. Baker, in order to have a talk with Hannah upon the subject. After a time, she went up to her room, and looked down into the garden, to observe the two persons in whom, for the moment, she felt most interest. She was very much gratified; her fondest dreams would be surely realized. There they were, husband and preacher, the unbeliever and the expounder of truth, in cheerful conversation on subjects of mutual interest; there they stood, like two old friends that had met once again, or more properly, like the meeting of a fond father and dutiful son, who had been long parted. What but good could she expect from such a beginning? How different was the manner and bearing of the young preacher compared with that of his superintendent. Whenever Mr. Baker ventured to call on her, and that was as seldom as possible, though treated with the greatest courtesy by her husband, his words to him were few and commonplace; and during a short stay, he was reserved and moody while in his presence. No wonder that she felt pleased; and now, as she stood at the dormer window, with the light of the pure, bright evening sky around her, burnishing the gilt picture-frame, and flashing on the mirrors of her room, and thus mingling with the radiant smile upon her face, she looked like a happy wife, and the mistress of a happy household.

Every one in Heath Cottage that afternoon was pleased at the arrival of Mr Capel. Robert, the trusty man of all work, was quite satisfied. He fully expected to see some dark-visaged, morose person drive up, and cast a shadow about the place, dark as a thunder-cloud. "But, Lor, bless you!" said he, as he was rubbing down Mr. Capel's horse, which was, for the time, to be an additional charge, "Lor bless you, Master William, no one would take him to be one of these Methodees. Least-

ways, I wouldn't. Why, he bean't no more like one than I am; that is to say, if he hadn't that ere white choker on him. I hope as mistress won't be disappointed. He don't look like a moping chap, that's always a praying and looking miserable. You'd think that them ere coves what brings us the tracts on Sunday morning, were under sentence of death, and had nothing to do but go straight to old Bailey, and get tipped off. He's not like them; he'd do better for one of these big parson chaps, only he's a great bit too civil."

"I like him very much, indeed I do," said William; "and so does ma and pa; and Mary says he has got such a nice face and curly hair. Oh! yes, we all like him—Hannah and all, and Mary, too."

"Does she? Well, that's a go!" said Robert, giving a curious wink at the wall, and stroking his whiskers during a little pause. "Oh! yes, may be Miss Mary will like him a bit, as well as yourself; quite natr'l like."

"She does," replied William, in all simplicity; "she says that she's very glad he came, and we expect to have some pleasant walks together. You know, Robert, the summer time is coming, and we shall have plenty of nice evenings and mornings, and, you know, if I am poorly, she will have some one to go out with her; that is, if pa is away."

"Yes, so I'm thinking," said Robert; "but may be mistress may keep him a praying all the day, leastways, when he's here. You know those Methodees have to be a praying or preaching more than half the time, and the other half they're begging. But I think he won't do much that way. Your pa will keep him busy. Yes, I think he'll have some sport with him;" and Robert, who was not strictly orthodox, kept brushing and rubbing away at the preacher's horse, which found himself in good quarters.

Hannah and Mrs. Baker had been in conversation together for some time before Mrs. Mannors again joined them, and when the latter made her appearance, she looked delighted, and began to tell how her husband and the young preacher had become such friends, and how she thought that, instead of having to travel away alone any more to hear the "Word," they might before long witness a great change. It would be something wonderful to see Mr. Mannors a regular attendant, and may be a member of a class, or even a class-leader. Would it not be a great thing to see him start away early every Sunday morning to distribute tracts among the ungodly, instead of remaining at home as he now did, reading newspapers, and magazines, and dreadful books against religion, or talking about politics, or reform, to people of his own sort, who called to see him? No, it would not be too much to expect to see him occupy a place on the missionary platform, either in their own church, or, on greater occasions, at Exeter Hall. "I feel certain," said Mrs. Mannors, "from what I witnessed the other morning, that Mr. Capel will be able to influence all within this house; and may God grant it."

"Well, ma'am," said Hannah, "I never saw a person I could be more pleased with than our young preacher; it is, you know, only a short time since I first laid eyes on him; he is the one we need. He is the evangelist that is to lead poor Christian to the city gates. I believe he will yet work a miracle in this house. I feel like poor Hopeful in the 'Pilgrim's Progress,' when Christian was ready to sink in deep waters. I can now say, 'Be of good cheer, sister, I feel the bottom, and it is good.' Let Mr. Capel have his own way awhile, and all will be right.'

"Goodness knows, I'm sure I hope you have got to the bottom of your trouble, any way," responded Mrs. Baker. "What a blessed thing it is to be able to trust in the Lord; when all fails, one can rely on him. Have faith, an everything else will follow. Oh! what answers I have had to the prayer of faith. I remember once, when I lived with my brother, that it rained for nearly three weeks in harvest time, and his sheafs of wheat were almost rotting in the field. I went to my room and pretended to be sick, and fasted a whole afternoon, and oh! how I prayed to the Lord for dry weather. Well, my dear, I slept that night in full faith, and in the morning when I awoke, bless the Lord! there was the sun shining right in on the bed-clothes. There was the answer to my prayer. When I got up, I was all praise; I read the one hundred and third Psalm, and, bless the Lord! ate a most hearty breakfast. It was afterward dry for a full week."

"Well then again, dear, but you know I wouldn't tell this to any one else, I was a kind of dependent on my brother, and I was anxious to get settled in life. I wanted to get married, and day and night, and night and day, I prayed to the Lord without ceasing. Bless you, how I *did* pray! I prayed for a good husband. Well, I went at once and joined the church, attended class, distributed tracts, attended Sunday-school, made good collections, and went to every tea-meeting in the circuit; and as soon as I laid my eyes on James, and found that he wanted a good wife, I worked and prayed harder and harder, and, again, bless the Lord! he answered my prayer, and we were married. Now I give you these as undoubted proofs of what prayer and faith can do;" and then, giving Hannah a sly wink and a little punch on the ribs, she leant over and said to her in a half whisper, "Go thou and do likewise." "Yes, my dear," continued Mrs. Baker, "I hope your trouble is nearly over. The Lord can work wonders through the lips of his chosen servants; but we must not forget prayer. 'Prayer moves the hand that moves the world.'" And this pious hand-maid concluded by repeating an appropriate verse from one of Wesley's hymns.

While these friends were trying to assure each other, Mr. Capel entered the parlor to hear a duet. Miss Mannors had just taken her seat at the piano, and, at that moment, one of the latest sunbeams of that beautiful evening shot in slantwise through the shining window, and rested on her golden brown hair and on its waving curls like a nimbus around the head of an angel. Mary never looked more radiant. There she sat, the folds of her white dress falling around her in graceful lines, and developing a form perfect, at least in the eyes of the young preacher, who now stood nervously by her side prepared to turn over the pages of music.

During the performance of the piece, Mr. Capel would have liked to mingle his voice with the sweet strains which now met his ear and charmed him away once more to his old home and to other endearing scenes, but, he must remember, was he not a preacher? were not all such recreations allurements which might draw him aside from the path of duty, as they had drawn others? No; these things must be avoided, must be even despised for the *Cross*. Alas! was it not a heavy cross to carry, to be obliged to reject and condemn what he could not help feeling was intellectual and humanizing? Was it not a heavy cross for one of excellent taste, to be content with the many dry, dreary, droning, and naked intonations embodied in church music, and to seldom rise above "Cambridge," "Devises," the "Old Hundredth," or above solemn or mournful anthems, sometimes sung, but seldom well performed? But, on the other hand, if he ever willingly gave way to the seductive power of secular music, it might be only the first step downward in a course of spiritual ruin.

For the time, there was a rebellion between nature and grace. Could it be sinful to indulge in harmony that was so elevating, so pure? Were not the angels in heaven thus engaged, and was it not one of the enjoyments of the blest in their home of eternal rest? Would it be wrong for him to mingle his voice with the soft sweet music made by that innocent girl? It could not be; and as he stood, listless as a statue, he never felt a restraint more galling than that which now prevented him from joining in such a delightful exercise.

Song after song was sung by Mr. Mannors and his daughter, and the poetry and musical composition were most suitable for the time and place. The sunlight had faded away, but so gradually that the mellow moonbeam was now its mild substitute. And the oblong patch of silvery light that was then seen on the carpet beneath the window was an agreeable evidence of the quiet transition.

"Well," said Mr. Mannors, during a pause after the piece was concluded, "I do not know how it may be with others, but music has the happiest effect on me; to be a day without it would be a deprivation I should feel very much. Morning and evening, for years, I have had music as regularly as other people have had prayer. Indeed, what they say prayer is to the devotee, music is to me; it is *my* religion, it is my prayer; for the heart may want words that music alone can supply; and when I worship nature, I worship her in music. Then, under its inspiration, I have often soared away in fancy. I often wish that I could leave the world and its discord forever, provided I could find some poet's happier sphere, and if I only had those I love to accompany me. Isn't that the way, Pop?" and he laid his hand upon the head of his fair daughter, and then looked into her blue eyes as if to read her thoughts.

"Indeed, pa, I have no doubt as to your mode of worship, and I think you are sometimes inspired. You dream in music as well as in sleep. I know for certain that you travel away occasionally where I could not follow. The other evening, after I had finished one of Mendelssohn's 'Songs without Words,' you must have started off somewhere, for when the modulations died away, there was a hush, and you stood mute and absent for nearly a minute; waiting, I suppose, to return with an echo from—"

"From the Summerland," said her brother quietly. William appeared very delicate, and had hitherto sat gazing in a kind of musical revery at his sister's beautiful face. "How I should like, Pop, if I was dying, to be allowed to go away by the light of such moonbeams, and that you and pa would sing that nice lullaby for me before I left for the spirit-land. I like to hear that song when I am falling asleep. If I have to go, won't you sing it for me? Yes, Pop, you must sing with pa, and I will hear your voices in the Summerland, won't you?"

"What is my darling saying?" said Mrs. Mannors, rushing over to him and clasping him in her arms. "What is my darling saying about the spirits, or about the Summerland? You shall not, you shall not go, dear; you must stay with me. Why, my dear child, do you speak that way?" said the already terrified mother; "who said that you should ever leave me? We will never part, my dear, never, never, never!"

He still sat and looked up at her with a faint smile; the moonlight was upon his face, giving it a strange pallor, and then an expression of seriousness, as if he understood what he had said, and wished to give a warning.

These remarks made by William so unexpectedly, and at such a time, had a singular effect upon every person present, especially upon Mary who was much overcome; and it required all the persuasion which Mr. Mannors could use to induce his wife to suppress her feelings. Her agitation was great; she had but just entered the room, and had heard every word of the boy's strange request. Her emotions were such only as a mother could feel.

"You know, my dear," said Mr. Mannors, "that William is often very much depressed. This infirmity will wear away as he grows older; he requires more exercise in the open air. A boy's mind is easily affected. Hannah has been telling him about the spiritualists, and about circles and manifestations; and about Bunyan's heroes, Christian, Evangelist, and Faithful; and about the Summerland or Happy-land. And you remember you told him only yesterday about the beautiful island you had seen in your dream, and how you saw him there, walking in a garden where there were such beautiful flowers, and then resting under the shade of such fine trees by the side of clear, sparkling streams, among happy children who had been many years dead, and most of whom you had known when you were a child. You know that such dream-stories can only leave a melancholy impression; even older persons have been sadly controlled by similar imaginations. Indeed, I am rather surprised," said he, somewhat gayly, "that we are not all in the same dreamy mood. Here we have been for the last hour with music and moonlight, and you ought to know something of their influence by this time." He addressed the last remark to Mr. Capel, and then sung in an undertone the first lines of the old song,

"Meet me by moonlight alone,
And it's then I will tell you a tale.'

This happy turn had its desired effect, and nearly brought back the cheerfulness which had been interrupted. In a few minutes, every shadow had disappeared; and when the lamps were lighted and the heavy curtains let fall over the windows, the moonlight disappeared from the room also. But, ah! there might be shadows lurking that the brightest light could not dispel; there might be gloom that the noonday sun could never chase away. What a pity! Already a shadow was stretching out that was destined to rest upon Mary's fair brow, and already the first faint trace of care had left a little furrow nestling close to the golden ringlets which hung from her classic head in such rich profusion. It was affecting to witness the efforts made by Mary to enliven her brother. Like a true, loving sister as she was, she resorted to various little methods to cheer away his temporary depression. She sat close by his side and ran her fingers through his hair, and put her lips to his ear repeatedly, whispering something that made him smile; and then she led him from the room to talk to Hannah and Robert in the kitchen. During the remainder of the evening, she scarcely left him; she would not allow him to brood alone for a moment; and it was not long before her winning ways and loving smiles restored him to boyish forgetfulness.

In a short time afterward, when all were seated in the pleasant room at the supper-table, and when the bright lamp-lights where reflected in a circle of smiling faces, Mr. Mannors, as the genial friend and hospitable host, appeared to great advantage. He had the faculty of making people feel happy, and now he related several anecdotes which were both humorous and instructive.

Mr. Capel's first evening in his new home was one which he said he could not forget: his first meal was most appetizing. Even Mrs. Baker, who was generally rather cold and formal toward Mr. Mannors, now, for once, relaxed her frigid demeanor. There was no remark made that could offend her religious sensibilities; there was no unpleasant innuendo. Mrs. Mannors might tell of her dreams or visions, or allude to the disturbance at the Bible meeting, or speak of ministers, or of ministers' wives, of missions or Mohammedans, just as she pleased, without eliciting a word from Mr. Mannors that might be taken as a slight upon organized piety. The preacher's wife therefore en joyed herself more than she had for a long time. So much was this the case, and so much more had she inclined toward her host, that she secretly wished her husband had but an opportunity to see him as he then was, even to witness but a few of the excellent qualities which, in spite of all prejudice, she must acknowledge were possessed in such an eminent degree by this reputed despiser of the Gospel.

The cheerful hours passed away, and Mrs. Baker had to return home. She left the cottage highly pleased with her visit. The piano had given its last note for the night, and Mrs. Mannors and Mary and William had retired. Mr. Mannors and his guest sat by the smouldering fire, talking freely about many things, as if the various topics could not be exhausted. Mr. Capel referred to the Bible meeting, with the view of hearing his opinion, and then to cautiously try and draw him out on the subject of religion. Mr. Mannors had read the account of the disgraceful scenes which had been enacted in Mr. Howe's church, and he alluded to the singular conduct of the majority of ministers and hearers who had openly encouraged what might be called a religious riot. The shameful proceedings had been talked of far and near, and he knew of many pious persons who exulted in the defeat of a certain religious body on that occasion.

"I must acknowledge," said Mr. Capel, "that the whole proceedings were most discreditable, most shameful, most injurious to our common Christianity."

"Or rather a common phase of Christianity," returned Mr. Mannors. "I see you wish to know my opinion on the subject, and I will give it plainly. I know you will listen without offense. Religious people seem to exist in contention ; it seems to be their normal condition ; they claim to monopolize all the virtue, honor, and morality which elevate humanity, and tell us that without the Bible man would be worse than a brute. What, then, has the Bible done for these men whose professed calling is said to be to promote in an especial manner peace and good-will? What has the Bible done to appease the clamorous sects around us who can violate, most deliberately, every principle of honor or justice to obtain an ascendency? How is our nation plundered and our people impoverished to sustain a class of men who from pulpit and platform shout out, 'The Bible, the whole Bible, and nothing but the Bible,' and yet—astonishing fact—the very rapacity of these persons, the same now as in all time, has been more depleting to our country than the support of another abuse—the payment of a large standing army. Look at the pomp, and splendor, and state of our national priesthood! Is this right? Look at the violent upheaving and struggle for precedence among the dissenting churches! What is the great actuating motive? is it the ultimate benefit of the people? Alas! you, as well as I, must answer, No. There is a ceaseless craving for more, more ; there is no appeasing the insatiable appetite of our religious teachers. There is an everlasting mania for the erection of pala-

tial churches, for ministerial endowments, for the printing and circulation of thousands of Bibles, and for sending men called 'missionaries' away to the ends of the earth, while we at home are infested with an ignorant, vicious multitude, even in the very midst of a crowd of priests. There is always something to demand the child's toy, the widow's mite, or the poor man's pence, at the time that thousands, yes, millions of human beings are kept languishing in poverty, and vainly struggling for the actual necessaries of life. There is always some gulf in which the resources of the nation are swallowed up in behalf of this terrible despotism called 'RELIGION,' which, while ostentatiously claiming to be the handmaid of charity, exhibits its sordidness by its unjust distribution of pence to the poor and pounds to the church, rags for the pauper and robes for the priest. This has been the result of its influence ; it has consecrated imposition, and almost dethroned humanity.

"On all sides of us we see churches towering up, the most magnificent and costly buildings in the land. In every city, town, village or hamlet in Christendom, the most prominent object is the sanctuary. A house must be provided for the Lord, though the poor perish on the highway. All sects, while preaching humility, seem to delight in a rivalry for fine churches ; the extravagance in this respect is unbounded. There are now, nearly or about a thousand of such edifices in London alone, erected at a cost of millions.* These magnificent piles are but seldom used, and, save a few hours every week, they remain closed to all the world. According to the arrogance of clerical opinion, it would be desecration to devote them to anything else than religion. Were the opinion not so prevalent, Science would not have to tremble so often in a shed, while Religion was exalted under a gilded canopy. Throughout the land, you will find a church where no proper refuge for the poor has been provided, or where no public school has been yet erected. You will find poor, homeless wanderers, for whom no adequate provision has been made ; hopeless men, forlorn women, and shivering children, who would gladly find a shelter within such walls. Our poor-house prisons are not homes for the poor, they are prisons ; and the man who is once forced to enter their walls feels forever degraded. They are a disgrace to our age. The splendid religious temples, so numerous around us, have never yet been devoted to the beneficent purposes of humanity. The night sha[d]ows of bleak winter may fall heavily around St. Paul's Cathedral, the cold winds may blow, and drifting snow or torrents of rain may fall on the frozen earth, but the desolate and wretched who wander through the streets, and who know not where to lay their heads, may look longingly in vain at that great Christian monument. It will be no asylum for them ; they are our

* St. Paul's Cathedral, London, is over five hundred feet long, covers two acres of ground, and cost the nation £1,500,000 sterling—about $7,500,000—which was collected by a tax on coal !

national vagrants, for whom nobody cares. They may rest their wearied limbs where they can, under door-steps and porches; they may lean against dead walls, or crouch into corners, or creep into filthy drains or sewers; but St. Paul's can not be polluted by such a rabble. Our religious civilization will not stand this; such noble structures are evidences of national taste—of our homage to superstition. They are consecrated and dedicated, but must not be desecrated by over-done efforts of practical benevolence; it would do violence to religious feeling, and be, simply and plainly, sacrilege. The rich cushion made for the knee of wealth must not be used as a pillow for the poor man's head."

Mr. Capel felt surprised at the vehemence of his host; there was a certain amount of truth in what he had just heard, and which he could not deny. Pious extravagance in the erection and ornamentation of churches was most remarkable. He had had positive evidence, time after time, that Gospel ministers were not all saints, were no better than other men, but in many respects far less liberal and intelligent; that the numerous sects were not charitably disposed toward each other, or always governed by just principles; but he thought that religion was not to blame for this; it was rather the want of it. He felt embarrassed as to how he should reply, relative to the so-called desecration of churches. The idea advanced by Mr. Man nors was new to him, and his better nature incl ned him to think that it could not be an unholy act to give such shelter to the poor, where shelter was so much needed. The temple in which active charity was displayed could not be less agreeable to the Lord than that which was reserved for a mere pompous exhibition of faith without works. It would be difficult, however, to reduce such a theory to practice; clerical opinion was stubborn on this point. He would think more on that subject.

"You imagine it is rather a want of religion," said Mr. Mannors. "I shall speak to you concerning this again; but, I ask, is there not something wrong in so much religious ostentation? Is not the accumulation and display of ecclesiastical wealth significant? The history of religion in this island is a national disgrace; its race of intolerance and oppression is nearly run; but it has been a galling fetter upon the noblest impulses of our people. Witness the cupidity of the priest-power of this nation at the present day. All must succumb to the fraudulent exaction of church rates, and to the ceaseless importunities of the so-called voluntary systems, which are almost as extortionate. There is something wrong in all this. With the immense sums annually expended for religion, we have in our British cities as much crime and destitution as you will find in an equal number of heathen cities in any part of the world. We may boast of our civilization, but we are still as obdurate, as selfish, and as inhuman as those who have never yet opened a Bible. We have enough for all, yet thousands are starving. A few monopolize the wealth, a few more the land. Passive

obedience is preached in our churches, and the poor are driven to desperation and crime. We boast of British law—laws that are based upon the principle of revenge instead of reform. If a man can not pay his debts, we imprison him; if he commits a certain crime, we take his life; we still have an eye for an eye, and a tooth for a tooth. Religion has never had any great regard for human life. In ancient times, by its sanction, men were robbed of their existence for trifling offenses; and until lately, even in this civilized kingdom, death was the penalty for offenses a conviction for which may now bring but a few month's imprisonment; and still, notwithstanding the efforts of the humane, a painful death is the legal remedy for misdemeanors made crimes, and for crimes made capital, by the persistency of Christian legislation."

"I must differ from you," replied Mr. Capel. "I think Christianity has mitigated the rigor of our laws; it has humanized our legislation, no doubt of it; and I think that we, as Christian people, have good reason to boast of the influence of religion in this respect."

"I fear you have forgotten. It is well known that Christianity has claimed to be the author of reforms which the church at first opposed; this is characteristic of its course. When a few reformers aroused the nation against the enormities of the slave-trade, who was it that upheld the system? Who was it that waved aloft the lash of the task-master, and tried to smother the humane, the merciful impulse under a cloud of texts?—The national priests! During the agitation of that question, some years ago, the late Lord Eldon sarcastically said, in the House of Lords, ' that he could not bring himself to believe the slave-trade was irreconcilable with the Christian religion, as the bench of bishops had uniformly sanctioned by their votes the various acts of Parliament authorizing that trade.'[*] I must remind you that when petitions were sent to Parliament against the death penalty, many of our ministers and preachers denounced the movement from the pulpit, and successfully used their influence against its abolition. ' Whoso sheddeth man's blood, by man shall his blood be shed,' is still the favorite text in support of legalized murder.[†] If Christianity has mitigated the rigor of our laws, the same excellence was claimed for it when Catholic and Protestant inquisitors endeavored to enforce their mild doctrines through the medium of the wheel, the rack, the thumbscrew, and the boot; by roasting and disjointing, by pressing, tearing, crushing, and defacing, and by mutilating and torturing the human body in every imaginable way! And it can not be denied that these cruelties were entirely of Christian origin. This, my friend, is a dreadful history; and if our laws are becoming more lenient, it is because humanity has triumphed over the scruples of religion."

Mr. Capel paused for a few moments before

* Note C.

† "Rev Chas. B. S—— gave his views on marriage and divorce, at the Cooper Institute, New-York, on Sunday evening. He thought the only penalty for adultery was the death of the guilty parties." From a Philadelphia paper, 1867.

he replied. He could not positively deny what had been asserted, and he hesitated, in the hope that he might be able to find some plea. "I do not," said he, "admit that Popery is Christianity. The inquisition was a disgrace, for which our purer faith should not be held accountable."

"I make but little distinction," said Mr. Manners. "The leaven of intolerance is in the whole lump, each in turn persecuting the other. You surely can not forget the enormities of the Star Chamber; you can not forget the fierce vindictive persecution that raged for years among the Protestant sects—Episcopalian against Dissenter, Puritan against Quaker. I will not recall the enormities, they are too painful. But I will ask you, plainly, after all our church-building, and preaching, and praying; after all that has been extorted for the maintenance of thousands of priests, of all denominations—what is the result of our boasted Christianity? Has it lessened the brutalities of war? Has it made men more humane, more generous, more self-denying, more forgiving, than those of re-mote times, who had never heard the Gospel sound? What have we as the grand result?"

"People who can resort to persecution have never been imbued with a true Christian principle," replied Mr. Capel. "I care not how they are called; the man who persecutes for opinion's sake is not a Christian. I can not admit that Christianity is answerable for the enormities of which you speak."

"Then," said Mr. Manners, "I do not understand where Christianity is to be found, if not among those who preach and those who profess it; if I can not find it among the tried and true believers who are, and have been, as ready to die for the faith as they have been to persecute—where is it to be found? Ah my friend! do not mistake your natural sense of justice for the gift of faith."

"If we look for pure Christianity," answered Mr. Capel, "we must look for it in the Bible alone. Were men to be entirely guided by its divine teachings, our world would be different from what it is. Professors of religion are, I admit, too often governed by angry passions; they exhibit a want of forbearance. The Bible denounces error, but has no plea for persecution. There is not a text between its covers that favors such a principle."

"Then I do not understand the Bible," said Mr. Manners, "I consider its teaching essentially intolerant; and when I read such texts as this, 'If there come any unto you and bring not this doctrine, receive him not into your house, neither bid him God-speed,' (John 2: 10,) I am justified in believing that it favors persecution. The *anathema-mara-natha* is ever ready. But as it is now getting late, we shall not pursue this subject any further at present. It is a pleasure to converse with you, and I hope you will bear with me hereafter if I venture to give you my opinion of the Bible more plainly."

"I am ready," said Mr. Capel, "to listen to any argument, either for or against the di-

vine word. Truth can not suffer by discussion."

"I am much pleased to hear you say so. I feel that I have spoken warmly on this subject, I am obliged to do so; and I well know the penalty which must be paid for the free expression of opinion. Our ministers are ever ready to denounce any person who may venture to question what you call 'Divine Revelation.' Instead of courting investigation, they try to avoid it. They are a popular and influential body, and it is not always safe to hurl a stone against a popular idol. It requires no small share of moral courage to smite the image; but if the duty falls to my lot, then it shall be performed; I am willing to strike the blow alone. I was once a believer, as you now are; I can believe no longer. I know that it requires much patience and fortitude to contend against a popular error. I respect the honest opinions of men of all creeds; I interfere not with them; but if any are desirous of approaching the light, they shall have my sympathies. It is hard to be maligned by men who profess to have been regenerated, yet who have not learned the lesson of charity. For years I have been misrepresented by certain of your preachers, because I can not bring myself to a passive belief of all that is recorded in the Scriptures. The late meeting of your Bible Society ought, I think, to satisfy you that some who profess to be ministers of Christ are wicked and designing. I know of but one who was at that meeting who is actually infamous. I know of one who is courted and smiled upon, and treated as the principal pillar of one of the great religious bodies, whose voice has charmed many in the sanctuary, but whose fierce intolerance has brought sorrow to his own home; and there may be yet one poor broken heart to cry out against him, 'How long, O Lord! how long!'"

CHAPTER X.

EARLY next morning, when Mr. Capel looked from his window, he was delighted with the fine panoramic view which he obtained of the distant city and surrounding scenery. Faint streaks of red light in the east betokened the coming glory of the rising sun, and in a short time those early harbingers of the day god were spread around in all directions, illuminating every object, crowning the distant hills with ruddy light, and sending golden rays over ancient tree and castle, and then flashing on a hundred glittering spires of the proud metropolis. The great cross of St. Paul's was again visible in the morning sky; and that which had been observed by Mrs. Manners as a cause of so much superstitious reverence was now only more noticeable from its great altitude, not from any thing peculiar in its appearance. He mused as the sunlight rested on the window-sill, and threw a glimmer on the rustling ivy that was creeping upward with silent progress. He still looked toward the city, and felt a degree of surprise at the vast number of towers and steeples which were looming up, as if trying to leave the smoky gloom, and the darker objects by which they were surrounded. These numerous structures called to his remembrance the remarks of his friend Mr. Mannors. What vast sums must have been expended in their erection! and the question again came, What was the result? Could it be that the world was in reality no better than if they had been so many heathen temples? Could it be that these numerous sanctuaries, dedicated to God, had not made the mass of the populace of London any better, but had been erected and consecrated to provide wealth, ease, and distinction for a horde of religious stock-brokers and professional imposters? Yet this was the opinion of thousands, who assert that they are forced to tolerate an unscrupulous priesthood. He was willing to admit that there was a portion of truth in the supposition; still he thought that such an extreme view could not be justified. There were, no doubt, many stately churches which had been built as much for the adornment of the city as for temples for worship; but were there not many other places in which the pure word of God was regularly expounded by faithful, persevering men, who, in the very midst of the pride and pomp of this mighty Babylon were not ashamed to go out into the highways, and into the streets, lanes and alleys to call upon the reckless and abandoned?

But why, thought he, with all these churches crowded into every quarter, why is there still such a complaint of "religious destitution"? With so many hundred places of worship, several of a gorgeous and imposing appearance, and with a multitude of priests, from the princely archbishop, lolling in his luxurious carriage, down to the most humble dissenting itinerant, there was yet an amount of vice and ignorance in London that was almost overwhelming. By the immensity of aids and appliances which Christianity had at its command—wealth, power, and authority—any religious system, Mormonism or Mohammedanism, or any other ism, no matter how monstrous, absurd, or debasing to human reason, might be inculcated and established by resolute men. Yet even with these very means, to an enormous extent, the complaint still was, that the national faith was languishing, and that many, even among priests and pious literati, began to doubt, just as if Christianity was behind the age—a drag upon science, and as if it contained no intrinsic excellence that could not be made sufficiently manifest without the persuasive aid of gold, legal enactments, and priestly pensioners.

Almost every city paper contained, periodically, accounts of some great meeting, got up by the clergy, for the purpose of making pious appeals to the benevolent for fresh means to meet the spiritual wants said to be so fast increasing. Did these wants arise from an increase of sinners, or an increase of priests? Every possible method was used to induce the people to resort to places of worship; and to effect this more particularly, the ministry united, almost to a man, in making pulpit appeals against Sabbath desecration. They loudly decried against a resort to public parks, gardens, libraries, or museums, but all to no purpose; the great mass of the working people would not come under the clerical yoke; and if debarred from such favorite places, many might wander away among green fields or pleasant highways, while too many others would defiantly resort to dram-shops, gin palaces, or dens of depravity. It was proved by official returns, that the numerous churches and chapels already erected were on the average not more than one third filled by regular attendants; and it was a well known fact that, with regard to the Established Church, not more than one third of the number of its clerical incumbents ever did more for religion than go through the occasional formality of reading liturgical prayers, or delivering a languid sermon—often the composition of some needy author. Yet still these very incumbents who live in ease, and revel in such ducal incomes, or draw such exorbitant salaries, are, without the least compunction, among the very first to shout out, "More money, more churches, more priests, and more Sunday restrictions."

These circumstances were degrading to religion. The truth was not preached, but it was made merchandise of by unscrupulous men, whose priestly trade was but a source of wealth to themselves and a tax on the nation. The Queen, Lords, and Commons united in support of that great religious imposition called "The Church;" and our legislators stood agape if any one dared to question such a palpable outrage. The church must be protected even though blood should be daily shed in support of its exactions.

But then, thought he, the dissenting ministers are a different class; were it not for them, Christianity in Britain would be almost extinct. These ministers might in reality be called the "successors." They were persons who cared not to preach for the sake of filthy lucre; the souls of men were of more value to them than rich livings or ecclesiastical preferments. But, alas! even among dissenters, there were only a few such preachers. They, too, had undoubtedly become more worldly. The strife and bitter feeling among the various sects seemed to grow with their growth, and strengthen with their strength. This continued strife was quite sufficient to counteract all the good that had been done by the most successful revivalists. And now, at the present day, while places of worship have been quadrupled; when preaching has become a lucrative trade; while the younger sons of the British aristocracy are foisted into bishoprics—taking precedence of merit in the church as they do of valor in the army—when clergymen and preachers of all ranks and conditions are aiming after popularity and distinction, while sects and denominations of all kinds have become wealthy and influential, and while the Christian creed has an aegis of protection in the strong arm of the law, the religious world is actually retrograding, and religion itself is held among many of the most gifted and intelligent to be only a delusion.

These were strange thoughts for a young preacher to indulge in, but they were such as had obtruded upon him at the time. He could not reject the evidence that had forcibly presented itself day after day. Again he tried to turn from these unpleasant cogitations; beneath him was the smiling garden, and the fresh fragrance of the morning ascended to where he stood. Spring flowers were flinging their incense to the young day, and buds of beauty that had been cared for by the hand of a fair girl were blushing in the early sunbeams. What peace seemed to rest upon the dwelling! When he thought of his friendly host, it was with a feeling of sincere pleasure, and he felt grateful that his lines had fallen in such pleasant places. He thought of Mary Mannors; her song seemed to linger in his ear; her image was before him, and her sweet smile rose like radiance in his memory. Mrs. Mannors he considered an excellent woman—good, pious, and charitable, but far behind either father or daughter in mental qualities; and already to him did that daughter appear as the special angel of the household.

Indeed, Mr. Capel might be justified in granting that position to Mary Mannors. Almost every thing that was beautiful or attractive in or about Hampstead Cottage bore traces of her superintendence. In fine weather, she spent much of her time in the garden. She trimmed the shrubs, trained the vines, nursed young, delicate plants, and petted the birds in the hall; and when she approached the cages, the little inmates became at once vocal. With William as her almost constant attendant, the flower pots, the flowers, the fountain, the rock work, and even the neat graveled walks, were all kept more trim and orderly by her industrious care. She was also quite competent to superintend household affairs.

What a blessing, thought Mr. Capel, she might be to her mother were she only brought under the full influence of religion, and not to her mother alone, but to her father; for she might be a missionary, whose gentle teaching would be more persuasive to a mind like his than that of the most skillful polemic, or than the argument of the most learned pulpit oration.

The events of the previous evening passed rapidly before him, and he began to reflect upon the duty which he had undertaken. He was greatly pleased with the frank, courteous disposition of Mr. Mannors; but he feared it would be a difficult task to make him believe that the sentiments which he held upon religious subjects were erroneous.

Mr. Capel, as well as other preachers, often had troublesome doubts arise in his own mind, he often felt confused about various ambiguous passages in the Bible, and about their various interpretations. He was often perplexed by contradictory chapters, verses, and texts; and the bare idea of *eternal* punishment was most repulsive, and conflicted greatly with his conception of divine benevolence. It would not, however, be prudent to mention these doubts to any one; least of all to the person whom he was now desirous of reclaiming from error.

I have been, thought Mr. Capel, too much like a doubting Thomas, ever ready to stumble over the slightest obstruction. I have allowed my frail reason to interfere with my faith, and if I do not suppress these rebellious thoughts, as others in the faith make it a duty to do, I may go on forever doubting and reasoning and reasoning and doubting, until I shall have stepped over the precipice which has brought destruction to so many. Why should I set up my opinions against those of the most able and intellectual that England has produced? Why should I hesitate to accept that which has been tried by a Wesley, a Clark, and a Paley? Great minds have submitted to revelation, and surely *I* can not refuse the truth which has been so apparent and conclusive to them. To doubt what Newton believed would be folly and presumption.

Before he left his room, he decided to be more prayerful, to try and banish every doubt, and to place full trust in the Lord. He would speak to Mr. Mannors in all sincerity; he would tell him of his lost state by nature, and how he might be enlightened by the Divine Spirit, and how he might be saved by placing all trust in the propitiatory sacrifice made for every child of Adam. He would in this matter boldly take up his cross, and the Lord would not be forgetful of his promise, but would reveal himself, and establish his own truth. That truth must be irresistible, particularly to one who, like Mr. Mannors was a sincere inquirer, and who could in calm discussion throw aside every prejudice and submit to honest conviction.

As Mr. Capel entered the parlor Miss Mannors had just commenced to play one of Beethoven's beautiful sonatas; she was not aware of the presence of the young preacher. She sat in her loose morning dress, and every motion was the perfection of grace. Her unbound golden hair hung around her snowy shoulders, and her delicate fingers ran along the keys with finished touch, sending out the most exquisite harmony. What little seraphs had once seemed to his boyish mind, Mary was now to his manhood; and as she still played, her presence and her music had such a magical effect that neither by word nor action could he interrupt the fair performer, and he listened delighted and spell-bound for the time.

When the piece was finished, he addressed Miss Mannors. She was a little surprised, and a faint blush overspread her face, greatly adding to her personal attractions, and rendering the clear blue eyes which she had now turned toward him singularly fascinating. She had not the least idea that he had been a listener in the very room; and now that they were alone for the first time, she felt slightly embarrassed. But with her, such a feeling could be only momentary; she looked up at him confidently, and said: "I hope I played one of your favorite pieces. Pa says you are a good judge of music, and indeed I think so too. I fancy I heard your voice last evening, you sang for a minute or two, and then quit suddenly as if you were afraid. Let me see, Quakers, I believe, never indulge in music. How strange! Is it sinful to sing?"

"Oh! not at all; we sing in our worship, we praise God in music."

"Yes, of course you sing hymns ; but such songs only. Now, you are a minister, and I think you will acknowledge that no one can be very bad who is readily touched or affected by music. Ma used to tell me when I was a child, that little angels were continually singing delightful melodies. Music, therefore, must be a heavenly acquirement."

"Heaven would not, I think, be perfect without it," said Mr. Capel. "Angels are always musical ; and I find that some of our earthly angels are very like their sisters in paradise."

Miss Mannors again blushed slightly ; she was perhaps a little confused by the reply, but she continued as if she had not heard it.

"I can not on that account," said she, "be a very great sinner. I don't pretend to be a saint, but I find that even some of our most religious persons are always deploring their own vileness, as they call it. Now really, Mr. Capel, don't you think that many of our pious people exaggerate a great deal with such religious phraseology of self-condemnation ? Now, my mamma is one of the best and kindest hearts in all the world, yet she is given to bewail her own sinfulness ; and she has told us over fifty times that we in this quiet place are all wicked and sinful, and very bad in most respects. Can this be so ? And Mr. Wesley, who, as you know, was a very good man naturally, and I suppose much better for having been such a devoted minister, often boasted—if I may use that expression—that he was the 'chief of sinners'! Was not such an assertion truly and positively wrong ? It was not only a very absurd exaggeration, but almost if not quite a—of course I won't say what. Don't you think so ?"

This question, simple as it was, and put with such naïveté, really disconcerted him for a few moments ; but the usual orthodox reply came to his rescue, and he said :

"According to the Scriptures, Miss Mannors, we are all sinners by nature. We are told that there is none good, no, not one. I acknowledge that there seems to be an apparent incongruity in the assertion to which you allude. As fallible beings, we are not truly capable of judging as to what is right or what is wrong.

"We think favorably of those whom we believe to be good and virtuous ; we may be partial, but there are no degrees of sin in the sight of God ; all alike are under condemnation. And until a man becomes regenerate, and freed from the curse of the law, he has no right to expect the favor of God, or consider himself any thing but a sinner of the deepest dye."

"Under the curse of the law! Dreadful, dreadful!" said Mary, with an arch smile ; "why, really, I think religious persons must be very unhappy. Just to think of having to believe that all the good, kind people we see around us are such terrible wretches as to deserve such condemnation! And then to believe that God, who is said to be so loving and merciful, is to be always so unforgiving and vindictive toward creatures which he himself is said to have created. I can not believe this. You must remember that it was

after his conversion that Mr. Wesley used to presume to be the 'chief of sinners.' You can not believe that he was. Ma and Hannah are almost always telling us of his goodness ; and to read his interesting journals, you could come to no other conclusion than that he was a favorite with God and man. Yet how mistaken good men can be sometimes!"

"Mr. Wesley was certainly a blessing to the world," said Mr. Capel ; "he was particularly successful as a preacher of righteousness, and no doubt many are now among the redeemed whom he can claim as seals to his ministry. He now enjoys his heavenly reward."

"And yet, wonderful to relate, he was all the time the 'chief of sinners.' Well, I declare, Mr. Capel, there is something very inconsistent in such an idea. Then you believe that the Almighty thinks every person fit for condemnation but the regenerate ; and that until we are what you call 'born again,' we are all equally guilty, and must all perish alike under the curse of the law? What injustice to make me answerable for the sins of another! Why did God permit Adam to be tempted, when he knew that he could not resist? Then if I am under this curse, how am I to get free ? I remember a text which I learned at Sunday-school, 'No man can come to me except the Father which hath sent me draw him.' If we can not repent until we are drawn, punishment for non-compliance would seem unjust. There are some other singular passages in the Bible which go to prove that the Deity is partial, 'blinding the eyes' and 'hardening the hearts' of some, lest they should be converted. This is hard to believe ; it may be orthodoxy, but it is not humanity. Such a doctrine is opposed to the better feelings of our nature ; it is most repulsive. We fallible creatures readily admit that there are degrees of guilt, and our reason and common sense lead us to believe that there ought to be degrees of punishment. Our reformatory laws are based upon such a principle ; but to condemn all alike may be divine justice according to Scripture ; it is certainly not consistent with human jurisprudence."

While speaking thus, Mary Mannors looked him full in the face, and her emotion spread a glow over her beautiful countenance. He paused in admiration and astonishment. She had given him a specimen of precocious reasoning which he did not expect ; he had never before heard a person of her age express sentiments so fearlessly, or with such a feeling of thorough indifference to orthodox censure. His immediate impulse was in sympathy with her opinions, but that impulse was but momentary. As like others anxious to believe, Faith was ever ready to whisper, "Beware of reason," and Faith with him still had the ascendency.

"I am aware, Miss Mannors," said he with some diffidence, "that there are passages in the Bible hard to be understood ; but there is enough sufficiently plain to teach us our duty. I trust you will some day view these matters as I now do. We know by experience how difficult it is for human tribunals to decide the claims of justice. What injustice has been done where justice has been the aim? We must submit entirely to the claims of revelation. Without the Bible, our reason would lead us far astray, and the world would be sadly bewildered."

"Upon my word," said Mary, laughing, "without desiring to speak irreverently, I think the Bible has sadly bewildered those who pretend to expound it. If there are, as you say, passages in that book hard to be understood, and liable to produce error and uncertainty, what necessity was there for them? They could not have been written for our instruction or edification. I am inclined to think that while we ignore reason in these matters, we shut out the only light we have. I fear you will think that I presume too much; but from the variety of opinions, the number of creeds, contradictions, and conflicting doctrines—all said to be derived from the same inspired source, and all claiming the same infallibility, those who are determined to stick to the Bible as being an inspired book must ever remain in a wilderness of doubt and speculation."

"Why such passages are included in the Bible is at present beyond our comprehension; we must only assume," said Mr. Capel, "that they are intended for some good purpose. It would be folly to reject all, because a portion is beyond our reason. The Bible, as it is, is the only revelation from God to man. In it we have sufficient instruction, and if we are governed by its precepts, we need not fear the designs of the Evil One, we need not be afraid to die."

"Well, well," said Mary, "I can not understand these things. I fear no evil one; and, when my time comes, I shall not be afraid to die. But apart from this, if you say that until we become regenerated we must consider ourselves sinners of the deepest dye, I can not agree with you. Now, do you think," said she, smiling, and giving him an arch look, "do you really think that I am such a wretched sinner, and that I deserve such terrible punishment? I do not feel that I am. I do not believe that I am. I never did the least harm to any one in my life; indeed, I would much rather do a kindness than an injury. And to say that I should be obliged to consider pa and William, whom I love, and many other excellent persons whom I know and regard, as vile degraded creatures, full of all kinds of sin and mischief, I would rather be vilified and despised as a downright unbeliever; as far as that goes, I am an unbeliever. I would not on any account submit to such a doctrine. I think you will find it difficult to do so yourself. If, in order to be a good Christian, you must believe that a few of us, quiet, unoffending people in this house, are as bad as even some of the ministers we read of in the papers, why then," said she, smiling, "we shall never be of one mind."

"That's right, Pop, that's right," said Mr. Mannors, who now entered the room, carrying William on his back. "I have overheard what you have just said, and if Mr. Capel is right, I must, like Bunyan's Pilgrim, get rid of this little bundle of sin;" and he placed William on a chair near his sister. "You see, Mr. Capel, when I am away, my daughter is my representative, and if you tell her we are all such bad people, then you must expect to get some hard blows. He tries to imagine that we are as wicked and corrupt as your mamma and poor Hannah fancy we are, does he?" said he, addressing Mary; and while he stood smiling behind her chair he began to smooth down her glossy ringlets with his open hands.

"Indeed, Miss Mannors is a very good exponent of the doctrine of self-righteousness," said Mr. Capel pleasantly. "I am afraid she is under the impression that the saints are a very exclusive set of beings. I trust, however, that before long she will be better acquainted with their sentiments."

Mary now stood by the piano, and again her fingers ran over the keys in a careless manner; and the notes that she awoke came in response to the gentle feelings of her own bosom. She had no dread of future misery; she had no fear of a Deity who created her for purposes of vengeance. She felt no condemnation for any thing she had done, and had it been in her power, she would have willingly banished care, and distress, and sorrow from every human being. She was not possessed of one truly selfish feeling, and had no higher ambition than to try and make the little circle in which she moved radiant with happiness. What, then, had she to fear? Ministers of the Gospel might frighten others about the "wrath of an offended God," and about the "death that never dies," and about flames and tortures, and the horrors depicted by Baxter, Edwards, and Doddridge,* she would believe in no such vengeance—of no worse fiends than some of those in human shape. She would still hope and trust in the great Being who made this beautiful earth, and the blue skies; who smiled in the sunlight, and gave fragrance to the flower. She would trust that Being who had given her a heart to feel, and who had given to her, and to them she loved, faculties for enjoyment; and who, above all, had endowed her with reason to resist teachings which would portray the Omnipotent Power as a barbarous divinity, influenced by malignant passions—capricious, arbitrary, tyrannical, and revengeful.

Her fingers still wandered over the instrument, bringing out snatches of favorite airs; and as she stood with her head turned to the sunlight, and her eyes directed toward some dew-spangled flower in the garden, she looked more like the impersonation of true womanly dignity and worth than the deluded abbess immured in a convent; or than many of her Protestant sisters who pay a silly worship to popular priests, and who neglect the duties of home to go on a round of collections for the purpose of erecting churches, circulating tracts and Bibles, or for providing funds and an outfit for Utopian missionaries to the frantic Feejees or treacherous Tongataboos.

*See Note D.

CHAPTER XI.

Mrs. MANNORS had a triumph! This morning, for the first time in many years they had regular family devotion; the domestic altar had again been raised in the good old fashion. A chapter was read, then a few words by way of explanation, and then there was prayer. What was more wonderful to her, Mr. Mannors had actually graced that triumph by his presence. He and Miss Mannors attended, as well as William and Hannah. All had assembled in the breakfast-room, and the greatest attention was paid while Mr. Capel was occupied in the performance of that service. Mrs. Mannors was in the best of spirits; she had brought this thing to pass; she felt like blessing the Lord all day long; and during breakfast, she entertained them with cheerful conversation about preachers and brethren, and about pleasant tea meetings in contemplation. And then she dwelt in anticipation upon the glorious time they were going to have in their grand assault on the stronghold of Satan, at the protracted or revival meeting that was soon to take place; many stubborn sinners were to be subdued, and the Lord was to be mightily magnified by the conquest. Then she told them about the busy preparations that were making for the great meeting of the British and Foreign Bible Society, to be held in Exeter Hall in the month of May; and about the ship load of idols, and Indian chiefs, and converted cannibals that were daily expected from foreign parts, and that were to be openly exhibited at a subsequent missionary meeting — genuine Gospel triumphs! She was not troubled this morning by the effects of any particular dream. William looked much better; she smiled most benignantly on Mr. Capel, and altogether she was in a most satisfactory state and very happy.

There were others also that morning, at Hampstead who to a certain extent might be said to be in the enjoyment of as full a measure of contentment as Mrs. Mannors. The young preacher could scarcely fancy that he was not among his own dearest relatives. He was almost persuaded to believe that Heath Cottage had once been his home, and that he had now returned to it after an absence of many years. He became communicative, and spoke about Ireland, and gave a description of the unrivalled natural beauty of the environs of his native city, and then related anecdotes of his younger days, and then revealed a little of his family history. He told them of the death of his mother and brother, and how lonely the world appeared to him afterward, and how he had been induced to enter the ministry. While he mentioned these things, he could not help perceiving that he was winning the sympathy of his new friends, and when he told them of his last visit to the old churchyard, where his parents and his little brother rested, and how he planted a rose-tree at each grave, and how wretched he felt when he had to leave all and go out into the world among total strangers, he saw that beside Mrs. Mannors's there was one pair of

soft eyes almost suffused with tears, and the solemnity on William's face was remarked by his mother as being strangely serious. Even Mr. Mannors was sensibly affected by the simple recital, and he spoke such warm words of encouragement as to make Mr. Capel truly feel that he was not without a home and friends.

During the conversation in the breakfast room, Hannah indulged as usual. Her voice from the kitchen could be heard singing lustily one of Wesley's hymns. She, too, seemed to be under the prevailing influence of the time; she was in the spirit, and although a good-natured laugh of mockery from Robert, who was working in the garden, could also be occasionally heard, Hannah seemed to pay no heed to the interruption, but resolutely continued until the entire hymn was finished.

Mr. Capel had yet a week to remain before he was required to recommence his itinerant visitations on the circuit. He would have been much better pleased had it been a fortnight; he was, however, determined to enjoy in the mean time all the happiness he could, and to make his stay at Hampstead agreeable to his new friends. He intended to embrace the first opportunity that offered in opening his mind to Mr. Mannors on the subject of religion, and if possible try and wean him from his erroneous views. He felt that he was but a weak instrument to effect much good. He knew his own inability to deal with a person of such mental calibre as his hospitable friend; but, fully trusting for aid from on high, he would undertake the duty in all humility, conscious that many eyes were fixed upon him, and that if he succeeded his success would be a triumph for the Gospel that might make scoffers and skeptics pause on their downward road. He would do his best, not for the purpose of obtaining any credit for himself, but for the further illustration of the potency of the Divine Word. He had already been considering some of the objections urged by his friend, and he thought it possible to meet them in a satisfactory manner. He had no faith in the subtleties of argument or controversy; he knew that prayer and faith would remove every mountain of unbelief; the result he would leave in the hand of the Lord.

The opportunity sought for by the young preacher was not long waiting. Mrs. Mannors had that day to visit Mrs. Baker, and she wished Mary and her brother to accompany her; the visit might benefit William. An early start was desirable, and in a short time Robert drove up with a plain, comfortable vehicle. Mr. Capel assisted Miss Mannors to her place, and was rewarded by one of her sweetest smiles. All was ready, and the parting between Mr Mannors and his wife and children was as affectionate as if they were not to meet again for a month; and when the carriage drove away, he and Mr. Capel stood at the gate, and looked after them until they were entirely out of sight.

It might not be difficult to speculate upon the young preacher's thoughts at the moment. It might not be hard to guess who it was that monopolized the most prominent place in his imagination, and who it was in particular that he missed when the sound of the wheels died away in the distance, and when the light clouds of dust that rose up behind them grew thicker and thicker. Although the sunlight was as bright as ever, yet already there was something shadowy in the appearance of Heath Cottage—there was a want of life about the place; even now, he really thought that the flowers were drooping their delicate heads, as if their queen had taken flight; that the little fountain had almost ceased to play, as if its gushing jets could only leave mere bubbles upon the surface of the limpid water; and that the yellow birds which looked up so often from their handsome prisons to the blue sky were more silent, just merely giving an occasional note, as if to let you know that they were yet alive. In spite of all he could do, a feeling of loneliness crept over him, and he was not much enlivened when Mr. Mannors said, in a kind of regretful mood, "There goes all my earthly treasure."

As they walked toward the house, Mr. Capel remarked, how happy they must be who had not their entire treasure upon earth, but who had their chief store laid up, where neither moth nor rust could corrupt nor thief break through to steal. What a privilege those enjoyed who could give up all, and forget all, for heaven. "Suppose," continued he, "that you should lose that treasure which you have reason to prize so highly, what consolation would you have left?"

"None, that I know of, but my tears—nature's own soothing. I would have to bear the affliction as best I could; we know by experience that such losses are among the contingencies of life, and are sure to follow in the course of human events. I envy no one the selfish privilege of forgetfulness. To be in such a place as heaven itself could not induce me to forget those I love—may I never be so selfish! My treasures are, however, upon this earth, which is now my heaven; and should I be so unfortunate as to lose them, I shall, no doubt, be delighted if I can again meet them in any happier place, or in some future state of existence."

The young preacher then endeavored to assure him of the certainty of such a meeting; it was that certainty which sustained the pious in afflictions or bereavement; and he then quoted several passages of Scripture in support of his assertions. Mr. Mannors, however, stated his regret that such passages were not sufficient to assure him, having had good reasons to question their authenticity; and as doubts were thrown on leading texts which Mr. Capel endeavored to explain, Mr. Mannors suggested that they should retire to his study where he had some books bearing on the question, and where they would be able to converse without interruption.

"Well," said Mr. Mannors, when they were quietly seated, "you and I are, I think, different from most persons who meet for discussion. We are about to approach the matter in a proper spirit, not like so many others who wage a war of words for the mere sake of a victory. We meet here for the more noble purpose of endeavoring to ascertain what is truth. Could I believe that you were determined to resist conviction and stick to cherish-

ed dogmas, whether right or wrong, I would not sit here a moment longer. We know that the pursuit of truth is attended with much difficulty, and that the sincere inquirer is often denounced as the enemy of his race. History has abundant proof that the high priests, and those in high station whom they could influence, have been ever ready to defame and persecute those who have refused to bow down and worship a popular error; or who have dared to brush away the antiquated excrescences which have impeded human progress. It has been truly said that 'reformers, in all ages, whatever their object, have been unpitied martyrs, and the multitude have evinced a savage exultation in their sacrifice. Let in light upon a nest of young owls, and they will cry out against the injury you have done them. Men of mediocrity are young owls; and when you present them with strong, brilliant ideas, they exclaim against them as false, dangerous, and deserving punishment;'* and another writer† says, 'An original thinker, a reformer in moral science, will thus often appear a hard and insensible character. He goes beyond the feelings and associations of the age; he leaves them behind him; he shocks our old prejudices; it is reserved for a subsequent generation, to whom his views have been unfolded from infancy, and in whose minds all the interesting associations have collected round them, which formerly encircled the exploded opinions, to regard his discoveries with unmingled pleasure.' Men man should be afraid of doubt; it has been called the 'beginning of philosophy,' and 'the accusing attorney in the court of truth.' No true man should hesitate to grapple with falsehood; for from the midst of the dust and confusion of the struggle, truth is sure to ascend more brilliant and triumphant. Any system, theory, or principle, no matter how antiquated or popular, that dreads or forbids investigation, bears witness to its own fraud, and is already stamped with its own condemnation. Grote says, 'To ask for nothing but results, to decline the labor of verification, to be satisfied with a stock of ready-made arguments as proof, and to decry the doubter or negative reasoner who starts new difficulties, as a common enemy—this is a proceeding sufficiently common in ancient as well as in modern times. But it is nevertheless an abnegation of the dignity and even of the functions of speculative philosophy.' We have thousands around us at the present day who dread this 'labor of verification'—mental drones, who swallow a creed as they would a pill; who are far behind the age, and who strut about like resuscitated mummies bearing their worm-eaten coffins on their backs as fancied emblems of distinction; and who are ever ready to erect a warning pillar of hieroglyphics in the way of every scientific, social, or moral improvement. These are they who, with haughty assumption, denounce the living, thinking men of the present day, who spurn their rotten bandages, and refuse to have their free limbs swathed in the musty conservatism of an ancient puerility. But the noble, liberal minds of all ages have been the unflinching advo-

* Adventures of a Younger Son.   † S. Bailey.

cates of free inquiry, even should the investigation lead to the abandonment of ideas long and tenderly cherished. Locke says, 'Those who have not thoroughly examined to the bottom their own tenets must confess they are unfit to prescribe to others, and are unreasonable in imposing that as truth on other men's belief which they themselves have not searched into, nor weighed the arguments of probability on which they should receive or reject it.' 'A mistake is not the less so, and will never grow into a truth, because we have believed it for a long time, though perhaps it be the harder to part with ; and an error is not the less dangerous, nor the less contrary to truth because it is cried up and had in veneration by any party.'

"Investigation should be commenced and continued without any dread as to its results ; a proposition which requires tender handling is possessed of some inherent rottenness. Harriet Martineau observes that 'No inquirer can fix a direct and clear-sighted gaze toward truth who is casting side glances all the while on the prospects of his soul.'

"When Galileo asserted the truth of the Copernican system, he was scoffed at and persecuted by the flaunting arrogance of old ideas ; and when he offered to give some of the wise ones of his day actual, positive proofs of the truth of his recent discoveries, he was not only denounced as a heretic, but actually imprisoned, for presuming to think beyond others. The ecclesiastical mummies of that period, like those of the present, declined the labor of verification, preferring to hug an antiquated error rather than permit the radiance of truth to expose their ignorance. Writing to his friend Kepler on this subject, he good-humoredly said:

"'O my dear Kepler! how I wish we could have a hearty laugh together. Here at Padua is the principal professor of philosophy, whom I have repeatedly and urgently requested to look at the moon and planets, through my glass, which he pertinaciously refuses to do, Why are you not here? What shouts of laughter we should have at this glorious folly.'*

"This is a fair illustration of blind, obstinate prejudice ; and that such prejudice still exists is glaringly manifest on every side. We have now a multitude of persons loud in their laudations of truth. Yet if you dare to doubt *their* idea of that principle ; if you venture in all humility to hint the possibility of their being in error; if you should benevolently

cast the most simple lamp-light across their path, in order to reveal, even to the least extent, the mud and mire through which they proudly and resolutely plunge—eager to follow in the slushy track of venerated predecessors—then you are an innovator, a disturber, an infidel, and a wretch.

"Daily experience goes to prove that such is the treatment which many of our most eminent benefactors have received from monopolizing blind guides, who persistently obtrude themselves as teachers of truth, and who as persistently stand in the way of progress. Even scientific Christian men have had to acknowledge that such is the case. Agassiz says, 'There are few of the great truths now recognized which have not been treated as chimerical and blasphemous before they were demonstrated.' Yet, after all this, the anathema is hurled at reform, and where priests can not persecute with the rack, as of old, they resort to social degradation."

"You can not deny," said Mr. Capel, "that many of our greatest reformers were sincere Christians. Newton, and Bacon, and others whom I might mention, gave eminent proofs of their ability and desire to enlighten mankind ; *they* were not afraid of advanced opinions."

"They were not ; but Lord Bacon's orthodoxy was, however, very questionable, and he was looked upon by many with distrust. Newton's great discovery of gravitation, and other discoveries of his, were strongly opposed, and were not fully understood by learned Christian men for more than fifty years after their announcement. These cases, however, do not affect the general correctness of what I have stated in relation to men who have departed from the beaten track of old opinions. We know that free inquiry has been proscribed from time to time, and we still see the necessity for perseverance. No matter how some may rage, or how base may be their detraction, let him who is on the side of truth be fearless, and he is sure to triumph. My object, so far, is to show the necessity for investigation ; and before I quit this preliminary, I will read you an extract bearing on the subject.

"Samuel Bailey, in his *Essay on the Pursuit of Truth*, says : 'The great interests of the human race, then, demand that the way of discovery should be open, that there should be no obstruction to inquiry, that every possible facility and encouragement should be afforded to efforts addressed to the detection of error and to the attainment of truth ; nay, that every human being, as far as he is capable, should actively assist in the pursuit ; and yet one of its greatest discouragements at present existing among mankind is the state of their own moral sentiments. Although he who has achieved the discovery of a truth in a matter of importance, or rescued an admitted truth from insignificance and neglect, may justly indulge the reflection that he has conferred a benefit on his fellow-men, to which even time itself can prescribe no limits, he will do well to prepare for the odium and persecution with which the benefit will be resisted, and console himself with a prospec-

---

* Luther, the hero of the Reformation, in the fullness of his priestly presumption, was as ready to rail at the discoveries of scientific men as were some of his late *confrères* of the Romish Church. In condemnation of the Copernican system of astronomy, he thus commits himself:

"I am now advised that a new astrologer is risen, who presumeth to prove that the earth moveth and goeth about, not the firmament; the sun and moon, not the stars—like as when one sitteth in a coach, or in a ship that is moved, thinketh he sitteth still and resteth, but the earth and trees do move and run themselves. Thus it goeth ; we give up ourselves to our own foolish fancies and conceits. This fool (Copernicus) will turn the whole art of astronomy upside down ; but the Scripture showeth and teacheth another lesson, when Joshua commandeth the sun to stand still, and not the earth."

tive reliance on the gratitude and sympathy of a future age. It is impossible to deny the fact, that in some of the most important departments of knowledge, the bulk of mankind regard novelties of doctrine—a description under which all detections of error and acquisitions of truth must come—as acts of moral turpitude or reprehensible arrogance, which they are ready to resent on the head of the promulgator.'"

"I regret," said Mr. Capel, "to be obliged to admit the full force of what you have just read. From my own limited experience, too many of our Christian teachers are ready to decry doubt and forbid inquiry. I fear no investigation; let truth and falsehood grapple. I am willing to submit Christianity to its severest test. I have had my doubts on many points, and some of the most thoughtful are troubled this way. I have been told that doubts were but temptations; they may be, but they generally tempt me to seek for an explanation. I have often said that there are many things in the Scriptures hard to be understood; but on the whole, I still accept them, as containing more truth than I can find anywhere else. I have full reliance on their authenticity, and do not fear to hear all that can be said against what the Christian world has accepted as Divine Revelation."

"This, then, is an honest conclusion," replied Mr. Mannors. "If men are hereafter to be punished for the rejection of that revelation, the subject becomes more momentous, and they should endeavor by all means to ascertain whether the Bible contains that pure truth which is claimed for it. No just Being can be offended if we submit the Scriptures to such fair tests as reason and common sense may suggest.

"Now, to proceed, we find that the earliest records concerning the human family lead us to believe that men in almost every age and clime have inclined to some form of religion, and have worshiped some particular idol or divinity, or a number of such, peculiar to their own race or nation.

"There are, it is said, a few very degraded tribes who have no conception of supernatural beings, and who do not, therefore, practice any form of worship; but, as a general fact, it may be accepted that religion has been a prevailing idea amongst mankind.

"It is not necessary to our purpose to try and trace the origin of the religious idea; it is merely sufficient to state, that the most ancient religious ceremonies are said to have been first practiced in Egypt; and from thence the whole world has become indoctrinated with forms and ceremonies almost innumerable.

"Religion has been always surrounded with mysteries; and, for the purpose of disseminating its principles, the order of priests was instituted.[*] They have generally assumed to

have been possessed of superior information, and to be able to regulate the intercourse between man and his Deity. Religious teachers, as a class, are mostly men who have ever been supported in luxury and power, and whose interest it is to persuade others that they alone are capable of giving or imparting religious information. An able writer[*] on this subject says: 'There were such bodies of professional priests in ancient Egypt, in Babylon, in Persia, in Gaul, in Phœnicia, in Judea, in Etruria, and in Greece. There are such priests now in Japan, in Hindostan, in Thibet, in Arabia, in Russia, in France, in England, and in Utah, and among many other civilized and barbarous nations. The several classes of priests of no two of the lands specially mentioned taught or teach the same creed. There have been at least two hundred different religious creeds taught, and extensively received among men, different from, and inconsistent with each other.' And he further says: 'History tells us that, in ancient times, the people were very ignorant and superstitious, and easily imposed upon, and the priests were numerous, and so influential that they could induce the people to believe or do almost any thing. It was the common belief among the political rulers, that government could not be firmly established, or morality preserved without the aid of superstition, the terror of the gods, and an implicit faith that the laws were of divine origin; and this belief frequently governed their action. Numa, Lycurgus, Zaleucus, Pythagoras, and scores of other lawgivers asserted that their codes were communicated to them by the gods. Diodorus Siculus tells us that the purpose of these claims to divine origin for human laws was to insure the supremacy and permanence of constitutions which would have been much less secure without the mighty protection of superstition. The laws of Egypt, Hindostan, Persia, and Babylon were all ostensibly dictated or written word for word in heaven.'

"It is a singular fact that the priests and propagators of almost every religion claim for their own particular belief a divine revelation. The Egyptians asserted that their mysterious rites had this authority. And, at the present day, so do the Brahmins, and the Buddhists, and the Jews, and the Christians, and the Mohammedans, and the Mormons—this is the latest revelation, one of our own times—and all who can boast of a written creed claim that their books are inspired, which to doubt would be to imperil salvation.

"Creeds, then, have been established, and human beings are found in every country professing some particular form of faith, and certain parts of the earth are almost entirely governed and influenced by peculiar religious prin-

---

[*] The author of the *Celtic Druids*, a learned work published in London, says: "Of all the evils that escaped from Pandora's box, the institution of priesthoods was the worst. And if we admit the merits of many of those of our own time to be as preëminent above all others as the *esprit de corps* of the most self-contented individual of the order may incite him to consider them, great as I am willing to allow the merits of individuals

to be, I will not allow that they form exceptions strong enough to destroy the general nature of the rule. Look at China; at the festival of Juggernaut; the Crusades; the massacres of St. Bartholomew; of the Mexicans and the Peruvians; the fires of the Inquisition; of Mary, Cranmer, Calvin, and of the Druids! Look at Ireland; look at Spain; in short, look everywhere, and everywhere you will see the priests reeking with gore. They have converted populous and happy nations into deserts; and have transformed our beautiful world into a slaughter-house, drenched with blood and tears."

[*] Hittel.

ciples. Let a man but name his religion, and you can tell whether he is an Asiatic or an European; let him name his country, and you can almost tell to a certainty to what subdivision of faith he belongs. Certain zones favor the production of a certain fruit; and particular parts of the earth have each a particular creed. In one quarter of the world, the worship of Brahma or Buddha may prevail; in another, that of Confucius or Christ; in another, that of Mormon or Mohammed. The fact is, most men get their creeds in their cradles; by early inculcation, men are to be found in the degrading worship of idols and animals, of mountains and rivers, of sunlight and of darkness, and of imaginary deities, benevolent or otherwise, corresponding with the moral perceptions of their worshipers. The God of one nation may be kind and benevolent, while the God of another may be depicted as influenced by ungovernable passions—fierce, exacting, capricious, and revengeful. To use the words of Schiller, 'Man paints himself in his gods.'

"Hereafter, then, we shall consider what the influences of religion has been to mankind, but for the present, I shall merely state that human beings, in almost every part of the habitable globe, have submitted to its control. According to an estimate made in the year 1844, the number of followers of the principal creeds were: Buddhists, 380,000,000; Christians, 230,000,000; Mohammedans, 160,000,000; Brahmins, 150,000,000; Pagans, 70,000,000; Jews, 10,000,000; in all, 1,000,000,000.

"The creed or belief with which we have now to do," continued Mr. Mannors, "is the creed of Christendom, known as Christianity. The adherents of this faith tell us that their religion is derived from a book called the 'Bible,' and that this book is a divine revelation, written many centuries ago, by inspired men, and contains in itself the essence of divine truth.

"It therefore appears that what the *Shaster* is to the Brahmin, or the *Koran* to the Mohammedan, the *Bible* is to the Christian. Now, if the Bible is truly a revelation from God, for the instruction, edification, and reformation of man, there can be no possible impropriety in a critical examination of its contents. This was the view taken by many eminent men, who from the earliest times—century after century—had submitted the scriptural books to a careful investigation; and notwithstanding the claims to inspiration made for the Bible by its theologians, it has been rejected time after time by many learned men and distinguished writers who were cotemporary with the supposed scribes both of the Old and the New Testaments.

"Without going back to ancient ages for authorities in support of this assertion, we find in modern times, and more particularly in our own day, a widespread and increasing opposition to the pretensions of Christianity. That opposition has not arisen from the ignorant, uneducated masses, but from several of the most intellectual, scientific, and distinguished men, who, with a vast number of other thinkers, also brought up in the Christian faith, now boldly, and with no small share

of moral courage, reject its doctrines as spurious, and as degrading and inconsistent in relation to the attributes and perfections of an all-wise benevolent Being. Not only have distinguished laymen repudiated the Scriptures, but actual priests of the altar, like the late Rev. Robert Taylor of the Church of England, have nobly resigned a living of ease and luxury, and have left a sanctuary where they could worship no longer, perhaps to enter a prison as alleged blasphemers. But from within the walls of Oakham jail, and from the able pen of the same Robert Taylor, came forth in due time the *Diegesis* and *Syntagma*, works which have caused hundreds to investigate more closely the presumptuous tenets of his reverend persecutors.

"Since the Reformation, when men could dare to speak and act more freely, unanswerable arguments have been published against the validity of the so-called sacred writings of Christianity. But instead of a fair reply having been granted, or a fair open discussion tolerated by the trained and paid religious teachers, misrepresentations have been printed, defamation has been used, penalties have been inflicted, and books containing calm, reasonable argument against the Christian Bible—not written under the idiotic afflatus of inspiration—have been systematically proscribed, to such an extent that not one bookseller out of fifty will venture to offer them for sale. Few indeed, dare to oppose Christian prohibition. Protestant toleration in this respect is strangely suspicious; and its boasted liberality singularly spurious and deceptive."

"To some extent, I acknowledge that such has been the case," said Mr. Capel. "I have often regretted that works published against Christianity were not allowed the privilege of as free circulation as the excellent books of Paley, Butler, Gregory, and many others, written in defense of the Bible. As far as I can learn, such writings are fully able to counteract any publications against the Holy Scriptures; candid investigation ought to make truth more apparent."

"Then," continued Mr. Mannors, "why do priests assert so confidently that the writings and arguments of unbelievers are but trivial and worthless, yet take such wonderful pains to prevent their coming under the notice of pious eyes? I will now ask you in all fairness, have *you* ever read any of the works written against the pretensions of the Bible? Have you ever read the *Age of Reason*, Greg's *Creed of Christendom*, Hittel's *Evidences*, the *Diegesis*, or any of the able works of De Wette, Strauss, Hume, Rev. Robert Taylor, Knelann, and others? You have no doubt read several, if not all of the books in favor of Christianity; now have you read any against that system?"

"I have not; in fact, I have never seen one of the books you mention."

"Then you can have no correct idea of the objections which have been urged by distinguished persons against your faith. You have had merely the pulpit, or tract, or orthodox burlesque, or misrepresentation of the statements made by prominent unbelievers."

"Perhaps so; yet I scarcely think that religious persons would misrepresent to the extent you imagine."

"As it would be impossible for us in a limited discussion to do more than give a partial investigation, will you read any of the denounced books, if I procure them for you?" said Mr. Mannors.

"Most certainly; I will readily do so, I have no fears in that respect."

"I am glad to hear this; I will not frighten you at first," said Mr. Mannors humorously, "with either Paine or Voltaire, or any other such terrible name. I will give you a small work, as a commencement, which can not be surpassed for the fair, plain, unpretending manner in which it deals with the Bible." Here he opened a book-case, and handed Mr. Capel a small volume entitled, Greg's *Creed of Christendom*. "You will," continued he, "be pleased with the style in which it is written; and afterward, if you desire, I will give you other books which go more thoroughly into the subject. And, now, in return, if there are any books in favor of Christianity which you would wish me to read, I shall do so, and by such means be better able to come to a more thorough conclusion."

"This is very fair," said Mr. Capel; "there can be no objection to such a course. I have one book which I will then ask you to look over—that is, Gregory's *Evidences*."

"Agreed; I have already perused Paley and several others, it may be that Gregory will offer something new. You see, however, that neither Christianity, nor any other system can force belief by denouncing free inquiry; for, at the present day, no prudent or intelligent man will scoff at the arguments of unbelief, or look with contempt upon the religious opinions of Hume, Gibbon, Shelley, Paine, Fronde, Bentham, Carlyle, Jefferson, Greg, Parker, Volney, Voltaire, Rousseau, Buffon, Comte, Spinoza, De Wette, Taylor, Colenso, and a host of such others. Nearly all of the persons I have named have written against the received *Divine Inspiration* of the Bible; and it is poor evidence of justice to pronounce an unlimited condemnation against their deliberate opinions, or even against the opinions of the multitude of cautious doubters, who for want of moral courage still remain nominal Christians.

"We will leave the subject for the present; one day's calm perusal of the books we have chosen may be better than a week of discussion. We shall compare notes from time to time, and see what advance we shall have made toward the great luminary, truth, which we both desire to worship."

During this his first conference with Mr. Mannors, the young preacher felt more inclined to listen than to speak; having never before had an opportunity of discussion with an unbeliever, he wished to elicit the leading views of such an opponent. He was surprised at the fairness and candor of Mr. Mannors; and when they left the room together, to take a walk along the pleasant highway, the prayer of Mr. Capel's heart was for light—more light.

CHAPTER XII

SHORTLY after the stormy Bible meeting which had taken place in the Baptist Church, the leading members of the congregation of St. Andrew's who were then present, and who had been obliged to witness the rudeness and discourtesy which had been manifested to Dr. Buster on that occasion, felt that some demonstration in his behalf was necessary, in order to give a quiet rebuke to those who had endeavored to lessen that esteemed minister in public estimation; as well as to satisfy that devoted Christian that the rude trial to which his faith and patience had been subjected only served to endear him still more and more to his own people; and to prove to the world that he was superior to the low motives of cunning and jealousy which had evidently actuated the vulgar, uneducated aspirants of other denominations.

A committee of ladies was soon formed, and after various preliminary meetings and deliberations, it was decided that, as a corresponding addition to the fascinating eye-glass with which he had been previously presented, a superb gold-headed cane should now be furnished the doctor. It would be a small but significant token, or rather emblem, of the staff he was to them, as well as to assure him that he would find his numerous friends united like a pillar of strength in the day of trouble.

In fact, Dr. Buster had in many instances received valuable testimonials of such attachment. He was a gifted individual, a moral hero, a stickler for the pure Calvinistic doctrine, who had won the esteem of ministers over whom he presided, and through them, as well as by other influences, he was exalted in the eyes of the people; so much so, that many particularly the female members of the church, never seemed tired of lavishing favors and distinctions upon him, all of which the worthy man received with due and humble acknowledgment. Indeed, so often and so refreshing had these evidences been, that the pious doctor more than once feelingly stated, that he was quite overcome by these unexpected and undeserved proofs of spiritual affection. He would then reiterate his entire unworthiness, and his utter inability to do any thing of himself; he would jiously tell them that his sole reliance was upon God, in whose mighty hand he was but a very weak and unworthy instrument.

He might have thought so; the gifts however were not declined, but were gratefully accepted, not of course for their intrinsic value, but as mere remembrances of how much his weak efforts had been overrated. They would be incentives to fresh zeal in the cause of orthodox principles, and would make him more anxious to advance the interests of the true Calvinistic church. He could look around, and see many of these presentations, but, strange to say, he did not seem to value them. There was more than one richly bound Bible; there were gilt-edged volumes from the Fathers, and valuable works by various religious authors; and comprehensive and learned commentaries, sufficient to enable him to give some meaning to doubtful passages;

and miscellaneous gift-books piled up in such profusion that the worthy man had scarcely more time to spare from his various duties than merely to read the presentation page, where his own name was proudly conspicuous. Then there were scriptural subjects on canvass, in rich, heavy frames; there was his massive gold watch, to remind him of fleeting time, besides little articles of *virtu* an l chaste specimens of *bijouterie*, from pious, individual, female friends; but above all, there was the splendid service of plate, presented to him but a few months before he had been forsaken by her who should have been his helpmate; on the principal piece of which his name and worth had been inscribed, surrounded by a halo of flourish and ornamentation. This rich service was now, alas! useless; it was laid aside. Was not his home desolate enough? The glare of the rich metal might only serve to remind him, the afflicted pastor, of the vanities of life, and of what he was called upon to suffer in the cause of the Gospel.

On this particular evening, however, the Rev. Theophilus Buster was very happy; at least, those who met him at the house of the Rev. Mr. Campbell thought so. Since he had been so unexpectedly deserted by his wife, Dr. Buster never asked any person to his house. It was now to him like a prison; for appearance' sake he merely lodged in it, and he took his meals here and there, as most convenient, not having yet decided on any particular place. He could not let the gloom which surrounded his late home affect his children; he had them removed from its dreary influence, and properly cared for in another quarter. He could not bear to hear them ask for the mother who had abandoned them; or even to mention her name.

These were depressing circumstances; but when the reverend doctor was asked to meet any friends at Mr. Campbell's, he endeavored to join them with a smiling face, like an upright Christian. He did not desire to obtrude his sorrows upon others, and he generally succeeded in making his visits very agreeable; and in making many—particularly pious ladies—believe that his light affliction only served to make his discourse more heavenly.

As usual, when the doctor was in the case, a very numerous and select party had assembled at the Rev. Mr. Campbell's, and after a most sumptuous repast, the presentation of the gold-headed cane was made by one of the most affluent and influential ladies of the congregation of St. Andrew's; and the pretty speech which she read on the occasion, referring to the great services of the reverend moderator, and of his still greater trials—delicately alluding to the peculiar domestic affliction under which he at present labored—was rapturously applauded.

In responding to this fresh evidence of their regard, the learned doctor, as usual, disclaimed any merit in himself. He was duly sensible of his own unworthiness, and he was almost unmanned by the gentle words spoken in reference to his forlorn condition. No doubt these trials have their good effects; they enable the ministers of God the more fully to alienate their affections from the things of this world, and to devote themselves more freely to the work of their Heavenly Master.

In connection with this subject the reverend doctor reiterated his disinterested opinion regarding the bestowal of costly gifts upon the servants of the Lord. "Of what value," he asked, " were such things to those who had renounced the world and its vanities? How much better it would be were the minister forgotten, and the humble poor held in greater remembrance." He felt it his duty to state that, agreeable as it must be to any person to receive such tokens of esteem, it would be to him much more so, were the money which was lavished—he used this word emphatically—to obtain costly articles, placed in his hands for charitable purposes. *He* did not care for these things. How grateful it would be to him were he enabled by such means to relieve, to a greater extent, the sufferings of the uncomplaining poor which his daily visitations had led him to discover—sufferings with which he deeply sympathized, but which, alas! too often pained him to the very heart to be unable to mitigate."

Such expressions from the reverend doctor under the circumstances, could not fail to win for him a still greater degree of consideration. Such abnegation was a rare virtue; it was a triumphant refutation of the malicious slanders that had been heaped upon this exemplary man. And so great was his influence at that moment, so great was their generous impulse toward him, that a single hint would have sufficed to urge every lady present to fling around his neck her rich gold chain and jeweled locket, as an offering to his worth and self-denial, and as a sacrifice on the altar of charity.

A few hours had thus been spent, and all present were highly pleased and edified. It was getting late, and as Dr. Buster was as methodical in his habits as he was punctual in his engagements, he signified this to his friends. His dwelling was several streets distant from Mr. Campbell's, and as he had an appointment with a friend on his way home, he refused to allow any person to accompany him. At his request, the Rev. Mr. Campbell offered up a parting prayer, and, at the conclusion, the moderator never looked more inspired than he did, when with closed eyes and upraised hands he devoutly gave the usual benediction. And when he went away, it seemed to many as if some pure spirit had departed, and for some time afterward the theme of those who remained related to his piety, his virtue, and his sufferings.

The night was dark when the doctor left the house, and when he got a short distance beyond the light that was flung out from the windows of Mr. Campbell's residence, he hurried on. It had just then commenced to rain, not in a dripping shower, but it came in pattering drops like the regular precursors of a down-pouring. The doctor increased his steps, and walked faster and faster. He wore a heavy cloak, and kept his face well muffled; he went along at a quick rate, and now commenced to mutter to himself; and, in a little time, the words became almost distinct and audible. He walked on in this manner for some minutes; it was now raining heavily, and he suddenly turned into an arched passage through which a street lamp, directly in front, sent sufficient light to make objects dimly visible. Here the doctor stopped; he still muttered, and then he drew the handsome cane from under his cloak, and held it out at arm's length before him. But stay, hark! What were the words he now uttered, sufficiently loud, sharp, and distinct, to be plainly heard? This person surely could not be the reverend moderator: these foul, passionate words could not certainly have proceeded from his lips.

He still held out the cane, and its polished smoothness, and massive gold carving flashed in the lamplight; he looked at it as if every moment he expected to see it become some shining reptile, or that he intended to fling it contemptuously against the rough wall, and break it to pieces.

"I say again, blast their stupidity! I have told them time after time that I did not care for their baubles; and the miserable dolts fail to perceive that I ever want money. Here is this thing—fit only for a Regent street dandy—put into my hand instead of—gold! If I were to be exhibited like a wax figure at Madame Tussaud's, this pretty piece of foppery might help to set me off; but, my God! just to think of the fools spending the money I want so badly for the like of this—twenty guineas! My heavens, how provoking!"

He had now balanced the stick on his open hand, and as he said these words he gave it a smart toss in the air, and caught it in its descent as he would a penny piece.

"Well, may confusion seize them! here's that cursed note for over a hundred pounds to be met in less than a week, and these finical jades throw almost as much away for this as would have enabled me to get a renewal. Well, well, it is hard to appear content before them; I have a mind to sell this precious bit of trumpery to the first Jew I meet, if I should only get a third of its value."

He paused a moment, and then muttered again; the rain was falling fast; he looked around, and peered into the dim passage as if he feared the presence of some person. For a few minutes longer he remained perfectly still and thoughtful, with eyes bent steadily on the ground; he drew a long breath, looked at his watch, and again said audibly, "Quarter past ten—they are waiting," and muffling his face once more, he started down the dark street seemingly indifferent to the drenching rain, or the starless sky.

The doctor had scarcely left where he had stood when two persons stepped from a doorway that was at the dark end of the passage, and rushed forward to look after him. One was Robert, who lived at Hampstead with Mr. Mannors; the other was a stranger, an American relation of his, who had been only a few days in England. Robert had come down to the city to meet him, and show him the sights of London, and here was one—an unexpected scene—that made Robert himself stare with surprise.

"Skeered, Bob, an't you?" asked the stranger humorously.

"Well, I'm blowed if that is'nt old Buster," said Robert. "I've seen him before, and I've heerd about him, the precious hypocrite. He beant about for nothing; he wants gold, does he? I'll lay that chap is up to summat. I say, Sam, I'd just like to find out what that fellow is about; let's after him a bit, he's going our way."

"All right—go ahead, steamboat—there an't no time to talk, that ere man is streaking it right through. I want to turn Jew, and get that pretty stick o' his'n; but stop what's this?" and he stooped and picked up a folded paper from near the spot where Doctor Buster had been standing, and taking it to the light, read—"A. M. North street, near Jewish cemetery"—"This is something o' his'n," said he, handing Robert the paper; "just put that away, it might come a kind o' handy after a while."

Robert put the paper in his breast pocket, and off they started. As they hurried along, he gave his friend a little of what he knew of the history of the reverend doctor, to whom they were now paying such attention; he was still well ahead of them, and had he turned either to the right or left, he might have escaped their curiosity altogether.

Robert's friend, whom he called Sam, was a slightly built, wiry-looking young man; he was a true Yankee, fond of adventure, was delighted with this little chase, and like his enterprising countrymen, he was determined to find the bottom of the well, and strike ile before he gave up.

They were gaining fast upon the doctor; he could now hear their steps, and he turned round once or twice, which caused them to come to a dead halt, lest he should become suspicious. He went on again, and turning down a lane to his left disappeared; and when they got to the corner, and looked down the dark, narrow street, the doctor was nowhere to be seen. They stood irresolute for a short time. Robert was for hurrying on, but his friend, laying his hand on his arm quietly, said, "Take it easy, Bob; 'tan't no use crowding the critter too hard; he an't far, he's a looking for gold, I reckon; maybe he's got a little Californy hereabouts; guess we'll fish him out presently."

The third house from the corner of the street was a small tavern; the gas lamp over the door displayed the rather common sign of the Swan Inn. The lights from within shone brightly through the windows, giving an exhibition of glasses, and painted kegs, and casks, and rows of bright pewter mugs. There were no lights to be seen in the houses close by, and this led Robert to suspect that the doctor had entered the tavern. There was but one door in front, and they did not think it best to go in for a while; he might have only taken a temporary refuge from the rain; he was not likely to be known in such a place, and if he did not come out soon, they might then enter and see for themselves.

It was agreed that Robert should walk a little way up the street, or lane, while Sam remained opposite the tavern; a small porch afforded a shelter for this purpose, and before Robert started, he thought it best to look closely around the house. There was no one to be seen outside; the place at best was not a noted thoroughfare, and now, in the darkness and rain, it had an unusually deserted appearance. He cautiously approached the front window, and saw a woman mixing something in a few tumblers. He went to the side of the house; there was a passage from the street to a back yard, and near the end of the building there was a side door, evidently a private entrance. He stepped carefully toward the first side window, a kind of red screen covered the lower half; it was not quite drawn across, and there was sufficient space for him to see three persons in a small room. They were sitting at a table, one of them with his back to the window, and when he spoke, Robert thought it was like the voice of the man they had heard soliloquizing under the archway. In a little while the speaker turned his side face, and Doctor Buster was immediately recognized. Robert at once signaled Sam, and they both stood outside, and had a fair view of what was going on within.

In front of the doctor a lady-like person was sitting; she was dressed in black; she wore a bonnet and cloak, as if prepared for a journey. The other person could be plainly seen; he sat at an end of the table; he was a stout, low-sized man, well dressed; he was partly bald on the front part of his head, his hair and heavy whiskers were turning gray; there was an expression of cunning on his face; but altogether he looked respectable.

They were talking in a low voice, and although Robert and his friend Sam listened attentively, they could not hear a word; the conversation was mostly between Doctor Buster and the other gentleman.

The landlady now brought in a tray with three tumblers holding some hot liquid; and when the door was again closed the conversation was resumed.

The gentleman who sat at the end of the table appeared very thoughtful, and stroked his bushy whiskers while he leaned back in his chair and looked vacantly toward the ceiling. He sipped the contents of his tumbler leisurely while the doctor was speaking. The lady seemed to be a quiet listener; she spoke a few words once or twice. Robert watched closely to try and discover who she was, but a heavy dark vail hung over her face, completely hiding her features.

In a little time Doctor Buster stood up; he continued to address the gentleman who was sitting; he was more excited, and soon spoke sufficiently loud to permit the listeners outside to hear every word. "Now," said he, "I have told you all; had I allowed her to roam about at large among all kinds of people, she would not only have circulated the most scandalous reports against myself, but against every friend I have. For over eight months, I have kept her quietly confined, but this moderate restraint has only made her worse. She has been well treated, and I have made my house like a prison to keep her, if possible, from the poisonous influence of others; but all to no purpose. I have tried to reclaim her by argument, by persuasion, and by other reasonable means; she will not be convinced, but blasphemes

under my very roof! How can I stand this? If I reason with her, she will not listen; and now she demands separation, she demands her children, and she demands an establishment for herself, to teach them her own errors. Just think! she is bold enough to denounce the Bible, to scoff at religion, and I found by mere chance that she has been actually in communication with a person named Mannors, one of the most infamous characters in or about London, a wretch, who by all accounts fears neither God nor man!"

As the doctor spoke, he held out both hands, and regularly emphasized his words by bringing his shut fist down upon his open palm; and when he spoke of Mr. Mannors, he did so with such extreme bitterness that Robert groaned with suppressed indignation; and the curse which he then muttered, like an angry growl, is not fit to be recorded.

"I can not," continued the doctor, "stand this any longer; she demands an establishment for herself, and," said he, lowering his voice, and bending significantly toward the individual he was addressing—"with your assistance, I shall provide her one. Several pious friends have told me that the woman is insane. I have tried not to believe this, but I believe so now; she must be made submissive, if not to me, at least to the Gospel; and the most influential missionary for her case will be found in an asylum. Now, Doctor Marks, as a member of our church, I wish you to assist me, I want you to see this unfortunate woman yourself. You will find her just what I have told you, and your certificate will be sufficient to place her where she will be better cared for; and," said he, with a peculiar smile, "she may at last find a minister that may bring her to a sense of her duty. This lady," pointing to the female before him, "is one of ourselves; she belongs to Mr. Campbell's congregation, and has been a matron in a private asylum. She is satisfied that there are symptoms of insanity; I have asked her to meet us here, and she can inform you."

"We have seldom had many worse cases," she said; "there is a peculiarity about this poor lady that I don't know how to explain; she is no way violent, but is all for argument. Lor bless you, no one could resist divine grace, and say that religion is a delusion, and have a sound mind. She has done this—and it is not long since she was a church member; a sudden change like this ought to be conclusive. Doctor Marks can see for himself."

The lady pronounced these last words with a kind of self-sufficient air, which she seemed satisfied ought to settle the business.

"I admit," said Doctor Marks, trying to look very devoutly impressed, "that the sudden change of which you speak, from piety to profanity, is often a marked symptom of mental disease. Her deplorable hallucination seems to be, that the Bible is false; as to her partial insanity, therefore, there can scarcely be a doubt; the case, however, is rather singular."

"Yes," said Doctor Buster, "it has been gradually coming to this; she first commenced to rebuke me for preaching eternal punishment;

then she insisted that there must have been interpolations or wrong translations ; then she disbelieved in scriptural inspiration ; and at last suddenly became an open defender of the Secularists. Could I submit to this? Could you?"

" Well," said Doctor Marks, " I see how it is. If you are ready, we will go, and in a short time I will try what can be done ; as it is, I am inclined to think that her mind is affected."

Doctor Buster went to the door, and spoke a few words to the landlady, and in a little time a vehicle from the back yard was heard approaching ; it was a cab ; it stopped at the front door, three persons entered it, then the driver at once mounted his seat and drove quickly away.

" By the 'tarnal, Bob, we came upon them a kind o'sleek ; let's follow that crowd, there's something up. We can keep alongside that cab o' his'n better than trying to track them afterward—we can go it like a streak."

Robert, however, was ahead already. On they ran, without saying a word, for some time. The rain had partly ceased, but heavy blasts of cold wind swept along the deserted streets, whisking into mist the pattering drops that fell from projecting eaves, threatening rickety sign-boards, and penetrating the thin wretched covering of the homeless wanderers who were then trying to find shelter. Wide and narrow streets were passed ; corners were turned ; and gloomy looking houses seemed to be gliding further away into the darkness. The night-watch as he peered from his cover might not have wondered at the rattling speed of the vehicle, but he no doubt felt a degree of suspicion upon seeing two persons, one at each side, following it up so closely, and running through street-pools with the most reckless indifference.

" Guess they're a going to hitch up here," said Sam, in a low, hurried voice and almost out of breath, as the pace began to slacken, and the horse's head was directed toward a row of gloomy buildings in a quarter of the city that was not the best lighted or most populous. Near the centre of this row there were two houses, older looking, and nearly a story higher than those on either side ; they had a deserted appearance, and the vehicle was brought to a full stop at the further house. There was not a light to be seen ; the lower windows were well secured by strong shutters, while dark, heavy curtains prevented the least ray from being noticed in the upper part of the building. Three persons ascended the stone steps ; a bell was rung, the strong front door was cautiously opened, and they quietly entered, leaving the cab to remain as if it were to be shortly required again.

—◆—

CHAPTER XIII.

SINCE the rumored departure of Doctor Buster's wife, very few persons had ever entered his house. It was a desolate place ; in the principal apartments, the furniture was covered, the mirrors and pictures were shrouded, and

already the rich rugs and carpets were fast becoming damp. Almost every thing in the other rooms was bundled up and stowed away, as if for an auction sale, while the kitchen fire, though not actually put out, was merely kept alive ; and the savory odors that had often ascended with appetizing qualities were now replaced by less fragrant fumes from the homely fare of the solitary care-taker of the premises.

There were two apartments, however, in that lonesome house that were still used : one was the doctor's library and study, situated on the first floor. Though he visited this place every day, it was not always to read, or spend an hour in religious contemplation, but often for the purpose of transacting business, and to receive visits from a few ministerial brethren and others, who were granted that privilege. It was allowed to remain in a very disorderly state ; books and papers were lying about, torn scraps of writing were scattered here and there, and almost every thing else was tossed and misplaced in the most negligent manner ; and there were times, when, if one could have entered this retreat, evidences of the doctor's occasional partiality for a little brandy and tobacco might be easily detected.

The other apartment was one that only the doctor and one or two other persons ever entered. It was a large upper room, old and dilapidated, in the back part of the house ; it was cold, bleak, and dimly lighted ; there was but one small window at the end, through which a gleam of sunlight never entered, and which looked into a kind of yard ; and, although this window was many feet from the ground, yet it was secured on the outside by iron bars, which were but a comparatively recent precaution against burglars. There was scarcely any thing to be seen in this room save a few things requisite for its solitary occupant. There were a small table and a little wooden stool, and a wretched straw bed spread out upon the floor in a corner. Close by, there was a small closet, in which was hung some patched and tattered articles of clothing. It was a melancholy place for one to spend long nights and tedious days and dreary months in, brooding in loneliness and sorrow, and wishing for death, like the poor forlorn creature—the victim of an arbitrary priest—the prisoner of religious tyranny—who was weeping away her life, recalling the sorrows and joys of the past, and thinking with suspicious dread upon the bleak, bleak future.

She sat upon the hard bed in the black darkness of the night, listening to the rain, and to the wild wind that ripped up the loose, fragile roof-slates and sent them flying into the street. The window shook, and the thin panes trembled as the cold blast rushed through some crack or crevice into the wretched chamber. She sat and listened to the wild commotion of the night ; and the wailing outside was in unison with her own desponding thoughts. She wrung her thin hands, and then placed them over her wan face that was once so fair ; her scanty brown hair fell around her shoulders. It had lost its rich luxuriance, and, already, threads of silvery hue, wrought in through its darker folds by early grief, could be traced, to correspond with the lines of care that were prematurely and indelibly marked upon her brow.

She rose and knelt upon the straw pallet, and raised her hands imploringly; she remained in this position for awhile, heaving heavy sighs, and struggling with painful emotion, and then exclaimed, "O God! O God! why do I suffer thus? What is to become of my poor children? What is to become of me? I can not exist here much longer. Am I never to see them again? O dear, dear, dear, the dreary winter I have spent! How I wish my sorrow was buried forever in the cold grave!" And then, as she felt some sudden pang, she pressed her hands over her fluttering heart, and said, "I wish it would break—it will, it will, but not till I see them again; let it not be until then. O my poor children!"

Once more she listened, as if waiting for some friendly voice of sympathy to whisper hope; as if looking up for some kind hand to lift her from out the dark, angry waves in which she was struggling. The hot tears chased each other fast and faster down her fevered cheeks, the storm-wind still reveled in the dark night, and its wild and swelling wail was the only response to the poor sufferer. Yet, strange to say, she paused to hear the melancholy sounds more distinctly; even at that lonely hour there was something soothing in them, something which kept her a moment from thinking of her own grief. She was not afraid; those spirit-like wails showered down no heavy curses upon her defenseless head, like the dreadful mutterings of that other voice which she too often had heard in that very room.

While thus pitifully waiting—waiting for something—for any thing—for the merest symptom of day-dawn to her long night of trouble—for the faintest ray of light, or hope, to cheer away any of the dreadful gloom that was around her like a thick, dark shroud, she was startled by a low rap at the door. She held her breath, her ears might have deceived her, she heard the rap again, but louder; there was a pause, and then a voice said:

"Are you awake, madam?"

"Yes."

"I am Mrs. Pinkley. I have a message for you; a person wishes to see you, if you will please to arise and dress; I will bring a light and the key."

"I will, yes, certainly; I will be ready in a moment."

The sight of any human being, save one, would now be a welcome intrusion; neither the lateness of the hour, nor the unusual time for such a call, made any difference; she would see one of her own sex; she was yearning to hear a woman speak to her then, no matter if even indifferent to her sufferings.

She had scarcely time to hurry on a few things before she heard the woman's step, and saw a light stream in through the key-hole. The door was opened, and Mrs. Pinkley entered; she had been there several times before, and consequently was not like an entire stranger. Though looked upon with suspicion, and many of the ungodly and uncharitable were of opinion that her intimacy and devotedness in connection with the pious and circumspect Doctor Buster was not exactly in accordance with strict Presbyterian rule, she was, however, one of the flock, a steady church member, and in the eye of many of the elect this was sufficient to cover a multitude of sins.

"I am sorry to disturb you," she said, placing the small lamp upon the table, and leisurely taking off her bonnet. "I know it is rather late; but I will assist you to dress, and to put things in a little order. A gentleman below wishes to speak to you. O my! don't start—it is not your husband, although he will be here also; the person I mean is his friend, and—"

"Alas! may be my enemy."

"Oh! not an enemy, by no means; he is a friend; yes, he comes at the request of your husband. I think they wish to remove you from this dull place," said she, bowing and smiling; "the change you will find much better—don't you think so? Indeed," said she, looking around her, "this place is not fit for you—not at all."

The poor woman shuddered when she heard this, at least when she heard that her husband was coming. He never entered but to threaten and reproach; but then, thought she, he will not be alone, he will not surely curse or try to terrify me before others. Still she trembled; and then suddenly, as if thinking of her great wrongs, she looked up defiantly, and said:

"Let him come! he can do little more than he has done already; perhaps the sooner he strikes the final blow the better."

"O my! madam, don't talk so! He won't injure you, no indeed." Yet Mrs. Pinkley was no way disconcerted; she smiled, and was very complaisant. She was a tall woman, slight but well proportioned; she had dark hair, a red face; there was something hard and repulsive in her cold gray, wandering eye, and her mouth was decidedly sensual. She had quite a professional address, and, as she moved about, the touch of her cold, delicate hand now made the poor victim before her shrink, as she would from the smooth, chilly contact of a reptile, or as if she had felt the hand of an executioner.

"I think, madam, we will do now"—she made a slight survey—"yes, we're ready," said she, bowing and gracefully backing toward the door; "I will just hint that we can see them." And placing her soft white hand to the side of her mouth, she gave a peculiar cough, twice or thrice, and presently she ushered in the two gentlemen with the stately ceremony of a duchess.

Doctor Buster entered first, with a heavy, formidable stride, and, despite of her resolution, his enfeebled wife became nervous when she saw his malicious frown, and she turned her eyes away from the unfeeling determination that was concentrated in his gaze. Doctor Marks, who was the other person, advanced toward her with the easy address of a gentleman, and very politely said how much he regretted to be obliged to make a call at so unseasonable an hour. "In fact," he said, " he was about to leave town, and her husband, who was anxious about the state of her health, requested him to pay her a visit at once." His manner was very insinuating, and his soft words seemed as harmless as the prattle of an infant.

She heard these words; they might have given her confidence, but she heeded not the speaker. She became at once self-possessed, and quietly folding her arms, sent a steady look of scorn upon the scowling countenance before her. She seemed for the moment bereft of all fear or dread whatever, and totally indifferent as to personal results.

" My husband—my health—did you say? Ha! ha! my husband! Yes, this is what an arbitrary, unjust law may call him; this is what our social barbarous conventionalism may designate him—but to me, what is he? I know him to be my unfeeling tyrant, and persecutor, and he may yet be my murderer. My health? Here is a proof of his anxiety for my condition," said she, spreading out her hands, as if directing their observation to the room; and then she drew up her sleeve and exhibited her attenuated arm. " Here I have been the victim of his intolerance, and in this place I have had terrible proof of his pious attention and care for nearly a year. While he has been preaching like an apostle, and praying for the souls of others, almost unknown to the world he has been heartlessly persecuting my frail body in this prison. My health! What a mockery! Did he care for my health when he robbed me of my children, and thrust me into this place? I have been treated like a criminal, and debarred liberty; he now seeks to deprive me of my senses, and it may be that he will yet take away my very life."

She directed these last words with such deliberation that they went stinging around the reverend doctor's ears like the touch of scorpions, and his Christian restraint became so impotent, that were it not for his own actual safety he would have annihilated her with one mighty blow.

" Yes, strike," said she, " I too well know the brutal fury of your passion; but I fear you not—what do I care for life? But even while it lasts—while I can still speak, I will tell some one of your infamy; I have been silent too long. If I can tell no others, these people shall hear of it. I will place you in their power—they may be yet witnesses against you."

Mrs. Pinkley here became very much affected; she was actually shocked; she found some relief, however, in a pious ejaculation, and muttered some inanity about falling from grace.

" Pray, madam," said Doctor Marks, " do not allow yourself to become so excited; your husband is anxious about you, and we are here to serve you, if possible."

" That is easily done. If he is anxious about me, let him give me my children and my liberty; let him cast me out upon the world from this very place, and I shall need no other physician. If you wish to serve me, if you are here as friends, then," said she, lowering her voice to tenderness, " plead with him for me—plead with him, kind friends; let him restore me to my little ones, and I will never trouble him more. I will go away, far away, where my name shall never bring him a reproach." She fell on her knees, and seized the hands of Doctor Marks, and looked up to his face most appealingly through her tears. " Oh! do, good sir, pity me; will you be my friend? I am an afflicted woman who has been sorely tried; be my friend, lead me to my children, and the sea shall divide me from that man, and its trackless mountains shall remain between us forever."

Doctor Marks had a heart, it was touched by this natural appeal, he felt embarrassed, and he gently raised the weeping woman, and made her sit on the low stool; while Mrs. Pinkley affected to require an application of her handkerchief, to keep back tears which were yet frozen.

" Woman," said Doctor Buster, trying to suppress his rage, " woman, be silent, if you have any reason left. You shall never utter blasphemies in your children's ears; they would only live to curse you for blighting their hopes of eternity."

" Reason! That is what you have always denounced; it is because you have despised that noble faculty that I am here now. " Friends," said she, addressing the other persons, " were it not for reason, I might have been, as he is, a shining light in the church. I might have still been a believer in that inspired revelation that has made him so chaste, so forgiving, and so exemplary. I might have remained a priestly instrument to disseminate what I now believe to be error. My reason rebelled against a doctrine that would depict a divine Being to be as cold, as heartless, and as revengeful as that man before you. I could not believe in the eternal punishment which he preached, and which he would relentlessly practice upon me."

" Wretch! what mercy can you expect either from God or man after uttering such impious sentiments? you shall have none from me! If your boasted reason has led you to this state of degradation, if it has led you to trample upon Christian truth, then, by Heavens! it must lead you out of this to a place where it may be better cultivated. I will not foul my hands any longer with your leprous carcass; prepare and leave this house, and may your days be spent in weeping, and your nights be as woeful as the terrors of the damned!" As he said this, the shadow of his raised fist could be seen like a death's head on the opposite wall.

Doctor Marks stood almost appalled when he heard these imprecations; Doctor Buster's face was livid with rage; he looked more like a ferocious maniac than a human being, and at the moment he was more fitted to become the shackled inmate of a mad-house than the awe-struck woman whom he denounced. Even Mrs. Pinkley, trained and accustomed as she had been to scenes of uproar and confusion in such places, became fearful. She could feel collected and indifferent when she heard the ravings of a disordered intellect in an asylum, but she could not witness this wild ungovernable fury of a sane man, and he too one of the called and ordained preachers of the Gospel, without a shudder. Yet she could excuse this excess of zeal on the part of the moderator. The determined contumacy of a self-opinionated woman was very provoking; he was a preacher of truth, and Mrs. Pinkley, as long as God spared her, would be always an humble upholder of that principle.

She followed the reverend doctor from the room. She no doubt thought it her duty to try and soothe away his anguish; his passion was too great to allow him to remain with safety in the presence of her whom he detested. His anger might have led him to commit some act of violence which would cause publicity, and this he dreaded more than any other result. Doctor Marks felt relieved when he saw him leave the wretched chamber and its helpless inmate; she, poor unfortunate! was weeping, and her pitiful sobs were an irresistible appeal to his better nature. He was, however, strictly orthodox, and was ready to doubt the sanity of any person who professed to disbelieve even the most mythical story of the Bible, but he could not persecute. The insight he had just obtained of the moderator's character and motives did not exalt the latter in his estimation, and as he had been requested to come there for a professional purpose he now promptly decided how it was best to act under the circumstances.

Mrs. Pinkley's returning steps could be heard; there was not a moment to spare.—He hurriedly whispered, "Leave this place, submit for the present, and I will see what can be done for you."

It was long past midnight when the cab drove quickly away with Mrs. Pinkley, and the doctor's wife, and a coarse-looking man, in whose pockets something like keys, or handcuffs rattled as he entered the vehicle. In a short time afterward, Doctor Marks and the moderator left the desolate house. They were seen by Robert and Sam, making their way along the dark splashy streets through the wind and rain, and it was with a feeling of disappointment that these watchers had to retire for the night without being able to do more then than avow their determination to make a discovery as soon as possible.

CHAPTER XIV.

THE red lion which hung outside the tavern bearing that name could scarcely be seen next morning through the heavy fog which enveloped every object. Masts on the Thames, huge buildings, royal and episcopal palaces, and ambitious steeples were but dimly visible, and pedestrians as they hurried on occasionally jostled each other in a very unceremonious manner. The red lion, crowned and rampant as he looked in the bright sunshine, now appeared rather subdued; and the large drops which accumulated on his bronzed sides fell with pattering sound on the pavement, being occasionally intercepted by the heads, great and small, of early street plodders. The good-natured landlord sat smoking a long clay pipe near the tap-room door, and as he now

and then looked up with pride at the dripping representative of his house, he had often to smile at the manner in which the said lion administered spiritless drops, so different from the more reviving ones contained in the circle of bellied and painted kegs which stood around him, like sturdy little bacchanalians awaiting his orders.

The Red Lion tavern was one of the oldest established places of its kind in London. Generation after generation had crossed its threshold, stood on its sanded floor, and had partaken of the generous cheer for which it was famed. Even up to this period, it had kept pace with the times, and its good ale and tender-loins could not be surpassed within the bounds of that old city. It was a peculiar resort; although generally frequented by the middle, or rather by the intelligent trading and working classes, yet authors, professors, and occasionally a stray waif of nobility, might be seen to enter. For the traditions of the house had it, that more than once, at irregular intervals of relaxation or revelry, the highest in the land drank in its cozy parlor, and looked on the Thames through the diamond panes of its great bay window. And good John Hollis, the present landlord, would point with pride to the stout arm-chair which held the last scion of royalty that honored his house; and it would be a favor indeed, were you permitted to drink out of the "King's cup," a cut and flowered glass tumbler, which more than once had touched the lips of a certain Prince Regent, who had afterward become "The Lord's anointed" as "George the Fourth."

To a person of leisure, who wished to hear the news of the day, or make short excursions through the city from a central point, the Red Lion was the spot. Not only was it well supplied with city and provincial papers, but it could boast of an excellent library, which was enlarged from time to time by gifts of rare and scientific books from its generous patrons. And works treating on the merits of the state church, and popular theology, which were proscribed from the shelves of respectable Christian booksellers, could here be found to satisfy the curious, stimulate investigation, and expose pretension. Adjoining the library was a large room in which guests could meet; and friendly discussion, mostly on politics and religion, might be often heard from an early hour in the afternoon until late at night.

Close to a front window in that room, and looking demurely into the fog that half hid the rampant lion, sat Samuel Styles; he was thinking of the events of the past night, and seemed in momentary doubt and confusion as to the reality of the dreary incidents of that period. And though he knew but little as yet either of the truth or falsehood of what he had heard Dr. Buster relate concerning his wife, still he was strongly suspicious that all was not right. From the moment he laid eyes on the reverend doctor, he took an instinctive dislike to him; he had not yet seen Mr. Mannors, whom Robert held in such esteem; but he heard him alluded to as being an "infamous character," and he had also heard Dr. Buster attribute insanity to his own wife, on account of her religious opinions, and threaten her with an asylum. And now, as he believed that threat had been carried into effect, it forcibly reminded him of a similar case of persecution that had lately been exposed in his own country.* He felt a glow of indignation, and as he was an ardent lover of fair play, and had time and means at his disposal, he determined to see justice done, and if possible rescue an oppressed woman from the clutches of an unfeeling priest and sanctimonious tyrant. He made up his mind that when Robert called that day, to go with him to Mr. Mannors, and reveal all to him; then, after a sudden thought, he snatched at his pocket and drew from it the paper which fell from the hands of the reverend moderator under the archway, and which Robert had picked up.

Samuel Styles, or rather as he chose to call himself "Sam Styles," was an enthusiastic native American, as proud of his country and of the "glorious Stars and Stripes," as ever Briton was of the Red Cross or Union Jack. He was, according to his own account, "raised" on a farm in Pennsylvania, and having lost his parents at an early age, entered a printing-office in Philadelphia, where he remained for two or three years. He was very sober and industrious; and during one of the great religious excitements which periodically occur in that city of gospel palaces and celestial ambassadors, he got converted and joined the church, and being esteemed for his sincerity and zeal, was appointed a tract distributor; his district in the city being varied occasionally from the streets known as—

"Chestnut, Walnut, Spruce, and Pine,
to
Mulberry, Cherry, Race, and Vine."

Having proved faithful in this respect, he was afterward called upon by a wealthy evangelical society to fill the more important position of colporteur, at a fair salary, and sent to dispose of Bibles, and Testaments, and to circulate other religious books in the country. In this capacity, he visited several places and studied the effects of religion upon the minds of different classes, from the slow "aborigines" of Cape May to the more enterprising and intelligent natives of Pennsylvania and New-York. And whether it was that he became dissatisfied with his own efforts, or that the general ideas of those most wedded to the Gospel were not sufficiently liberal and progressive, he grew discontented with his vocation and resigned. And while he left Moses and the prophets to grope their way among the unregenerate as best they could, he, being fond of adventure, commenced business "on his own hook," and traveled with horse and wagon from State to State, as the vender of small wares and fancy articles. After a time he became a doubter in matters of faith; he was surprised to find, that wherever he traveled, a large majority of the most intelligent persons were skeptics or downright unbelievers, and having found a great demand for those liberal books so regularly denounced from the pulpit, and so formally condemned by certain leaders of the press, he added them to

* Mrs. Packard's, of Illinois.

his stock, and became an active agent for the circulation of secular and spiritual journals. For so doing, he met with many reproofs, received some insults, and was more than once threatened by respectable church-members with personal injury. But Samuel Styles was not the man to be intimidated, and while governed by his own free thoughts, he would come to no decision on any question of importance until he had heard both sides; and now being as strong in his opposition to the popular faith as he was truly sincere while a believer, he felt it his duty to try and counteract that which he had once striven to propagate. Like most of his countrymen, he was a great reader; but not of the trashy, sixpenny literature—as greedily devoured in the United States as pea-nuts or painted candy; he was well informed on general subjects, great on statistics, and in argument was prepared to defend his position with obstinacy. When asked for the cause of his apostasy, he would state that the prevailing cupidity of Gospel ministers, who claimed and received exorbitant salaries, was the first matter which caused him to reflect. While a boy, forced like others to attend a Sunday-school, and wearied with the endless routine of texts and catechism, hymns and prayers, none of which he could truly understand, a minister would attend at stated periods, and after having given a lecture, would make the application result in forcing the boys to give, as a voluntary contribution, the few pence they might have accumulated as pocket-money.* Thus after he had grown up and joined the church, he found one great systematic method for collection. Cash was required for the minister's fund, for a church fund, for a building fund, for a missionary fund, and for a superannuated fund. There was a fund for Bibles, and a fund for tracts, a fund for special matters, and one for general purposes; and it seemed to him like one concerted shout from pulpit and platform, of "give, give, give, eternally give." And the rich gave of their wealth, and the poor of their poverty; and still the reverend pensioners cried for more, until they made Christianity, in this respect, the most oppressive and expensive system in the world.

Then in the churches were held tea-meetings and soirées, fairs and festivals, pious lot-

* In general, children are very reluctant to attend Sunday-schools, and still more so to give up their scanty supply of pocket-money: but by the peculiar pressure of the "voluntary" system, the money is obtained, as may be inferred from the following paragraph taken from a Philadelphia paper of Sept. 26, 1866:

"A MISSIONARY VESSEL.—On Saturday last, at Boston, a vessel called the Morning Star was launched in the presence of 5000 spectators. She cost $24,000, and was paid for entirely from the contributions of Sunday-school children in about 2000 Sunday-schools in different parts of the world. This vessel is to be fitted out by the Missionary Board at Honolulu in the Sandwich Islands, and is to be engaged wholly in missionary work."

Who can believe that "Sunday-school children" ever deliberately planned this unwise expenditure in their anxiety for the conversion of Honolulu heathen? This priestly scheme produced the desired excitement, however; five thousand witnessed the display—this waste for Honolulu; while the priests have good reason to believe that, in the winter, necessity may drive more than five thousand of the Boston poor shivering to their hard beds.—AUTHOR.

teries and religious revels, in which fashion and flirtation had full sway ; where ministerial potentates, who lorded it over the reason and consciences of their adherents, were noted for making a peculiar distinction between those who had much to give and those who had not ; and where the priest, who formally preached humility and the vanity of wealth, was too often worshiped as the god of the temple, ever ready to receive the rich gifts of his votaries. Samuel Styles saw these things, and found that Christianity instead of being, as it strangely claimed to be, a despised thing, was in fact a haughty power, pampered by rulers, and regal in wealth ; an authority that could exalt, or depose, or persecute.

But what of the Bible, once the idol of his soul, the centre of his hopes and aspirations, revered and worshiped by millions trained to its belief ? A book, or collection, by whom written, or when, or where, none could determine ; teeming with contradictions and absurdities ; in conflict with science, reason, and humanity ; a fearful record of crime, lust, and brutality ; depicting a divine Being as governed by the basest of human passions, full of wrath, and hurling destruction on the fallible beings whom he had created. A horde of sects professed to be guided by its maxims, and these have been notably exhibited in mutual persecution ; and, like the Bible, almost every page of their acts and records is sprinkled with blood.

These discoveries were painful, and suggestive of deep reflection ; then followed a strict investigation, and, like many others who have yielded reluctantly to conviction, Samuel Styles at last became an unbeliever.

After a time, and, contrary to the predictions of many of the faithful, his circumstances became much improved. He had a genius for invention, and succeeded in obtaining a patent for two or three very dissimilar articles, the sale of which placed him in a good position. By his straightforward intercourse among the people, he earned a good reputation ; and though many doubted his orthodoxy, yet no one doubted his word. He was intelligent, humorous, and communicative, and in his frequent sojournings was a welcome visitor to many a rural homestead. And it often happened that while trading among settlers in the far West, he was entertained at the same board with the traveling preacher, whom he generally managed to draw into a friendly discussion—thus, as he said, "casting his bread upon the waters." When the rebellion broke out, he joined the Union army, was wounded at Manassas, and after having remained in hospital for a long period, his health being much impaired, was honorably discharged.

For his restoration, he decided to risk a sea-voyage. In his younger days, on the "glorious Fourth of July" he had heard declamatory orations against Britain, but he could resist prejudice ; he knew that she was a mother of nations, the parent of his own, and the progenitor of European liberty. And though, as a republican, he believed that that great country was terribly blighted by its royal government and state church, yet he sympathized with the pluck and free spirit of its common people—the true nobility of the land. After due preparation, he left New York for "the birthplace of his grandfather ;" and the only relation he as yet found was Robert, his cousin.

Samuel still stood at the window of the Red Lion tavern looking intently at the paper he had drawn from his pocket, and as he gazed at the cramped words, they seemed to move about and arrange themselves into curious forms. He saw the fierce features of Doctor Buster, then the outline of a pleading woman, then again they changed to the shape of a heavy-barred window ; and while trying to peer into the darkness of a cell, and just as he imagined he could discern some dim, withering form in its depths, the words resumed their places, and he again read "A. M. North street, near Jewish cemetery."

"Darn me if that an't strange ; if my eyes were spirit mediums, they could not have changed that writing better ; all there ! bars and bolts and Doctor Buster to boot." He turned the paper, looked at both sides, then held it from him, and then aside, as if it were a veil or screen which hid some object from his view. " Yes, these are the words, words that may give me a clew. I'll try and unravel them, and if I have to hover about the Jewish cemetery as a medium or resurrectionist, I may disentomb some critter either dead or alive. I'll try hard, and if the great doctor feels spiritually inclined, and calls upon me, I'll answer that call with such a rap as will make him feel like being in the very centre and embrace of a corkscrew thunderbolt."

Having thus soliloquized, and while leisurely folding the paper, his attention was called by shouts and hooting almost immediately across the street. He could just distinguish a number of persons outside a shop door ; a carter was unloading some pieces of furniture, and two or three persons in official costume, like policemen, were superintending the delivery. A motley gathering stood around, and as piece after piece was shoved into the building, the jabbering crowd gave a shout, and one voice louder than the rest cried out,

" Och ! success to the 'stablishmint, divil a scrimmage we'd have on the ould sod at all at all widout it ; sure, it keeps the boys busy ; and the parsons, and peelers, and hangmen makes a fine livin out of it." Then there was a loud laugh, another shout, and the jeering officials, who really appeared ashamed of their work, made a show of threats. Then the voice cried again,

" Arrah ! that's right, make the haythins behave themselves, keep away wid ye, sell 'em out bed and blanket ; sure, the divil must have his due." Shouts and laughter again followed, and there were more threats ; but it was all in vain, big and little remained, and save the jeering and occasional shout, no interference was offered. The furniture was stowed away, the more orderly of the assemblage had entered the shop, and Sam, having his curiosity excited, crossed the street to see what was going on. He looked in from the doorstep, and near a corner, close to where some household articles were piled, he saw five or six members of the society of Friends, commonly called "Quakers." There they stood, with the utmost gravity and decorum, and the majority of those inside seemed to regard them with deference. Some proceeding was about to take place in which an interest was manifested, and while many outside were vehemently discoursing, the expressions," "national church," and "national curse," could be heard most often; those within kept tolerably still. In a few minutes, a kind of beadle or tithing-man stepped upon a platform. He was a stout, coarse-looking fellow, evidently well adapted for his business; he leisurely took from his pocket a paper, and having spread it before him on a desk, glanced first at the attendant Friends in the corner, and then with stolid indifference at the upturned faces of those around him. After a preliminary cough, he lifted the document, which was a kind of distress warrant or execution for the non-payment of church rates, and said, "I have here authority from the church wardens of this parish to offer for sale at public auction the goods and chattels of Mary Wilkins and others, for the non-payment of lawful rates due to the reverend rector; and now unless the cash is paid, with costs, forthwith, I shall commence. Well, what do you say?"

He paused, there was no reply; but a heavy sob was heard from one poor woman who with bent head stood clutching the handle of a little trunk which was placed on a table before her.

"I don't want to be in haste; I'll just give you five minutes to think," said he, chucking out his big silver watch, "five minutes to pay the legal dues of the church."

He then coolly stuck his thumbs in the armholes of his waistcoat, and began to whistle to himself unceremoniously while he kept time with his foot on the platform.

"Friend, thee need not delay on our account. We do not recognize thy claim to be just; we neither enter the church nor hear the parson; therefore we have no right to pay. Thee must enforce thy unjust tax; the society of Friends in England will never submit to thy legal extortion. Thee hast seized, and thee may sell."

"Bravo!" cried one; and a murmur of approbation was heard around. The beadle was getting nettled, and hastily replied: "Oh! you broad-brimmed chaps are very particular, very conscientious. The church is there for you, and if Quakers won't go near it, that's their own fault. If you want to go to heaven your own way, why, then you must pay for it. If you are so chock full of the Gospel as to resist the law year after year, the same law will just as surely prosecute." A hiss could now be heard over the place. A policeman called out, "Order!" and the irritated beadle, with a "Here goes!" snatched up the little trunk, and placed it on a stand before him.

"I have here," said he, looking at his warrant, "a claim against Mary Wilkins of one shilling and eight-pence for church rates, and half a crown for costs; give me a bid for this," and he tossed about the trunk, making its contents rattle. It was locked, and he applied his big thumb to the hasp to try if it would give way. "How much for this? She has the key, and won't let us see the contents. I'll lay

there's something good in it," said he, with a chuckle, and giving a peculiar wink at one of the policeman. "What do you say for this trunk and its contents, no matter if it holds Bank of England notes?"

"Indeed," said the sobbing woman, turning a pleading look toward the audience, "there's nothing in it but my dead boy's clothes, some of his school-books, and other things of no value to any one now but myself. He made that little trunk for me, and it's all I have belonging to him." She was a widow, and had lost her only child.

"Come, give me a bid; how much for this —clothes, books, bank-notes and all?"

Yet no bid came, the suppressed feelings of all present scarcely let a sound louder than a whisper be heard; and as the poor woman stood silently weeping, with head still bent and her hands upon her face, even the rough crowd turned toward her many a pitying eye, some of which were already brimful of tears.

"Can I hear no bid, not one bid for this? then if you don't, I shall have to give one myself. Forbes," said he, turning to one of the policemen, "can't you do something for the church? Just start this."

The man thus appealed to only shook his head, as if his heart and emotions were all the other way. There was another pause, tho beadle looked perplexed; the woman stood close by, and her sobbing was heard, as if her sobs alone could now sufficiently plead her case, or protest against the wrong.

"I will give thee a bid for that poor woman," said one of the Friends, moving toward the beadle.

"No, you don't, I guess," said a strange voice; the people turned around, and Samuel Styles was seen elbowing his way manfully through the crowd; he soon reached the desk, and laying hold of the little trunk, and giving a comical look at the beadle, said, "Well, old stingo, what do you want for this?"

The act was performed so quickly and with such nonchalance, that the beadle himself stood looking in gaping wonder at this assurance, and the affair had such a ridiculous aspect that the general laugh which followed almost completely disconcerted the church official.

"Give you a dollar; guess that's about right, an't it, eh?"

I don't know any thing about your Yankee dollars," said the beadle, now plucking up, having discovered his man; "if you say a British crown, and no other bid, 'tis yours."

"Can't give you a Yankee one anyhow; guess we han't got such trinkets on the other side of the mill-pond; if there was fewer crowns round these diggins, there might be more money, and your occupation would be gone. Now an't that strange?"

The gruff beadle was in no mood for argument; no other bid was given, and Sam became the purchaser of the little trunk for a "crown." He immediately restored the poor woman her property; she was full of grateful expressions, and the audience applauded so loudly that the crowd greatly increased, and those who passed along the street wondered at the sudden acclamation.

Order being restored, the sale again commenced ; one by one of the goods and chattels of the Friends was then put up, but quickly purchased by their owners for just sufficient to pay the clerical or parochial demand against them. The society of Friends have ever resisted, and still continue to resist the iniquitous claim for tithes or church rates, and the annual formality of such a conscientious protest is still to be witnessed, and still the pious and legal atrocity is as regularly consummated in free old England.

Samuel Styles had now witnessed one effect of the practical workings of the British State Church ; a degrading instance of clerical extortion and rapacity. He felt the most utter disgust at such a vile resort to plunder a community, and he was amazed to think that the intelligence, civilization, and freedom of that great country should, at the present day, submit to such infamous oppression. But he did not consider at the time how the masses in Britain have struggled against priestly power, or how the great minds of the nation have declaimed against such usurpation. He did not then remember that that terrible incubus on the resources of the country—the State Church—was shielded by a royal and aristocratic influence which was almost absolute ; and that that influence, by its potency and wealth, still controlled Parliament ; still thrust its mercenary bishops in the House of Lords ; and still degraded British legislation before the world, by leaving unrepealed among its statutes authority for ecclesiastical monopoly, a code of laws partial, arbitrary, and unjust.*

Dwelling on these things, he wandered moodily along the street, and crossed Waterloo bridge with the intention of going to Hampstead. He went on, and soon found himself in front of a large brick building, before which a number of stylish vehicles were drawn up. It was Exeter Hall ; some one of its great public meetings was in progress ; people were yet going in, and he felt half disposed to follow. For many years he had heard of this great arena where liberty had been proclaimed to many, but where others were drawn into bondage ; where the shackles o. the slave were broken, but where the human mind was bound by fetters of a different kind, and led into servility.

While standing here, he was surprised at the evidences of wealth and poverty which met his eye ; the contrast was extreme. Aristocratic equipages passing and repassing, coachmen, footmen, and postillions, laden with rich lace and heraldic trappings were seen in every direction ; while at the same time could be observed the sunken eye and hollow cheek of numerous wretched and forlorn creatures, who were listlessly lingering around, or moving here and there like passing shadows through the glittering crowd. He was impressed by the great difference of circumstances, and was trying to philosophize upon a remedy, when his attention was directed to a movement of the people who had been standing idly about the great hall. Policemen were busy trying to get the loiterers to stand aside, a lane was soon formed, and presently a stately equipage

* See Note E.

moved slowly away from the building and turned toward the Strand. As it came along, the policemen raised their hats deferentially ; it was evident that one of the numerous great personages of London was present, and, upon inquiry, Samuel was informed that it was the "Lord Bishop of London," a great name there. He had just presided at some meeting in which the church was interested, and as that great and humble "successor of the apostles" was wheeled away after his arduous duty, he was followed in formal and regular order by the principal and minor grades of metropolitan clergy, who, although less splendidly conveyed, yet gave palpable evidence to the poor and hungry, who looked wistfully at the display, that to many "Godliness is great gain," even in this wicked world.

Satisfied in his own mind with this conviction, and while attracted by the long line of moving splendor, his eyes rested upon a clerical vehicle of a different kind. In a neat carriage drawn by a pair of fine horses were four persons, two young ladies in front, one of whom was driving, and behind sat a lady and gentleman. The ladies were richly dressed, the gentleman was in spotless clerical black, and was a distinguished and popular preacher. He was blandly smiling to some whom he recognized ; and while his heavy features seemed distorted by a continued unnatural effort to wear a smile, Sam caught at a glance the cold, soulless eye of Dr. Baster. Even there, in the bright sunlight, in the midst of favorable surroundings, seated by fashion, and in the hurly-burly of actual life and business, there was in that look something that gave even to Sam a momentary doubt of his own resolution. Were he alone and possessed of treasure, he would not like to meet such a countenance in a desolate place. But see ! the features relax, the smile is gone, there is a frown, and suddenly a scowl of hate, which the doctor as suddenly hurled into the benevolent face of—Martin Mannors.

Samuel, following the direction of the doctor's eye, saw Robert at a few yards distance ; he was driving a small neat vehicle, and by his side sat a person whom he immediately took to be Mr. Mannors, and who had his calm eye unflinchingly fixed upon the lowering features that already seemed to shrink and wither beneath his mild but steady gaze. The doctor had thus unexpectedly met one for whom his dread had generated a deadly hate ; he hurriedly reached over and struck one of the horses with his cane, and as they rushed onward he made some frivolous excuse to the ladies about becoming nervous in a crowded thoroughfare.

"There he goes," said Robert, looking after them, "there goes a saint as I hope to see elevated nearer heaven one of these days." And saying this, he quickly and significantly wound the end of his whip-lash around his own neck. He now observed Sam who stood close by, and was glad they had met. "This is my cousin, sir, this is Yankee Sam, sir, all the way from America—a wildish chap in his way."

Mr. Mannors was much pleased to meet Robert's friend ; he had heard of him, and of the adventure of the preceding night. He gave him an invitation to Hampstead, and made him promise to call there with Robert the next day. He was now on his way to town, and might not return before night. A few remarks were then made about the unexpected meeting they had just had with Dr. Buster. Mr. Mannors said but little, yet there was a meaning in his look that could not be misunderstood.

After they had driven away, Sam felt in a rambling mood ; he was quite indifferent as to his course, and walked through several streets, often stopping before gorgeous shop-windows to look at the rich goods and splendid wares exhibited, then halting to guess the dimensions of some immense church or public building. He loitered near gardens and wealthy mansions ; then in a park, and, going on still further, got in the neighborhood of an old churchyard. It was not a cemetery on the modern plan ; it was a crowded acre or two in the midst of dwellings, like some of those he had seen in Philadelphia — charnel-places, which are yet allowed to pollute the air of that city. The burial-ground in question was inclosed by an iron railing and surrounded by some squat-looking buildings, and tall lodging houses ; and even there, at short distances, were places where strong liquors and London stout could be had ; it seemed as if the proximity of these resorts to the dead often induced mourners to test the oblivious qualities of such liquids.

Outside of one of these places, some distance up the street, and nearly in front of the principal gate of the cemetery, a great number of persons were assembled ; others came on every moment ; some remained near the gate, while many went into the graveyard. Anxious to see what was going on, Sam hurried to the place ; the crowd was getting larger every moment, and boys clung to the iron railing ; while others were busy climbing such lamp-posts, or trees as would afford a view. Thinking some great funeral was expected, he asked a by-stander, a plain looking workman, if such was to be the case ; the man at once replied, " No, it beant no funeral. We had one hereabouts yesterday—Tom Jones's child—there's the grave yonder," said he, pointing to the cemetery. The end of the little mound could be seen, and close to it stood the father and a number of men armed with sticks and clubs—a resolute dare-devil set, that were ready to bid defiance to law or gospel.

" Now," continued the man, " Tom is a Methodee, and the parson don't like such, and says 'cause the child wasn't baptized, it shan't lie there."

" Why, you don't mean to say they're going to take it up again ?"

" Yes, that's it, they're coming here to-day, coming now to do it. The parson is high-church—a high-flyer—and wants that bit of pasture for his own flock. See, here they come —damn them !"

Another crowd was now moving down toward the churchyard, but neither the so-called " high-flyer " nor his expected assistants could be seen. It was another funeral ; the aged mother of one of the parish workmen had died, and they brought her body to the old resting-place for interment, and, as she had been some kind of Methodist, several said that bringing her there would be the cause of more trouble. For some years past a sect of Methodists called " Ranters " had been established in certain districts of the city—a sect very plain in its way, but very noisy and uproarious in its religious demonstrations. Its members were almost entirely belonging to the poorer working class, which great missionary societies in their anxiety for the conversion of foreign heathens had overlooked. Now, the Ranters looked upon the pretensions of the church with great indifference ; and the church, or at least the high-church, still assuming control over the souls of English sinners, claimed to dictate, and would not allow an unbaptized thing to moulder side by side with " the faithful ;" nor should any who had left the bosom of the church for a conventicle find interment in a parochial grave, unless the formal burial service was read at the place by an authorized minister. No, the church could never forget its authority ; it would still hurl its legal anathemas, and deny to the foul weeds of dissent Christian burial in " consecrated ground."*

The funeral now arrived at the gate ; the bearers were ordered to halt ; a line of constables stood across the entrance, and a clergyman with a very little head, very little eyes, and a very large nose, pompously warned the intruders to keep off. He held a folded surplice on one arm, and flourished the other with clerical determination. A number of other constables kept moving about, and matters looked serious ; some were for an immediate resort to force, while others advised a more peaceable method. The bearers now lowered the coffin on the pavement, and one of the relatives asked that permission might be given to bury the deceased in the same place where her husband and two of her children had been laid years before. But the parson was inexorable ; none, he said, should have the privilege of burial in that place but deceased members of the church ; those who resisted its authority should be as the heathen and the publican. The body of every schismatic found in that churchyard should be disinterred, and buried where they ought to be — in the common highway. Yells and groans followed this reply ; a hundred indignant faces could be seen around, and already some were collecting stones and other missiles for a pitched battle. One or two persons, however, seemed to have control, and an old workman stood upon the coffin, and, after having called the attention of all present, said

" Friends, we all know that this is an un-

* Perhaps one of the latest specimens of this kind of clerical intolerance is exhibited in the following, from an English paper—the London *National Reformer* : " The Rev. Mr. Mirehouse, Rector of Colsterworth, has been displaying his Christian charity by refusing to bury a child, because it had not been baptized at his establishment, but had had its sins remitted at the Wesleyan Chapel. When the funeral procession arrived at the church, the gates were locked, and it was not until the mother of the child fainted in the street that this 'Christian gentleman and humane man' allowed the funeral to enter the 'consecrated' ground."

christian proceeding ; we know that there is no religious equality yet in this land ; much as we may boast of our free laws, there," said he, pointing down to the coffin, " is an evidence of their partiality, and some, as we now see, would have no equality even in the grave. But it matters not where this poor body beneath my feet is to be hidden, whether in a field or highway, neither does it matter what is said over her remains. I may not live, friends, to see it, but, remember," said he, lowering his voice, " there's a good time coming, and England will yet be free. I would now advise that if the clergyman permits us to bury the body here, her friends shall consent to allow the ' church service ' to be read, and so end further trouble."

After some contention, this prudent advice was followed ; it was a triumph for the church. The minister, after a show of hesitation, consented, and in a few moments afterward he was heard in sonorous tones consigning to the grave " the body of our deceased sister," and she was thus laid in the same earth with her mouldering relatives.

While this ceremony was taking place, and while most of those present stood around the grave, the constables formed a circle about that of the child, two men tossed aside the mound, and commenced to disinter the body. These proceedings were not noticed for some time ; but soon word was passed from one to another, and the incensed father, followed by a hundred others, rushed upon the constables, and in less than a minute three or four of them were bleeding profusely, and the two men who had been digging at the grave were leveled to the earth and shouting for mercy. Sticks and stones were flying in all directions ; one fellow was seen tramping furiously on the minister's hat, while another tore his surplice into ribbons. The parson however was strong in the faith, and though pressed back, step by step, by the reckless crowd, he feared no mob, but continued to urge the police to support his authority. At this juncture, some one with truer aim than the rest flung a large sod at the head of his reverence, and he was seen to tumble backward across the little grave which had been already violated by his orders.

The scene at this time was one of great confusion ; yells, oaths, threats, and even blows were still heard, just as if a legion of demons had been let loose among the tombs. The constables were powerless, their main effort now seemed to be to protect the minister ; but their help to him would have been of little avail, were it not for the old workman who had spoken at the gate, and a few others. The parson was with some difficulty dragged away from the place, the constables retired, but the crowd remained, and the triumph this time was with the people. Samuel Styles, who had witnessed the whole proceedings, was now thoroughly disgusted ; he had often heard and read of similar scenes, but he had no idea that such clerical intolerance would be attempted in England at that period of the nineteenth century. He had now seen enough of it in one day to last him for life ; and a rumor having spread that the constables would

return with reënforcements, he left the " consecrated ground " and place of contest. That night, while sitting in the large room of the Red Lion, the principal theme was the innate tyranny of priestcraft.

Early next morning the papers teemed with conflicting accounts of the proceedings at the cemetery ; and journals in the interest of the church commented vehemently on the savage outrage which had been perpetrated by a heathenish mob against a " defenseless servant of God." There was no word of extenuation in these religious papers for the outraged feelings of the people. Clerical correspondents suggested that some immediate action must be taken ; a line of demarkation should be drawn in every cemetery to distinguish the " faithful " from dissenters. Some argued that a dividing wall should be built in each churchyard, others thought a hedge might answer, while others would be content with a gravel walk ; it would be quite sufficient to enable all to distinguish where lay those who had been blessed by England, or cursed by Rome, damned by dissent, or saved by the State Church.

CHAPTER XV.

MR. CAPEL had been absent several days, and had visited every station on the circuit. In his missionary wanderings, he traveled through a picturesque country, rich in landscape scenery, reminding him of the rock and river and mountain of his native land. He passed by pleasant meadows, where lazy cattle fed and rested, scarcely moving at his approach. He rode through shaded lanes, fragrant from hawthorn blossoms on either side ; then by some quaint old place which had given a page to history ; by little brooks and shining rivers ; by woodman's cottage, nestling among trees ; and then he wound around some grassy hill-slope, towering above which might be seen a hoary, crumbling castle, crouching under the sheltering ivy, as if waiting for the final stroke of time. Yet, attractive as these would have been to him at other times, he scarcely glanced at the magnificent grouping ; he was in deep thought, thinking of what he had lately read ; and during his abstraction, the horse walked slowly along, often even stopping to pluck at the fresh grass which grew by the road-side. Now and then he would arouse, and urge his beast onward ; he would look around for some object on which to feast his eye, in order to rid himself of doubts and harassing speculations ; but while seemingly intent on some picture of rustic scenery, or the commingling of shadow and sunlight beneath the rough branches of some old oak, he would relapse again, and again his thoughts would wander away, away, far from their wonted track, and then return but to transform into hideous images the ideas which he once considered so fair and beautiful.

It was only when he was actively engaged among the people to whom he was sent that he, in a measure, got rid of this embarrassment ; and he applied himself perseveringly.

He tried to obtain a fair knowledge of the wants, wishes, and mental status of the people among whom he was destined for a time to labor. He was very punctual in his ministration; preached once, and often twice, each day, and was diligent in the performance of his other duties. For the time, he devoted himself very assiduously to these matters, and tried hard to think of little else. He found Methodism there much like what it was in Ireland; but the people were rather more demonstrative in their religious exercises, accepting the peculiarities of their creed as pure gospel, and rarely ever doubting the propriety of any rite, doctrine, or exposition bearing the sanction of the revered Wesley. Indeed, the credulity of some would have approved of any absurdity, provided it had his indorsation, thus acting like thousands who continue to pin their faith to the sleeve of others.

Mr. Capel kept busy; every suitable moment was one of industry. He wished to ascertain the state of religion on the circuit; to know the state of every class, and the qualification of every class-leader; was particular to learn who were the most exemplary members; gave a word of encouragement to some, and a suitable rebuke to backsliders. But ah! the thought then came, Who was it that might yet rebuke him? Even here, among the few who had once been faithful, there stepped aside out of the beaten track daring skeptics. He had heard of this, and felt alarmed lest even he, the preacher, should yet follow them in their terrible descent. Still he worked; he did not want to think; he had been near the precipice, and had just looked over its dreadful brink, and shrunk back, as if fearful that some sudden impulse would urge him to destruction.

For nearly a week he thus struggled with the mutiny of his own thoughts—thoughts that *would* obtrude themselves; frightful forms, which he tried to hurl into oblivion. But the trial came at last; he could be active during the day, he could then form sage resolutions to cling forever to the ark in which so great a number had found refuge, and which had borne him thus far through storm and sunshine so safely and pleasantly. He would pray more—would urge the Lord—would assuredly find the promised help, would find more strength to resist, and more determination to follow on in the narrow way, without looking to the right hand or left, until he attained "eternal life." Thus it was with him in the busy daytime; but then came the night —night again, with its shadows—not a time for him of quiet contemplation or calm repose, but a season for wild conjectures and fevered dreams, and for alternate feelings of hope and despair. Now, again, came those thoughts which one by one sought to rob him of some treasured idea, some glittering little idol that he worshiped from infancy. Why was he troubled thus, why doubtful of the Word of Life? Could he not be content with evidences and assurances that had satisfied a Wesley, a Whitefield, a Clark or a Paley? He had read and re-read their learned expositions, and now by such aid he sought to banish those obtrusive fancies which kept him restless and wavering; but those expositions, once considered so lucid and satisfactory, had now, alas! for him, degenerated into mere assumptions, or speculation. He had all his life been hearing and reading one side of a history, and had but just glanced at the other side, to find that that structure, the erection of which had taken centuries, was already crumbling to ruins. He would lie awake thinking of his conversations with Mr. Mannors, of the history of Christianity, of its rapacity and persecution; of Romish and English popes, and of their respective state-churches; of the wealth and blood that had been expended to secure their establishment, and of the salaried armies of bishops, priests, and preachers yet required to keep the world from relapsing into paganism.

Against this array, Science had now lifted its mighty arm. Reason was boldly asserting its rights, while Truth was silently pointing to the throne from which it had long been excluded by an usurper. There was the "Inspired Word" which he had been taught to revere, and which had for centuries been held in awe by multitudes, now treated by the intelligence of the age as a myth. The "sacred" narrative had been subjected to impious criticism, and its assertions tested, like those of any other book, by Reason and Philosophy. How had it stood the test? Thousands had thrown it aside as worthless. Should he do so, might he not make a fatal mistake? He was taught to believe that the greatest attainment of reason was to know that there was an infinity of knowledge beyond its limits. Might not this knowledge be centred in the Bible, and might not erring, presumptuous man misinterpret its teachings? But why misinterpret?—why, if written for man's guidance and instruction, should it be so contradictory to reason?—why should it so bewilder both wayfaring man and philosopher? He had expressed to Mr. Mannors a willingness to investigate the Bible, and he had scarcely commenced before he became startled, and was almost ready to recede. He had already discovered enough to leave him in a labyrinth of doubt and perplexity.

He found that there was no evidence to show that the books said to have been written by Moses were ever penned by him; on the contrary, there was the most conclusive proof within their own pages to establish that they were the production of other persons, hundreds of years after the death of their reputed author! Had they been written by Moses, they could have contained no descriptive account of his own death and burial; they would not have been written in the *third* person, as, "The Lord said unto Moses—" "Moses said unto the people;" nor would he have referred to himself in the fulsome terms mentioned in Numbers, 12th chapter, 3d verse: "Now the man, Moses, was very meek above all the men which were upon the face of the earth." But the most positive evidence against the assumption that Moses was the writer is the numerous anachronisms which occur. Moses is made to relate in the *past tense* events which did not happen in his lifetime, nor indeed for centuries afterward.

The poor plea can not be made that he was speaking prophetically; it is a plain relation of occurrences, said to have taken place previous to the time of their record. In the 14th chapter of Genesis, there is an account of how Lot was taken prisoner in battle and carried off, and that Abraham and his followers marched to rescue him, and followed his captors as far as *Dan*. Now there was no place known as *Dan* in the Bible until over 300 years after the reputed death of Moses; consequently, it would be as absurd to state that Moses mentioned such a place as it would be to assert that a writer of Shakespeare's time had mentioned an incident of Waterloo. Thus, concerning the burial of Moses, the writer states, "And he buried him in a valley in the land of Moab, over against Beth-peor: but no man knoweth of his sepulchre *unto this day.*"

"And there arose not a prophet *since* in Israel like unto Moses."

The 36th chapter of Genesis gives the genealogy of the descendants of Esau called "Edomites," and a list of these kings; and the 31st verse says, "And these are the kings that reigned in Edom before there reigned any king over the children of Israel." These passages could not have been written by Moses. The latter verse must have been written at least after the time of David; there were no *kings* in Israel in the days of Moses, consequently the writer of that particular passage must have lived in the time of King David, or during a subsequent reign: for if at this present day a writing without date should be discovered, and which, in speaking of past events, should say that such and such an occurrence took place during the reign of Queen Victoria, the inference as to the writer would of course be, that he lived and wrote *after* her accession.

These texts, then, are proof positive that Moses was not the writer; that they either must be interpolations—which, to get rid of the difficulty, some would admit—or the whole book is an anonymous tradition of absurdities.

With regard to the other books said to have been written by Moses, similar evidence can be had in abundance, to prove he was not the writer. In Exodus, 16th chapter, and 35th verse, it is said: "And the children of Israel did eat manna forty years, until they came to a land inhabited; they did eat manna, until they came unto the borders of the land of Canaan." As this account extends *beyond* the life of Moses, it is plain that he could not have related it.

The curious instance in Deuteronomy, 3d chapter, verse 11, shows the fabulous notions which prevailed at the time. One concerning a race of giants says: "For only Og, king of Bashan, remained of the remnant of giants; behold his bedstead was a bedstead of iron, is it not in Rabbath of the children of Ammon? nine cubits was the length thereof, and four cubits the breadth of it, after the cubit of a man."

According to this measurement, the bedstead was over 16 feet in length, and more than seven feet wide. This singular relation could not have been made by Moses, for he knew nothing of Rabbath, nor of what was in it. It was not a city owned by this giant. The knowledge, therefore, that this bedstead was at Rabbath, and the particulars of its dimensions, must be referred to the period when Rabbath was taken, which was not until 400 years after the death of Moses, according to 2d Samuel, 12th chapter, 26th verse: "And Joab fought against Rabbath of the children of Ammon, and took the royal city." News was then sent to King David; and the 29th verse says that "he gathered all the people together, and went to Rabbath and fought against it and took it;" and then, after robbing the king of his crown, and sacking the city, a proof of King David's lovingkindness and tender mercy toward the miserable inhabitants is given in the 30th verse:

"And he brought forth the people that were therein, and put them under saws, and under harrows of iron, and under axes of iron, and made them pass through the brick-kiln; and thus did he unto ALL the cities of the children of Ammon. So David and the people returned to Jerusalem."

If such infamous brutalities could possibly meet the approval of a *merciful* God, it must have been the savage and revengeful Deity of the Jews, not the more *humane* and considerate God of the Gentiles.

The same objections that are urged against the credibility of the books of Moses, or the Pentateuch, also appear against the book said to have been written by Joshua, as well as against many other of the strange books which compose the Bible. In the 24th chapter, 29th and following verses, he is made to give an account of *his own death and burial*, and of events which followed.

An astonishing fact respecting the books of Moses shows that the *first* certain trace of the Pentateuch in its present form was when one Hilkiah, a priest, said he had found the *book of the law* in the house of the Lord. This discovery is said to have been made as late as 624 years before Christ. The finding caused a great sensation. The alarmed menarch, King Josiah, "rent his clothes," went to the temple, and read "*all* the words of the book;" and a great reformation immediately commenced. It is evident that if these books of Moses had been *previously* known to the Jews, they would not have manifested such surprise and alarm upon their discovery by Hilkiah. That discovery stands upon his mere assertion. He might have written "the book of the law" himself, or, if there were any ancient records that he knew of, he might have made such alterations as he pleased; it is evident, however, that at that period there was but *one* copy of the law in existence, the validity of which depended entirely upon the veracity of this priest. The story is to be found in the 34th chapter of 2d Chronicles.

Here, therefore, appears a strange contradiction. We are told in 31st chapter of Deuteronomy that about 1450 years before Christ, when Moses, it is said, made an end of writing the words of the law in a book, he said to the Levites, "Take this book of the law and put it in the side of the Ark of the Covenant of the

Lord your God, that it may be there to witness against you." Now if this book of the law was faithfully kept with that reverential care which the Jews are said to have had for it, why was it not in the same ark 450 years afterward, at the time the great temple is said to have been dedicated by Solomon? It was not then to be found, and no mention is made of such a book; for in the 8th chapter of 1st book of Kings, it is said: "There was nothing in the Ark save the two tables of stone which Moses put there at Horeb."

It is impossible to reconcile these discrepancies. Errors of this kind implanted in a book claiming to be inspired seriously affect the credibility of the whole. But why should an almost unknown barbarous tribe like the ancient Jews be the sole recipients of favors and communications from the Deity? As a race, they were perhaps the most vindictive, cruel, and blood-thirsty monsters that ever lived; their God was but the reflection of themselves, and their law-giver Moses, called *meek*, possessed such a character as the civilization of the present day would pronounce thoroughly cruel and depraved. His first prominent act was the deliberate murder of an Egyptian, whom he buried in the sand; and afterward he was the hero of a number of murders and robberies almost too dreadful to recite; and the writings which bear his sanction are records of fearful atrocity. While assuming to teach his countrymen purer doctrines, and a more correct notion of a Divine Being, he followed the example of surrounding nations by the slaughter of poor dumb brutes, as a sacrifice to appease the imaginary wrath of his Deity. He incited the Jews to be faithless and implacable to their enemies, and to rob and murder them whenever an opportunity offered. Not only was he cruel to strangers, but by his commands, *death* was the penalty to his own people for comparatively trivial offenses, as well as for a difference of opinion with regard to worship.

In Leviticus, 24th chapter, 13th to 16th verses, there is an evidence of great disregard for human life: "And the Lord spake unto Moses, saying, Bring forth him that hath cursed without the camp, and let all that heard him lay their hands upon his head, and let *all* the congregation *stone him*." "And he that blasphemeth the name of the Lord, he shall surely be put to *death*, and *all* the congregation shall certainly *stone him*: as well the stranger as he that is born in the land, when he blasphemeth the name of the Lord, shall be put to *death*."

The 13th chapter of Deuteronomy, 6th to 9th verses, contains a sad proof of the intolerance and inhumanity prevailing among "God's chosen people."

"If thy brother, the son of thy mother, or thy son, or thy daughter, or the wife of thy bosom, or thy friend which is as thine own soul, entice thee secretly, saying, Let us go and serve other gods which thou hast not known, thou nor thy fathers; namely, the gods of the people which are round about you, nigh unto thee, or far off from thee, from the one end of the earth, even unto the other end of the earth, thou shalt not consent unto him nor hearken unto him; neither shall thine eye pity him, neither shalt thou spare, neither shalt thou conceal him. But *thou shalt surely kill him*; thy hand shall be *first to put him to death*, and afterward the hand of *all* the people." Will the liberality of the nineteenth century accept of such teaching? The bloody code of Draco was mildness in comparison.

The "divine law-giver," Moses, also inculcated revenge by numerous precepts, as in Deuteronomy, 19th chapter, 21st verse: "And thine eye shall not pity; but life shall go for life, eye for eye, tooth for tooth, hand for hand, foot for foot."

His savage treatment of enemies was most frightful. In the 7th chapter, 2d verse: "And when the Lord thy God shall deliver them (their enemies) before thee, thou shalt smite them and utterly destroy them; thou shalt make no covenant with them, *nor show mercy unto them*."

A fearful instance of butchery by the command of Moses is given in Numbers, 31st chapter, from 13th verse. The Jewish army were sent to "avenge" themselves of the Midianites; to effect this, they slew "ALL the males," together with five of the kings of Midian. The women and children were taken as captives, their cities were burnt, and their cattle, flocks, and goods taken as spoil. Upon the return of these chosen avengers, with their captives and prey, "Moses and Eleazar the priest, and all the princes of the congregation, went forth to meet them without the camp." "And Moses was wroth with the officers of the host, with the captains over thousands, and captains over hundreds which came from the battle."

"And Moses said unto them, Have ye saved all the women alive?" "Behold these caused the children of Israel, through the council of Balaam, to commit trespass against the Lord in the matter of Peor, and there was a plague among the congregation of the Lord."

"Now, therefore, *kill every male among the little ones, and kill every woman that hath known man* by lying with him: but all the women children that have not known a man by lying with him, *keep alive for yourselves*."

Humanity shudders to think that such an atrocious command could be given by one divinely appointed; yet it is orthodox, and meets the approval of Christian priests unto the present day, even this murder and debauchery!

The Mosaic account of the creation, and the Mosaic cosmogony in general, are singularly false, leading to the grossest errors and absurdities, and contradictory to well-established principles of modern science. In this account, it is said that *light* was created on the *first* day; that grass, herbs, and fruit trees were created and made to grow on the *third* day; while the SUN, the only source of natural light, and the great agent of vegetation, was not made until the *fourth* day.

Now, there could not have been an evening, or a morning, or a first, second, or third day, without the natural revolution of the *earth*;

neither could there have been any vegetable growth, to cause a tree to grow and yield seed, without its direct influence.

The 14th verse of the first chapter of Genesis says: "And God said, Let there be lights in the firmament of heaven, to divide the day from the night, and let them be for signs, and for seasons, and for days, and years."

Yet three days and three nights had already passed without a single planetary revolution. The account states that on the fourth day the stars were made also, merely "to give light upon the earth." How different to what astronomy has proved! Sir J. Herschel, in his philosophical transactions, proves that some of the nebulæ are at such an immense distance from the earth that their light, traveling at the rate of 200,000 miles in a second could not have reached the earth in less than about two millions of years. Later discoveries of Lord Rosse fully corroborate the estimate, and it is now well established that thousands of stars, which Scripture asserts were made as if but "to give light upon the earth," are in reality SUNS to other systems, so vast as to reduce our *solar system*, by comparison, to almost insignificance.

After the creation of fishes, fowl, and great whales on the *fifth* day, the beginning of the *sixth* day was devoted to the production of cattle, creeping things, and beasts of the earth; and then God said, "Let *us* make man in *our* image, after *our* likeness, and let *them* have dominion," etc., etc. The plural number is introduced into this verse as applicable to both God and man.

So God created man in his own image, in the image of God created he him; *male and female*, created he them. And God blessed *them*; and God said unto *them*, be fruitful and multiply," etc., etc. The 27th verse of the first chapter of Genesis, above recited, declares in positive terms that God created man *male and female*; and this is confirmed in the next verse, when *they* were blessed and bid be fruitful. It is evident from this, that God was addressing Adam and his wife, whom he had just created.

The 30th verse states: "And to *every beast* of the earth, and to *every fowl* of the air, and to *every thing* that creepeth upon the earth, *wherein there is life*, I have given every green herb *for meat*; and it was so." This is directly at variance with what is known of the habits of animals of prey, which are nearly all carnivorous. Naturalists have proved that such animals can only exist by feeding on flesh. The lion, tiger, wolf, and other animals would quickly perish if left to the sole sustentation of green herbs for the text includes *every* animal.

The chapter thus concludes: "And God saw every thing that *he* had made, and behold *it was very good*. And the evening and the morning were the sixth day."

The second chapter begins with the declaration: "Thus the heavens and earth *were finished*, and all the host of them. And on the seventh day God ended his work which he had made, and he rested on the seventh day from all his work which he had made." The creation, therefore, *was finished*; God had pronounced *every thing very good*, and rested from his labor.

Great surprise has been manifested by many, anxious to believe the Scriptures, that the plain statement respecting the creation of man—male and female, in the first chapter, should be as plainly contradicted in the second. In this latter chapter, we are told that, after the creation, God "took the man and put him into the garden of Eden, to dress it and keep it; but at the same time forbade him to eat the fruit of *one* particular tree, after having previously told him that *every* tree "yielding seed" should be to him "for meat." And the Lord said, "It is not good that the man should be *alone*, I will make him an helpmeet for him." A deep sleep then fell upon Adam, and, while in that state, the story says: "that one of his ribs was taken out, and God made a *woman* of it"!

From this, it appears, that, although in the first chapter, God made man *male* and *female*, and even addressed them as in the text, yet, in the next chapter, after God had ended his work and rested, no woman had been created until he made one out of Adam's rib! A tradition so inconsistent would be readily treated as a myth by any others but those who seem determined to believe all and every thing included in the Bible.

The 2d verse of the 5th chapter of Genesis is confirmatory of the *first* account of the creation of man; thus "*male* and *female* created he *them*, and blessed *them*, and he called *their* name Adam" in the day when *they were* created.

Another inconsistency appears as to the satisfaction which the biblical Creator derived from his own work. The first chapter of the Bible records that he pronounced *every thing* he had made *very good*; in the sixth chapter, after having discovered the great wickedness of man, the record says: "And it repented the Lord that he had made man on the earth, and it grieved him at his heart."

Truly the prescience and omniscience of the Mosaic Deity must have been very circumscribed; and his instability, his repentance, and his grief like unto those same frailties of mortals!

The account of the "fall" is one which has sorely puzzled the best and wisest "divines." Adam, whom the Lord had but just pronounced perfect, falls at the very first temptation, and his posterity are unjustly cursed and degraded by the commission of that act.

If Adam was not perfect, it seems like trifling with human infirmity to place him in such a position as to be unable to resist the inducement to sin; for it was not until after he had committed the offense that he was able to discern between good and evil.

For eating this apple, Adam was expelled from Paradise, and condemned to earn his bread by the sweat of his brow; his wife was cursed, and both made sinful and unhappy; the ground was cursed, and ordered to produce thorns and thistles; and a special malediction was pronounced against the serpent: "upon thy belly thou shalt go, and dust thou shalt eat all the days of thy life."

The question arises, if the serpent was then cursed, it must have previously had some other means of locomotion. In what way did it travel, as serpents were never known to have had legs? It had never eaten dust, neither does it at the present day. The whole story has been pronounced most absurd, and commentators have been at their wits' end to render it plausible, or, as having been derived from "inspiration."

The learned expositor, Dr. Clarke, has suggested that it might have been an APE that tempted our first mother! To such an extremity has learning and intelligence ever been reduced, when submitting to the incongruities of fiction.

To hide the nakedness of Adam and Eve, the Lord, it is said, went and made coats of skins, with which he clothed them!

The tradition concerning the fall, like many others in the Bible, can be traced to the legends of a more ancient people than the Jews, and to an antiquity far more remote than any recorded in Bible history.*

Among other curious recitals of the "word of truth" is that of the 2d verse, 6th chapter of Genesis. "The sons of God (angels) saw the daughters of men that they were fair, and they took them wives of all they chose." Here is something for "doctors of divinity." Angels descending to *wed* the daughters of *men!* The Egyptians and Persians have allegorized the same doctrine, and Thomas Moore has founded his beautiful poem, *The Loves of the Angels*, on such an idea.

The depravity of mankind had already become so great that the Lord determined to rid himself of them. "And the Lord said: I will destroy man whom I have created from the face of the earth, both man and beast, and creeping thing, and the fowls of the air, for it repenteth me that I have made them," verse 7, chap. vi. But Noah having fortunately found favor, in order to save him and his family, and preserve animals to stock the earth anew, the Lord commanded him to make a large vessel called the ark; it was to be about 540 feet long, 90 feet broad, and three stories high—made according to specific directions from the Deity—and a careful estimate has given its capacity as about 90,000 cubic yards.†

Noah was then to take seven of every kind of bird, male and female, and seven also of every clean beast; and two each of every other kind of animal. An orthodox authority gives the number of birds of all kinds at 8000. Seven of each kind, male and female, would make 112,000 birds, and allowing less than one cubic yard to each bird, they alone would *more than fill the ark;* for many of the birds of that period were of an immense size. There are 1658 species of beasts, two of each kind would be 3316; but then there are 166 of

these clean beasts; and seven of each of these make 1162; making in all, 4478 beasts large and small. Of reptiles, there are 657, multiplied by two, gives 1314; and yet further, of insects and creeping things there are 750,000 various kinds, which, doubled, would make over one and a half millions! An important element in the calculation is yet to be considered. Noah was required to put into the ark sufficient food for all the living creatures to be taken. But even to supply grass-eating animals alone, numbering about 2000, the ark itself could not contain the quantity requisite.

Some animals would require flesh, others fish, others grain, others fruit, and others insects. How was it possible to obtain supplies for all these? The food necessary for ten or twelve months would make an immense bulk, far beyond the capacity of the ark; neither could even a vessel of its size contain the indispensable supply of water, as the ocean of the flood would be salt.

Assuming that the immense collection could be cribbed and confined within the ark, the question then comes, how could they breathe? There was but *one* small window in the ark, which was closed; and how could eight persons only attend to all these animals, and supply them with food and water?*

But whence the flood itself? The mere raining of forty days and nights would be comparatively nothing toward it. The Andes are supposed to be 20,000 feet above the level of the sea; the vapors of the atmosphere, if condensed, could not deluge the earth to the height of an ordinary house. Modern geologists deny that there ever was, or ever could be, a universal deluge; the marine shells found on the tops of mountains have been deposited by changes of the earth's surface, and there is proof incontestable that these changes have been produced by the *gradual* operation of water and heat; Egyptologists assert that monuments have been found in the valley of the Nile which bear evidence of having been erected at a period long before that assigned to the flood.

This part of the Mosaic history has been the cause of much embarrassment to professional theologians; numerous explanatory theories have been formed but to confound each other; and many intelligent Christians have wished that such a record had never existed. The Rev. Dr. Pye Smith admits that—"the flood could not be universal," that it could not have "resulted in the destruction of *all* animal life," and "that, connecting the question with physical causes, it appeared to him, that unless we resorted to miraculous agency (against which he protested) it was impossible to imagine the ark capable of containing parts of all the animals whose exist-

---

* See Note F.

† As to the materials of which the mythical ark of Scripture was composed, learned Christian commentators have formed various opinions. Thus our modern "authorized" version makes it *gopher-wood*; Onkilhos, of *cedar*. The Arabic commentators declare it to be *box-wood*; the Persians, *pine wood*. The celebrated Bochart declares it was *ebony*; Dr. Geddes affirms it to be *wicker work*; while the distinguished Christian, Dawson, contends that it was made of *bulrushes daubed with slime*.

* Bishop Wilkins tries to get rid of the difficulty by "reducing the number of *species*;" but the 19th and remaining verses of the 6th chapter of Genesis are conclusive as to the meaning and intention of the angry Deity according to his "Inspired Word." There was to have been two saved of every *sort*, of every living thing, of all flesh—plain enough in this case for a "wayfaring man." Assuming, however, that there had been a flood, and that almost every living thing *on land* had been destroyed, the deluge could not have affected the inhabitants of the "*great deep*."—AUTHOR.

ence must depend entirely upon their exemption from inundation." Then, having detailed the great variety of species in the animal creation, he admits the impossibility of stowing them in the ark.

The great Dr. Burnet says that the quantity of water it would take to cover the highest mountains, "must at least exceed the magnitude of eight oceans;" that no such quantity could be found, or, if found, ever removed, and that, therefore, "our present earth was not subject to a deluge, nor is it capable of it by its shape or elevation." (*Archeol. Philos.* chapter iv. p. 40.)

Scientific evidence bears so strongly against the theory of a general deluge that the whole story has long been given up by many as being the issue and result of downright ignorance.

After the subsidence of the flood, the Lord made another covenant, and promised not to destroy the earth again by a deluge, and "set his bow in the cloud for a token." Again, science confutes this rainbow novelty, and proves that there has always been rain and sunshine, and that the rainbow had not then appeared in the heavens for the *first* time.

Passing the strange relation about the tower of Babel, and the confusion of tongues, the discrepancies in the accounts of how Abraham made his wife appear as his sister, we find that the destruction of the flood having failed in its expected results, the Lord appears *again* as a destroyer. He visits Abraham in his tent upon the plains of Mamre accompanied by two angels. It seems his foreknowledge was at fault; for he came to try and find out whether the iniquity of Sodom was as great as had been represented. "I will go down now, and see whether they have done altogether according to the cry of it which is come unto me; and if not, I will know." The Lord and his heavenly messengers having had their feet washed, and having partaken of refreshments—cakes, butter, milk, and veal—made a promise to Sarah, then a very old woman, that she should have a son; and one to Abraham, that he would not destroy Sodom, provided ten righteous persons were found in it, and took his departure! This account is to be found in the 18th chapter of Genesis, and portrays the Lord and his attendants in every respect as very like ordinary mortals.

In the continuation of the history of murders, which forms such a large portion of the Old Testament, the 10th chapter of the book of Joshua contains a record of that great miracle, the standing still of the *sun* and *moon*. The slaughter of the nations around them seems to have been a favorite pastime of the "chosen people." Joshua was their leader after Moses, and he did not fail to indulge and encourage the pious recreation of exterminating the "enemies of the Lord."

The men of Gibeon having sent for aid to Joshua, against the Amorites, he went out with his mighty men to give them battle. There were five kings to be overcome; but the Lord, as usual, promised "his people" the victory. The slaughter commenced at Gibeon; and as the poor wretches fled for their lives, "the Lord cast down great stones from hea-

ven upon them, unto Azekah, and they died." But lest the day should not be long enough to complete the butchery, then spake Joshua: Sun, stand thou still upon Gibeon, and thou, moon, in the valley of Ajalon. And the sun stood still, and the moon staid until the people had avenged themselves upon their enemies. Is not this written in *the book of* JASHER? "So the sun stood still in the midst of heaven, and hasted not to go down about a *whole day.*"

Had such an event ever occurred as the sudden stopping of the earth in its swift revolution, every living being, and every work of man upon its surface would have been instantly destroyed; even the earth itself would fly into fragments. Yet it is known that there are buildings now standing in Egypt erected before the alleged time of Joshua. Were it possible that the sun or moon could have stood still, such an extraordinary event would have been known over the whole world; yet neither in China, India, Persia, or Egypt, more ancient countries, where astronomy was studied, is there any mention made of it. The narrative was never penned by such a person as Joshua; for the unknown scribe quotes the *book of* JASHER as authority to corroborate the miracle! This book of *Jasher* was then considered as one of the "inspired" books, and as it was not written until the *time of the kings,* centuries after the *death of Joshua,* he could not have been the writer. The *book of Jasher,* like many others still quoted in the Bible, has long been enumerated among the *lost books* of Scripture; it can not now be found.

This is another of the so-called miracles that theologians would be gladly rid of. There is no concurring testimony respecting it. In barbarous ages, every pretender was a miracle-worker, and this particular one has been foisted into the "word of truth" by some one ignorant of the first principles of astronomy.

The whole story is a fable, a relic of some ancient myth, on which are founded so many of the Bible miracles, to eclipse science and common sense, and to cast a shadow over reason and intelligence.

As a further proof of the humane disposition of the people of God, the story continues, that after the great slaughter, the five kings who had taken refuge in a cave were dragged out by order of Joshua. He said, "Come near, put your feet upon the necks of these kings. And they came near, and put their feet upon the necks of them." "And afterward Joshua smote them, and slew them, and hanged them on five trees, and they were hanging upon the trees until the evening."

Not satisfied with the bloodshed of this notable day, he went on smiting; he took seven other kings, which he treated to the same kind of death. "So Joshua smote all the country of the hills, and of the south, and of the vale, and of the springs, and all their kings: he left none remaining, but utterly destroyed all that breathed, as the Lord God of Israel commanded."

The next chapter continues the fearful record; even the poor brutes taken from the enemy were gashed and *hamstrung* by order of the Lord! "And Joshua did unto them as the Lord bade him; he *houghed their horses* and burnt their chariots with fire. For it was of the Lord to *harden their hearts, that they should come against Israel in battle*, that he might destroy them utterly, and that they might have *no favor*, but that he might destroy them, as the Lord commanded Moses."[*]

What a frightful picture! A " benevolent Deity" deliberately hardening the hearts of creatures whom he had created to war with others to whom he was partial! No wonder that these cruel tales have become so revolting, and that humane Christian ministers try to avoid reading them from their pulpits. No wonder that more missionaries are required, and that money is squandered in vain attempts to bind down humanity and generous impulses to such "*truths*;" and it was no wonder that Mr. Capel, while he dwelt upon such a history during many a weary night, trying, like many others, to reconcile himself to its belief, was tortured by dreams in uneasy slumbers, and, on awaking, to be shamed by doubts, and—to wish himself dead.

CHAPTER XVI.

THIS was a busy week at Mrs. Baker's, a week of bustling preparation. Not only was there to be the regular class meeting but there was also to be a prayer-meeting every evening during the week, in anticipation of the great anniversary at Exeter Hall. These pious sisters were like light skirmishers in a corps of volunteers, determined to be in advance of all others, and to do battle as it were on their own account against the enemies of the Lord. The grand object of this special attack was to gain supplies from the enemy; and the Lord was to be importuned to loosen the grasp of the miser upon his hoards, the rich man upon his wealth; and high and low, old and young, were all prayed for in succession, so that abundance might flow into the spiritual treasury, and that the Bible might be scattered, thick as hail in a storm, among deluded Papists and blind unbelievers.

Then after these little sorties, the sisters retired into the cheerful parlor, where trifling chat, the rattle of tea-cups and the fragrance of young Hyson made these religious meetings so decidedly agreeable.

Apart from any excellence attributed to religion, one of its greatest attractions for woman is the opportunity it affords for pleasant reunions and social intercourse. How tedious the Sundays would pass were there no place to go, to see and be seen. Christian, or rather intensely Protestant Christian laws and customs, have made it improper and unpopular, even sometimes actually criminal, to devote any part of that sombre day either to

science, secular discussions, or convivial meetings. The ding dong of bells on the early Sabbath has a reviving effect in a community thus deprived; even going to church is a relaxation. Those who have lived apart during the week have now a chance of meeting some old friend—the maiden her lover, the youth a companion. There is a quiet pleasure in being able to look around upon an orderly, well-dressed assemblage of worshipers, to see a display of fashion, to hear fine music, and to sit in somniferous ease, while the well-trained minister performs in peculiar clerical tones the religious service; which, whether rendered at the shrine of Moses, or Mohammed would be a matter of indifference to many were it only popular.

To woman, religion offers free scope for usefulness. She is foolishly debarred from interference in most other matters; she is made a child in intellect, and denied a profession; she is lampooned in politics, and ridiculed as a sage; and though the church ignores her as a teacher, yet she is placed on an equality as a co-worker for its support; and to her powerful aid, religion in every land is indebted for its greatest supplies, and for its numerous adherents.

Mrs. Mannors was one among the number who went heart and soul into the work. She was a believer of the right kind. For her, there was nothing outside Christianity worth living for; she believed that she had an important part to perform, and now she never felt so contented as when actively engaged in some religious duty. She also felt that while her husband was without the ark of safety, it behooved her to redouble her exertions on his account, whereby she might propitiate God in his favor; for, although hopeful of his conversion, she would relax no effort until it was accomplished.

She had been at Mrs. Baker's all the week; she took but little interest in her household affairs; every night she had a spiritual dream, and every day she formed new plans in order to accomplish the conversion of sinners; and now, as the Bible cause was about to receive a fresh impulse, she would wait for the return of Mr. Baker and Mr. Capel, and then she and her class-mates in a body would go with them to Exeter Hall. She could remain from home safely, for she could depend upon one trusty servant, and she knew that Miss Mannors was quite competent to see after the wants of her father and brother.

Hannah had also a busy week. She was occasionally afflicted with a mania for house-cleaning; and whenever an opportunity offered, and very often when it did not, she would upset every piece of furniture in the house; beds, bedding, chairs, tables, bureaus, and cupboards would be put outside, and one passing might imagine that the tithe proctor was going his rounds, or that there was to be a hasty removal. Mr. Mannors had been so accustomed to this kind of thing that he good-naturedly submitted, and let Hannah have her own way. Miss Mannors never interfered, for she knew her mother would not; and on such occasions, while Robert generally kept out of the way, William and Flounce would sit in a corner together, watch

---

[*] Among the terrible scenes of pious butchery recorded of "God's people," few can exceed in barbarity that related in the 2d Book of Kings, chapter xv. verse 16.

"Then Menahem smote Tiphsah, and all that were therein, and the coasts thereof from Tirzah; because they opened not to him, therefore he smote it; *and all the women therein that were with child* HE RIPPED UP!"

ing the proceedings; or, if it was a fine day, would perch upon some elevation in the sunlight, as if expecting that after the last piece of furniture was thrown out, the next operation would be the pulling down of the whole house.

Hannah was never so happy as she seemed to be on such occasions. She acted as if she had full control, and more especially in the absence of Mrs. Mannors, she did just as she pleased, quite irrespective of the inconvenience she might cause; and, while tugging at some heavy article, or striving to eject some stubborn piece of furniture, or while scouring away at something that would persist in looking black or brown in spite of all her efforts, she would sing all manner of hymns that she could remember; and if her memory failed her, as it often did, she would improvise tunes and words, sometimes very irrelevant, for the part that was wanting; and it was only when she was forced into a regular breakdown that she would pause for a moment or two, to renew her efforts, or commence to soliloquize upon some household affair, or other matter, then more particularly on her mind.

Now Hannah, though somewhat beyond maidenly years, that is to say, between twenty-five and thirty, was yet fresh, and rather good looking. Strange to say, she never considered herself a beauty, and scarcely ever thought of matrimony; no, not since she left her dreams of eighteen. She seemed entirely devoted to her mistress, to her household duties, and to John Bunyan. Now and then, while in the very midst and bustle of her work, with moistened brow and sleeves tucked up, she would pause for a moment, and steal away to a certain corner in the pantry, to take a peep at the object of her thoughts. There, on a little shelf close to a small window lay the *Pilgrim's Progress*; she would take up the treasured book, read a little here and there, turn the pages over and over, and seem delighted with the engravings. There was the poor pilgrim, heavily laden with his pack between his shoulders, leaving house, wife, and children to flee from the "City of Destruction." Then he was seen toiling up the hill toward the little "wicket gate." There was "Vanity Fair," "Christian and Evangelist," and other such pictures at which she appeared to be never tired of looking; and she would gaze in admiration at the plate which represented the Pilgrim with his heavy pack conversing with "Good Will," at the arched gate, over which was written, "Knock, and it shall be opened unto you;" while on a tower, at one side, could be seen Beelzebub with bow and arrow, bat-like wing, and crooked forked tail, ready to shoot down pilgrims ere they entered, or, as in the words of Bunyan, "From thence both he and they that are with him shoot arrows at those that come up to the gate, if happily they may die before they enter in."

Thus it was with Hannah; while other damsels similarly situated would leisurely survey their good looks in some piece of looking-glass, privately stowed away, she, on the contrary, only went to consult her favorite John Bunyan. Often, when she was in the midst of such a turn-out, Mr. Mannors with

Mary would steal on tip-toe and watch the operations unobserved from behind a door, or from some other favorable spot. He would humorously say, that Hannah's particular vice was that of scrubbing, and that neither tin pans, nor britannia tea-pots would live out half their days through the scraping, rubbing, and polishing they were destined to suffer under the influence of her restless arm.

But now Hannah's labors for the week were nearly brought to a close. The clean cages and fluttering canaries were hung up, pictures were replaced; even the shining brass pendulum of the clock in the hall seemed to look laughingly at you through its polished glass casing, while it swung steadily to and fro, as if determined to pull up for lost time. Things were getting in order; Mr. Mannors might venture again into his study, and Hannah, still watched by William, could be seen manfully backing in and dragging to its place the great heavy kitchen table, that one would think held back as if it felt inclined to put her to all the trouble it could.

"Well, I declare, if missus was here, she'd make that good-for-nothing Robert help me in with this. He's—he's always away when he's wanting." Then she put an air to this verse of Bunyan's:

"'What danger is the Pilgrim in! how many are his foes!
How many ways there are to sin no living mortal knows;
Some in the ditch spoiled are, yea, can die tumbling in the mire;
Some, though they shun the frying-pan, do leap into the fire.'

Ah me! just so; foes within and foes without in this horrid world.

'When I can read my title clear
To palaces —'

Well, I ought to know that verse; but our vile nature is always a thinking of something else.

'Hark! how the watchmen cry; attend the trumpet's sound,
Stand to your arms! the foe is nigh, the powers of hell surround.'

Yes, if them fallen angels couldn't stand him, how can we? but—"

"Hannah, here comes Ma and Robert," said Miss Mannors, entering the kitchen. Hannah had fortunately got through with present difficulties; chairs, tables, and cupboards were in their proper places, and seemed to rest content that they should not get such another overhauling again for some time.

"Why, bless me, missus, how glad I am that you are back; I am so glad you did not come until I got over my hurry; and there goes that lazy fellow," said she, as she saw Robert driving round to the stable.

"Hannah, poor girl," said Mrs. Mannors, tenderly, as she looked around the shining kitchen, "you have been doing too much, too much entirely; you are, I am afraid, too anxious about these trifling matters and—"

"Oh! not at all, ma'am," broke in Hannah. "Why, we were getting in such a state here that I was ashamed myself to look at the dust and cobwebs; but I thought, ma'am, that you were going to wait for Mr. Capel."

"So I was, Hannah; but we heard to-day, at Mrs. Baker's, that he was going to call here first on his return from the circuit, and I thought I would be home to meet him."

Mary and William, and Flounce whisking his bushy tail, now followed Mrs. Mannors from room to room. She soon encountered Mr. Styles, who had called there that morning to pay a short visit, and Mr. Mannors, to interest his wife, told her that their visitor had been formerly a traveling agent for the American Bible Society; he knew that Mr. Styles could give her a great deal of information about the state and prospects of religion in America, but he was very careful for the present not to shock her by relating how the same person had fallen away from his first love.

Mrs. Mannors was very much pleased; she forgot many other things for the time, and asked fifty different questions about the progress of Methodism in his native land; whether all the Indians and black men were converted, and whether many of the American saints were to be at Exeter Hall. Samuel, having learned her tendencies from Robert, was careful just then to say nothing which might cause her to regret his presence at Hampstead. She told him how pleased Mr. Capel would be to have an opportunity of meeting him—he was a devoted minister, in whom she had great hopes. And then, best of all, she assured Mr. Styles that, as he was just in time for the great anniversary meeting, he would learn at Exeter Hall what the British Christians were doing, and what sacrifices were annually made by them for the circulation of the "Word," and for the conversion of poor benighted heathens—she, of course, meant the foreign ones.

During that quiet forenoon, Mr. Mannors and Samuel had a long conversation; various topics were introduced—the merits of the respective governments of Great Britain and the United States, the progressive liberality of ideas, and the terrible rule of priestcraft which still kept its icy gripe upon the generous impulses of the people of both countries, forcing the great majority yet to succumb to the puerilities of a superstition which would have been long since effete, were it not for the constant supplies that it extorted. Samuel related the evidence he had at the sale for church rates, and the instance of priestly intolerance, by describing the scene at the cemetery. Mr. Mannors was but too familiar with such acts on the part of the state-paid priests; and though America is as yet almost free from such gross usurpation, still, even in the new world, there can be found occasional instances of the same spirit, one of which Samuel remembered to have taken place at a churchyard in Pennsylvania.*

Among other things, he was particular to give Mr. Mannors a more detailed account of his night adventure in company with Robert. He told him they had seen Dr. Buster under the archway, how they had followed him un-

til the carriage drove away after midnight—and when he handed the paper which he believed the doctor had dropped, Mr. Mannors scrutinized it very closely, and pronounced the writing to be Dr. Buster's.

"This," said Mr. Mannors, with a slight emphasis, "may serve as an important clew to his transactions. He has completely evaded me for some time; this very paper may, perhaps, enable us to take the first step toward a discovery. Dr. Buster is a popular man in London, but he shuns me; very few know him as I do, and he knows me. He is a saint to some, while in truth, a monster of cruelty."

"I saw that he recognized you yesterday on the Strand, I kind o' think you'll not forget the heavenly smile he gave you."

"No, not readily; it is seldom indeed that I can get an opportunity of seeing that gentleman, unless I choose to enter his church. I never did the man any harm, but I believe he is a tyrant, and will yet commit some diabolical act if he is not legally restrained, or humanized by some other means."

"Just so, or by a trifling assistance from brute force."

"Well, any suitable force, or any proper means that will prevent him from accomplishing his purpose might almost be resorted to; I have learned, partly by mere chance and partly from his own wife, that he persecutes her, hates her, and will soon end her days, unless she finds some deliverance; and this I fear he will manage to do in such a way as to escape legal responsibility."

"That will be his game. But he must be watched, tracked, circumvented, and finally squashed. You see chance is against him; it has led you to find one of his qualities, it has partly shown me another, and I want no better pastime at present than a chance to follow him up until I can tree him sky high."

"Indeed, I think you will be an excellent agent for that purpose; and we shall try and devise some plan to entrap him, for I have long determined to step between him and his victim. I only await the opportunity. We have a wily, unscrupulous man to deal with, and must be very guarded in our approaches, or he will defeat the best laid plans. He has caused it to be circulated that his wife has forsaken her children and himself; there has not yet been a trace of her whereabouts, but it has been suspected by myself and a few others, that the unfortunate woman has been deprived of her liberty, and from what you have lately discovered I am strongly of that opinion."

"Well, we came upon him rather close, I imagine; he ain't alone, though—he's got his tools, male and female. Now, just give me the credentials. I want to be a kind of walking gentleman, or any thing else that comes handy, for a month or two. This little circumstance interests me a trifle; just put me on the track, and I'm off." So saying, Mr. Styles quickly whisked one hand across the other, as if to illustrate the celerity of his intended movements.

"I stated," continued Mr. Mannors, "that the first knowledge I had of Dr. Buster's ill treatment to his wife was by chance. About

* In Chester.

two years ago, I was crossing the Bristol Channel in a steam packet; it was during a fine summer's night; several of the passengers remained on deck; but as it grew later, one by one went below, until I thought I was left alone. The air was delightfully fresh. I felt no inclination for sleep, and, having paced up and down for some time, I stretched myself on a seat or bench close to the wheel-house and was trying to compose myself, when I heard a discussion between two persons on a religious subject. They sat or stood around a corner, out of my view, but I could hear every word distinctly. A lady's voice asserted that King David, of the Old Testament, was, if any thing, a greater monster of cruelty and wickedness than either Moses or Joshua; and after reciting some of his murders, treachery, and misconduct, declared that she could not believe that a Supreme Being had ever connived at such infamy, or declared that such a wretch could be 'a man after his own heart.'

"A man's voice testily replied that such things were beyond our comprehension; that we must take the account as we found it in the Bible. It was inspired, consequently correct; that whether David repented or not, God could select whom he pleased to work out his designs; he could make one vessel to honor and another to dishonor. David was referred to in the Scriptures as a progenitor of the Messiah, whose coming was established by prophecy. Prophecy was the thing that had spread confusion among sneering infidels.

"The lady contended that these so-called prophecies had no direct reference whatever to a Messiah, and that even such a conclusion had been formed by certain commentators.

The man then replied in a passionate tone that such commentators would meet damnation, and all who believed as they did. He then told her she had better give up the Bible altogether; and he raised his voice sufficiently loud to let me hear imprecations and words of anger, and then, after the lady had made some reply, I was startled by the noise of a heavy fall on the deck, and I ran to the spot in time to see the stout form of a man descend the cabin stairs and to assist in raising the lady, who had evidently been thrust off her feet. She was bleeding and was partly confused, and she looked around and at me as if greatly ashamed. I assured her that I was the only person that knew any thing of the matter, that I had overheard the conversation which led to such violence, and after having assisted her to a seat, begged her to allow me to get some water to wash away the blood. She thankfully declined, she was anxious to retire unseen, and, folding a shawl over her face, permitted me to lead her as far as the cabin stairs. In about two or three minutes afterward, the same stout person came on deck again, and, when he saw me, was, no doubt, suspicious that I had witnessed his unmanly act. I stood near and watched him, and my indignation at his conduct was so great that I could not refrain from telling him that he ought to be punished for what he had done, and that I would inform the captain before

we left the vessel. It was sufficiently light to enable me to see his features; he made no reply, but gave me one angry look and went quickly away.

"Upon inquiry next morning, I learned that the person whom I recognized as the probable aggressor was one Dr. Buster, and that the lady was his wife. On her account, I did not think it prudent to mention any thing about the violent act which I was satisfied he had committed. I saw that he tried to avoid me, but when we arrived in London I stood at the ship's side and watched him pass out; he recognized me and frowned, and as he strode hurriedly away he left his wife to follow as best she could.

"It was some months afterward, and I had almost forgotten the circumstance, when I happened to read in one of the numerous religious papers of the city that a course of lectures on the Apocalypse and on the prophecies of Daniel were to be delivered by a certain Dr. Buster. The paper lauded his piety and ability in the highest terms. The name recalled the circumstance on the vessel, and, curious to learn whether it was the same person, I went to town and purchased a ticket—it was not a free lecture; and as I loitered outside the church-door, a carriage drove up, out of which stepped the identical doctor that I expected. He looked me full in the face; I saw a change of expression; but he passed in, determined not to know me, or to make me believe that it must have been some one else—that he could do nothing derogatory to his character as a minister. I was, however, satisfied, and did not remain to hear the lecture.

"You might have heard at the Red Lion that there are a very great number of Secularists in and about London. I profess to be one of that class; we have several halls and lecture-rooms in which religious and utilitarian subjects are freely discussed in an orderly manner. These discussions have been productive of great benefit, and many church-members and other persons, troubled with religious doubts, or curious to learn our particular views, attend such meetings; sometimes privately, in order to hear our objections against Christianity, occasionally to try and refute them, and to ascertain what we think on relative subjects; for of course you are aware, that so careful are the priests of their creed, in such dread do they hold free investigation, that books written against them or their faith are denounced, and their authors calumniated. Among the many who attended, there was one lady who appeared anxious to remain unknown, and she might have done so were it not that she was recognized one evening leaving the hall by some devout church-members who were watching outside, for the purpose of discovering who were falling away and proving recreant to the faith. Great was the surprise when it was learned that the lady was the wife of one of the principal dissenting ministers of the city, and true to their mission, the orthodox detectives made an immediate report to her husband; and the Rev. Dr. Buster appeared to be greatly depressed, greatly humiliated, and in deep affliction by this woeful proof of his wife's religious degeneracy.

"As for her, she had been long suspected of indifference to church matters. Church-going ladies said she was not like a minister's wife; she was never seen at prayer-meetings, never at Sunday-schools, was no tractarian, did not get up missionary tea-meetings,' or, in fact, interest herself in any of the numerous devices for raising money for the spread of the Gospel, or to increase the slender resources of her pious husband. She was known to be studious and thoughtful, of an inquiring mind, and very benevolent to such needy applicants as craved more for actual food than they did for the scriptural 'bread of life.'

"In her domestic capacity, she could not be excelled. She had two children, and proved herself a most affectionate mother; but alas! her want of faith had robbed her of any love her husband might have had for her, and though affecting before members of his church to be most considerate toward her, it was well known that his dislike grew stronger and stronger, until at last his hatred made her life miserable. It was then rumored that her mind was affected; insanity could be traced in her family; for the idea was considered most absurd, to suppose that a person religiously brought up as she had been, carefully trained in youth, and then daily and hourly the recipient of spiritual knowledge under the teaching of such a husband, could ever possibly become skeptical while under the guidance of a sound mind.

"There would be no great difficulty in tracing the authorship of such a reputed mental frailty. In deference to the feelings of the reverend doctor, the rumor was charitably accepted as truth, but alas! how uncharitably for his wife. She well knew that this subterfuge, if not counteracted, would accomplish her ruin; and as week after week passed, when she found herself neglected, spurned, and treated with contempt, she was almost on the verge of despair. She knew there was but little if any sympathy for unbelievers among the positive class of Christians which were under her husband's control, that at best she would be treated as a kind of monomaniac, when she bethought her of the secularists; she had heard of my name in connection with that organization, and I received through the post this letter." Here Mr. Mannors took a letter from a small drawer, and read:

"'DEAR SIR: One who is greatly persecuted on account of her religious opinions, and who fears actual violence, would wish to consult with you. An interview is particularly desired. A letter addressed to E. C. M., 32 Tottenham Court Road, will reach me.

P.S.—If convenient, an interview on Thursday next, between two and five P.M., would be most suitable for me.   A FRIEND.
"'June 17th.'

"I sent a reply, I think the same evening; and on the following Thursday I met her at the house of a private friend, and I was surprised to find that she was the very person whom I had so singularly met on the steamboat. She would not have recognized me from that circumstance, but when I mentioned it, she again expressed her thanks, and told me that the treatment which she had then received was but the commencement of far worse outrages; that not only was she abused herself, but, to add to her agony, her husband would threaten and terrify the children, until they actually dreaded his approach. She said it was evident that he wished to make her out insane, and unfit to be left without some restraint. He had already sent the children away, and she had good reason to fear that some evil toward herself was premeditated.

"I gave her the best advice I could at the time, told her if any further violence was committed, or any probability of such, to make her escape at once; that I would leave word with John Hollis, at the Red Lion, to take her under his protection, until he could send for me; and that afterward I would use every possible method to secure her from molestation. She was very grateful. I told her that before I went home I would consult some friends, and write to her more fully next day, and that I would meet her again in a week; but if any thing happened in the mean time, she was to do as I had directed.

"I called on the landlord of the Red Lion the same evening, and had every thing arranged. I also met a few friends in town, and related as much of the matter as was necessary to enlist their protection in case it should be required. Next day I sent her another letter, and, at the appointed time when I called again, instead of meeting the doctor's wife, I actually met the doctor himself!"

"A very agreeable surprise, no doubt," said Samuel.

"Not so agreeable as I could have desired. With the coolest assurance he told me that I had brought a scandal upon the once fair name of his wife, that my vile teaching had corrupted her mind, and that he supposed she had already taken refuge in that very respectable rendezvous, the Red Lion, in accordance with my letter of instructions; and here to my surprise he coolly unfolded the letter, and I saw my own signature."

"I took a moment for reflection; I supposed that both she and I had been betrayed. The woman in whose house we were, and who was present during my interview with the doctor's wife, was now absent, and I felt somewhat embarrassed by the awkwardness of my position. I, however, replied that he must know he was stating what was not correct, that I had but two interviews with his wife in the course of my life—the first on board the Bristol packet when he had abused her, the last but a week ago in that room. When I mentioned that he had abused, or had struck his wife, he jumped up and violently exclaimed while holding his shut fist before me in a threatening attitude, "It's false, it's false, you never saw me do it."

"'Well, sir,' said I, 'if I did not see you do it, I heard something of your violence, and I afterward saw the effects of your mode of argument, and I now believe that you intend to follow up that particular method of combating error by persecuting one whom you should cherish.'

"'See here,' said he, holding out my letter at arm's length, 'I possess in this damning evidence against *your* principles of honor. If you dare to deal in vile misrepresentations, I have *this* fact to refute your assertions, and your honored name subscribed in attestation. Now, proceed if you dare.'

"His teeth were clinched fast when he uttered these words, and as he waved the letter violently before me, he looked like one of Milton's fallen angels, or the impersonation of Satan himself.

"'I know not what your threat means,' I replied, 'nor how you may distort the meaning of that letter; but remember, you will yet be held responsible for the crime you are about to commit; or, if the act has been already perpetrated, there may be sufficient evidence to test your religious scruples in a court of law.'

"'*You* talk of religion or law,' said he, giving the mock laugh of a fury, while his eyes seemed like skulking fiends ready with some fulminating substance for my annihilation. 'You, with an infidel heart and body without a soul, you talk about crime! Go,' said he, pointing to the door, 'go and teach virtue to the wretch who has sought your protection, teach her more of your infernal principles, until she is fit to graduate among a class of Tom Paines, and Voltaires and Bolingbrokes, and like them, die in the pangs of remorse, and meet with their final damnation.'

"If his curses were blessings in disguise, they could not be more harmless so far as I was concerned. I saw what he was drifting at, he wished to make *me* think that his wife had left her home, and that he believed she was under my protection. Before I went out, I told him that I was not deceived, that I well understood his object, and that there might be a reckoning between us at some future day.

"How he became possessed of my letter, I know not. Unfortunately, I did not keep a copy of it, it was written in haste, but I am not aware that there was any thing in it that could compromise me. I think I recommended her to leave her prison like home for a time, and that I would see that she had suitable protection from the designs of her husband.

"Something must have happened to her; I never heard from her afterward. Since that time, it has been circulated that she left her husband and children. Inquiry was made for her among her relatives in Bristol, and search was made at other places, but no trace of her could be found. As she had sufficient means of her own, some of the pious ladies and members of her husband's congregation suppose that she is living privately with some friends, or perhaps among the Secularists; while many, outside the pale of the doctor's influence, think that he has her securely under lock and key, either to shorten her existence, or force her to abjure the errors of an unbelief which has brought so much misery to her, but which has gained so many prayers, and so much sympathy for him.

"I did not see the doctor afterward until the day we encountered each other on the Strand; you were a witness of that friendly recognition. If I ever meet him again, it may be to assist in convicting him of such inhumanity as will truly exhibit the meaning of his piety to the world."

"Guess I'll try and meet him again," said Mr. Styles; "I tracked him once in the rain and dark, but it didn't amount to much. I'll try him again, and see if I can't trot him out in broad daylight, so that his admiring female saints, when they see his elegant qualities in perfection, may wish him away up out of sight, with Elijah; or up, or down, or anywhere else, but in the velvet-cushioned pulpits they made so soft for him in the Presbyterian churches of London."

CHAPTER XVII.

THE evening sun sent its red beams slanting down upon Hampstead, and nearly every window in Heath Cottage blazed in the ruddy light. Troops of children were at play by the roadside, and workmen, after having partaken of their frugal meal, sat each by his open door in the sunset, enjoying that calm hour after the labors of the day. Lowing cattle in the distant fields could be seen winding homeward, followed here and there by cheerful milkmaids carrying their white pails while humming some favorite air as they went along. A thousand birds sung and fluttered in gardens and among orchard blossoms, and the mellow notes of the thrush, and robin could be heard, as if bidding farewell to the fading day.

It was a calm hour, one which predisposes for rest or for soothing thought. At such a season, even care seems to loosen its hold, and, under the milder influence, the heart which has long been burdened with sorrow dreams of hope again. In the tender light of eve, memory loves to wander back once more to the mountain, or stream, or green field of youth, and the faces and smiles of friends of earlier years return again to greet us.

Looking down upon Hampstead—as Mr. Capel now was from the brow of a small hill which he had just ascended—one might have lingered a moment or two, as he did, to survey the rich landscape spread out before him. The view obtained was very attractive, and while musing upon the variety of combinations which formed the natural picture, the young preacher forgot temporary troubles, and his memory also wandered—but not to a very remote period—neither was his fancy as excursive as at other times. He glanced at the village church with its ivied walls, glowing windows, and old gray steeple; at houses and gardens, fields and mansions; at the shadows on the distant hills, and then back again to Heath Cottage, where his eyes remained fixed. He could gaze without tiring on that quiet spot; it was the principal object in the picture to him, and, while thus looking, he thought of its inmates, and of their different characters; of the credulous visionary, Mrs. Maunors, of her generous, noble-minded husband, and of one other, to whom his thoughts would stray even while he tried to keep them confined to the mental problems which often kept him restless and wavering. He could not but admit that were all the matrons to become like Mrs. Mannors, there would be a sad retrogression—she could now boast of having become more alienated from the world, and it was evident that her worldly affairs, as far as she was concerned, were to be allowed to take care of themselves. What a contrast between her and the reasoning utilitarian, Martin Mannors! It was his desire to improve matters in this sublunary state as to make every human being as happy as possible. Were there more of his kind, the query arose, whether mankind would or would not be better prepared for a future existence than they are now, under the influence of a class who formally denounce "pomps and vanities," but beneath whose sway for centuries crime has so increased, and human misery become so extended. And then he thought, were the "angels of light" as pure and noble and as disinterested as the angel within that dwelling (but he shrunk from the profane idea) that heaven would be more worthy of his aspirations.

"Begorra! Harry, but you're in a brown study," said a friendly voice, almost at his elbow. "Faith, if preaching adds such a lamblike expression to your countenance, you may expect it to approach downright sheepishness by the time you're fit for the apostolic Swaddlers to lay hands upon you."

Mr. Capel turned suddenly round, and was surprised to see his old friend, the Rev. Father Thomas McGinn, with his cheerful red face, sitting in a gig, surveying him from head to foot, while a good-natured smile lit up his jovial countenance.

"Why Father Tom, I'm very, very glad to see you."

"I know you are, Harry, but you blush like a girl. Sure, you don't mind what I say. I'd blush too, I think, if I had such a pair of saddle bags dangling behind me. Barring them things, you put me a good deal in mind of your poor father, God rest his sowl!"

"Amen, Father Tom. I know you and he were great friends, and I often wished to see you. I went down the other day to find you, but I heard you had gone over to Ireland for a few days. I was so sorry I didn't know of your intention sooner."

"Faith, I wish you had, but I went off in a hurry. I got a letter stating that poor Billy Doolan of Blackpool was in the last stage of consumption—you knew my cousin Billy—and sure the divil a one but my own four bones would do him to administer *Extreme Unction* to him; well, if it did the poor crayther any good, I don't begrudge the trouble."

"I knew poor Billy well, and am glad you went to see him; it was just like what you would do, Father Tom; but you can scarcely doubt the efficacy of your own rites?" said Mr. Capel, looking with affected surprise."

"Oh! no, oh! no, not the least," said Father McGinn, giving a slight cough, while the tips of his cheeks became if possible a little redder than usual. "You know I sometimes talk at random, Harry; your poor father knew that. There's but one true church, and whatever she directs is right." He spoke these words in such a manner as if intended to reassure himself. "But, Harry, different as our creeds or calling may be, you and I must never discuss religion. There was a solemn agreement of the same kind between your father and myself, and, faith, it worked well—anyhow he didn't bother his brains much about hell or heaven or purgatory, and God knows I wish we had more like him."

"I wish there were more like him, I wish there were, Father Tom. I think of him now oftener than ever, and oh! how I many a time have wished that some Christian men and ministers had even the hearts of so called pagans, what a gain it would be for humanity!" Mr. Capel's eyes almost filled with tears as he said this, and Father McGinn stared at him a moment or two in evident surprise.

"'Pon my sowl, but that smacks a good deal of your father; you've got his features, and I think you're rising to his ideas. Go on that way a little longer, *arick*, and you'll know something of the Bull *in cœna Domini*, at least the Methodist interpretation of it. But tell me, Harry," continued the priest, in a tone of great kindness, "do they use you well? where do they keep you? and is that what you're at every day?" said he, pointing significantly to the horse and saddlebags.

"Not every day; I have just been over the circuit. I left here about ten days since, and am now returning. I may not go out again for another week—perhaps longer;" and the priest noticed the troubled look which almost forced him to articulate the words—"perhaps never."

"I fear they don't use you well," interrupted Father McGinn. "The English don't like us, Harry—never will like us—they haven't the same warm feelings that we have. The ravenous clergy of the Establishment have robbed and plundered poor Ireland until there's little left, and take my word for it they're going to do the same here, or I'm much mistaken; though there's some hope, as the Chartists aren't all dead yet. But tell me, how do they treat you?"

"Indeed, Father Tom, I can't complain of bad treatment; on the contrary, I have found the people very kind. 'Tis true they exhibit their friendship in a different manner from what our country people do, but, so far, I have nothing to say against English hospitality—nothing indeed. But, Father Tom, don't you think the clergy of one church would be just as bad as those of another, either for Ireland or for this country, or for any other country—that is, if they all had the same chance—all on an equality? I've thought the matter over lately, and I am inclined to this opinion."

"Lately, have you," said Father McGinn, musing; "and do you include the Ranters and Swaddlers among the rest? You know *we* look upon these as bastards—upstarts—but faith they're beginning to hold up their heads as high as the best of us—the Swaddlers are at any rate. Sure it's only the other day I heard of—och! bother—what's his name—I can't think of it now—but, anyway, a chap that calls himself a 'Methodist *parson*,' marching into his conventicle with all the airs of a cardinal, and stepping up into his elegant pulpit decked in *gown* and *bands*. Why, God bless the mark! I would just as soon expect to see a Quaker in regimentals. Now, with all their mock humility, and sanctity, and their pity for the deluded of England and Rome, only give these same creatures wealth and numbers, and then, *ecce signum*, they acquire the clerical animus, and the inflated Swaddler who may have begun life on a kish of turf now turns up his nose if you call him a '*preacher*,' and hobbles into the sunlight as a 'reverend *clergyman*.' What d'ye think of that?"

"You are very severe! but 'tis too true—too true—all from the same spirit of arrogance. But, Father Tom," said Mr. Capel, after a pause, and suddenly changing the conversation, "I want to have a long, long talk with you some day. I do not hesitate to say to you that you are far better informed on many subjects than I am, and there are many questions which have troubled me lately—problems which you may be able to solve, and doubts which perplex me very much, that your superior knowledge may remove. I'm not afraid to tell this to you."

"Questions, problems, doubts, all troubling you, and lately too. Pray," said Father McGinn, straightening himself up, and assuming to be very particular, "do these partake of a scientific, metaphysical, or theological tendency? if of the two former, I shall have much pleasure in a rehearsal with you; if of the latter, of course you would not consult *me*—a Papist." And here the priest made a low bow of mock humility.

"I will consult you," said Mr. Capel eagerly—"I will know what you think. I would rather go to you, Father Tom, than to the Archbishop of Canterbury. My doubts *are* theological, and I know you will set me right, if you can. I will go to you; I would rather confess to you, now, than to any one else in the world."

"Well, then, my child," said the priest, speaking very tenderly, "if you confess to me, you will be sure of my poor absolution; such as it is, you shall have it, and then," said he, in a low, confidential tone, "I may make a more startling confession to *you*. But who is to absolve me? Who? You will. Ay, but the Pope won't. You must never doubt *his* form of truth; if you do, you're damned! Ah! Harry, twenty years ago I learned some of my doubts from your poor father, and I have carried them along with me ever since; and I suppose I shall forever and ever."

"Father Tom," said Mr. Capel after a moment's pause, "when can I see you after to-day?"

"When? Any time you like, almost. Sometimes they send me out to jails and prisons, and such places; for I'm no great favorite with the bishop, and he adds these appointments, I suppose, by the way of penance. But I don't mind knocking about in the fresh air, if I hadn't to visit cells, and gloomy places, among criminals and half idiots. I'll tell you

Harry, could you ride out with me some day?"

"I could. What day do you say?"

"I don't know yet, until I get back. If you come to Moorfields, ten chances to one but we'd have half a dozen priests around us; and as they are a little suspicious of me at times, they'd be more so if they saw me cheek by jowl with you and your white choker; lave that thing off. No, Harry, 'twould be a bad place for a priest and a Swaddler to meet."

"Name your day, then, Father Tom. We can ride. I would prefer it."

"Let me see—Monday, Tuesday, Wednesday. Where do you live, Harry? hereabouts, somewhere, isn't it? I think we may try it on Friday. You'd have no objection to a beefsteak on that day, neither would I for the matter of that; but we must keep this to ourselves. So we can have a long chat and a beefsteak and trimmings somewhere in town in the evening, eh?"

"That will be excellent. Friday will answer me better than any other day next week. See, there's where my temporary home is, Father Tom." And Mr. Capel pointed to Heath Cottage, with its burnished windows, fine shade trees, and pleasant garden; and just as they were admiring the cheerful homestead, the sun's lingering rays struck the spray of the little fountain, forming a beautiful tiny rainbow, and now and then as the jet gushed higher, it seemed to beckon a welcome to Mr. Capel and his friend, Father Tom.

"Heath Cottage, you call it. Well, now, may I never, but if I was going to choose a snug little spot where I could spend the remainder of my days, I wouldn't want a sweeter little place than that. 'Pon my sowl, perfectly charming." And the good priest put up his hand to shade his eyes, in order to get a better view. "Why, Harry, how in God's name did you strike upon that place? The owner is, of course, a Swaddler? Do I know him? What's his name?"

"It is all what it appears to be, Father Tom; it is better even inside, and you will wonder that its owner is not a Methodist nor a Swaddler, as you call them; in religious matters, he is something like my father; but his wife, Mrs. Mannors, is a Methodist, and—"

"Mrs. what?" eagerly interrupted the priest. "Mrs. Mannors, did you say?"

"Yes, Mrs. Mannors, wife of Martin Mannors, or, as he ought to be called, the *honorable* Martin Mannors, one of the noblest men living."

The priest looked at his friend in blank amazement, and then repeated slowly, "The honorable Martin Mannors, of Hampstead, Commander-in-Chief of the Secularists in and about London, and Great High-Priest of the same." And then, still looking at Mr. Capel, he gave a long, low whistle, so ludicrous that Mr. Capel actually laughed aloud.

"O faith! you may laugh, *ma bouchal*, but he's got one. I've heard of that name before, and if that's the same Martin Mannors that shines in the *National Reformer*, and in the *Westminster*, occasionally, no wonder you'd be troubled with doubts and problems. Why, man, for a plain, logical writer against churches and creeds, he can't be surpassed in London, nor may be, in all England. He's murder all out, when he begins."

It was Mr. Capel's turn now to be surprised; not that he was unacquainted with the peculiar opinions of his host on the subject of region, but he had never heard of him as a leader or writer, and he assured the priest that a more unassuming person he had never met

"That's the man, Harry; not a bit of pretension about him—but och, murder! he's down on the whole of us, root and branch. I've never seen him, but I know this from a particular friend. And bad luck to half the clerical thick skulls, instead of facing him like men and refuting his fair arguments, they try to attack his character; but, by all accounts, that's beyond their reach, and they can't do with him yet as they have done to Paine and others. Well now, 'pon my sowl, priest and all as I am, I'd like to meet him. True genius has a passport to every heart, whatever its character."

"Father Tom, there is nothing I would like better than that you should get acquainted with him. You will be very much pleased; drive on with me, and if he's at home, you shall have that gratification in less than five minutes."

They drove up to the garden-gate, and Mrs. Mannors, being as usual on the look-out for Mr. Capel, saw him outside, accompanied by another person whose clerical habit, as he stepped out of the gig, rather puzzled her. The priest wore his *soutane*, over which, when driving, he drew on a light or heavy outside coat, as the weather might require. Mrs. Mannors therefore did not venture out, but Robert came to take charge of the horses; even he also felt nonplussed as to the real character of the priest, and at last concluded that he must be some great man among the Methodists, or some novel importation from "abroad" to delight the vision of Mrs. Mannors and other pious sisters at Exeter Hall.

"'Pon my word, Mr. Mannors," said the priest, after the introductions were over, "I'm very happy, very happy indeed to meet with one so distinguished as yourself, and I am entirely indebted to my friend Mr. Capel for this unexpected pleasure." And the honest red face of the Rev. Mr. McGlinn was beaming with smiles, while he continued to look with admiration upon the genial countenance of Mr. Mannors.

"You flatter me, Mr. McGlinn, indeed you do; but flattery from a clergyman, to one *not* so distinguished, but rather so noted as I am, ought to be, and really is very gratifying. It is a rare pleasure for me to be honored with a visit from either priest or parson, except in the case of our friend Capel; and I shall treasure this event as one worthy of particular record."

Mrs. Mannors had only just then entered the room; and her husband, upon presenting Mr. McGlinn, stated that he was a Roman Catholic priest, and a very intimate friend of Mr. Capel. Had some wicked imp quickly thrust a pin into her arm, she could not have held back more suddenly. She had almost as

great a passion for reading Fox's *Book of Martyr's* as Hannah had for reading John Bunyan; and as her prejudice against Popery was very strong, she really fancied that there was nothing too perfidious for a Romish priest; and to meet one thus so unexpectedly in her own house produced the violent nervous effect—actual dread.

Scarcely one present, not even Mr. Mannors himself, could suppress a smile. Mr. Samuel Styles had to cough quickly and loudly several times to keep from bursting into an open laugh; and the farcical expression on the priest's face just meant as much as if he had said, "Don't be afraid; indeed, I won't eat you at all, at all, ma'am!"

In a moment or two, however, she became reassured, and having bowed politely, forced herself to utter some expressions of satisfaction; but the tantalizing burden remained on her mind, how Mr. Capel, a preacher of the Gospel, could be really and truly the intimate friend of a Popish priest. After a glass of wine, and the interchange of a few commonplace remarks, as it was getting late, the priest reluctantly said he should have to leave; but he received a warm invitation to pay another visit, and he took his departure, mentally flinging his best blessing on the head and shoulders of Mr. Mannors and upon his whole household. As he drove off alone in the fast waning sunlight, he felt delighted at having crossed by chance such a flowery, fragrant oasis in the dreary desert of his clerical life.

During Mr. McGlinn's stay, he made inquiries about some old friends residing in Philadelphia, whom Mr. Styles happened to know, and made some flattering observations on the prosperity of the great republic; and when Samuel, in return, thought to gratify him with an account of the immense Catholic cathedral in course of erection in that city; of the great wealth of the hierarchy of his Church in the United States, and of the influence which the Catholic body exercised throughout the country, he was surprised at the indifference manifested by Mr. McGlinn, and set him down as an exception to the general rule among Catholic clergymen.

"Father McGlinn is an oddity," said Mr. Capel, in reply to a remark of Mr. Styles; "he is looked on by his own people as very eccentric and independent, but he is a great favorite, and a more charitable man does not exist; his kindness in this respect is never regulated by creed, color, or country."

"That's an admirable trait," said Mr. Mannors. "If his face be the representative of his heart, his generous impulses will never be circumscribed by such ideas. He would never make an inquisitor; I hope we shall meet him soon again."

Mrs. Mannors could attend to no household affairs that evening; and while her husband was engaged in a conversation with Mr. Styles, she drew Mr. Capel toward a seat near the back window of the room, where they could chat more quietly, and asked him fifty questions about priests and Catholics, and about the state of religion on the circuit. She told him all the local news concerning class-meetings, prayer-meetings, tea-meetings, and expected revivals, and what she anticipated at Exeter Hall; told him about a controversy which had been commenced on the subject of baptism; how Mr. Baker, when he returned from the district meeting, would overwhelm the immersionists; said something of Dr. Cumming's new exposition of Daniel's vision of the ram and he-goat; and then related a curious dream which she had had three nights in succession, and in which he and Mr. Mannors were the principal actors; and how her hopes were growing stronger and stronger that her husband should soon be clothed in his right mind, and get rid of the delusion of unbelief.

Mr. Capel listened to these desultory recitals with patience; he made but few remarks. He knew she would be more content if he sat and heard all she had to say; and while she tried to make him feel interested with her religious burden of eccentricities, his mind was preoccupied with other matters. He thought of Father McGinn, and of the shadows of skepticism which were already closing around him; a little longer, and *he* too might fall, to be maligned and despised by those who now held him in such respect. Then he reflected upon his own condition; how wavering, how undecided. Should he yet be subjected to the scorn of the "faithful"? What would Mr. Baker say to *him*? how should he ever again hold up his head and be called an apostate, a renegade, a wretch? Then there came a little gleam of hope: how many thousand of the learned and intellectual in all ages had given their assent to Christianity, never doubting the Bible or its teachings. He must try and resist this growing incredulity, he must abandon those speculations, and curb the towering pride of his reason. How many in the heyday of health and prosperity had professed to reject inspiration but to submit and bewail their error in a dying hour. He knew there were such; but then again, he knew that the reputed death-bed scenes of Paine, Voltaire, and others, which had many times made him shudder at a doubt, were but gross fabrications of unprincipled men, who, like other priests in all ages, believed that if truth could be advanced by the aid of a lie, it would be proper to do so. Then again, how uncertain was this death-bed testimony; how many instances were there at such times of Protestant converts relapsing to Catholicism, and of men in every age and country accepting, in the feebleness of senility, the very errors which they had rejected under the influence of a sound mind.

The shadows of evening fell upon the sombre features of Mrs. Mannors, as she looked with indifference upon the sleeping flowers beneath her window. She had ceased speaking, and seemed in one of her pious reveries, and sat, listless and languid, with passionless face, like one weary, very weary of herself and the whole world. Just then her busy, joyful daughter flitted into the room like a ray of light; she was followed by her brother; and Mrs. Mannors, having kissed the delicate cheek of her little son, led the way to the tea-table in the next room.

Half an hour afterward, and before Miss Mannors had time to commence one of her favorite pieces, Mrs. Mannors remarked, when they had reassembled in the parlor:

"Oh! you have not heard all that Mr. Styles has to say about America. You must hear all he has to tell us of the missionaries and wild Indians, and what the Gospel has done for the poor black men in his native land. He has traveled for the Bible Society, and knows every thing about those interesting matters." And she led Mr. Capel toward Mr. Styles, and looked delighted to see her husband apparently so interested in private conversation with the American stranger. What a positive miracle she thought it was now to see Mr. Mannors entertaining a minister of the Gospel, and the agent of a Bible Society. Even the presence of a Catholic priest would be evidence, however trifling, that her husband had yet some regard for religion.

"Mr. Styles must know a good deal; he could even tell your priest friend, Mr. Capel, what they were doing to advance the interests of his church—that terrible Popish system. The cathedral they are putting up in Philadelphia must be a wonderful building. What a pity to waste so much money in an endeavor to delude so many poor ignorant people!"

"Guess it is, ma'am," said Samuel Styles, with great sincerity; "just see what good might be done for the poor with the pile of dollars which it will require to complete the building. Fancy one million thrown away—yes, worse than thrown away, for such a purpose. But Philadelphia, like New-York and other American cities, is a great place for churches, and ministers, and misery. Some of the preachers contend so hard with sinners, and, said he parenthetically—so often with each other—during the cold dreary winters, that by the time summer comes round they are used up, and then the ladies go about among the converted and collect money enough to send the broken-down ministers away upon an European tour to recover their health and appetites. Then, when they get back in the fall, ready for another brush with the enemy, the women folks go around again, and get more money to buy what they call a service of plate—that is, a silver tea-pot and a lot of cups and saucers—to encourage them to work harder, and sometimes your tip-top men get a gold watch or two thrown in. These women are charitable to the ministers; if it wasn't for them, I guess the preachers would once in a while come out at the small end—guess it's a kind of so all the world over. While the men squabble and make money, the women take care of the church."[*]

"You see," said Mrs. Mannors approvingly, "that the Lord often chooses the weak things of the world to confound the wise. He, in his own peculiar way, selects the weaker ves-

* A religious paper—the New-York *Ambassador*, of Aug. 10, 1867, stated that the Fifth avenue Presbyterian Church, New-York, had presented their late pastor, Rev. N. L. R——, with a purse of twenty-five thousand dollars, and also one year's salary of six thousand dollars; that this poor, worn-out pastor had purchased a farm near New-Brunswick, N. J., where he intended to recruit his health.

sels, the Marys and the Marthas, to effect his great purposes."

"Just so, ma'am. If the women don't rank equal to the ministers in church usefulness, I kind o' guess they follow immediately next."

"So they do. The Lord has made his hand-maids serviceable; I hope he will continue to do so unto the end."

"Yes, ma'am; the United States has made great strides in religious matters; but here I think you are yet a leetle ahead of us just yet. You know we've got no 'state church,' but, Lord bless you, we've got pious edifices at every street-corner—splendid ones too; the whole country is studded with them, almost as thick as tombstones in a graveyard. We have now about fifty-four thousand churches in the United States, valued at one hundred and seventy-two millions of dollars, affording accommodation for nineteen million persons. Why, in New-York itself, there are over three hundred churches of all kinds, which to support, including ministers' salaries, costs about one million dollars per annum. Many of these churches are richly endowed, producing, according to a careful estimate, an annual income of eighteen millions of dollars—all, too, free from any kind of tax. Trinity Church alone is possessed of vast wealth.* Then we have a spiritual army of over fifty thousand well-paid ministers, going to and fro throughout the land, preaching and praying; yet poverty and crime, especially in cities and among churches, is on the increase; and though ministers use all their influence to have museums, public libraries, and places of amusement shut up on the Sabbath day, yet not more than one sixth of the population can be induced to attend a place of worship. They once tried in Philadelphia to put a stop to traveling on Sunday, by putting chains across the streets in front of church doors, and even now they object to let a street-car run on that day—the poor man must walk, while the rich can drive with impunity; but the multitudes won't be forced, and the churches are no better filled than usual; still they go on building more, but with the same result; and unbelievers boastfully say that the money it costs to erect stylish sanctuaries† and pay an

army of preachers would be more than sufficient to banish every trace of poverty from the land; that the money which is annually squandered for religious purposes would be more than ample to provide homes for the homeless, and food and clothing for all in need; thus reducing motives to crime, and increasing a general contentment and morality."*

Mrs. Mannors felt a little surprise at such admissions from Mr. Styles, and seemed doubtful as to the propriety of this mode of upholding religion in the presence of her husband. He and Mr. Capel sat quietly by, listening with great interest to the recital; and she came to the rescue by saying that she thought such facts were the best proof of the depravity of the human heart in resisting divine grace. It was so all the time. Some will never do more than ask. "What shall we eat, what shall we drink, or wherewithal shall we be clothed?" As long as their perishing bodies are cared for, they feel indifferent about providing for their immortal souls.

"But," said she, making a diversion, "you can tell us about the Bible Society. The American Christians get credit for great liberality in trying to circulate the glorious Gospel."

"So they ought, ma'am," said Mr. Styles, pulling out a little memorandum-book. "I guess there an't a race of people on earth fling their money away faster than they do. Just get steam up pretty well, make some loud talk about 'the Book,' and then they go it like a streak. I rather think I can give an illustration of their excitability—guess it's about the same in piety as in politics. The American Bible Society has done a good deal in its particular way. In about fifty years," said he, consulting his memoranda, "they have collected over ten millions of dollars, issued over twenty-one millions of Bibles, and have published over seventy editions of 'The Word' in forty-three different languages; and last year again the society raised over six hundred thousand dollars!"

These tremendous figures made even Mrs. Mannors gasp, and she brought her hands together in a perfect ecstasy. "Oh! what indefatigable men you must have in your native land, what wonderful liberality, in such a new country, what a conscientious regard for the Bible! Your nation must prosper. The Lord loveth a cheerful giver."

"That regard may be another matter, ma'am. I have assisted in the distribution of some thousands of copies of the Scriptures; every family thought it but right to have a Bible; but then it was mostly laid aside if it was a plain affair; but if it had good binding and gilt edges, it would be put among trinkets, where it could be admired with the rest. This kind of Bible-purchase used to remind me of the great number of pious folks who regularly attended church to hear fine music and go to sleep." Then, after a pause, he continued, "It was a mystery to me; the money kept a

* With respect to the vast wealth of Trinity Church, New-York, an American paper gives the following item of news:
"The Claim of Trinity Church, in New-York City, to about SIXTY MILLIONS OF DOLLARS worth of real estate is about to be tested in the Courts of that State. —— is one of the counsel for the heirs of Anneke Jans who claim the property."
After reading this, one is almost forced to rub his eyes, to see if he be not deceived; but the fact is too notorious. The characteristic greed of the Christian craft has enabled even that one church to monopolize enough to furnish a home for every poor family in the great State of New-York! O shame! where is thy blush?—Author.

† FASHIONABLE CHURCHES.—A writer in the Atlantic Monthly, for January—says: "The design of the fashionable church-builder of the present moment is to produce a richly-furnished, quietly-adorned, dimly-illuminated ecclesiastical parlor, in which a few hundred ladies and gentlemen, attired in kindred taste, may sit perfectly at their ease, and see no object not in harmony with the scene around them. Every thing in and around the church seems to proclaim it a kind of exclusive ecclesiastical club, designed for the accommodation of persons of ten thousand dollars a year and upward."

* From the New-York Christian Advocate, (1868,) we learn that the Centenary contributions of the M. E. Church now foot up to nearly eight and a quarter million of dollars, with four conferences yet to hear from.

coming in, and out went loads upon loads of Bibles; but the fact is, they're not read; and if white folks won't read them, neither will the black; but then, they all must have Bibles, just like the papist his cross, or the witch her charm, and so it goes on from year to year, and the world won't be converted. It is all a mystery—ten millions of money and twenty one millions of Bibles!"*

Having made these statements, Mr. Styles assumed a reflective attitude, and Mrs. Manners again put in a defense.

"It may be a mystery to us for a while, but a glorious result will follow—the Lord has promised it—therefore we need not doubt. The missionary reports give us glowing accounts of what the Lord is doing among the heathen; and his divinely appointed ministers of our land and of yours are going forth like spiritual Samsons, overturning idols and routing the enemy."

"There is unfortunately a great difference sometimes between these missionary reports, One says, that, beside the actual cost, it takes about six missionaries to convert one Hottentot; that is, it takes six lives; six of them die off, and then the Hottentot won't stay converted if you don't feed him well. You know the heathen parishioners often eat their minister! The *Missionary Herald* won't publish such facts, or will gloss them over, and make it appear as if things were going on swimmingly; but the truth leaks out by degrees; and I often think it is such a pity that the millions we spend—including many a widow's mite—should be flung away while we have so many poor, and ignorant, and heathenish at home."

"No matter, these things may be disheartening, but the command is, 'Go forth, and proclaim the Gospel to every creature!' and it must be done. What is the wealth of earth compared to the value of one immortal soul! Our missionaries have contended with the powers of darkness in foreign lands; have had fierce struggles, but glorious triumphs. Even one solitary rescue from the grasp of Satan more than compensates for the millions we spend. The cross has been raised and the crescent is waning, and devils tremble, while the idols of the heathen lie scattered in the dust. Come to morrow, come with me and see a proof of these glorious triumphs at Exeter Hall."

<hr/>

CHAPTER XVIII.

It was the fourth of May, 1861, and a vast number of persons thronged the streets of the metropolis. The many houseless and homeless

*MAGNIFICENT BIBLE.—Mr. Mackenzie, of Glasgow, has printed a small number of what he calls his "Hundred Guinea Edition" of the Holy Scriptures—an edition with which his name will always be associated. It is the most sumptuous and best printed Bible ever produced. The size is atlas folio; the type used is a beautiful, sharp-cut great-primer, set up in two columns, with two narrow central columns of reference; a thick red border line is printed outside the text; the paper made use of is very thick, made especially by Dickenson, costing, we believe, as much as fourteen pence a pound. Twelve copies only have been printed, and the probability is, that whenever a copy turns up for sale it will fetch some fabulous price.—*English paper.*

wanderers that lurked here and there, or sat listlessly in some recess, looked with moody indifference upon the gay crowd that flitted by, though often shadowed by the diseased and limping poverty that hobbled by its side. English lords and foreign barons passed and repassed, and now the gay retinue of a wealthy peer moved proudly by; while, not far distant, the fluttering rags of a British beggar could be seen, as he watched with scowling aspect the approach of a policeman who would prevent him asking the charity which he so much needed, or warn him off as an unclean thing, unfit to be seen. And then, at intervals, could be observed drifting wrecks of frail and famishing womanhood, moving slowly but surely down, down, to that deep, dark gulf of infamy, out of which not one in a hundred is ever rescued.

Neither fog nor cloud interposed this day to frown upon the flaunting gayety of heartless wealth, or shut out the sad condition of those harassed to temptation and crime by the heavy load of poverty and affliction which flung out such dreary shadows of despair upon the future. The sun shone down brightly on all alike, as if in reproof to the imposed distinctions which religion and exclusiveness have ever advocated, and which have robbed so many of nature's free gifts, spreading such misery and desolation over the whole earth.

Onward went the crowd; and those who, from long observation, could readily distinguish between the every day appearance of the stream of life which pours through a London thoroughfare and one of an unusual kind could this day notice the foreign faces and quaint and provincial costumes which moved toward Waterloo bridge. The throng here was very great, and it required all the exertion of a host of policemen to keep the thoroughfare from being completely blocked up. Pedestrians and equestrians, soldiers and civilians, cabs, coaches, and omnibuses followed each other in quick succession; and a great number of clergymen, a few statesmen and philanthropists, made the medley almost complete.

Farther toward the Strand the current of people seemed to flow, but a crowd was kept from forming in that place by the tens and dozens which went off together in the direction of Exeter Hall. Equipage after equipage was ranged around the building, in waiting for the great personages they had conveyed thither. Surely some extraordinary business must be on hand; it might be supposed that a convocation of the great, the wise, the humane, and charitably disposed of the world was about to take place to concert one grand measure to relieve the necessities of every human being, and that an experimental attempt was to be made among the hundreds and thousands of poverty stricken wretches struggling out a miserable existence in that great city of wealth and privation, and afterward to be extended to the children of misery throughout the kingdom. Or it might be an immense gathering of the kind and merciful, to abolish, first of all, those pauper prisons and bastiles of poverty which ought to bring a blush of shame to the cheeks of British legislators—prisons and bastiles, in which human beings are degraded for the crime of penury—where the child knows no parent, and where the venerable couple who have walked together nearly to the very foot of the hill of life are here separated forever, and imprisoned because of their mendicancy!*

Were these people about to meet to establish some great system of free education, or to improve the condition of the overwrought working classes? What benevolent object could there be in view which could thus induce the reputed wise of the earth to hurry together from its four corners to meet in a distant city? Alas! simply but a matter which fancifully relates to the soul alone, and to another state of existence, and to the tedious and exorbitantly expensive dissemination of a so-called revelation from the offended deity of Christendom!

The stranger or citizen of London on that fine May morning could not but observe the numerous placards and large posters put up in conspicuous places, side by side with bills about Drury Lane, Covent Garden, and other noted places of amusement; and, as he went along, he would see, wandering about the gay streets, brutalized and sottish men, earning sixpence or a shilling by carrying the same placard on their shoulders, and then, as with staggering step, one thrust himself in the way, the pedestrians could read—

"EXETER HALL!
GREAT MEETING OF THE BRITISH AND FOREIGN BIBLE SOCIETY,
THIS DAY!"

Those who chose to follow the stream of life toward the Hall could notice the great number of loungers and idlers in front of its entrance; that is, if men who are willing to labor but can not find employment may be called such, and coarse jokes and rough comments, made by the pauper crowd, could be heard as a stately carriage drove up, or upon the appearance of some clerical celebrity, against whom these comments were more particularly directed.

"That's a rum cove, Bill; that ere fellow's a Sandwicher, I'll bet."

"No, he beant, Tom; if it's that lantern jaw with the gold swag, just going in, it's Parson Rockett, with his five hundred a year. Dare say he's taken in more sandwiches in a week than we ever did in our blasted lives, and yet he's slim about the belt."

"Here's a swell, boys! my eyes, what a well-paid Christian! there's a corporation for you!"

"Who's he, Jack?"

"Dunno; I'll lay it's a bishop; 'tis too. Fine coach that! dare say he's got the dibs. I'd damn sight rather have his purse than his prayers. Ay, that's Bishop of Winchester; he's a big 'un, and will stick to the Bible as long as it brings him from ten to twenty thousand a year, the blasted state cormorant!"

"See, Bill, here's another on 'em. Good heavens! what I'd give to be a bishop; another fine coach, lots o' flunkies and plenty of brass. That's Ripon. My Lord Bishop of Ripon, ha, ha! Damn me, but I could like to be him; some thousands a year, plenty to eat, nothing to

* See Note G.

do, plenty of beer, lots o' fun. Good God, what a life!"

"Jack, this next fellow an't a bishop; the mope is afoot, and looks as if he had just lost his mother."

"That's one of them 'ere preachers, a Methody, reg'ler blue-face. Jest hear him once, when he's set a'going. All hell, hell! He knows more about it than the best on 'em."

"Who's this grinning ape, Tom? This cove with the umbreller?"

"And the big teeth? don't you know, Bill?"

"No, but blast it, I think I ought! Blow me, but it's Spurgeon! so it is. He's got jawbreakers, and uses them too. He'll make 'em finger the dibs to-day, and send another batch of Bibles to the forriners."

"Say, Bill, didn't you get a Bible once from one of them hired chaps? One of them—what do you call 'ems? What did you do with the Bible, Bill?"

"Sold it for beer and bacca—same as you and Tom Brown did."

"But you never read yours, you blasted heathen!"

"Didn't, 'cause I couldn't—wouldn't if I could."

"O Bill! Then you never knew any thing about the ass that talked for a full half-hour to Jonah before the cock crew at him."

"Wouldn't bleeve it if I did; that's all gammon—bishop's gammon."

"Them chaps going in bleeves it, Bill—eh? Pays well."

"So they says, but I knows better than that—they may though, cause they're paid—'tis their trade, and they'd bleeve any sich rubbish for money."

"Stand aside, here's another one of the spouters, swellish like. Them's a nice pair of grays. I don't mean the reverend old buck, nor the lady, nor of course the young uns in front, but the horses—slap ups, an't they? 'Tis a'most as good as a bishop's. Lord, how this praying business does pay! See him, how he blinks, and bows—that's your style, old boy."

"Jack, if that fellow has the face of a converted saint, there's hope for you and Bill."

"What the devil do you know about it? You wouldn't compare me to that chap, would you? Who is he? Just see him hand the ladies. O Lord!"

"Who is he, Bill?"

"Why, that's Buster, Dr. Buster, as they calls him—one of the most certain, immortal saints in town, great among the female angels!"

"Buster—Buster, I've heerd o' him some place afore; he's big and ugly enough to bust into hell without a passport."

"Well, if he's a saint, there's hope for me!"

On this particular day, Exeter Hall was filled to its utmost capacity; one would think that the élite of the wealth and fashion of Britain had deputed its most stylish to attend, in order to convince the distinguished foreigners of the earnestness and orthodoxy of the wealthy and high-born of the United Kingdom. Eminently credulous men, full of faith, from distant lands, could be seen in the brilliant assemblage, and there were great anticipations that this day would furnish another triumphant proof of British benevolence, and that another check would be given to the increasing skepticism and presumptuous infidelity of the age.

While the spacious platform was crowded with many of the most famous defenders and expounders of the Bible in Great Britain, America, France, Germany, and other countries, it was remarkable that the higher dignitaries of the Established Church were not to be seen amongst them. Where were the spiritual princes of York and Canterbury? Where was the regal fisherman of Lambeth Palace? It might be, however, that it would not comport with the dignity of an arch bishop thus to expose himself to vulgar gaze, along with the numbers of once wild chiefs and cannibals that were to be exhibited on that and the following day, as triumphs of the Gospel. But when the Bible has done so much to inculcate a regard for the "powers that be," and has so particularly secured for the English hierarchy such an overflowing of worldly ease and comfort, it might be only within bounds to expect that, if for no other reason, even an assumed veneration for that holy book should induce "His Grace" of Canterbury to appear there among other humble Christians, and personally advocate its circulation.

However, the embodiment of piety and religious talent which was this day to add such additional lustre to "Gospel triumphs" seemed to sit together like lambs of the same flock, dutiful children of the same father—a spectacle of love and humility, on which men and angels might gaze forever with delight. What an exhibition! A spiritual fraternity, docile and submissive, striving not for precedence, nor for the unholy superiority of creeds, but all met again in the fear of the Lord, to assist in the propagation of the "glorious Gospel." Men of every nation and clime here met in fraternal embrace on this spacious platform, as living proofs of Bible regeneration; and the skeptic or infidel might well look confused when he saw a titled and mitred bishop sit as contentedly side by side with a converted Caffre or Ojibbeway chief, as the Rev. Dr. Buster then and there sat between his reverend friends, James Baker and Jonah Hall.

As soon as the noble and distinguished president of the society, the Right Honorable the Earl of Shaftesbury K.G., took his seat on the platform, there was a murmur of applause from the vast assembly, and the great organ swelled forth its strains of solemn but exquisite music; and, now, as wave after wave of harmony swept through the great hall, it had its usual preparatory influence upon the feelings of all present.

A clergyman then opened the proceedings with prayer, and read the forty-fifth Psalm. An abstract of the society's proceedings for the year was then read, showing that the receipts for the year, applicable to the general purposes of the society, were nearly £90,000 sterling, being nearly £6000 over the preceding year, and greatly exceeding the annual collections of any former period. The amount received for the sale of Bibles and Testaments was £80,000, while the total receipts from the ordinary sources of income amounted to about £169,000, being more than in any preceding year; and during the year the society had issued from its depots at home about 1,000,000 copies of the Scriptures, and from the foreign depots 645,000 copies.

The grand total of copies issued by the society up to its sixtieth anniversary amounted to over *forty-five and a half millions* of copies of the word of God, at an expense of *several millions sterling!* The total expenditure for the year was over £151,000, leaving the society still under engagements to the extent of about £110,000.*

It is quite probable that the issues of the British and Foreign Bible Society now extend to over fifty millions of copies of the so-called "word of God." Actually more than one Bible for *every minute* of time of the last sixty years, or since the establishment of the society. Who can fairly prove that the world is any better for all this expenditure?—millions worse than wasted in an insane idea to elevate humanity by the degradation of reason? Half of what it has cost to circulate Bibles and teach religion within the last fifty years, properly disbursed for humane or educational purposes, would have almost banished every trace of poverty, and have given a more correct idea of "what is truth" by leading men to see the vicious principle of the false ideas, false honor, false patriotism, and spurious benevolence which still govern and actuate priests and rulers of all kinds throughout the world. Talk of a religion of *peace*, while it seems that *war* is the great idea of the human race at the present day! Nations which claim to be eminently Christian are generally first in the field of contest, and are continually making preparations for a further reliance on providence by increasing their store of bullets, bayonets, and bombshells. It has been asserted, as a melancholy fact, that during the sixty-eight years of this century, more human lives have been sacrificed to the Moloch of war than in any five centuries of history. The present century may be said to have opened with the French Revolution, while the year (1865) closed the stupendous war of, the rebellion among Christian Americans; and now, Christian Europe is again ablaze with the pomp and circumstance of war, there being already over three millions of Christian men under arms, awaiting a signal from the great destroyer to commence their pastime of havoc; ecclesiastical history, more than any other, is a dreadful record of atrocity. The sentiment of the age is for war; impress the gilded and glittering word "patriotism" upon the human heart, and it almost blots out every trace of the imprint of humanity left there by the better feelings of our nature. There is no confidence between Christian nations. Christian diplomacy is but a system of polished duplicity—suspicion lurks in every cabinet—and, as proof, the armed peace of Christian Europe annually costs the enormous sum of over £300,000,000 sterling. Talk of war, and the school-boy, with "paper cap and wooden sword, plays the

* See British and Foreign Bible Society's report for June, 1864.

general;" while the *bishop* lays down his Bible, and marches from the pulpit to command a brigade.* In every gallery of art, the busts of our "national heroes" obtain the most conspicuous place; and our numerous costly monuments are nearly all for the purpose of enthroning in equestrian marble some military demi-god, and elevating him nearer to heaven. Shakespeare may remain perched on a stool, while the column erected to a York or a Nelson can almost touch the cross of St. Paul's.

After the report was read, the president, Lord Shaftesbury, addressing the ladies and gentlemen, said, "That nothing had occurred during the year to render it necessary for him to interpose between them and the business of the meeting. He had only to thank God that this unhistorical, uninspired, unfortunate and unnecessary book had been demanded with redoubled avidity. They had upon that platform proof of what he said. Among others, they had ambassadors from the distant island of Madagascar coming to record the triumph of God's holy word in their own land, ready and rejoicing to carry back to their country a narrative of the triumphs, which they had witnessed *in this*. But he would not, by saying any more, interrupt a far better speech from a far better man, and he therefore called upon the Lord Bishop of Winchester to move the first resolution.†

The noble chairman, whose address, if it possessed no other merit, had that of brevity. Like most other Englishmen, he could not refrain from alluding to the "triumphs" of his native land. But as those to which he more particularly referred were "of the Gospel," it might be well to notice a few of the complaints of missionaries respecting their want of success in foreign lands, and to show that the "triumphs of God's holy word" in distant climes are not altogether such as to justify so many confident assertions from the mighty spirits of Exeter Hall.

As to the achievements of missionary enterprise, what forlorn accounts are regularly received, and how often has the terrible fact been recorded of Christianized cannibals devouring their minister! In India, and China, and among distant islands, missionary zeal has sacrificed many votaries; and the accumulated offerings—often made up of widows' mites and gleanings from the poor—have been lavished without any commensurate results. Yet the delusion is still kept up in England and America; and though pious periodicals make urgent appeals for the "poor heathen," and continue to gloss over actual failures, yet some of these papers are forced to admit that there are, occasionally, very depressing reports.

The *Missionary Herald*, of the American Board for Foreign Missions, for June, 1863, dolefully gives the following particulars:

* In the late rebellion in the United States, Bishop Polk, a Southern churchman, was a Lieutenant-General in the confederate army, and was killed in action on Pine Mountain in Georgia, June 14th, 1864.
† This is a slight abridgment of Lord Shaftesbury's address at the meeting of the British and Foreign Bible Society, in Exeter Hall, London, on May 4, 1864.—*Author.*

"That only seven per cent of the population of Ceylon (2,000,000) should profess Christianity, and that only *two* per cent should be *Reformed* or *Protestant* Christians, will be melancholy facts, pregnant with solemn reflections to many of our readers. But so it is, after all that has been done to preach the Gospel and distribute the Bible. The darkness of the picture in our case is only relieved when the contrast presented by continental India is regarded. In Ceylon, it may be said that *something* has been done, not merely to sap the outworks of heathenism, but to build up the edifice of Christianity. If ours is the day of small things, what are we to say to India (British and independent) with her *two hundred millions* against our *two*, and her *less than half a million* of Christians, say *one fourth of one per cent* against our seven per cent! When we say half a million, we allow for 120,000 *European* Christians, including the civil service, army, navy, merchants, planters, etc.; and we give the most liberal margin for Romanists, papal and Portuguese, Syrian, Armenian, etc. Subjected merely to the numerical test, Christianity may be said to have made but *small progress either in India or Ceylon.*"

What an overwhelming waste of money these missions have involved; and according to the *Herald*, what "*melancholy facts*" are the return—*two* per cent in Ceylon, and *less than one fourth of one per cent in India!* In a subsequent issue of the same journal, giving an account of the Mahratta Mission, in which during the then last fourteen years over $20,000 had been expended by one society alone in efforts at conversion, it says, "The account which Mr. Munger (the missionary gives of the present state and prospects of missionary efforts in the Mahratta Mission *is not encouraging. Less than a dozen* persons constitute his stated Sabbath audience, and these *are from his own family*, and the Christian household connected with the mission. His opportunities for preaching, during the week also, he says, are *less encouraging* than they were *three years* ago. There are fewer persons who attend upon these religious services, and they manifest much less interest in the facts of Christianity. He seldom meets the young men who then were accustomed to come in his way, and *seemed* disposed to become acquainted with Christian ideas. It is *now fourteen years* since the work of the Gospel was commenced in this place. Much labor has been undertaken: we have much desired success, and still we sow, and pray, and hope. I hope I may be able to do something."

And this is all! While missionaries "hope and pray to be able to do something," the poor unconverted heathen die and go to perdition—according to Christian theory—and the God who has promised to "answer prayer" will not open the eyes of the blind, but will witness with indifference their gradual approach to the precipice of destruction!

With respect to Chinese missions, another American paper, the *Herald* says, "The pigtail celestials of the 'flowery kingdom' do not take very kindly to Christianity. With *twenty-four* missionaries and *twelve* native helpers in China, the American Foreign Mission organization reports the '*baptism of a first convert*,' a man who was of 'respectable condition.' Millions of money contributed in the United States to convert the Chinese, and the result is a solitary baptism! Half the money would have secured the baptism of ten thousand worse heathens here at our own door."[*]

From this statement, it is to be presumed that the twelve "*native helpers*" are interpreters—mere hirelings—each of whom, in the intervals of service, burns incense before a "family god" in his own particular Joss-House.

British journals have, time after time, admitted that several missions to Papists, Jews, and heathens have been deplorable failures. And still restless visionaries continue to encourage the religiously romantic to wander 'from pole to pole" in costly and wasteful attempts to supplant one absurdity by the propagation of another, as if oblivious of the personal and intellectual misery that broods around the thousands of heathens at home.

That distinguished London clergyman, Dr. Pusey, admitting the folly of this pious romance, says, "There are places in London, as I have myself seen, where for generation after generation the name of Christ has never reached, and their inhabitants had much better have been born in Calcutta than in London, because the charity which sends forth Christian missionaries would the sooner reach them."

So much, then, for my Lord Shaftesbury's Gospel triumphs in foreign lands."

We are also told by the President of the Bible Society, that the ambassadors from Madagascar would be ready and rejoiced to carry back to their own land a narrative of the triumphs which they had witnessed in England. Now for a recital of some of these, which are

[*] Dr. Livingstone, in one of his latest works on Africa, said that *forty* missionaries had been sacrificed to the deadly climate of that continent, even before the first heathen had been converted!

As a set off, however, to the depressing missionary reports given in this chapter, a late religious journal (Feb. 1868) states that, "Sixty years ago, there were no Protestant Christians in Travancore, Southern India. Now, what do we behold? There are at this point alone 27,000, and 500 native assistants, and 11 ordained native ministers. At Nagercoil, the principal station in the district, there is a large Christian village of 800 souls, a printing office, girls' boarding-school, native church, and boys' school, with theological classes, with three European and two native ordained missionaries. Wonderful triumphs of grace!"

And again: "There are now twenty-five Protestant missionary societies that are laboring in India. Of these, three are organized in Scotland, eight in England, one in Ireland, four on the continent of Europe, and nine in America. These societies maintain about 550 missionaries, and expend annually in that country not far from $1,250,000."—*Montreal Daily Witness*, Feb. 1868.

These successes, after *sixty years'* labor, are said to be "wonderful triumphs of grace!" but could less be expected from such determined efforts to Christianize? And what more meagre result could be reasonably anticipated where 550 native intelligent missionaries, sustained by an annual amount of $1,250,000, are left among an unreasoning multitude—already superstitiously prepared, to keep them from relapsing into their native paganism? Triumphs of grace! Why, the first Mormon church was organized only *thirty-eight* years ago, (in April, 1830;) it has sent its missionaries to almost every part of the civilized world, and it already claims about 300,000 converts, "rescued" from Christianity! Are not these triumphs of the Mormon gospel a greater wonder?—*Author*.

alas! too openly displayed within the boundaries of the Christian city of London.

Religion in that great metropolis has about one thousand costly temples to accommodate a wrangling multitude of contending sects, whose mutual denunciations are often rather startling. It has several thousand trained priests—divinely chosen—who are willing to manifest great anxiety for the "salvation of sinners," and conduct them by various short roads to heaven for—ready pay. And as an evidence of the great benefit arising from the teaching and practice of these devoted men, there are to be found among the vast number of metropolitan sinners one hundred thousand prostitutes, over one hundred and fifty thousand thieves, robbers, and vagabonds; while, according to the estimate of an eminent coroner, Dr. Lancaster, the result of a hidden frailty is twelve thousand cases of infanticide annually. There is, then, a large portion of a standing army to intimidate into submission a majority of the people, who would otherwise resist oppressive laws over which they are denied a controlling voice. Then there are thousands of policemen required to detect crime, and numerous prisons, and judges, and hangmen to deal with offenders! The death penalty is strictly scriptural; therefore *true* mercy is not yet the quality of Christian legislation.

But London is the headquarters of the state church. What evidence can that church give of its usefulness? While some, like Lord Shaftesbury, can boast of imaginary triumphs, that particular and favored corner of the "Lord's vineyard" can exhibit tangible trophies; and while like a mockery it can affect to despise "the pomps and vanities of this wicked world," its *two* princely archbishops can conscientiously accept and divide with each other £25,000 sterling, (over $120,000) *annually* for their spiritual superintendence, and its *twenty-six* other bishops can as unscrupulously demand and distribute among themselves, in the same way, over £135,000, (about $650,000,) as compensation for their pious services, and these exorbitant sums are independent of what is derived from other numerous sources of ghostly profit. Then add to these the immense amount paid to the increasing horde of the minor clerical adherents of the Established Church, and its usefulness seems to consist in perpetuating a monstrous fraud, and in impoverishing the nation.[*]

Let the ambassadors from Madagascar witness *these* "triumphs," and upon their return to their native land, where even pagan savages do not as regularly die of starvation, let them narrate the sad tale of the ineffectual efforts of 100,000 wandering paupers of London in

[*] A Philadelphia paper makes the following remarks: "PAYING POSITIONS.—It makes people's mouths water to think of the revenue of some of the English ecclesiastical functionaries. The net revenues of the Bishopric of London, for the year 1865, were $100,335 in gold; of the Dean and Chapter of St. Paul's Cathedral, London, $54,350 in gold; and of the Dean and Chapter of Westminster Abbey, $143,635 in gold."(!!) Yet this very paper is noted for its obsequiousness to the horde of wealthy sectarian priests in that Gospel-blighted city, and does not utter one word against such priestly swindling.—*Author*.

their feeble endeavors to provide food, clothing, and shelter. Let them witness the struggle between hope and despair of these baptized Christians, and how sad and how reluctantly many, very many of these let loose their last hold on virtue to be hurried onward and downward to *crime* by the extortion and rapacity of priestcraft, and by the usurpation of a selfish, unfeeling aristocracy. Perhaps the narration of these triumphal woes might even suffuse the eye of some dusky savage, and tears might wear a channel on his painted cheek. Yet, behold! See our Christian bishops, and priests, and merchant princes, and nobility stand by and look complacently on these reputed "triumphs," and while ostentatiously giving a liberal donation for the "spread of the Gospel," dole out but an insignificant pittance for the relief of their famishing countrymen.

CHAPTER XIX. *

THE president took his seat, and all seemed anxious to hear the speech on the first resolution, especially as it was to emanate from one of the mitred faculty whose veneration for "The Word" had gradually increased with his salary, and whose dower as a prelatical bridegroom of the church militant is paid to him in *annual* installments of *ten thousand five hundred pounds sterling*, (about $52,000.)

When the applause subsided, the Lord Bishop of Winchester, said, that he stood there as having been an old friend of the society for more than half a century, and had the privilege to be numbered among its vice-presidents. He had often reflected with pleasure upon the second part of the description of their society, [it was the British and Foreign Bible Society,] and when he had heard the list of places in which the word of God had been circulated during the past year, the importance of the foreign branch was more forcible. Error, like some of the disorders which affect the human body, seemed to return from time to time with periodical recurrence. The errors of the present were the errors of the past. There was nothing new in skepticism and free thinking. The Voltaires of another country, and the Paines of their own, or the *daring spirits of modern times*, over whom they had to lament, and of whom they were ashamed, but of whom they were not afraid, they had said nothing in that day which had not been said in times past. The Bible and the society had suffered from recurring attacks, and sometimes among other disputes the Trinitarian controversy divided their friends. He wished, as an old member of the society, very humbly, and with much deference, to make a suggestion—to maintain with the most unflinching resolution the supremacy of "*divine* revelation. Unsettle that principle, and you shake the foundation of your faith; sap that pillar,

* The speeches contained in this chapter are an abridgment of those delivered at the annual meeting of the British and Foreign Bible Society, held in Exeter Hall, London, May 4th, 1864.

and you have nothing on which to rest the sole of your foot." We lived, he said, in an age of controversy; he did not regret it, for he thought that the more they inquired into and searched the Bible, the more they would find in it the true manna of the soul, that which they needed for time and eternity.

After this specimen of prelatical support and assumption, the resolution was seconded, in a short but unmeaning speech, by Lord Charles Russell.

A Methodist minister was then permitted to move the second resolution; he made a very prosy display—a mixture of pomposity, pedantry, and egotism, which was highly applauded by his own particular denomination, but which otherwise seemed to produce a wearying effect upon those who were compelled to listen.

He was followed by the Bishop of Ripon, who stated that he had observed from one of the papers that a subscriber for the present year had doubled his donation, *because* the Bible had become *so much dishonored*. He sympathized with that feeling, for to him it was a positive relief to express his unabated confidence and undiminished attachment, when the Bible had been dishonored by its professed friends. This innuendo against a brother bishop—Colenso—was received with loud applause. But, he continued, if the Bible had been dishonored by man, it has been honored of God, as was manifested in a greater amount of contributions than the society had ever before received in one year! It was to him delightful to think, that amidst all the contentions and divisions by which the visible church of Christ was unhappily so much torn and divided, there should be one sacred platform, upon which Christians of every denomination could meet together, and where all could agree that the Bible was the word of God, to which one and all would unitedly bow, and to which they rendered homage as the supreme and only infallible source of all-saving truth. They had met there because they believed that the Bible was the most blessed gift of God to a fallen world, and it was the bounden duty of all who possessed that inestimably precious treasure to endeavor to communicate it to those who had it not. He believed that they had nothing to fear from the attacks to which the Bible was exposed; there was nothing new in them, nothing that had not been often started before; there was nothing, he believed, which the word of God did not prepare them to expect in the last days. As was once said to one who was sneering at the word of God, and ridiculing the Bible as an imposture, "It is the existence of such men as you that makes me believe the Bible is true; for the Bible tells us, that in the last days there shall come scoffers, and if it were not for such persons as you, we should seem to want one credential for the truth of the Bible." (!)

Verily if this be a valid claim for the truth of Christian inspiration, it is one easily made, and one which has often supported other tottering systems of error. God, continued the Bishop, had made the Bible to be its own witness, and had thereby placed within the reach of the humblest inquirer the means of ascertaining *to his own satisfaction the divine authority of the message.* (?) But they were not to give up external evidence by which it may be as satisfactorily established that the Bible is the word of God; that, with respect to the Bible, while it was not given to man in order to teach science, there was not a single sentence in the Bible contrary to *true* science; and that whatever appeared in science to contradict the word of God is rather to be spoken of as "oppositions of science falsely so called!"

If put to the test, the dogmatism of this bishop might lead him into difficulty to find a proof equal to his flippancy of assertion. How doctors differ! particularly those who claim to be genuine successors—even through a popish parentage, of the inspired twelve. Yet truly they may be apostolic in one sense; for we find by the revered Gospel records that *their* authors were by no means unanimous on points of faith and doctrine, and their inspired contradictions, as to time, place, circumstance, and other essentials, have been a heritage of perplexity to the more learned, dignified, and assuming "right reverend fathers in God" of these latter days. If God made the Bible to be its own witness to the "*humble* inquirer," the beneficed bishops can not claim to be of that class: for no other body of men in Christendom have tended to mystify the alleged "plain meaning" of Scripture more than the lordly prelatical teachers of Rome and England. Ah! but science has dared to witness against inspiration! Science, that never errs, but with the torch of truth in its good right hand flashes down upon the deformity of error, and upon its darkness, its mystery, and its pretension. My Lord of Ripon, however, is not abashed; he still hugs this "best gift of God," with all its glaring inaccuracies, rather than admit the opposition of this "science falsely so called."

To men of determined faith, nothing is truth that will expose an error in the Bible. Similar to the wisdom of an Indian prince, who, it is said, trampled a microscope to pieces because it revealed to his astonished view living animalcula in the food and water from which he had just partaken. Like many others, the Bishop of Ripon tells us, in one breath, that the Bible was not given to man to teach science—evidently in doubt himself of its scientific correctness—and yet that there was nothing in it contrary to *true* science! Now, were philosophers to admit such an anomaly as *false* science, we wonder where it could be found more elaborately displayed than among the "sacred pages" of "God's most blessed gift to man."

However, the bishops are not all so incautious. Many excuses and explanations have been framed for the extraordinary legends of biblical cosmogony; and if the superior intelligence, or more general investigation of the age has forced a reluctant assent from many of the clerical *savants*, it is satisfactory to find one so spiritually and temporally endowed as the right honorable and right reverend the Lord Bishop of London yielding so graciously. In one of his discourses, published about the very time the steadfast Ripon spoke so confidently as to the agreement of the Bible with *true* science, he said, "it is satisfactory to feel assured that no clergyman of the Church of England can be called on to maintain the *unwarranted position*, which indeed scarcely any hold, that the Bible is an *infallible guide* in questions of *physical science.*" What an admission! Until lately, the almost universal orthodox cry resounded that the Bible was absolute truth, in whole or in part; that it should lead in science as in principles of faith; and now, alas! for its worshipers! able *clerical* disputants contend for and against the validity of its science and its inspiration, and even venture to question its entire credibility.

The Rev. "Cannon" Stowell next addressed the assemblage. He said, that although it had been his privilege to attend the anniversary meetings of that institution, he never remembered to have taken part in one of so profoundly interesting a character, especially so on account of the gathering assault that was making on the great citadel of their faith—the inspired word of God. Not, alas! simply from without, but from within the visible church. If there were any originality at all in the attack, it was not found in the arguments, but in the men who employ them. It was this which gave such an apparent authenticity to those arguments, not from any intrinsic weight that belonged to them. The British and Foreign Bible Society was giving such men one of the best refutations. It was showing that to simple, humble, honest, believing men, those arguments were without power or conviction. That society had written upon its colors: "The Bible, the whole Bible, and nothing but the Bible;" it was truth without a mixture of error. He considered the question of the inspiration of the Bible as the question of the day; the one on which his reverend brethren more particularly ought to be established. He thanked God that that society held strenuously to the *whole* Bible; for they never could sever the Old and New Testaments; they stood or fell together. The New rested on the shoulders of the Old; if they struck down one, they infallibly brought down the other. The Old Testament was the divine porch to the temple of the New, and he who did not enter the temple by the *front* door could never find the eternal truths of God. The Old Testament Scriptures were not superseded; on the contrary, they were, if possible, more intelligible, more impressive, more vital than ever. Then let "the Bible, the whole Bible, and nothing but the Bible" be the watchword of that society. The more the evidences of Christianity were examined, the more they would be found impregnable, insubvertible. The martyrs knew the Bible to be true. They had heard much of the leaders of the noble army of martyrs—their Cranmers, Latimers, and Ridleys; but they had heard too little of *poor peasants,* and *mechanics,* and *simple women* who had died for their Bible. What a noble testimony it was, that men who could not write for it, or could not argue for it, yet could die for it; and, by dying for it, could give the noblest evidence of its truth. He would beg of them not to be disturbing their minds by the doubts and objections that were floating about; they had only to wait, and truth must come forth triumphant from the struggle. The suggesting difficulties of art, history, and arithmetic need not be met until they were worth meeting; silence was often the best answer. Let scientific objections, novel speculations, and vain calculations bend to the Bible; they could not consent that the Bible should bend to them. It would indicate a sense of insecurity, were they always endeavoring to meet objections. One beautiful passage in the word of God was worthy of all acceptance at that juncture, "Let God be true, and every man a liar." Let critical ingenuity find out, *as it could*, various difficulties and doubts, yet "let God be true, and every man a liar." That was still their confidence. There might be errors of translation; passages that ought to be eliminated, there might have been introductions of *slight mistakes*; but still, the word of God in its integrity, as it came from those guided by the hand of God, contained "the truth, the whole truth, and *nothing but the truth*." (!) "They should spread it wherever man was found; they should trust in the Bible, rest on the Bible, live by the Bible, die in the faith of the Bible, and it would carry them safe to a land where there was no more doubt or darkness."

Were it necessary to obtain the testimony of a blind believer in "divine revelation," it would be difficult to find one more explicit or satisfactory than that contained in the priestly harangue of this reverend canon of the British State Church. It might be uncharitable to assert that such persons are, perhaps, as much influenced on behalf of the Bible by the certainty of worldly comforts and distinctions, which it has insured to priests as a class, as they are by the promises of a future reward in another state of existence, where neither benefices, pluralities, nor dignities come into view to distract the head or burden the conscience. But when we reflect that it is comparatively but a short period back in history since the clerical predecessors of the reverend canon, like the "sainted Cranmer," were, for the sake of earthly endowments, just as ready to rise into oratorical flights concerning the infallibility of popish decrees and tradition as they are now to denounce the "Man of Sin," and stupidly cry out, "The Bible, the whole Bible, and nothing but the Bible," one might not be far astray in imputing this vacillating zeal to their characteristic greed, instead of to their more particular or conscientious regard for truth. For gain, theology has canonized many popular absurdities.

But then we are told that there is "*nothing original*" in the attack, nothing novel in the arguments. What a subterfuge, what consolation! It would indeed be a lever in the hands of priests were they truly able to assert that the infidel objections of the present day were but novelties—witnesses which had never testified before; but because these objections are *old*, and have thereby acquired additional force; because they have been the protest of reason against superstition century after century, even from the beginning, they

are, therefore, according to the decree of our present clerical prodigies, to be considered but mere trivialities, and only deriving "apparent authenticity" on account of having been reiterated by a new race of skeptics. Another specimen of priestly quibbling. It is well known that the chimeras of religion have ever been made to appear more worthy of veneration while shaded and festooned by the cobwebs of antiquity.

Were the objectors to Christianity none but "simple, humble, honest, believing men," such as were so paternally referred to by the reverend canon, how boastfully the church could speak of the intelligence of *its* adherents; but because those who venture to judge the Bible according to its wild but positive statements and extravagant narration are really among the most enlightened and discriminating, we are sagely told, that the "best refutation" of their arguments against revelation is that "poor peasants, *and mechanics*, and simple women" remain steadfast and "had died for their Bible." One might wonder at the temerity which could lead his reverence to try to intellectually degrade *mechanics* by including them in such a classification. It is well known that the artisans of Great Britain, like most of those in other countries, are generally found siding with the intelligent objectors to a domineering superstition; and a large majority of those very mechanics continue stubborn and determined in their resistance to clerical oppression. Of this, there is abundant proof. So much for the mechanics.[*] But assuming that the reverend canon had confined himself strictly to the truth, could the fact of there being, or having been, any number of "poor, simple, humble women," or peasants, or mechanics, awed, mystified, or deluded by the "foolishness of preaching" be fairly claimed as a refutation of the sound reasonable arguments against biblical assertion? It is obvious that such a concession to the misty logic of Exeter Hall would grant equal stability to the pretensions of popery or paganism, or of any other ism which could produce a multitude of "poor, simple, humble," ignorant

[*] In an article on "The Working Classes and Christianity," the London *Patriot* says: "That not *fire per cent* of the working classes—that is, of the true handicraftsmen, from the skilled optical instrument maker and engineers, down to the bricklayers' laborers—ever enter the churches and chapels with which this professedly Christian land is covered. Perhaps it is true; certainly it must be something near the truth. Very few artisans are to be seen in the fine churches of the establishment, or in the chapels of the Congregationalists. In some parts of the country, and amongst some classes of laborers, the Wesleyans have had their successes; but the very large majority of attendants at Wesleyan chapels are, we take it, gathered from the small shop-keepers also."

A clergyman—the Rev. Edward White—anxious to discover the cause of this "religious indifference," resolved to go among the working-men and ask them personally, "Why they never went to church?" He gives the replies as taken down. The following are specimens: "The parsons are a bad lot." "It's their living, that's why they preach." "The parsons are at the bottom of all the villainy." "They preach, but very few of them practice." "There's not a worse class of men on earth than bishops and parsons." "It's all done to frighten the people, and to keep them down." "I had enough of religion and imprisonment at the Sunday-school." "I went to church to get married, and that's enough for me." Such ready replies from several "*simple mechanics*" are full of meaning.

supporters. If simplicity and credulity are sufficient to counterbalance intelligence and investigation, then Christianity and cognate forms of superstition have gained the day.

The Bible is such a "tower of strength" to believers that its arrogant and mercenary teachers are never tired of asserting its "impregnability." Assault and undermine this crumbling fortress of inspiration as you may, its reverend Goliaths will rave away as loftily as ever, and furiously brandish their broken weapons; and as they proudly strut about on the ruins of the "older and outer works" of the fated citadel, will boastfully shout of its "insubvertibility," even while the calm and impartial spectator can observe the sinking or overturning of its very foundations.

We are told from the platform of Exeter Hall that the "suggesting difficulties of art, history, and arithmetic need *not* be met; that silence was often the best answer." What an evidence of weakness! If the professed learning of our mitred heads and apostolical successors, "legitimate" or "spurious," can suggest nothing better than that *science* "must bend to the Bible," it is but too plain that they are reduced to the last extremity. *They*, proudly confident, do not feel themselves called upon to argue with unbelievers; "it would indicate a sense of insecurity!" Pressed by their adversaries, however, they now admit that "there may be errors of translation!" How many? "*Slight* mistakes!" What number? Superfluous passages! To what extent? Alas! how reluctantly these forced admissions are laid at the feet of truth—admissions, which, to make but a few years since, would be looked upon as a shipwreck of faith, almost sufficient to insure expulsion from the fold. The time is fast approaching when the hired advocates of a withering error shall be exhibited to the world in their proper character.

While Christian teachers are thus obliged to change their position and resort to successive new modes of defense, every assertion on behalf of their "divine book" seems to involve a fresh contradiction; and when confronted by the "suggesting difficulties of art, history, arithmetic, and science," our pulpit demi-gods, after the manner of their pagan prototypes, enshroud themselves in mystery, and cry out incoherently from behind their shifting cloud, "The Bible, the Bible; let God be true, and every man a liar."

Other speakers followed in praise or defense of the "grand old story of the Pentateuch;" but nothing particular was offered—a mere clange of futile assertions. One would expect, however, that from such a celebrity as the Reverend C. H. Spurgeon some powerful reasons would be given in support of the "Book of Books;" but when we extract his ideas from the cloud of verbiage which he exhibited, we find but the merest trivialities.

With regard to objections against the Bible, he said, that for his part he did not undertake the task of refuting them, because he believed the logical faculty in him was too small; that if he were to talk against arithmetical objectors, he should be like the boy in the churchyard who whistled to keep his courage up. He did not think it was his particular

work, and he believed that ninety-nine out of every hundred Christians were not called for the defense of the Gospel against infidel objectors, so much as the pressing of that Gospel home to men's hearts. He took it that while it was necessary to show the true quality of the Bible, it was also necessary to show the true answer to objectors. His metal was of such a kind that he thanked God when the adversaries of truth were loudest. A slumbering devil was more to be feared than a roaring devil. Let the devil roar; he should but wake them up from their slumbers, and make them more earnestly contend for truth. Why were there no objections to the Bible twenty years ago from high and eminent places? Because they were not necessary to Satan's ends.(!) He wished them to go and evangelize London, to scatter light in the dark alleys, to carry the Gospel to the South Seas and Africa, and make the whole world ring with it, and they need not stop to answer objections. That was the best logic—that was the noblest argument—the application of the word. The way to secure the masses would be to secure them *when young*.

He remembered being greatly puzzled when he was a child. On a shelf in his grandmother's parlor was a little vial, containing an apple just the size of the largest part of the bottle. He got the vial down, and tried to find out how the apple could possibly have got down that narrow neck. He thought that the vial must have had a false bottom. But it happened, quite accidentally, that this great mystery of nature became unraveled. One day, as he walked in the garden, it occurred to him that his grandmother had put a little apple inside the bottle while it was growing, and it had grown there to its present size. He could not but think of that while standing there. They could not get men under biblical influence very readily after they were grown up; but if they could be put inside the bottle when they were little ones, he was sure they would be following the analogy of nature. He found commentaries very useful; but, after all, many a text that would not open to a commentary would open to prayer. Just as the stone-breakers went down on their knees to break the flints on a heap, he believed they often broke up texts better on their knees than in any other position.

They should cultivate the highest reverence for God's word, especially as to their obedience to it. The Bible was to be the great pacificator of all sects, the great hammer of all schismatics. The Bible was to be the end of all disunion.

It is evident that, like many others, this last speaker had attained his popularity by special appeals to the feelings, instead of to the reason. The fine, studied, pulpit oratory of the day is mostly a grand display of flashing metaphors, a meeting of fancy and ideality in the regions of cloudy splendor, depicting as realities the castellated piles and numerous beautiful forms that rise up and appear in golden and roseate hues on the aerial mountains of the imagination. Here, the preacher is at home; here he delights his excited audience. But let him descend to the solid earth, let him come down to hard facts, and he may say with the Rev. Mr. Spurgeon, that he dislikes the task of refutation. Like the Mohammedan, he is satisfied with the inspiration of *his* book; he heeds not objections, and is only anxious for its circulation, "to make the world ring with it."

But even then, notwithstanding all the glory which Exeter Hall has tried to fling around the Christian Scriptures, we obtain another admission, "That old birds can not be caught with chaff!" The masses must be secured "*when young*," or not at all. You must catch them, and *bottle* them, and mould their ideas within the circle of theology, and by that means secure a new generation of Christians. The Jews, the Brahmins, and the Mohammedans succeed admirably on the same principle; while skepticism alone obtains *its* reënforcements from the vigorous ranks of maturity.

Many of the sturdy preachers of the present day were bottled into theology by their grandmothers, and they have never yet been uncorked. These are the class who, like Spurgeon, overcome theological difficulties on their knees; and the flinty text that will neither yield to commentaries nor common sense, is sure to be reduced to powder beneath the potent influence of *faith*. These are they who believe that the Bible, which has been for generations dividing and subdividing, and which has been claimed as their justification by opposing ranks of furious zealots—truly a sword on the earth—is yet to be the great hammer of all schismatics—the end of all disunion! Assertions of this character will gain more credence upon the exact fulfillment of the prediction which states that, "The *wolf* shall lie down with the *lamb*" and "the lion eat straw like an ox"! But, as the question of prophetical inspiration remains yet undecided, it is probable that the fulfillment may be deferred to an indefinite period.

Every one of the speakers at Exeter Hall, on referring to the Bible, affirmed its *full and entire* inspiration in the most positive manner. The Bishop of Winchester asserted that the divine inspiration of the Scripture "should be maintained with the most unflinching resolution;" that to unsettle that principle was to shake the foundation of faith, and leave nothing on which to rest. Strange that his immediate predecessor, Bishop *Law*, should have held such a different opinion. This prelate, in his work on the *Elements of Christian Theology*, says:

"When it is said that the Scriptures are divinely inspired, we are not to understand that God suggested *every word* and dictated *every expression*; it appears that the sacred penmen were permitted to write as their several tempers, understandings, and habits of life directed; and that the knowledge communicated to them by inspiration on the subject of their writings was applied in the same manner as any knowledge acquired by ordinary means. Nor is it to be supposed that they were thus inspired in *every fact which they related*, or in *every precept which they delivered*."

One would think that such an opinion from a mitred head and learned theologian would have a great tendency to "*unsettle*" the question of scriptural inspiration and to "shake the foundation of faith."

Another bishop—Hinds of Norwich—says: "It is not, therefore, truths of all kinds which the Bible is inspired to teach, but *only* such truth as tends to *religious edification;* and the Bible is consequently infallible as far as regards *this*, and *this alone*." This is another blow against plenary inspiration, and leaves us completely in doubt as to whether the account of the creation of the world, or scriptural history, be true or false.

Bishop Hampden, of Hereford, says: "So independent is the science of ethics of the support and ennobling which it receives from religion that it would be nothing *strange* or *objectionable* in a revelation were we to find embodied in its language *much of the false ethical philosophy* which systems may have established!" Archbishop Whately favors this view in the following passage:

"In matters unconnected, indeed, with religion, such as points of history or natural philosophy, a writer who professes (as the apostles do) to be communicating a divine revelation imparted to him, through the means of miracle, *may be as liable to error as other men*, without any disparagement to his pretension!"

Le Clerc, a great Christian writer, in his disquisition upon inspiration, remarks: "It may be said that the books in the Jewish canon ought to be acknowledged as divinely inspired, rather than the Apocrypha, that were never in it. I answer, first, that no clear reason is brought to convince us that those who made the canon, or catalogue of their books, were *infallible*, or had any inspiration whereby to distinguish *inspired* books from those which were *not inspired*."

And the great Neander writes, "It must be regarded as one of the greatest boons which the purifying process of Protestant theology in Germany has conferred on the faith, as well as science, *that the old mechanical view of inspiration has been so generally abandoned!*"

Among other prominent orthodox writers, Arnold, Coleridge, Kingsley, Morell, Maurice, and Macnaught are clergymen who sustain the same views.

A large number of the orthodox, however, are shocked at these opinions; and one, the Rev. Mr. Noble, in supporting *plenary* inspiration, asks:

"Now, how do the free thinkers receive these concessions so liberally made? The advocates of revelation may be regarded as saying to them, 'See! we have come half way to meet you; surely, you will not obstinately refuse belief, now that we require you to believe so little.' What does the free thinker answer? He says, 'You are admitting, as fast as you can, that we are in the right. If you, who view the subject through the prejudices of your profession, are constrained to give up *half* of what we demand, unbiassed persons will augur from the admission that truth would require a surrender of the *whole*.'" The reverend gentleman then exclaims, "No, my friends and brethren. He who would effectually defend the Christian faith must take his stand on higher ground than this. What! tell the world that to escape the increasing influence of infidelity they must surrender the *plenary* inspiration of the Scriptures! As well might we tell them that to obtain security when a flood is rising they should quit the top of a mountain to take refuge in a cave at its base.

"Assuredly this is a state of things calculated to fill the breast of the sincere and humble Christian with profound concern if not with deep alarm. On the one hand, he beholds divine revelation assaulted with unprecedented fury and subtlety by those who avow themselves its enemies; on the other, he sees it half betrayed and deserted by those who regard themselves as its friends. Every devout believer in revelation feels an inward predilection for the opinion that the inspiration of a divinely communicated writing must be plenary and absolute. He feels great pain on being told that this is a mistaken notion; that he must surrender many things in the sacred writing to the enemy to retain any chance of preserving the rest; that he must believe the writers of the Scriptures to have been liable to error, as a preliminary to his assurance that the religion of the Scriptures is true. Surely, every one whose heart does not take part with the assailant of his faith must be glad to be relieved from the necessity of making surrenders so fatal."

If men trained to theology and "*called*" to preach the Gospel can so dispute among themselves concerning the full or the partial inspiration of the Christian Scriptures—a very essential matter—how are "poor peasants and simple women" to decide the question? Either they must blindly believe—as, indeed, many do—all that is recorded in "divine revelation" about the creation of the world, the flood, and the other strange events, or else doubt the whole. It is positive stupidity to follow priestly "blind guides," who are themselves merely groping in the dark, not only on the question of inspiration, but on other points of equal importance; and it is a delusion to countenance any longer that broad farce of "infallibility," which presumptuous teachers still set up for their respective churches. With all the glaring defects of their religious system, these men periodically attend at Exeter Hall, and unblushingly demand more money to continue the circulation of a so-called revelation, as being "truth without a mixture of error," but which "science, art, and history" have proved false, and which has been already rejected as spurious by a vast number of the thoughtful and intelligent in every part of the world.

As an evidence of public opinion on this subject, about the time the great Bible Society meeting took place, the London *Morning Mail* published the following remarks:

"The May meetings of Exeter Hall are now in full blast. Sanctimonious pride walks the stage, and blatant hypocrisy invokes the sympathy and material aid of assembled thousands for objects impossible of accomplishment. Under pretense of forwarding these objects, a host of secretaries replenish their purses, and missionaries, ministers, and agents of all sorts draw fat and easy salaries. From real misery at their very doors, these men turn away, and fix their gaze on objects perfectly ideal. As to so-called missionary operations in other countries, experience has shown how little dependence is to be placed on the representations made by saintly secretaries, and by the pious movers and seconders of resolutions who figure on these occasions. Missionaries are not content merely to thrive upon the credulity a portion of the British public afford them. In New-Zealand, as we know, they have been the great instigators of the Maori insurrection; in connection with the Chinese rebels, they have played a part by no means creditable, and have sought to mislead public opinion as to the objects had in view by those murderers and cut throats called the Taepings. As to the home objects represented by the Exeter Hall fanatics, we would only be too glad to point to any results proportionate to the amount of money placed at their disposal. It is humiliating to see such a superabundance of false sentimentality in the community—such readiness on the part of thousands to become the dupes of designing men. As long as a set of benighted spinsters can be found to contribute to the support of these vagrant Spurgeons, so long must the Exeter Hall gatherings prosper. They enjoy a certain amount of excitement, and pay the price. We should be glad, indeed, could we disabuse them of the idea that Exeter Hall is the straight road to heaven."

CHAPTER XX.

ALTHOUGH the meeting in the regular Baptist church failed to appoint a delegate to the great Bible Society anniversary at Exeter Hall, yet, as has been noticed, it did not deter the rival heads of the antagonistic sects from making their appearance on that occasion; and it singularly happened that, from the unusual crowd of clergy and foreigners, the moderator, Dr. Buster, was forced to take a chair between his reverend opponents, James Baker and Jonah Hall. This was rather a trying position; there could be no friendly side whispers between them as among others. Within two inches of his right elbow, his Methodistic friend Baker sat rigid and stern; while equally close, on the other side, the humorous Jonah seemed to enjoy his proximity to so much greatness: and though he tried hard to assume the conventional gravity of "the cloth," yet occasionally his eyes would turn obliquely on the portly form of the moderator, and a faint smile would appear as he thought of his late discomfiture.

The doctor, indeed, could have wished himself any where else; he looked crest-fallen, and it was to him a particular trial of human nature to wear that lamb-like expression so requisite under the converging gaze of Christian eyes from all quarters of the great building. He felt greatly mortified, especially as he knew that a crowd of admiring friends and many devoted ladies wished to hear his sonorous voice on behalf of the Bible; but the mean jealousy of the very men between whom he was now placed prevented the delivery of the eloquent speech which he had prepared with such labor, and had saved infidelity from the withering rebuke which he felt himself able to give, and which might have exalted him in the opinion of the foreign deputations of true believers. Yet, were there no such jealousy, were that obstacle to his usefulness removed, and were he even surrounded on that platform by such trusty male and female saints as usually greeted him in the pleasant parlor of his subordinate, the Rev. Alexander Campbell—it would not avail. He could not command a word or arrange an idea on any subject while there was one man unexpectedly present who he believed could guess at his thoughts, who knew something of his motives, and who might have witnessed an act which an enemy could turn greatly to his disadvantage. That man he feared and hated, and were it possible to have annihilated him with a scowl, the reverend doctor would have done so.

Almost immediately in front of the platform, Martin Mannors, and his wife, and daughter were seated. Mr. Capel and Samuel Styles were also present. Mr. Mannors seemed in a complacent study of the different faces before him, and no one listened with greater attention to the several speeches delivered on the occasion. But when his look happened to rest for a moment on the moderator's face, that dignitary appeared to be affected with a nervous twitching of the right eye, which caused him repeatedly to adjust his gold mounted glass as if merely desirous of scanning the vast assembly. His situation was evidently very unpleasant, yet the doctor sustained the part he was forced to act; and, on the evening of that day, when again in the house of his friend, the pastor of St. Andrews, the moderator once more wore the saintly smile of a martyr. He expressed the satisfaction he had felt in having been permitted to take even a secondary part at the great meeting; it was the part he most admired. To sit at the feet of the eminent Christians who had spoken, and to hear and learn from them was most in accordance with his own feelings; and as he lisped Gospel promises to the pious sisters who were present, he rubbed his hands in ecstasy and blessed the Lord for what had been done that day in Exeter Hall for the further spread of the "glorious Gospel."

While Mr. Mannors and his friends were listening to the prominent and distinguished expounders of the Bible at the great meeting, Hannah and William remained at home; and after she had bustled through her morning's work, and put things in order all through the house, she and William—and John Bunyan of course—retired from the busy outer world, and, like humble pilgrims, took refuge in the summer-house. There, surrounded with young, aspiring vines and tender creeping plants, they sat, side by side, on a low seat. The young flowers in the pleasant garden bent gently as the fragrant air passed through their blushing petals, and the dull sound of busy life from the city reached the ear like the lulling flow of distant waters. Flounce

stretched his lazy length across the sunlit doorway, and William, who was more delicate than ever, laid his head in Hannah's lap, and looked up through the lattice-work at the bright blue sky, and watched the flitting clouds as they passed along; while she, with monotonous voice, read, for their mutual edification, passages from her treasured little book, the *Pilgrim's Progress*. Now and then, as some particular part concerning Christian or Evangelist, or some other of the many characters depicted in that popular similitude needed explanation, and while still looking up, he would ask Hannah; and often after she had tried to unriddle the mystery, she would leave it more unintelligible than ever. She seemed, as usual, to be wonderfully interested in the rehearsal of the narrative; she must have read it over and over more than twenty times, and he would be a fool indeed who could seek to rob her—simple soul—of the pleasant emotions which its perusal afforded by trying to convince her that it had no reality. There are certain minds more pleased with the shadow of mystery than with the broad light of naked fact.

After a long pause in his inquiries, during which William seemed to have been speculating on the height of the clouds or the depth of the blue sky, he suddenly asked:

"Hannah, why does ma pray—why do you pray?"

She raised her eyes from the book, and, looking down at his pale face, said: "Pray? Why, God tells us to pray, we must pray for what we want; we can't get to heaven unless we do so. Wicked people never pray."

"Never? Then won't God give us what we want, or let us go to heaven unless we pray?"

"No; never. We must all pray—all, every one."

William thought awhile, and then said: "Why doesn't *pa* pray—he never prays. Is he wicked, and won't he go to heaven?"

Hannah hesitated for a time, and then replied, "Oh! your pa will soon pray, God will make him do so; he will, and then, when you die you'll see him with ma in heaven."

"Will Pop be there, too?"

"Yes, Miss Mary will be up there with the angels."

"Why doesn't God make every one pray, why didn't he make every body good?"

"Oh! well," said Hannah, pausing, and somewhat perplexed, "I don't know—I don't, indeed."

"If pa doesn't pray, then he won't go to heaven?"

"No."

"Nor Pop?"

"Nor any body?"

"Then I won't die—I don't want to go to heaven!"

"Oh! dear child," said she tenderly, "don't say that; 'twould be very, very wicked not to wish to go to heaven. What would your ma say?"

But William heeded not; he was again busy watching the clouds, or looking for some opening in the sky to peer right into paradise. In a short time he again asked:

"Is every body in heaven good; do no wicked or bad people ever get there?"

"Impossible!" said Hannah, astonished, "impossible! God lives in heaven, that's his home, and all his bright and holy angels are up there with him. All the saints, and all the martyrs and poor pilgrims, and all the holy people that ever died are in heaven with God; your ma, and you, and I will be there; and I hope your pa, and Miss Mary, and a great many others;" and then, raising her extended hands and looking fervently upward with a bright smile, she continued: "Oh! yes, up, up on high with God, forever, and ever, and ever."

An expression of solemnity rested upon the boy's face as he still inquired: "Are you sure that no bad people ever got into heaven or ever lived there, Hannah?"

"Oh! nothing sinful or wicked can be where God is—nothing impossible! every thing in heaven is so good and happy."

"But ma says that God is everywhere; that he is on this earth, which she says is so very wicked, and that we are very wicked too."

"Oh! yes," followed Hannah somewhat abstractedly; "yes, we're very, very wicked indeed."

"And then," continued William, "how did Satan and all his wicked angels get into heaven? Ma told me that they once lived there with God, and that they got very wicked, and that there was a war in heaven, and that God sent Michael and his angels to fight with them, and then that God cast Satan and his angels down out of heaven. Didn't these wicked angels once live in heaven, and wasn't there fighting up there, too?"

Hannah now looked more confounded than ever; she laid her book aside and remained thoughtful for a time, while the boy's large, inquiring eyes were still fixed upon hers.

"Well, dear child, I'm sure I don't know how these wicked ones got into heaven; they were there I suppose, for the Bible says so. 'Tis a mystery we can't understand, but it will be all made plain to us some day."

With this comfortable assurance, she resumed her book, but not to read; she looked over a few pages here and there, then closed it again, and commenced, in a soft, low voice, to sing one of her favorite hymns—

"There is a land of pure delight,
    Where saints immortal reign;
Infinite day excludes the night,
    And pleasures banish pain.

"There everlasting spring abides,
    And never-withering flowers;
Death, like a narrow sea, divides
    This heavenly land from ours."

She had scarcely finished the second verse, before William's weary lids began to close, and as the last words he heard distinctly were about the "heavenly land," he went away there in his mid-day dream—even Flounce followed him. There was soft, heavenly music, and he wandered about those "sweet fields" with his father and mother, and Mary and Hannah, and he told them how blissful he felt to have them with him at last, and that they should never, never go back to earth, never more be wicked, nor ever part again.

While William thus slept, Hannah, poor kind creature, tried not to disturb his quiet slumbers. She watched the pale and wearied features of the sleeping boy, like some hovering, compassionate angel—yet only an angel of the earth—and for nearly two hours longer she felt almost perfect happiness, while softly singing hymn after hymn, and verse after verse, in her own simple way, and comforting herself with delightful thoughts of the pilgrim's land, of which her anticipations led her to think that

"No chilling winds nor poisonous breath,
    Can reach that healthful shore;
Sickness and sorrow, pain and death,
    Are felt and feared no more."

She ceased at last, and, as she closed, her voice died away with the sound of the evening bells from the distant city.

"Why, Hannah, my goodness! how still you keep," said Mrs. Mannors looking into the doorway; she had stepped lightly along the garden walk and gave her maid such a pleasant surprise. "And is my poor boy sleeping?" said she, stooping and tenderly kissing his forehead. And then, looking affectionately at Hannah, who had watched over his slumbers, cried, "O you good, kind, loving Hannah! God bless your tender heart! what should we do without you? Wake up, my dear," said she, gently taking William's hand, "wake up, until I tell you all about what we saw to-day in the city."

"O ma!" said William, stretching himself, "I have had such a nice dream, I never wanted to wake again; but where's Pop?" said he, looking around.

"Here I am, you lazy fellow," said Mary, gliding in with the sunlight. "Have you been sleeping all the time we were away?" She seated herself by his side, and ran her fingers through his brown silken hair.

"Indeed, he has not," said Hannah; "we have had such a long talk about many things —things that you should talk about sometimes, Miss Mary; and then, when he grew tired, he slept a little, while I sang."

"I'm sure you were very happy; of course you were," said Mrs. Mannors; "the Lord was with you. I left you under his protecting care during my absence. And then we had such a glorious time in Exeter Hall—such a crowd of people; such a number of ministers and pious foreigners. The work of the Lord has surely prospered this day—I know it. But let us go in, and I will tell you all about the meeting after tea."

Mary and William, followed by Flounce, led the way to the house, while Mrs. Mannors and her faithful maid walked slowly after, talking about the great sums which had been poured that day into the treasury of the Lord.

Mr. Mannors returned very much pleased that he had attended the great Bible meeting; he had heard all that the principal ministers of different sects had to say concerning the spread of the Gospel; he had heard their futile insinuations against skepticism, and their admission of its growth and influence in high places, among eminent men—even within the "visible church" itself! And he felt satisfied that, though they spoke of the present and future with such lofty confidence, they sometimes feared that the whole structure of Christianity was growing more and more insecure. Samuel Styles did not accompany them to Hampstead, but went to the Red Lion, where he agreed to meet Mr. Mannors the next day.

Mr. Capel, of all others, seemed to be the most dissatisfied. He, too, had heard all the great speeches and all the news which Mrs. Mannors had emphasized as "glorious;" still he seemed demure and thoughtful; even Mr. Mannors felt a share of surprise, and once or twice tried to rally him, but with little effect. Latterly, indeed, an occasional abstraction was observable, but it was of short duration; his natural cheerfulness was like a rainbow over every cloud; but now the cloud was there, and no rainbow could be seen, nor glimpse of blue sky beyond. Mrs. Mannors also noticed his unusual gravity, and, of course, attributed it to religious emotion. He was, no doubt, pondering upon some of the truths he had heard that day, and was probably affected concerning the state of the perishing millions which he had been told were yet in heathenish darkness—doomed to eternal misery. Such a state of mind, she thought, was all very proper in a minister; she was rather pleased than otherwise; for, contrary to all expectation, she had begun to think that he was not quite as diligent as he might be; but lest she should misjudge one of God's servants, she only very cautiously mentioned her doubts to one confiding heart—to Hannah alone; and now again she believed that, in answer to her prayers, God was about to manifest himself and increase the usefulness of one of his human agents—of this she had no doubt.

Mr. Capel sat near the open window, and watched the beautiful sunset, and saw the evening shadows gather around the drooping flowers; the distant, motionless cloud looked like a mountain of sapphire in the waning red light. How peacefully nature approached with its season for slumber, and how he envied the calm which seemed to rest upon the inanimate world. But his mind, at that still hour, was like the stormy ocean, and his heart was heavy in anticipation of the approaching trials which he feared he had to undergo. Still he had courage to face any ordeal in a just cause; but, just or unjust, he felt that a trial of some kind was unavoidable. Then, again, he thought it might be kept off, he would try and avoid a collision; and then, when he thought of his position—a reputed preacher of the Gospel—he drew a heavy sigh, and muttered to himself, "It is inevitable."

He was now alone, and he heard Mrs. Mannors's voice in an adjoining room. She was busy giving a relation of all she had seen and heard that day at Exeter Hall; she dwelt especially upon the many remarks made against the growing infidelity of the day, and how the "word of God" was to triumph over every adversary. But to him who went

there too in search of hope, how different was the feeling! In support of the Bible, he was treated to a rehash of flippant assertions, and a round of the usual orthodox assumptions. The clerical defenders of revelation did not attempt to establish scriptural truth on the basis of reason or science, but more as the result of faith evidenced in the feelings and affections of "poor peasants and simple women;" while science, art, history, and arithmetic were frowned upon as the trusty allies of skepticism.

"You have become more serious since your visit to Exeter Hall," said Mr. Mannors kindly, as he placed his chair near him. "You are not, I presume, entirely satisfied with all you heard on the occasion."

"To be candid, I am not."

"Well, I can not say that I feel disappointed. Of course, we could not expect to hear a learned defense of the Scriptures at such a time; but one would think that we should have heard better reasons for a continuation of the heavy, voluntary tax on the pockets of believers. Circulate the Scriptures, is the great cry at Exeter Hall; but the speakers entirely failed to prove that that circulation had resulted in any permanent benefit, so far, either to Jew or heathen, or even to the nations so long under its influence. The priests alone are the great gainers. It might not be too much to assert that the united incomes and salaries of the state bishops, and priests, and other clergymen on the platform to-day, would be more than sufficient to rid one of our most populous parishes of the want and nearly actual famine which drives so many to crime. No other class who profess to labor do so little or get so much as the priests of Christendom at the present day. No wonder that their united aim is against skepticism, which is so vigorously denouncing their pretensions. Let Christianity prevail again as it did once in Europe, and once more we should have gloomy fanatics, intolerance, and an inquisition; then, alas! for human progress or liberty. We should again have bigoted Puritans, and men like Doctor Buster lording it in a Star Chamber; and a tribe of bishops as greedy as Winchester, who, while advocating the spread of the Gospel, would tax the poor man's bread to increase benefices and to double or treble their present exorbitant incomes; and again we should have reënactments for the enforcement of test-oaths and religious penalties."

"Then am I to be one of that class you reproach? Shall I remain as I am, and be considered the ally of such men as Doctor Buster and the bishop of Winchester—even a co-worker with James Baker?" Mr. Capel was still looking out at the flowers, and a shadow had already overspread his face.

"Yes, if you think you're right; if not, leave the narrow track in which you have been treading, and move out boldly upon the great highway of progress. Be free!" Mr. Mannors spoke with unusual energy, and when Mr. Capel turned to reply, he saw that emotional glow, the emblem of sincerity, resting upon his features.

"I may have been on that highway for

some time; I have ventured out stealthily, like one afraid to meet a traveler—afraid to ask whether I was on the right road. I know not where I am now. You asked me to investigate, and, when I commenced, I left the beaten track in which I had so long paced backward and forward without making an advance. Yes, I have read and re-read the books which you mentioned, and have read others for and against the creed which I was trained from infancy to believe as truth; now I am like one confused, like one blinded by the dust which he has raised about him—uncertain which way to move. I have gone back for aid to Paley, and to Butler, and to others, but to return more disappointed than ever. I have searched the most learned expositions without avail; and to-day I attended at Exeter Hall, only to be mortified at the pretensions and self-sufficiency of the very class to whom I am supposed to belong. I am harboring terrible doubts, and am therefore in a false position."

"And yet how much better than to be like an owl at twilight, content to hoot and flap within the ivied ruins of a church tower. You have dared to doubt; that is a step toward freedom; even one pace outside the charmed circle of theology. Doubt is but the dawning of truth. Be not afraid to advance; walk out into the broad highway; look up at the light, and then go on; for progress may be eternal."

"One step outside that circle would make me an apostate, to be laden with reproach. Apostasy is but infamy in the eyes of the faithful; even once made a *crime*, to be punished with death. That penalty can not now be exacted, but the ostracism of religion will remain. I can not avoid my doubts, but I dread the ordeal which may follow."

"Take courage; have freedom at any price. Mental slavery is the most degrading. If in bursting your fetters you should receive a wound, time will heal it; and though bigotry may point to the scar as a mark of degradation, it will be to yourself and to the progressive a proud mark obtained in the cause of true liberty."

It was late that night before these friends retired: but had Mrs. Mannors stood by and heard all they had said, she would have been amazed at the want of faith in him who was to have wrought such a change in her household, and she might have exclaimed, "O Ephraim! what shall I do unto thee? O Judah! what shall I do unto thee? for your goodness is as a morning cloud, and as the early dew it goeth away."

That same evening, after their return from Exeter Hall, Mrs. Baker entertained a few friends—some members of her class besides Mr. Wesley Jacobs, the local preacher, Thomas Bolster, and one or two other influential church members on the circuit. Nearly all spoke in praise of the Bible Society, and of the pleasure afforded them in witnessing such unanimity among members of different persuasions. One and all were, however, particularly delighted that Doctor Buster's pride had been humbled; and Mr. Baker wore a smile of quiet satisfaction at the thought that the result of his counter-plot had been so successful, and that the great Presbyterian champion and his allies had been forced to submit. Indeed, he felt as satisfied of his own individual prowess in the achievement of this victory as he did of the supremacy of Methodism over every other ism of the day.

"What a pity, friends," said he, "that such a distinguished hero of Black Presbyterianism should be obliged to sit so meekly between myself and Jonah Hall, and never get a chance to say more than *Amen* the whole day. I fancy they won't send me another invitation in a hurry to attend at brother Caleb Howe's Baptist wash-house; but we'll watch them for the future, and if they catch me asleep, why, then, they're welcome to all they can get."

"I declare, brother," said the local preacher, "the doctor did keep unusually still to-day; he has assurance enough, he can be bold if he likes but I thought there was some other influence at work to keep him quiet. A popularity hunter like him is not easily silenced, especially when he could not fail to notice so many of his admirers present."

"It was rather strange; he fancied, I suppose, that none of us humble preachers would have the assurance to appear on the platform alongside of his dignity, and that he would have it all to himself, whether or no. Wasn't he mistaken though? However, I think the doctor was not himself; he was as fidgetty as a sick bear, and for some reason or other he seemed to keep a watchful eye, either upon that sedate impostor, Martin Mannors, who was right in front of us, or upon his wife or daughter; while he, in turn, stared back as defiantly. There's something, I think, between that precious pair; I must find it out from brother Capel."

"I almost forgot," said a pious sister, "How is sister Mannors likely to succeed? Do you think that brother Capel will add another seal to his ministry by the conversion of her husband?"

"The Lord alone can tell," meekly replied Mrs. Baker, "the work is in his hands. Our poor sister is still hopeful; but her husband is yet puffed up with the pride of his heart. Alas! his day of grace may be already passed; he may be left to the sole comfort of his weak reason. You know what the Scriptures say, 'My spirit shall not always strive with man.' He may yet bewail, and say,

'Ah! wretch that I am! I can only exclaim,
Like a devil tormented within,
My Saviour is gone, and has left me alone
To the fury of Satan and sin.'"

"Let him go," said Mr. Baker testily. "I never had any hope of his submission to truth. Let him go with the rest. I place but little confidence in what our state bishops say on behalf of true religion; they are greedy impostors; but I was glad to hear them rate infidelity at its proper value; and that, too, in the presence of such an upholder. Psha! brother Capel has no more influence over that man than I would have over the Pope of Rome."

"And yet," pleaded one of the youngest sisters, "you see he had sufficient influence to induce him to attend at Exeter Hall."

"Not a bit of it, sister; it was all a matter of mere curiosity. Martin Mannors went there te criticise—to hear what could be said; I know him."

"I didn't think much of the speeches, any way," said Mr. Thomas Bolster, a very strong Methodist. "We all know what the bishops are: Spurgeon and his little apple were very much alike. I think our secretary made the only speech worth hearing."

"Wife," said Mr. Baker suddenly, after a moment's thought, "was brother Capel here lately?"

"No; not for some days; not, I think, since you returned from district meeting."

"Very strange! I do not know how it is, I see him but seldom. I had scarcely time to say, 'How do you do?' to him after the meeting to-day before he was off again with his friends. He ought to have called here upon his return from the circuit. He must be greatly devoted to sister Mannors, or to her husband, or some one of her family. I have heard that he entertains a most exalted opinion of his friend Mannors; it can not be on account of his religious principles. Then," continued he sharply, "what is it for; what is the nature of the bond? This must be looked after." But suddenly checking himself, he adroitly turned the conversation on Doctor Buster and the bishops; he was too cautious to scrutinize the conduct of the junior preacher before any of the flock; he would have a long talk with his wife about him when the friends went home.

After sundry cups of tea and other more solid refreshments had been piously consumed, Mr. Baker, with brothers Bolster and Jacobs, stealthily retired to light their pipes in the kitchen, while the sisters were left chatting agreeably at the tea-table. In about half an hour, they all reassembled in the little parlor. Mr. Wesley Jacobs gave a peculiar sigh, and made a favorite allusion to the presence which would be manifested where two or three were gathered together in the name of the Lord. There was then a round of prayer for the spread of the Gospel and the conversion of the world; and Mr. Baker made a closing and pathetic appeal for the increase of the Wesleyan Church, for all who were in trouble, for all who were in error, for the poor benighted heathen, and for missionaries far, far away.

CHAPTER XXI.

ONE evening, a day or two after the Bible meeting, Samuel Styles entered the large room of the Red Lion. He found it well filled with a number of intelligent shop-keepers, clerks, artisans, and other persons. Good John Hollis, the landlord, moved with cheerful look from table to table, stopping now and then to give a word or two of welcome to one or another, or to pause, in order to catch more fully the remarks made by some more fervent speaker than usual. Many of those assembled were quietly sipping the stout ale for which the Red Lion was noted; others were looking over the daily papers, or reading to those near by passages from some popular or favorite author; while the majority seemed to be earnestly engaged in familiar discourse, in which much

thought and interest were manifested. The prevailing theme related to the peculiar efforts resorted to for the propagation of Christianity and its eleemosynary system of taxation; and in the buzz of conversation one could easily detect that the State Church, the aristocracy, the Bible Society, and Exeter Hall, bishops, parsons, priests, and preachers came in for no small share of animadversion. Samuel watched the face of more than one eager speaker, and he soon became satisfied that though several of those around him had a somewhat rough exterior, they had manly hearts, and were men who had read and thought for themselves—were a type of the free and progressive spirit of the British nation; men who could not be intimidated by royal threats or lordly frowns, or made tamely submissive to the prejudiced and oppressive acts of any servile or aristocratic Parliament.

A notice, placed in a conspicuous part of the room, stated that the regular weekly meeting of the Secularists of the Strand district would be held at their large hall, in a street within a short distance of the Red Lion. In about half an hour, there was a general movement of all for the place; and Samuel, being anxious to go, and having previously formed a friendly acquaintance with several of the visitors, was particularly invited to attend the meeting. Taking the arm of the secretary, he followed the crowd, and in a few minutes was conducted to a seat in a spacious and well-lighted hall, capable of accommodating seven or eight hundred persons, and which was already more than two thirds filled when he entered. The speaker's platform was elevated about two feet above the floor, and mottoes or trite phrases, printed in large letters, could be seen in several conspicuous places. One over the platform read: "Reason, our most intellectual guide." Another, "Hear all sides," and above these, and almost touching the frescoed ceiling, the word "TRUTH," in golden text-characters, flashed down upon the assembly.

The hall was soon crowded, and a number of well-trained singers in front commenced the following liberal song, which, from the peculiarity of the words and harmony of the air, and excellent manner of performance, seemed to have had a most animating effect upon all present. Nearly every one appeared to know the words and their purport, and, as they followed the leading singers in swelling the strain which now filled the place, Samuel Styles was forcibly reminded of his younger days, and he almost fancied himself again at a Christian meeting in his native land:

SECULARIST'S SONG.

We've been waiting through the night,
  And the dawn will soon appear;
And the mountain's misty height.
From the clouds shall burst out bright;
  And the eagle in his flight
Reach a radiant atmosphere;
  And the toiler on his way
Shall look up and see the day.

O bleak time when hope seemed dead!
  Ages lost in doubt and gloom;
And whole centuries of dread
By dark superstition led,
  Until reason almost fled
    From a throne into a tomb;

Till the mind in frenzied flight
Darted deeper into night.

But the dawn on every side,
  The gleam of glorious day,
Will be seen while shadows hide:
Then the priest in towering pride,
And the prophet who has lied,
  Shall forever lose their sway,
And the despot and the slave
Shall lie mouldering in one grave.

At the close of the song, the chairman, a venerable gentleman, introduced the speaker, and when the name of Martin Mannors was mentioned, the demonstrations of welcome were so great that it was some time before a word could be heard. As soon as an opportunity offered, Mr. Mannors commenced:

"Mr Chairman and my friends: As this is the period when various religious societies, and those interested in the circulation of the Bible, or what they call the 'word of God,' hold their annual meetings in Exeter Hall to collect more money for pious purposes, it will be a proper time for us to ask, what the Bible is, and on what is its surprising claim to infallibility founded. Such a claim, however, is not peculiar to the Christian Bible; the Buddhists, the Mohammedans, the Mormons, and others insist on that characteristic for their so-called inspired books, and are as positive in asserting that they have the evidence of prophecy and miracles to as full an extent in support of their warranty to a divine revelation as that so authoritatively demanded by Christians. In as few words as the nature of the subject will permit, we shall make some observations on the Bible; and it is to be hoped that those who feel interested in ascertaining, 'What is truth?' will make a fuller inquiry, and be satisfied as to the correctness of our assertions: no amount of scrutiny can injure truth.

"It is a curious fact, that the Jews, who are said by Christians to have been the first privileged with a message from the deity, and who are or were once known as the 'chosen people of God,' only came into notice after the time of Alexander the Great; and that the historical monuments preceding that period make not the slightest mention of any Jewish transaction; and that the Jews were unknown to the world as a nation until they were subjected by the Romans. This has been fully established by the celebrated Wyttenbach. Professor Cooper, of America, also writes, that no authentic historian of ancient times, Josephus excepted, has ever mentioned the Jews as an independent nation or state, or as being in possession of Palestine, or any part of Great Syria before or in the time of Alexander. As a nation, they appear to have been entirely unknown to Herodotus and all other Greek historians! In view of these facts, another American writer* has said: 'But what confidence can be placed in the *ancient* writings of a people so insignificant and obscure as to be, as it were, totally unknown to other nations till at least a *century* after all the facts, real or pretended, therein recorded were said to have been written? Who ever knew any thing about King David, or King Solomon and the splendid temple built at Jerusalem by

* Kneeland.

the latter, except the Jews?' Writers who have made their history a study assert that the Jews, as a people, were a rude, barbarous, cruel, blood-thirsty tribe; and Apollonius, quoted by Josephus, said that the Jews were the most trifling of all the *barbarians*, and that they were the *only* people who had never found out any thing useful for life. The great Doctor Burnet, in his *Archæologia Philosophica*, admits that they were of a gross and sluggish nature, of a dull and heavy disposition, bereft of humanity, a vile company of men. Even Josephus concedes that his countrymen were so illiterate as never to have written any thing or to have held intercourse with their learned neighbors. Indeed, no people of antiquity were more ignorant, credulous, intolerant, and wretched than the Jews. While the ancient Chaldeans, Arabians, Egyptians, Grecians, and Romans produced their men of science and erudition, the Jews added nothing to the glorious pyramid of human knowledge; and yet we are to believe, even in the nineteenth century, that a being said to be 'all wise' and 'all good' selected such a race as his 'chosen people,' the people who were *solely* and *specially* intrusted with his divine word? What a mockery!*

"It is a singular proof of the want of correct information among believers in the Christian Bible that, with very few exceptions, they are of the opinion, that that book always retained its present form; whereas, in truth, there was no proper canon or collection, even of the books of the *Old* Testament, until, about two hundred years before the time given for the birth of Christ. Previous to that period, a great number of 'holy books' were scattered about, occasionally altered or amended, just as priests, or prophets, or rulers might determine. The early history of the Bible is shrouded in almost impenetrable darkness. As we now have it, the Old Testament is composed of thirty-nine books, exclusive of a number of others called '*apocryphal*,' but which are still received by the Roman-Catholic Church as canonical; and the New Testament has twenty-seven books. Therefore, the whole number of books composing the orthodox or English Bible is sixty-six; and these are accepted by the Reformed Church of the present day as *inspired*. Now, although it is strongly asserted by the clerical defenders of the genuineness of the Bible, that the Lord has miraculously preserved the 'sacred writings,' yet, without particularizing any of the forgeries, interpolations, or corruptions discovered, we find that there were several other inspired books, referred to in the Bible as authoritative, which have been *entirely* lost, and which are alluded to by commentators as the 'lost books.' We find passages in the Bible relating to about *twenty* of these; but, for the sake of brevity, we shall enumerate texts which only refer to a few of them—such as '*The Book of the Wars of the Lord*,' '*The Book of Jasher*,' '*The Acts of Solomon*,' '*The Book of Gad, the Seer*,' '*The Prophecy of Ahijah*,' '*The Visions of Iddo*,' and '*The Book of Shemaiah, the Prophet*.'

* R. Cooper, of England.

"I will read extracts from the Bible as proof:

"'Wherefore, it is said in the book of the wars of the Lord what he did in the Red Sea and in the brooks of Arnon?' Numbers 21: 14.

"'Is not this written in the book of Jasher?' Josh. 10: 13. 'Behold, it is written in the book of Jasher!' 2 Samuel 1: 18.

"'And the rest of the acts of Solomon, are they not written in the book of the acts of Solomon?' 1 Kings 11: 41.

"'Now the acts of David the King, first and last, behold, they are written in the book of Samuel the seer, and in the book of Nathan the prophet, and in the book of Gad the seer.' 1 Chron. 29: 29.

"You will perceive that this verse alone refers to more than one of the lost books.

"'Now the rest of the acts of Solomon, first and last, are they not written in the book of Nathan the prophet, and in the prophecy of Ahijah the Shilonite, and in the visions of Iddo the seer, against Jeroboam, the son of Nebal?' 2d, Chron 9: 29.

"This verse also mentions *three* of the lost books:

"'Now the acts of Rehoboam, first and last, are they not written in the book of Shemaiah the prophet, and of Iddo the seer concerning genealogies?' 2 Chron. 12: 15.

"Here two others of the lost books are spoken of; and I think we have sufficient evidence that the Bible is deficient in one particular respect: it does *not* contain all of the so-called 'inspired word.'*

"You will remember that we stated that there was no proper form or collection of the books of the *Old* Testament until about 200 years before Christ; we will now state that there was no regular satisfactory collection of the books composing the *New* Testament until the middle of the *sixth* century, over 500 years after the death of the reputed founder of Christianity! Up to the period of the council of Nice, A.D. 327, a great many Acts, Gospels, Epistles, and Revelations were circulated, and received among the faithful as of equal authority.†

"There were, of course, conflicting opinions as to their credibility, and serious contentions arose in consequence; the book which one priest rejected, another would accept; to settle the dispute in some way, a selection of

* Du Pin, Professor of Philosophy at Paris, and author of a *Complete History of the Canon and Writers of the Books of the Old and New Testaments*, says:
"St. Eucharius says, 'it is evident why we have not the remaining books which the Holy Scriptures approve of, because Judea, having been ravaged by the Chaldeans, and the ancient bibliotheque being burnt, there remains only a small number of the books which at present make up the Holy Scriptures, and which were collected and reëstablished by the care of Ezra.'
"Simon, in his *Critical History of the Version of the New Testament*, quotes St. Chrysostom thus:
"The Jews, having been at some time careless and at others profane, suffered some of the sacred books to be lost through their carelessness, and have burnt and destroyed others."

† Among the apocryphal books of the New Testament were the *Gospels* of St. Peter, St. Thomas, St. Mathias, St. Bartholomew, St. Philip, Judas Iscariot, Thaddeus, and Barnabas. There were the *Acts* of St. Peter, St. Paul, St. Andrew, St. John, St. Philip, and St. Thomas, and the *Revelations* of St. Paul, St. Thomas, St. Stephen, and the *Great Apostle*. These and many others were at one time considered as of "divine authority," but now rejected—*though not yet even by all*—as spurious.

the true from the false was made by the assembled bishops at Nice; and Papias, the Christian father, informs us as to the manner of that selection. We shall give his own words: 'This was done,' said he, 'by placing all the books under a communion-table, and, upon the prayers of the council, the inspired books jumped upon the table, while the false ones remained under!' After a time, however, many mocked at this manner of selection, and priestly wrangling continued as fierce as ever.

"About the year 363 A.D., another council, called the council of Laodicea, was held, to make a more perfect selection of the holy books. This time, the manner of doing so was by *vote*; and it is said a list of the books of the New Testament, nearly as we now have them, was then chosen, but the book of Revelations was excluded. And St. Chrysostom, who died A.D. 407, informs us that in his time the book of the Acts of the Apostles was little known. After this, two other councils were held, one in the year 406, and the other about the year 680. The council of 406 rejected some books deemed canonical by the council of 363; but the council of 680 restored them. Thus, until a late period, did contending priests leave the settlement of the 'divine word' in doubt and confusion. A writer says: 'Thus were the "sacred writings," the "word of God," tossed like a battledoor from sect to sect, and altered as the spirit of faction might dictate.'

"As an evidence that 'ordained heads' at these councils did not always conduct themselves in a proper spirit, we shall quote the words of the great Christian writer, Tindal, on the subject: 'Indeed,' says he, 'the confusion and disorder were so great amongst them, especially in their synods, that it sometimes came to *blows*; as, for instance, Dioscorus, bishop of Alexandria, *cuffed* and *kicked* Flavianus, patriarch of Constantinople, with that fury that within three days after *he died!*' And, speaking of their doctrinal consistency, he says, 'For though they were most obstinate as to *power*, they were most flexible as to *faith*; and in their council, complimented the Emperor with whatsoever creeds they had a mind to, and never scrupled to *recant* what they had before enacted, or refusact what they had before recanted.'

"If these men were inspired to select the true from the false out of such a number of books—and it would require 'inspiration' for the purpose—the godly priests proved rather flexible.

"That no doubt may exist as to the period when the New Testament was compiled, we shall give the statement of another distinguished Christian; the learned Dr. Lardner says: 'That even so late as the middle of the *sixth* century, the canon of the New Testament had not been settled by any authority that was decisive and universally acknowledged, but Christian people were at liberty to judge for themselves concerning the genuineness of writings proposed to them as apostolical, and to determine according to evidence.' Vol. 3, pp. 54-61.

"The Rev. T. H. Horne, in his second edition

of his *Introduction to the Scriptures*,* says:
"The accounts left us by ecclesiastical writers
of antiquity, concerning the *time when* the
Gospels were written or published, are so
vague, confused, and *discordant* that they
lead to no certain or solid determination.
The eldest of the ancient fathers collected
the REPORTS of their own times, and set them
down as *certain truths,* and those who followed adopted their accounts with *implicit
reverence.* Thus tradition, *true* or *false,* passed
on from one writer to another without *examination,* until, at last, it became too late to
examine them to any purpose."

"It must not be imagined, however, that the
final selection of the books of the New Testament gave general satisfaction; evidence is
to the contrary. Many learned Christian men
of *recent* times have expressed themselves
strongly in favor of several of the discarded
books, even going so far as to consider them
as genuine as any of the canonized version;
and to silence every cavil on this subject, we
shall confine ourselves to Christian authority.

"The learned Dr. Whiston, on page 28 of
his *Exact Time,* declares that *twenty-seven*
of the discarded books are genuine; he says,
'Can any one be so weak as to imagine Mark,
and Luke, and James, and Jude, who were
none of them *more* than companions of the
apostles, to be our sacred and unerring guides,
while Barnabas, Thaddeus, Clement, Timothy, Hermas, Ignatius, and Polycarp, who
were *equally* companions of the same apostles, to be of *no authority at all ?*'

"In his *Rationale of Religious Inquiry,*
the Rev. J. Martineau says, 'If we could recover the gospels of the Hebrews and that
of the Egyptians, it would be difficult to give
a reason why THEY should not form a part of
the New Testament; and an epistle actually
exists, by Clement, the fellow-laborer of Paul,
which has as good a claim to stand there as
the Epistle to the Hebrews or the Gospel of
Luke. If none but the works of the twelve
apostles were admitted, the rule would be
clear and simple; but what are Mark and
Luke, who are received, more than Clement
and Barnabas, who are excluded?'

"Bishop Marsh observes that, 'It is an undoubted fact that those Christians by whom
the now rejected gospels were received, and
who are now called heretics, were in the right
in many points of criticism where the fathers
accused them of willful corruption.'

"Archbishop Wake, who actually translated
St. Barnabas, St. Clement, St. Ignatius, St.
Polycarp, and St. Hermas, fathers of the first
century, recommends them to the world as
'inspired' and as 'containing an authoritative declaration of the Gospel of Christ to us.'[†]

"And William Penn, the celebrated Quaker,
in an argument against the positive acceptance of the Bible as the rule of faith and practice, says, 'I demand of our adversaries, if
they are well assured of those men who
first collected, embodied, and declared them
(the Scriptures) authentic, by a public canon

which we read was in the Council of Laodicea,
held 360 years after Christ—I say, how do
they know that *these* men *rightly* discerned
true from *spurious?* Now, sure it is that some
of the Scriptures, taken in by one council were
rejected by another for apocryphal, and that
which was left out by the former for apocryphal was taken in by the latter for canonical.
Now, visible it is, that they contradict each
other, and as true that they have erred respecting the present belief.'[*]

"We could multiply such admissions, but
every candid hearer will agree that we have
produced sufficient to establish the fact that
the orthodox Bible was not completed, or reduced to its present form until between five
and six hundred years after Christ. As it is, we
have now *two* distinct Christian Bibles, the oldest or Catholic Scriptures, which include the
Old Testament Apocrypha, and the Protestant,
or King James' version, which excludes them;
some, indeed, say that the Bible of the Greek
Church is still different. Now, a large majority of Christians are Roman Catholic, and they,
as a church, denounce the Protestant Bible.
In 1816, the Pope declared it 'pregnant with
errors;' and the Protestants, in return, though
not wholly rejecting the Catholic book, say it
is very imperfect.

"The honest investigator will furthermore be
astonished to learn that the Jews themselves,
even their priests and kings, were ignorant of
any 'divine law,' until a priest named Hilkiah said that he 'found the book of the law
in the house of the Lord.' This wonderful
discovery is said to have taken place only 628
years before Christ, centuries after the death
of Moses, its supposed writer! The 34th chapter of 2d Chronicles relates the matter, and
tells of the surprise and dread caused by the
finding.

"The inquirer will be still more astonished
to hear that that same 'divine book of the law'
was, a few years after its discovery by Hilkiah,
completely lost (some say burnt) during the
Babylonish captivity, and *never afterward
recovered;* and that the Old Testament books
which we now have were re-written by Ezra,
or Esdras. Hittel says, 'The ancient Jews
had a tradition that the Mosaic law had been
burned at the time of the captivity, and that it
had been republished by Ezra; and the tradition was received as trustworthy by Irenæus,
Clement of Alexandria, Chrysostom, and The-
odoret.' In the Hebrew Apocrypha, Esdras
says:

"'Thy law is burned: therefore no man knoweth the
things which thou hast done, or the works that are to
begin. But if I have found grace before thee, send
down the Holy Spirit into me, and I shall write all that
hath been done in the world since the beginning,
which were written in thy law, that men may find thy
path.' 2 Esdras 14 : 21.
"'And it came to pass, that when forty days were fulfilled, that the highest spake, saying, the first that
thou hast written publish openly, that the foolish and
unworthy may read it; but keep the seventy last, that
thou mayest deliver them only to such as be wise
among the people.' 2 Esdras 14 : 45.

"Alluding to this, the Christian father Irenæus says, 'that, they (the books of the Old
Testament) were *fabricated* seventy years
after the Babylonish captivity by Esdras'

And Dr. Adam Clarke, without venturing so far, says, 'All antiquity is nearly unanimous in giving Ezra the honor of collecting the different writings of Moses and the prophets, and *reducing* them into the form in which they are now found in the Holy Bible.'

"Bagster admits that Ezra, '*perhaps* assisted by Nehemiah and the great synagogue, corrected the errors which had crept into the sacred writings through the negligence or mistake of transcribers,' and that 'he occasionally *added*, under the superintendence of the Holy Spirit, whatever appeared necessary for the purpose of illustrating, completing, or connecting them.' This appears to have been a very extensive license. God, it is said, first inspired men to write his law, and had afterward to inspire Ezra to correct the errors of transcribers, and yet a thousand admitted errors still exist! Ezra '*added*' to the Scriptures, in order to 'illustrate' what God actually meant! Could more have been said as to the ambiguity of human laws? To what deplorable shifts have *our* semi-inspired priests been reduced!

"The Bible, having attained its present form, does not, however, give satisfaction. While the Samaritan Jews, and ancient Sadducees rejected all but the Pentateuch, those same books, and many others now included as canonical, had been discarded by some of the primitive fathers, and by priestly heroes of the reformation, as well as by many bishops, priests, and learned commentators of these latter days.

"Belsham in his *Evidence*, page 117, declares that, ' of the law of Moses, that which is *genuine* bears but a small proportion to that which is spurious.'

"The celebrated Bishop Usher says that our present Septuagint is a *spurious* copy! 'The Septuagint translation continually adds to, takes from, and changes the Hebrew text at pleasure; the original translation of it was lost long ago, and what has ever since gone by that name is a *spurious copy*, abounding in omissions, additions, and alterations of the Hebrew text.'

"Origen, the first learned Christian of critical ability, doubted the genuineness of the Epistle to the *Hebrews*, the second of *James*, second of *Peter*, second and third of *John* and *Jude!* but considered the book of *Hermas* as inspired.

"Luther, the apostle of the reformation, doubted the truthfulness of the following scriptural books, namely: Of the Old Testament, *Chronicles*, *Job*, *Ecclesiastes*, *Esther*, and *Isaiah*; of the New, *Hebrews*, *James*, *Jude*, and *Revelation*. We shall quote Luther's own words as evidence. He says: 'The books of the *Kings* are more worthy of credit than the books of the *Chronicles!* Job spake not therefore as it stands written in his book, but hath had such cogitations. It is a sheer allegory. It is probable that Solomon made and wrote this book. This book, *Ecclesiastes*, ought to have been more full; there is too much broken matter in it; it has neither boots, nor spurs, but rides only in socks, as I myself when in the cloister. Solomon, therefore, hath not written this book, which had been made in

the days of the Maccabees, by Sirach. It is like a Talmud, compiled from many books, perhaps in Egypt, at the desire of King Ptolemy Euergetes. So also have the *Proverbs* of Solomon been collected by others. The book of *Esther*, I toss into the Elbe. I am such an enemy to the book of Esther, that I wish it did not exist ; for it Judaizes too much, and hath in it a great deal of heathenish naughtiness. *Isaiah* hath borrowed his art and knowledge from the *Psalter*. The history of *Jonah* is so monstrous that it is absolutely incredible. That the Epistle to the *Hebrews* is not by St. Paul, nor by any apostle at all is shown by chapter 2: 3. It was written by an exceedingly learned man, a disciple of the apostles. It should be no stumbling-block if there should be found in it a mixture of wood, straw, hay. The Epistle of *James* I account the writing of no apostle; it is an epistle of straw. The Epistle of *Jude* is a copy of *St. Peter's*, and altogether has stories which have no place in Scripture.

"'In the revelations of St. John, much is wanting to let me deem it scriptural. I can discover no traces that it is established by the Spirit.'* Such is the opinion of the great high-priest of the reformation of books now deemed inspired.

"Of the book of *Daniel*, the learned Dr. Arnold speaks, 'I have long thought that the greater part of the book of *Daniel* is most certainly a very late work of the time of the Maccabees ; and the pretended prophecy of the kings of Greece and Persia, and of the north and south is mere history, like the poetical prophecies in Virgil and elsewhere. In fact, you can distinctly trace the date when it was written, because the events up to that date are given with historical minuteness, totally unlike the character of real prophecy, and beyond that date all is imaginary.'

"What a pity it is that some of our mad priests do not take the same view ; our semi-prophetic lecturers would not have so many 'rams' and 'he-goats' skipping through their brains and scattering their senses. Neander also took the same view of the book of Daniel. Doctors Aitken and Eichhorn have repudiated the books of *Jonah* and *Daniel* as mere 'legends and romances.' Doctor Whiston denounced the Canticles as 'forgeries;' and many other of our learned priests, who, while accepting certain books as canonical, yet admit that they contain spurious passages, interpolations, false translations, sufficient to mislead and bewilder the multitude.

"I would ask, how, then, is it possible for an 'unlearned' man, a 'simple, humble believer,' to 'stand fast and continue in the faith,' surrounded by such a babel of opinions? The only way he can do so is by resolutely shutting his eyes and stopping his ears, determined neither to hear nor see any thing likely to produce a single doubt; he must be guided entirely by the advice of interested priests, who 'affectionately' caution against 'unbelief,' and then threaten 'that he that

---

* Dionysius, Bishop of Alexandria, Erasmus, Calvin, and Zuinglius also doubted the genuineness of Revelation.

believeth not shall be damned;' and this threat is, with thousands, an extinguisher to investigation; it is the most convincing orthodox argument.

"Now, with respect to the books included in the present canon of the Old Testament, there is no satisfactory evidence to prove when, or where, or by whom they were written, or in what language. On the contrary, there is abundant proof to show, that such of those books as bear the name of certain authors were never written by such persons. The book of Genesis, and other books of the Pentateuch, are plainly the production of two or more persons. Genesis contains two conflicting accounts of the creation. The story of the deluge is twice told; the relation as to how Abraham passed off Sarah as his sister is repeated with discrepancies; and the circumstance which also obliged Isaac to call his wife Rebecca his sister, in order to escape from the lust of Abimelech—evidently the same monarch who, by one of the accounts, had been years previously smitten with the beauty of Isaac's mother—are all related in the same book, manifestly confused accounts of the same legend.

"There are also two conflicting reasons given for the institution of the Sabbath, and *two* distinct codes of the ten commandments.

"Several matters recorded in the Pentateuch are nearly exact fac-similes of the mysteries of the Babylonians. The creation in six days is a perfect copy of the Gahans of Zoroaster; the particulars of each day's work are also the same. The story of the serpent and the fall was long known among that people. The mythological deluge of Ogyges is just the same as Noah's flood, and the story of Adam and Eve in paradise is a mere copy of Zoroaster's first pair. The Talmud expressly declares that the Jews borrowed the names of the angels, and even their months from the Babylonians.*

"It is a great mistake to believe that the Bible is the oldest book; at the very time we are told that all the inhabitants of the world, except Noah and his family, were drowned, the Hindoos existed as a great nation, and Egypt and China had their learned men—their philosophers, their architects, their astronomers, and historians; and their vast cities, burdened with an overflowing population.

"So palpable, indeed, are these facts, that eminent Christian writers have declared their disbelief in the authorship of such a person as Moses. St. Jerome confesses that he 'dares not' affirm that Moses wrote the Pentateuch, but, like the Talmudists, he ascribes it to Ezra, (Esdras.) Sir Isaac Newton affirms, that it was neither Moses nor Ezra who wrote the five books, but Samuel. Lord Barrington asserts the same. The Rev W. Fox, in his sermons, published in 1819, remarks, 'That the early part of Genesis is a compilation of ancient documents, and *not the writing of Moses* has been the opinion of some of the most able divines and sincere believers.' The distinguished Christian pro-

fessor Du Pin is positive that 'we are not certainly assured of the true authors of most of the books of the Old Testament.' These are only a few of the authorities who openly disbelieve in the authorship of Moses. Almost every book of the Bible has been in turn doubted and defended; and while Jewish rites can be traced to a more ancient heathenism, nearly every thing of Christianity is of Egyptian origin.

"It would," continued Mr. Mannors, "be a difficult task to give, within the limits of a single lecture, any lengthened review of the other books of the Old Testament. We shall merely say, that several of them are mostly occupied with trifling details of silly observances, by no means edifying. Kings and Chronicles contradict each other in almost every chapter; while other books are but such accounts of atrocity, debauchery, and gross indecency as to make humanity shudder and sh ck all delicacy and refinement. Any other book but that called the 'Holy Bible,' c ntaining such abominable records, would be stamped forever as infamous. Yet, wonder of wonders! though a great number of these 'inspired texts,' are too impure to be read or quoted from pulpit or desk, or even breathed to 'ears polite,' Christian priests will still uphold the imposition, and positively tell us that *every word* was written for our improvement! Who can truly believe this?

"But then we are vauntingly pointed to scriptural miracles and prophecies as a glorious refutation of the slanders of unbelief. In boasting of such evidences, Christianity but follows the practice of far more ancient superstitions. Religious imposture in every age fortified itself with magic and miracles to overcome doubt and opposition; and with prophecies which were as clearly and often more intelligibly fulfilled than any that the Bible can yet claim. Prophets have been a prolific race, the raving and incoherent dreamers and enthusiasts of ancient and modern times. Does not even the Bible admit that some of its prophets were false and lying, and drunken men, who 'divined for money,' and were jealous, of each other's success; who became as often 'inspired' through the influence of wine, or music, or dancing as they did by the insane idea which governed their feeble minds? Micah, 3d chapter, speaks of prophets who 'divined for money,' but modestly speaks of himself as being 'full of power,' Jeremiah in second chapter, 14th of Lamentations, says, 'Thy prophets have seen vain and foolish things.' Isaiah, in chapters 9th and 28th, that they 'teach lies' and are 'drunken.' These passages do not particularly refer to foreign or heathen wanderers, but to the recognized 'fortune-tellers' of the time. (Jeremiah 20: 7.) As a prophet, he complains, 'O Lord! thou hast deceived me, and I was deceived:' and in the 14th chapter of Ezekiel, 7th verse, God himself is made to say, And if the prophet be deceived when he hath spoken a thing, '*I the Lord have deceived that prophet.*' Comment on such prophets and on such a deity would occupy too much of our time at present. While we have but just shown that many of the leading Chris-

* See "Age of Reason," p. 13.

tian priests had no confidence in the asserted prophecies of Isaiah, Daniel, and Jonah, we find that others of them, such as Dr. Keith and Bishop Newton, have waded through a vast mass of useless learning, to try and establish the fulfillment of certain prophecies ; yet it is now fairly proved that the greater number of such predictions have failed. It has also been placed beyond doubt that many of the so-called prophecies were written *after* the event happened to which they related ; while others have been singularly falsified.

"But what of the famous prophecy regarding the coming of the Messiah? We reply that no part of Scripture has been more unfairly twisted to accommodate the desire of priests than that which it is said relates to such an event. We can now only notice the principal prediction in Isaiah, which some tell us is beyond all cavil:

"The kings of Israel and Syria, having united in a war against the king of Judah, the latter was much alarmed, but the prophet Isaiah assured him that they should not succeed against him. The Lord told the king to 'ask a sign,' but the king declined, stating that he would not 'tempt the Lord.' Isaiah then said:

"'Therefore the Lord himself shall give you a sign : Behold, a virgin shall conceive and bear a son, and shall call his name Immanuel ; for before the child shall know how to refuse the evil and choose the good, the land that thou abhorrest shall be forsaken of both her kings.' Isaiah 7 : 14-16.

"This, then, was the sign promised to assure the king of Judah of his ultimate success over the two who had conspired against him ; and, in order to secure the fulfillment of this 'prophecy,' we are told in the very next chapter, 2d verse, that Isaiah himself got a prophetess with child, and that she afterward bare a son. This is an abridgment of the absurd story, and had no more reference to Jesus, who is said to have appeared several hundred years afterward, than it had to Cæsar or Peter the Great.

"The assurance of success which Isaiah gave to the king of Judah proved, however, that Isaiah himself was one of the 'lying' prophets ; for, in the 2d book of Chronicles, chapter 28, it is recorded that, instead of the two hostile kings being overwhelmed, Ahaz was completely defeated ; the usual godly slaughter of one hundred and twenty thousand of his people having taken place in one day, followed by the captivity of two hundred thousand women, with their sons and daughters: so much for the infallibility of Isaiah.

"Several enlightened Christians are inclined to abandon this once favorite prophecy as untenable. Michaelis, the learned Christian professor, p. 212, says, he 'can not be persuaded that the famous prophecy in Isaiah, chapter 7, verse 14, has the least reference to the Messiah.' The church has been sorely troubled to get rid of the difficulties arising from the alleged prophecies relating to Christ. Whiston, the successor of Sir Isaac Newton as mathematical professor, published a book to prove that in early times the Jews had altered the passages of the Old Testament referred to as prophetic of Christ. If such were really the case, the Old Testament could not

be relied on in any particular. Whiston's theory was, however, much approved of, until an actual comparison with the ancient Jewish Scriptures proved them to be alike in their predictions. Dr. Arnold tried to avoid the prophetic difficulty by saying, 'We find throughout the New Testament references made to various passages in the Old Testament which are alleged as prophetic of Christ, or of some particulars of the Christian dispensation. Now, if we turn to the context of these passages, and so endeavor to discover their meaning according to the only sound principles of interpretation, it will often appear that they do not relate to the Messiah or to Christian times, but are either expressions of religious affections generally ; or else refer to some particular circumstances in the life and condition of the writer or of the Jewish nation, and do not at all show that any thing more remote, or any events of a more universal and spiritual character, were designed to be prophesied. Every prophecy, as uttered by man, (that is, by an intelligent and not a mere mechanical instrument,) and at the same time as inspired by God, must, as far as appears, have a double sense—one, the sense entertained by the human mind of the writer ; the other, the sense infused into it by God. We may even suppose the prophet to be totally ignorant of the divine meaning of his words, and to intend to express a meaning of his own, quite unlike God's meaning.' This reasoning of the learned and pious Dr. Arnold in favor of a 'double sense' to prophecy, and to assume that prophets did not know the meaning of their own words, is very like taking leave of common sense altogether. The doctor further says, 'Generally the language of prophecy will be found to be hyperbolical, as far as regards its historical subjects, and only corresponding with the truth exactly *if we substitute for the historical subject the idea of which it is the representative.* It will be found, I think, a general rule in all the prophecies of Scripture, that they contain expressions which will only be adequately fulfilled in their last and *spiritual* fulfillment ; and that as applied to the lower fulfillments, which precede this, they are and must be hyperbolical.'

"Upon this, Greg remarks, 'It is difficult to grapple with a mode of interpretation such as this ; equally difficult to comprehend how an earnest and practical understanding like Dr. Arnold's could, for a moment, rest satisfied with such a cloudy phantom. Our homely conceptions can make nothing of an oracle which says one thing but means something very different and more noble ; which, in denouncing *with minute details* destruction against Egypt, Babylon, and Tyre, merely threatens final defeat to the powers of evil ; which, in depicting, in precisest terms, the material prosperity reserved for the Israelites, only intended to promise blessings to the virtuous and devout of every age and clime ; and which, in describing ancient historical personages, did so always with an *arrière pensée* toward Christ. If Dr. Arnold means to say that the Old Testament prophecies signified primarily, chiefly, and most specifically the ultimate triumph of good over evil—of God and virtue over the world, the flesh, and the devil, (and this certainly *appears* to be his meaning)—we can only reply that, in that case, they are poetry and not prediction. To conceive, therefore, this to be the meaning of the God who is alleged to have inspired them is to imagine that he used incompetent and deceptive instruments for his communications; and it is certain that, had the prophecies been perfectly and unquestionably fulfilled in their obvious sense, the secondary and recondite signification would never have been heard of.'

"The double meaning which Christian priests have advocated for Bible prophecies is just what they have so often condemned in the pagan oracles—it was a way of escape for the sibyl or prophet. In endeavoring to make the so-called prophecies applicable, some of the greatest minds have become puerile and prostrated. Some have boldly asserted that the prophecies are ' plain and explicit;' but Sir Isaac Newton, who was a believer, states that ' God gave these, (revelations,) and the prophecies of the Old Testament not to satisfy men's curiosity by enabling them to foreknow things, but that, after they were fulfilled, they might be interpreted by " the event." ' Hittel says, ' Sir Isaac thus admits that the biblical prophecies furnish no evidence of the truth of the Scriptures or of the Messiahship of Jesus ; for a prophecy which does not enable men to foreknow things, but which is to be interpreted by " the event" is a pitiful affair, in no way superior to the predictions "of the heathen oracles.' "

" In his discourse, page 31, Bishop Sherlock says, ' That many of the latter prophecies are still *dark and obscure*, and so far from evidently belonging to Christ and Christ only that it requires much learning and sagacity to show, *even* now, the connection between some prophecies and the events.'

" The Jews, who should best understand their own book, have ever denied the application of the prophecy to Jesus. They charge the Christians, in order to accomplish their purposes, with having ' changed in the original nouns, verbs, tenses, and meanings.' In a work called *Israel Vindicated* they say, ' These prophecies have repeatedly been shown by our rabbins to have a different meaning from that given them by the Christians, which it is impossible for any one to mistake whose mind is not predisposed to shut out the light of truth.'

" That the Jewish imputation against Christian priests, of having ' changed in the original nouns, verbs, tenses, and meanings,' was not undeserved or unjust, we shall show from the words of the great commentator, Doctor Adam Clarke. Speaking of the quotations usually made from the Old Testament, he says, that many of them ' are accommodated' to the New Testament story, ' their own historical meaning being different, may be innocently credited; but let it always be remembered that these accommodations are made by the same spirit by which the Psalms were originally given. Many passages of the Old Testament seem to be thus quoted (as predictions) in the New. And *often* the words a little *altered* and the meaning *extended*, to make them suitable to existing circumstances.' If

this is not a palpable evidence of pious fraud, we wonder where a plainer one can be found. Words actually ' altered' and their meaning ' extended '! The doctor, ' innocently ' however, places the burden on the ' spirit ;' that is the spirit which first directed the prophet to say, *while* should afterward influence the transcriber or translator to say *black!*

We can not in the present discourse refer any further to the prophecies ; another opportunity may be offered for that purpose. It has been said that prophecy is ' prose run mad,' and it is plain that its study has greatly distracted the reasoning powers of some devout thinkers. What erratic fulfillments have learned priests extracted from the prophetic word! The Pope, and Luther, and Napoleon have each in turn been made to stand godfather to the wild creations of Daniel : and lesser lights, such as John Hawkins, Esq., prove that Britain is the kingdom which, according to Daniel, God will set up! Captain Maitland illustrates Daniel by Revelation! J. H. Frere proves that Daniel, Esdras, and St. John found their accomplishment in Bonaparte! and the exking of Sweden asserts that Bonaparte is the beast of Revelation ! Dr. Whiston, professor of mathematics at Cambridge, of whom we have spoken, believed that the bringing forth of rabbits by one' Mary Tofts, according to the then popular delusion, was the accomplishment of a prophecy in Esdras! and among many others at the present day, we have a Cumming, or a Bagster, who, in silly lectures or in prosy pamphlets, opens the ' seven vials,' or wrestle with ' the beast with seven heads,' or with the ' red dragon,' or marches with triumphant pace to the great battle of Armageddon ; we all know that these tedious expositions, so far, have been about as lucid as that of a certain Irish legislator, who, while in a supposed state of derangement, insisted that Armageddon really meant Armagh, ' because in the apocalyptic version something is incidentally said about *fine linen*.' It truly seems that one is about as near the mark as the other. We shall finish our present remarks on prophecy by a brief quotation from that greatly traduced, but noble and benevolent man, Thomas Paine.

" ' According to the *modern* meaning of the word prophet, and prophesying, it signifies foretelling events to a great distance of time ; and it became necessary to the inventors of the Gospel to give it this latitude of meaning, in order to apply or to stretch what they call the prophecies of the Old Testament to the times of the New ; but, according to the Old Testament, the prophesying of the seer, and afterward of the prophet, so far as the meaning of the word seer was incorporated into that of prophet, had reference only to things of the time then passing, or very closely connected with it ; such as the event of a battle they were going to engage in, or of a journey, or of any enterprise they were going to undertake, or of any circumstance then pending, or of any difficulty they were then in ; all of which had immediate reference to themselves, (as in the case already mentioned of Ahaz and Isaiah, with respect to the expression, *Behold a virgin shall conceive, and bear a son*,) and not to any distant future time. It was that kind of prophesying that corresponds to what we call fortune-telling; such as casting nativities, predicting riches, fortunate or unfortunate marriages, conjuring for lost goods, etc.! and it is the fraud of the *Christian* church, not that of the *Jews*; and the ignorance and the superstition of *modern*, not that of *ancient* times, that elevated those poetical, musical, conjuring, dreaming, strolling gentry into the rank they have since had.

"Those who have leisure will find priestly speculations on prophecy a very amusing study.

CHAPTER XXII.

"THE New Testament is said to contain the last written revelation from God to man. It now includes but twenty-seven separate tracts, called books. Formerly, as was stated, there were a great many more, over fifty different *gospels* having been received at one period; but as it seems that various degrees of inspiration were imparted to certain contending councils, who undertook to make a selection, the books considered necessary for man's salvation were, as we have shown, very prudently reduced to the present number.

"Among the principal books of the New Testament are the four gospels, said to have been written by the persons whose names they bear; but for this, there is no evidence whatever, neither can it be shown when, or where, or at what time they were written; there is not an original manuscript of any of them in existence, nor can it be proved that any such were seen during the first century;* and it is a remarkable fact that Christ himself, the real hero of the New Testament, never wrote a line of it; all we have of his reputed acts or sayings is mere hearsay. These gospels, however, profess to give a true history of the birth, life, and death of the Christian Saviour; and so much has been said as to their entire harmony, as synoptical records, that one is amazed in discovering how widely they differ where it is presumed they ought to be in perfect agreement.

"Matthew commences by giving the genealogy of Christ from David up through Joseph, the husband of Mary, and makes *twenty-six* generations; Luke also gives a genealogy from Christ through Joseph down to David, the same progenitor, but records *forty-three* generations, through a different line of ancestry. Now, if Matthew was right, Luke must have been wrong; and as equal inspiration has been claimed for both, if one is wrong, both may be wrong.

"The *annunciation* is not mentioned in the gospels ascribed to Mark and John, but is differently related in Matthew and Luke. The former says, that the angel appeared to *Joseph*, the latter that it was to *Mary!*

"Matthew alone mentions any thing concerning the destruction of the children by Herod; upon this important matter, the other Gospels are singularly silent; no historian of the day makes the slightest allusion to such a circum-

stance; neither does Josephus (and he would not have spared Herod) say a word about such a cruel act. There is no proof that such a slaughter by Herod ever took place, and the story has been pronounced apocryphal. An atrocity of this kind would have caused a great sensation, and would have been noticed by historians. Sir William Jones, in his *Christian Theism*, page 84, gives reason for believing that the whole story is probably of Hindoo origin,* and Greg says, 'Luke's account entirely precludes the sojourn in Egypt.' He says that *eight* days after the birth of Jesus he was circumcised, and *forty* days afterward he was presented in the temple, and that when these legal ceremonies were accomplished, he went with his parents to Nazareth.' There is a strange discrepancy between Matthew and Luke as to where Joseph and Mary originally lived. Luke says they lived at Nazareth *before* the birth of Jesus, Matthew declares they did not reside there until *after* that event.

"Matthew, in particular, has been noted for a tendency to 'accommodate,' or find in Jesus the fulfillment of supposed prophecies; and to 'alter' and 'extend' words and meanings for that purpose. To effect this, he has narrated circumstances respecting which the other evangelists remain silent. His repeated expressions, 'That it might be fulfilled,' 'For it is written,' and others of a similar kind, were used to adduce passages which had no possible reference or application to Jesus, but merely to show the dogmatic purpose of the writer; and we have already shown that eminent Christian men do not accept such application.

"At the birth of Christ, Matthew tells us (chapter 2) that *wise men* came from the East to worship him, and were directed by a *star*; Luke states (chapter 2) that they were but *shepherds* from a field, led by an *angel!*

"Matthew (chapter 8, verse 5) informs us that a centurion came *personally* to Jesus, and begged him to heal a servant; Luke (chapter 7) says that the centurion did not *go* himself, but sent '*elders of the Jews*' to request the favor!

"Matthew's frequent amplification, or rather multiplication, is quite apparent. In chapter eight, he gives an account of the healing of *two* furious demoniacs whose unclean spirits entered a herd of swine; but Mark and Luke

---

* The oldest we now have are of the fifth century.

* Many centuries before the birth of Christ, the Hindoo scriptures contained the following legend connected with the Incarnation of Chrishna, the favorite god or "saviour" of India:

Chrishna, a god-begotten child, was the son of Vishnu, the principal god of the Hindoo Trinity, by a woman named Devaki, the wife of Vasudeva. Shortly before the birth of Chrishna, a mighty demon called Kansa, being apprised that a child would be born that was forever to overthrow his power, summoned his chief, Asuras, and ordered: "Let active search be made for whatever young children there may be upon the earth, and let every boy of unusual vigor be slain without remorse."

The sacred child, Chrishna, was, however, saved by Nanda, a cowherd, whose wife had a child of the same age called Rama, or Bala Rama, and spoken of as the brother of Carishna.

This very ancient legend was, it is said, derived by the Hindoos from a tradition still more remote, and is, no doubt, one of those upon which is most certainly founded the myth of Herod's slaughter of the innocents.

say there was only *one* demoniac. This story, however, is one of the most wretched scriptural absurdities, and has cast a leaven of doubt into the mind of many a believer.

"In the twentieth chapter of Matthew, there is the repetition of a miracle related in the ninth chapter, giving sight to *two* blind men near Jericho; but Mark (10th) and Luke (18th) mention the cure of only *one* blind man, and only on *one* occasion.

"Matthew and Mark give *two* variable accounts of the feeding of the multitude; while Luke and John tell of but *one* feeding. Matthew (chapter 14) says there were about *five* thousand men, besides women and children, and only ' *five* loaves and two fishes,' and that after all had been fed, *twelve* basketfuls remained. In the next chapter, he repeats the miracle—*four* thousand men, 'besides women and children,' were then fed; there were '*seven* loaves and a few little fishes,' and *seven* basketsful remained. Neither Mark nor Luke say there were any 'women and children;' and many commentators believe that there was but *one* feeding of a multitude.

"According to Matthew, Mark, and Luke, Jesus, 'immediately' after his baptism in the Jordan, 'was led (or driven) by the spirit into the wilderness,' where he remained *forty* days 'tempted of the devil.' This is truly one of the most improbable stories in the New Testament; even John the evangelist must have disbelieved it, for his gospel altogether excludes such a conference. John, in his first and second chapters, gives a positive contradiction to the narrative. He states that on the first day *after* the baptism, Jesus remained with John, (the baptist;) that he conversed on the second day with Peter; that he attended the marriage of Cana on the third day; after that, he went to Capernaum, and afterward to the pass over at Jerusalem; leaving it therefore impossible for Jesus to have been at all in the wilderness, even for a single day!

"At the baptism of Christ, John 'bare record' of him, and 'saw the spirit like a dove descend upon him,' heard the recognition of his sonship in a voice from heaven, 'and, looking upon Jesus as he walked, he (John) saith, Behold the lamb of God!' Yet, strange to say, shortly afterward—Matthew, chapter 11, Luke, chapter 7—the very same John, when in prison, 'sent disciples' to Jesus to learn whether he was the true Messiah! 'Art thou he that should come, or look we for another?' Much priestly ingenuity has been used to shield John the Baptist from inferred obliviousness, but the record is too plain.

"We must overlook numerous other discrepancies—we shall not have time to examine them on this occasion—and we will only refer at present to those relating to the crucifixion, and to subsequent events recorded by the apostles.

"When Christ was brought to execution, Matthew says, 'They gave him vinegar to drink, mingled with gall;' Mark says, 'Wine, mingled with myrrh!'

"Matthew affirms that the *two* thieves who were crucified with Christ reviled him at the time; Luke writes that but *one* 'malefactor'

did so, and was rebuked by the other for so doing!

"The four evangelists differ as to the exact words of the superscription on the cross.

"The discrepancies respecting *Judas* are remarkable. According to Matthew, (27th chapter) Judas *repeated*, *returned* the thirty pieces of silver, and then *hung* himself; and that the *priests* took the money and *bought* the potter's field with it.

"Acts 1 : 18 implies that Judas did *not* repent, that he did not return the money, that he was *not hung*; but states that *he* 'purchased a field with the reward of iniquity, and falling headlong, he burst asunder in the midst, and all his bowels gushed out!'

"Matthew relates that extraordinary occurrences took place immediately after the death of Christ. 'The vail of the temple was rent in twain, the earth did quake, the rocks rent, graves were opened, bodies of the saints which slept arose and came out of the graves *after his resurrection*, and went into the holy city, and appeared unto many.' What a fearful time, and what dreadful appearances! All quite public! Yet Matthew alone makes such a record. No other writer of the New Testament makes any allusion to such an earthquake or opening of graves.

"The account is very confused. Verse 52 of the 27th chapter leads us to believe, that the dead arose and appeared on the very day of the crucifixion, but the next verse says, that they came out of their graves '*after* the resurrection.' These statements are admitted to be irreconcilable. Greg says, 'There can, we think, remain little doubt in unprepossessed minds that the whole legend was one of those intended to magnify and honor Christ, which were current in great numbers at the time when Matthew wrote, and which he, with the usual want of discrimination and somewhat omnivorous tendency which distinguished him as a compiler, admitted into his gospel.' [*]

"When Christ was put into the sepulchre, Matthew states that the Pharisees applied to Pilate for a guard to be placed over it, to prevent the body being stolen; and that a watch was therefore set and the sepulchre sealed. Yet none of the other gospels say any thing of such an application, or of any watch or guard, or of the sealing of the sepulchre, or of the earthquake. According to their accounts, there were none of these things.

"After the resurrection, Matthew says that Jesus *first* appeared to Mary Magdalene and the other Mary, on their way from the sepulchre, who '*held him by the feet*, and worshipped him.' He next met the eleven disciples, by appointment, upon a *mountain* in Galilee.

---

* Similar prodigies were said or supposed to accompany the deaths of many great men in former days, (long before Christ,) as in the case of Cæsar. (Virgil, Georg. 1, 463. *et seq.*) Shakespeare has embalmed some traditions of the kind, exactly analogous to the present case. See *Julius Cæsar*, act ii., scene 2. Again he says, *Hamlet*, act i. scene 1:

"In the most high and palmy state of Rome,
A little ere the mightiest Julius fell,
The graves stood tenantless, and the sheeted dead
Did squeak and gibber in the Roman streets."

Greg, p. 188.

"According to Mark, 'He appeared first to Mary Magdalene;' next, 'in another form, to two of them;' 'afterward to the eleven as they sat at meat!'

"By Luke, first, 'toward evening' as he sat at meat with *two* at a village 'called Emmaus, which was from Jerusalem *about* three-score furlongs.' Next, he appeared in the midst 'of them' at Jerusalem, where he ate 'broiled fish and honey-comb.' After this, he led them out as far as Bethany, and, having blessed them, 'was parted from them and carried up into heaven.'

"According to John, he first appeared at the sepulchre to Mary Magdalene, whom he *forbid* to *touch* him; afterward, on the evening of the same day, at Jerusalem, in the midst of his disciples, in a closed apartment, the doors being shut; eight days afterward, in the same place, when Thomas was present, who *was permitted to touch him;* and again, for the last time, to his disciples, at the Sea of Tiberias.

"The startling descrepancies in these accounts as to when, where, by whom, and how often Jesus was seen after his death should, one might think, entirely disqualify them from being received as evidence. Those who will take the trouble to read the passages in full from the Testament will discover the utmost confusion as to time, place, and circumstance; we shall just look at two or three of them. One account says that Mary Magdalene and the other Mary *held Jesus by the feet;* another, that he would *not* permit himself to be touched by her, because he had 'not yet ascended to his Father'! And yet another account certifies, that he allowed Thomas to *touch* and examine his *hands, feet, and side!*

"One account states that Christ first met his disciples, after the resurrection, upon a mountain in Galilee; other accounts state that he met them at meat, in a closed room, at Jerusalem! One account leads to the certain inference that he took final leave of his disciples at Bethany, and ascended to heaven the very day of his resurrection; another states that he remained and *ate and drank* with his disciples for several days after his resurrection; and Acts 1 states that he ascended from Mount Olivet! It would be impossible to compile more glaring contradictions.

"The several accounts of the conversion of Paul are at variance; and, had we time, we could furnish a list of palpable discrepancies and contradictions, such clashing, repugnant, incompatible, and inconsistent histories, statements, and doctrines, all given as 'inspired truth,' that we venture to say no other book yet printed can exceed the Bible in this particular in the same number of pages.

"Even after all the inspiration said to have been given, and after all the great care taken to make the present selection of biblical books perfect, yet many chapters, parts of chapters, and verses have been declared spurious! In the New Testament, the first and second chapters of Matthew; the first and second of Luke; the last twelve verses of the sixteenth chapter of Mark; besides certain verses, here and there, in gospels, acts, and epistles. In this scientific, enlightened, and inquiring age,

there can be no greater fraud than to continue to assert that such an incongruous mass as that contained in the Christian Bible is a reflection of the divine mind or a revelation from a Supreme Being to man.

"The doctrines of the Bible are *not original.* Many nations of antiquity had similar religious creeds and ceremonies, long before the alleged time of Moses. The wonderful resemblance between the religious doctrines and ceremonies of the Jews and Egyptians have led believers in the Bible with peculiar assumption to assert that the Egyptians were but mere copyists from Moses; but at the time when it is said that Abraham entered Egypt, the few score Jews that then existed were rude, wandering shepherds; dwellers in tents, ignorant and unskilled. Then, at that very period, Egypt was a proud, ancient kingdom, with a dense agricultural population; it had its learned and scientific men; it had houses, and palaces, and temples, and of many of these the rich and significant ruins still remain. Those who have investigated the antiquities of that country assert these facts. Kendrick, in his *Ancient Egypt*, says, 'It is a remarkable fact that the first glimpse we obtain of the history and manners of the Egyptians shows us a nation already far advanced in all the arts of civilized life; and the same customs and inventions that prevailed in the Augustan age of the people, after the accession of the eighteenth dynasty, are found in the remote age of Osirtasen, the cotemporary of Joseph, nor can there be any doubt that they were in the same civilized state when Abraham visited the country.'

"We shall look at the similarity of a few of the ceremonies. The Egyptians had an ark, boat, or shrine carried in procession by the priests; the Mosaic ark was born by the Levites. Gods of the ancients were said to travel, and were provided with such an ark for conveyance; the Jews had an ark of the covenant, into which their god occasionally entered. Speaking of the ark of the covenant as being but a model of the Egyptian shrine, Kendrick says, 'The mixed figures of the cherubim, which were placed at either end and overshadowed it with their wings, has a parallel in some of the Egyptian representations, in which kneeling figures spread their wings over the shrine.' Kitto, in his *Biblical Cyclopedia*, furnishes indirect evidence as to which was the more ancient religion; in order to illustrate what cherubim were, he gives engravings of Egyptian sphinxes! Who will assert that Judaism is older than such Egyptian sculptures?

"Hittel states that 'The religious ceremonies of the Hebrews bore a remarkable resemblance to those of the Egyptians. The Jews considered Jerusalem a holy city, and attributed great religious merit to pilgrimages thither. In the valley of the Nile, there were holy places also. The great temple of Artemis, at Bubastis, was visited by 700,000 pilgrims annually, if we can believe the report of Herodotus, who visited Egypt while the ancient superstition was still in full favor with the people.'

"The Egyptians offered sacrifices of vegetables and animals to the gods, and so did the Jews. The Jewish and Egyptian priests slew the sacrificial animals in the same manner, by cutting the throat. The Egyptians preferred red oxen without spot for sacrifice, and Moses directed the selection of a red heifer. (Num. 19 : 2.) The custom of the scape-goat (Lev. 16 : 21) was common to both nations. A sacred fire was kept continually burning in the temple of Thebes as well as in India. (Lev. 6 : 12, 13.) Egyptian priests took off their shoes in the temples, and Joshua took off his shoes in a holy place. (Josh. 5 : 15.) The Egyptian priests danced before their altars, and the same custom prevailed in Jerusalem. (Ps. 149 : 3.) The practice of circumcision, claimed by Moses as a divine ordinance communicated to Abraham, is proved by the monuments of Egypt to have been fully established there at a time long antecedent to the alleged date of Abraham. Herodotus wrote that in his time ' the Phœnicians and the Syrians say they learned it (circumcision) from the Egyptians.' The Egyptians had their unclean meats, including pork, as well as the Jews. The Egyptians anointed their kings and priests long before there were any kings or priests in Israel. The Urim and Thummim, (Ex. 39 : 8, 10 ; Lev. 8 : 8,) which play a stupid part in the books of Moses and Joe Smith, were once not inappropriate figures of Re, the god of light, and Themi, the goddess of justice, (whence the Greek *Themis*,) worn on the breasts of Egyptian judges.

" The Jews reverenced the name of Jehovah precisely as the Egyptians did the sacred name of Osiris. It is even known that Herodotus, after having been at Memphis, when writing about that divinity, would not use his name.

" Certain writers in favor of the Jews have had the temerity to assert that the idea of *one* supreme God originated with them. The Rev. Robert Taylor, in his *Diegesis*, says, ' The notion of one Supreme Being was universal. No calumny could be more egregious than that which charges the pagan world with ever having lost sight of that notion, or compromised or surrendered its paramount importance in all the varieties and modifications of pagan piety. This predominant notion (admits Mosheim) showed itself, even through the darkness of the grossest idolatry.' *

" That the worship of Egyptian, Jew, and Pagan was in many respects very absurd, few are now inclined to doubt ; but the Egyptian was more speculative and philosophical. Much has been said concerning their worship of the onion. The Rev. Robert Taylor says, ' The respect he (the Egyptian) paid to it referred to a high and mystical order of astronomical speculations, and was purely emblematical. The onion presented to the eye of the Egyptian visionary the most curious type in nature of the disposition and arrangement of the great solar system.' This learned author, in his *Diegesis* proves, we think to a certainty, that the Jews' plagiarized

the religious legends ' and ceremonies of other nations, particularly from the Egyptians, and that their ancient and mystical theology forms the grand basis of the Jewish patch-work of rites and ceremonies, so often mistaken for the original creed, and so lauded as the 'divine porch to the temple of the New (Testament) by the clerical autocrats of Exeter Hall.*

" But what of Christianity ? Was not that something original ? Was not the idea of a God-begotten child, ' of a celestial Saviour, entirely new ? Surely, there was something in this ' wonderful plan,' of which man had no previous conception. Let us see. It was a common idea in ancient times to fancy that great men or great heroes were descended from the gods. Jesus Christ had prototypes in Æsculapius, Hercules, Adonis, Apollo, Prometheus, (who it is said was crucified,) Chrishnu, and many others. Of Æsculapius, the Rev. Robert Taylor says, (*Diegesis* p. 149.) 'The worship of Æsculapius was first established in Egypt, the fruitful parent of all varieties of superstition. He is well known as the god of the art of healing, and his Egyptian or Phœnician origin leads us irresistibly to associate his name and character with that of the ancient Therapeuts, or society of healers, established in the vicinity of Alexandria, whose sacred writings Eusebius has ventured to acknowledge were the first types of our four gospels. The miracles of healing and raising the dead, recorded in those Scriptures, are exactly such as there superstitious quacks would be likely to ascribe to the founder of their fraternity.

" ' By the mother's side, Æsculapius was the son of Coronis, who had received the embraces of God, but for whom, unfortunately, the worshipers of her son have forgotten to claim the honor of perpetual virginity. To conceal her pregnancy from her parents, she went to Epidaurus, and was there delivered of a son, whom she exposed upon the Mount of Myrtles ; when Aristhenes, the goat-herd, in search of a goat and a dog missing from his fold, discovered the child, whom he would have carried to his home had he not, in approaching to lift him up, perceived his head encircled with fiery rays, which made him believe the child to be divine. The voice of fame soon published the birth of a miraculous infant ; upon which the people flocked from all quarters to behold this heaven-born child.

" ' The principal result, however, of this resemblance is the evidence it affords that the terms or epithets of ' our Saviour'—*the Saviour being God*, were the usual designations of the god Æsculapius ; and that miracles of healing and resurrection from the dead were the evidence of his divinity for ages before similar pretenses were advanced for Jesus of Nazareth.'

" Middleton, in his *Free Inquiry*, says : ' Strabo informs us that the temples of Æsculapius were constantly filled with the sick, imploring the help of GOD ; and that they

---

* All the inferior deities in Homer are represented as then addressing the supreme JOVE—

" O first and greatest God ! by gods adored,
We own thy power, our Father and our Lord."
　　　　　　　　　　　　　　　　　　　　　Iliad.

* The religious ceremonies of the Egyptians and Jews were so similar, that the Roman law, in the time of the emperors, to prohibit the worship of Isis in the capitol, spoke of the Jewish worship as though it were not distinguishable from that of the Egyptians.— *Millet.*

had tables * hanging around them in which all the miraculous cures were described. There is a remarkable fragment of one of these tables still extant, and exhibited by Gruter in his collection, as it was found in the ruins of Æsculapius' temple in the island of the Tyber in Rome; which gives an account of two blind men restored to sight by Æsculapius in the open view and with the loud acclamations of the people, acknowledging the manifest power of the god.' It was said that Æsculapius not only cured the sick, but raised the dead; and that Jupiter, having become fearful or jealous of his power, 'slew him with a thunderbolt.'†

"We shall pass over the others, to call your attention to the remarkable coincidence there is between the history of Christ and that of Prometheus. The name corresponds with that given to the Christian deity, *Providence.* Prometheus, it was asserted, was both god and man. His character and attributes are depicted in the beautiful tragedy of Æschylus, *Prometheus Bound,* written over five hundred years before the Christian era, the plot being then taken from 'materials of an infinitely remote antiquity.' Prometheus was, it is said, crucified at Mount Caucasus, as an atonement for others. At his crucifixion, there was great darkness and a terrible storm; rocks were rent, graves were opened, and all left him except a few faithful women! The story will be found more detailed in the *Diegesis* of the Reverend Robert Taylor; or, had we the *lost* 'gospel to the Egyptians,' it might shed some light upon that great forerunner of the Jewish Logos.‡ In connection with this, we might mention that the *cross* is of pagan origin. Taylor says, (*Diegesis,* p. 201,) 'It should never be forgotten that the *sign of the cross,* for ages anterior to the Augustan era, was in common use among the Gentiles. It was the most sacred symbol of Egyptian idolatry. It is on most of the Egyptian obelisks, and was believed to possess all the devil-expelling virtues which have since been ascribed to it by Christians. The monogram, or symbol of the god Saturn, was the sign of the cross, together with a ram's horn. Jupiter also bore a cross with a horn, Venus a cross with a circle. The famous *Crux Ansata* is to be seen in all the buildings of Egypt; and the most celebrated temples of the idol of Chrishna in India, like our Gothic cathedrals, were built in the form of crosses.'

* Tablets.
† Ovid, who wrote before the time of Christ, gave in his *Metamorphoses,* second book, this prediction concerning the life and actions of Æsculapius, the great physician:

"Once as the sacred infant she surveyed,
The god was kindled in the raving maid,
And thus she uttered her prophetic tale:
Hail, great physician of the world! all hail!
Hail, mighty infant! who in years to come
Shall heal the nations and defraud the tomb.
Swift be thy growth, thy triumphs unconfined,
Make kingdoms thicker, and increase mankind;
Thy during art shall animate the dead,
And draw the thunder on thy guilty head;
Then thou shalt die, but from the dark abode
Shalt rise victorious and be twice a god."
Addison's versification.

‡ See Potter's translation of Æschylus.

"'On a Phœnician medal found in the ruins of Citium, and engraved in Dr. Clarke's Travels, and proved by him to be Phœnician, are inscribed not only the cross, but the rosary or string of beads attached to it.' The cross was also found in the ancient temple of Serapis. A pious writer, Mr. Skelton, says, 'How it came to pass that the Egyptians, Arabians, and Indians, *before* Christ came among us, paid a remarkable veneration to the sign of the cross is to me unknown; but the fact itself is known.'

"Another very marked resemblance is to be found between Sakya Muni, the Buddhist saviour, and Christ. Hittel says, 'The life of this saviour, Sakya Muni, bears much similarity to that of Jesus. He was an incarnate god, and was born of a married virgin of royal blood. He spent six years in the wilderness as a hermit, and, having been purified by penance, he went to the populous districts of Hindoostan, and to the sacred city of Benares, where he preached the gospel of Buddhism, wrought miracles, and made numerous converts. Sakya did not commit his doctrine to writing; his disciples composed numerous sacred books, containing records of his life and teachings.'

"Huc, in his book *Journey through the Chinese Empire,* chapter fifth, states, 'If we addressed a Mongol or Thibetan this question, "Who is Buddha?" he instantly replied, "The saviour of men." The marvelous birth of Buddha, his life and instructions, contain a great number of moral truths and dogmas professed in Christianity.' And yet these 'moral truths' were disseminated ages before Christ.

"Father Booris, a Catholic missionary to the Buddhists of Cochin China, in the sixteenth century, was astonished to discover rites and ceremonies among that people similar to those of his own church; and upon this he wrote, 'There is not a dress, office, or ceremony in the Church of Rome to which the devil has not here provided some counterpart.' And Murray, in his *History of Discoveries in Asia,* alluding to Father Booris, says, 'Even when he began inveighing against the idols, he was told that these were the images of departed great men, whom they worshiped exactly on the same principle and in the same manner as the Catholics did the images of the apostles and martyrs.' In fact, while Christianity has been called a 'revamp of Buddhism,' 'the Buddhism of the West,' Milman and Remusat speak of Buddhism as 'the Christianity of the East.'

"Were we not limited for time, we could give you numerous other coincidences, and also prove that many sayings attributed to the Christian Saviour were maxims uttered centuries before his birth. The most noted plagiarism of this kind is that of the golden rule of Confucius, whose 24th maxim runs thus: 'Do to another what you would he should do unto you; and do not unto another what you would not should be done unto you. Then only needest this law alone; it is the foundation and principle of all the rest!'

"We find that there are three principal characters in the Christian Bible: the 'Almighty,' or spirit of good ; 'Satan,' the spirit of evil ; and the person known as the 'Redeemer.' There is no account given us of the creation of Satan or of the numerous angels, good and bad, which are said to exist. We are told that this desperately wicked being and his adherents were once denizens of heaven itself, and, consequently, must have been pure and 'holy.' Satan is now known as the wicked and designing one, 'going about seeking whom he may devour.' The Divine Being is said to have created all things, and to have pronounced them 'very good.' How, then, came he to create such a fiend as the 'devil,' and permit him to have such perfect freedom, even to thwart Heaven's designs, and with sufficient influence to counteract the 'atonement' and successfully urge frail humanity down to 'eternal ruin'?

"Bible worshipers tell us that that book is plain and easily understood ; that it is the pure, unadulterated 'word of God.' Yet, upon examination, it is found false in its history and science, gross and impure in its morality, and full of absurdities, contradictions, and anachronisms. Priests, with lengthy and learned commentaries, then endeavor to explain. When they find a palpable error, they say, 'It must be a mistake ;' when a glaring discrepancy is discovered, then they find an 'interpolation.' Show them a plain contradiction, they will make it a 'false translation ;' point them to grossly indecent passages, they are 'figurative.' Question them about absurdities of doctrines, they will call them 'mysteries.' Tell them of the violence and inhumanity of God's chosen rulers and people, and they will find you a ready excuse. They will find a plea for indecency, treachery, and blood ; and were the Bible stamped on every page, as it is in many chapters, with assertions contradictory to science, reason, and common sense, the plea will be, 'it is because they are above our finite comprehension !' And the unmerciful, revengeful deity of the Jews —'the assassin of humanity'—will be represented as a God of compassion, 'full of pity and loving-kindness, whose mercy endureth forever !'

"To submit to the teachings of the Christian Bible, you must believe that there is a Supreme Being, pure, just, loving, and merciful : that he is at the same time partial, wrathful, and unforgiving. That he created all things and pronounced them good, and afterward repented having made them because they were evil. That man was created pure, and holy, and in the likeness of the deity ; and, that afterward, without being permitted to know good from evil, he 'fell,' and became sinful and wicked at the very *first* temptation. That Adam and his posterity were condemned and cursed for the offense of his ignorance ; but that in the course of time a deity came down from heaven, assumed human form, and died, 'the just for the unjust,' to satisfy the 'justice' of a loving Creator. That the deity who suffered, called the *Son*, was just as old as his father. That there is but *one* God, and that there are *three* Gods. That, notwithstanding the power of omnipotence, there is a devil having freedom to go about 'like a roaring

lion, seeking whom he may devour,' doing, with a certain impunity, all the harm he can. That God, desirous of revealing his will to man, did so, through the agency of men whom he inspired for that purpose, many of whom were grossly wicked characters. That a God of pity, whose mercy endureth forever, in anger drowned the world in a great flood, and burnt Sodom and Gomorrah. That he chose, in preference to all others, a wretched and barbarous race, the Jews, to whom he was especially favorable ; that he assisted them to conquer, rob, murder, and utterly destroy other nations ; and that yet 'there is no respect of persons with God.' That God, sometimes alone and sometimes in company of attendants, visited men, talked with them, and ate and drank in their presence ; and yet that 'no man hath seen God at *any time.*' That David, a robber and murderer, was a man 'after God's own heart ;' that Solomon, proud and licentious, was a 'wise' man. That God made the sun and moon stand still, in order that a greater number of 'his enemies' should be slaughtered. That Elijah, in a chariot of fire, drawn by horses of fire, went up *alive* to heaven 'in a whirlwind ;' and yet that 'no man hath ascended to heaven but he that came down from heaven.' That a witch raised and conversed with the dead Samuel. That Nebuchadnezzar 'ate grass like an ox.' That Balaam's ass spake. That a whale devoured Jonah, and that he was afterward cast up alive and unharmed. That Lazarus, dead and in a presumed state of decay, was brought to life. That a herd of swine became possessed of devils. That there is a hell where a 'merciful' Creator will torture 'the condemned' with 'fire and brimstone' forever, and that his 'redeemed saints' shall look upon such atrocious cruelty with satisfaction and approval.

"This, then, is the revelation about which interested priests and those they can 'convert' keep up such an excitement ; they tell us, with professional effrontery, that it is a 'free gospel,' while we all know that Christianity is the most costly of all religions, exorbitant and unceasing in its demands. During the last fifty years, the British and American Bible Societies boast that they have circulated '80,000,000 of copies of the word of God among the *heathen*.' Who can truly prove that in so doing they have served the cause of humanity ? In Britain, we have four million sermons annually to explain conflicting doctrines, and a crowd of jarring sects to retard human progress and perpetuate strife. It is said that at the birth of Christ the temple of Janus was closed ; there was then universal peace ; but since that period, the Gospel has been 'a sword' upon the earth and religion a greater woe to mankind !"

CHAPTER XXIII.

THERE was a great shadow moving toward Hampstead Cottage—a shadow that was destined to rest there, and lie bleak and cold upon the hearts of some of its inmates forever !

The darling of the household had a few days previously taken a severe cold, and inflammatory symptoms had increased. The delicate boy was very low; and as he lay restless and feverish in his sick chamber, his sister and Hannah were indefatigable in their gentle attentions. The attack was rather sudden; and though Mrs. Mannors felt quite alarmed at first, she "poured out her soul in prayer," and recovered her equanimity. She had now no fear; she would have no physician, but was willing to leave results in the hand of God; she was assured he would not take her child from her. Each day she would repeatedly look in upon her afflicted son, and would pray a short time at his bedside, and then move about from room to room humming pious tunes, and muttering to herself encouraging texts and promises made to the faithful; and after listening to expressions of anxiety from Hannah, she would reproach her for want of faith, and even hint that she was falling from her high estate; and then she would go on humming again, in a state of the most cheerful resignation.

Her disposition in this respect was unusually strange. Since the meeting at Exeter Hall, she had attended revival or protracted meetings at Mr. Baker's church, and for over a month past her absent manner had been noticed, and she would say, that, while "dwelling upon the promises," her soul seemed to leave its earthly tenement and wander toward Calvary; and that she was becoming more and more indifferent to the things of earth, almost weaned from every tie—husband, children, home. This condition she insisted was the best evidence of her entire devotion to Christ. Formerly, the least mishap to William touched her maternal feelings to the quick; and if it were of a serious nature, she would become almost distracted; but now, when Mary wept in secret over the sufferings of her brother, when even Hannah could scarcely find consolation from John Bunyan, Mrs. Mannors was perfectly calm and confident; her matured faith came to her rescue from despondency in the hour of trial.

The stillness around the whole place was very great. Outside, the sunbeams seemed, as it were, to steal down timidly upon the ivy, among the trembling leaves, and upon the cages at the door, inducing slumber instead of awakening the sprightly melody of the little prisoners. The flowers appeared to signal sad tidings to each other, and then mournfully bend down their pretty innocent heads; and the soft, sad wind came along in whispers, as if cautioning you not to speak above a breath. Flounce missed his companion, and even when resting upon the smooth garden walk, his silken head between his fore-paws, would look up whiningly toward the curtained window where William first greeted him each morning; and people as they passed, heard neither laugh nor song, and wondered at the unusual quietness. Within the house, there was almost a perfect hush; the ticking of the clock alone could be heard in the lower rooms; while the quick, heavy breathing of the patient, and the sigh of his loving, sympathizing sister were distinctly audible in the upper apartments; and no sound was allowed to disturb any momentary slumber that might weigh down the weary lids of the poor sufferer. Mr. Mannors felt the affliction very keenly; the doctor had but just left without having given any great encouragement, and the owner of Hampstead Cottage now sat alone in his quiet study, thinking painfully of the brooding trouble that seemed to approach like the first great cloud over the sunshine of his life; the first entry of sadness into his pleasant home. Though very anxious, he was, however, still hopeful, and trusted that, with proper treatment and attention, William might be again restored. But this was not his only care; he was a keen observer, and had noticed the gradual indifference shown by Mrs. Mannors, not only toward himself, but to every one in the house; she did not seem to realize the danger of her child. Even Hannah felt that her mistress was getting, as she said, "like another person," seldom speaking to her about household matters, and still more seldom on religious subjects; all was most unaccountable. She saw her mistress go about alone, and heard her pray alone; often saw her sit an hour or longer at a time in the garden or summer-house, apparently thinking, or brooding upon some dark, mysterious subject, yet seemed to take no more pleasure in communicating her thoughts to her; this to poor Hannah was a sore deprivation, the reason of which she could not fathom. Notwithstanding all this, Mrs. Mannors was more devoted than ever to her religious duties. Night after night she would attend "meeting," and would keep by herself upon her return; she seemed indeed to forget that she had ever communed with Hannah about future blessedness.

This conduct astonished Mr. Mannors very much, and now, as he sat thinking, he experienced an unusual depression of spirits; visitors could not be received. Mr. Capel had been away for several days, and might not return very soon, as he knew nothing of William's illness; there was no friend near to sympathize; the house seemed desolate, and as he turned his eyes toward the garden, every thing was as gloomy as his own thoughts. Never before had he felt so dejected; but, after pacing the room for a few minutes, he again sat down, determined to meet every trouble like a brave man—neither to cower in adversity, nor despond in misfortune. "These trials," said he, "are incident to human life; no matter how severe, I shall try and meet them in a becoming manner, and act my part to the best of my ability."

It was getting toward evening, all was yet still, and Mr. Mannors, having taken but little rest for several nights past, dozed in his study; he sat in his cushioned chair, with his arm under his head, resting upon his desk, and his short slumber brought consolation as well as refreshment—it gave him a pleasant dream, a dream of William's restoration; and in that mirage of the desert, sleep, he saw William and Mary sit again among the sun-lit hills, and watched the clear stream sparkling and running at their feet. He was suddenly awakened by a slight noise in the adjoining room; he looked up, and Mrs. Mannors stood before him. There was a wildness in the expression of her face, and she held out a Bible at arm's length, and her other hand was raised in a threatening manner. He was a little startled, and, without replying to his inquiry about William, his wife, in slow and solemn voice read from the book of Job, "How oft is the candle of the wicked put out! and how oft cometh their destruction upon them! God distributeth sorrows in his anger. They are as stubble before the wind, and as chaff that the storm carrieth away. God layeth up his iniquity for his children; he rewardeth him, and he shall know it. His eyes shall see destruction, and he shall drink of the wrath of the Almighty."

"Emma, Emma," said Mr. Mannors quickly rising, "what does this mean?"

But she heeded not; as he approached her, she stepped back, and again read, "This is the portion of a wicked man with God, and the heritage of oppressors which they shall receive of the Almighty. If his children be multiplied, it is for the sword, and his offspring shall not be satisfied with bread. Those that remain of him shall be buried in death, and his widows shall not weep."

"O Emma! why do you read this? Do sit down," said he tenderly, and he tried to lay his hand upon her upraised arm. Again she retreated; a frown settled upon her troubled face, and, looking sternly at him, repeated this verse from the fourth chapter of Hosea, "Seeing thou hast forgotten the law of thy God, I will also forget thy children." So saying, she flung the Bible with great force at his feet, and turned to leave the room. He seized her arm, and begged of her to be seated, to be calm, and talk to him in her accustomed manner. "Talk to you," said she, turning upon him with a scowl; "talk to you! Have I not spoken to you, and entreated you for years without avail? Talk to you! My God! Have you not rejected the promises and threatenings of the Gospel, and despised God's sanctuary and his ministers? Have you not lived without God and without hope in the world? and," said she, lowering her voice, "you will die in despair; and your blood—yes, your blood—be upon your head, be upon your own head."

She again tried to get free, but the strong arm of her husband held her in the chair. "Let me speak to you, Emma," said Mr. Mannors, getting alarmed. "Let me speak to you. What is the matter? why do you speak to me in this way?"

"Unbeliever, be gone! We have been unequally yoked! Oh! how I have sinned by remaining here so long! What if God has withdrawn his Spirit, has withdrawn his Spirit eternally, eternally? I must flee from this city of destruction—I must, I must!"

Hannah, hearing the unusual exclamations, just then rushed into the room, and saw her mistress in an excited state, struggling to get away. The poor girl was dreadfully alarmed, and tried to soothe her the best way she could. It was of no use; Mrs. Mannors only reproached her again, and told her that she was in league with the evil one and giving encouragement to an unfaithful man. "Yes," cried she, now standing out on the floor and stamping with her foot, "Unfaithful, unfaithful to me and to the God who made him! I will abide among ye no longer."

Mr. Mannors, pale and calm, looked with pity upon the woman for whom he would readily have laid down his life; he seemed to realize at once the dreadful woe that had fallen upon her—a woe almost as dreadful to him, who understood its nature. Fearing that any alarm might, at this critical time, have a fatal effect upon his child, he whispered to Hannah, who now almost bewildered, stood weeping, and trembling, and pleading before her mistress, and left the room to enter the sick chamber.

Just as he was about to step upon the stairs, a pale-faced young man, with an extravagant shirt collar, a person whom he had seen somewhere before, and who might have been standing or waiting at the door some time unheard, handed him a letter; it was from his Solicitors, Vizard & Coke, Gray's Inn; and as Mr. Mannors hurried up to the sick-room, the young man lingered a moment or two, and with sinister expression leered into the parlor where Hannah and Mrs. Mannors were yet standing, and then, when he was walking away, he muttered, "Unfaithful! unfaithful! What! such a paragon as Martin Mannors lacking virtue!"

About seven o'clock that evening, many persons were seen moving toward Mr. Baker's church, at Hampstead; a great revival was in progress, and for several successive nights a motley crowd of saints and sinners had been collected, and it was said, as it always is said, that a great deal of good had been done; "the Lord was making bare his arm," that sinners were "struck down on the right hand and upon the left," and that "many precious souls" were now able to sing and rejoice, having obtained "the blessing," and been fully restored to divine favor. In about an hour's time, the church was crowded; those who were "under conviction," mostly women, occupied seats and pews nearest the pulpit; while it was manifest that those who selected the back seats, or loitered around the doorways, belonged to the "unregenerate," of whom there were still a sufficient number to excite the sympathy and start the spiritual activity of the most skilled and energetic gospel workmen. Two preachers occupied the pulpit, and two others, supernumeraries, sat within the railing which enclosed it and the communion-table, ready at the proper time to perform their parts toward the spiritual renovation of such sinners as might be brought within their reach. Indeed, it was plain to be seen that they need not remain idle for want of material; for, by the looks, and gestures, and whispers of a large number of the congregation, there were many who appeared to attend but for mere pastime, or more probably to enjoy a scene peculiar to revivals.

The Rev. James Baker now stood up in the pulpit, and, having looked around with a kind of clerical scrutiny at the congregation, said, "Let us begin the worship of God by singing to his praise the hymn to be found on page

27, common metre ;" and then, with slow and doleful voice, read out one of Wesley's hymns of six verses, commencing,

"Terrible thought! shall I alone,
Who may be saved, shall I,
Of all, alas! whom I have known,
Through sin, forever die ?

"While all my old companions dear,
With whom I once did live,
Joyful at God's right hand appear,
A blessing to receive.

"Shall I amid a ghastly band,
Dragged to the judgment-seat
Far on the left with horror stand,
My fearful doom to meet ?"

During the time occupied in reading the hymn, several other persons entered the church, and every seat was crowded. Having finished, he read again, and gave out the first two lines of the first verse ; the choir, who were in the gallery, commenced to sing the hymn to the tune of "Mear ;" an organ led, and as the player fancied that the occasion required its most thundering tones, so he performed, and the air rushed through the stentorian pipes nearly loud enough to drown all the principal voices ; it would be next to impossible to combine the clipt words or mutilated lines in any intelligible form. During this particular part of "divine service," most of the congregation turned from the preacher in the pulpit, and almost one and all gazed up at the harmonious assemblage in the gallery. A person might think that the dreary music was to them the most important and attractive part of religious duty, and that they came specially to hear a pious song instead of a long sermon ; several, however, who stood in front, nearest the railing, "raised their voices in praise" and joined in the singing with particular fervor.

At the conclusion of the hymn, the preacher began his prayer in a low and tremulous voice at first ; then with more spirit ; then the words came faster and louder ; yet louder still ; then loud, long, and vociferous—his hands being extended in front, and sometimes waving over his head—while every word seemed to fall like a shaft from a thunder-cloud among the trembling sinners of the congregation. The preacher strained his voice to the very utmost, until at last he became hoarse, croaky, and incoherent ; he rather gasped than shouted, and when he could scarcely articulate any longer, he suddenly descended from the *fortissimo*, and panting from the terrible efforts he had made, closed the prayer in his natural voice.

The appeal itself was as exciting as the manner of him who was interceding ; he depicted the state of the lost sinner ; the wrath of God and the terrors of the damned ; and at irregular intervals, during the continuance of his invocation, cries and groans could be heard from those around him. Some would clap their hands in ecstasy ; some raise them in despair. Some would cry out suddenly, "Bless the Lord, bless the Lord !" "Lord, save, or I perish !" "Son of David, have mercy upon me !" "I am lost, forever lost !" "O God !" "O Lord !" till at one time it seemed as if each one of the whole congregation was shouting in a different key, in a different tongue, to a different God—a bedlam let loose—plunging the timid in apprehension, and forcing alarm upon the weak-minded, while many nervous persons were affected by the most painful emotions. Another hymn was then sung in a minor strain, and at its close it was evident that the feelings of most present were in a sufficiently plastic state, ready to receive any impression.

Mr. Baker's pulpit-companion then stood before the people ; he was an older man, mild-looking, and less robust ; his lank, gray hair hung down behind, covering his coat-collar, and in front it was parted in the centre. He waited with lugubrious aspect until all were settled in their seats ; until every rustle and cough had subsided ; then, drawing a long sigh, he gave out as his text, the three last verses of the third chapter of Lamentations, "Render unto them a recompense, O Lord! according to the work of their hands. Give them sorrow of heart, thy curse unto them. Persecute and destroy them in anger from under the heavens of the Lord."

The sermon which followed—though not a fair illustration of the text—was a terrible picture of the woe which would surely result from "wickedness and unbelief ;" these words he repeated several times, as being synonymous. The wicked man might grow up and prosper for a while, and might consider the wretched enjoyments of this world as only worth living for ; who could see no sin in their delusive attractions, or, if he did, would put off repentance ; who was willing to procrastinate, in order to dally a little longer with the vanities of life. Such a one might perhaps find himself suddenly cut off, cursed by God, and bewailing his misery in the lowest depths, in company with scoffers and unbelievers. It was "a terrible thing to fall into the hands of the living God." To secure heaven, every idol should be struck down. No sacrifice should be considered too great to insure eternal happiness. The treasures of the heart, friends, home, children, were unworthy to be permitted to stand in the way, and, if necessary, these—even these—should be forgotten for the "Friend of sinners."

During the discourse, the preacher at times became most excited ; his voice was loud, and his gesticulation often wild and rapid, stamping, thumping the desk, or clapping his hands. He used a battery of threatening texts, and a profusion of sounding words, to depict God's anger ; and after he had drawn a lively picture of eternal torments, he lowered his voice, and cautioned, beseeched, entreated, yea, commanded, his terror-stricken hearers to "flee from the wrath to come," to accept "God's plan of salvation" ere it be forever too late. Alas! they might now hear the voice of pleading—the voice of God's minister for the last time ; and it might be that ere the rise of another sun, some now present might stand terror-stricken at the bar of an offended God. But, he said, there was still hope, another opportunity yet offered ; they were as yet, thank God, out of hell—here he raised his voice again, and thumped the pulpit ; and lowering it to a hush, said, "The

Mediator is still pleading ; *now*, yes, *now*, is the accepted time, and by presenting yourselves this night before the mercy-seat, God, even our God, may be yet gracious."

When the discourse was ended, there was a feeling of relief ; some began to breathe more freely, but many others were deplorably cast down. The preachers left the pulpit and joined their brethren below. An invitation was then given to all those who felt a desire " to flee from the wrath to come" to approach, and openly present themselves before the Lord, in order that the people of God might unite with them in prayer for their deliverance.

"Come, friends, come!" said one of the preachers, rubbing his hands in a business-like way, "come to the Lord ; he is waiting to be gracious—yes, poor sinner, he is waiting for *you*! We shall now sing a few verses, and, as we do so, let every one who thirsts draw nigh."

When he was speaking, a great many did go forward and kneel at the railing ; four out of every six of the "penitents" were women, a majority of whom were young ; there were also several young men. Others remained in their pews, as if to await a more direct and pressing invitation from the preachers, who were sure to move about among the congregation, and urge repentance upon such as might be found to be most easily entreated.

The old Wesleyan hymn,

> "Come, ye sinners, poor and needy,
> Weak and wounded, sick and sore,"

was now sung out briskly by preachers, penitents, and by all around the "anxious-seats ;" the choir in the gallery took no part. After a couple of verses were finished, prayer again followed ; one, very loud and special, was offered up in behalf of those "under conviction :" sighs, and groans, and mutterings could be heard in every direction ; and from those who came to mock, an occasional titter would follow the uncouth or extravagant manifestation of feeling by some more impressible penitent than ordinary. Presently, every one who could pray began ; the grave, the lively, the fearful, the terrified, the hopeful and the exulting, all were heard addressing the "throne of grace" together, in the most irregular and disorderly manner ; and high above all, in *alto*, resounded the prayer of one local preacher, whose powerful voice and still more powerful lungs were equal to such an emergency.

Near one poor sinner, who was shouting wildly for mercy, there sat another on the floor in the lowest state of despondency ; and then a pious brother or sister would stoop down and whisper, "Pray on, sister, pray on. God is willing to be gracious ; do not give up." And very often this peculiar process of conversion would force a shout for mercy, or a shriek of despair from many who almost thought themselves forever lost. Meantime, during the holy uproar, one or two preachers and a few of the converted and experienced members of the church went slowly about from pew to pew, now pleading with one, now entreating another, "to turn to the Lord ;" now making a fraternal inquiry as to the state of a sister's soul, or whispering a word

of encouragement to a brother struggling under his heavy burden of sin. Mrs. Baker and other matured female members were also engaged in the same way—tendering pious consolation.

At intervals, as some penitent professed to have found "peace," exclamations would follow from many—"Praise the Lord!" "Bless the Lord!" "Glory, glory!" "Hallelujah!" "Amen!" and others, under the impulse of the moment, would cry out and clap hands as if to signal the triumph. Then all would rise and sing again.

Mr. Baker, having passed from one to another in the mean time, now addressed a plain working-man, who appeared to be looking on with the greatest indifference ; he stood, his hands in his pockets, leaning leisurely against one of the pillars supporting the gallery, quite unmoved by the excitement ; evidently one of the many who regard this peculiar method of spiritual renovation as a delusion.

"Brother," said Mr. Baker, gently laying his hand on the man's shoulder, "how is the Lord dealing with your soul ? do you feel that you have no interest in— "

"See here," cried the man abruptly, "I want none of your gammon—no, I don't. Go on and make fools and idiots of them before you ; they are fools, but the knaves that make them what they are should suffer—ay, they should."

Mr. Baker started back as if stung by a scorpion ; he looked sharply at the man's face in the dim light ; it was a face not altogether strange ; he began to feel angry, and for a moment scrutinized every feature.

"Yes, look at me," said the man, with the same imperturbable coolness ; "if you don't know me, I know you—yes, I do ; and you'd know me better if I could put such chaps as you in the common Bridewell for what you've been doing ; you would know me then, you would."

"How dare you come here and speak to me this way in the house of the Lord ?" said Mr. Baker, getting very much irritated.

"House of the Lord ! house of the dev— !"

"Wretch !" cried Mr. Baker, without giving the man time to finish the last syllable of a profane word. "Did you come here to pollute the sanctuary, and interrupt divine service ? I shall have you arrested."

"To pollute the sanctuary," said the man, repeating the words scornfully ; "better call it a mad-house—that's what it is. Do you call *that* divine service ?" said he, pointing to the fearful religious confusion before him. "Do you call them poor creatures as ones havin' their common senses ? and do you call that poor raving lady yonder—as is walking up and down afore ye all—do you call her converted ?"

"Ah !" said Mr. Baker, "I know who you are now. Did you come here to scoff, at your master's bidding ?"

"I came, but it was not to listen to your stuff ; I came, at his bidding, to see after that poor lady ; you ought to be proud of your work—you ought. But the law is on your side ; only for that, yes—only for that. Well, if you were a man as had human nature in you, you'd have her away from here long ago ; but you're not," said Robert, now getting excited, "you're like the rest of your tribe; there's nothing good only what *you* have. You should be made to pay for your deviltry—you should."

Robert never flinched an inch as he gave his opinion so freely. His resolute manner somewhat cowed Mr. Baker, who now, as if struck by what had been said, or by some fancied eccentricity in Mrs. Mannors—upon whom he had steadfastly looked since Robert had pointed toward her—went quickly away without making any reply, and whispered to his wife, who was still busy among the penitents.

"Ay, you may go now," said Robert, in a kind of growling under-tone, as the preacher walked up hurriedly between the pews. "You may go, but you're too late. Your prayers will never more do her any good—never. She's not the first that's been here to save her soul and lose her reason—not the first."

At this time, and since the close of the sermon, Mrs. Mannors had been walking alone, backward and forward, in a passage behind the pulpit leading to a "class-room" or kind of vestry. Her bonnet was off, and her unbound hair fell upon her shoulders. She would occasionally stop and look at the confused scene before her with a frightened or bewildered gaze; or pause to listen for a moment to the tumult of dismal sounds, and then suddenly dart back, as if terrified at something she had heard. Her lips moved continually, and at times she would heave a deep sigh, and in a low melancholy voice would utter, "I am lost, I am lost; O God! save me."

It was noticed that the first few evenings of her attendance at the revival she went amongst the penitents and prayed with them, as did Mrs. Baker and other members of her "class;" she was rather more demonstrative than usual; then all at once became demure and reserved, and for the past night or two kept mostly by herself, doing nothing very particular to attract attention; indeed, if she had, the revival excitement being at its height would prevent even a very extravagant act from being observed; for where nearly all seemed for the time to abandon ordinary decorum, one perhaps more singularly afflicted than Mrs. Mannors might not be suspected.

Mrs. Baker, followed by her husband, went toward the passage where Mrs. Mannors was walking. They stopped at a little distance to watch her movements, and see whether they could be justified in assuming that her mind was impaired. The scrutiny must have satisfied them; a look of deep meaning passed from one to the other, and though they stood closer to her than at first, she paced on moodily as before, without raising her eyes from the floor or changing the sad expression of her face. It was pitiful to see this wreck; and the preacher, anxious to attract her attention and speak to her, now stood right in her way—the passage itself was rather gloomy—and when she suddenly came upon his dark figure, she started back in alarm, raised her hands, gave a wild cry, and fell trembling on the floor.

Mrs. Baker and one or two sisters raised the demented woman, and led her into the room back of the church. The cry, though piercing, did not seem to disconcert the revivalists for any time—it was taken to be one of the ordinary effects of that spiritual despair which is said to precede the assurance of heavenly reconciliation; and while fruitless efforts and prayers were made in the vestry to win back reason, and dispel the frightful apparitions of a frenzied brain, every means was used in the church to bring others to the dangerous verge of despondency; and the continued sighs, and groans, and shouts of alarmed sinners in the sanctuary, given to appease an "angry God," could now be heard in that closed room, like the wailing of a distant tempest, the rush of waves, and the doleful death-cry of struggling, drowning men.

CHAPTER XXIV.

It was late that night before Mrs. Mannors could be induced to leave the class-room. She had stealthily made her escape from her own house in the evening, and dreaded to return to her home. It was, she said, the "city of destruction," and she fancied she had committed the unpardonable sin by remaining there so long. She never spoke of her children, and was silent when their names were mentioned. She seemed to think that Hannah and her husband were but specious fiends, endeavoring to lure her on to perdition: her insanity was undoubted, and she could no longer be allowed to go about unattended, particularly as William yet continued in a very critical state. Mrs. Baker and another pious friend, however, remained with her until the next day, and, as she grew no better, it was deemed advisable to have her removed for a time; and Mr. Mannors consented that she should be taken to Mrs. Baker's residence; he felt satisfied that she would receive every attention, and that, in the mean time, it would be a friendly asylum.

Mr. Capel returned the day afterward, much to the satisfaction of all in Hampstead Cottage: he was astonished at the suddenness of the calamity that had fallen upon his friend, and no one could be more assiduous in endeavoring to mitigate the severe trials to which he was subjected. Mary, from watching day and night at the bedside of her brother, was sadly changed; and poor Hannah's eyes were red with weeping, as well for the woe which had fallen upon her mistress as on account of the disease which she believed was slowly but surely wearing out the young life of one to whom she was so much attached.

How lonely the whole place appeared; there was but little difference between noon and midnight. Ominous looking clouds came along, and streamed down upon the house as they passed away; and the trees around sighed audibly as if an October wind—a premature blast—were about to rob them of their foliage. The long hours of the day as well as of the night sped slowly by, as if they were willing to slacken pace and add a few moments longer to the lingering, limited existence of the young sufferer. Alas! thought Mr. Capel, as he sat alone in the once pleasant parlor, what a shadow is human life—how evanescent! It is but as yesterday since one, apparently happy and sound in mind, welcomed me like a mother to this place, told me of her dreams, and visions, and hopes, and of the bright future in the distance; now that mind is a blank, every pleasant and maternal recollection is blotted out, and she may go down to the grave without any dawning of reason. It seems but an hour since the gentle laugh of him who was her pride—but now in the clutches of death—was heard like music among the flowers, a laugh that came so oft with the sunlight, but which may never be heard again.

What a cloud, dark and unpropitious, settled already over this once happy home! misfortunes had come there together; and even now many of the pious were free to remark that it was a judgment—"just what might have been expected from unbelief!" But then it was one more calamitous to the believing wife than to the unbelieving husband; if the trial was sore to him, his reason was not withered, he was not doomed to be the living sepulchre for a "dead soul." O orthodoxy! how uncharitable are thy impulses!

The patience and manly fortitude of Mr. Mannors surprised Mr. Capel. He could see that his friend was cut to the quick, yet bore all most heroically. Now tenderly moistening the parched lip, or cooling the fevered brow of his prostrate child; now whispering hope and encouragement to his daughter, even when hope could scarcely find a resting-place in his own heart; and then trying to cheer up Hannah, whose generous nature was almost overcome. Her mental resources were insufficient under the stroke; the oft luminous pages of Bunyan were now dark and depressing. Mr. Mannors went about quietly, doing every thing in his power to heal the wounds of others, when it was but too apparent that the dart had entered deeply into his own bosom; and, though forced to taste of the bitter cup that fate had presented, yet, with great consideration for the feelings of Hannah, and of some religious friends who called from time to time, he never alluded to the particular cause of his wife's affliction, and never uttered a reproachful word.

Mr. Capel, however, was satisfied that that affliction did not arise from any latent disorder of the mind, or from any inherited tendency to aberration; it was the effect of unnatural religious excitement upon a too sensitive organization, inducing a faith in dreams and visions, and gradually producing some pleasing hallucination that lingered and was nourished, and became a reality, and which then shaped itself into a monster, a usurper, which overpowered reason and reigned supreme in mental devastation. It has been the fate of ten thousand others. Alas! what intellects have been crushed and ruined beneath the gilded car of a pompous and imperious superstition. How many enthusiasts have been broken under the ponderous wheel of the Christian Juggernaut; and the useless and maddening pageant still moves on, amid the groans of victims and the hosannahs of priests.

The unwearied Hannah still watched by the side of William; his sister, who was much fatigued, tried to snatch a little rest in dozing upon a sofa near by, and he had lain comparatively quiet for some minutes listening to the heavy rain which now pattered against the window-panes.

"Hannah," said he, in a very faint voice, "why doesn't ma come here? I want her now to tell me of the bright angels she used to dream so often about, I want her now to let me see them; she often told me how beautiful they were, and that I should know them, and they know me; I wish I could see them to-day—yes, to-day."

Hannah leant over his pillow to catch every word; she was painfully struck with the change in his manner and appearance, and her heart beat quickly with foreboding pulsations.

"Your ma is tired, darling, and is resting, like Miss Mary. She will soon be here, I hope; but she is tired now, very tired."

"Poor ma!—tired and asleep. I am tired too—very tired and weary—and must soon sleep. I would like to have her come soon and kiss me, and tell me about the angels again; for I am tired, and may sleep a long, long time."

She listened to his failing voice, and made no reply; she could not then speak, but one of her big tears fell upon his pale cheek.

By an effort, he raised his little thin hand, and let it rest upon her dark hair; he looked at her for a moment, and then said, "Poor, poor Hannah!"

"O my darling child! O my darling child! I've prayed for you, but now I wish my heart would break," she sobbed in a low voice. These were the only words to which she could give utterance, as the tears coursed down her cheeks; and she pressed the small hand to her lips as if she never intended to let it go again.

He looked intently at her for some time in silence, a look such as one of her blest ideals might have given to sorrowing humanity, and she in turn tried to restrain her tears and seem cheerful.

"Why do you cry, poor Hannah?—don't cry for me! you know we must all sleep. Ma often told us that we should all sleep, and awake again at the resurrection—what is the resurrection?"

"The resurrection, dear," said she, after some hesitation, "is when we get up to go to heaven, after we die."

"Up from where—from sleep?"

"Up from our graves! we shall all get up at the last day."

"From our graves—from our graves," he repeated the words slowly, and then pondered over their solemn meaning.

"Will every body get up to go to heaven?"

"I hope so, dear," said she, trying to evade a direct answer; "Oh! how I wish it was to-morrow! all to be together again."

He remained for a time in deep thought, during which he watched the wearied face of her who was now to him as a mother, and then said to her in a whisper, "Tell ma to come soon—very soon, I shall sleep to-night ; but I must sleep again to-morrow, yes, to-morrow. Hannah, stay near me until then, and I will come back at the resurrection."

There was a deep silence after this prophetic warning, and Hannah had to leave the room to stifle the terrible grief which tried to find utterance.

She soon heard his feeble voice again, and when she bent down low to catch his words, he whispered :

"Won't you bring me Flounce ? I must see poor Flounce to-day. Do, do let me see him again."

Presently the affectionate animal followed Hannah into the darkened room ; his head hung down, as if he anticipated a last leave-taking. A chair was drawn close to the bed ; he sat upon it, and, suppressing every joyful demonstration, looked mournfully into the large eyes of his young master, gently licking the hand that was now slowly extended toward him. The dog's subdued manner touched the tender feelings of the boy ; he would have wept, but the fountain of his tears was forever sealed.

Flounce left the room with reluctance, and after his removal he lay the remainder of the day outside in the wet grass, under the rain in the lonely garden, looking up at the curtained window of William's room and whining piteously.

It was the evening of the next day ; the sun was setting in glorious effulgence. A great white cloud, like a mountain of light, was moving slowly onward toward the east ; the red and golden beams which now rested upon it made it appear as if it were the throne of a divinity ; and to the imagination it might have been made the foundation for any sublime aerial structure. The robin's lone farewell-notes were heard in the garden ; but all else was still, not more still, however, than the living and dying who looked through the open window upon the beautiful mellow light of eve slowly fading away in the western sky.

At William's request, his bed was moved so that he could look out through the window and take his last view of earth ; and as his wan face was turned toward the sunset, the rays that fell around it only served to show more plainly the death-shadows that were already creeping in and resting upon his features — shadows that no morning light would ever more dispel. Hannah looked awe-struck ; it seemed then to her as if the very portals of heaven were opened to receive the pure spirit of a departing pilgrim. But Mary, pale and worn, could not turn her head away from her brother ; now burying her face in his pillow, now pressing her lips upon his cold forehead that was already damp with the dew of death ; she saw the flickering of the little lamp, and would watch until it was blown out forever.

Mr. Capel and Mr. Mannors stood silently by ; to one it was an hour of the darkest trial, and the heavy bursting sighs of that father's breast could alone truly tell how the deep fountain of his affection was overflowing ; and

Mr. Capel's eyes were suffused, as if he were waiting by the side of a dying brother ; it was a death-scene which should never leave his memory.

"Pop," said the dying boy, raising his feeble voice, and looking eagerly upward at the magnificent sun-lit cloud. "Pop, that is the summerland, and ma is there ; oh ! I see her among such a crowd of angels ! She is now beckoning to me — see, Hannah, ma is waiting ! how beautiful she looks ! but I'm getting very cold ; won't you sing again for me, Hannah ? I am sleepy—I must soon sleep—sing for me now."

Poor Hannah struggled to comply with his last request to her, and, while all were silently weeping, she sung in a low, broken voice a verse from one of his mother's favorite hymns—

"Lift up your eyes of faith and see
  Saints and angels joined in one ;
What a countless company
  Stand before you dazzling throne !"

When she had sung thus far, he made an attempt to raise himself from the pillow, but his head fell back powerless ; it was a last effort of his tender nature to offer all an embrace ; he could but just whisper, "Kiss me, pa ; kiss me, Hannah ; kiss me, Pop ; I am getting very tired, and must now sleep ; but I will come back again with ma at the resurrection—good night !"

The evening sun just then disappeared ; the great cloud stood alone in the ruddy sky, and William closed his eyes in that last sleep, and went off to the real or fancied summerland.

Days, dreary days, had passed since the fresh mound was raised in Hampstead churchyard, and fresh flowers had been almost daily scattered upon the little grave by a sister's hand. In the quiet evenings, when Hannah felt lonely, she would go and sit by the head-stone in the cemetery and watch the western sky, as if expecting some recognition from him who had departed ; but no signal appeared ; no token ever came ; no voice from across the lone sea ever reached her ear ; no secret was revealed ; but the future to her, as well as to many others still kept its own solemn mystery.

CHAPTER XXV.

ONE month after the sad scene witnessed by Mr. Capel in the house of his afflicted friend, he received a peremptory note from the Rev. James Baker, requesting his attendance at the quarterly meeting, to commence on the following Saturday in the Hampstead Methodist church. It had been mooted about for some time that Mr. Capel was strangely indifferent and lukewarm in his religious duties ; that his ministrations were irregular ; and that his manner indicated he had no heart in the "work." Some said that he was but a mere formalist ; others that he was foppish ; others that he was popish ; and many asserted that he was assuming clerical airs more like a high-churchman than comporting himself as an humble preacher of the Gospel ; and knowing ones were of opinion that he was preparing to follow other high-minded preachers, and desert the "old Wesleyan ship," to obtain a curacy in the state church, and swell out as a Church of England minister. There were a few, however, who had misgivings as to the true cause of his apathy; and confidential whispers to this effect were poured into the ear of the Rev. James Baker, superintendent of the circuit.

So far, indeed, from being vainglorious, Mr. Capel had made many friends on the circuit by his unassuming disposition, and several here and there stood up in his defense. The young lady members in particular were generally of opinion that no such servant of God had ever before appeared among them; and one sanctified spinster, of over thirty-five summers, said she would be willing to fight her way in his behalf through a whole conference of preachers, even were they as stony-hearted as the stern senior preacher of Hampstead. The ladies generally flocked in large numbers to hear the calm gospel expositions of Mr. Capel, and the female membership of the church greatly increased under his "word." Although he avoided every exciting theme, there were as many female "conversions" as if he had been one of the Boanerges class; and he had consequently "seals to his ministry" which might not have followed from the preaching even of a much older man—one who was more matured in "divine things"—such as the superintendent himself.

Whether the Rev. Mr. Baker grew a little jealous of his younger brother on this particular account can not be fairly asserted. He might have had good methodistic reasons for the course he was about to pursue. Mr. Capel kept aloof, and had not called at the parsonage for nearly a month; and when he did call, hurried away, giving no satisfactory statement of the affairs on the circuit. It was well known among the brethren that he never encouraged revival meetings; and when those anxious for a "special outpouring" made efforts to awaken slumbering sinners, he always managed to be absent, and often hinted that he would prefer to have every thing done "decently and in order." But it was not until after the sad derangement of Mrs. Mannors that he spoke out plainly. Sympathizing with her family, he felt indignant that such a sad result—one of many—should follow from the persistency of Methodism in religious excitements, and he had the temerity to state that revivals were but nurseries for lunacy. Besides this, it was well known that he spoke of Mr. Mannors as a person whose example, in several respects, might be followed advantageously by many gospel ministers, and he was ever ready to defend his character from the unscrupulous attacks so commonly made by the pious or orthodox against unbelievers; and certain expressions made from time to time conveying his doubt of eternal punishment alarmed not a few of the more zealous, whose Methodistic instincts led them to reverence the Bible, as much for its consignment of the wicked to eternal torments as for its perpetuity of glorious rewards to the faithful.

Mr. Capel had made preparations to leave Hampstead Cottage after the death of William; he had several reasons for so doing. He had been solicited by Mrs. Mannors to reside in her family, in order to accomplish a purpose which now could never be reached; his own religious views had undergone a complete change; his mission was therefore useless; and he felt that if it was proper to change his place of residence, it was much more so his duty to break off all connections with a society whose teachings he had ceased to believe. Yet, dreading the obloquy which was almost certain to follow a formal recantation, he was desirous of withdrawing gradually from Methodist membership, and he trusted that some opportunity would be afforded to make his exit unnoticed. He could not consistently teach a doctrine which he did not believe; for over a month he had neither been seen nor heard at any religious service—it was public talk—and the anomalous position he occupied made him very unhappy, and rendered it necessary for him to do something to release himself from a bondage which was so irksome.

He often met his friend, Father Tom McGlinn, often traveled with him whole days, had had long and interesting conversations on the subject of religion; and he found that his friend in Romish orders—a veritable priest of the "Mother Church"—was just "as much in the mud as he was in the mire;" that both were sliding—or rather had slidden—from doubt to unbelief; both reputed ministers of the Gospel, though of widely different and hostile sects, were each anxious to be free from the fetters of a religion which investigation had shown to be the more modern form of an ancient superstition; and both alike dreading the outcry which would be made upon their open defection, were consequently more and more in sympathy.

Father McGlinn, after all, thought it best that his friend should answer the summons, and appear in person at the quarterly meeting; and Mr. Mannors, who would not hear of Mr. Capel's change of residence, also advised him to go boldly and hear every accusation. There might be invidious charges, which it would be necessary to disprove. The orthodox seldom believe that religious doubts or openly avowed skepticism can arise from any pure motive—any abstract love of truth; or that any man can desire to be raised above a class of servile worshipers of any myth or creed but from a desire for sensual indulgence, an eagerness to be rid of the wholesome restraints of religion. Mr. Mannors therefore strongly urged that Mr. Baker should be met on his own ground; and that while Mr. Capel made such acknowledgments respecting religion as he thought proper, he should demand proof, or rebut charges against his character, upon which solely they might, and no doubt would try, to base a motion for his expulsion.

The Rev. James Baker, in the mean time, was very industriously circulating his opinion of Mr. Capel throughout various parts of the circuit. He well knew where he could discover pliant aids for his purpose, and he found them. He was exceedingly bitter in his denunciation of ministerial unfaithfulness, and he succeeded in depicting the conduct of the junior preacher as deserving the impeachment of the "church of God." He insisted that the "servants of the Lord" were bound to make the punishment of such gross perfidy a terror to evil-doers; and for days, while some of the young ladies dared to sympathize, the select "people of the Lord" were preparing to give an exhibition of Christian forbearance and magnanimity.

The dreaded Saturday came. The church was filled; and although many of the brethren had to leave their daily toil, they did leave it, to be present on such an occasion of importance. The ladies assembled in as great numbers as if there were to be a special revival, or a missionary meeting, or a public raising of some dead Lazarus. Local preachers, church stewards, and other official members were well represented; and besides Mr. Baker, there were three other preachers, among whom was the old superannuated itinerant, who had held forth in such a lively discourse at the late protracted meeting.

Mr. Baker, as superintendent of the circuit, preached a doleful, proxy sermon, in which ministerial backsliding was represented as one of the basest crimes against the church; and he simulated great regret at being compelled, much against his will, but as a matter of duty, to bring serious charges against a brother—an erring brother—for whom he once had such a strong and deep affection. He assured his brethren that this duty was most painful; but the cause of the Lord should not be influenced by our human feelings—the right eye should be plucked out or the right hand cut off, should dire necessity require the sacrifice.

Mr. Capel did not make his appearance until after these preliminary services were over. The eyes of many had wandered over the church, and much surprise was manifested when he could not be seen. Mr. Baker himself felt then like an Abraham without an Isaac; the altar was raised, he held out the shining blade ready for the sacrifice; he wanted to make an atonement, but no victim appeared. He began to feel as uncomfortable as a tiger robbed of his prey, when Mr. Capel was seen walking slowly up the aisle, the object of prominent interest to all; and it was evident that he was somewhat nervous under the concentrated gaze of so many firm believers.

He took his place quietly, however, and scanned the complacent faces of the sanctified row of church officials; not one of whom, in this trying hour, ventured to give him even a nod of friendly recognition. There was a flutter among the ladies, and one particular spinster applied her handkerchief very frequently, and looked quite woe-begone.

After some formalities, there was a great hush, when Mr. Baker stood before the brethren as an accuser. He reiterated that it was painful to him as a minister of the Gospel, and it was with much reluctance that he was obliged to call their attention to certain charges which he felt it his bounden duty to prefer against brother Henry Capel—he would still call him brother—the junior preacher under his superintendency. Indeed, one might imagine that at this particular time the worthy man had found difficulty in giving utterance to his words; he was very much affected, very, and the faces of the official brethren around were lengthened into the gloomiest solemnity.

Having adjusted his spectacles, he opened a paper, and read out the charges.

"1st. That he, Henry Capel, as junior preacher, has been negligent in his duties and irregular in his appointments.

"2d. That he has sneered at and reviled the practice, discipline, and teaching of our church and founder, and has spoken contemptuously of our holy religion.

"3d. That his private acts and his general conduct and morality have been discreditable to himself, and a reproach to the people of God."

With respect to the first charge, Mr. Baker said, it was well known that for a long time Mr. Capel had not kept his appointments. People attended at the regular time mentioned on the "plan," but no preacher came; some frivolous excuse having been given for non-attendance. Even when he did preach, it was but a mere lecture in favor of a cold, formal morality; not a stirring appeal to induce sinners to flee from the wrath to come.

He was then about to furnish evidence in proof, when Mr. Capel said that, for several reasons which he need not mention, his appointments were not regularly kept; he admitted the correctness of the charge, and regretted that he had caused the members any inconvenience. Any address or "lecture" which he had given was an effort to improve his hearers morally and intellectually; he had thought it best to appeal to the reason instead of to the feelings.

Mr. Baker said that the next charge was far more serious. He, Mr. Capel, on several occasions—privately, he admitted, but yet not less invidiously—had stated that God's Holy Bible was false and contradictory in several places. False in its history and science; false and even barbarous in its general teachings and tendency; false in its idea of a Supreme Being. Its prophecies were false, its miracles untrue, and that many parts of that blessed book were unfit to be read. "I can not, I dare not, my friends," said the speaker, much excited, "repeat the horrid blasphemies to which he has given utterance. The offense is of such a nature as not only sufficient to exclude any man from our confidence—to place him beyond the pale of moral society—but also to subject him to the pains and penalties wisely and properly provided against blasphemy by the laws of this realm. O my friends! I feel a dreadful responsibility for having permitted that man—that guilty, deceitful man—to go about among our people and betray us, while holding such sentiments."

The reverend gentleman grew very indignant; his assumed regret and forbearance disappeared, and he scowled upon the accused with a ferocity of expression which might have made even his pious brother in the ministry,

Doctor Buster, feel a little nervous. Yet Mr. Capel sat there unintimidated; he never flinched beneath the dark fiery eye that was now turned upon him; but it was particularly fortunate for him, at the time, that "brother" Baker had not full power to impose the aforesaid "pains and penalties so wisely provided by law." The rack or the thumb-screw, so necessary in other days for the propagation of one form of Christianity, might not then have been looked upon with such holy horror were this servant of God only permitted to apply them in defense of the "book of books."

Brother Wesley Jacobs and others of the elect were grieved in spirit, groaned audibly, and shuddered to find themselves in such proximity to an actual reviler of the Gospel: it was dreadful; and many of the faithful around raised their pious eyes toward the ceiling, and thanked God that they had not hearts of unbelief. Nearly all looked upon the junior preacher as one who had fallen—miserably fallen—from a high estate; yes, one whose condemnation was already sealed. Were he a criminal—a felon before a judicial bar—there would have been hope, pity, and sympathy, extended toward him; but for an awful unbeliever did not the word say, "Let him be accursed"?

Besides some of the ladies whose tender feelings were yet with the accused, "old Father White"—as the superannuated preacher was familiarly called—looked with compassion upon the young man, and yearned for his soul as well as for his restoration. Father White was loved for his kind, human impulses: the natural man was not yet entirely absorbed in the spiritual. He knew there was one text which said, "But though we, or an angel from heaven, preach any other gospel unto you than that which we have preached unto you, let him be accursed;" and another, "If there come any unto you and bring not this doctrine, receive him not into your house, neither bid him Godspeed;" still, under the influence of human frailty, he preferred the text which said, "Judge not, and ye shall not be judged; condemn not, and ye shall not be condemned; forgive, and ye shall be forgiven." And now, could he get his erring brother—or rather his erring son—then and there to make an open acknowledgment of his sin—to accept the divine word before all, it would bring confusion upon skeptics, and redound to the glory of the Gospel.

In natural dispositions, there was a great difference between the old superannuated preacher, Father White, and the Rev. James Baker, the superintendent. The influence of the spirit which would induce one to restore a doubting Thomas would actuate the other to cut him off root and branch. There was the mild impulse of humanity on the one side and the stern, unrelenting spirit of orthodoxy on the other.

"My son—my brother," said the old preacher, "do you not see how greatly you have sinned in bringing discredit upon the Gospel of our Lord? The guilt is greater on your part, having been a laborer in the vineyard. God looks upon unbelief, that hideous monster of the human heart, as involving the rejection of the Holy Spirit—a sin of such magnitude as to close the ear of heavenly mercy to all future appeals, and seal the offender to the doom of eternal perdition.

"The true Christian can not—dare not—look upon the rejection of the Gospel in any more favorable light. My brother, what saith the Scripture—Matt. 12: 31, 32, '*I say unto you, all manner of sin and blasphemy shall be forgiven unto men; but the blasphemy against the Holy Ghost shall not be forgiven unto men. And whosoever speaketh a word against the Son of Man, it shall be forgiven him; but whosoever speaketh against the Holy Ghost, it shall not be forgiven him*—neither in this world, neither in the world to come.'

"That is, ' all manner of sin '—crimes of the deepest die—ingratitude, murder, any thing may be forgiven but that woeful offense against the Holy Spirit—against high heaven—shall not, can not be forgiven, dreadful to contemplate! O my brother! I feel that the Spirit of God still strives with you, and that you are not as yet left to a reprobate heart, and cut off forever. Haste! hesitate no longer! He who willfully rejects the divine word rejects the spirit of grace, and insures his own condemnation. Mark your danger! you once received the Gospel, dare you now refuse it? Has not our Master said, ' No man having put his hand to the plow, and looking back, is fit for the kingdom of God.' And Paul says, in Heb. 5, ' It is impossible for those who were once enlightened, and have tasted of the heavenly gift, if they shall fall away, to renew them again unto repentance; seeing they crucify to themselves the Son of God afresh, and put him to an open shame.' ' If we sin willfully after that we have received the knowledge of the truth, there remaineth no more sacrifice for sins; but a certain fearful looking for of judgment and fiery indignation, which shall devour the adversaries.'

"These extracts from the word of God, my brother, ought to make you start in your sleep! Be not attracted and deceived by the world; the transitory things of time and sense are comparatively unworthy of our notice. Cling to divine revelation—it gives you an assurance of a glorious hereafter! How insignificant are the rulers or great men of the earth, when compared with the illustrious characters portrayed in the Holy Bible! Who can compare with David the sweet Psalmist of the Old Testament; or with Paul, the great apostle, of the New? Alas! what would the world be without the Bible? Where should we find our morality—where our civilization? Take away the Bible, and the world would be a chaos! Uproot our divine religion, and what can you give in its place?"

The old preacher again tenderly pleaded, and again repeated his admonitions. He would have cheerfully given up his few remaining years, and have died to save his erring brother; and when he sat down, though Mr. Baker and others, "steadfast in the Lord," remained stern and immovable, yet the greater number under his voice and exhortation were softened even to tears.

CHAPTER XXVI.

When Mr. Capel got up to speak, there was almost perfect silence; all were anxious to hear what he had to say in reply to the serious charges of the superintendent, and many were of opinion that the plea so feelingly made by Father White had turned the scale in favor of the accused; that he would most probably acknowledge his error, and submit to a reproof. Mr. Baker himself seemed rather disconcerted; he did not approve of tampering with an enemy; he would not have taken a single step toward the reclamation of a skeptic by argument. Unbelief to him was a crime that should be punished. He would rather follow the example of a class of inquisitors, who, in dealing with certain penitents, first granted absolution, but gave the body to the flames, lest the soul should be endangered by a relapse into heresy.* As it was, he neither wanted penitence nor pardon; he had the offender in his clutches—let the law take its course.

" I can not but feel," said Mr. Capel, " that the consideration extended toward me by the Rev. Mr. White demands my most heartfelt thanks. Viewing the matter from his standpoint, I have committed a most grievous offense against religion—against the church of which I was once a member, but to which I can never more claim to belong. I would fain have his good opinion; and, for his sake, and the sake of many others, I wish we could believe alike—I fear it is now impossible; but we all know by experience that that which at one period of our lives might have been estimated as true and beautiful, at a subsequent period may cease to possess that virtue and quality. What appears to be truth to one may be error to another; and, as our convictions in this respect are not voluntary, but are, or rather ought to be, the result of a mental process, this result should be accepted, no matter how painful to our own feelings or to the feelings of another.

" The second charge brought against me by the Rev. Mr. Baker is, in the main, correct; but I object to the terms which he has used. I have never ' sneered at ' or ' reviled ' any thing religious, nor have I spoken ' contemptuously ' of the founder of Methodism, or of any Christian doctrine. I admit that, for a long period, I had serious doubts—long rankling privately in my own bosom; these I tried, with all my power, to suppress; and if prayers or tears could have removed them, they would not have remained. If I ever ventured to mention them to any person, it was to some one whom I considered more experienced than I was myself. Upon my appointment to this circuit, I was surprised to find that many members of the church—generally the more studious and thoughtful—were troubled with nearly the same doubts which agitated my own mind, and sought occasionally to confer with me for an explanation."

* The inquisitors probably took their cue from St. Paul—1 Cor. 5 : 5. " To deliver such a one unto Satan for the destruction of the flesh, that the spirit may be saved in the day of the Lord Jesus."

" 'Tis false! 'tis false! Name them—let us know them!" cried Mr. Baker, jumping up, dark and angry; " let us have their names, and let them answer for themselves if they are present. 'Tis false!" he wildly reiterated, striking the palm of his hand fiercely. " No man, woman, or child on the circuit ever had doubts until you brought them. I say again, 'tis false!"

Some of the official members were becoming agitated, and others rocked impatiently in their seats, as if anxious for the word of command to " go in " and defend the faith; and were it not for the calm, tolerant bearing of good Father White, there might have been a scene worthy of a notice in the next morning paper.

" Friends," said he mildly, " I pray let there be no interruption. Let us hear Mr. Capel's reply to the charges; let him speak freely, and if what he says is not sufficient to exculpate him, the church can so express it."

Mr. Capel took no notice, however, of the interruption. He said, if permitted, he would give a simple statement of his views, and if he could be proved to be in error, he would cheerfully submit to their decision. Having, as he said, entertained serious doubts, he thought it his duty, as one on probation for the ministry, to inquire into the alleged errors, discrepancies, and contradictions said to have been discovered throughout the Bible, with a view of being better able to speak in its defense and refute the arguments of skeptics. In so doing, he had read the most distinguished authors for and against the Bible; he conceived that he could form no just conclusions by merely reading one side; that if the Bible were perfect truth, as its upholders asserted, no strictness of investigation could possibly affect its paramount claim. Contrary to his expectations, however, that investigation had but still further shaken his faith, and satisfied him that his previous doubts were but too well founded. He felt that this was a delicate subject to mention in a Methodist church; but, as his motives had been impugned, he thought it but proper to give the reasons for his unbelief.

" We want to hear none of your reasons. I dare say your so-called investigation was more confined to Tom Paine than it was to Paley; no doubt your distinguished friend, Mannors, gave you important assistance in the research."

" Patience, brother Baker," said Mr. White. " We should hear him out like Christian men—like men who are not afraid of the rock on which they stand."

" I know," continued Mr. Capel, " how deeply ministers and members of the church must feel when defects and inconsistencies are said to have been discovered in a book which they have been taught to believe ' inspired ;' I know personally the strength of such prejudices, and I know how positive the precepts of that book are against unbelief. But when a claim is made to infallibility, such precepts should not prevent investigation.

" If you shut out inquiry, distrust is sure to enter. I do not wish to particularize in this place, or to go into details as to what parts in the Bible I have found objectionable. I do not wish to utter any thing which might cause a moment's pain to any one present, but I wish to be permitted to give the reasons why I dissent from what has just been so kindly expressed by one for whom I shall ever entertain a high regard.

"Our reverend father has drawn a comparison between the great men and rulers of the earth, and two of the principal characters of Scripture, DAVID and PAUL—the psalmist and the great apostle. For centuries the pious have given these personages a prominent place in the history of the Bible—have lauded their many and noble virtues, and recommended them as distinguished patterns to all mankind. David, in particular, has been called 'a man after God's own heart' for his reputed excellencies and obedience to the divine will. The Bible itself goes far to establish this reputation; for it says that, 'David did that which was right in the eyes of the Lord, and turned not aside from any thing that was commanded him all the days of his life, save only in the matter of Uriah the Hittite.' It would be difficult to find a greater eulogy within the limits of that book. In reading this commendation, a person would think that David was one of the most estimable that ever lived. I can not believe so. I judge him by the records of the same Bible; and I have often thought that there must have been one of the many Bible interpolations, made to express a grave error—a blasphemy—in saying that David could ever be 'a man after God's own heart.' Who would choose a cruel, blood-thirsty, rapacious man—a deliberate murderer—to be his bosom friend? Let us glance at the history of David.

"His first principal act was the slaying of Goliath, whose head he afterward cut off. Anxious to obtain Michal, the king's daughter, for his wife, Saul, it is said, told David that if he brought him the *foreskins* of one hundred Philistines, he should have her. David, who had been made a 'captain over a thousand,' thereupon went with his men and slaughtered 'of the Philistines *two* hundred men,' one hundred more than was required; and he 'brought their foreskins and gave them in full tale, to the king, that he might be the king's son-in-law.' David, by this means, succeeded in getting his first wife. It strikes me that it was a most barbarous mode; no way inferior to the way in which brutalized savages purchased similar favors with the scalps of their enemies. Again, in a war, he 'went out and fought with the Philistines, and slew them with great slaughter.' To screen himself from the anger of Saul, he prevailed upon Jonathan to tell the king a falsehood. After he had fled from Saul, he told a lie to Ahimelech, the priest, as to the reason for his departure.

"When he went to Achish, the king of Gath, —being 'sore afraid'—'he changed his behavior before them and feigned himself mad, and scrabbled on the doors of the gate, and let his spittle fall down upon his beard.' Having escaped to a cave, he again became a captain over about six hundred freebooters—men who were 'in distress,' 'in debt,' and 'discontented'—ready for any enterprise; and the Lord, having delivered the Philistines into his hand, he brought away their cattle, and again 'smote them with a great slaughter.' After various adventures, David, on being refused a favor by Nabal, a herdsman, 'girded on his sword,' and went out with his men for the purpose of destroying him and his helpers. The oath he swore to this effect is too indelicate to mention. On his way, he was met by Abigail, Nabal's wife—'a woman of a beautiful countenance.' She brought presents to David, and entreated him to spare her husband, and his wrath was appeased. Ten days after her return, the Lord, it is said, 'smote Nabal that he died;' and when David heard it, he sent and took Abigail to wife—Michal, his first wife, having been taken from him by Saul—and at the same time he took another woman to wife, named Ahinoam.

"Were it not, therefore, for the intercession of Nabal's wife, David would have committed a cruel outrage, simply because he was churlishly refused a favor by Nabal.

"Dreading the enmity of Saul, David, with his wives and his six hundred adventurers, fled to the land of the Philistines, and again sought the protection of Achish, king of Gath. Not desiring to dwell in the royal city, he prevailed upon the king to give him 'a place in some town in the country.' Achish kindly gave him Ziglag; and, while dwelling there in safety from Saul, he violated the rights of hospitality; and, like a brigand, with his six hundred privately made incursions into certain nations, even allies of his protector. 'He smote the land, and left neither *man nor woman alive*; and took away the sheep, and the oxen, and the asses, and the camels, and the apparel.' When questioned by Achish as to his inroads, he deceived the king, by stating that he had been against other people hostile to him; and to support the untruth, he cut off every living being whom he had taken. The text says, 'And David saved neither man *nor woman alive*, to bring tidings to Gath, saying, lest they should tell on us.' Such wanton and unprovoked slaughter to hide deception was the extreme of human depravity.

"He again went to the king and gave evidence of his want of patriotism, by basely proposing to join the Philistines with his men in a war *against his own country*; but, being mistrusted, he was not permitted to go, and he regretted his rejection.

"Upon his return to Ziglag, he found that the Amalikites, whom he had wantonly despoiled, had, during his absence, entered and burnt his city, and had taken his wives and all that were therein captives; but they exhibited a greater humanity than David, for it is said 'that they slew not any, either great or small.' After bewailing his loss, he went and consulted God through the medium of an 'ephod,'—as a heathen would his oracle, and having received divine encouragement, he, with only four hundred of his men—the other two hundred being 'faint'—went out against the Amalikites. The text says, 'And David smote them from the twilight even until the evening of the next day; and there escaped not a man of them, save four hundred young men, which rode upon camels and fled.' If the Bible be true, this bloody restitution was awarded by the Almighty, and David was the meek avenger!

"When Saul was dead, David was recognized by the tribe of Judah as their king; but he soon began to intrigue for the house of Israel, over which reigned Ish-bosheth, the son of Saul; and he encouraged a traitorous proposal made by Abner, chief general of the army of Israel. Fierce wars were prosecuted between Judah and Israel—the select people of God. David finally succeeded in being established as ruler over both nations; but the means he used to accomplish this object were most cruel and unjustifiable. At this time, besides Michal, his first wife, he had six others; and six sons were born unto him at Hebron. Now, having obtained full dominion, instead of giving an example of self-denial, and making an endeavor to promote peace and good-will among men, the text says, 'And David took him more concubines and wives out of Jerusalem after he was come from Hebron.' Then, under direction of the Lord, he continued to war, dealing blood and destruction to different nations; and, following the brutal example of Joshua, he 'haughed' or hamstrung 'all the chariot-horses' taken in battle, save one hundred kept for his own use!

"When the 'ark of God' was 'set upon a new cart and brought out of the house of Abinadab,' David appears in a new character. Merely girdled with a linen ephod, he danced naked on the highway before the Lord and all present. The linen girdle must have been but of gossamer texture, as his first wife, Michal, sarcastically reproved him for the indecency in these words, 'How glorious was the king of Israel to-day, who uncovered himself to-day in the eyes of the handmaids of his servants, as one of the vain fellows shamelessly uncovereth himself!' For this deserved reproach, he repudiated Michal, who had been faithful to him when he was poor and unknown; and afterward, upon a mere pretense, caused two of her brothers and five of her sons by her other husband to be hung! Bishop Kitto, in framing an excuse for this terrible act, says, 'It was desirable for the peace of his successors that the house of Saul should be exterminated.'

"When David was about forty years of age, he saw a woman, who was very beautiful, washing herself; upon inquiry, he found she was the wife of Uriah, but he took her, and she became with child. To get rid of Uriah, who was one of his soldiers, he gave private orders to have him placed 'in the forefront of the hottest battle'—for battles were then of frequent occurrence—so that Uriah, being unsupported, was slain. David then took Bathsheba, the widow, and made her another of his wives.

"As David grew older, he was not content, but was anxious for more conquests; and he extended the boundaries of his empire from Egypt to the Euphrates. His treatment of the vanquished, always terrible, was at times very atrocious. Having taken Rabbath, the chief city of the Ammonites, and the great spoil it contained, the text says, 'And he brought forth the people that were therein, and put them *under saws* and *under harrows of iron*, and *under axes of iron*, and made them *pass through the brick-kiln*, and thus did he unto all the children of Ammon!'

"The indecent scandals of his household are recorded in the Bible; but all through a long life, he was a man of uncontrollable passion, his self-indulgence, even to licentiousness, being of the grossest character; for, when he was old and 'stricken in years,' the shameful chronicle was added against him. As he drew near his end, one would think that then, if at any time, he would have exhibited some redeeming qualities—some remorse—but the picture grows darker. In his last charge to his son Solomon, he betrays treachery and vindictiveness almost without parallel. Here are his words: 'Moreover, thou knowest also what Joab, the son of Zeruiah, did to me, and what he did to the captains of the hosts of Israel, unto Abner, the son of Ner, and unto Amasa, the son of Jether, whom he slew, and shed the blood of war in peace, and put the blood of war upon his girdle that was about his loins, and in his shoes that were on his feet. Do, therefore, according to thy wisdom, and let not his hoar head go down to the grave in peace.

"'And behold thou hast with thee, Shimei, the son of Gera, a Benjamite, of Bahurim, which cursed me with a grievous curse in the day when I went to Mahanaim; but he came down to meet me at Jordan, and I sware to him by the Lord, saying, I will not put thee to death with the sword.

"'Now, therefore, hold him not guiltless; for thou art a wise man, and knowest what thou oughtest to do unto him; but his hoar head bring thou down to the grave with blood.'

"Thus David passed away without one word of forgiveness for his enemies, or even one word of regret for his misdeeds. Overhung by the shadow of death, vengeance was upon his lips, and his last act was the violation of his solemn oath to protect Shimei.

"Who, then, at this later period, could expect to be regarded as righteous by following the example of such a life or of such a death? The humanity of these so-called degenerate days shudders at the idea! Who, with a true heart, would not prefer years of poverty and an unknown grave, rather than live like David and be called 'a man after God's own heart'?"

During this delivery, Mr. Capel was several times interrupted; Mr. Baker often became nearly outrageous. He would not permit persons weak in the faith to be contaminated by such heresy; and, to pacify him in some degree, Father White proposed that all present should be requested to retire except the church officials and a few others who could be depended on. After some discussion, this was agreed to; a great many went away, but a few yet lingered, here and there, as if their interest had been increased. So the ministers and officials had it nearly all to themselves.

"Brother," said Mr. White, in his usual mild
manner, "the character you have drawn of David is only such as the Bible gives him; it is
an evidence of its impartiality; it depicts man
with his defects as well as with his virtues.
It does not screen the offender, though it ex-
alts the penitent."

"I can not say," said Mr. Capel, "that the
recital of such defects can be profitable or
edifying; it, on the contrary, tends to give
men false ideas of what is right. The inhu-
manities of profane history claim no heavenly
sanction; no brutalized leader could exhibit
a divine commission; men acted under the
impulse of human passion, not as hordes
rushing out to execute the vengeance of a
deity. The actions of David, as recorded
in the books of Samuel, like other biblical
biographies, have rather a tendency to blunt
our feelings of delicacy and humanity than
to make them more sensitive. The man
who for the first time sees the dead and
dying stretched upon the battle-field is
shocked at the carnage; but sad experience
has proved that the most humane become indifferent by the frequency of such sights.
When we read numerous accounts in the Bible that conflict with the prevailing ideas of
purity and justice, we gradually learn to accept them when we are told that the Almighty
for some special purpose, *connived* at or *favored* such actions. In cruelties continuing from
the Waldenses to the Quaker, Inquisitors
and Puritans alike have emblazoned their persecuting banners with authoritative texts."

"The Bible does not exculpate David," said
Mr. White; "you know of Nathan's stern reproof. That David sincerely repented is fully
established by his Psalms."

"There are Christian men willing to admit that David committed many vile acts, but
the *Bible* accuses him in *only one* instance,
that of Uriah; it was for this that Nathan
rebuked him. But notwithstanding, he is defended in 'Holy Writ,' and the text which I
shall repeat is ample proof. But first, Solomon
and some of his people were threatened for
their idolatry; it is said in 1st Kings, chapter
11, verse 33, 'Because they have forsaken me
and have worshiped Ashtoreth, the goddess
of the Zidonians, Chemosh, the god of the
Moabites, and Milcom, the god of the children
of Ammon, and have not walked in my ways,
to do that which is right in my eyes, and to
keep my statutes and my judgments, *as did
David, his father.*'

"Here, while Solomon, the great and wise,
was threatened for his idolatry, David, his
father, was commended for his righteousness;
and when the Lord promised certain favors to
a successor, it was, the text says, 'Because
David did that which was right in the eyes
of the Lord, and turned not aside from any
thing that he commanded him *all the days of
his life,* save only in the matter of Uriah the
Hittite.' 1st Kings, chapter 15, verse 5. Language could not be stronger. The approval
of David's conduct is full and explicit, one act
alone being condemned.

'As to David's being the author of the Psalms,
commentators have differed. There is no evidence to prove who the writers were. The
137th Psalm could not have been written till
more than four hundred years after the time
of David, because it refers to the captivity of
the Jews in Babylon. If, however, such a
man of blood wrote the Psalms, no one could
excel him in dissimulation; they are a hete-
rogeneous collection, wherein sentiments of
piety and self-righteousness, imprecation and
vengeance, are freely commingled; and
though the Psalms have been ever lauded
with amazing obliviousness as to their defects, they would form but a wretched basis
for morality at the present day."

Mr. Baker made another effort to silence
Mr. Capel; he said the evidence they already
had from his own lips was sufficient to brand
the late junior preacher as a ravening wolf—
an out and out defamer of the word of God.
It would be sinful to listen any longer. Unexpectedly, however, the brethren, as if desirous of allowing the accused to commit himself to the fullest extent, consented to hear
his opinion of Paul; for he who could presume to utter any thing against one so de-
vinely inspired must be far, far on the high-
road to spiritual infamy. Father White, like
most preachers, could be very bitter at times
against revilers of the word; now, he manifested great patience. He was troubled, and
seemed to ponder upon what had been said;
perhaps a terrible doubt might have been in-
truding upon his own mind!

CHAPTER XXVII.

HAVING received permission to continue his
reply, Mr. Capel, to the surprise of Mr. Baker,
grew bolder, and proceeded to give his opinion
of one who is said to be the father of the
Gentile church—the thirteenth apostle, as
"born out of due time," yet who declared of
himself that he "was not a whit behind the
very chiefest."

"Paul, who was a Jew and a Pharisee,
though by no means so inhuman as David,
yet, as the reputed agent of the high-priest,
was undoubtedly guilty of murder; for this,
we have his own acknowledgment. In his
speech before Agrippa, he said, 'And I persecuted this way unto *death,* binding and
delivering into prisons both men and women.'
(Acts 22:4) He was an accomplice at the
murder of Stephen, (Acts 22:20,) for he stood
by and kept the clothes of those who stoned
him, 'consenting unto his death,' and he had
'breathed out threatenings and slaughter'
against the disciples of the Lord.'

"After his conversion, his fierce zeal was but
transferred; for when he considered it necessary, he could be rigorous enough, had he the
power, to crush his opponents and extermi-
nate heretics. In this respect, he must have
been the exemplar of Calvin and others of
similar views. From the beginning, he evinced
a strong desire to be a prominent ruler in
the church; he was arrogant, had disputations,
given offense, and had many enemies; and
though he inculcated charity, humility, and
submission to as irreconcilable an extent as is
followed by some religious teachers at the

present day, he was nevertheless in disposition intolerant and dictatorial, and caused no little strife among adherents of the new faith. Anxious to make proselytes in his own way, the means he used were often exceptionable; and it is to be feared that he had not a consistent regard for truth. If Peter cursed and denied his Master, if John was presumptuous, if James was vindictive enough to wish the destruction of an unbelieving village, and if Judas was such a wretch—if these, chosen by Christ, and in his very presence, were not free from sin and offense, surely we may admit that Paul, who was not so highly favored, might have gravely erred himself—as priests still do—though giving excellent admonition to others.

"That he was ambitious of being distinguished as a high-priest in Christianity, many consider evident from the fact that his alleged writings are said to have been the first formation of the New Testament. *Fourteen* of its books are ascribed to *him* alone, the other *thirteen* being the reputed production of *seven* persons, four only of whom were apostles, the remaining eight apostles having obtained no literary position in the present compilation. The admirers of the 'great Paul' wish, however, to make it appear that it was because of his peculiar fitness and education that he was inspired to become the initiatory scribe; but such a plea is untenable, for we are informed that on the day of Pentecost the disciples received the miraculous gift of tongues in order to qualify them to 'teach all nations.'

"The inference, therefore, is most conclusive that Paul, no matter how well or how early trained in the high schools of his nation, was not as well qualified for a mission among the heathen as those specially gifted and instructed for that purpose by a divine power, long before his conversion. His natural presumption, which led him to say, 'For I speak to you, Gentiles, inasmuch as I am the apostle of the Gentiles, I magnify mine office,' (Rom. 11 : 13,) is proof either of his entire ignorance that Christ had previously made special appointments for the Gentiles, or that he was determined to act quite independently, irrespective of the authority granted to others. That such appointments were made and such authority granted, I shall be able to prove from the Scriptures.

"Immediately before Christ ascended, he gave his disciples promise of the gifts which they subsequently received in a miraculous manner on the day of Pentecost, gifts which enabled them to speak the language of every nation; and his intention as to how the gifts or power should be used is apparent when we read the text, 'But ye shall receive power after that the Holy Ghost is come upon you; and ye shall be witnesses unto me both in Jerusalem, and in all Judea, and in Samaria, and *unto the uttermost parts of the earth.*' (Acts 1 : 8.) Again he told them, 'Go ye therefore and teach *all* nations.' (Matt. 28 : 19.) And again, 'Go ye *into all the world*, and preach the Gospel *to every creature.*' (Mark 16 : 15.) These commands are plain, precise, and positive; when the disciples were told to go into the 'uttermost parts of the earth,' to 'all na-

tions,' and to 'every creature,' no one can hesitate to believe that they were fully commissioned to the heathen; and it is more reasonable to believe that several persons should be required for such an extensive mission than that *one* man—Paul alone—should be set apart for that purpose. That he therefore usurped authority' must be the inevitable deduction of every unprejudiced mind.

"Paul is first spoken of in the Acts, a book written, it is supposed, by Luke. It is mostly a history of him, and tradition says that he supplied much or nearly all of the information it contains. There is not a shadow of evidence to substantiate the miraculous account of his conversion; the narrative is entirely his own, depending altogether on his mere assertion. He does not give the names of any who were with him; neither does he give place, nor date—simply, 'as I went to Damascus.' The story is, that about two years after the crucifixion, being on his way to persecute Christians, he suddenly saw 'a great light,' 'a light from heaven,' not the personal appearance of any one; he then fell to the earth, heard a voice, and was ordered to preach. This miracle, he said, made him a believer; the story, however, contains several discrepancies. The first account of this occurrence, in Acts 9th, says, that after they had seen the 'great light', *Paul* fell to the earth, but the *men* who were with him 'stood speechless,' *hearing a voice* but *seeing no man*; the second account, in Acts 22, Paul says, that the *men* heard *not* the voice; and in the third statement, Acts 26, he says, that when the light was seen, *all* fell to the earth! One account, therefore, says, that the men *stood* and *heard* a voice, another that they did *not* hear the voice, and a third that they did *not* stand, but that *all fell* to the earth! Which is the correct account?

"According to these different narratives, Paul saw no person, only a 'light,' which struck him with immediate blindness; but he subsequently wished to leave the impression that he had seen Jesus, for he reports him as having said, 'For I have appeared unto thee;' he made Ananias say, 'The God of our fathers hath chosen thee that thou shouldst know his will and *see* that Just One.' (Acts 22 : 14.) When the disciples were doubtful of Paul's conversion and afraid of him, his companion, Barnabas, to whom he related the miracle, assured them that 'he had *seen* the Lord by the way, and that he had spoken to him.' (Acts 9 : 27.) And Paul, in addressing the Corinthians, said, 'Am I not an apostle? am I not free? have I not *seen* Jesus Christ our Lord?' (1 Cor. 9 : 1.) And again, having declared that Christ was seen by many after his resurrection, he says, 'And, last of all, he was *seen* of me also, as of one born out of due time.' (1 Cor. 15 : 8.) To say the least, the ambiguity of these passages is very great, almost a contradiction.

"By the two first accounts, we find that, at the time of his miraculous conversion, Paul received no message, but was directed to go and be instructed at Damascus; by the last, we are informed that he received his instructions and authority from the Lord at the very hour of his conversion, and that he proceeded on his mission forthwith*—no way afflicted with blindness!

"Paul evinces a desire to be distinguished. He claimed to be an apostle, though not recognized as such by the others, the number of whom was limited to twelve. By his own statement, he did not go near them immediately after his reputed conversion, either for counsel or to manifest contrition for what he had done as a persecutor. He kept away for 'three years,' and boasted that his right to teach was independent; that he was not taught by man, he had 'conferred not with flesh and blood,' 'neither,' says he, 'went I up to Jerusalem to them which were apostles before me, but I went into Arabia and returned again to Damascus.' (Gal. 1 : 17.) Indeed, he declares that he was so little known in person either to apostles or disciples as to be 'unknown by face unto the churches of Judea which were in Christ.' 'But they had heard only that he which persecuted us in times past now preacheth the faith which once he destroyed.' (Gal. 1 : 22, 23.)

"It is surprising, however, to find this relation most positively contradicted in Acts 9. In that chapter, we are told that, after Paul was restored to sight, he remained 'certain days with the disciples which were at Damascus.' While in that city, his zeal led him to enter the synagogues 'preaching Christ' and 'confounding the Jews,' who, no doubt, were greatly annoyed by his intrusion as well as by his doctrine ; and, governed by a national impulse, 'they took counsel to kill him ;' but having heard of it, 'the disciples took him by night, and let him down by the wall in a basket.' He then went direct to Jerusalem 'and assayed to join himself to the disciples; but they were all afraid of him, and believed not that he was a disciple.' They, it appears, had only heard of him as a persecutor, and had no authority for his conversion but his own word. Barnabas, having assured the apostles that Paul was a believer, that he had 'preached boldly at Damascus,' they confided in him. 'And he was with them, coming in and going out at Jerusalem.' Again his indiscreet zeal brought him into trouble ; he 'disputed against the Grecians,' and they, most probably incited by the Jews, 'went about to slay him ;' and the 'brethren,' to save him a second time, 'sent him forth to Tarsus.'

"Furthermore, in his speech before Agrippa, Paul stated that, in obedience to the 'heavenly vision,' he went 'first unto them of Damascus and at Jerusalem, and throughout all the coasts of Judea, and then to the Gentiles.'

"If he, therefore, 'first' went to Damascus and Jerusalem after his conversion, how are we to reconcile this account with that which declares as positively that 'immediately' after the same event he went to Arabia, and did not go to Jerusalem until three years subsequently? Commentators have failed to produce an agreement ; such glaring discrepancies affect the credibility of the different narratives. If Paul thus contradicts himself, what reliance can be placed upon his statements?

* See Gal. 1 : 16, 17.

To account for these contradictions, some suppose that Paul felt annoyed at his reception by the apostles—at the indifference of them and of the disciples—and denied being near them.

"Having started, however, upon his mission, his constant endeavor was to impress others with his assumed authority. He never appeals to any gospel or record of the Jerusalem church, he never points to the true apostles, but seems to ignore their prerogative, and orders his own epistles to be read as sufficient for his converts. 'If any man think himself to be a prophet or spiritual, let him acknowledge the things that I write unto you as the commandments of the Lord.' (1 Cor. 14 : 37.) 'For I speak unto you, Gentiles, inasmuch as I am the apostle of the Gentiles, I magnify mine office.' (Rom. 11 : 13.) When giving certain directions, he concludes, 'And so ordain I in all churches.' (1 Cor. 7 : 17.) 'Wherefore, I beseech you, be ye followers of me.' (1 Cor. 4 : 16.) 'Be ye followers of me, even as I also am of Christ.' (1 Cor. 11 : 1.) 'Now, as concerning the collection for the saints, as I have given order to the churches of Galatia, even so do ye.' (1 Cor. 16 : 1.) 'To whom ye forgive any thing, I forgive also ; for if I forgive any thing, to whom I forgive it for your sakes, I forgive it in the person of Christ.' (2 Cor. 2 : 10.) 'Brethren, be followers together of me, and mark them which walk, so as ye have us (me) for an example.' (Phil. 3 : 17.) 'And if any man obey not our word by this epistle, note that man, and have no company with him, that he may be ashamed.' (2 Thes. 3 : 14.) Priestly arrogance could scarcely go further ! From these passages, it is plain that his desire was to be considered equal, or, indeed, more correctly, superior to any one else. No other writer in the New Testament presumes to such an extent ; the real apostles were comparatively modest and humble in their assertions. The writings of Paul can be distinguished from all others by the frequent repetitions of the pronouns I, me, my, and mine ; and the letter I, like an index-finger, is almost continually seen in his epistles as it pointing to the egotism and self-sufficiency of the scribe.

"Paul was jealous of other teachers ; certain disciples or preachers having visited the Corinthians, to whom he had partly devoted himself, he wrote, 'I am jealous over you with godly jealousy.' (2 Cor. 11 : 2.) And, like many an intolerant high-church and low-church Paul of the present day, he not only dealt in strong imputations against these teachers, but denounced them as 'false apostles, deceitful workers, transforming themselves into the apostles of Christ,' (2 Cor. 11 : 13,) without attempting any proof. He reminded the Corinthians that, as a teacher, he 'was not a whit behind the very chiefest apostles.' (2 Cor. 11 : 5.) 'I say again, let no man think me a fool ; if otherwise yet as a fool receive me, that I may boast myself a little.' (v. 16.) 'Are they Hebrews? so am I. Are they Israelites? so am I. Are they the seed of Abraham? so am I. Are they members of Christ? (I speak as a fool,) I am more.' (v. 22.) 'I am become a fool in glorying ; ye have compelled me: for in nothing am I behind the very chiefest apostles.' (2 Cor. 12 : 16.) The 11th chapter of 2d Corinthians is almost entirely taken up with his self-laudation, contrasting and denouncing. The teachers who went among the Cretans he also condemned, as 'unruly and vain talkers and deceivers, whose mouths must be stopped,' and, quoting the language of another, he abused the Cretans as being 'alway liars, evil beasts, slow bellies.' (Titus 1 : 12.) Yet, after all his anxiety to establish and control churches, the Corinthians and Galatians almost entirely rejected his teaching. The Christians at Jerusalem, it appears, did not approve of his course in suddenly breaking loose from the Mosaic law to please or gain adherents, and they sent out missionaries, with 'letters of commendation,' to counteract his teaching. (2 Cor. 3 : 1.) It was against such that Paul was so very bitter.

"As a preacher, he was obtrusive, given to contention, and vindictive. He repeatedly entered synagogues at Damascus, Jerusalem, and other places, disputing with Jews and Gentiles, giving offense, engendering strife, and causing such ill-will as often to place his own life in jeopardy; when forced to leave, or when obstinately confronted, instead of an act of conciliation, he would give some harsh rebuke, or defiantly shake the dust off his feet against them. (Acts 13 : 51.) Of those who spoke 'slanderously' against him, he said, their 'damnation was just.' (Rom. 3 : 8.) He contended with Barnabas, his fellow-laborer, and separated from him. (Acts 15 : 39.) According to his account, Peter, his senior in the church, was blamable, and he 'withstood him to the face.' (Gal. 2 : 11.) His intolerance against those whom he called 'unbelievers' or 'false teachers' proves that, though he changed his religion, his dogmatic spirit was as fierce as ever: he said, 'If any man love not the Lord Jesus Christ, let him be anathema maranatha.' (1 Cor. 16 : 22.) 'If any man preach any other gospel unto you than that ye have received, let him be accursed.' (Gal. 1 : 9.) Unbelievers were to be 'punished with everlasting destruction from the presence of the Lord.' (2 Thes. 1 : 9.) 'And for this cause God shall send them strong delusion that they should believe a lie, that they all might be damned who believe not the truth.' (2 Thes. 2 : 11, 12.) 'Alexander the coppersmith did me much evil, the Lord reward him according to his works.' (2 Tim. 4 : 14.) These denunciations are in direct opposition to the admonition of Christ, which said, 'bless and curse not.' Paul said to his hearers, 'Be ye followers of *me*,' and in this dictatorial mood too many of the priests have trodden in his very footsteps—even to the present day.

"Determined to gain proselytes, he was pliable and inconsistent; he says, 'Unto the Jew I became as a Jew, that I might gain the Jews.' 'To them that are without the law, as without the law.' 'To the weak became I as weak, that I might gain the weak; I am made all things to all men.' (1 Cor. 9 : 20 : 21.) To please some, he professed to disbelieve in the utility of the Mosaic law, and declared that

'by the deeds of the law, there shall no flesh be justified.' (Rom. 3 : 20.) 'Behold I, Paul, say unto you, that if ye be circumcised, Christ shall profit you nothing.' (Gal. 5 : 2.) Yet we shall see that on a certain occasion he agreed to dissemble, and make it appear that he 'walked orderly' and 'kept the law.' After having spent some time among strangers, he revisited Jerusalem and told the brethren of his great success among the Gentiles. The brethren, who gained many converts among the Jews by adhering to the law, incorporating it with their Christianity, said to him, 'Thou seest, brother how many thousands of Jews there are which believe; and they are all zealous of the law.' 'And they are informed of thee that thou teachest all the Jews which are among the Gentiles to forsake Moses' sayings, that they ought not to circumcise their children.' 'What is it therefore ? The multitude must needs come together; for they will hear that thou art come.' Here was a difficulty; the Christian Jews were sure to learn that Paul, who taught a violation of the law to gain the Gentiles, had come among them, and the teachers at Jerusalem anticipated trouble. What was to be done ? Could there be no compromise ? No! nothing but an open act of deception was suggested to preserve the peace! It was to be done this way—Do, therefore, this that we say to thee. We have four men which have a vow on them. Them take, and purify thyself with them, and be at charges with them (that is, to pay his proportion of the ceremonial expenses), that they may shave their heads, and all may know that those things whereof they were informed concerning thee are nothing; but that thou thyself also walkest orderly and keepest the law.' The deception was to be carried so far as not only to try and make Paul appear as a conscientious upholder of the law, but that the Gentiles among whom he had been were also observers of it; 'only keeping themselves from things offered to idols, and from blood.'

"Then Paul took the men, and the next day, purifying himself with them, entered into the temple to signify the accomplishment of the days of purification, until that an offering should be made for every one of them.' By this act, he therefore betrayed a total disregard for principle or truth. As to the culpability of the other teachers, we can not say, for the account was derived from himself; but he was not reliable, and he might have wished to make others appear as temporizing as he was himself. The deception, however, was of no avail; the Jewish Christians had been too well informed of his constant violation of the law, and before the end of the seven days—the time required for the ceremony of purification—'the Jews which were of Asia, when they saw him in the temple, stirred up all the people and laid hands on him.' The history of this discreditable conduct can be read in Acts 21 : 17–30. On other occasions, he also gave proof of his insincerity by a formal compliance with the Mosaic law. He had his head shorn, 'for he had a vow' (Acts 18 : 18 ;) he desired to have Timotheus accompany him on a mission, and to make him acceptable to the Jews, he with his own hands actually circumcised that disciple. (Acts 16 : 3.)

"His idea of the social state was absurd; his bias was strong against marriage. Though we find him at one time saying, 'Marriage is honorable in all,' (Heb. 13 : 4,) yet he repeatedly insinuates against it. 'For I (Paul) would that *all men* were even as I myself' (unmarried.) (1 Cor. 7 : 7.) 'I say, therefore, to the unmarried and widows, it is good for them if they abide even as I.' (1 Cor. 7 : 8.) 'Art thou loosed from a wife? seek not a wife.' (1 Cor. 8 : 27.) On this question, he displays further inconsistency by saying that a widow was 'at liberty to be married to whom she will.' (v. 39.) Yet he declares to Timothy that 'younger widows,' 'when they have begun to wax wanton against Christ, they will marry, having damnation because they have cast off their first faith.' (1 Tim. 5 : 11, 12.) Such reasoning is totally indefensible.

"He was in favor of *caste*. 'Let every man abide in the same calling wherein he was called.' (1 Cor. 7 : 20.) This is an unwise check to all commendable ambition. He was in favor of servile obedience to the 'higher powers,' asserting that, 'the powers that be are ordained of God,' concerning which nothing can be more false; all experience goes to establish the utter rottenness of such a proposition. The acceptance of such a sentiment would be the degradation of liberty. Despots might rule 'by the grace of God,' and men submit to every usurper! No wonder that the first seven verses of the thirteenth chapter of Romans have ever been texts and letters of gold to secular and ecclesiastical tyrants.

"Woman, too, he would keep in ancient slavish submission; in this respect, he adhered to Jewish ideas. 'Let your women keep silence in the churches; for it is not permitted unto them to speak, but they are commanded to be under obedience.' 'And if they will learn any thing, let them ask their husbands at home; for it is a shame for women to speak in the church.' (1 Cor. 14 : 34, 35.) 'Let the women learn in silence with all subjection.' 'But I suffer not a woman to teach nor to usurp authority over the man, but to be in silence.' (1 Tim. 2 : 10, 11.) These clerical dicta were based on what he wishes the ladies to accept as sufficiently profound reasons. 'For Adam was first formed, then Eve.' 'And Adam was not deceived, but the woman, being deceived, was in the transgression.' (!) Yet to make up for her disqualification and inferiority, he adds a word of comfort in another direction. 'Notwithstanding, she shall be saved in child-bearing, if they continue in faith, and charity, and holiness, and sobriety.' (1 Tim. 2 : 13, 14, 15.) The connection, however, is somewhat bewildering.

"In trivial matters, too, he presumes to govern women, and issues very frivolous commands as to how they should even dress and wear their hair; she should appear in 'modest apparel, not with broidered hair, or gold, or pearls, or costly array.' (1 Tim. 2 : 9.) She should have 'long hair,' but should not pray with her head 'uncovered.' He said, 'But every woman that prayeth or prophesieth with her head uncovered dishonoreth her head; for that is even all one as if she were shaven.' 'For if the woman be not covered, let her also be shorn; but if it be a shame for a woman to be shorn or shaven, let her be covered.' 'Judge in yourselves, is it comely that a woman pray unto God uncovered?' (1 Cor. 11 : 5, 6, 13.)

"Man, however, being in his opinion her superior, was more privileged. 'For a man indeed ought not to cover his head, forasmuch as he is the image and glory of God; but the woman is the glory of the man.' 'For the man is not of the woman; but the woman of the man.' 'Neither was the man created for the woman; but the woman for the man.' 'For this cause ought the woman to have power on her head because of the angels.' (1 Cor. 11 : 7, 8, 9, 10.) This verse has completely defied the ability of commentators. What she was to gain by the 'power on her head because of the angels' is perhaps wisely inexplicable; and like the meaning of many other texts will be made known when it can be understood.

"Doth not even nature itself teach you that if a man have long hair it is a shame unto him?' 'But if a woman have long hair, it is a glory to her; for her hair is given her for a covering.' (!) (1 Cor. 10 : 14, 15.)

"A popular author may impose a silly tale on the public, and it will be read with delight; while a far superior one from an unknown writer may not get a single notice of approval. Doctors of divinity, ministerial sages, profound theologians—all of them eminent scholars, burdened with the lore of distinguished universities, will gravely read these priestly absurdities of Paul, and—must it be believed? actually try to eclipse each other by writing enigmatical comments upon them!

"Though the women of our times, the most resolute church members, seem not to have yet recognized the domineering spirit which dictated such commands; and though women are the most active agents to promote their circulation, yet as to these mandates, none—positively none—will obey them. They are a dead letter to all; but as part of the 'sacred word' are still included in 'holy writ,' and disseminated for spiritual edification! And were a Paul or an Apollos to preach them again among us, our mothers, and sisters, and wives would spurn the idea of being degraded to the social condition of the women of the Bible.

"Like other ecstatics, Paul professed to have received communications in dreams and visions; he even went in a trance as far as the 'third heaven;' and to impress all with the fullness of his power, undertook to perform miracles, but the evidence of this gift depends upon his own report to Luke. He was 'crafty' and was, as has been shown, willing to practice 'guile' to gain converts; even were a falsehood necessary for such a purpose, he could excuse himself, and say, 'For if the truth of God hath more abounded through *my lie* unto his glory, why yet am I judged as a sinner?' (Rom. 3 : 7.) He was high-minded and presumptuous, and said he was 'not a whit behind the very chiefest;' he was humble, 'less than the least of all saints.' He was vindictive, and could curse his ene mies; he could assume a different character, and say, 'Bless them which persecute you; bless and curse not.' (Rom. 12 : 14.) He could say, 'For there is no respect of persons with God.' (Rom. 2 : 11.) Yet in his ninth chapter to the Romans is to be found the main prop of predestination. 'Therefore hath he mercy on whom he will have mercy, and whom he will he hardeneth.' 'Hath not the potter power over the clay of the same lump to make one vessel unto honor and another unto dishonor?' (Rom. 9 : 18, 21.) He wrote to the Hebrews that, 'it was impossible for God to lie.' (Heb. 6 : 18.) To the Thessalonians, he declared that God could delude others to believe a lie. (2 Thes. 2 : 11.)

"In many respects, as we have just seen, his precepts were contradictory and his conduct inconsistent and prevaricating. It would take me too long to recount other instances in which he appears to disadvantage. I would not, therefore, consider Paul a safe guide in morals; and in my opinion, neither David nor Paul was as well qualified to teach mankind as were many of the ancient philosophers and moralists who never even heard of Moses or of Christ."

There was a pause, Mr. Baker looked as fierce as an angry inquisitor; the brethren were astonished at the boldness of Mr. Capel; yet his calm declamation, if it did not convince, it perplexed; and before any could reply, he continued, "I have a few words more to say, and, if not trespassing too far, would like to make a fuller confession of my reasons for leaving the faith, which you must perceive I have already left. To be plain, I do not consider the Bible the inspired 'word of God.' I have labored in vain for some time to discover who were its authors, where written, in what language, and at what time; none can tell, all is speculation. Though immense expense has been incurred in the circulation of that book and to disseminate its doctrines, yet Christianity has failed to attract mankind; its adherents are but a small minority compared with the whole. I do not believe that God will punish the great majority for their ignorance or unbelief. I never could heartily believe that a benevolent Being, who made man so fallible, would inflict an eternity of torture upon him for *any* offense. The wrath of man may exist against his fellow for a time, even for long, long years; but, as a general rule, if no counteracting influences are thrust upon him, nature will interfere, and the plea which he oft refused to hear will at last bring pity and forgiveness; I ask, can God be less than man in this sublime virtue?

"I have been asked, where we could find morality or civilization without Christianity? how it could be replaced? Man in every clime gets his morality with his humanity—the source of his love, and his joy, and his hope; but these good impulses have been too often controlled and misdirected by superstition. The religion of the Bible never yet clung to humanity with fidelity. The human mind contains within itself the germs of goodness, which will generally increase with intellectual growth! Morality and noble virtues were as fully developed among the ancient Greeks and Romans as they ever have been since. Christianity is not progressive; for centuries it kept in its formal track; it did nothing to advance cotemporaneous civilization; where it could not repress the spirit of progressive innovation, it tardily followed, and then—as it still does —it unblushingly arrogated the victory. *

"In London and in Rome, in Turkey and in Japan, on the Ganges and on the Nile, creeds are widely different; yet priests of every belief alike demand, 'How can you replace religion?' I answer, by the diffusion of greater knowledge, and the establishment of less inequality among mankind. Crime exists; it is mostly the result of want or from the dread of it. Reduce distress, and let there be more rational information, and you increase human happiness; this can be done. The blessed task will remain for a more perfect and paternal form of government than man has at present; but it can never be accomplished by any form of religion.

"Man must be led to advance in morality, first out of a regard for the principle itself, next for the approbation of his kind; and to avoid the inevitable consequences of a violation of the principle which are sure to follow in *this* world, not because of the dread of future punishment 'beyond the grave.'

"My friends, I feel that the pursuit of truth is to me most painful. To some it is but the work of a moment to bend to conviction, and reject errors as soon as they are discovered; with me it is different, I yield reluctantly, but yield I must. I have read that Bible at my mother's knee when I was a child, and heard with pleasure the story of Joseph and his brethren, of Samson's power and Solomon's wisdom. I read of these in the full belief that all was true, that there could be no trace of error among the then luminous pages of that book; with what regret have I discovered the mistake! I must soon return to my native land, but I can not pass the old church to where my mother often led me, where I worshiped as a child, without a pang, to think that I can worship there no more. The Sabbath bell may reach my ear like the sound of some olden melody, but its influence will be gone forever. And when I visit that mother's grave in the quiet of evening, I can not again read the text upon her tomb as the word of inspiration. None can tell how deeply I feel these things; it is hard to exclude the pleasing illusions of the past, but truth is worthy of every sacrifice, and in making this public acknowledgment I give my first offering."

"Your regrets are very poetical, and, if report is true, you are to have your reward, the price of your apostasy. Well, well, friends," cried Mr. Baker, "such a blasphemous tirade against God's blessed apostle I never before heard! I am even now surprised that I could sit and listen to it so long. It is a miracle that the Almighty did not hurl a special shaft of his vengeance against him that uttered, as well as against us that could allow his temple to be desecrated by such dreadful profanity! It is over, I hope; and God's mercy to us is great! As for that man, let him go his

* See Note II.

downward road ; we will not curse him, but his blood be upon his own head !"

"I do not know to what reward you allude," said Mr. Capel, "but I well know what I am to expect from the church for my recreancy. I can not expect any more indulgence than has been granted to others who have been forced to submit to conviction. I have hidden nothing from you; I have taken the unpopular side ; it can not be from any sinister motive. As there is a charge against my character, I wish to hear it ; I desire to know of what act of immorality I have been guilty ; I ask what is to be the reward of my apostasy ?"

There was some whispering among the brethren. Mr. Baker was very pressing with one brother to get up and speak ; it was Wesley Jacobs, the local preacher, and he seemed reluctant to comply with the urgency of the superintendent, who now looked as if in no very gracious mood. Old Father White sat aside by himself, and he viewed the young man, the late junior preacher, with an expression of pity.

"I hope no person will hesitate to accuse me of what I am thought guilty ; I am here to answer, and I again ask, What has been my immorality, and what is to be my reward ?"

Mr. Baker sprang up quite irritated, and almost shouted, "You have been seen drunk with a popish priest in a tavern—that's the immorality : and the reward you expect for your shameful desertion of the faith is an alliance with the daughter of that arch-fiend, Martin Maunors !"

These words, uttered quickly by the angry preacher, took almost all present by surprise ; the cat was let out of the bag ; a burning blush mounted to Mr. Capel's cheek ; and the ancient spinster, who had pertinaciously remained, gave a little scream ; but whether it was caused by the abrupt accusation, or from a fright occasioned by the presence of a fierce-looking man, who rushed from a back seat close to her side, is not certain. The man at once raised his rough fist, and cried out loud enough to be heard over the whole place, "That's another hypocritical lie—it is !" This unexpected interruption caused great confusion. Some of the brethren were for laying hands on the intruder ; but when they found he was not a maudlin wanderer, they prudently refrained. Mr. Baker, however, violently demanded that constables should be sent for. "This is the second time that that man has been sent here to disturb a religious meeting. I say, let him be arrested."

"That's another of your lies, it is. Ha! ha! you call this a religious meeting ! The last time I was here it was a bedlam, and now it's a shabby police-court—just that. Stand off my man," said Robert to one of the brethren who was approaching him, "stand off ; if you come any closer, I'll—yes, I will ! so keep off."

The brethren, rightly judging that he would be perhaps as good as his word, were afraid that a very discreditable scene might be enacted in the house of God. Mr. Capel very fortunately interfered ; he called the man aside, and prevailed upon him to leave the place. Robert, who had a great regard for Mr.

Capel, was, like others, anxious to hear what charges were to be brought against him ; he was indignant when he heard Mr. Maunors spoken of so disrespectfully. When he left the church, at Mr. Capel's bidding, he was very much inclined to believe that Mr. Baker and many of the saints at Hampstead were occasionally influenced by a spiritual potentate to whom no good Christian would dare to offer up a prayer.

Order being in a manner restored, brother Wesley Jacobs, the local preacher, after some pressing, said that, having heard that one or two members of his class were in the habit of visiting the Red Lion tavern for the purpose of hearing religious discussions, as well as to read skeptical books, against which he had often cautioned, he went there one evening, and, to his surprise, among others, saw Mr. Capel sitting at a table with a stranger who did not appear to be in his sober senses. Upon inquiry, he found that the stranger was a Catholic priest. There was a bottle on the table, and each had a tumbler before him which he believed contained intoxicating liquor. He might have been mistaken, but he thought that Mr. Capel acted rather strangely — unlike his ordinary way. "Indeed," said Mr. Jacobs, assuming to be rather scrupulous, "I'm sure I can not say whether he was —" "Oh! it's no matter—'tis quite sufficient," struck in Mr. Baker. "Friends, you see that brother Jacobs is over-cautious ; but he has told us enough—or rather he has privately told me enough. Just think of finding a preacher of the Gospel sitting in a low tavern, side by side with a popish priest, and not, as I have discovered, one of the most abstemious ! To make a companion of an ordained agent of the man of sin, even if he were as sober as Father Mathew, would be bad enough ; but to be on intimate terms with one whose propensities are notorious, what is the inference ?"

"This, then, I am to understand as my act of immorality. Well, I was present at the time and place mentioned by Mr. Jacobs ; and, were it of any avail to bring witnesses here, I could prove that neither I nor the gentleman mentioned was in any worse state than I am at present ; but where charity is wanting, evidence will have little effect. I had been out in the country all that day with the Rev. Mr McGlinn, and accepted his invitation to take dinner, on our return, at the Red Lion : when there, we partook of nothing stronger than ale. If this act is sufficient to justify the charge, then I am guilty. As a matter of duty to myself and to others, I have attended here in obedience to your summons. I shall not reply to the offensive liberty taken as to my motives for disbelief. If Mr. Baker can conscientiously sustain the course he has pursued toward me and others, then I can not expect strict justice before his tribunal. I shall make no appeal against any decision he may recommend, but will now retire."

Just as he got outside the door, Father White, who followed him, seized his hand, and, with tears in his eyes, said, "Well, brother, you, I suppose, leave us forever ; I can not think that you are willful in opposing an ancient creed ; you believe you are right, I am sure you do." He kept his eyes fixed on the ground, and was silent for a moment, as if troubled, by some rebellious thought, and then, almost in a whisper, added, " You may be right, but it is too late for me now to think of these things ! For long years I have made religion my staff, my hope, and my light. I may linger here a few more winters, but I can not, at the eleventh hour, give up the lamp I have held so long ; and though its light may appear feeble to you, I must now bear it with me to the grave."

Among the records made at the quarterly meeting that evening, there was one to show that Henry Capel, late junior preacher on the Hampstead circuit, was expelled from the membership of the Wesleyan Methodist Church for " Immorality," and this was attested by the rough, cramped signature of " James Baker, Chairman."

CHAPTER XXVIII.

THE autumn had passed away, and the feeble ray of an evening sunlight in November rested upon the window near which Mary Mannors was sitting. She had been engaged for some time making alterations in a dress, and the heavy folds of crape which were added gave no token of returning cheerfulness. There was no formal or conventional "putting on" of that which she did not feel ; her deep black raiment truly indicated the grief which was around her own heart.

As the light grew less, she ceased her work, and looked up at the cold, gray sky, and at the shadows which were stretching over the distant hills, and over the bare, brown fields, and bending down as if to rest and remain over the dim city. It was from this very window that, some months before, her mother was awed by the appearance of the shining cross ; and now, as Mary looked in the direction of St. Paul's, she could just distinguish the same object, faintly brightened by the waning sunset.

Alas ! what a reverie that glimpse brought her ! Every phase of her mother's mind, every illusion, every event, culminating in insanity and in death—a grave in Hampstead cemetery, and a prison asylum, perhaps for life ! She looked care-worn and pale, as if the trials of years had been crowded into months. The course of her life had been almost completely altered ; she had new duties to perform, which she undertook cheerfully ; she could be reconciled to the sad bereavement and affliction, but the scandal which had been uttered against her father, and the uncharitable insinuations of the pharisaical grieved her sorely. Her mother had been for some time in a private asylum ; in her case, alas ! there was no room for hope ; the best advice in London had been obtained, but no skill could induce any improvement.

Well, among other passing thoughts—alternate vistas of the memory, dark and bright—it was possible, or rather probable, that she should think of Mr. Capel, he who had been

with them for so many months. Ah me ! for how many pleasant days—whose stay had been so agreeable ; who had been so like a brother ; and whose good, kind, generous disposition had so won the esteem of those who knew him best. She did think of him ; she was aware of his change of opinion, of his expulsion, and of the discreditable attempts made to injure his reputation and affect his prospects for life. She knew of these, and, could he learn the great depth of her sympathy for him, how cheerfully he would have borne every reproach, and braved every enmity to live and gain her favor. But there was another reason why her thoughts now reverted to him—she was even troubled—he was soon going to return to Ireland, to leave them, perhaps, forever. He had too much spirit to remain any longer like a dependent upon her father, more particularly as the busy tongues of Mr. Baker and some of the brethren had attributed his change of faith as well as his protracted stay at Hampstead cottage to a certain motive. For this reason he had left the residence of Mr. Mannors, and since his almost *ex-parte* trial had been staying with his friend, Father McGlinn ; under such peculiar circumstances, it would not, therefore, be prudent to press him to remain at Hampstead.

Mary might not have been told all this, but she suspected something of the kind and she appreciated his delicate consideration. She believed he was poor ; she knew he had no profession, trade, or occupation—perhaps no well-to-do relatives willing to aid him ; and, in imagination, she followed him from place to place in his wanderings for a position of some kind ; she knew how soon an evil word would bear against him. The *Watchman*, the Methodist organ, had already given its warning to the faithful ; she knew he would have the scorn and rebuke of the godly and the suspicion of the formalist. She fancied him buffeted about by misfortune—poor, and friendless, and hopeless—until at last he sunk in despair, meeting the fate of a thousand others. She then wondered, as she often did before, why she should be so troubled about a comparative stranger ; she shrank from the thought of making him one, she could not look upon him as such ; she, as yet, scarcely understood her own feelings toward him, though they were a fresh cause of anxiety ; yet, such as they were, she felt a kind of pleasure in their indulgence ; and now she sat considering how she could be of benefit to him, how she, poor thing ! unskilled in the rough matters of life, could advance his future prospects ; she did not want to see him borne out into the great contending crowd, and pass away forever.

By what means could she introduce the subject to her father ? What a relief it would be could she speak her mind to him fully and freely as in other matters, and tell him of her fears, and of the mountain of pious prejudice that would lie in the wanderer's way. How could she enlist him to act in behalf of that young man ? But alas ! she could not frame the most simple speech for her father's ear ; she could find ready words for any one else, for the greatest stranger, but not for Henry Capel—

why not for him? To find a proper answer for her own plain query caused her great embarrassment.

Mr. Mannors might have thought of the future prospects of his young friend, and most probably did. He was one of those who naturally anticipated the wants of others, and tried to provide for them; he was among the least selfish of the earth.

He perhaps knew that Mr. Capel had no resources, and he might have laid some plan for his advantage; but any thing he did, or intended to do, in this respect, he kept entirely to himself. Though his affliction was heavy, and though the tongue of scandal was busy, yet his old cheerful manner remained; and he tried to lighten the burden of others, hiding the care which was so weighty to himself. As for Mary, no daughter could have been more dutiful or affectionate; his first desire was to promote her happiness, and, as she was all now to him, he was determined to do every thing in his power to make her future as bright and as free from the bleak shadows of adversity as possible.

Mr. Mannors had the faculty of judging character almost at a glance. In an inquiry, he fixed his mild gray eye upon you, and if there was any wavering from strict integrity, if there was any lurking deceit, he knew it at once. It would be very difficult for one who was a pretender to escape detection at his hands. Now, Mr. Capel had been as one of his family for several months, and from the first hour that he entered the cottage, Mr. Mannors was impressed in his favor as being worthy of all confidence; and, day after day, as the character and disposition of the young preacher became more developed, so much the more was that confidence in him established. Indeed, it was one of Mrs. Mannors's peculiar enjoyments to hear her husband commend a minister of the Gospel as he did Mr. Capel; and every one in Hampstead cottage seemed to anticipate with pleasure his return from the circuit. Such regard did not escape the observation of Mr. Mannors; and he rightly judged that one so gentle and confiding, yet so discriminating as his daughter, could not be less appreciative. He was a close observer, and for some time he noticed symptoms, the least of which, he thought, indicated that deep down in poor Mary's heart there was a feeling which she tried to hide even from herself and from all others; but of this he was determined to be more fully assured.

"Well, Mary," said Mr. Mannors, entering the dusky room, "so we are going to lose Mr. Capel; I have just come in to say that he will call here to-morrow to bid us adieu. How sorry I am for this! I was very much pleased with his society, and few indeed will miss him as I shall. He tells me that he is going at once to Ireland. I question much if he well knows what he is going there for; however, it seems best to him, and though we may never see him again, I shall always remember him as deserving of my highest regard. I am sure we shall all regret his departure. I had hopes that the pleasing acquaintance we had formed would have continued for years; what a pity that our intimacy should

be so short! Thus it is, Pop; they will leave us one by one; one to-day and another to-morrow, and you and I are to be left alone."

How fortunate it was for her that the dim light prevented her father from observing the sudden pallor that blanched her cheek and brow! She could have fallen, but made a powerful effort to cling to the chair; as for words, she could find no utterance—the effort to articulate seemed to choke her. What would she not have then given to be alone?

"How cold your forehead is, child; and so are your cheeks." He passed his hand tenderly over her face and head, and she shrunk back at the touch. "Why, you almost tremble! Mary, you must, I fear, be ill."

She could just reply, "Indeed, pa, I feel quite well, only perhaps a little chilly. Don't you find the room very cold?" and she moved away from the open door.

"No, not particularly so; not for me, at least. You have been too much confined lately; after this, we must walk or drive out oftener. Since Mr. Capel left the house, you have been out very seldom. I have, I fear, been too negligent; but I will take you again over some of his favorite drives; it will renew him in our memory—at least it will in mine—when he is far away, poor fellow!"

That sad heart was again fluttering, beating, bounding, but it would not do for Mary to be silent; oh! what a struggle to appear calm; her mute anguish could have been eloquent in tears, but she dare not weep, she must now speak. "He leaves to-morrow, then, does he, pa?" said she, trying to assume a tone of indifference. "Well, I'm sure we shall all be very sorry. He may not be back again, you think?"

"No, I don't suppose he ever expects to return; he has no tie here; save our sympathy, he can have no inducement to remain. The Methodists are now his bitter enemies, and you know the slander of the godly is the most defamatory. He may, perhaps, think of going to America or to Australia, to any place where he may not be known as an apostate preacher. What a shame that he should be driven, for conscience' sake, like an Ishmael, away from home and friends; but alas! he has no home, and where are his friends?"

"Neither home nor friends! that is very sad, pa," said she, with tremulous voice. She could hardly control her feelings; she would have gladly rushed into her father's arms, and have wept and pleaded for the dear friend who was about to be cast out upon the world; but that dreadful, unnatural restraint kept her back, that uncontrollable influence which would now make her appear so different from what she really was; she still sat like a statue, merely repeating the bleak monosyllables, "No home nor friends!"

"Well, child, he is still young, and, though going out alone upon the stormy sea of life, like a bark into a tempest, he may yet reach some favored port, and find those who may learn to esteem him. I have no doubt of his success; it will be gratifying to hear of this. We shall see him to-morrow, and learn more of his intentions." And Mr. Mannors, having some business to transact, kissed his daughter's forehead, and bid her good-night.

When he entered his own room, he paced it backward and forward for some time, in deep thought; he then sat at his desk and drew from it a parchment, which he carefully read over; afterward he wrote two or three long letters, and then retired.

Poor Mary, left alone, sat for hours at the window, watching the glimmer of distant lights and looking up at the great black night-clouds, moving slowly over the leafless trees. She listened to every sound, as if anticipating some farewell step passing through the garden; and then, with her face almost touching the glass, she peered out into the darkness, like one watching for a bright star to cheer the rayless night. Like her father, she delighted in thinking and suggesting for the good of others; but now she was unable to shape any idea for the benefit of him she was so anxious to serve; and, totally failing in this, she, perhaps for the first time in her life, began to think of her own future.

The cruel morning came at last; a cold, drizzling rain had set in for some time, and the melancholy season imparted deeper gloom to every thing in and around Hampstead. The old clock in the church tower struck the hours, and the sound reached the ear like a distant wail—not like the full, clear, ringing tone it often gave in happier days. The trees in the small park stood up like a long row of silent mourners awaiting a great funeral, and an air of sadness seemed to pervade all. Even the very children who ventured to rush out into the splashy, guttered highways were discouraged from play by the chill, dreary sky, and ran back again to the more cheerful fireside.

Mr. Mannors awaited his expected friend; he sat in the parlor looking over the morning paper, and Mary, with pale face and beating heart, went briskly from room to room, bustling about as if she had scarcely a minute to sit and think of any thing in particular. Hannah, who had been for some time on the look-out for the visitor, was rather surprised at her unusual diligence; and as Mary occasionally passed her father, he would raise his eyes from the paper, and look thoughtfully after her, as if in doubt of his own penetration.

About eleven o'clock a carriage drove up to the gate; a small trunk was fastened behind, and two persons alighted. Robert, who was in waiting, warmly shook Mr. Capel's proffered hand, and bowed to the Rev. Mr. McGlinn, as he followed his friend toward the house. Mr. Mannors received them both at the door; and Mary quickly left the room, in the hope of being able to get a moment or two to compose herself, and to try and wear a look the very opposite of what she felt.

"Well, my friend," said Mr. McGlinn, "you see I have brought the truant back again. I suppose," said he, looking archly at Mr. Capel, "that he would have been inclined to take French leave, if I had not kept my eye on him. I know he hates leave-taking, and for some reason, he, I think, particularly disliked to pay such a *pro forma* visit here. You see nothing will do him but 'go back,' as the Irish say, to the 'ould sod,' and show his loving countrymen the *San Benito* which Father Baker, one of the Wesleyan popes, has thrown upon his shoulders. Faith, such an investment has the sanction of *my* church, any how; the good ould Christian way of decoration, so as a heretic might look a little more decent on his high-road to the—well, I won't say what in polite company. 'Twas a blessing in disguise, I suppose; ha, ha! much good may it do you, Harry, any way!"

"Indeed," said Mr. Capel, "I could never think of leaving England without calling here to acknowledge my obligations to one of the kindest friends I ever met. I can truly say that the period of my stay at Hampstead has been one of the most agreeable of my life—one that I shall forever remember, with pleasure."

"Now don't say any thing about obligations," said Mr. Mannors, "or you will make me your debtor. Mary," said he, as his daughter entered the room, "here is Mr. Capel, actually come to bid us farewell. I am sorry, very sorry for this; I wish we could keep him longer, for it may be some time before we all meet again."

Mr. Capel's cheek was flushed as he looked at Mary; he was surprised at the change; he had not seen her for several days, and now he perceived a sad alteration.

She was dressed in deep black; there was an expression of care upon her pale face which he had never noticed before. The delightful vivacity of her nature had given way, and traces of subdued grief were still apparent in her sweet submission. She sat near him on the sofa, and while her father and the kind priest held a conversation, she ventured to tell Mr. Capel that she hoped he would enjoy himself in Ireland; she supposed he had friends there whom he was anxious to meet after so long a separation.

"If you mean relatives, Miss Mannors, I really can not say whether I shall find any now willing to acknowledge me. I know of none who wish my return; they are, any that I know of, strict church members. I am under a *ban*. I would like to see my native city; but I never shall forget Hampstead and the few friends I leave behind."

She would have liked to hint that there might be other friends. Some particular one, perhaps, whose attractive power could hurry him away even from his good friend the priest, but she could not trust herself with words. There was no way in which she could venture to communicate any of the thoughts which disturbed her, or make herself understood. The embarrassment in this respect was mutual; and after talking, as it were, in a circle for some time upon indifferent matters—as remote as possible from the subject nearest the heart—there was an unpleasant pause, and either would have given a world to be able to make the least revelation or to obtain one word of encouragement. But the golden moments flew by; though each at the time considered them as moments of destiny, they were allowed to pass without improvement, and inexorable fate seemed to have fixed an eternal seal upon their separation.

"Time is nearly up, Harry," said Father M'Glinn—he often used this familiarity, and called him Harry—"time is nearly up; the Cork packet starts at six; we have yet to drive to the city, and to call upon Tom, Dick, and Harry ; and, even if we spend but half an hour with each, it will give me little enough time afterward to exorcise you and give you the benefit of my poor blessing. Friend Baker, you know," said he, turning to Mr. Mannors, "says that Harry is possessed. Ha! ha!"

"Possessed of more charity, no doubt," said Mr. Mannors. "Well, he leaves Hampstead, and we all regret it; don't we, Pop? But he leaves the limited round he lately traveled for that far more extensive circuit—the wide world. I trust he will henceforth preach the common brotherhood of all nations, and the great gospel of humanity."

"Faith, that is the real true gospel—you have me with you there! It is the one I best understand ; it requires no learned commentators to make it plain. There are no sects in humanity, no mercenary piety, nor heartless inquisitors. It is the great creed for all mankind! What a change *that* gospel will bring! Do not look surprised ; Harry knows that I am in a strait, but I am not the only ecclesiastic that is prepared to stand uncovered before the altar of reason. Yes, I am in a singular position ; but I will soon have my liberty. The dawn is coming, and we shall soon be surprised at the multitudes who will move out into the sunlight ; thousands who now timidly hide within the shadow of superstition long to see that day. When that pure gospel shall have been preached, we will have morality without creeds, reform without cruelty, national amity without threats ; the priest, and the soldier, and the executioner must disappear with other concomitants of Christian civilization. You must," said he, addressing Mr. Capel, "go on and not be easily discouraged. He who attempts to reform an abuse must expect calumny. If you attack an antiquated imposition, you are sure to be waylaid by the prejudiced and interested. They who love truth—not they who live godly—must suffer persecution. Take courage, and let your light shine, for even now there is a growing principle that will uphold the right."

Mr. Mannors then handed him a small package which he said contained one or two letters of introduction to old friends in Ireland, and a few words of advice from himself, which he was to read upon his arrival in that country.

The parting glass of wine was then taken, and tears rushed into the eyes of Mr. Mannors as he took his friend's hand to assure him of his unalterable friendship. Father Tom had to cough and strut smartly about to hide his emotion ; and Mr. Capel, as he looked out upon the garden-walks, and around the familiar walls, and then upon Mary's pale face, it might be, he thought, for the last time, felt his heart almost give way, and he had to hurry out of the house somewhat abruptly to escape an utter breaking down.

In the hall stood Robert and the good Hannah, holding her apron to her eyes ; and Flounce sat thoughtfully by her side, perhaps thinking of his young master who but a short time before had left them forever.

All assembled to bid Mr. Capel a kind farewell ; even the old clock, near the door, appeared in waiting like an ancient retainer, its pendulum swinging to and fro, as if waving adieu to passing time.

When Mr. Capel and Father Tom left the hospitable home of Mr. Mannors and drove away in the dreary mist, poor Mary hurried up to her window and watched the receding carriage. Oh! how eagerly she followed it ; and as it grew less and less in the distance, she strained her eyes to still keep it in view ; and when at last it was buried in the November gloom, she threw herself on her couch and burst into tears.

CHAPTER XXIX.

THE REV. DOCTOR BUSTER sat alone in his study ; he had been reading the morning paper, and had just laid it aside. Snow-flakes were falling and melting in the muddy streets; and as the weather was not sufficiently tempting to induce him to leave the cheerful fireplace, either for study or private prayer, he made amends by refilling a long clay pipe, and then, elevating his feet on the sides of the grate, leaned back in his easy-chair, puffed away leisurely, and seemed for a time only intent upon watching the ascent of the little whirling clouds of smoke which he blew out in long gray lines toward the chimney. He looked very thoughtful ; now surveying the grotesque forms into which his fancy shaped the glowing coals, now glancing at the array of authors quietly ranged around on the loaded book-shelves, as if awaiting his command to jump down in defense of the faith ; once or twice he paused to listen to passing footsteps, and then resumed his cogitations.

Was he thinking of his next sermon? Pshaw! that was not in his line ; he had, like other distinguished divines, a pile of the most select and orthodox discourses laid away, sufficient to last for a lifetime, should he require them. Indeed, his mind was not just then altogether bent on heavenly matters; generally, there was a large proportion of the earthly ingredient mixed up with his contemplations; but at the present moment things terrestrial were entirely running through his brain, and things spiritual were perhaps judiciously laid aside for a more convenient season.

The most notable and exemplary Christian ministers have occasionally to descend to worldly affairs ; human passions or emotions may not have been sufficiently subdued. Secular contamination has, alas! too often distracted the attention of many a saint, and the reverend doctor, like others of the "sacred calling," was often forced to turn his consideration exclusively to the weak, beggarly elements of the world, and to become harassed and agitated by the perishable things of time and sense. His religion never yet came to the rescue ; as a frail man, he grew more frail, until vileness was a characteristic ; he could never learn to love an enemy, or even to forgive one ; and dreadful thoughts of hatred, revenge, and blood alternately overwhelmed and controlled his impulses.

Minute after minute passed; at times, he would mutter and frown darkly, as he gazed at the red bars—he never smiled when he was alone—and he would turn frequently and look out as if exasperated at the disagreeable weather, which perhaps helped to detain him within that dull house.

After a time he got up, and, having knocked the ashes from his pipe, went and unlocked a small cupboard, took out a decanter of brandy, and, having nearly half-filled a tumbler, drank it off at once, without reducing its prime strength with any a mixture of pure water. He then commenced to pace the room, and would often stop at the window to look down the sloppy street, as if anxious to see some one approach, or as if expecting a visitor.

"Curse the brat! it is now nearly eleven," said he, pulling out his massive gold watch; "does he intend to keep me here all day? he must have got my note." And again the doctor looked up and down the street, growing at the same time more and more impatient.

A tap was now heard at a private door which led from the study into a small yard connecting with a back lane or alley. The doctor gently lifted a corner of the blind of the window which looked out into this place, and cautiously peered from behind it. In a moment he unbolted the door, and Mrs. Pinkley, well muffled up, entered.

"Ah Fanny! is it you?" and he actually hurried to hug the hidden form. "I did not expect you until evening. Any news?" said he, rubbing his hands together briskly, and drawing a chair for her toward the fire.

"Why, you've been away so long, doctor, I thought I'd drop in as soon as I could, when I heard you was back. We've been busy at the *Home* lately, and as I had a chance, I thought I'd run in. My! but it's a nasty day," said the lady, deliberately shaking her cloak, and placing it on the back of her chair.

"My visitation was much longer than I expected; I always have so many grumbling pastors to satisfy, so much petty jealousy to get rid of. Confound them, they are the most hard to please; and then there are so many disputes among congregations, that one's time is greatly taken up. Any way, I wanted to be out of the city for a while, though one or two weeks are not long passing. But tell me, what's the news? I've been expecting Bross all the morning. I sent him a line last evening to drop in to-day on his way to the office. I'm better pleased to see you any way; Fanny —draw closer to the fire."

"Oh! them clerks, you know, doctor, haven't always their own time at command. In fact, neither have I, just now; but, any way, I thought I'd call and tell you about the children."

"I'm satisfied enough about them, as long as they are under your charge; they are well enough, I suppose—you'll see to that, Fanny; but what of their good mother? the same old story, I expect."

"Well, just about the same," said Mrs. Pinkley, with a careless air.

"Ay, 'twill be so to the end of the chapter and I wish it were ended long ago; what a curse she is, to be sure!" And the venom that glistened under his bushy eyebrow, as he glanced meaningly at his companion, brought the least smile to the surface of the red face of the amiable Mrs. Pinkley.

"Things may soon come right," said she, giving a little cough. "Dr. Marks is very kind to her somehow—very kind; but yet—"

"But yet—the devil!" said the doctor, now rising and stamping angrily upon the hearth. "I told him more than a dozen times I wanted no mild work with her; what is she good for? what is her vile *life* to me? He knows what I want well enough. Does the fool expect me to commit myself to pen, ink, and paper? You must see to this, Fanny—*you* must help me. If Dr. Marks wishes to make his patronized *Home*, his famous *Maison de Santé*, more popular at my expense, he will find his mistake. I was a fool to send her there; we might have managed better, far better here, ourselves. If he can't serve me, others will. I'll see to this."

"Patience, doctor," said Mrs. Pinkley, with the mildest voice possible. "Things, you know, can't be done in a hurry, even there. Dr. Marks will never do what you want—never. Take care how you approach him on a matter of life and death! The *Home* is popular, and he intends to keep it so. You and I understand each other; then have nothing to say to Dr. Marks about *that*. I have a great charge; he trusts me with many of his patients, and I can not be too cautious for a while. Whom can *I* trust in that place? I can catch staring eyes and listening ears in every corner; better take time; better, far better, have her under Marks than where you would send her. There are few inquests held over his dead; no suspicion, no detectives on the hunt, no hue and cry in the papers; he manages all that. Come, what do you say?"

The doctor's face grew livid; there was something in the imperturbable manner of the woman that fairly awed him, savage as he even then was. He looked steadily at the fire for a few moments without opening his lips. Then, laying his hand affectionately upon the lady's shoulder, he said: "Yes, better take time; you're right, Fanny, you're right. I am too rash; I will leave this business to you; but when I think of what I have suffered by that wretch, I only wish that we had another Laud, and another Star-Chamber. —Well, tell me, what of that Hampstead ruffian; have you heard any thing?"

"Only there's been such a precious row among the Methodist saints; brother Baker, one of your kind friends, has excommunicated brother Capel, and Mrs. Mannors's household chaplain has left for parts unknown —some say for Ireland."

"Ha! ha! ha!" The doctor gave a loud sardonic laugh, and again rubbed his hands with positive delight. "The infernal hypocrites! I did hear some time ago that Capel, an Irish apostle, was imported for the special purpose of converting that fiend. Convert *him;* good God! To send a smooth-faced milk-sop to convert Mannors! He'd make perverts of a dozen such empty fools, of course, with the assistance of his virtuous daughter." There was a scowl on the doctor's face whenever it was turned toward Hampstead.

"You've heerd, I suppose, about his mad wife; about the raving Methodist saint? Them revivals are a help to Dr. Marks."

"Oh! yes," said the doctor, chuckling; "the meek Martin knows something of bedlam now as well as his neighbors; ha! ha! They tell me that that Jezebel he keeps in the house with him only wore a religious mask, like other Methodists, to effect her purposes. Hannah, I think they call her, professed to be one of the church militant, and her simple mistress was enraptured with her for a time, until she found out which way the wind blew; no wonder she had her brain turned. But tell me, Fanny," said he, suddenly recollecting and looking at her intently, "how can the Methodist revivals help Dr. Marks; how, tell me?" He seemed anxious for a reply.

She was silent a moment or two, as if pondering thoughtfully upon her answer; she then slowly bent over and whispered something in his ear.

As if stung by an adder, he sprang from his chair and stared wildly and savagely at the woman before him. But she never quailed like the poor creature he had so often abused; she returned his gaze as calmly as if some pleasing notion were then passing through her brain.

"God of heaven!" exclaimed he at last; "is it possible?" He could only then utter these passionate words.

"Just as I tell you; she is there, she is with us at the *Home*, as comfortable as heart could wish." And Mrs. Pinkley's little smile was again making its appearance, as if she had communicated the most agreeable information.

"Heavens and earth! the fellow must be mad—raving mad," roared the doctor, in a perfect fury. "Gracious Saviour!—well, may the eternal—"

"Oh! fie, fie!" quickly interrupted Mrs. Pinkley, and laying her hand upon his shoulder, "Don't swear, doctor, don't swear, even in *my* presence; 'tisn't worth your while; tut, tut, 'tis but a trifle." And she met his angry eye with the most provoking amiability.

"Let me go, woman, let me go," said he, stepping back, pale and wild with rage. "Did you come here only to bring me this damned information? Did you come here to bid me curse you, and him, and everybody? Did you come to hurry me on faster and faster to misery? Have I not been harassed enough with that living devil which you *will* keep alive? Are you in league with that fool, that imbecile, that knave, to say that you can remain with him after he has almost betrayed me by accepting as a patient the very wife of my greatest and most dangerous enemy, Martin Mannors? Just think of his demented Methodist wife raving her unmeaning prayers alongside of mine; just think of the same treacherous, incorrigible infidel walking in and out of that place daily, and then making

his grand discovery. Did you come here, like a Job's comforter, to tell me of this?"

She did not even then condescend a reply; she seemed like a physiologist in a study over some inferior animal; she watched the expression of his face and eye, and then glanced at his nervous, twitching fingers, as if she expected to see him suddenly grasp something and tear it to pieces

"I came here partly for that purpose, and if I didn't tell you, how could you find it out, eh? You might go in and out there every hour of the day and be none the wiser. If I did not stay with Dr. Marks, either as a day or night attendant, he might be inclined to fancy your good wife quite restored, and within less than a month she might walk out, sensible of her own wrongs and armed with the *law*. How would that please you, doctor?" said she, still studying every rough feature. "You are a great man in the pulpit; you have great influence in the General Assembly; but, la me! what a simpleton I have found you—a perfect child in some things—a great big buzzing fly, that would be entangled in many a skillful web if I did not put in my finger and take you out." When saying this, she gently placed her forefinger within the angle of the wall, as if in the act of rescuing a veritable blue-bottle.

"This," continued she, "has been so for years; you overrate your influence with many. Dr. Marks won't be caught; he won't leave himself in your power, or in mine, or in the power of anybody else. As you desired it, he allows me to attend upon your wife; of course, I make my daily report, and he believes she is a little crazy—just a little only—so little, that she would be out, yes, out, before now if it hadn't been for—now, who do you think? And you would curse me for serving you this way, would you?"

The cool, collected Mrs. Pinkley moved back and surveyed him with a feeling akin to scorn, as he kept demurely near the window, frowning out at the massive black clouds away in the distance.

"Do you think," she again said, "that Dr. Marks would refuse patients merely to please your whim? He wants money as well as others, and he couldn't afford it. There may be fifty patients in together, and not one know the other; and fifty different fathers, or mothers, or husbands may call to visit, and not find out that their next door neighbor was there under treatment. I have been there now for some time, and as yet don't hardly know who's who; I have tried to find out secrets in that place, but, sharp as I think I am, I often get completely foiled; I told you there were eyes and ears all around."

"Then how did you learn that Mrs. Mannors was one of the ornaments of the institution; you did not know her before; perhaps you are so fortunate as to have control of the religious department; perhaps Marks has great faith in your prayers?" said Doctor Buster sarcastically.

"I knew that she was there, because I saw her husband call on more than one occasion, and I soon found out his errand."

"Then he found out you; no doubt he

quickly ascertained the full value of your indispensable services, in case his wife should want consolation," sharply retorted the doctor.

"There again you're mistaken; he has never laid eyes on me since I managed to bring you and him together at Tottenham Court road; you don't forget that I put you in possession of his letter to your wife?"

"I remember."

"Well, it's a wonder you do. I am not so simple as to let him recognize me since that. I have watched his coming, and kept clear of him. What if you were in my place? Good Lord! what a mess you'd make of it. I'll take care of Martin Mannors. You induced me to enter Dr. Marks's service; if I leave, so will your wife. Then you may go, for you will be undone."

It is said that certain powerful and ravenous beasts have often been controlled by weak and insignificant animals. The lion may entertain a partiality for a poodle dog, and indulge its gambols, and he may suffer his flowing mane to be pulled and tugged at with impunity. Whatever the nature of Mrs. Pinkley's influence over the doctor might be, it was evident that she, as the weaker vessel, had almost absolute rule; he submitted to her when it might be dangerous in a measure for any one else to approach him; and when his temper at times grew savage, she had only to speak, or rebuke, or threaten in her own way, and he became as docile as a child.

"Fanny," said the doctor now, in his blandest manner, "I sometimes think I'm mad; I must be nearly so to speak to you as I have. But I was startled by what you told me—it was so unexpected, so cursedly provoking; but it is no fault of yours, I see that. It is unfortunate that Marks took such a patient; we must, however, make the best of it; but you must stay there now, you must be for the future as *her* shadow. It is obvious that I can not visit that place, it might be fatal to our plan; but Mannors will go, and so will his daughter; you must now catch every word, see every motion—watch him, watch her, watch every body."

"Now you are more reasonable," said the lady, in a complimentary tone; "I knew that we should have a little storm, that you would bluster awhile, it was only bluster after all. It is now over, and we must look at the business quietly and consider what is best to be done." They were again seated before the fire—Mrs. Pinkley as if perfectly at home, and the doctor was tamed down to the standard or quality of a rational being.

"Fanny, I know how deeply I am indebted to you, I can never forget that. I know how faithfully you have served me in times past; I know what you have risked for me, and how powerless I might often have been without your ready aid; and hear me, Fan," said he, drawing closer to her, "I know my promise to you, I remember it well, and, by heavens! just as soon as I am at liberty—ay, the very day I am made a widower, that promise shall be renewed and carried out in due time."

Whether it was the gentle oath—gentle, of course, on such an occasion—that the doctor then swore, or the unnatural tenderness that seemed to wander about his hard features, like a lost sunbeam in a desert, that made the amiable Mrs. Pinkley blush a deeper pink, she did really blush; it came to that, and then bashfully as it were raising her hand to shade her eyes from his ogre-like glances, she looked modestly down at the hearth, as if overcome by a very peculiar emotion.

"Well, doctor," said she, with eyes still bent down and emphasizing her words, "I *did* want to hear that promise again, I did. I sometimes have been foolish enough to think that you might forget me for some favored one of the rich, proud, pious ladies that swarm around you. I have made sacrifices for you; for your sake I got rid of Pinkley and became a widow; for you I have remained so, and am willing to wait. Ay," said she, lowering her voice almost to a whisper, and regarding him with singular interest, "you know what I have done and am still willing to do to join our fate. Yes, I wanted that promise renewed. I wanted your most sacred word—even your oath, your solemn oath."

"You shall have my word, or my oath, or any thing else you desire. Have I not trusted all to you, and put myself in your power, as you have placed yourself in mine? Can you doubt? Our interests are one—not my interest alone, but my inclination is toward you. Never think of the brainless butterflies that flutter around your gospel luminaries. I know their value, the full value of such very pious ladies, and I know yours. You have ability, Fan; tact, shrewdness, caution, courage—true courage; that's the quality! never think again of those moths. I tell you I have promised, and will perform. I must do so; I can not do without you. You are my legal adviser, Fan; my faithful pilot in every storm, but I am still in bonds; when, when shall I be free?"

"That's an important question to answer; it won't do to be in too great a hurry. I am, I know I am, more anxious than you, but I am more cautious. Oh! how I wish this affair was over? Pinkley's was bad enough; will this be worse? There are some imps in the *Home* that I must get rid of. I have spoken to Marks about a change, and have given him some plausible reasons. I think he is willing; we have already engaged a new keeper, and if I can only get a few other total strangers in place of some of our present inquisitive attendants, I shall, I think, be able to avoid all suspicion."

"That's the point, Fan; beware of that rock!"

"Your wife is cautious with me; I made up a story to explain about how that letter from Mannors got into your hands, still she is cautious. She has, I am sure, one confident that I will get rid of, and then—"

There was a pause. What a terrible revelation might have been made by the full, free completion of the sentence. Even an unwonted gravity settled upon the doctor's face—not in dread of the commission of actual crime, but of the terrible detection which, in spite of all, might possibly follow. He thought of this, for he knew the determination of her who had just spoken.

"But tell me, doctor," she continued, "we are now, I may say, talking practically; supposing every thing all over as you could desire; you say that you would not stay here very long afterward; so far, so good. But what are your means? You have got through a lot of hard cash, sure enough. You are always complaining of a want of money. All I have saved is about one hundred and fifty or sixty pounds—a great deal to me, but, goodness! only a mere trifle to you. Now, what are your means? Then there's the children, think of that."

"Now, *you* are the simpleton. Why, did you for a moment think that I have been forgetting the main point? Not I; I never forget that. You know I lost heavily by that stock I purchased, but that will be soon made up. I have already got a full score of your pious butterflies at work for me. I can always depend upon them. They believe I have robbed myself to give to the poor; let them think so. Of course, I have had to throw away a good deal that way for appearance' sake. I have, however, told my silken saints this time, in plain English, that I wanted no presents—neither gilt-edged books, nor shining plate, nor baubles of any kind; that cash, hard cash, was necessary for certain pious purposes; and already there have been a number of tea-meetings, and bazaars and fairs are still in progress—every thing in full blast. I have managed to start a nice little rivalry, and cash *will* come in this time."

The fair Mrs. Pinkley seemed very much interested in these details, and her reverend gallant rose greatly in her estimation; she admired him in the character of such a deluder.

"Then I can get Wilkins, the banker, one of our church, to discount a note for any amount. I have managed to be clear on his books for some time, and I can arrange to take a cool thousand there; I will see about that to-day, and, when I am gone, the Rev. Andrew Campbell, my indorser, can afford to lose it. He has, to my knowledge, nearly double that amount to his credit; and he may thank me for his present good position. I intend to make *him* grateful."

"Well, doctor," said the lady, in the prettiest manner she could assume, "I always heard among our church members that you were good at finance, as you call it; popular ministers—indeed, preachers of all kinds—have the real knack of getting money—raising the wind, as they say—filthy lucre! he! he! he!"

"That's not all, Fan," said the doctor, flattered by her approval; "see here! this is a sub-scription-list for the erection of a new church near Highgate; just look! one, two, three of them down for a thousand pounds each, and five others for five hundred a piece. Now, the contract is not to be let until five thousand of this sum is placed in my hands. Yes, in mine, as treasurer for the trustees." And his fist closed tightly at the pleasant idea.

"Now, if I should be, say, so unfortunate as to lose the money, or have it st'len—a thing, you know, of common occurrence—and if you should happen to find it—a thing equally pos-

sible—I can, of course, lament the loss; but, bless your heart, it won't be felt. What's a thousand or ten thousand to some of them? Put on a little pressure, and they will come down again; but we need not wait for the result. Will that answer, Fan?" said he, gently laying his hand in hers.

Good Mrs. Pinkley counted over the strong names on the list which the doctor had taken from a small drawer; and, having after a little time succeeded in adding up the three for a thousand and the five for five hundred, she clutched the paper as if she then and there had hold of the princely amount which the doctor partly predicted she might be so lucky as to stumble over out of the sum total.

"That will do," said she, highly delighted; "that will be the very thing. Prince! excellent! if it's only managed well. Let that be your part—mine, I fear, will not be so easy. Then there's the children—we may have trouble with them; there will be trouble any way with that boy, he'll be as stiff and as positive as ever his mother was. You must look after him in time; he has strange notions."

"The children will be a nuisance—well, a difficulty," said he, correcting himself; "but we may be able to make some arrangement; there's time enough, however, for that. Frank is getting positive, is he? he shall never be like his mother, if I can help it. I'd rather see him dead and in his grave first. I'll regulate him, don't be afraid of that. How glad I am now that you called, Fan—you do manage things so well. Yet, one more, just one more cautious act, and you know the rest; one more, and I shall fulfill that promise."

Just then a smart rap was heard at the street door. "This is Bross," said the doctor. "I shall hear something now about Mannors." And then, having promised to call and see her and the children as soon as possible, he tenderly pressed her hand as she retired by the private entrance. Quickly arranging his hair by running it back through his fingers, he then approached the door, and, wearing his most benevolent and sanctimonious expression, he meekly smiled as he received his expected visitor.

CHAPTER XXX.

MR. THOMAS BROSS was the young gentleman with extensive shirt-collar, who called at Hampstead Cottage to deliver a letter, and who, at the time, happened to overhear Mrs. Mannors, under the influence of her hallucination, reproach her husband for his unfaithfulness; and this incident he, as a moral man and good Christian, immediately construed into its worst sense, and, with slight additions, retailed it in his own way where he thought the story would be most acceptable.

Mr. Bross was a junior clerk in the office of Vizard & Coke, Gray's Inn; in his own estimation, rather clever, but his fellow-students considered him a parasite, a syco-phant, any thing to ingratiate himself with his employers, or with any one else whom he fancied had influence. He was a strict Presbyterian, a member of the Rev. Andrew Campbell's church, and he distributed tracts after breakfast on Sundays until church time.

He had a class in the Sabbath-school, and was particularly obsequious to the lady teachers, who found an agreeable pastime in co-operating with such prepossessing young gentlemen for the illumination of younger Christians.

The ladies of the congregation he, of course, knew esteemed Doctor Buster very highly; he had heard them speak of his great talents and exalted character, and Mr. Bross was not slow to insinuate himself into the good graces of the moderator; and the doctor found in the very moral young man a very convenient tool or agent.

It was the low, stumpy form of Mr. Bross that entered the study of Doctor Buster after Mrs. Pinkley's retreat; he was greeted by the genial smile of that distinguished pillar of the church.

"Ah! my very dear young friend, I am most happy to see you; I was beginning to fear that you had not received my note. I trust I have not put you to much inconvenience by requesting you to call so early to-day; I like to see all my friends when I return to the city."

Mr. Bross leered with his prominent eyes at the doctor; he was delighted at the complaisance of the great man before him, and paused a moment in grateful admiration ere he could find a reply.

"Not the least, doctor, not the least; there could be no inconvenience. O my! not at all, sir—'tis such a privilege to be here; I would have called sooner, but it so happened that just as I was about to leave the office last evening, your very respected friend Manners walked in, and I thought I could make my visit more interesting by waiting a little longer."

"He did, indeed! how very opportune! pray be seated, my dear friend. Ah! pardon me, how is your excellent mother? You see," said the doctor, piously raising his eyes, "what we sometimes might only consider a fortunate occurrence is often, in reality, an act of Providence—the mysterious hand guiding our destinies, the luminous finger pointing out the hidden danger, the vast intelligence graciously counteracting evil designs. Ah! my friend, this has been my experience; I cannot be too thankful. Undeserving as I am, even you have been an agent in the hand of the Almighty for my benefit."

The eyes of the delighted Bross fairly glistened to hear such words from the mouth of such a chosen vessel. The bare idea of having been acknowledged as the selected instrument to serve this meek, exemplary pastor was almost overwhelming! What would he not have then given to be able to weep a little gratitude for so much condescension?

"Yes, my dear friend, you have proved an unexpected aid to me with regard to the evil designs of that bad man. I have already made you acquainted with the nature of his calumnies, of his unholy attacks against me, yet I care not for myself. He is, as you are aware, an unbeliever in our divine faith; and,

as an humble instrument in upholding the truth of God, I have had to reply to the specious and dangerous reasoning which he has circulated through the debased columns of the *Westminster Review* against the Scriptures. I have had to neutralize the poisonous error with which he had infected many feeble minds, and for this, as well as for other similar reasons, I have incurred his hatred. Since my unfortunate domestic affliction, his base insinuations and intermeddling have been to me a painful persecution. But the ministers of God should esteem it a privilege to suffer in his cause. 'Our light affliction, which is but for a moment, worketh for us a far more exceeding and eternal weight of glory.' The Lord will, I humbly trust, counteract the intentions of this wicked person."

After this delivery, the doctor was evidently much affected, and when he stooped down to apply his handkerchief, the feelings of the sympathizing clerk were overcome, and in a similar manner he tried to hide the tears which it is to be presumed filled his eyes on the occasion.

"He will—he will, no doubt, reverend sir," said Bross in a faltering voice. "I am aware of all that that evil-disposed man has done against you. I can assure you, nothing will give me greater satisfaction than to be of the slightest service to you in any way. I am but a humble individual, sir; but if my very humble services can be of the slightest assistance, pray do, sir, command me; it will be such a pleasure to obey."

"Ah!" said the doctor, as if soliloquizing, "what great faithfulness and amiability we discover where there is least pretension." Then, after a well-regulated pause, he continued: "He calls at your office very often then, you say; he must be rather litigious? no doubt of it."

"Yes, sir, he calls occasionally. We do his business—at least the respected firm of Vizard & Coke have the management of whatever matters require legal attention. We conduct his legal affairs when he has any; they can't be much, for we never had a case of his in court; yet he calls, it must be for advice."

"What business can he then possibly have to require attention in your office? what advice can he require if he is neither plaintiff nor defendant? Can you find out? I am anxious to know, and I will explain the reason some other time."

"Explain! Of course you need explain nothing to me, sir; I shall only be too happy to be of any—"

"Never mind, never mind, my dear friend; I am quite aware of all that; just find out his aim, he must have some sinister motive in view; he is one whom we must distrust."

"Well, it is so difficult to find out what he is after. He is generally in close consultation with Mr. Vizard, all that is, of course, lost to us; he must have a design—indeed, I suspect him already. You remember the conversation which I told you I overheard between him and his wife?"

"Ah! yes—that where she accused him of unfaithfulness. Poor woman! Let me see, I think you said the maid, or rather his favorite, was present at the time," spoke the doctor suggestively.

"There was another person—a wozan, a female, a favorite—no doubt just what you say," stammered the compliant clerk.

"Alas! she was the certain cause of all the misery that has since fallen upon his unhappy wife. But what better could be expected? What faithfulness, or honor, or principle, or morality could follow from one who would ignore religion? The tree is known by its fruit."

"Very true indeed, sir. What faithfulness or honor, or morality could follow?" echoed the correct Mr. Bross.

"Now that I think of it, perhaps it would be well that you should clearly remember what took place at that time; it may be of service hereafter. No doubt it then occurred to you that the trouble was caused by domestic jealousy," again suggested the doctor.

"I think it did, sir; yes, I think that was my impression—of course it was. You are perfectly right, sir; it was jealousy."

"Oh! it is quite apparent, it could be nothing else. And you have no idea of the real nature of his business at the office?"

"I can not say for certain; I often take an opportunity of going into the private room to make an inquiry—this is a great liberty—and I once overheard Mr. Vizard say something as to the law regulating the confinement of insane persons."

"Insane persons! Ah! I see," said the doctor stoically. Yet the sudden pressure on his temples at the moment was rather oppressive; and his face became suddenly flushed.

Mr. Bross continued, "Lately, I had reason to believe that he had some business of his own. There was, I think, a settlement, or will, or instrument drawn, by which his daughter was to be benefited. The copy of this I have not yet seen—I will get hold of it if possible; but a scrap of memoranda which I saw in the waste-basket, related to such a conveyance."

"A scrap not worth keeping, I suppose?" said the doctor carelessly. "The matter, however, as to lunatics must have been in relation to his own wife. Methodistic excitement and jealousy, and the misconduct and immorality of her husband, all, no doubt, combined to overpower her weak mind."

"Most probably, sir; but there was nothing on the piece of paper which could be of any advantage; I looked it over carefully. Perhaps, though, there may be something in this; I saw it upon one of the office chairs after they went away." And Mr. Bross handed the doctor an open envelope.

Two small pieces of paper were all it contained; one was written, the other printed, but even these were sufficient to drive the blood into the doctor's face and then suddenly back to his heart, leaving him in a state of pallor; and though he tried to appear very calm, he was evidently much agitated. The print and the writing took but a minute to read, yet like some powerful spell, or as but a single drop of a potent drug, the effect was sudden and stupefying. On one piece of paper the doctor read, in his own hand-writing, "A. M., North street, near Jewish Cemetery," and the other was an advertisement cut from the *Times*.—"Wanted, two or three steady and intelligent persons, suitable for attendants in a private hospital; strangers to the city preferred. Address Dr. A. M., 1322 North street.

For the time, Mr. Bross seemed to have been entirely forgotten. The eye of his reverend friend still rested upon the advertisement, then it glanced at the writing, and then there was a contraction of the brow, as if some deep problem required the most powerful concentration of thought. The doctor had never missed the memorandum which he had dropped, he could not tell where; but there was his own writing, sure enough, and how this scrap ever got into the hands of Martin Mannors was the mystery. Then the connection which had evidently been established between the writing and the advertisement caused him the greatest anxiety. Through the small opening already made, an enemy might see a great, great distance. Were his plans known? Were his schemes detected? Was he already discovered, and the hated infidel already upon his track to crush and expose him before the world? He looked half bewildered around the room, and then askance with tiger eye even at Bross, as if he had already suspected him of being an emissary. Suddenly collecting himself, he assumed his blandest tone, and said carelessly:

"I hardly understand the meaning of these items; there may be something in them, yet scarcely of any consequence. Are you sure that they were left by Mannors?"

"Oh! yes, sir, quite certain; at least, either by him or the person who was with him—one or the other."

"Person with him! Was there any one with him when he called?"

"Indeed, I forgot to mention that there was a stranger—a person I never saw before." And Mr. Bross gave the best description he could of the unknown individual.

With all his caution, the doctor could not hide his uneasiness. Who this new actor was that had, as it were, just entered on the stage, or the part he was to perform, created much embarrassment. There was an alliance or secret combination formed which disconcerted him very much, and every attempt must now be made to discover the nature of this fresh source of danger. However, it would not do to appear in the least intimidated; there should be no evidence of weakness or wavering, and the doctor for the time simulated the greatest indifference.

"Well, my dear friend, I feel greatly obliged to you for your kind attention to my interests. I do not, of course, understand to what these papers refer; however, they may, perhaps guide us to something. But if you can possibly ascertain who this other person is, or where he resides, or what business there can be between him and my enemy, it may be serviceable. It is probable that this envelope and its contents were left behind, as being of no service. I can not see that they are of any consequence; any way, I shall keep them in my possession; insignificant as they now are, they may, perhaps, be useful at another time."

The doctor again thanked Bross most graciously. He then gave a pious turn to the conversation, and feelingly commented on the great refuge of the Christian in troublous times. What was this world but the vanity of vanities—a fleeting show, a snare? He spoke of the glorious privilege of Sabbath services; he urged punctuality at the weekly prayer-meeting and regular attendance at the Sabbath-school. Every effort should be made to spread a knowledge of the Lord over the whole earth. The beauty of holiness was a theme upon which he said he loved to dwell. Oh! how it made his heart expand in love to all. What reproach he would be willing to suffer for the truth! Words of affection seemed to flow from the lips of the holy man, and from the manner in which poor, devoted Mr. Bross hung his head, it was evident that the doctor's pious remarks made a due impression.

Time was fleeing fast, and the punctual Bross hinted the necessity of returning to his post; and just as that hopeful young Christian and law-clerk was about to take his leave, the doctor drew from a recess a bundle of assorted religious tracts and handed them to his young disciple for distribution. Here was a means for the most unassuming to make themselves useful. He complimented Bross for the diligence he had already shown, and urged him to continue in the good work. Scattered here and there among the careless and profane, these little leaves might cause some to pause on the downward road, and bring reflection to many a careless sinner; and what a gratification it would be for one to know that he was a privileged agent in such a work.

Mr. Bross reverently received the orthodox package. He was delighted at such manifestations of confidence from one of such established piety; he stammered many promises; and took his departure, asserting his determination to renew his exertions in the cause of the Lord—and Doctor Buster.

The day continued gloomy, and the doctor stood at the window for some time and vacantly watched the retiring form of Bross through the thick mist. The morning, so far, had been unpropitious, the moderator felt strangely uneasy; every visitor as yet had brought him but ill news—how would the day end? As he still looked out, he clutched the envelope, and, having given his wandering conjectures full scope for some minutes, he again read the writing and advertisement.

"Well, what a cursed fool I must have been to let this out of my hands! How the devil did Mannors get it—or was it given him by another? Well, damn them, let it go! what can they make of it? nothing! They may do their best, Marks and Fan will be able for them. But stay, she has not yet seen these waifs; this has wandered back to me," said he, looking at his own writing; "and as for this advertisement, I must show it to her at once. No doubt she will be their match—she never fails."

Having thus soliloquized, the doctor again fortified himself with an increased dose of his favorite liquor, and, muffling himself up carefully, left the lonely house to make a few calls, and then to visit Mrs. Pinkley, and counsel with her as his chief friend and adviser.

When Mr. Bross reached the office of his employers, he was immediately dispatched with a message to Hampstead. He was very much pleased at this, and trusted that an opportunity might offer of being able to serve his reverend patron, Doctor Buster. On his arrival at Heath Cottage, he was met at the garden gate by Miss Mannors, and admitted into the house by her whom he then thought one of the most beautiful beings on which his eyes had ever rested. Mr. Mannors was absent, but was expected home every minute, and in the mean time his fair daughter, Mary, kept his visitor in conversation. The blushing, blundering Bross was sadly stricken, and for a full half-hour made the most desperate and agonizing efforts to appear collected and in his ordinary senses; but at the end of that time, when Mr. Mannors returned, he could scarcely make himself understood. He was almost hopelessly lost—a victim to love at first sight.

What a change had already come over the fickle Bross! The maligned Martin Mannors was now a hero, for whom he would have consigned the great Doctor Buster to the remotest ends of the earth; and Miss Mannors was a sweet divinity, for whom he could have forsaken his Sunday-school and its feminine attractions; she was an angel, for whom he might be possibly persuaded to lay down his very life, or even resign the coveted honor of being secretary to an extensive and distinguished branch of the Young Men's Christian Association of London. Alas! what a sudden fall from grace to nature. Poor Bross was already a willing backslider, already contemplating further strides upon the downward road.

CHAPTER XXXI.

AFTER Mrs. Pinkley had accepted a situation from Dr. Marks, she found it necessary to remove to a dwelling more convenient to his celebrated Home, in which she might be said to be the principal attendant. She had to search for some days before she could find a suitable house, yet the one which she had at last secured was not the style she wished, nor was it the most pleasantly situated; but it answered her purpose for the time, as she did not expect to remain in it very long. The building was one of a row of old, dilapidated structures which had, perhaps, two centuries before given victims to the great plague, and had subsequently escaped the great conflagration. Any way, it bore the marks of age, if cracked and crumbling walls, spreading door-jambs, and sunken lintels were evidence to that extent; its late occupant, an old trading Jew, having resided there for over fifty years, until he was at last transferred from his garret to his grave, and deposited in the cemetery—only just across the street—to moulder and mingle with the mortal remains of others distinguished as the descendants of the great, ancient Abraham.

As cleanliness is said to be next to godliness, Mrs. Pinkley, therefore, as a pious woman, could not but exhibit a due regard for appearances; and it was not many days before she had the lower front room—long used as the general store-room for the odds and ends upon which the old Jew advanced petty loans—cleared of its cobwebs, and, with the remainder of the house, cleansed and renovated as much as possible. Indeed, after the operation, the old store-room, decked out with its new carpet and old furniture, now looked more like the quiet parlor of some country inn; and it was the principal reception-room for the very few who ever called or gained admission at the particular hours when Mrs. Pinkley was likely to be found at home. During her absence, the outer door was generally kept locked, and the entire place left in charge of a trusty hump-backed girl called Bessy—a waif, who had been deserted in childhood, who never knew a parent, and who, one would think, seemed neither to know nor care for any one else but Mrs. Pinkley; how she came by her, none could tell, but she claimed to have adopted her simply through a humane motive. This unfortunate being had been trained for a special purpose—trained to be trusted; every act was to be in strict conformity to the wishes of her mistress; the training part was, no doubt, peculiar, for if she did not learn to love the protector she had found, it was evident that fear had a powerful influence in rendering her obedience perfect—Mrs. Pinkley had a slave whom she could govern at will. Bessy was allowed to grow up in the grossest ignorance; she took to house-keeping, however—it was all she had been ever taught; she knew nothing of religion, except that she was told that there was a hell, where, after the woes of this life were ended, she would find multiplied misery if she did not render faithful obedience to her mistress; but in the matter of house-keeping, she could manage things pretty well, and Mrs. Pinkley felt satisfied that while she was away Bessy could take care of the house, and control her tongue and her appetite according to instructions.

The December day had been gloomy; it was now getting toward evening, and in the upper front-room of Mrs. Pinkley's domicile two children, a boy and girl, stood silently together at one of the windows watching the flight of the dark clouds, or speculating upon the probable number of graves in the Jewish cemetery right in front of the house. The room was a cold-looking apartment, scantily furnished; there was an old, rickety table, a few old chairs, and leaning against the rough wall was a kind of book-shelf, upon which lay scattered a few old school-books, a Testament, and a number of religious tracts; there was not the simplest picture or engraving to attract the children's attention, and when they grew weary looking at the bare walls of the room, they could look out and see graves and little mounds in the burial ground.

There were yew-trees along the walls of the cemetery, and though monuments were few, still Jewish affection could be traced by the number of willows which bent like mourners over the last resting-place of many of those who had departed this life resolute unbelievers in the mission of the Christian Messiah. While the children watched vacantly from the window, they noticed a man standing under one of the large trees—or rather behind it—and he seemed as if looking at them or toward the house. He peered cautiously from time to time, and then drew back as if to escape observation. Was he, too, a mourner? He must be. After he stood behind the tree for some time, he commenced to pace slowly backward and forward, treading down the dead leaves, and while still watching the house, he went and sat upon a new grave. He wore a heavy shawl and muffled up his face as if he were weeping, but still he looked at the house; and the children, in their simplicity, pitied the sorrowing Jew.

"Dears, how quiet you are," said Bessy, stealing up behind them, and placing a hand upon the shoulder of the boy and girl. "How still you do keep! Ma'am is away again." She always called Mrs. Pinkley "ma'am," and mostly in a subdued voice. "Ma'am is away, Miss Alice—we can laugh now." And Bessy made a wailing kind of attempt at laughter which almost startled the children. "Don't be afeared of me, dears." Why, Master Frank, you look frightened! Poor Bessy loves you both, and you know I can only laugh when you are with me. Ma'am is away again, and I want to laugh; it does me good—it does."

"We were looking at that man," said the boy, pointing to the cemetery; "he is a poor Jew—may be crying for his children."

"Why, dears, Jews have got no hearts—ma'am says they're such wicked bad uns. She would kill 'em and burn'em, I know she would. She says they are worse than—" and Bessy pointed downward significantly, as if afraid to utter the name of the evil one.

"Jews have tender hearts, like other people," said Alice, "for you know, Bessy, how it made us all cry the other day when we saw the poor old Jew so sorry at the big funeral. Oh! how sorry he was; they could scarcely get him away from the grave; may be that poor man over there is crying for somebody that's dead."

"May be," said Bessy, "but a man goes to that place very often just like him, and he keeps a looking over this way—see, he's looking at us now! Ma'am doesn't like un, and she told me to watch un, she did, and to keep the door fast, and to let no one come in but the doctor. You know how she beat me the other day for letting the man in with the lot of toys—oh! such beauties;—and when he got in, he peeped here and there, and asked if there was any children, and I said, no, because ma'am told me—she did."

"Oh! I wish we had seen them," said Alice; "I wish we could see something, I wish we could get out to see somebody—to see the nice green fields in the country, only just for an hour."

"Dears, dears, ma'am would kill me if I was to let you out, or let any body come in again

—she would. How I would like to go too! what are green fields like, Miss Alice—like that?"

"No, Bessy, not like that—that's a grave-yard, full of graves; but the green fields that I remember are away, away from streets, and houses, and noise—so very quiet; away in the country, where the sun shines, and where we could see cows and little lambs, and could pick daisies and buttercups in the springtime and—"

"O Miss Alice!" interrupted Bessy, and clapping her hands in ecstasy, "do, do tell me about the fields; I often heard of fields—green fields—tell me what they are like." Bessy had but a faint conception of what they were; she had never been outside the gloom of the city, still she had an idea that the country and its hills and fields might be part of heaven, about which the children spoke sometimes.

In her eagerness to hear, she sat upon the floor, as she often did when she was alone with them, placing one on each side of her. They formed a strange little group in the dull light before the window. Bessy's pinched and worn-looking face made her appear old; though she was scarcely seventeen, she might have been taken for thirty; she seemed to have had no childhood, but to have passed from infancy to maturity at one dreary bound. Her life so far had been but a bleak period of drudgery, hardship, and oppression, and the only real joyful moments of her existence were those spent in the society of these children; they were the only beings that had ever been truly kind to her, and they pitied Bessy in her desolation. Unknown to Mrs. Pinkley, they taught her to read; for though that stern Christian woman professed to be a patron of knowledge and of Sunday-schools, yet she never permitted her dependent to waste a moment with books—Bessy in gross ignorance served her purpose better. The children, however, were not suspected, and they took pleasure in imparting to Bessy a share of their little stock of knowledge, and Bessy, in return, loved them with all the intensity of her benevolent nature; they seemed to be, like herself, the inheritors of affliction. Alice, the older child, was about ten years of age, a delicate-looking girl; she had beautiful brown hair, which Bessy took great delight in twisting into long curls. Frank might be two years younger; he was a healthy boy, very intelligent for his age, and singularly independent in his manner of thinking. For more than a year Bessy had been almost their only companion. Mrs. Pinkley was generally away during the day and often during the night, and, when thus left alone, as soon as Bessy hurried through with her work, they would all sit together in the upper room, and the children would tell of what they had seen of the world outside of London, and tell of their mother, and of the nice home they once had; and when they wept, as they often did, for that mother and home, Bessy would weep too, and be their only comforter.

After Alice had delighted Bessy with a description of the fields, trees, hills, and streams of the quiet country, and had contrasted cottages and gardens with old houses in dirty, crowded city thoroughfares, Frank did his part by hearing Bessy spell her hard words, and then he assisted her to read the last tract which had been left with him by Mrs. Pinkley; it gave a terrible description of the final judgment, and of hell, and of the woeful doom of the wicked; and it was completed by the three following verses, from one of the most orthodox hymn-books: *

"The great archangel's trump shall sound,
    (While twice ten thousand thunders roar,)
Tear up the graves and cleave the ground,
    And make the greedy sea restore.

"The greedy sea shall yield her dead,
    The earth no more her slain conceal;
Sinners shall lift their guilty head,
    And shrink to see a yawning hell.

"We, while the stars from heaven shall fall,
    And mountains are on mountains hurled,
Shall stand unmoved amidst them all,
    And smile to see a burning world."

Poor Bessy shuddered; she looked in the boy's face, but she saw no change—no terror; neither did his sister seem to be much affected.

"Dears, are you not afeared? Isn't that dreadful? Don't let's read any more of it, Master Frank. O my! O my! Ma'am says it's all true—she does; better we'd never been born—never been born."

"Bessy, it's not true," said the boy, trying to assure her; "my ma often told me so; she said there was no such place as hell, and that God was good and loved everybody, and would never burn them up."

"He won't? O dears, dears! I hope he won't; dears, I hope!"

"He won't, Bessy," continued the boy; "God never made such a horrid place; it was the priests who made hell—ma said that, too."

"O Miss Alice! isn't it dreadful to think on? I could love God better if there was no hell—I could. I wouldn't want to hide from him so if he was as good to me, dears, as you are—I wouldn't."

"I'm not afraid of God, Bessy," said Frank. "I remember that ma used to tell us that cruel men make a cruel God; if I was very, very sick, and going to die to-morrow, I wouldn't be afraid."

"God loves all good people, Bessy," said Alice; "I think he loves everybody; he loves you, for you are good—I am sure he does."

"Oh! but I'm very wicked, dear—I am. I would like to be very good, Miss Alice—I would, but I'm a very bad un, I suppose; for ma'am says I'm so terribly wicked—she does; but you know I didn't make myself; if I did, I'd be a good bit better—I would, Miss Alice. God pity us all!"

"God will pity us all, Bessy," said the children solemnly.

During the pause which followed, there was a loud thump heard at the front-door. The children were startled, the boy became rather agitated, and grew suddenly pale; and as Bessy moved off on tip-toe, she beckoned significantly and whispered, "Hish, hish, dears! 'tis th' doctor, 'tis th' doctor."

---

* Wesley's Hymns.   † See Note D.

The children instinctively drew into a corner of the room, and the man in the cemetery moved from the grave on which he had been sitting, and stood looking at the house again from behind the big tree.

Before Bessy had time to reach the door, another loud knock was given. She had no occasion to look through the side-lights to be assured of who was waiting for admittance, for already she could hear Doctor Buster muttering either prayers or curses at her delay, and, as soon as the door was opened, he stamped in rudely past her, and in a gruff, impatient voice asked for Mrs. Pinkley."

"She be out, sir," said Bessy, almost trembling.

"Out? the devil! How long has she been out? When will she be back?"

"More'n an hour or two, sir; she's a coming back soon—soon, sir."

"When is soon, you jade—you damned Lump? Where are the children?"

The doctor was evidently annoyed, irritated. He did not expect to find Mrs. Pinkley out, and her absence and may be other matters had ruffled his temper. He did not wait for Bessy's answer, and, as he mounted the creaking stairs, the children tried to crouch further into the corner, and the man in the cemetery moved closer toward the house.

The room was gloomy, and as the doctor paused in the doorway, his dark form loomed up in the dusky light like a great spectre, and when his eye rested upon the little fugitives in the corner, he seemed to get rather angry, and said in a sharp, upbraiding manner: "Why, what do you hide there for, you stupid fools? Whom did you expect to see coming? Come out of that—come here!"

The frightened boy sat still, but Alice moved toward her father; yet she approached him in a hesitating manner, which did not tend to make him more amiable.

"Come on, girl—go. Am I an elephant?"

"O ya! we were a little afraid; for a man came into the house the other day, you know, and—" and the girl hesitated still more in trying to frame some excuse.

"A man in the other day! I know that. Was he here again? Did that cursed humpback let him in a second time?"

"No, pa; no, sir, Bessy did not, she didn't, indeed, pa; but we saw a man over there this evening, and we were afraid." And Alice pointed to the burial-ground across the street.

The doctor went quickly to the window, and looked eagerly out toward the place, but the man in the cemetery suddenly drew back behind a tree, and, as it was getting dark, the doctor made no discovery.

"I see no one; you mustn't be afraid of your shadow. What are you skulking there for, sir? Come here! What is the brat thinking of?"

"Frank was afraid too, pa," said Alice, trying to be cheerful. "Come, Frank, pa has got a nice book for us."

The boy left his corner rather reluctantly. Alice took his hand and led him on, and, when he ventured to glance upward at his father, he saw him standing near the window frowning, and holding his gold-headed cane.

"What have you been doing, sir? You look as if you had been guilty of something," said the doctor.

"Oh! nothing, sir, indeed, nothing; but I said my lessons to Alice, and we read a tract for Bessy."

"You like tracts, do you?" said the doctor ironically, and he glanced at the latest doctrinal effusion of the society, the reading of which had so alarmed poor Bessy. "Anything rather than read your Testament—tracts or any thing."

"We read it every day, pa, we do, indeed," said Alice.

"You read! Yes, you read, but do you believe—does he?"

"He does, pa, I believe, and so does Frank, almost all—almost every thing." And Alice nearly trespassed on the truth to try and conciliate her father.

"Almost!" retorted the doctor; "those who almost believe will be almost saved, think of that! Almost won't do; it must be a full and entire belief. I have heard that this wicked brat almost believes—almost; that won't do for me. If he doubts that God will be revenged, if he doubts that there is a hell, he may find one, as I hope all unbelievers will do. He must believe it." The doctor stamped upon the floor as he uttered the last four words, and the boy trembled as he stood before him.

"Indeed, pa," pleaded Alice, "we read a good deal every day; we like the Testament very much. To-day we read such nice chapters—we read of how Christ preached forgiveness, of how he fed the multitude, and of how he cured lepers, and poor, sick people, and of how he blessed little children, and of how he wept at the grave when he raised the dead Lazarus. You know, pa, that every one would like to believe these things—and we would too."

"Yes, yes, I see; like a good many others, you would like to believe in all mercies, in all forgiveness, but what of divine justice? God must be avenged. Now, let me see what you know on this point." The doctor drew a chair and sat down, as if prepared to catechise. "I have ordered you to read the Bible, now let me test your knowledge.

"What is said in the Old Testament with respect to the vengeance of the Lord? Will he be avenged?"

Alice gave the answer out of the book of Nahum, 1st chapter, 2d and 6th verses: "God is jealous, and the Lord revengeth; the Lord revengeth, and is furious: the Lord will take vengeance on his adversaries, and he reserveth wrath for his enemies. Who can stand before his indignation? and who can abide in the fierceness of his anger? his fury is poured out like fire, and the rocks are thrown down by him."

"What are the divine threats against the disobedient?"

She answered from Leviticus, chapter 26: 27, and from Isaiah 34: 3: "And if ye will not for all this hearken unto me, but walk contrary to me: Then will I walk contrary unto you also in fury, and I, even I, will chastise you seven times for your sins. And ye shall eat the flesh of your sons, and the flesh of your daughters shall ye eat. And I will destroy your high places, and cut down your images, and cast your carcasses upon the carcasses of your idols, and my soul shall abhor you.

"Their slain shall be cast out, and their stink shall come up out of their carcasses, and the mountains shall be melted with their blood." (Isaiah 34: 3.)

"Were they not to be cursed by the Lord? What were the maledictions?"

Again she answered, reciting several verses from the 28th chapter of Deuteronomy: "But it shall come to pass, if thou wilt not hearken unto the voice of the Lord thy God, to observe to do all his commandments and his statutes which I command thee this day, that all these curses shall come upon thee: Cursed *shalt* thou *be* in the city, and cursed *shalt* thou *be* in the field. Cursed *shall be* thy basket and thy store. Cursed *shall be* the fruit of thy body, and the fruit of thy land, the increase of thy kine, and the flocks of thy sheep. Cursed *shalt* thou *be* when thou comest in, and cursed *shalt* thou *be* when thou goest out. The Lord shall send upon thee cursing, vexation, and rebuke, in all that thou settest thine hand unto for to do, until thou be destroyed, and until thou perish quickly: because of the wickedness of thy doings whereby thou hast forsaken me. The Lord shall make the pestilence cleave unto thee until he have consumed thee from off the land, whither thou goest to possess it. The Lord shall smite thee with a consumption, and with a fever, and with an inflammation, and with an extreme burning, and with the sword, and with blasting, and with mildew; and they shall pursue thee until thou perish." She paused, as if wearied with the weight of cursing, and the doctor seemed to exult in the proofs.

"Ha! that's it; no silly tempering of mercy here, no weak relenting, no robbery of divine justice! Now, what is to be the doom of unbelievers and wicked?" And he rubbed his hands in anticipation of the answer.

"The wicked shall be turned into hell, *and* all the nations that forget God." (Psalm 9: 17.) "Upon the wicked he shall rain snares, fire, and brimstone, and a horrible tempest; this shall be the portion of their cup." (Psalm 11: 6.) "I will be unto them as a lion; as a leopard by the way will I observe *them*. I will meet them as a bear *that* is bereaved *of her whelps*, and will rend the caul of their heart, and there will I devour them like a lion." (Hosea 13: 7, 8.)

"Prove that God's wrath will not be finally appeased."

"Mine eye shall not spare, neither will I have pity." (Ezek. 7: 9.) "I also will laugh at your calamity; I will mock when your fear cometh." (Pro. 1: 26.) "When your fear cometh as a desolation, and your destruction cometh as a whirlwind, when distress and anguish come upon you, then shall ye call upon me, but I will not answer." (27: 29.)

"Give me a few texts from the New Testament in proof of eternal punishment."

She answered, "The Lord Jesus shall be revealed from heaven with his mighty angels, in flaming fire taking vengeance on them that know not God, and that obey not the Gospel of our Lord Jesus Christ. Who shall be punished with everlasting destruction from the presence of the Lord, and from the glory of his power." (2 Thes. 1: 7, 8, 9.) "The smoke of their torment ascendeth up forever and ever." (Rev. 14: 11.)

"Will not these judgments be approved of by the righteous?"

"He that sitteth in the heavens shall laugh; the Lord shall have them in derision." (Psalm 2: 4.) "The righteous see it, and are glad; and the innocent laugh them to scorn." (Job 22: 19.) "The righteous shall see, and fear, and shall laugh at him." (Psalm 52: 6.) "Let Mount Zion rejoice; let the daughters of Judah be glad, because of thy judgments." (Psalm 48: 11.) "The righteous shall rejoice when he seeth the vengeance; he shall wash his feet in the blood of the wicked." (Psalm 58: 10.)

"Here is sufficient evidence! Nothing about mercy or forgiveness, no yielding to pleadings for pity; and *you* dare to doubt these denunciations," said he, turning savagely to the boy.

"O pa!" again interceded Alice, "he does not understand it; he will believe all soon."

"Soon! he *must* believe *now*; curse him, does he want to follow his mother? does he ever say his prayers?"

"I pray, and Bessy prays, pa; we all pray sometimes." And Alice now began to tremble as she stood before her angry parent.

"Does *he* pray, I ask? Have you prayed to-day?" said he, scowling down upon Frank.

The boy could not utter a word; he held his sister firmly by the hand, bent his head, and remained silent.

"Pray, you infernal imp! none of your mother's doings here—quick, or I'll make you pray."

The little fellow could scarcely stand; he looked up imploringly, his eyes were filled with tears; he knelt down, he tried to remember a prayer, a verse, a text, or any thing, but could only utter, "Our Father—deliver us from evil; God be merciful to me a sinner!"

O dear! dear child, God ha' mercy on you now," said Bessy, clapping her hands together and looking into the room.

"Begone, you beast," said the now infuriated doctor, banging the door in Bessy's face. And while the poor creature stood upon the dark stairway, wringing her hands and sobbing, the doctor rushed back, and shouted almost loud enough to be heard across the street, "Pray, damn you! imp of your mother; if you don't pray at once, I'll take your cursed life."

Alice was almost ready to faint; she still held her brother's hand; he could not speak; he tried to get up to recede a step or two, but before he could move away, his father struck him several quick blows and smashed his cane. Alice screamed, and fell fainting. Bessy rushed in, but before she had time to shield the prostrate boy, the doctor seized the cane by its broken end, and, with one mighty blow,*

* See Note I.

buried its heavy golden handle in the child's head.

The man in the cemetery heard Bessy's wild wail; he bounded over the wall and rushed toward the house. Mrs. Pinkley had just hurriedly entered before him; he heard the commotion in the upper room, and her sharp accusations upon the discovery of the crime.

"O madman, madman! you've done it now; what shall we do?" she cried; "is all forever lost? What shall we do? I cautioned you this morning; see how you have ended the day."

Muffling his face closely, the man stole up the stairway and peeped into the room from the dark lobby; he drew back in horror! There lay the dying boy in a pool of blood—his sister was in a swoon. Bessy knelt wailing at his side, and Mrs. Pinkley stood before the bewildered doctor, hurling bitter reproaches and cursing his madness. The man remained but a few moments; he left the house as quietly as he had entered. He went his way undiscovered; he did not again enter the burial-ground. See, he hurries away! Who is to hear his terrible tidings?

It is nearly dark; there is another great funeral in the Jewish cemetery. Death stalks about the place, and people are in sorrow. Is it his grim carnival? The night wind begins to moan through the leafless willows and to mingle with the sobbings which are heard around. But stay; 'tis the triumph of woe—here is another victim! Is it a Christian corpse? Ah! how poor Bessy weeps. Say, who shall weep for her? Hearts of pity! see those closed eyes and that little pale, upturned face, see that little hand clutched in gore! Alas! how that little form already stiffens in death. Wrap it up hastily in its shroud; hide it, 'tis a foul sight; get ready its grave—take it out stealthily—take it out in the night, that none may ever know the tearless mourners.

CHAPTER XXXII.

NIGHT had set in for some time; it was very dark; the large street-lamp in front of the massive door of a large, dreary-looking house flashed upon the polished door-plate, and the wayfarer who could read might trace, almost at a glance, the words, "Doctor Andrew Marks's Private Asylum." This was his celebrated *Home*, his *Maison de Santé*; there was a stillness about the place, and but few lights could be seen in its upper barred windows. Many of the afflicted ones had already been obliged to retire to their narrow rooms to rave or scramble upon narrow beds, and kings, beggars, emperors, and messiahs, the hopeful and the desponding, were again secured by bolt and bar, and left alone to sing or whine, command or implore, according to the mood of a disordered imagination.

Doctor Marks was alone in his study; he had visited his patients, and was now looking over the evening papers. A few attendants moved noiselessly about, and the keeper of the wards,

who was to be on duty until after midnight, paced leisurely up and down the long hall between the prison-like dormitories. Now and then the stillness would be broken by the whimpering complaints of some neglected monarch strutting in his den, or by some desponding penitent moaning for mercy. But the keeper heeded not; he had often been besought by potentates, and was now getting accustomed to their appeals, and could allow their humble petitions to remain unanswered with all the indifference of a god. But the keeper was not, however, as hard-hearted; he often stopped at one end of the dim hall to listen sadly to the mutterings of spiritual despair which fell in doleful words from the quivering lips of one who fancied that God had utterly forsaken her, and that her day of grace had forever passed; and day and night, through bright hours, or solemn darkness, the sad burden of "Lost, lost, forever lost" could be heard in the same sad monotone almost continually. He had just been listening to the doleful repetition; all else had become tolerably quiet, as if one great grief had silenced all the rest. Looking carefully around, he then lessened the light in the hall-lamp and proceeded cautiously along the passage; at its end there was a short stairway; this he ascended, and went along a narrow way leading to a few rooms at the back of the building. Mrs. Pinkley generally occupied one of these; she was now absent; and the keeper, having paused a moment or two, and finding that all was quiet, gave a peculiar tap at the door of the adjoining room; then drawing a note from his pocket, he hastily thrust it under the door-way, and returned to his station in the lower hall.

It was nearly ten o'clock; the night-bell was rung briskly, the front-door was opened, and Mrs. Pinkley entered. She went into Doctor Marks's study; she looked flurried and excited, and, throwing her cloak aside, stood in front of the table at which the doctor was sitting. He had been writing; he laid his pen aside, and looked up at his visitor; she was mute. Mrs. Pinkley seemed unable to speak; the doctor began to feel surprised; there she stood like a statue, and he was about to question her, when she at last managed to exclaim, "O doctor, doctor! I have such dreadful tidings! dreadful tidings! Oh! yes, yes, yes; dreadful, terrible, fearful; what shall be done? what shall be done? O doctor, doctor!"

"For heaven's sake!" said the doctor, becoming alarmed, "what is the matter? You look frightened; sit down, try and be calm, let me know what is the matter." The doctor drew a chair, and almost forced the woman into it. "Sit down, sit down, and tell me what is wrong."

"O good God! 'tis terrible! How shall I begin to tell you—how am I to commence? 'Tis a death story, a story of blood!" And while Mrs. Pinkley was making efforts to appear distracted—indeed she actually fancied some impending danger—a man was looking in, and listening from the outside; he could see into the room through a small opening in the shutter; he heard her passionate words; he was well muffled up, and as he heard the step of some wandering policeman, he moved away from the window until it passed; he then resumed his position, as if determined to catch every word and watch every motion.

"Mrs. Pinkley," said the doctor, assuming the calmest possible tone, "pray tell me what has happened; is medical aid necessary? let me know at once."

"O doctor! you can be of little service now; 'tis, I fear, too late, too late; let me think a moment, and I will tell you all." She stooped and hid her face in her hands, as if afraid to look at the light or at the man before her. "You remember, doctor, that I told you this morning I wanted to see Doctor Buster; I heer'd he was back. He was away for some days, and I thought he might want to know about the children, and I wanted to tell him how his wife was troubled with these spasms, so as in case any thing happened that he might be prepared for the worst. Well, I saw the doctor, but I was delayed longer than I expected. I hurried back, but before I came here, I just looked into my own house to see if things was all right. I met Bessy at the door; there was something wild in her look. O that unfortunate girl, that I tried to save from misery and starvation! Years ago I took pity on her; she was a humpbacked foundling, and I brought her up as if she was my own child. I've had a world of trouble with her, doctor; I tried to teach her something, but she was only a half-idiot at best. 'Twas in a place like this she ought to have been—I see it now when it's too late. However, when I got the doctor's children to my charge, she seemed to take to them for a time, but she was often very cross, and headstrong, and cruel; but of course the children wouldn't tell me, the poor things bore with a good deal that I never heerd of. Anyhow, lately—and it was by mere chance I discovered—I found that she got acquainted with some man who she kept about the place, and I also found that she sometimes actually let him into the house; just think of that. I missed some things; he was, I suppose, one of our street thieves; what a companion for an honest girl! She said he was some kind of a peddler; and when I reproved her for her vile conduct—I only said a few words—she grew terribly angry, and began to threaten, as she always did when I made the least complaint. I often heerd her say that if I scolded her she would make away with herself, or take poison, or do something very bad; you know, doctor, that I am but a poor scold, but I got accustomed to Bessy's threats and I didn't mind them. I mentioned this matter once, I think, to Doctor Buster, but he only treated it as a silly joke; in fact, he is too kind-hearted a man to think bad of a creature that seemed so forlorn at times; indeed, he pitied Bessy as much as I did. However, when I left the house this afternoon to come here, every thing appeared quiet enough, except that I noticed that Bessy had but little to say—she was rather surly. Ah! what a confiding fool I was; for when I returned to the house, just

about dark, what did I see? O doctor! 'twas terrible. When I went in, I could see no person; every thing was very quiet, as I said. I called, no one answered, no Bessy could be seen. I began to grow alarmed, I called again and again; I ran up-stairs at last, and, when I looked into the room, gracious God! what did I find? I thought I would drop; little Frank lay on the floor, the blood streaming from him, and when I screamed and tried to lift him, he was dead! Oh! yes, doctor, dead! A heart of stone would then pity me; I must have fainted. When I got able to move about again, I laid the poor child on the bed, and put a covering over him. While doing this, my suspicions was provoked; I thought of the wicked girl, and of her bad companion—I guessed the truth at once! I thought of that horrid Bessy, and of the vagabond she was encouraging. I saw at once that I was robbed; and while looking here and there in the room, I was terrified by a loud scream. I heard a noise or struggle in Bessy's room; I ran in, and there she lay on her bed, as I thought, in some kind of fit. She was foaming at the mouth and grasping at the bed-clothes. She had taken poison. The cup was on the table by the bedside, and there was sufficient left in it to satisfy me that she had committed a double-murder—I almost felt certain of this. O the unfortunate wretch! I forgot to tell you, that when I went to see Doctor Buster this morning, I took Alice with me to see her father. It was fortunate, for I am sure if she had been left with her brother she would, no doubt, have shared his fate. What a providential escape! See, doctor, I brought this paper with me, 'twas on the table near the cup; it contains the remains of a white powder—I'm sure 'tis arsenic. Bessy was dead in about ten minutes after I got into her room; I tried to do all I could to save her, but 'twas no use. What was I then to do? I did not want to alarm the neighborhood. I fastened the door, got a cab, and drove at once to Doctor Buster's. I told the poor man the sad story; he went almost distracted, God help him! he did; and we had, of course, to keep it as secret as the grave from poor Alice; she is very delicate, and such horrid news might bring her to death's door. I got a good woman of my acquaintance to remain with her, and the doctor came back with me. He is alone now with his dead child, and his heart is ready to break. 'Tis a dreadful providence, Doctor Marks; something must be done. Doctor Buster wants to see you at once; he knows you can feel for his affliction."

"This is, indeed, dreadful," said Doctor Marks. "Are you sure they are dead? Is it not possible to do any thing for them? I am sorry you did not run here for me at once, before you went for Doctor Buster; I might have been in time even then."

"O doctor! I was so distracted, I'm sure I scarcely knew what to do. They were dead—yes, dead—before I left, and I thought it best to tell the child's father at once."

"Well, well, 'tis a sad business, Mrs. Pinkley. I can do but little now to lessen the grief of the bereaved father; but I will see him, I will do what I can; 'tis a sad, sad affair with his other troubles."

"Very sad, doctor; afflictions seem to follow that poor man—they do follow God's people. 'Twas bad enough before, as you know, now 'tis death—and such a death! I dread to go near the place again."

"I can understand your feelings. Were it an ordinary visitation of Providence, one might be in a measure prepared; but here we have sudden deaths! not one alone, but a foul murder—a suicide—a double calamity! Were it even such as could only affect yourselves, it might be more easily borne; but it is a matter that can not, must not, be kept secret. The news of this will startle the whole community. There will be comments in the papers, vexatious rumors and speculations, the public inquest, and the harrowing notoriety which will follow."

Inquest! The word darted through her brain like fire. She never thought of that horrid ordeal. The room commenced to turn round, its rotary motion increased, her sight grew dim, and she would have fallen from her chair were it not for the prompt assistance of Doctor Marks. The man outside the window still listened; he now scarcely moved, and he heard every word.

"Did you say 'inquest,' doctor?" said she, striving to appear calm; "not surely an inquest? They died like others—not surely an inquest, doctor?"

"This outrage has upset you—no wonder. It would require strong nerves and a wicked heart to remain indifferent. A deed of blood has been committed, an inquest is indispensable. You would, of course, be anxious to discover the perpetrator."

The respectable dead of the Home had often been delivered to mourning relatives; there was nothing secret in their manner of removal, there were few inquests held over the defunct of Doctor Marks's establishment; they were shrouded and coffined and publicly taken away, and no one cared to ask a question. Mrs. Pinkley knew this, and now she wanted her dead hurried out. What did she care in this case for Christian burial? There were the bodies, dreadful to look at; she would readily take them across the way, and thrust them underground by the side of dead Jews. She wanted no inquest, and her charity was sufficiently expansive at the time even to forgive the murderer.

"'Tis bad enough as it is—what good will an inquest do? Think of a father's feelings; but you know best, Doctor Marks, you know best. We will see him about it, let us be guided by what he says; he will advise for the best, if he can advise at all in this extremity."

Mrs. Pinkley began to pluck up her latent courage; she had been taken unawares—the case was desperate. No; she would never flinch now, but was resolute and already determined to resort to a desperate remedy.

Doctor Marks at once prepared to go out. Mrs. Pinkley left the room, she had some instructions to give to the attendants, and would be back in a few minutes. She went into an adjoining apartment, whispered to a waiting-woman, and then went up-stairs to her own room. The keeper sat in an arm-chair, and seemed half asleep as she passed through the long hall; but as soon as he thought she was out of sight, he looked sharply around and went on tip-toe to the end of the upper stairs and stopped to listen; when he heard her returning—she remained but a minute or two—he resumed his place in the chair, and affected to be startled when she gently tapped him on the shoulder.

"Oh! is that you, ma'am? I declare I didn't hear you; I—"

"Never mind, Staples, I just wanted to tell you that I have to go out again; the doctor wants me to attend him in a case not far off; I may be away an hour or two. The patient in No. 19, next to my room, is very restless to-night; she is, I'm afeard, sinking, and I want you to remind Mrs. Jenkins to attend to her in about an hour's time, punctual. 'Tis not eleven yet; you stay in here until the doctor returns—he may be back before me, he may want me to stay out longer for all I know. Anyway, Staples, don't forget—I'll be back as soon as I can—that's a good fellow."

Just as she was about to leave the hall, plaintive murmuring was heard in one of the rooms; there were words of woe and despondency, and then a melancholy voice droned out:

"Behold! with awful pomp,
　The Judge prepares to come.
Th' archangel sounds the dreadful trump,
　And wakes the general doom."

She was startled, unusually so; her natural firmness seemed to have been a little shaken at the moment; the keeper noticed her trepidation, but it quickly passed; she felt slightly annoyed at her own weakness, and, as she left him, her thin lips were compressed and her step more determined.

When she went down, she called Mrs. Jenkins, the nurse, into a kind of dispensing-room; there were shelves at one end and several drawers and bottles with latinized labels; but Mrs. Pinkley generally exercised a prudent caution, she knew nothing of Acet. Plumb., Ant. Tart., Bac. Junip., Hyd. Submur., Pulv. Potass., or Pil. Rhei.; and was, therefore, careful how she ventured to compound, lest a fatal mistake should follow through her ignorance. Sad occurrences of this nature often took place, she knew they were quite common; but as she was known to be extremely particular, and very cautious about touching drugs, she was trusted in this respect more than any other person in the establishment. There were a few simples, however, which she could venture to handle. Doctor Marks had these placed so as to be within reach at any time; and as sedatives were often required, she as often prepared them without reference to her principal. While her attendant was engaged at a little distance, Mrs. Pinkley drew from her bosom a small package, and took from it one of a number of small papers folded up like those containing medical powders; she then emptied a few grains of a white substance into a bottle, then poured in some water, added a little coloring, shook all up, and, having corked the bottle, handed it to the woman.

"You see, Nancy, I leave a good deal to you at times. I told the doctor that I have great confidence in you, and your allowance is to be increased from the beginning of next month ; he did so on my recommendation, and I can do more for you yet. I'm sorry I have to go out again; I want you to look after No. 19, give her this in about an hour's time ; see that she takes it—now don't forget ; here, take this too." And she handed Mrs. Jenkins, the nurse, a half-crown, and left a sedative for one patient which was intended to heal mental and bodily ailments forever.

While Mrs. Pinkley was engaged outside, Doctor Marks examined the contents of the paper which she left on his table. He touched his tongue to the white powder, he then applied a chemical test, and was satisfied that arsenic had been taken or administered. He folded up the paper, laid it carefully in a drawer and locked it up ; but he thought it useless to prepare an antidote, as no doubt the potent poison had already done its work.

Mrs. Pinkley was now ready, and they went away together to the house of death ; but before they were hidden in the gloom of the dark street, they were watched and followed by the man who had been looking in at the window.

The large front door of the Home was again securely bolted, the keeper heard their departure ; he now stood in the long hall close to the lamp, and was examining the contents of a small folded paper which he had picked up. The light shone full upon his face, displaying sharp, shrewd features, evidently those of an active, intelligent man. Having satisfied himself with the scrutiny, he put the paper carefully in his pocket, and went quickly to the upper apartments. Looking closely into a little recess near Mrs. Pinkley's private room, he withdrew a key ; this he applied to the lock of the adjoining chamber, the bolt flew back, he moved quietly away, and in a few moments the patient, known in the Home as No. 19, stood in the passage ; and while there, the same melancholy voice which was heard almost continually recommenced its doleful pleadings for mercy. In the dim light she looked like a midnight spectre. She wore the dark dress allotted to the female patients of Doctor Marks's establishment, her hair was partly loose, and her face deadly pale, while her faltering step indicated great feebleness. She looked anxiously after the keeper, as he went slowly on before her, and, by placing one hand against the wall, she managed to follow him through the long hall, then slowly down a back-stairs, at the foot of which she was obliged to take his arm, and in a few steps more she was conducted into the private reception-room of the Home.

It was a neat, carpeted apartment, well-lighted up. Oh! how the cheerful fire, the papered walls, the pictures and polished furniture reminded her of a home now almost remote in her memory. She sat upon a sofa, a dimness grew before her eyes, and she could scarcely see. She had not as yet perceived any person, and when her hand was gently raised from where it hung by her side, and when she heard the mellow, tremulous, sympathizing voice of a friend—a voice she must have heard before—she leaned back and sobbed pitifully, like a child ; and then, when she found her sight restored, and when she looked pleadingly upward anxious to discover a compassionate face, Martin Mannors stood before her trying to hide his manly tears.

"Dear lady, how I have pitied you—how I have sought after you for dreary months, but I have found you at last. What a gratification it is to know that even in this place, even in this prison, you have so far escaped the designs of your persecutors. I am indebted for a knowledge of your existence here, and for this interview, to a generous friend who has devoted his time and his means for the purpose of counteracting the vile projects of an inhuman man. You have had a sad trial, yet with your restoration you may but find another grief. Oh! that with liberty I could bring you happy tidings. How am I to tell you all? Alas! I may but darken your existence, and cause you to wish for the deep sleep which knows no waking. But still you must live ; there is one who will still look up to you and call you 'mother'—for her sake you must make an effort."

"For her sake, did you say?" said the startled woman, who now stood up and looked with intense earnestness into the face of Mr. Mannors, "for her sake! Ah! think, kind friend, there are two pretty ones. Yes, I will live for my children! For her sake, say you? What of my boy, my pretty child —there are two, kind friend—what of my darling boy? Oh! tell me, tell me all, or I will go mad at last." She seized Mr. Mannors by the arm and trembled violently.

"Good God! you make no reply. Heaven pity me now! O my child! my child! my boy—can it be this at last?"

"I do pity you, poor lady, we all pity you ; but you can live for one—we trust that one is still left."

She could hear no more ; the black shadows of woe gathered around her, and she was about to sink in a swoon before him. She was just able to exclaim, "Oh! that this were death!" and then fell heavily at his feet.[*]

"Hark! she prays for death—he is near, for here is his messenger. Come, nurse, grant her request."

Mr. Mannors was startled, the deep stillness of the few preceding moments totally unprepared him for this interruption. He turned around, the keeper stood looking in from the door, the nurse was by his side, and she held the bottle of medicine which Mrs. Pinkley left with her to be administered. The woman seemed rather timid, she hesitated, but the keeper was urgent.

"Come, nurse, you may be too late—I was told to remind you. If a spark of life remains, you have that which will do death good service. See, we brought her down here for you ;

---

[*] See Note J.

'twill save trouble—she will be nearer her grave. Psha! woman, are you afear'd? what will Mrs. Pinkley say?"

The woman was bewildered; what did it all mean? She looked from one to the other for an explanation; she did not know that there was a stranger in the house at that time of night, and could not account for the scene before her. Just then the back entrance of the house was opened, and another stranger entered—he was a stout, plain-looking man. She began to grow afraid, and lest the bottle should fall from her hand, the keeper took it from her. The person who had last come in was Robert, the trusty servant of Mr. Mannors, who had been acting as a detective, and she felt relieved when she was called to assist in placing the lady upon the sofa. Restoratives were immediately applied, and while the poor lady still seemed in a kind of stupor, she was carefully attended. The nurse, upon being questioned, acknowledged that Mrs. Pinkley had given her the bottle, that she had mixed the medicine, and had cautioned her particularly to get the patient in No. 19 to take it as a draught that night. She declared that she did not know herself what the bottle contained, only that she was told it was a "draught."

"'Twould be a final draught," said the keeper; "but I rather guess we'll keep it for the benefit of some one else. Now, nurse, I'm in command here at present; I want you to take good care of that lady, we are just going to the doctor's study for a few minutes; I will send in one of the other women to stay with you; we will be back soon." He then left the room, Mr. Mannors and Robert followed, but he was cautious to lock the doors, and take the keys, so that none could find egress from the establishment.

Ever since his wife had been placed in the Home, it was the custom of Mr. Mannors to visit the asylum about once every week; his daughter and Hannah often accompanied him—sometimes they went there by themselves during the intervening time. He had this day paid his usual visit; Robert was with him, and he remained in conversation with the doctor longer than he generally did on other occasions. He was anxious to see the keeper—he did not let the doctor know this—but that attendant had received permission to go out that evening, and had not yet returned. It was nearly dark before Mr. Mannors left the place, and they had proceeded but a short distance when they met Samuel Styles, the very person for whom they had been waiting at the Home. He had been running fast, and was nearly out of breath. He looked excited, and during his quick respiration he hurriedly communicated something which seemed to affect his hearers and to decide Mr. Mannors to return with him at once to the Home.

"She is away now, she has only just got there. I know she'll be back soon for the doctor—she must tell *him*; she won't tell the detectives—but I've already done that for her, I've just been at the station—they've scented blood already. I'll just run ahead, you follow; I can let you in privately, and we'll see what turns up."

It must have occurred to the reader that Samuel Styles was the new keeper at the Home. From the moment that he became determined to counteract and expose the plans of Doctor Buster, he was, to use his own words, "continually upon his track," and he spared neither time nor pains to obtain all necessary information, or at least such as could be got by the most artful expedients. By means of the memorandum which Doctor Buster had carelessly lost, together with the advertisement taken from the *Times*, a sufficient cue was obtained to lead to the important discovery that the moderator's wife was immured in the private asylum of Dr. Marks. By his good address, he managed to secure the situation of keeper under the name of *Staples*, and subsequently, by great tact, secured the high opinion and good-will of an important personage, Mrs. Pinkley, who was the principal female attendant at the Home. In a few days, without causing the least suspicion, he learned the ins and outs of the whole place. The female patients were kept in the upper rooms; he soon discovered the occupant of No. 19, and managed to establish a communication with her by which she was encouraged to be hopeful, and assured her that she had one watchful friend, who merely waited for an opportunity to secure her freedom and punish her oppressor. Dr. Marks he found to be an easy-going man, considerate enough; but Mrs. Pinkley was callous and indifferent to the sufferings of others, particularly to those of her own sex. The patient in No. 19 was kept within hearing of the most violent lunatics, as if to hurry her to madness, and the dreary wailings of Mrs. Mannors could be heard by her almost continually; in fact, he already detected that the treatment she had received was specially intended to shorten her existence.

Having made the discovery in the asylum, his next object was to ascertain whether Doctor Buster's children were in the actual charge of Mrs. Pinkley. According to his engagement, however, his time was rather limited; his hours of duty were from nine o'clock A.M. until four P.M. during the day, and from six P.M. until midnight. He was required to confine himself strictly to the Home during the night, but the hours between four and six in the afternoon might be spent either in or out of the place, as he liked; special permission was necessary to enable him to leave the Home at any other time. Mrs. Pinkley's residence was but a short distance from the asylum; through the influence of Doctor Buster, she had the privilege of lodging in her own house after a certain hour at night, unless some urgent case required her attention. Her nightly absence, however, enabled the new keeper to make his most important discoveries, and often after midnight, when off duty, instead of seeking repose, he would steal out, contrary to rules, and if he saw no light, or heard no sound about her place, he would listen, to try and find whether she slept, and then he would speculate upon the nature of her dreams ere he returned to indulge in his own.

Anxious to gain admittance to Mrs. Pinkley's house, he once or twice succeeded in becoming the bearer of a message to her from Doctor Marks; but though she did not mistrust, she was very guarded, and baffled every effort he made to gain admittance—she was sure to meet him at the door, and keep him outside until she sent her answer. He saw that it would not do to excite her suspicion; this might destroy his plans. At last, it struck him that by watching from the Jewish cemetery opposite her house, he might be able to discover who were the actual members of Mrs. Pinkley's household, and perhaps ascertain at what particular time Doctor Buster paid his visits.

Day after day, then, the keeper visited the cemetery, and faithfully spent his two leisure hours watching Mrs. Pinkley's house. The door was always kept shut, the lower windows were closely screened, and the upper ones had half-curtains. Once when she was out, the upper curtains were put aside, and he saw three persons—Bessy and the two children. The next day he came disguised and with a basket of toys; he did not go into the cemetery, but loitered at a corner of the street until he saw Mrs. Pinkley leave the house; he hurried to the door and rapped, and the girl, thinking that her mistress had perhaps forgotten something and had returned, opened it; the peddler pushed his way in, but, as the children were up-stairs, and silent as usual, he merely asked a few questions, looked sharply around the place, and then left, lest by some chance he might be discovered.

Lately, however, he had not seen Doctor Buster. What could have detained him? Were the rumors of his suspected visits after all but an envious scandal? Night and day, for more than a week, he had been closely watched, but so far his shadow had never darkened the doorway. The keeper was nonplussed. Was he watched himself? and had some churchyard imp given the doctor a timely warning? His fears, however, were in this respect ill-founded. The devoted moderator was away at the time, ostensibly upon a visitation to certain churches or congregations as a peace-maker. Sometimes even where prayers and sermons are most plenty the enemy of souls will intrude, and children of the same church will wrangle, and lambs of the same fold will lose their spirituality and become like ravening wolves, ready to devour each other, and pious pastors will desert a congregation for one more deserving of their sympathies; who can say whether the fresh "call" is so promptly answered because a stipend is to be increased, or because others are in greater spiritual destitution? Anyway, the call is generally answered, old ties are rudely sundered, pastors often leave their old flocks to take care of themselves, and the moderator had often much to do to suppress schism, to keep the sheep from wandering away into other folds, and to reconcile deserted sinners to their temporary abandonment.

At last he came! The keeper was again in the cemetery, it was a gloomy evening and drawing toward dusk. He saw Doctor Buster enter the house; after a short time he heard a scream, he rushed toward the place. Mrs. Pinkley, who also heard the scream, had just got in before him, and in her alarm neglected to fasten the door. He followed, he heard her reproaches, and witnessed the scene of blood which sent him shuddering away.

It was long past midnight, the afflicted lady in the parlor of the Home still lay almost unconscious upon the sofa. The three men yet remained in Doctor Marks's study. Samuel Styles had given Mr. Mannors a full account of how he had acted since his engagement as keeper, and how his last fortunate discovery was the attempt to administer poison, which was to have been made that night. There was the bottle, its contents could be easily tested, and there was the additional paper of white powder which he had picked up in the hall, and which had been dropped by Mrs. Pinkley at the time she was startled by the premonitory words of Mrs. Mannors, for it was she who spoke.

The relation of these things, together with the events of the day, had a saddening effect upon all, and now they sit demurely in the stillness of the night, listening to the bleak, wintry winds which rush and moan around the building, and make the long poplars sigh mournfully in the desolate cemetery. They are aroused! Footsteps and voices are heard at the door, the night bell resounds through the silent building. They enter—not Doctor Marks alone—Mrs. Pinkley with drooped head is safely escorted by two detectives! She enters the study, and stares wildly at the men who are there to meet her. They look at her now in silence. Ha! she knows that face—'tis the infidel! She turns to the keeper, she frowns, she scowls, her hand is clinched, and she bites her lip. Oh! could she but force him now to swallow the contents of that bottle. But he holds it out at arm's length, and exhibits the paper of poison. "See," he exclaims, "she is saved!"

"Saved!" She stood erect before him as if suddenly petrified. A deadly pallor overspread her face. "Saved!" She was growing very faint. Was she lost herself? She revived again, and her hopeless, wandering gaze rested upon Mr. Mannors. "Yes, 'tis but an infidel plot—I see it all now—a vile plot, Doctor Marks, an infamous lie. But I am weary, and 'tis very late. Let me rest here to-night, let me think, and I will prove it all to-morrow."

The gray dawn of the wintry morning stole in through the curtained window of a small upper room in the Home, and, as the light slowly increased and struggled for admittance, the dim outlines of a chair, a table, and a bedstead could just be discovered. Every thing was still; and, as the light grew stronger, an empty cup could be seen on the table and the muffled form of a wearied sleeper on the bed. But now the stillness is broken, and a voice at a short distance wails out, "Lost, lost, lost." It is quiet again, and not the faintest sound of breathing can be heard. What a lethargy! Even the drowsy watcher outside the room door is listening to the silence. Still the torpid form lies stretched upon the bed—it never moves—its last breath has been drawn. Ah! how had death entered? The fatal draught had at last been given! and—Mrs. Pinkley had made her escape.

———

CHAPTER XXXIII.

THERE was to be a public inquest at the Home! one unlike any that had ever taken place there before. A posse of ignorant jurors would soon be assembled; they might take it into their heads to extend their judicial privileges, and to go tramping through the whole place, causing confusion; and after that, their blundering verdict might bring financial ruin upon the entire establishment. It was very provoking to one of Doctor Marks's staid and precise respectability. He was very much agitated, he felt himself singularly compromised, and that his position would be considered rather questionable. He was already conscience-stricken. Danger seemed to be looming up around him. Was he not liable to be accused as being an accomplice in a shameful system of persecution toward one who had been placed in his power? Would he not be looked upon as one so thoroughly base, as to have acted in coöperation with a heartless, infamous woman, in order to carry out an inhuman design, or for the sake of the paltry sum which was to be the reward of systematic cruelty? Friends of the patients, and other persons who had already called and obtained admission that morning were, he thought, rather shy toward him; and, as he went about from place to place, he was followed by curious eyes, and in imagination public curiosity seemed to be already drifting into public suspicion. In this trying time, he had scarcely a single friend in whom he could confide, and he was obliged to assume a calm demeanor while he was agitated by wild and conflicting emotions. Oh! how he could have cursed his own pliability and that clerical impostor whose specious piety had lured him into this vortex of trouble. He was very anxious; as yet there was no accusation made against him, but he felt every moment as if the hand of justice was about to be laid on his shoulder. What if some vile endeavor should be made to blast his prospects? What if his patients should see that stiffened body lying in the hall, and should get startled back to sanity at the sight of its distorted features? There was trouble on every side, and his hopes, and his honor, and his respectability seemed to have almost withered away. The terrible news of the murder and poisoning of the previous evening had been heard all over the city, and early in the day a crowd of idle persons had assembled outside the Home, in expectation of being able to get a chance sight of the noted woman who was supposed to be the accomplice of Doctor Buster, if not, indeed, the very principal in the horrid crime which had been committed. Already several palliating circumstances and many excuses were framed in behalf of the reverend moderator; and a number of sturdy Christians were quite prepared to assert that Doctor Buster could not possibly be guilty of

a crime, but that it was a deep-laid plot, an infidel design, against a well-known servant of the Lord. The blind confidence of the pious would not be easily shaken, and soon as the religious papers made their appearance they would defend him in thunder tones and hurl defiance at his accusors. Large bail was promptly tendered, and he was still at liberty.

Any way, there was to be a judicial examination. Mrs. Pinkley, and Doctor Buster, and Samuel Styles, and others would be brought face to face at the police court. It would be a feast for the press, and reporters made early preparations so as to be able to send full accounts to their respective papers. Doctor Marks had pledged himself for the appearance of Mrs. Pinkley before the magistrates or at an inquest, and as a matter of greater security, two detectives were to have her under surveillance; she should get no chance to slip away. The investigation was to take place in the forenoon, and other officers of justice had already arrived at the Home for the purpose of procuring certain witnesses and to conduct the accused to the legal tribunal.

They had been waiting there for some time, the hours passed quickly; punctuality was necessary, and there could not be much further delay. It was, however, very late when the accused woman had been permitted to retire; no doubt she had great need of rest—that is, if repose were possible to one in her position. The detectives watched in turn outside her room during the night. It was now nine in the morning, and she had not yet made her appearance, neither could the officer who kept watch at the time hear the least sound of preparation. Excitement, shame, and mortification must have kept her awake during the night, and heavy sleep must have at last overpowered her. But justice could not wait—it is a petulant thing. Minos or Rhadamanthus would brook no delay. Ate stood claiming retribution, and should she not have it?

Is not the justice of Christian civilization more rigid in its demands? It is ever eager for its prey, it is righteous; vengeance is its handmaid, and reformation is but a step-daughter which it elbows aside to be nurtured by visionary philanthropists. It must feel no pity—tears can not affect its purity; they may drop unheeded forever upon its marble bosom; the quality of mercy might be degrading to its dignity. It must have no human sympathies. It frowns upon the wretched culprit in the dungeon; and when its decree has gone forth, when even *human life* is the sacrifice to be laid upon its altar, it will not waver. It can heed no natural emotion, but it will stalk away from the scaffold with haughty tread, severe brow, and fingers dripping in gore—for, alas! is it not more noble than humanity? Ah! who is to arraign justice for its cruelties? Who is to blot out its texts and statutes of blood? Who is to stop its legalized atrocities forever?

As yet, there was no stir in Mrs. Pinkley's room; the detectives rapped—there was no reply. A woman was sent for to demand admittance and to hurry her out; and though the woman rapped and called lustily and long enough, still no answer came; the sleeper was not aroused, and, after many other unsuccessful attempts had been made, the officers grew impatient and suspicious, the door was burst open, and when the nurse entered and uncovered the sleeper's face she started back in affright—behold, Mrs. Pinkley was dead!

The discovery was quite shocking; the excitement throughout the place was very great. Those who had assembled outside the house were much disappointed; they became clamorous and unruly, and tried to gain admission; they were anxious to see the Jezebel living or dead, and when they could not succeed in effecting an entrance, they muttered curses against her who had eluded justice.

Doctor Marks was agitated, the keeper seemed confounded, and maids, nurses, and attendants appeared frightened or bewildered. There were ominous whispers among visitors; there were strange preparations; the frowning corpse was stretched out in the long hall—it did not receive tender handling—there was no solemnity. The curious gazed with unfeeling eye, the timid stood aloof, and, while it lay uncared for in the gloom, messengers were dispatched for the coroner.

In consequence of this unexpected act in the drama, the magistrates who had assembled in order to hold a preliminary examination had to adjourn. Three inquests were to be held that day, and Doctor Buster might perhaps be able to have another day or two to prepare his defense, and to bless and pray for his sympathizing friends. They came in a little crowd; he was again in the pleasant parlor of his reverend friend, Mr. Campbell, and, though he was but slightly flushed, and to all appearance perfectly resigned to meet what certain pillars of the church called his fresh ordeal of persecution, those only who looked at him sharply could detect the traces of great anxiety which were visible on his countenance. But he managed, however, to receive the numerous visits of clerical and legal friends, and to smile benignantly upon dowagers, spinsters, and other sighing sisters who came to proffer their stock of pious sympathy.

Yet all this could not last, he was again alone. He said he needed a little rest, and so he did; but when alone, then came his brooding thoughts, the most cheerless and harassing of all intruders. What dire despondency they brought! Could it be that she with whom he had so cheerfully conversed the previous day, before whom he had laid his future plans, was already a suicide, lying perhaps at that very moment under the cold gaze of an investigating jury? Oh! that unfortunate blow; and as he looked down at his right hand, he could have wished it withered from his arm. Still he felt but little remorse for the death of his child, but he felt a deep dread of hopeless loneliness. His mainstay had been cut down. Within the short period of one wintry day, his future had been blasted, and his shrewd, unprincipled, courageous confident had been balked, baffled, overreached, and driven to destruction. And when he then almost met the calm, defiant look of Martin Mannors, and almost heard the reproaches of his outraged wife, and when in the terror of imagination he beheld the prostrate form of his paramour, and saw the fixed stare of her sightless eyes, and saw her clenched hands, compressed lips, and distorted features, the very shadow of death seemed to encompass him—he shrunk and crouched in horror and dismay, and wished for sudden annihilation.

An hour of misery had passed—how he dreaded the future! He could find no rest. Were he only secure of being left alone, and within reach of some strong opiate, he might be tempted to follow her who had proved so resolute in self-destruction. Even then he admired her infamous courage—courage which his overbearing disposition could not, however, equal. She, in possession of her faculties, took the desperate plunge when she saw no chance of escape. He might be aroused to do so were his senses sufficiently blunted, and were he satisfied that his infamy was about to be detected and exposed. Still his love of life was strong; as yet he stood fair in the eyes of many—he was one of God's ministers—and many scoffed at the accusation. They demanded proof—where was the evidence? It was but an infamous plot—they dreaded no investigation.

But the doctor did dread such a proceeding; it could not be now avoided. He was still in deep thought; there was a faint ray of hope, and he clung to this like a drowning mariner to a plank. "What is the evidence? who is to prove against me? The humpback alone saw the blow, but her account is settled. Poor Fan did not see me, but she knew all—she too is beyond their reach. Then who is to prove? Law is law, they must convict legally. A man's life should not hang upon mere circumstantial evidence. Who is to testify?" He pondered for a few moments; his emotions of hope and fear quickly came and went, bringing assurance or despondency, and were as visible on his face as freaks of lightning across a thundercloud in the darkness of midnight. But suddenly the mental illusion disappeared; his hopes again seemed prostrated. Was there not another present when the blow was struck? Had not Alice seen all? Would it not be dreadful were his own child obliged to speak in evidence against him? He was struggling again with despair and he almost writhed in mental torture. Yet once more there came a flickering of hope. He started—where was Alice? In the midst of his own troubles, he had never given her a thought! Where was she? he felt but little doubt of her safety, but could she not be put beyond the reach of his ferocious inquisitors? Could she not be tutored to lie—to deny all knowledge of the fatal blow? Could she not be sent away, or confined, or any thing—he did not care what, so as she could be kept out of sight? Ay, in this desperate case, and in his present mood, he would not object to have her strangled, were he only able to find an accomplice; but the trusty hand that might have lent him ready aid was now powerless forever.

The accused man was in an extremity; time was pressing, he would be obliged to appear that afternoon or early next day at the inquest which was to be held over the body of his own son and also over that of the poor humpbacked girl. The sudden death of Mrs. Pinkley had caused delay. Fortunately, he was not required to appear at the asylum; but no plea of indisposition, nor any other plea whatever could save him from a horrid notoriety; he would be forced to attend, he would have to view the remains of his dead child, and to meet his accusers face to face. Still he could do all this, he could view his bloody work without a shudder; yes, he could go and boldly defy all, could he but get Alice out of the way; that girl should be disposed of, and it should be done at once.

She must be found, no matter when, or where, or how. Caution required, however, that he should not appear too anxious concerning this matter before others. Then whom could he trust? Where could he get one to be faithful and to do his bidding? He would pay a princely price for the work; he had ample funds, for on the previous day, anticipating the happy flight he expected to take with Mrs. Pinkley, he drew a thousand pounds upon the indorsement of the Rev. Andrew Campbell. With a full purse and a willing agent, he ought to be able to do much; where could he find the right person? Stay! he feels relieved, he has been trying to think who among the faithful was worthy of his confidence at this critical time—he feels again assured. There is another gleam of hope, he has hit upon the right one—he has found an ally—he would send at once for Bross.

The inquest at the Home was over; it was a tedious post-mortem case, but, after all, the jurors had not much to do. The evidence was direct, and went to prove that the late principal female attendant of the Home had retired at a certain hour on the previous night apparently in good health, it might be a little weak or fatigued, and that' in the morning she had been found dead in her bed. It was proved that the cup found upon her table contained arsenical sediment, that she had taken such poison, and that several small papers of the same substance had been found in a private drawer in her room. Everything went to prove an evil intention on her part. Her design upon the life of a female patient in the asylum was made manifest. It was therefore believed that she had taken poison to escape the legal penalty for murder; the verdict was in accordance, and in the eyes of many the case looked brighter for Doctor Buster.

There were loiterers around another door! How gloomy the place seemed! It might have been caused by the cold shadows of the tall, leafless trees in the cemetery across the way. It was chilly, and the wintry wind howled mournfully through the branches. Look in! There they still lie—the boy in his gore, and the poor girl with a placid smile on her worn features, but stamped there in the marble rigidity of death. Her untold, her unpitied sufferings had ceased, and her little term of patient endurance had ended. There were sighs of real pity; many of the strong men who stood silently around could have shed honest tears; and there were women present —pious ones, too—who could have prayed, but to what purpose? They might pray, it

would be but a formal muttering. Prayer without faith, like a body without a soul, would be dead. In these latter days, when organizations for prayer are so numerous, petitions may constantly ascend, but the most orthodox never hope for a notable miracle. The dead may be raised at the general judgment, but not sooner. The inspired word might be true, and its promises very cheerful and consoling, but, alas! these promises may be now read by the most confident Christian, and there is still a sad lack of faith. Of what avail are those which say, "Verily, I say unto you, that whosoever shall say unto this mountain, Be thou removed and be thou cast into the sea, and shall not doubt in his heart, but shall believe that those things which he saith shall come to pass, he shall have whatsoever he saith. Therefore I say unto you, What things soever ye desire when ye pray, believe that ye receive *them*, and ye shall have *them*." Mark 11 : 23, 24.

"These signs shall follow them that believe: In my name shall they cast out devils; they shall speak with new tongues; they shall take up serpents; and if they drink any deadly thing, it shall not hurt them; they shall lay hands on the sick, and they shall recover." Mark 16 : 17, 18.

"Verily, verily, I say unto you, He that believeth *on me*, the works that I do shall he do also; and greater *works* than these shall he do, because I go unto my Father—and whatsoever ye shall ask in my name, that I will do." John 14 : 12, 13.

"If two of you shall agree on earth as touching any thing that they shall ask, it shall be done for them of my Father which is in heaven." Matt. 18 : 19.

It is asserted that these and other scriptural promises are applicable for all time. Where are the true believers? Where are they, even among the earthly sanctified, who can truly accept these promises, whose faith in them never falters? The lip may utter its prayer, yet the heart has no hope. The inspired promises may be read, but the church must have degenerated. *Our* Israel has not the faith of the ancient saints. At the present day, faith will neither walk upon the water, remove the mountain, nor raise the dead. Lazarus might have been called from the tomb; Jairus might have had his little daughter restored; the widow of Nain might have been weeping near the city gate, and following in the mournful procession which bore her only son to the grave; her sobs might have suddenly ceased, and she might have been permitted to clasp his living form once more to her bosom. He who is said to have done these works also said to his disciples, that those who had faith in him should perform greater. Has that word lost its power, or is faith in it merely theoretical? Who now can raise the dead?—There they lie! let the miracle be performed. See that girl! bring back the smile again to her wan face, and let the pulsations of her loving heart return. Reanimate that little form, and give back the boy to his weeping mother. Alas! they move not! Of what worth are these assurances? to what intent? Neither promise, nor prayer, nor faith hath power to do this thing! Even those who still cling to belief hope not for a miracle, neither for the restoration of such as these. Their faith may be " the substance of things hoped for, the evidence of things not seen ;" yet though they acknowledge no existing doubt, they must feel content to wait for the actual evidence until the " last great day."

All were in waiting. Doctor Buster came with rather reluctant steps. The minister of St. Andrew's and members of the church—wealthy members, too—followed, prepared to renew their bonds for the moderator were it necessary. Legal friends came also, who could cross-question, perplex, and almost demolish the evidence of any ordinary witness. Every arrangement had been made to give aid and comfort to one so wantonly harassed and accused. The doctor entered ; the place was familiar, but *she* was not there to greet him. There were strange faces—the coroner and his assistants, police officers and jurors—who looked suspiciously at him, as if eager to give the verdict which he feared. There were others, perhaps accusers or witnesses ; and now, while he tried to assume the air of an injured man and to appear greatly affected, he looked searchingly around for one girlish countenance. He could not see it, neither was that dreaded infidel present. Hope came again and grew stronger. He could look with comparative indifference upon that other little face, bruised and blackened, that was there before him—yes, he could look, for Alice was not there whose living visage he feared still more to behold. A great point was gained. Bross must have received his message, and acted promptly. His daughter Alice was not there, thanks, no doubt, to Bross. He began to breathe more freely, and to feel himself saved.

The jurors were sworn, they went to view the bodies, and the legal gentlemen who appeared on behalf of the crown stated that evidence would be produced to show that the deceased girl had been in the employment of the late Mrs. Pinkley, that she was not of a vicious disposition, as had been improperly reported, and that it was not at all probable that she had committed self-destruction. Evidence would also prove that she was very much attached to the children of Doctor Buster, and that she had never committed the least act of violence toward one or the other ; but that, on the contrary, when the boy had been struck down by another, she was heard to bewail him as if dead ; and that there was strong reason to believe that her own death had been effected in a very short time afterward by persons who were then present, and anxious to get her out of the way.

" Persons who were then present !" The moderator grew nervous—who could prove that *he* was there? He whispered to his legal adviser, and that gentleman begged permission to interrupt his learned friend by asserting his doubts as to his ability to procure such proof. Then the doctor looked eagerly around again, yet Alice could not be seen.

The interruption met with no reply ; the counsel for the crown merely told the jurors that they would not be kept waiting for the evidence ; he would first call on Samuel Styles. This witness was entirely unknown to Doctor Buster—he applied his eye-glass. Samuel Styles! Who is he? He was sworn. In order to explain his position more fully, he gave the jury his reasons for entering the Home as keeper, and how he had detected the plans of the moderator and Mrs Pinkley ; how he had discovered the doctor's imprisoned wife, and how he had watched for the children, and, at last, how he had entered the house, when he heard the scream, on the very evening of the murder. He could not say who had actually struck the blow, but, said he, pointing to the accused minister, " That man was present, and I heard Mrs. Pinkley accuse him of the act, and reproach him for so doing." The doctor turned ghastly pale, and trembled from head to foot. " It is infamous," muttered the Rev. Andrew Campbell, " an infamous plot !"

" I beg to draw your attention, gentlemen, to the fact," again interrupted the doctor's legal friend, " that the witness was rather on intimate terms with the deceased girl—what proper business could he have had there at the time ? Might it not be asserted, that he is now only acting like a criminal, who, to shield himself, would accuse others ? He is a stranger—one to be suspected—where is his proof that my accused friend was in the house ? surely we are not to take the *ipse dixit* of a man in the very equivocal position of this precious witness."

" You shall have evidence presently," replied Samuel Styles ; " I may be a kind of strange in these parts, but I guess I know a thing or two. I can prove that I engaged in the asylum as keeper by the advice of one, perhaps known to many present—one, anyway, whom to know is to trust. I followed Mrs. Pinkley into her house that evening unperceived ; I saw who were there—guess I saw too much. I didn't wait a minute, I limbered up and put, and in less than an hour I told my story to the authorities ; that poor girl lying there, was made away with before they got here, she was kneeling by the side of the boy when I left. Anyhow, I'm about right in what I say, and that child coming in will prove the rest."

All eyes were now turned to the door. Mr. Thomas Bross entered obsequiously—he had already transferred his allegiance. The moderator as a priest, and the moderator as a prisoner were to him two distinct individuals ; there was no personal identity—he knew neither. Though pious, he was a worldly-wise man, a time-server, and knew where the sunshine was, and there he would bask. The doctor was in the shade—there let him stay ; Bross would now follow the fortunes of his great opponent.

The moderator's heart failed him. Was *she* coming? He dare not look up—a sight of that living child would be more terrible than the sight of the dead one. He heard her weeping, and the prayer of his heart then was, " Oh ! that with her tears her eyes might melt away and her tongue refuse its office. Oh !

that the sight of that mangled body might put her reason to flight, or stop the throbbing of her heart forever."

She came weeping, poor thing! Oh! how sadly. She was led in tenderly by Mr. Mannors, and at the moment, the intense gaze of pity from nearly all present seemed to bring a hush followed by a deep silence. Men held their breath, and tried to keep back their tears —the mute eloquence of nature. They stood aside to let her approach; her slight form was bent with grief, and she drew near, crying and sobbing as if her heart would break. She approached the table, and then, for the first time, looked up; what a sight met her eyes! She seemed suddenly overwhelmed; she was sinking, but ere she fell she was seized and then taken fainting from the crowded room. Had her father's prayer or curse already had its accomplishment?

They waited for some time, but a medical gentleman who was in attendance gave it as his opinion that, as the child had received a dreadful shock, it might prove fatal were she again brought in that day. If her evidence was necessary, it must be taken in some other place and at some other time. The coroner was of the same opinion; and, as it was getting late, he suggested that other evidence might be taken, and that they would then adjourn until the next day.

A witness was called, and Mr. Mannors answered to his name. "I beg respectfully to object to that gentleman's evidence," said Doctor Buster's legal friend, addressing the coroner. "I am sure that you will concur in the opinion that his evidence is not admissible."

These remarks caused some surprise.

"Not admissible! Why so?"

"Because he is not a believer in our holy religion. He treats the Holy Scriptures with contempt. He is an infidel—a blasphemer."

The counsel for the crown interfered; he could not imagine that such a disqualification existed. Were he to judge by appearances, there was not a person present before the court on whom he could more readily depend for a truthful evidence.

"The learned counsel must, however, admit," retorted the other, "that appearances are sometimes very deceptive. Truth from prejudiced lips is too often equal to falsehood. However, if the gentleman is truthful, a plain answer to a plain question will settle the business."

As it was, the coroner felt rather ashamed of the objection. "Mr. Mannors, you have heard what has been just stated; will you be good enough to say whether you believe the Holy Bible to be the revealed word of God, binding on all men? Do you believe in a future state of rewards and punishments?"

"Will my answer be satisfactory? I am not sworn; will my mere word in reference to this be believed?"

"Certainly."

"It seems, then, that the evidence which I may give against myself will be accepted, while that which I could give against a criminal will be refused. Let it be so—it is the result of Christian liberality. I do not believe that the Christian Bible is the revealed word of any God, or of any being superior to man. I can not say whether there is or will be a future state of rewards and punishments. I can neither affirm nor deny; but I never yet have had any proof of a *post-mortem* existence. Still, my fondest hopes are in that direction."

"Then," said the coroner in a hesitating manner, "I regret that we can not accept any statement from you as legal evidence."

Well might the coroner and those around him have blushed at such a declaration, and well may intolerance point with pride to its recorded triumphs. There is a statute included among British laws—a usage in British practice—whereby honest, thoughtful, incredulous men can be wantonly insulted in a public court and unjustly ostracized for their adherence to honest opinion. The exercise of this antiquated bigotry in the nineteenth century should bring the blush of shame to the cheek of every liberal man.

"As the court has very properly refused that person's evidence, before we adjourn I trust I may be permitted, on behalf of my accused friend, to show that a deep design has for some time existed against him; that the very individual whose word or whose oath would not be trusted by honest men, or received in an ordinary court of justice, has not only destroyed the domestic happiness of my client, but has hounded and persecuted him down to the present moment. Not only have the infidel sentiments of that man caused him to be a blight to the happiness of his own wife, so much so as to cause her to be immured in an asylum, but here is evidence to show that he has been the principal agent in leading a once worthy woman down to infamy." Having said this, he held out the letter or note which had been hastily written by Mr. Mannors to the moderator's wife at the time she was trying to escape from persecution.

"HAMPSTEAD, June, 1863.

"MY DEAR MADAM: I shall meet you again next Thursday at the place appointed. I have already made arrangements for your temporary stay at the Red Lion. In that place, you can be perfectly private. I think you should leave your husband at once, and be free for a time or forever from his vicious control. Yours sincerely,

"MARTIN MANNORS."

"Gentlemen, comment is almost useless, but I consider this letter to be damning proof of the infamy of that man."

"As I have not been permitted to give evidence," said Mr. Mannors in a mild tone, "I trust that I may be allowed to explain why that letter was written, and to prove by others that the persecuted lady first sought me. She is at present beneath my roof and under my protection, and were it not that she is greatly enfeebled, and that it would be worse than cruelty to bring her here, she could give such a rebuke to her detractors and to mine as would silence them forever."

"So she could, sir, so she could," interrupted Mr. Bross; "I can prove that when—"

The counsel for the crown rather abruptly stopped the law-clerk's flow of eloquence, by stating what had been just read or said was irrelevant; it was no matter for the consideration of the jury. Direct evidence was required, and he had been but a moment or two since assured that if the little girl, Alice, was kept quiet and free from any further excitement for a few hours, she would be able to give evidence to-morrow; that evidence was all that was now required before the matter was left to the jury.

"I guess here's a piece of evidence you won't refuse," said Samuel Styles. "I rather think 'twill speak conclusively. I shall leave it with you before we part; it can be cross-questioned at leisure. He handed the Queen's Counsel a handsome cane, which had been broken in halves; it was of ebony, and its massive gold handle was covered with blood, which had dried and crisped in its rich chasing. In searching Mrs. Pinkley's room that morning, he had found it under the mattress of her bed.

"Now," continued he, pointing to Doctor Buster's legal friend, "that gentleman a kind of hinted that I was a stranger in these parts, and might be acting like a criminal, by trying to throw the load on others. Just ask him if he ever saw that fancy article before, and if he knows who is the owner. I rather hope that his position just now won't be quite as equivocal as he hinted that mine was a spell since. If he can't exactly turn it through his mind, perhaps that other gentleman"—and he pointed to the Rev. Andrew Campbell—"might refresh his memory, and help him to make a clean guess: not that I exactly want the information myself, 'tan't of no great consequence to me—guess I'm sufficiently posted—but these twelve men here might be just a leetle curious and might like to hear their sentiments."

It was lucky at the moment for Doctor Buster that the broken cane was the object of such general interest. He sat crouched in a corner of the room, and the policeman, who stood close by, could see him tremble, and could mark the knotted veins swell out upon his forehead. Were it possible for that dead boy to arise from his clotted bier and give evidence against his father, it would not be more conclusive to many present than the sight of that blood-marked witness. The owner of it was well known; neither the doctor's advocate, nor the Rev. Andrew Campbell made any reply—a dawning of the terrible truth had even now come for them.

The shadows of the wintry evening had already begun to make their appearance; an adjournment was asked for. The doctor, it was pleaded, felt much harassed and fatigued; he would be able to give a satisfactory explanation to-morrow. The coroner was very considerate—he did not wish to be too rigorous with a distinguished clergyman; but it was with difficulty that the counsel for the crown was prevailed upon to consent to renew the doctor's bail—he did not deem it just to draw nice distinctions in favor of clerical offenders. However, promises and importunities prevailed, and the moderator was again saved from commitment. In leaving the place, the accused man was without hope, but he made a desperate effort to appear calm; he smiled, and leaned upon the arm of his reverend friend, and he walked away as complacently as a sanctified criminal on his way to execution.

For obvious reasons, Alice was consigned to the care of the medical attendant until the next day, and a posse of constables were to be left in charge of the place. Samuel Styles joined Mr. Mannors, and they once more turned their faces toward Hampstead.

The dreary December night had passed away, and the cold, gloomy dawn was slowly making its appearance. The moon was in its last quarter; it now shone through a small opening in the heavy clouds, and a few stars in the interminable distance stole glimpses at the bleak earth. One of the homeless urchins of the city, who had taken refuge during the night in an outhouse or shed adjoining the stable belonging to the pastor of St. Andrew's, peeped out from under his bundle of rags. He was trembling, there was snow upon the ground, and the pangs of hunger had already robbed him of any chance for the continuation of his wretched rest. Would he live another day, he must be active; he must go out again into the wilderness of streets, and pick up and swallow such garbage as could be found. Perhaps it might be a lucky day, he might find a shilling, or get a chance to steal one—it made no difference which. Pinched and straitened as he was, theft to him could not be crime, but suicide was; in his great extremity, he had never yet thought of that. But was it not right to steal? else how could he live? He wanted bread; it was in his last thoughts at night when he lay down in hunger—bread was in his dreams, and bread, or rather want of it, came again with the dawn. He must live; forlorn as he was, there was hope—there was yet a charm in his bleak, unblessed existence which he would not exchange for death. The cold moonlight was streaming down, and a colder blast was rushing about, and now, as this poor starveling indulged in felon thoughts toward large brown loaves, he noticed a long shadow moving backward and forward at the end of the shed furthest from where he lay. He looked listlessly at it for some time, but its motion in the moonlight was so unusual that he watched it more closely. He had often taken refuge in that place before, but no such vision had ever until now disturbed his waking moments or banished his thoughts of bread. Wrapt in his rags, he hobbled out, then went toward the stable-door; the end of a beam projected a couple of feet from the wall; he looked up in the gloom somewhat frightened: a rope had been attached to the beam, the body of a large man hung at the end of the rope, the wind swung it to and fro, and the long spectral shadow which followed the body was the shadow of the late Doctor Theophilus Buster.

———•———

CHAPTER XXXIV

It had been blowing a keen sou-wester all day, and the Atlantic waves, as they entered the passage leading to Cork harbor, rushed wildly toward Fort Carlisle, and then, as if repulsed, seemed to be diminished, and to slacken their speed as they bounded by Spike Island on their flushing and sparkling course to the most spacious and beautiful haven in Ireland. Some miles out at sea, a large steamer from Liverpool was heading for this port; it had struggled nobly all day against adverse winds and waves, and now, as day drew to a close, there was a lull, and an April sunset flung a glory along the coast, and its waning red rays could be seen wandering away over the distant hills, and then, as if resting on the very verge of earth and heaven, gradually mellowed into the most delicate blush ere sinking into repose.

Several passengers had assembled on the deck of the vessel; some who were in a hurry to land had already been packing trunks and carpet-bags; a few mercantile men were discussing the chances of an increase or falling off in business; politicians talked of the reform bill, of Fenians, and of the gloomy prospects of the confederates in America; while others, who had been a longer or shorter period away from their native land, gazed thoughtfully upon the distant headlands, or traced the dim outline of some mountain whose summit was lost in the clouds, but by whose base, perhaps, stood the sheltered valley cottage that was—*Home.*

Apart from the other passengers, two persons stood leaning against the ship's side toward the forward part of the vessel. There was a pause in the conversation, and they were gazing on the panorama of beautiful scenery which moved slowly by. One was a stout, low-sized man of middle age, he had a reddish, good-humored face, and there was something clerical in his appearance; the other was younger, taller, rather slight or slim, and of no particular complexion.

"And that's the Green Isle, the Island of Saints? Well, now, I fancy 'twould be much better for all parties if it had never gained that name. Saints! my present idea of that particular class is something like what I used to have of bears or wild-cats. They're mild and glossy at times, well enough to look at; but 'tis just as well to keep hands off, and not cross their track or interfere with their doings; if you're risky, and keep within reach, they're not mighty particular about hurtin' your feelings. Well, now, that's a kind of natural looking right across the way—green and brown fields, and them old blue hills away off; you han't much timber, rather too much of a clearance, but how green! green and garden-like, that's a fact. Yes, there's no mistake about it, I rather fancy that that *is* the Emerald Isle."

There was another pause for a few moments, and then his companion, while looking at the approaching shore, said reflectively, "Yes, sir, that's *ould* Ireland," and he seemed to lay particular stress upon the adjective.

"Well, old or new, 'tis about as good a place for raising saints as any I know of. It takes a certain kind of folks to make good saints—such as are ready to believe all they know, and a good deal of what they don't know. Anyhow, they ought to prosper over there; but some say they've been as bad for the land as Canada thistles."

"Just as bad. We've had saints of all degrees from Palladius or Patrick, its reputed patron, down to Cullen. If religion has been a blessing to others, it has failed altogether with us; we've had it in almost every shape and form—Pagan, and Popish, and Protestant; it has been fed with blood, and pampered with gold. The crown, and the cross, and the Bible have each in turn exercised an influence only adverse to humanity. Then we've had a dominant church and its holy apostle—*the sword;* but all to no purpose. It seems to me that the Irish will never be converted by Christianity, it wants something more pure and undefiled than that to soften their hearts and end their strife. In this respect, I think they are but a type of our common humanity. Yes, sir, the Gospel has been a woe to that island; its ancient Druidism could not have created more superstition, caused more contention, or produced greater mental degeneracy; and sure I myself have helped them down; well, *nabochlish,* I'll undo what I can before I die."

"I guess we've all a little to undo in that way; still 'twas no fault of ours, we were hitched to the thing in early years: that's the Gospel plan you know—catch them while they're green—they can't begin with thinking, reasoning men; secure the young ones and the women folks, and the rest are more likely to follow. But now that we're free, let us try and help those in bonds. 'Tis a tough task, I admit; but the ball is rolling, and time will do the rest, that's certain.—See them green hill slopes! every thing so fresh looking, an't that fine? If a man had any poetry in his nature, he ought to be able to find it somewhere about here. Well, how I should like to have a few thousand of them Irish acres, and then, if I could only get the right kind of settlers, every one of them as ignorant of all religion as a rhinoceros, and have common-sense laws, good schools, and freedom from the extortion of priests and parsons, I rather think we should make the thing work, and make out to live, and prove to the world what could be done on Irish soil."

"So you might, but, alas! for poor Ireland; its soil has been enriched mainly by blood. For centuries the battle of creeds has continued, until almost every foot of its surface has been trodden over by armies, and factions, and religious freebooters of all kinds. First the pagan was routed, then came Palladius, or Patrick, or some other pious pretender, upsetting one idol and erecting another, then Christianity was called civilization, and the converted poor were plundered and made poorer by continued imposts for the erection of cathedrals, and abbeys, and monasteries, and for the support of a horde of idle priests; then came the Reformation, with its alien clergy and rapacious gospelers, eager for prey and for proselytes, and these were soon followed by Cromwell and confiscation. The old form of Christianity was called idolatry, the next was avarice; both, in their results, were mercenary and inhuman. The exactions of the one were bad enough, but the extortions of the other have been the main cause of rebellion and murder, legal and illegal, for the last three hundred years. Rome in its palmy days quietly fleeced the Irish flock, but the voracious English state church has rushed down upon them like a wolf, and, behold its effects! religious despotism, religious strife, and a pauper population."

"Just so, the boasted effects of a religion of peace and good-will; but what of the dissenters—you an't forgetting them?"

"No, they are our chief beggars—a hungry race. They are foxes that gnaw the very bones; they are the Pharisees of our day, praying for humility, yet eager for power. But no wonder we have continued discord and rebellion in Ireland—religion has been its greatest oppressor. The state church, with less than one seventh of the population, demands support from the remainder who reject its teachings. That institution, established by violence and fraud, still exacts for the maintenance of its archbishops, bishops, priests, and ecclesiastical commissioners about £700,-000 annually; besides, it has rents and revenues from 100,000 acres of land, and other enormous emoluments, sufficient if expended in humane and charitable purposes to give vast relief to the deserving poor. What but rebellion can be expected from such wholesale plunder? Irish Catholics, who are heavily taxed to pay their own priesthood, naturally feel indignant at such base oppression, and justly offer it a continual resistance. Between Papists and Protestants, orange and green, the spirit of the nation has been almost crushed out, and kings, popes, prelates, and priests may well exult; they have brought misery on a land that might have been a region of happiness."

"This is, you know, what they call propagating the Gospel; but, according to your idea and mine too, they have had too much of a good thing—I guess they'd better take up again with the Druids."

"They might, for the matter of that; ay, propagation of the faith and spread of the Gospel are ready expressions, but what have they cost the world? A frightful amount. Every fanatic has a mission of some kind or other—one has a patron saint, and importunes to decorate its shrine; another starts off to the ends of the earth to carry a Bible to the heathen. What with churches and priests, saints and shrines, Bibles and tracts, the world has been agitated and impoverished, and the necessities of the poor made only a secondary consideration. Instead of trying to eradicate poverty, the whole machinery of Christendom is kept in ceaseless operation for the purpose of extracting money—not of course for the relief of actual distress, but under the pretense that, unless you teach religion, or spread the Gospel, souls will be driven to perdition; the real woes of this life are considered but trivial, while the imaginary ones of a future state must be averted at any cost."

"You mustn't forget that it requires eternal diligence to counteract the designs of the evil one; the operations of priest-folks lie in that direction. 'Tis something of a task to clip the wings of the old dragon, and something of a triumph to keep the critter from gobbling up all creation—an't that so?"

"Ay, that's a triumph, to be sure; we hear constant boasts of the triumphs of the true faith—but which is true? The Papist boasts, and so does the Protestant, and every sect, no matter how great or insignificant, tells you of Gospel triumphs; and then what are they compared with the efforts that have been made, or the sums which have been lavished on the insane idea of making all men have but one faith, and forcing Christianity on the world? After all that has been done, what is the actual progress? Why, after nearly two thousand years of praying and preaching, begging and compelling, other systems have not only remained intact, but have gained adherents. Mohammedanism has superseded Christianity in the East; Judaism still scorns its pretensions, paganism is proud in a vast control; while science, and secularism, and spiritualism are winning and drawing thinking men away from the worship of the cross and from the idolatry of the Bible. The magnificent efforts of Exeter Hall are unavailing; the torrent of unbelief rushes on. During the last sixty years, the Bible Society of Britain alone, has printed and distributed over fifty-three millions of copies of the Christian Bible, and yet it has been calculated that even at this rate it would take 1140 more years, and one hundred and twenty millions more of money, to give a copy of this so-called *free* Gospel to every human being! and though millions have been already spent to circulate the Scriptures, not one person in twenty has yet been favored with the perusal of this strange message from God to man. If the Gospel, as has been alleged, was once preached to every creature, the inhabitants of the earth must have been very few, or else they must have quickly rejected its teachings; if it was indispensable for man's salvation, what indifference and cruelty to let its circulation depend upon the uncertain efforts of a few believers, while vast multitudes are in the mean time left to perish through lack of knowledge—what a sad reflection upon the benevolence of a supreme Being! Christians, however, continue to boast of the triumphs of grace—meagre triumphs according to the means used. Give me money and men, give me but one fiftieth part of what is actually wasted in efforts to Christianize, and I will Mormonize Manchester, Brahminize Bristol, and the praises of Mohammed and the Koran shall be sung in the streets of London. Give me ample means and resolute men, and I can establish any system! Christianity has already had full sway for centuries. Kings have been its nursing fathers, it has had almost unprecedented popularity, and has become imperial in wealth, power, and intolerance; yet even now, refulgent as it may seem, let candid men but fairly investigate its claims, and they will as surely reject its authority.

"The best years of my life have been spent

in an endeavor to make others believe what I could not understand myself. What years of trial many of these have been to me! and what mental torture I have suffered contending with theological absurdities! Investigation has, however, satisfied me, as it has a host of others; and as soon as the fallacious pretensions of the Christian creed are more fully examined and exposed, they will be rejected, and will follow the course of other popular delusions which have had their day."

"That will be the case. I was once as great a stickler for them venerable chapters of inspiration as any man living; the Bible I imagined was law, physic, and divinity, and every thing else; what I couldn't understand at one time, I thought I'd be able to make out at another. I used to read and read, and felt mighty cheap at times when I couldn't riddle out the meaning; still I b'lieved, and still I doubted; then, after a time, I began to think that something wasn't all right—'twas I, of course, was rather slack—and soon as a doubt came, so soon was I bound to find out the exact truth. Guess I had a lively time of it for a while; but at last truth came, and truth in the end was too much for the Bible. I've been among Christian men and women since I was so high, through York State, and Pennsylvania, and New-Jersey, and many other places—among Episcopalians, Methodists, Presbyterians, Baptists, and twenty other different kinds; good Lord! they're all alike, the people never think; religious folks, in one way, are all of a stripe—they just, nine out of ten of 'em b'leeve what they're told, pay little or much right down, and ask no questions. And then there's the preachers or ministers, or whatever you like to call them, pretty well stuck up, most of them living at their ease—despots and exclusives in a small way—I won't say all of them, but pretty much all; some of them are sincere enough, but others are chuck full of the old Adam; they hitch right on and take to sinning quite natural-like; they an't often stuck when they want to start, they pitch right in, and then when they fall from grace, they talk about remorse and make out to feel rather cheap; but when there's a general row, and when it gets into the papers, or if the business is pretty scaly, they sometimes quietly slip cable, make tracks, or go off, just like our friend the moderator."

"No doubt Harry was surprised when he heard of that—he must have seen it in the papers. Ah! sure I know something of the clergy, but let them go for the present. Here we are in sweet old Cove once more; but sure now 'tis Queenstown—still the place is all the same—they can't change that. See, there's the guard-ship, and that one over the way is the hulk or prison-ship. I'll warrant they've got more than one Irish rebel on board for exportation—well, God help the poor fellows! and there's vessels, big and little, bound 'or the four quarters of the world. Isn't this a harbor fit for paradise? 'tis, faith, if there is such a place, and I hope there is. Look at that old church away up on the hill, and streets and houses, like huge steps of stairs, rising up from the water. You're sure to find churches wherever you go; like the clergy, they are fond of elevated positions. 'Tis no great matter in Ireland whether there's a congregation or not—where there's a church, there must be a salary. But what have I got to do with churches now? I'm no longer a priest, but a poor pariah; I will no more urge the erection of temples, but do what I can to undermine the stately fabric of superstition. Ay, there's the old sod, the fine green fields again; I some way think it does one good to step on native soil Psha! how hard 'tis to get rid of old notions. What is country or creed to me now? just old notions, nothing more. A subdivided world is hostile to humanity. Henceforth, I shall humbly tread in the footsteps of that true friend of man, who said, 'The world is my country, to do good my religion.'"

After Mr. Capel left England, his loss was not only felt by the family at Hampstead, but also in a particular manner by the Rev. Mr. McGlinn. That tottering pillar of the Roman Church found himself almost alone. Mr. Capel was a companion to whom he could freely unburden his mind, and from whom, he well knew, he would receive sympathy. An apparent conformity to the doctrines and ceremonies of his church had already become insupportable, and a thorough investigation into the claims of the Bible had satisfied him that Christianity was based upon a false foundation. He never studied the problem which no doubt deters many others—how am I to live if I resign my charge? but, true to his own honest nature, he decided to leave the church and renounce the faith, to take his chance among thinking men, and to warn others against the pretensions of creed and authority of inspiration. Yet, though he loved truth, he dreaded the obloquy which would follow his desertion of the faith. Surrounded as he was by thorough adherents of the church, he had not one in whom to confide; and when he mentioned a doubt, or threw out a hint respecting his unbelief, he was only laughed at by brother priests, who could not admit that he was serious.—Wasn't he an eccentric—sure he was controversial Tom, and drunk or sober he had a leaning for argument; when the Protestant was routed, he would attack the Papist—any thing for argument. So the priests of Moorfields still thought; but Father Tom was in some respects a very changed man—he had become abstemious, and instead of festive debates or post prandial polemics, he ventured on skepticism; but were his clerical friends even satisfied of his total unbelief, they would have had more consideration for him than if he had merely changed his faith. To leave the mother church for "Luther's bantling of apostasy" would, in their opinion, be an ecclesiastical crime, not to be forgiven in this world or the next. Anyway, Mr. McGlinn was determined to be free; and, as he had business in Ireland about that time, he notified the bishop, and received the usual permission. He desired to depart in peace, and let the anathema of excommunication afterward follow.

Having therefore made up his mind to leave London, he wrote to Mr. Capel, from whom he had lately received a letter; their positions were similar. He had not yet decided as to his future course; he was comparatively poor, so was Mr. Capel; not only would people of his late creed look coldly on him, but Christians as a body would mark their distrust, and perhaps attribute any thing but the purest motives for his rejection of the faith. He would now be obliged to stem the current against which he had faced; this he was willing to do; and as something must be done to earn a livelihood, he wrote to consult his friend, who himself was rather irresolute; it might be that they could unite in opening a school or seminary, or in establishing an institution of the kind; and if the spirit of intolerance interfered with their success in their native land, why, the world was wide, and they could cross the sea. This was the purport of the letter which he had dispatched to Mr. Capel; he had about a week yet to remain before he could complete his arrangements, and in the mean time he thought it his duty to pay perhaps a last visit to his friend Mr. Mannors, whom he had not seen but once since the departure of Mr. Capel.

No one could have received a greater welcome at Heath Cottage. Mr. Mannors, cheerful as ever, met him at the garden-gate, and after a hearty shake of the hand, gave him a good-natured reproof for what he called his desertion. What a pleasant home! even after the dreary visits of sorrow, the sunlight streamed down and seemed to renew happiness within the dwelling. Still there was a want—Harry was away; Mr. McGlinn had never been there before but in his company, and, though it was springtime again, he thought of the gloomy November day when they both left the place together. And then how changed Miss Mannors looked; there was a sadness in her appearance, yet how warmly she pressed his hand, and how earnestly she asked him if he had often heard from Ireland, and then, after a little hesitation, how she had even ventured to mention Mr. Capel's name.

"Oh! he has forgotten us," said Mr. Mannors," as you almost did yourself. What do you think, only one solitary letter from him since he left us—indeed, that was scarcely a letter, a few expressions of gratitude for all I had done for him, but at the same time positively declining the only little favor I ever tried to bestow. Indeed, it could scarcely be called a favor; when he was going away, I inclosed a check for a hundred pounds—merely as a loan if he liked. I did not tell him at the time what it was; I told him not to open the letter until he got to Ireland, but in less than a week after he left, back came my check, and we have never heard from him since. Now, Father McGlinn, isn't that ungrateful?"

"Well, upon my sowl, I rather like it. But begging your pardon, Mr. Mannors, don't *father* me any more—I'm done with all that. When you saw me last in town, you might have guessed at what was going to happen—you remember what I told you. Well, sir, at this blessed moment I'm an independent heathen at your service; faith, in one sense not very independent either, but any way free from all ecclesiastical bonds, and quite indifferent to interdicts. Well, even that's something to boast of, after nearly fifty years of servility to an idea. Yes, I admit it looks ungrateful on Harry's part, but, Lord bless you! you don't know him. Poor fellow! the day he left here with me was, I'm sure, the most miserable one of his existence; I saw it, he could scarcely speak, and when the big tears stood in his eyes as we were parting, he spoke of you as having been a most generous benefactor, and of you, Miss Mannors, as being an angel of light—faith, he did. Ungrateful! not a bit of it. He may be troubled perhaps with a little Irish pride, or he may have too much spirit, but nothing like ingratitude. If you were to see his letters—indeed, I once told him he should direct them to you instead of to me—nearly all about Hampstead and Heath Cottage, and Mr. Mannors, and his angel-daughter."

"Well, well, he's a strange fellow; I hope we haven't got rid of him altogether. Yes, Mr. McGlinn, I remember our last conversation in the city, and I am not surprised at the result—I sincerely congratulate you upon your mental freedom; and now I trust you are going to remain with us a few days, and not leave us in a hurry, as your friend Capel did."

"Remain! there's not much for me now but leave-taking; sure, I daren't stay here, besides, haven't I Harry's last letter hurrying me away? Somehow, I don't think he's at all happy in Ireland; he wants to try the other end of the world, and wishes to consult me about going to Australia."

Miss Mannors had to blush once or twice during the conversation; now, from some sudden cause, she grew pale and faint, and a dimness affected her sight.

"Australia! Why, who ever heard the like of that? Just think, Pop, of the man going away, away to Australia, like a romantic missionary, perhaps to be devoured by Christianized savages! How long has he had that notion?"

"'Pon my word, I can't exactly say—not long, anyway. You see he hasn't been very successful—many of his old religious friends gave him the cold shoulder. He's very sensitive, and, to my surprise, has lately become rather anxious for wealth. I know that since he left here, Hampstead has been often in his dreams; and now, as if there was some connection therewith, he dreams of gold, he would like to grow suddenly rich—yet a thousand pounds will do him; and as there is no possible chance of finding or making such a sum here, he is willing to seek it in far-off Australia."

"Ah! what a foolish dreamer, when he might be, perhaps, much more successful nearer home. How does he know but some well-to-do relative would turn up, and save him such a long voyage? Well, we must see to this; I do not want to have members of *my* church scattered about; we, too, have a labor of love to perform, we must act as missionaries in a noble cause, but let us first attend to the enslaved and uncomforted in Britain—here is the stronghold of the enemy. And now, Mr. McGlinn, while you and I try to devise some plan to keep our increasing flock together, perhaps you, Miss Pop, might consult your legal adviser, should he favor us with another visit.   Mr. Bross might be able to suggest how we can lawfully prevent Mr. Capel from wandering away to distant lands."

Depressed as Mr. McGlinn must have been at the time he called to pay this last visit, the short stay he made at Hampstead served greatly to cheer his spirits, and to give him confidence in the future.   His benevolent host was ever hopeful, and ever anxious to forward the interests of the deserving.   It was most gratifying to learn that the health of Mrs. Mannors was very much improved, and that there was every probability of her complete and speedy restoration ; during the last month, there had been a marked improvement.   He had also the pleasure of meeting his American friend, Mr. Samuel Styles, the late keeper at the Home.   Doctor Buster's career was freely discussed ; his death had caused a great sensation in the religious world, and almost to the last, a certain pious journal in the Presbyterian interest persisted in asserting that the untimely end of the estimable and talented moderator was the sad result of insanity, induced by the systematic persecution of certain noted infidels, aided, it was to be deplored, by a few jealous sectarians who claimed to be ministers and servants of the living God.   The Rev. Andrew Campbell also favored such reports ; but his opinion was somewhat altered when he made the very unpleasant discovery that he was held responsible to the city bank for a thousand pounds, drawn by the late Doctor Buster a day or two before his death.   Other revelations also tended to place the defunct moderator in no very enviable light, and for some time afterward when church-members, and brethren, and sisters, still strong in the Lord, ventured to allude to their once renowned preacher—their denominational idol—they were wont to exclaim, "Alas! alas! how are the mighty fallen."

Before the ex-priest took his departure from Hampstead, it was arranged that Mr. Styles, who was desirous of visiting Ireland, should accompany him ; this was most agreeable. And as Mr. Mannors was recommended to give his wife the benefit of change of air and change of scene, being anxious to see Mr. Capel again, he thought a trip to Ireland would be just the thing.   To the delight of Mr. McGlinn, he therefore promised that he and his wife and daughter would meet them in Cork on the first of May.   The afflicted widow of the late Doctor Buster and her only child had been kindly cared for at Heath Cottage ; about two weeks previously, they had been taken by friends to Bristol.

The two travelers who had held a conversation on the deck of the steamer have no doubt been recognized as Father Tom and his American friend, Styles ; they landed in Queenstown, and, having remained a day in that favorite resort, started again on a fine spring morning.   As they passed up the river, the scenery along the banks of the "pleasant waters" seemed enchanting ; in an hour or two they heard the melody of the Shandon bells, and found one true friend to give them a cordial greeting on their arrival in the "Beautiful City."

CHAPTER XXXV.

MRS. MANNORS was at Hampstead again, mentally restored, but still rather weak and worn after months of dreary confinement, and after the peculiar treatment to which she had been subjected in that other Home, out of which comparatively few indeed had ever escaped.   Oh! how grateful she felt for the blessing of reason.   She had but a dim recollection of her long restraint, yet she guessed at the sad truth ; painful to her memory, it recurred like a confused, dismal dream. Yes, she was home and restored, and at times she almost wept at what seemed to be to her a fresh evidence of mercy.   Another glorious morning had again appeared, she could look up to the mild heavens and see the early lark soaring in the blue sky.   Springtime had again returned with its budding beauty ; she could see the garden-walks fringed once more with the variegated, ornamental work of nature, and she could even look calmly upon the distant glittering cross of St. Paul's, and watch the sunlight flinging beams over the Surrey hills ; yet nothing visionary came to disturb her imagination—it was happiness.   She was again in her own pleasant cottage ; there were those around her who showed the most affectionate care, and nothing was left undone to win her back to cheerfulness ; even Flounce seemed doubly attached ; he followed her about, and in short, quick barks tried to make her understand his delight.   She was still religious, but that feeling came back in a subdued form, more under the control of her reason.   She had an increased regard for her husband, but as yet none of her old anxiety concerning his conversion.   At first she wondered what had become of Mr. Capel ; it seemed strange that he should not be there to greet her, and she fancied that he was still away on the circuit calling sinners to repentance ; and then often as she thought of her dear, lost boy—her great bereavement—her true maternal nature paid its repeated tribute to his memory.   As for poor Hannah, she was delighted ; what pleasure she anticipated in again being privileged to give a relation of her spiritual trials and conflicts to her best friend, and though particularly warned to say little or nothing to her mistress on the subject of religion, she could scarcely withhold pious ejaculations, and, as soon as she was alone, she would commence with renewed vigor to praise the Lord and take a look at John Bunyan.

It was now the end of April ; in a few days they would start for Ireland.   Mr. Mannors had made every necessary arrangement, and he anticipated good results from the excursion.   His wife would, no doubt, be greatly benefited, and for certain reasons he was particularly desirous of meeting Mr. Capel ; indeed, what he had heard from Mr. McGlinn only made him more anxious in this particular, and it did not lessen him in his estimation ; he was rather more strongly impressed with the idea that his daughter's happiness depended a good deal upon the course which that generous young man might determine to pursue. He never mentioned this matter to Mrs. Mannors; he felt somewhat reluctant, he wished to wait until it was perhaps more matured. He well knew that she had been very partial toward the young preacher, and though she had heard of his resignation and expulsion, still her discrimination led her to believe him in natural disposition to be one of the excellent of the earth. She, of course, regretted his apostasy; however, she could make an allowance for his defection, for she was inclined to think that Mr. Baker had been too peremptory and severe; but, notwithstanding what had passed, she entertained hopes that at some future day Mr. Capel would return to the church like a repentant prodigal.

Time flew by; they were to leave home next day. Hannah, and another pious woman, and Robert were to remain in charge of the house; the family might be a week or two away. One who was to be left thought such a chance a godsend, and she had resolved to make the most of it. Hannah privately determined that when she had the place to herself she would disregard all protestations from Robert or any one else, and tumble out, scrub, and overhaul every thing she could lay hands on; she anticipated a term of delightful confusion, and, eager for her task, she was impatient to have full control of the premises.

Trunks and boxes had at last been packed, and every one had retired for the night; repose came to all others, but Mary Mannors could not sleep. It was an hour of stillness; she sat at her window and looked out pensively upon the calm, moonlit scenery. The tall trees were motionless, and their young leaves scarcely stirred in the soft whispers of the night air. What were her thoughts? Perhaps in less than another week she would know her fate—she would learn that which might make her either happy or wretched forever. She loved—was it a flower that was doomed to wither prematurely? She hid the flame from all, and now it was consuming her own bosom. Alone she could think of Henry Capel, and she was thinking of him now. What if he had truly determined to leave all and go to a distant land? She well knew that if one word from her could bid him stay: she could not speak it—she could not even by one word avert her doom. Yet she had hopes; she had been greatly encouraged by what Mr. McGlinn had said about his friend. Did he not write often about Hampstead, and allude to her as being an angel, and then was he not anxious to get rich? What could that be for? She had often and often heard him say that he cared not for wealth, that he could be satisfied with a modest portion, with a humble home and peace of mind. Could it be possible that he wished to get rich for her sake? Would that that were his desire! She would then tell him, yes, tell him how—but, alas! her lips would be sealed; she could never tell him how dear he would be to her, even were he in the most abject poverty. No; it might be that at their next interview, should he tell her of his intended voyage, she would seem only a little surprised, might appear quite indifferent, and then that wretched simulation might drive him away forever. Poor Mary! she soon forgot her troubles in quiet slumbers,

and bright dreams again brought visions of happiness.

They had been nearly a week in Cork. What a meeting of true friends! It was a week of happiness to Mr. Mannors, a week of great restoration to his wife, and a period of almost perfect bliss to two young persons who spent much time together. Mr. McGlinn began to see matters in a different light; the proposals he had made to his friend Harry concerning a seminary were likely to be rendered futile by the proposal which he fancied that that young gentleman would very probably soon make himself to another person. He began to suspect something of this kind, and at the first opportunity he gave a sly hint to Mr. Capel, which made him blush like a girl. Samuel Styles evidently understood what was going on, and rather increased the young man's diffidence by telling him with the most serious face to go ahead, at the same time giving a side nod toward Miss Mannors; and it was plainly seen that Mr. Mannors favored the intercourse which he saw was so satisfactory to all, and which for a long time it had been his own desire to establish.

The strangers were delighted with the city and its attractive environs; they had been from Black Rock to Ballincollig at Glanmiro and at Sundays-Well, and at other places of resort; everywhere the scenery was most charming. Mr. Mannors proposed to visit an old friend in Mallow, but as Mrs. Mannors wished to see the Lakes of Killarney, it was agreed that Samuel Styles should accompany Mr. Mannors, while Mr. Capel, much to his satisfaction, was to escort the ladies. Mr. McGlinn had business to detain him in the city, and he would await their return.

In a few days they all met again. Mrs. Mannors could scarcely speak of any thing else until she had told the same story over and over about the beauty of the far-famed lakes and of the exquisite scenery of the neighborhood. Miss Mary had nearly filled her portfolio with sketches; her devoted *chaperon* had pointed out the most attractive landscapes, and she was entirely guided by him in the selection of views; as it was, she somehow found singular difficulty in transferring them to paper; but they would answer well enough to remind her in after-years of some of the happiest days of her life. During their stay, they had sailed upon the crystal waters from one fairy-like spot to another, they had had little private picnics on romantic islands, and had visited retreats sacred to lovers' vows. Whether Henry Capel ever had an opportunity of taking any advantage which such retreats might have afforded and of finding sufficient courage to make an avowal on his own account has not been made known; as far as this was concerned, he was rather reticent; but if words did not reveal the secret, there was a tell-tale expression in his face which might fully satisfy even such as were not very close observers that he had most probably asked some particular person a very particular favor, and that it had been granted. Any way, after he had returned, nothing more was heard about crossing the stormy sea or of going to Australia; instead of that, his excursive notions wandered no further than "*Blarney*"— to that place he proposed a visit. Father Tom recommended him to be sure and kiss the famous stone, for the sake of good luck ; after that he would acquire a peculiar kind of assurance, and might venture such an attempt upon a softer and more impressive substance.

They were at Hampstead once more. During their absence Hannah had worked wonders— every thing around the place had a shiny, smiling appearance ; every piece of furniture looked brisk and polished, just as if it were inclined to laugh ; the garden appeared to yield its greatest profusion of flowers, the birds to sing sweeter and louder. The fountain gushed up higher, sparkling in the clear air like liquid light, and the tall trees, crowned with azure, seemed to whisper joyful news to each other—murmuring softly, lest the listening black-feathered rooks in their branches should overhear the tidings. Nature seemed to have come out in holiday garb ; the earth and the heavens were alike serene and beautiful.

Hannah had received a hint that there might probably be a great day at the cottage, and she did her best to meet the occasion. Truly she had succeeded so well that Mr. Manners himself was surprised at the change ; upon his arrival he gave her a gold coin, which, with a nice present from her mistress, greatly pleased the industrious maid.

Although Henry Capel had given up the notion of crossing the wide sea, yet he readily crossed St. George's Channel to link his fate with one whom to gain he would have willingly braved the dangers of a thousand oceans, in order to try and procure that thousand pounds, the possession of which might embolden him to plead for the hand that was soon to be his. Mr. Manners had long discovered his true worth, and felt assured that one so noble in mind, so honorable in conduct, and so unselfish as he had already proved, would be more likely to make his daughter happy than a wealthy suitor without such sterling principles ; and soon as he was convinced that Mary Manners had more than an ordinary regard for Henry Capel, he made a legal settlement in her favor, securing to her sufficient property to place her in easy circumstances. He had lost his only son, and to a certain extent no one could so well fill his place as the person on whom his daughter had fixed her affections.

The day had been named when the wedding was to take place. Father Tom—his friend Harry would call him nothing else—had been prevailed upon to return with the little party ; Mr. Manners would hear of no excuse. Samuel Styles would be there, and a select few—every thing was settled. A beautiful day dawned ; the sunbeams rushed down like invited guests, they danced in the garden, flung the fragrance from the flowers, and then lingered around the doorway, looked in at the windows, and peeped into every place where a shadow might hide, as if to chase it away ; and then they seemed mingling and gliding through the pure air as if weaving a garland of light for the brow of the bride.

The benevolent Martin Manners never looked more happy ; he was radiant with smiles, and his wife was serene and cheerful. Father Tom felt an inspiration of wit, and Mr. Samuel Styles threatened matrimony on his return to America. The young people were married, there was a sumptuous repast, others were not forgotten, every poor family in the neighborhood had a better dinner than usual on that day, and many of the homeless ones were seated in the garden and fed bountifully ; and when Henry Capel and his bride entered the carriage to start upon a wedding tour, a number of persons—young, old, healthy and decrepit—who had assembled on the road-side, regarded the married pair with the greatest interest, and the murmured wishes for their happiness and long life could be heard around ; and when at last the vehicle moved off there was an impulsive cheer, and Father Tom, who stood at the gate, gave a lusty shout, and then, with considerable force, flung an old shoe after the open carriage, which most fortunately just escaped the bridegroom's head.

The May meetings at Exeter Hall had again taken place. The great Bible Society had once more made its annual effort. The same distinguished chairman had presided, many of the lordly and reverend speakers had made their fresh appeals, and almost a repetition of the same glowing speeches had been delivered exalting the Great Book, and showing what had been done for the benighted during the past year. The widow's mite, the peace of the poor, and the gold of the wealthy had been poured into the treasury of the Lord, even in excess of previous years, but still the receipts were wretchedly deficient. Sacerdotal ingenuity was again set to its task, and the omnipotence of words was required to overwhelm reason and conquer hearts. Studied metaphors, perfected flashes of oratory, and skillfully prepared fulminations— matured masterpieces of burning eloquence, as if fresh creations of a semi-inspired imagination—had been flung like thunder-bolts among the mass of awe-struck hearers, and had again aroused the echoes of the great Hall, and, with culminating grandeur, evoked the feelings of an almost breathless assembly. The effect was produced ; help, more help, was required in the cause of the Lord against the mighty, and liberal aid had again been secured to fortify priestcraft and intolerance.

Since the last anniversary, thousands, it was said, had perished for lack of knowledge, and alas! thousands who knew not the Lord were now on the road to eternal ruin. The mournful cry, Save us, save us! came from afar ; it was a shriek of woe, an alarm that should awake to powerful action entire Christendom. Infidelity was still defiantly holding up its accursed head ; let it not defile the land. British Christians were adjured to unite in a greater effort for its overthrow, and they were implored to occupy and retain their present advanced and distinguished position in the cause of the glorious Gospel.

Such were the delusive repetitions of Exeter Hall. Princely prelates and richly endowed priests in eloquent flights entreating the orthodox on behalf of those in foreign lands assumed to be perishing for lack of knowledge, while the increased number of those in their very midst, who were known to be actually perishing for lack of food, claimed but a secondary consideration, and were too often left to depend upon the humane impulses of the "ungodly," or upon the charitable efforts of unbelievers.

In conversation with his friends on this subject, Mr. Mannors said :

"It has been the cause of great surprise to many why there should be so much poverty even in the very midst of abundance, and comparatively few have ventured to ask why there should be any at all. It is taken for granted that indigence is the necessary condition of some, and divines have ever encouraged the notion that poverty is often a blessing in disguise ; for they assert that the poor belong to the Lord—'Hath not God chosen the poor of this world?' Yet, while lauding destitution—for beggary favors humility and dependence—the church, as a general rule, has shown its worldly wisdom by the most contemptible pandering to wealth and power.

"The rapid increase of pauperism has astounded the benevolent. The millions of victims to starvation in Ireland, in India, throughout Europe, and almost in every part of the earth where Christianity and its fostered civilization have control, have startled many to serious thought, but have scarcely affected the equanimity of rulers or priests. In times of great privation, instead of immediate retrenchment, armies are increased as if to avert a threatened danger, and while famine gloats over its thousands, priests ply their trade and collect for missions; and these funds, accumulated for the spread of the Gospel, must not be diverted from their legitimate course, even to allay the pestilence of want. Priestly policy, to be sure, assumes to lead in efforts at benevolence, and as ostentatious charity has subserved the interests of religion, institutions were founded in which the poor might find temporary refuge, but such wretched relief only engendered a dependency upon the priesthood, and gained a spurious reputation for a class who gave back but a tenth of what they had extorted in the name of the Lord. *

"The great question occurs, Why does so much destitution exist? The prominent cause arises from the pauperizing tendency of religion ; the insatiable greed of priests has been too well established. A great portion of the wealth of England is absorbed by them, and what do they give in return? They have impoverished Ireland as well as Italy, and the present condition of Austria, Russia, France, Spain, and other countries of Europe fully attests that where a nation has to support such vast numbers of non-producers called ecclesiastics, priests, or preachers, drones claiming exemption from labor, and in most cases from taxation, an additional burden must of necessity be placed upon the shoulders of the people. It may be fairly asserted that throughout Europe, for every priest you will find ten soldiers, and for every soldier ten ac-

tual paupers. Religion must have priests, nationality soldiers, and poverty is the common offspring of both. Religion and nationality, the theme of moralists, poets, and transcendentalists, have been in my opinion the most fertile sources of misery to mankind."*

"Well, I rather guess they have," said Samuel Styles. "I imagine I know a little of what religion has done to delay progress and turn things in general upside down. Nationality has parceled out the whole earth into little garden-patches, like a great field divided and fenced off into acres. The man squatted in the north corner fancies that the man in the south is a kind of inferior crittur; and if they make out to quarrel about nothing—say on a point of honor—why then they go at it and rob and plunder each other all they can—and that's so much to the account of national glory! If the man in the east boasts that the sun rises for his sole advantage, the man in the west feels called upon to resent the insult and cut a foreign throat if he can. That's called—patriotism. That's just how it works. What bosh ! A streak of mean selfishness exalted to a virtue. Yes, sir, religion and nationality have worked harmoniously together for the benefit of kings and priests, but have just left the world where it is."

"Those who have thought most on the subject," said Mr. Mannors, "admit that subdivisions, nationalities, and creeds are favorable to despotism—the world united would be free. Continue the distinction of races, tribes, clans, and caste, and you keep mankind forever in bonds, and you as surely perpetuate the jealousy, hatred, and strife which have arisen from such conditions. Another evil is the unfair distribution of land. If the state claims to own the land, and apportions it only to a few, those who own no share of the soil, and who can not therefore produce food, should not be allowed to suffer in consequence. The unequal distribution of land throughout Britain is infamous. Every man who has a desire to cultivate a portion of the soil should have an allotment of the same for that purpose. Talk of vested rights—rights secured to one at the expense of deprivation and destitution to hundreds! The people should own the soil in as fair and reasonable proportions as possible. But how is it here ? A vile monopoly. There are in the United Kingdom seventy-one millions of acres, there are about thirty millions of inhabitants, and yet the entire land is in the hands of less than thirty thousand landlords, a vast quantity of the same being vested in the State Church. One hundred and fifty men actually own the half of England, and twelve men own the half of Scotland ! Of the whole quantity, less than nineteen millions of acres are under tillage and over thirty-five millions of acres entirely uncultivated. Were no person permitted to own say over a thousand acres—which would be quite sufficient for all reasonable purposes—what a vast improvement it would be to the nation as well as to the individual! But mark the selfishness of some, particularly of the *aristocracy*. The Duke of Cleveland has an

* See Note K.

* See Note L.

estate *twenty-three miles* along the public highway; the Duke of Devonshire owns *ninety-six thousand* acres in the county of Derby alone, besides other immense estates throughout the three kingdoms; the Duke of Richmond has *three hundred thousand* acres at Gordon Castle, and *forty thousand* acres at Goodwood, besides vast estates at other places; the Duke of Norfolk's park in Sussex is *fifteen miles* in circumference; the Marquis of Breadalbane can ride a *hundred miles* in a straight line on his own property; the Duke of Sutherland *owns an entire county* in Scotland, from sea to sea. Other instances of such rapacious monopoly could be given, but the list is long enough. Two thirds of the land owned by such persons is totally unimproved, and those already in possession of immense estates are eager to acquire more. The late Marchioness of Stafford took from her tenants over *seven hundred and ninety-four thousand acres*, which had been held by them or their fathers for centuries! What can be expected but discontent and poverty when good land is thus monopolized and diverted from cultivation for the purpose of enlarging private parks, or of being made into forests or sheepwalks? Is not this another fertile cause of discontent? Should such exclusive possession be allowed to continue? Attempt to reform the abuse for the benefit of the plundered masses, and religion will side with the rapacious, will pervert ideas of justice, and cry out for vested rights; attempt a revolution, the church will preach obedience to power, it will stand by the oppressor, and grow frantic in denunciation."

"Well, I often heard," said Mr. Styles, "that they used to hold pretty considerable estates down South; but for one man to hang on to a hundred miles of land right along in a straight line, is about the tallest kind of ownership I ever heerd of. I like your idea of limiting a man to a thousand acres. Even that's too much of good, arable land; yet 'tis a great improvement, and I hope to see it carried out yet, even were it in Old Virginny."

"'Tis dreadful to think that such a state of things should continue to exist," resumed Mr. Mannors. "There should be no such thing as actual poverty; there is enough for all; yet what deplorable suffering from mismanagement and injustice! Many schemes have been advanced to rid the world of paupers. Civilization often lets them perish. Communists, socialists, and moral and political reformers of every degree have been perplexed with the problem of poverty—but to what effectual purpose? Unfortunately it has been too frequently assumed that privation is normal. Whence is ghastly pauperism that prolific parent of crime? It stalks through the land with blanched face and hollow cheek, sifting the garbage of cess-pools, and living—yes, *living*—on refuse and rottenness, and watching with wolfish scowl for plunder, or, it may be, for blood! Whence this phantom of moral and physical disease? It is the offspring of fraud and oppression, the certain result of a deprivation of human rights. Poverty is simply the effect of a continued wrong; yet, if governments were based on just principles, the

remedy would be plain and simple. The first great move in social reform should be a restoration of natural rights. Every brute creature free from man's control finds a bountiful supply in the lap of nature. Was less provision made for man? Every human being is entitled to light, air, food, clothing, and shelter; these are *natural rights*, of which to deprive any man is to despoil, to rob. Every government should guarantee those rights and make them respected; this should be a first and principal duty. Our poor-law system is based upon the principle that human creatures must not be allowed to starve, that they have a right to food; but instead of properly recognizing this beneficent law, we delay in most cases until they are reduced to the most abject want before relief is offered; then charity becomes a mark of degradation. How does the state assent? It seldom interferes until famishing men are driven to pauperism or crime, and as soon as they have become disreputable or infamous they are fed and cared for. The uncomplaining poor may suffer without relief until terrible hunger has overcome their good resolves; but when at last they become debauched by poverty, and trained to felony by want, then they are qualified for the grateful shelter of a prison and entitled to the food and protection for which they had perhaps reluctantly bartered their honor.

"How deplorable! To prevent this, all should have their natural rights, rich and poor alike. Those in need should be able to avail themselves of the food, clothing, and shelter ready to be dispensed by the state. Of course, there should be a limitation until the system became general; a country or nation could only afford to keep its own people, just as a parish now keeps its own poor. What was given should of necessity be plain, but good and sufficient; it should be furnished as a right, not doled out as a charity. That which the rich or prosperous might decline to accept could be estimated, and an allowance made for the same on any claim held against them by the government. Those who wished for better than the state had to furnish should gain it by their own industry. Thus, while all were insured against positive want, there would yet be an incentive to labor; those who wished to advance in social position would have to be diligent in order to improve their own condition. In connection with this, a liberal education perfectly free from sectarian bias should be placed within the reach of all.

"In such a plan of benevolence fairly in practice there need be no obtrusive socialism; every one, as circumstances permitted, would be at full liberty to accept or refuse that which the government had for distribution. Every industrious person could acquire property, live in his own house, and improve his own condition, just as at present, independent of all others; but the state should make no class distinction in the appropriation of simple necessaries, just as no distinction or exemption would be made among those liable to pay a rated proportion of taxes. There is generally an abundance of food to be had, if not in one country, in another, and the government storehouses should always be amply provided. It is not probable, however, that even a third of the population of any country would ever avail themselves of such assistance.

"The establishment of any such system would, in my opinion, be a remedy for the evil of pauperism, and the only certain one of which I can conceive. It might be made very simple, and, in the long run, less or no more costly than even the heavy penalty resulting from the wretched and unjust governmental policy, and the disreputable diplomatic shifts and stratagems which have obtained for centuries, and which, besides creating innumerable woes, have vastly increased national obligations. The rich could not reasonably complain, for all would be privileged to partake alike, and heavy imposts, for which the wealthy are now mainly liable, would be, no doubt, greatly reduced, and many others entirely abolished. The poor would be made more virtuous, and would not be the humiliated recipients of a stinted, morose charity. Hunger, that great incentive to crime, would be appeased. Even if actuated by no higher motive, prevention would be better than cure, and man would feel more dignified, more grateful, and more inclined to do what was correct when he learned to know his rights, and found them respected; when he was cared for by his parent state, instead of being shunned as an outcast, prostrated by poverty, and treated in many respects worse than a beast. And then what a happy result to the state itself—less misery, less discontent, less degradation, less crime, and perhaps, eventually, far less expense! Indeed, what it now costs to keep up additional armaments, armies, police, and numerous aids to suppress the turbulence created by wrong legislation, besides that which is required to put numerous pains and penalties in force, and the immense sums wasted for many unworthy purposes, would do much to meet this new and just demand for national benevolence; and as there is generally an excess of officials in government employ, none in addition would be required.

"I can not go into details more fully at present; but the management regarding plain buildings, with gardens or grounds to cultivate if possible, to be called, say, public homes, not 'poor-houses' or 'houses of refuge,' and that concerning the distribution of food and clothing, could be made very simple; honest and careful legislation is only required to start the great experiment. And satisfied am I that the names of those who supported such a measure of justice and humanity would be recorded on millions of living hearts and registered for the gratitude of future ages."

"I fancy I see what you're at," said Samuel Styles. "Every man belonging to a national ship feels that when he turns in at night he is sure of his grub next day—no need of pilfering to get it. And you would liken the state to a great ship, and feed and clothe every man on board. Somehow I like the notion—guess 'twill bear some calculation. I'll figure

it up; for even in Yankee land, though we may be a leetle ahead of all creation in some matters, we an't yet quite perfect. Our government is yet but an elective monarchy; we must get rid of the 'one-man power;' we want no uncrowned kings—our presidential elections are sinks of political corruption, into which all parties plunge. We need no costly presidents to guide our ship of state—they mostly rule for a party; and before we are entitled to be called the 'Great Republic,' we must first be a *true* republic; we must have an economical government, more simple—like that of the Swiss, than that of flashy, imperial France. 'Twould do our senators and congressmen no harm to take a friendly hint once in a while from such a liberal British cousin; it might give us a fresh start in advance and do many a world of good; and, acting at once on your idea, we might still lead on in the cause of human progress."

Father Tom, who had been listening attentively to all that had been said on the subject, seemed to have been much struck with the benevolence of the plan. He remained silent and reflective for some moments, and then, looking up at Mr. Manners, exclaimed, "Were Britain to lead in this matter, what a post of honor it would occupy in the world!"

"It would, no doubt," continued Mr. Manners; "but some of our so-called great statesmen are so wedded to their prejudices that it will be difficult to move them in a new direction. I am aware that difficulties exist which may be urged against bringing such a system to a practical issue; but those difficulties are more imaginary than real. Timid politicians may probably elaborate as to the expense, without making a just estimate of the great advantages to be gained; they may draw a line of distinction between the country and the people, and while heedless and extravagant in upholding the honor of the one, may be still almost indifferent as to the poverty and degradation of the other. They may continue to take a wrong idea of what is right—just as false notions are still entertained as to what is virtue or what is crime. However, until a full measure of justice is meted out to all, until there is a full restoration of human rights, it should be the great duty of the nation to make suitable provision for all of its people in actual need, sickness, or distress, and for the children of such, until they are educated and able to do for themselves. Those who are willing to labor, but who can find no employment, should not be left a prey to hunger. If the state continues to sanction and uphold an unfair distribution of land, it should either provide work or food for those who have no land to cultivate. And next to a security from degrading poverty, there should be a free education for all.

"Pauperism is a disgrace, a pestilence which should be stamped out were it to take the crown jewels or national treasures to find food, or had every church in the kingdom to be opened and used as a shelter for the homeless. No nation can claim to be truly great while thousands of its people are obliged to go supperless to bed. Governments must become more paternal, and not remain as some, like the shadow of despotism upon the land. Advanced ideas have had their effect upon legislation, and the conservatism and exclusiveness of the past will no longer be tolerated. And, kind friends, hoping on, may we live to witness the fraternity of nations, and may we see the priest and the soldier, who have kept them so long divided, obliged to turn to occupations more in the interest of humanity."

This was Martin Mannors's prayer ; he held out his hand and looked upward as he spoke, there was a short pause, and then, as if with one voice, they all exclaimed, *Amen.*

In due time, Mr. and Mrs. Capel returned, to the great joy of Mrs. Mannors, and to the thorough disgust of the aspiring Mr. Bross, who, regretting having ever entertained a favorable opinion of any person known to be skeptical, had rejoined the church and Sunday-school and commenced a redistribution of tracts. The industrious Hannah, in the fullness of a happy spirit, grew more fascinated with John Bunyan ; but Robert hopes to be able to alienate her affections to some extent from that dreaming pillar of orthodoxy and perhaps to legally monopolize the greater share of them himself. Father Tom had to leave for Ireland, but engaged to return in a short time and embark with his friend Capel—who with his wife had already become active Spiritualists—in the publication of a paper intended to advocate human rights and to expose popular superstition and priestly fraud. Samuel Styles, who was a great favorite among the Secularists and Spiritualists of London, was honored by them with a public dinner at the Red Lion, and soon afterward took passage for New-York, bearing to the liberal bodies of that city the fraternal greeting of their brethren in England. He promised, however, to pay Hampstead another visit within a year, provided Mr. Mannors would, in the mean time, cross the Atlantic and hail the friends of free thought in America. This proposal is likely to be favorably entertained, and Martin Mannors may expect an enthusiastic reception.

How long still is the human mind to remain in the bonds of superstition ? How long is the great delusion to continue ? Shall men learn hatred through nationality and religion, and shall Christian priests pursue their systematic extortion and maintain their mischievous rule for yet another century ? Shall annual meetings continue to be sustained in order to promote the circulation of that dreary volume of " inspiration," and shall cunning words and mystic threats drain further millions from the credulous ? It may be so for a time ; but there are even now hopeful signs of a rescue. After a trial of over eighteen hundred years, Christianity has so far failed in its mission. The triumph of reason and humanity must be accomplished, and there are those now living who may witness their ascendency and celebrate their union and installation as the great ruling guide and power of EXETER HALL.

APPENDIX.

NOTE A.

In Puritan Massachusetts, during the period which Cotton Mather called the "golden age" of the Pilgrims, it was enacted with regard to heretical books:

"It is ordered that all and every one of the inhabitants of this jurisdiction that have any books in their custody that go under the names of John Reeves and Lodowick Muggleton, (who pretend themselves to be the last two witnesses,) and shall not bring or send in all such books to the next magistrate, shall forfeit £10, and the books shall be burnt iff the market-place at Boston, on next lecture day, by the common executioner."

And respecting infidels and skeptics:

"Any one denying the Scripture to be the word of God shall pay not exceeding £50, and be severely whipped not exceeding 40 strokes, unless he publicly recant, in which case he shall not pay above £10, or he whipped in case he pay not the fine. And if the said offender after his recantation, sentence, or execution, shall the second time publish, and obstinately and pertinaciously maintain, the said wicked opinion, he shall be banished *or put to* DEATH, *as the court shall judge.*"

PURITANISM.

It is recorded in the early history of the Puritans of New-England that—

"The Quakers were whipped, branded, had their ears cut off, their tongues bored with hot irons, and were banished upon the pain of death in case of their return, and actually executed on the gallows."

It is also recorded in the same history:

"The practice of selling the natives of North-America into foreign bondage continued for two centuries. The articles of the early New-England Confederacy class persons among the spoils of war. A scanty remnant of the Pequod tribe in Connecticut, the captives treacherously made by Waldron in New-Hampshire, the harmless fragments of the tribe of Annamon, the orphan offspring of King Philip himself, were all doomed to the same hard destiny of perpetual bondage."

The same history also says:

"Where are now the numerous and flourishing tribes of Indians which once peopled New-England? Where are the Narragansetts, the Pequods, the Pokanokets, the Mohegans, and the Mohawks, to say nothing of other tribes? All have disappeared from the face of the earth, thanks to the cold-blooded policy and heartless cruelty of the Puritans! They all vanished at the first dawn of Puritan civilization! First overreached in trade by the cunning Yankees, then hemmed up within restricted territories, then goaded into war, and then exterminated with fire and sword. . .

"The Pokanokets were the first tribe to shelter the Pilgrims after their landing on Plymouth Rock, and they were the first to fall victims to their insidious and ungrateful policy."

It is further recorded in the same history:

"At the two sessions of the court in September, 1693, fourteen women and one man were sentenced to death on charge of witchcraft. One old man of eighty refused to plead, and by that horrible decree of the common law was pressed to death.

"Although it was evident that confession was the only safety in most cases, some few had courage to retract their confessions; some eight of them were sent to execution. Twenty persons had already been put to death, eight more were under sentence, the jails were full of prisoners, and now accusations were made every day."

Among the laws recorded in the early history of New-England, were the following provisions:

"No one shall travel, cook victuals, make beds, sweep house, cut hair, or shave on the Sabbath-day."

"If any man shall kiss his wife, or wife her husband, on the Lord's day, the party in fault shall be punished at the discretion of the court of magistrates."

"No woman shall kiss her child on the Sabbath or fasting-day."

To these provisions of the law the historian appends the following note:

"A gentleman, after an absence of some months, reached home on the Sabbath, and, meeting his wife at the door, kissed her with an appetite, and, for his temerity in violating the law, the next day was arraigned before the court and fined for so palpable a breach of the law on the Lord's day."

NOTE B.

THE following report of the proceedings of a Bible Society meeting, held in December, 1863, at the city of Hamilton, in the Province of Upper Canada, speaks for itself, and shows that little, if indeed any, exaggeration has been used in the narrative of the Bible-meeting at Hampstead. Were it not for the reliable account of the one, the other would be asserted a libel against Christian unity, and what strong language might be used by "reverend gentlemen" and pious hearers against its reckless author.

HAMILTON BIBLE SOCIETY MEETING.

IT ENDS IN A FREE FIGHT.

(From the Hamilton Spectator.)

In accordance with the circular issued by Edward Jackson, Esq., one of the Vice-Presidents of the Hamilton Branch Bible Society, a meeting of the members was held in the Mechanics' Hall yesterday evening. The public were also admitted, but the front seats were reserved for the members, so as to distinguish them from the rest of the audience. There were from a hundred to one hundred and fifty members present, and about four hundred of the general public.

On the platform, to the right of the chair, were the Rev. Messrs. Burnet, Pullar, Cheetham, and Irvine; and Messrs. C. D. Reid, Wilson Kennedy, and A. Milroy; on the left were the Rev. Messrs. Ormiston, Rice, and Inglis, Mr. Sheriff Thomas, and Messrs. E. Jackson and James Watson.

Shortly after seven o'clock, the Rev. Mr. Burnet rose and said that, as it was now past the time at which the meeting was called, he would move that Mr. A. Milroy take the chair.

Mr. Kennedy seconded the motion.

Mr. Sheriff Thomas said he supposed the object of the motion was to test the feeling of the meeting, but decorum dictated that, in the absence of the President, the vice-president should take the chair. He would therefore move, in amendment, that Edward Jackson, Esq., be chairman.

Rev. Dr. Ormiston said it was unnecessary to say one word in favor of the propriety of the course proposed by the sheriff. He seconded the amendment.

The sheriff then put the amendment to the meeting, and declared it carried amidst cheers and hisses.

Mr. Jackson came forward and took the chair.

Mr. C. D. Reid rose, and was received with loud cries of "Chair! chair!" He attempted to speak, but so great was the uproar that it was impossible to hear him. All that reached us was, "I protest against Mr. Jackson taking the chair."

Rev. Mr. Burnet next took the stand, and was greeted in a similar manner. He said, "I have just one word of explanation." (Uproar, which continued for some time.)

Rev. Dr. Ormiston tried to say something, but was not permitted to be heard.

Rev. Mr. Burnet continued, amidst interruptions, "As mover of the motion, I am entitled to one word of explanation. This meeting has been called by Mr. Jackson, and it did seem to him proper that the one calling it should take the chair.

The chairman said he had been placed in not a very pleasant position, and he would need all their sympathy and forbearance. They had assembled to hold a meeting of the Bible Society, and they ought to respect the principles of the Bible. Before proceeding to the business of the evening, he would request Rev. Dr. Ormiston to implore the divine blessing.

Rev. Dr. Ormiston offered up prayer.

The chairman said he would say a few words on the occasion of their being called together. It had been the custom for the last twenty-five years to arrange the business of the annual meeting in committee. This year they had failed to do so, in consequence of a difference regarding the appointment of certain officers. The minority of the committee determined on carrying the matter to the annual meeting, and to that course he attributed all the subsequent inharmonious proceedings. He was persuaded that Exeter Hall would not tolerate an amendment at an annual meeting, for there all the business was arranged in committee. However, at their annual meeting, after the list of officers had been proposed and an amendment offered, it was thought by some that they could not arrive at a just conclusion, it being a mixed meeting, and a resolution was therefore passed adjourning the election of officers to a meeting of the members of the society, to be called by circular a fortnight afterward. The circular was issued, but on account of appearances, to which he would not now allude, it was thought proper to postpone it indefinitely. The present meeting was based on that postponement, and had all the powers of the annual meeting. They could propose amendments to the constitution, (and he believed some gentlemen intended doing so,) elect officers, or dissolve the society if they pleased. He would now call on the Rev. Mr. Inglis to address the meeting.

Rev. Mr. Cheetham started to his feet, holding a paper in his hand, and Rev. Mr. Inglis also rose.

Then commenced a furious uproar, which continued without cessation until the breaking up of the meeting. Cries of "Cheetham, Cheetham!" "Inglis, Inglis!" alternated, and neither speaker was allowed a hearing.

Mr. Cheetham was the first to make the attempt, but was met by so great a noise that it was useless to persist.

Mr. Inglis—Mr. Chairman and friends—(cheers and hisses.)

Mr. Cheetham—I move that, as this meeting—(uproar.)

The chairman rose and said that he decided Mr. Cheetham to be out of order.

Mr. Cheetham again tried to speak, but with a similar result as previous attempts.

Mr. Inglis—Will this meeting allow me just one moment? ("No, no," and continued uproar.)

Mr. Cheetham—Just one moment. (Laughter and hisses.)

The chairman, having obtained a hearing, read a letter from John Young, Esq., requesting that his name be withdrawn from the list of vice-presidents, as he was disinclined to continue associated, even in name, with a society, the committee of which acted in such a disgraceful manner.

Mr. Inglis and Mr. Cheetham again attempted to address the meeting, but all attempts were in vain, for the hooting and yelling was at once commenced when either of them opened his mouth.

Mr. James McIntyre rose in the body of the hall, and inquired of the chairman who had the right to the floor.

The Chairman—Mr. Inglis.

Mr. Cheetham—I have the right; and I intend to have that right. (Cheers and hisses.)

Mr. Coombs said he had come to the meeting, as he had no doubt many others had, to see fair play. The first one on the floor had the right to speak, and as Mr. Cheetham was the first, if the other had any sense of propriety, he would sit down. (Cheers.)

Mr. Cheetham—Allow me just one moment. (Cries of "Shut up!" "Go on!" etc.)

At this stage of the proceedings, Mr. Hugh McMahon, amidst loud cheering, went upon the platform, and took a seat behind the chairman, but higher up.

Mr. Sergeant-Major Brown, seconded by W. Powis, Esq., moved that the meeting adjourn sine die.

The chairman said it was of no use for any one to occupy the chair when no respect was paid to it. As he despaired of restoring order, he would declare the meeting dissolved. (Loud cheers.)

We may state that the motion Mr. Cheetham was desirous of moving read as follows: "That, as this meeting is wholly illegal, we adjourn."

Notwithstanding the declaration of the dissolution of the meeting, the crowd still lingered in the hall, as if expecting something else to occur, and their expectations were not long ungratified. A swaying to and fro of a knot of persons in the centre of the hall attracted our attention, and on proceeding thither, we found Hugh McMahon and a Mr. King struggling for the possession of a walking-stick. The origin of the disturbance, as near as we could ascertain, was as follows: McMahon went up to Mr. James Walker, who had the books of the society under his arm, and took hold of them. Mr. King went in between them, and pushed away McMahon, Mr. Walker making his escape in the mean time. McMahon seized hold of King's stick, one or two others joined in, and soon there was quite a disturbance, but it would doubtless soon have been quelled had it not been for the introduction of another element. Some five or six Irishmen (and Roman Catholics, we believe) armed with shillelahs, dashed into the crowd with wild whoops and yells, and laid about with their sticks in the most promiscuous manner, the leader crying out, "Clear the way before you, boys!" The seats were scattered in all directions, and a scene of the wildest confusion ensued. After a time the gang of rowdies went out of the hall, smashing at the seats with their bludgeons, and yelling like savages. The excitement continued for some time after their disappearance; and it was not until the superintendent prepared to turn out the gas that the crowd was persuaded to leave the hall.

A LATER PIOUS SCENE.

"At a Methodist chapel in Yorkshire, England, on a recent Sunday, (April, 1869,) there was a regular battle between the trustees and Sunday-school teachers, who had been ordered out of the building by the trustees. One of the teachers had a large piece bitten out his thumb, and another person was seriously injured by a buffet being thrown at his head from the pulpit. Bibles and hymn-books were freely used in the fight."—*Extract from Brooklyn Daily Paper, May 3d, 1869.*

NOTE C.

It is well known that the clerical defenders of slavery in the Southern States of the American Republic invariably sought to strengthen their position by an appeal to Holy Scripture, as fully authorizing the establishment and propriety of *slavery*. Independent, however, of the sanction deduced from the Bible, it also seems that they could see "God's providential care" manifested on behalf of the inhuman system. The pious Bishop Elliott, of Savannah, Georgia, in a thanksgiving sermon, thus alluded to slavery. He said:

"It is very curious and very striking in this connection to trace out the history of slavery in this country, and to observe God's providential care over it ever since its introduction. African slavery had its origin in this country in an act of mercy, to save the Indian from a toil which was destroying him: but while the Indian has perished, the substitute who was brought to die in his place has lived, prospered, and multiplied. Behold the providential interposition! Then, when the slave-trade was destroyed, the inability any longer to obtain slaves through importation forced upon masters in these States a greater attention to the comforts and morals of their slaves. The family relation was fostered, the marriage tie grew in importance, and the 800,000 slaves who inhabited these States at the closing of our ports in 1808 have, in the short space of fifty years, grown into four millions."

How widely different have been the conclusions drawn by Northern and other Christian teachers from the same inspired word respecting slavery; and how plainly they can *now* trace the finger of Providence in its total abolition! Yet, strange to say, the American Religious Tract Society, during the existence of slavery in the South, never permitted the publication of any thing reflecting upon that vile oppression; and, in its republications, generally expunged all that had been written against slavery by others!

Slavery has caused the greatest disunion among Christian ministers as well as among Christian people. Since the close of the American rebellion, a proposition for reunion among Northern and Southern Methodists was promptly rejected, and the organ of the latter body, the *Episcopal Methodist*, the leading Southern journal of that denomination, published at Richmond, made the following remarks on the subject:

"A formal reunion with Northern Methodism is to be deprecated as the most intolerable calamity that could befall our Southern Zion. To consent to it on the terms suggested, we must abjure our principles, sacrifice our position of usefulness, consign the memory of our brethren and fathers to infamy, pronounce the sentence of self-condemnation upon our whole communion, and accept a feature in the moral discipline of a dominant Church which dooms to death and damnation all who have been connected with what it denominates 'the great evil'—'the detested sin of slavery.'"

How "kindly affectionate" are such exhibitions among the divinely enlightened!

NOTE D.

THE following extract from that greatly admired work, *Baxter's Saints' Rest*, (unabridged,) will give a fair idea of the revolting orthodox opinion concerning the vengeance of God:

"Your torments shall be universal. The soul and the body shall each have its torments. The guilt of their sins will be to damned souls like tinder to gunpowder—to make the flames of hell take hold of them with fury. The eyes shall be tortured with sights of horror and hosts of devils and damned souls. The ear shall be tortured with the howlings and curses of their companions in torment. Their smell shall be tortured with the fumes of brimstone, and the liquid mass of eternal fire shall prey on every part. No drop of water shall be allowed to cool their tongues; no moment's respite permitted to relieve their agonies."

What a hideous picture! And yet poor Baxter believed his God to be merciful and gracious—" Whose mercy endureth forever!"

A terrible "Sight of Hell," from a *Catholic* point of view, will further illustrate the fearful teachings of religion:

"HELL DEPICTED FOR THE YOUNG.

"At present, (says the *Pall Mall Gazette*,) when there is so much discussion about what all children should be taught, it is useful to know what some children are taught. We have before us the tenth of a series of books for children and young persons,' composed by the Rev. J. Furniss, C.S.S.R. and published by authority, for it is stamped '*permissu superiorum*.' Its title is *The Sight of Hell*, and its contents are quite as startling as the title. The children who are instructed out of this work will learn, 'It seems likely that hell is in the middle of the earth;' and the Rev. J. Furniss adds: 'We know how far it is to the middle of the earth. It is just four thousand miles. So if hell is in the middle of the earth, it is four thousand miles to the horrible prison of hell.' Down in this place is a terrible noise. The children are asked to 'listen to the tremendous, the horrible uproar of millions and millions and millions of tormented creatures, mad with the fury of hell. Oh! the screams of fear, the groanings of horror, the yells of rage, the cries of pain, the shouts of agony, the shrieks of despair from millions on millions! There you hear them roaring like lions, hissing like serpents, howling like dogs, and wailing like dragons There you hear the gnashing of teeth and the fearful blasphemies of the devils. Above all, you hear the roaring of the thunders of God's anger, which shakes hell to its foundations. But there is another sound. There is in hell a sound like that of many waters. It is as if all the rivers and oceans of the world were pouring themselves with a great splash down on the floor of hell. Is it, then, really the sound of waters? It is. Are the rivers and oceans of the earth pouring themselves into hell? No. What is it, then? It is the sound of oceans of tears running down from countless millions of eyes. They cry forever and ever. They cry because the sulphurous smoke torments their eyes. They cry because they are in darkness. They cry because they have lost the beautiful heaven. They cry because the sharp fire burns them. Little child, it is better to cry one tear of repentance now than to cry millions of tears in

hell.' It is hardly needful to follow the Rev. J. Furniss through all his ghastly pictures. The foregoing passage is a fair specimen of his style, and the substance of his remarks is not so attractive as to induce us to quote at great length. We can not, however, withhold the following picture of what is to be witnessed in the third dungeon—that is, in the lowest depths of hell. 'The roof is red-hot; the walls are red-hot; the floor is like a thick sheet of red-hot iron. See, on the middle of that red-hot iron floor stands a girl. She looks about sixteen years old. She has neither shoes nor stockings on her feet. The door of this room has never been opened before since she first set her foot on the red-hot floor. Now she sees that the door is opening. She rushes forward. She has gone down on her knees on the red-hot floor. Listen! she speaks. She says, "I have been standing with my bare feet on this red-hot floor for years. Day and night my only standing-place has been this red-hot floor. Sleep never came on me for a moment that I might forget this horrible burning floor." "Look," she says, "at my burnt and bleeding feet. Let me go off this burning floor for one moment, only for a single, short moment. Oh! that in this endless eternity of years I might forget the pain only for one single moment." The devil answers her question: "Do you ask," he says, "for a moment, for one moment, to forget your pain? No, not for one single moment during the never-ending eternity of years shall you ever leave this red-hot floor." "Is it so?" the girl says, with a sigh that seems to break her heart; "then, at least, let somebody go to my little brothers and sisters, who are alive, and tell them not to do the bad things which I did, so that they will never have to come and stand on the red-hot floor." The devil answers her again, "Your little brothers and sisters have the priests to tell them these things. If they will not listen to the priests, neither would they listen even if somebody should go to them from the dead."' The concluding sentence proves that the 'mocking fiend' can twist Scripture to his own ends. It is clear, also, that the Rev. J. Furniss has no scruple in accepting the devil's advocacy of 'the priests.' It is permitted to the upholders of any creed to spread it abroad without opposition; but those who use such questionable methods as the Rev. J. Furniss deserve censure even while they enjoy toleration. Lest it be supposed that we have selected an obsolete work for comment, we may add that the copy before us was published in 1861. On the cover his author is styled 'Father' Furniss. Were he really a father, he would never have penned such a work, nor would he have enjoined on others the duty of teaching its doctrines to children."

Religious tract societies circulate similar pious blasphemies for the edification of women and children, and large sums are regularly expended in order to terrify the "unconverted" and bring them to "belief" by stereotyping such savage and inhuman threats.

NOTE E.

A PROOF of the tender mercies of the state form of Christianity was given in the London *National Reformer* of April, 1861, about four weeks previous to the great Bible Meeting held in Exeter Hall:

"It is, we are assured, unquestionably true that on Thursday, the 10th instant, the church-wardens of Broseley (near Birmingham) levied a distraint on the goods of James Clark, a poor laboring man, for the non-payment of the sum of one shilling and threepence halfpenny, which the said James Clark was called upon to contribute toward certain expenses which are annually incurred by the congregation that worships in Broseley parish church; the articles seized in satisfaction of this claim consisted of a clock, an oak chest, an oak cupboard, two tables, seven chairs, a tea-tray, a looking-glass, a smoothing-iron, and a straw mattress: and that Clark has a family of six children, who, together with his wife, bed-ridden mother, aged eighty-three, and his idiotic relative, aged forty-three, constitute the household which has been deprived, at an inclement season, of so many humble, but to them valuable, necessaries in order that the church of the state may get the munificent amount of fifteen pence halfpenny. Who can read such an account of Christian charity as this without being filled with the greatest indignation and disgust at the system which is the cause of such disgraceful and cruel proceedings?"

The same paper, in its weekly issue in May, 1861, thus alludes to a scene at a collection for church-rates in Edinburgh:

"CHURCH RATE.—There was a terrible scene in

Edinburgh on Tuesday week, in consequence of a sale by auction of goods seized for minister's money. About four thousand people assembled round the place of sale, and the goods seized were taken possession of, smashed, and burned in St. Andrew's street. Surely it is time the authorities of Edinburgh saw the injustice of such a rate. This is not the first 'scene' that has been produced in Edinburgh through the enforcement of what is justly considered an unjust tax; and unless the rate is abolished, we fear it will not be the last."

Just about the very time of the above disturbance, reverend and princely church magnates were in Exeter Hall glorying in the humanity of Christian civilization; and, while begging for the benighted heathen in Borneo, were plundering their own Christian poor in happy Britain!

NOTE F.

THE more ancient cosmogony of the Jews has every evidence of decided Egyptian origin. Of the curious representations in one of the principal tombs at Thebes, Miss Martineau says:

" It is impossible to look upon these representations of the serpent, of the tree of life, of which those who ate were made as gods, of the moving spirit of the Creator and of the universally prevalent ideas of the original spread of water, the separation of the land from the water, the springing of vegetation, and the sudden appearance of animals on the new surface, and the separation of the upper air into regions of abode, without seeing whence was derived the first of the two accounts of the creation given in the book of Genesis."

And again: " In their theory of the formation of the world, they (the Egyptians) believed that when the formless void of eternal matter begun to part off into realms—the igneous elements ascending and becoming a firmament of fiery bodies, the heavier portions sinking and becoming compacted into earth and sea—the earth gave out animals, beasts, and reptiles; an idea evidently derived from their annual spectacle of the coming forth of myriads of living creatures from the soil of their valley on the subsidence of the flood. When we remember that to them the Nile was the sea, and so called by them, and that they had before them the spectacle, which is seen nowhere else, of the springing of the green herb after the separation of the waters from the land, we shall see how different their view of the creation must be from any which we could naturally form."

NOTE G.

TERRIBLE ABUSES IN COUNTRY WORKHOUSES.

From London Christian World.

THE *Lancet* has done good service in directing public attention to the horrors of Farnham workhouse, and thereby leading us to ask whether the same scandalous neglect may not be possible elsewhere. Within sight of Aldershot, not far from a bishop's palace, and under the eyes of guardians and inspectors, official and amateur, such abominable cruelty has been perpetrated that it can only be characterized as " a reproach to England, a scandal and a curse to a country which calls itself civilized and Christian." For fourteen years cruelties almost incredible have been practiced, although the visitors' book bears no evidence of a single complaint having been made. On the contrary, the statement perpetually recurs, " The wards are clean and every thing very satisfactory." Under the guidance of the *Lancet's* commissioners we know what Hampshire visitors mean by " clean " and every thing being " very satisfactory." The workhouse premises are badly constructed, the wards gloomy and comfortless, and dirty beyond description. The accommodation provided for old and young, for tramps, male and female, and especially for the infirm, is intolerable. The casuals are locked up all night in noisome " cages " without food. A short time since, a poor woman, on the verge of her confinement, was imprisoned in this manner, and when the porter unlocked the cage next morning, she was found to have been already four hours in the pains of child-birth. The inmates of the infirmary are also locked in all night, and the cruelty of this can only be rightly imagined when it is remembered that every convenience is out of doors. Persons mortally sick are left day and night without any nursing attendance except what they might or might not succeed in summoning by ringing a bell for a nurse, who might be in any part of a large and

straggling building. The nursing staff for from sixty to ninety patients consists of one paid nurse and one male pauper assistant—an invalid, who has been tapped five times for dropsy. Until Dr. Powell, the medical officer, who has waged a good and persistent fight against the evils of the place, insisted that towels should be allowed, the inmates, after washing or bathing, dried themselves on the sheets of their beds. The master of the workhouse, who has since been dismissed for gross immorality, several times threatened the doctor with personal violence because he persisted in proposing reform. When the doctor ordered a ' mutton ' dinner, thick lumps of tough beef and bacon were served out to poor old men and women without a tooth in their heads. The children did not fare any better. The ' nursery ' is a gloomy, damp, brick-floored room, with absolutely no furniture except one low wooden bench, on which seven or eight little children were sitting, in front of the fire. They had no toys, no amusement, and no education." Such are a few of the horrors which the *Lancet* has laid bare. A more deplorable state of things can hardly be imagined. The question is, Are other country workhouses in a similar plight? It is evident we can no longer rely on the reports of poor-law inspectors. Even independent visitors appear to have been afflicted with blindness in part. Having begun the work, we trust the *Lancet* will pursue it with unflinching fidelity.

THE LONDON POOR.

Distress always reigns in London, the very rich and the very poor being close neighbors in the great metropolis. The London *Times* notices that at certain doors of some of the districts of the city crowds of men may be seen jostling, striving, almost fighting each other for admission; and the admission, when once secured, is not to see a favorite actor or hear a popular preacher, or to witness a prize-fight or rat-bait, but to gain the privilege of breaking hard stones in a cold, muddy yard attached to the parish workhouse, for the reward of threepence and a loaf of bread. " These men," it adds, " are not clad in the usual stone-yard apparel; they wear good coats—rags are scarcely to be seen. They are men who not very long ago were earning from $6 to $13 weekly, to whom the very mention of the workhouse would have been contamination; and here they struggle and wrestle for its most meagre advantages." The journal referred to then makes some comparisons of the relief afforded to the poor. During the winters of 1865-6, the average daily number of laborers in the Poplar stone yard, attached to one of the London poorhouses, was 200; but in the week ending January 9th, 1867, the daily average was over 1000. In the last week of 1866, that poorhouse gave out-door parochial relief to 4840 persons, as compared with 1974 in the last week of 1865. This establishment is now giving relief to its utmost capacity, and this fact, together with the announcement that nearly all the funds have been drawn out of the London savings banks—the working-classes having been from four to six months without regular wages—shows that at present there is greater distress in London than has been known for a long time.—*American Paper.*

NOTE H.

CHRISTIANITY is imperious in its assumptions; it claims to be all that is truthful, noble, and magnanimous; it boasts of its humanity and of its moral and civilizing influence; but what a burlesque upon its pretensions is its actual history—sectarian enmity, gross intolerance, and bloody and inhuman persecution. Can Christianity, with its arrogance and cupidity, show a purer record than that exhibited by ancient paganism? Christian nations are preëminent for their love of war, plunder, and devastation; and so great is their mutual distrust that, even during the uncertain periods when there is no actual war, the *armed peace* of Europe alone costs, as has been stated, about £300,000,000 sterling ($1,500,000,000) annually! Can Christian people claim to be more upright, more honorable, and more exemplary than Buddhists, Mohammedans, or Parsees? In numerous instances the ethics of China or Japan might bring the blush of shame to entire Christendom. What among the deceptive transactions of Bible-worshipers—who boast of a purer theology—is still most common? Frauds, in castle and in court, in state affairs and in church matters; frauds in national intrigue, in diplomacy, and in naval and military affairs; frauds in senate-chambers and in law tribunals, in elections and in appointments;

frauds by word and by oath, in buying and selling, in giving and receiving; frauds by weight, and frauds by measure, and frauds by adulteration, and increasing frauds in every imaginable shape and form that may escape the penalty of crime!

But it may be said that a majority of such persons are not true Christians. Well, if they are not, let us go among the reverend clergy; they, if any, are surely of the right stamp; nearly all of them have sworn or solemnly declared that they have been called—moved by the "Holy Ghost"—to preach the Gospel. Then what of the priests? Alas! with all their spiritual endowments, they have proved to be but frail and fallible men; and though there are many excellent persons among them, yet, as a class, in proportion to their numbers, it may be said that they excel all others in sensuality; and so notorious have they become in this respect that one can scarcely read a newspaper that does not bear a record of their vileness. To avoid scandal, much is connived at, and many of the clerical culprits permitted to escape where others would be held accountable; yet so heinous have been some of their crimes that the law has had to take its course, and felon priests are now paying the penalty in prisons and penitentiaries, and even the scaffold itself has often had to close a career of clerical infamy. The latest case of the kind at present remembered is that of the Rev. Mr. Hardin, a Methodist minister, who, for the sake of a paramour, murdered his wife in New-Jersey a few years since and was hanged for the crime.*

Indeed, of late so frequent and scandalous have been priestly amours that the secular press in many places has been forced to notice the fact and to issue a warning to over-pious and confiding females; and in consequence of the caution thus given against the wiles of the ordained servants of the Lord, the *Pulpit*, for November, 1857, a religious magazine, makes the following extraordinary comments in palliation of clerical fallibility:

A CURIOUS ARGUMENT FOR A RELIGIOUS MAGAZINE.

"We infer from what we hear in private conversation, and what we read in the public journals, that the public think it very marvelous that so many of the clergy are wrecked upon the rock of sensuality. The astonishment is not astonishing. People who do not make a habit of thinking will hardly be thoughtful enough to know the fact in reference to this matter. The fact is, there is no profession, class, or avocation so exposed to or tempted by the devil of sensuality as the ministry. The very sanctity of their office is an occasion of their stumbling. The office is confounded with its occupant. The sanctity of the former is made the possession of the latter. Now, the office is an invulnerable myth; its occupant is a man of like passions with other men. No temptation is sufficient to overcome the other office, while so stout-faithed an occupant of it as Peter the apostle may fall grievously at the first approach of the adversary. Unthinking women may seem to be only tempting the office, when they are unwittingly laying snares for the occupant. By their persistent exhibition of confidence in the office, they are confiding persistently in its occupant. And so it comes to pass in this way that the minister, with all his flesh and blood about him, has the door of temptation thrown open to him and then closed behind him. Blind confidence on the one side, and unguarded sociability on the other, lead to equivocal circumstances as to both. No man in the world has so few conditions imposed upon him at the threshold of society as the clergyman. His passport to society is almost a *carte blanche*. Women of both states and all ages are his companions, socially and professionally. The rules of social intercommunion between the sexes are, in this case, virtually suspended. What would be indiscretion with other men, is a matter of course with him. He shares or is alternately admitted to the privacy of the sick-room with the physician.

"Whenever spiritual advice is called for, there he reigns alone and unmolested. And he is a sedentary man, of nervous, sanguine temperament, and, like all men of this sort and life, feels the law of his flesh warring against the law of his religion. None have such passions as those of sedentary life. In proportion to the idleness of the muscles is the activity of the passions. The devil tempts the industrious; idle men tempt the devil. The clergy should give more earnest heed to 'muscular Christianity.' But not only is their life afflicted with deficiency in bodily exercise,

* Between the years 1860 and 1862, *four* Protestant priests were hung for murder in the United States.

but it is additionally accursed with the temptations that take advantage of this physical feebleness. Considering, then, this sandy-haired composition, this nervous combustibility, this superabundance of sexual heat from a deficiency in physical exertion, and this extraordinary exposure to the wiles of the wicked, and the insinuative influences of unsuspicion, the marvel, nay, the miracle is not that so many, but so few of the clergy fall into the sins of sensuality. The wonder is, not that so many yield, but that so many stand firm!!

"While we regard a sudden trip into sensual sin as comparatively the most excusable of the obliquities of which the clergy can be guilty, we certainly advise all those who are thus guilty, or feel themselves in danger of being, to quit the pulpit at once and forever. And let none go to the sacred office who are not strong in the flesh as in the Lord, and let the physically feeble who are in it leave it, lest a worse fate comes upon them. Divine grace will not make amends for physical infirmities.

"And so far from these clerical sins of sensuality being the inexplicable lapses they are represented to be by the public press and private Grundys, they are not only the least surprising, *but the most excusable sins the clergy can commit!* But we do not excuse, we explain them. We are giving their comparative and not their actual criminality.

"As for seduction, that is a crime than which none is more heinous, infernal, and damnable, let who will commit it. The man who is convicted, deserves every twinge of the torture to which he can be subjected by the retributive laws of the divine government. Nor is there any explanation to be offered for that terrible species of the genus sensuality, of which several clergymen in this country *recently have been found guilty*, and which shall be nameless here. Such offenses are very peculiarly odious and abhorrent in view of the fact that sensual gratification is possible without adding more than one to the number of the debauched.

"Let all these putrid brethren be cut off and put away, and let there be a vigorous endeavor to lift the standard of clerical purity in the above as well as in every other respect; but let it also be remembered that the steadfastness of the clergy is a matter of amazement, when the considerations we have named are taken into the account."

Not only does the church in many cases try to screen the foibles of its clergy, but with genuine craftiness it can connive at or mildly reprove the sins of certain of its members in good standing—that is, good paying members.

Neal Dow, during his recent visit to England, gave evidence in corroboration of this; in one of his lectures he said:

"I was to be received at a great tea-meeting in Edinburgh. In the afternoon before, one of the magistrates took me in his carriage for a ride around that ancient town. As we rode up the famous Canongate, he stopped, 'This,' said he 'is the house of John Knox, very much as he left it. It is now the property of the church of the Rev. Mr. ——, one of the leading Presbyterian churches in this city. The upper stories are occupied as dwellings, and the ground-floor as a low and vile grog-shop, the rents going into the church treasury.' A little further on, he said, 'There is a grog-shop, kept by a son of an eminent Scotch doctor of divinity of this city. The capital furnished by the father, of whose church the son is a prominent member.'

"Further on he said, 'Look at that shop; it is one of the vilest in Edinburgh, and is kept by the leading elder of the leading Presbyterian church in the city. A little while ago he was convicted before the police court and fined for harboring thieves and prostitutes; but his standing in the church has not been compromised in the slightest degree. Shortly after, he presented to the church for the pulpit, a splendid Bible and hymn-book, which are now used there.' Many other similar places were pointed out to me, kept by church-members in good standing, one of whom had taken from a poor ragged woman, in exchange for a pint of gin, a pair of shoes stripped from the feet of one of her children."

Other evidence might be added, but this from Neal Dow ought to be sufficient for the present. Were infidels to countenance and profit by such infamy, what poisoned shafts the priests would gladly hurl against them; priests will vilify them any way; but, were it not for the reproaches of infidels and spiritualists, these abuses might be more generally tolerated by the pious; and, were it not for the efforts of reasoning skeptics, Britain might not even at the present day be able to boast of its temperance organization. The infidel has brought reform to the Christian church; extirpate him with his advanced ideas, and intolerance will be followed by increased hypocrisy, and orthodox morals may become again so degenerate that Christian people may be glad to copy the more honest and upright conduct of pagan nations.

The Rev. Dr. Burt, who visited Egypt in 1867, states that, though nearly all the Egyptian boatmen and attendants along the Nile were wretchedly poor, and though they had ample opportunity to pilfer, yet he asserts that not an article of the slightest value was ever missed by himself or by any of his companions.

A writer, giving an account of a heathen people says: " Take the Japanese as a whole, high and low, rich and poor, they are the best fed, best clad, best lodged, least over-worked, and most genial and happy people on the face of the earth. Food is abundant and cheap, imaginary wants rare, and thus temptations to crime are less than with us, though the land is no Utopia.

" There is no such thing as squalor to be seen in Japan. In the houses of the very poorest, a Fifth avenue belle might sit upon the matted floor without soiling her dress. The streets are admirably sewered; all offal and garbage are removed for manure.

" There is no bigotry. The people are wonderfully open-minded. There is no hatred of Christianity as such: only it is feared as an engine to cause political changes."

What Christian state can boast of so much worldly happiness?

NOTE I.

THE very dreadful deed—the sudden murder of his son—which Doctor Buster is represented to have committed, is far exceeded in cruelty by the deliberate and fiendish act of an ordained servant of the Lord, the Rev. Joel Lindsley, a Presbyterian minister near the village of Medina, in the State of New-York, in the United States of America. In June, 1866, this clerical monster cruelly tortured to death his little son—only three years old—because the child would not say his prayers! The fearful account of the murder is truly one of the most revolting ever brought to public notice, as the following extracts from American papers will sufficiently show:

A REVOLTING AND OUTRAGEOUS CRIME.—A CLERGYMAN WHIPS HIS CHILD TO DEATH!

The Rochester Union, of Thursday, gives the following particulars of one of the most revolting and outrageous crimes we ever read. It almost staggers belief, That a father—a clergyman—should deliberately whip his little son to death for refusing to say his prayers, is one of the most remarkable as it is revolting of crimes.—Boston Sunday Herald.

" We learn from railroad men who came from Medina this morning that there was a great excitement in that village arising from a report that a Presbyterian clergyman, named Lindsley, residing a mile south of the village, yesterday whipped his son, three years old, so severely that he died two hours afterward, because he would not say his prayers. Report adds, that the child's fingers were broken by the blows administered. The report seemed so monstrous and unnatural, that we telegraphed to Medina to learn if it was true, and received an answer that it was.

" The telegraph states that the minister was two hours whipping the child with a heavy rod, and it died within the time stated above. Lindsley had not been arrested at the time the dispatch was sent, but we learn that an officer from Albion has gone to Medina to take him into custody. For the sake of common humanity, we hope the story is exaggerated, and it may be possible that it is.

" Since writing the above, we have received by special telegraph the statement of Mr. Lindsley, the father of the child, made to a jury summoned by Coroner Chamberlain: ' On the 18th of June, the child disobeyed his step-mother, and I commenced correcting him, using a shingle for the purpose, and continued to chastise him for more than two hours, when the child began to show signs of debility; and I ceased to punish him, and laid him on a couch and called my wife. When she saw the child, she said he was dying, and before twelve o'clock he was dead.' The coroner's jury returned a verdict yesterday, ' that death resulted from chastisement by the father.' "

THE MEDINA MONSTER!

The following, from the Rochester (N. Y.) Union, gives further particulars of the minister-monster near that city, who whipped his child to death for not saying his prayers.—Boston paper.

" The account of the whipping to death of a child three years old by its father, a clergyman, because it would not say its prayers, near Medina, awakened the greatest indignation of our citizens against the inhuman father. The report was hardly credited, so unnatural and monstrous was the crime committed. We blush to say it, but the most sickening and dreadful part of the unparalleled horror was not published.

" Lindsley's (that's the monster's name) statement before the coroner's jury was corroborated by other witnesses before the jury. The body of the child told more plainly and pathetically than words could of the terrible punishment it had undergone. Several of its fingers were broken, and the blood had oozed from every pore. To conceal the crime, the father tied the little one's hands behind its back and placed it in its coffin. While physicians were making a post-mortem examination of the body, he sat by, coolly looking at the proceedings. After a while he spoke, and asked them if they had not carried ' this thing about far enough?' The physicians discovered no disease about the child; it died solely from excessive and cruel punishment. The little one would have been three years old next August—whipped to death because it would not say its prayers.

" We are told that Lindsley justified his horrid work! He thinks it was his duty to punish the child until his will was broken and he obeyed. Lindsley was arrested and committed to jail in Albion. It was with the utmost difficulty that the officers who had him in charge could keep the citizens of Medina and neighborhood from lynching the murderer on the spot. Lindsley is a man about five feet eight inches in height, well proportioned, has black whiskers, and dark complexion. He has the appearance of a man of violent temper."

A telegram announces that Rev. Joel Lindsley, who beat his child to death, was released from custody on giving bail in the sum of $10,000.—Journal.

A CLERGYMAN CONVICTED.

The Rev. Joel Lindsley, like the Rev. Mr. Babin, has been on trial charged with murder, but the result has been less fortunate for him than that of the Aylmer trial for the Canadian clergyman. Lindsley, who was tried at Albion, N. Y., was accused of whipping his little son to death, and the jury finding him guilty of manslaughter, he was sentenced to be imprisoned in the state prison for four years and a half. A thrill of horror went through the court-room as the physicians testified as to the condition of the child's body as seen by them after it was laid in the coffin. One witness swore that the boy must have received several hundred blows; that the body was covered with black and blue marks, the skin broken in many places, the nails of the hands and feet torn upat the sides, and even the soles of the feet and the backs of the hands laid bare in places. Lindsley acknowledged that he had alternately beaten and " reasoned with " the child for two hours, when, observing a change, he laid him on her bed. The poor mother cried out, " Why, Johnny's dying !" On this, the father took him from the bed, and the boy died in his arms.—Leader.

THE LINDSLEY WHIPPING CASE.

This is a case of great peculiarity. No one, taking a natural view of the matter, can for a moment suppose that this father intended to kill his own child. If premeditation is an ingredient of murder, Lindsley is not a murderer.

Heretofore, we are informed, this clergyman has sustained a spotless reputation, and was considered an inoffensive man; therefore, we can not class him with those depraved wretches whose evil deeds are a terror to the community in which they live. Nor can we suppose he was so inflamed by anger toward a little child, three years of age, that he deliberately pounded it to death.

Mr. Lindsley has probably been a man of austere piety—a piety that is intolerant to the opinions of others and uncompromising in its dealings with the world. There are thousands of such persons in the country; they are men of impracticable minds, who claim that they should " do right though the heavens fall," and they are unwilling that any thing should be considered " right " unless they indorse it. This was a peculiarity of the early settlers of New-England, who pierced holes through people's tongues, and hanged them on the gallows, and banished them from the country, all in the name of their austere orthodoxy.

These peculiarities of religion are mostly the fault of education. Men are so impressed with the "duty" they owe to God, that they commit the greatest outrages against humanity in the name of their Creator. Such religion is worse than no religion at all.

But thus has it been from the foundation of the world, not only with the Christian religion, but in all forms of idolatry. How many victims have suffered because of their intolerant spirit!

This man who has killed his child is to be pitied as well as condemned. He is to be pitied because he is so narrow-minded and full of bigotry as not to be able to understand the divine truths of the Master whom he professes to serve.

He is condemned before trial, by all classes of the community—even by those who, some of them, are as bigoted as he is, and by disciples of Jesus who profess charity for all men. While we all must cry out against this frightful cruelty, let us speak a word against those false systems of religion that permit the beating of the life out of a tender child.

The above is from the Orleans (N. Y.) *Republican*, and it gives as good a defense of Lindsley as probably can be given. But it is nonsense to say that he is not a "depraved wretch," when he could beat a little child two hours, even if he did not mean to kill it. Such cruelty is the best evidence of depravity.—*Boston paper.*

NOTE J.

THE persecution and forcible confinement in an asylum of Doctor Buster's wife, on account of her liberal opinions, is not such a picture as may be merely drawn from the imagination ; like other charges made in this work against priestly characters, it can be sustained even too well by actual fact.

The case of Mrs. E. P. W. Packard, of the State of Illinois, one of the United States of America, affords a good illustration. She was the wife of a minister of the Gospel, "in good standing;" her religious ideas were too liberal for the cramped orthodoxy of her bigoted husband; she not only believed in, but actually taught, Universalism ; and for this alone she was harassed and persecuted by her reverend tyrant ; and at last was forcibly imprisoned for a long time in an insane hospital.

The following letter from Judge Boardman will explain more fully:

To all persons who would desire to give sympathy and encouragement to a most worthy but persecuted woman:

The undersigned, formerly from the State of Vermont, now an old resident of the State of Illinois, would most respectfully and fraternally certify and represent:

That he has been formerly and for many years associated with the legal profession in Illinois, and is well known in the north-eastern part of said State; that in the duties of his profession, and in the offices he has filled, he has frequently investigated, judicially and otherwise, cases of insanity; that he has given considerable attention to medical jurisprudence, and has studied some of the best authors on the subject of insanity; has paid great attention to the principles and philosophy of mind; and therefore would say, with all due modesty, that he verily believes himself qualified to give an opinion entitled to respectful consideration on the question of the sanity or insanity of any person with whom he may be acquainted.

That he is acquainted with Mrs. E. P. W. Packard, and verily believes her not only sane, but that she is a person of very superior endowments of mind and understanding, naturally possessing an exceedingly well-balanced organization, which no doubt prevented her becoming insane under the persecution, incarceration, and treatment she has received; that Mrs. Packard has been the victim of religious bigotry, purely so, without a single circumstance to alleviate the darkness of the transaction—a case worthy of the palmiest days of the Inquisition.

The question may be asked, How this could happen, especially in Northern Illinois? To which I answer: That the common law prevails here the same as in other States where this law has not been modified or set aside by the statute laws, which gives the legal custody of the wife's person into the hands of her husband ; and therefore, a wife can only be relieved from oppression, or even from imprisonment, by her husband, by the legal complaint of herself, or some

one in her behalf, before the proper judicial authorities, and a hearing and decision in the case, as was finally had in Mrs. Packard's case ; she having been in the first place taken by force, by her husband, and sent to the insane hospital, without any opportunity to make complaint, and without any hearing or investigation. But how could the superintendent of the insane hospital be a party to so great a wrong? Very easily answered, without necessarily impeaching his honesty, when we consider that her alleged insanity was on religious subjects. Her husband, a minister of good standing in his denomination, and the superintendent, sympathizing with him, in all probability, in religious devotions and belief, supposed, of course, that she was insane. She was legally sent to him by the authority of her husband as insane. Mrs. Packard had taught doctrines similar to the Unitarians, Universalists, and many radical preachers, and which directly oppose the doctrines her husband taught and the doctrines of the church to which he and Mrs. Packard belonged. The argument was, that, of course, the woman must be crazy; and as she persisted in her liberal sentiments, the superintendent persisted in considering that she was insane ! However, whether moral blame should attach to the superintendent and trustees of the insane hospital or not for this transaction, other than prejudice and learned ignorance, it is quite certain that the laws, perhaps in all the States, in relation to the insane and their confinement and treatment, have been much abused by the artful and cunning, who have incarcerated their relatives for the purpose of getting hold of property, or for differences of opinion as to a future state of existence or religious belief.

The undersigned would further state, that the published account of Mrs. Packard's trial on the question of her sanity is, no doubt, perfectly reliable and correct ; that the judge before whom she was tried is a man of learning, ability, and high standing in the judicial circuit in which he presides; that Mrs. Packard is a person of strict integrity and truthfulness, whose character is above reproach; that a history of her case, after her trial, was published in the daily papers of Chicago, and in the newspapers generally in the State, arousing at the time a public feeling of indignation against the author of her persecution, and sympathy for her; that nothing has transpired since to overthrow or set aside this verdict of popular opinion; that it is highly probable that the proceedings in this case, so far as the officers of the State hospital for the insane are concerned, will undergo a rigid investigation by the Legislature of this State.

The undersigned understands that Mrs. Packard does not ask pecuniary charity, but that sympathy and fraternal assistance which may aid her to obtain and make her own living, she having been left by her husband without any means or property whatever.

All which is most fraternally and confidently submitted to your kind consideration.

WILLIAM A. BOARDMAN.

WAUKEGAN, ILLINOIS, Dec. 3, 1864.

NOTE K.

DISTRESS IN EUROPE—SUFFERING IN LONDON AND FRANCE.

THE London *Examiner* says of the distress among the poor at the East End in London:

"The most populous quarter of the metropolis is craving for food, and *Civis Britannicus* has to fall back on public and private charity for the means of keeping body and soul together. It is deplorable to find such a state of things coexistent with and contiguous to an accumulation of wealth such as was never aggregated before within the same space. A world of coined gold in the banks and a world of skilled labor in the hovels, and no employment for either the one or the other—Midas and Misery in perilous proximity. Let us not be unjust, however, to Midas. The gold which he can not use to profit for himself he gives with an unstinting hand to save his poor neighbors from starvation. The mischief is, that the demands of poverty rise with the supply of charity. Craving want pursues willing wealth as the shadow follows the substance. The willingness of wealth teaches want to crave; and in this lies the great danger of the situation."

The London *Daily News* says:

"Every winter the dry and rocky bed of human misery in this rich man's country becomes a torrent and almost an inundation of distress. Instantly and invariably society sets itself to work in an irregular and bewildered fashion to arrest by dikes and drains this devastating deluge of unknown and unnumbered fellow-creatures who have drifted from penury to starvation. Our English public prides itself on its philanthropy, and rejoices in the subscription-lists spread before its eyes every morning like an oblation. Hundreds of thousands of pounds are distributed by checks, to the great relief and satisfaction of the charitable donors, to all sorts of committees and lists of secretaries and collectors. Nothing was ever comparable to the organization and abundance of British charity. But where does all the money go to? Still the cry of want rises up, and the torrent overflows, and men, and women, and children starve and are forgotten, and still the checks are poured in. Then comes the over-lasting confession of incompetence to deal with such an unexampled amount of suffering.

"Every year the amount of suffering is 'unexampled.' Is there no possibility in this classic land of men of business, of colossal industry and enterprise, of obscure but enormous opulence, of arriving at some tolerably direct and effective system of charitable assistance and relief? There is no other country in the world that professes, as England does, to find bread for every man who is willing to work, yet leaves hundreds of men and women willing to work to perish for want of clothing and a loaf. There is no other country in the world that has so many millionaires—good men, for the most part, and church or chapel-goers. And among them all there has been one Peabody; and he is not an Englishman, but an American, philanthropist."

Returns up to the present year (1869) go to prove that pauperism in England is on the increase by five per cent annually. The total number of paupers in Great Britain being now over a million—another "triumph" for the reverend Princes of Exeter Hall.

Advices from various parts of France speak of the great misery of the poorer classes. The *Avenir National* says that the accounts from the north, centre, and south are deplorable. The general disquiet occasioned by the uncertainty of the government policy, and augmented by divers circumstances in which politics do not much enter, paralyzes industry and commerce. The *Gironde* mentions that in Bordeaux the number of those who demand bread and work is greatly increasing; that the guards at the townhouse are doubled, and a squad of *sergents-de-ville* stationed before the gate, "round which a famished crowd gathers." At Lille, Auxerre, Limoges, and other towns, the charitable boards (Bureaux de Bienfaisance) have been obliged to adopt "exceptional measures" to maintain tranquillity. In Paris, the boards of public relief have received nearly 400,000f. from the Minister of the Interior, and even this hardly suffices. M. de Girardin pertinently asks whether such a state of things is not a supreme warning to Europe that it has something more useful and more urgent to do than to augment its armies. If it be not to make war, why are they increased? If it be to make war, why is there any delay about it? "Between amputation before gangrene sets in and amputation after it, who but a madman would hesitate?"

In other countries of Christian Europe the terrible details of poverty and suffering among the masses are most lamentable.

NOTE L.

It is a pleasure to find that the idea advanced in this volume against *Nationality* has already occurred to others. The following article from the *Northern Press*, as published in the London *Public Opinion* of March 21st, 1868, is sufficiently clear on that subject:

"NATIONALITY.

"Throughout all our history, an Englishman has but to cross the Straits of Dover or the Irish Channel to find a man, fashioned by the same God as himself, but speaking a different language and having another history, to find one whom it was justifiable to rob and honorable to slay.

"Compared with savages, Christians have only been better in degree. In the Sandwich Islands cannibalism used to be sinful only when the victims were Sandwich Islanders. An Englishman or a New-Zealander could be eaten and relished with impunity. We have stopped short of the eating; but there is little else we have not deemed excusable when our victim has been of a race or of a religion different from ourselves. The doctrine of nationality, misapplied as it has been misapplied by the cannibals of Otaheite, in days gone by, has really been the origin of the evil. Englishmen pray earnestly to heaven to save them from a contest with a kindred nation, and English statesmen grow as eloquent as Chatham did in his last great speech, depicting the awful sinfulness of a war with our brethren. When Chatham delivered that memorable oration, our subsidized Indians were scalping our French enemies on the banks of the Mississippi in hundreds, and the pitch-cap and triangles were in the hands of every British officer in Ireland. But there was not a word about the sinfulness of our policy. And in these latter days when the danger threatens of a conflict with men of the same race as ourselves, and the conscience of England is shocked at the prospect, it never occurs to Englishmen to question whether there was not just as much moral guilt in rushing to the slaughter of Muscovites in the Crimea, and in blowing rebel Sepoys into fragments from the mouths of our cannon, as there would be in carrying into Charleston harbor an iron-clad full of the horrors of war.

"What has this false idea of nationality produced through the long ages during which it has been held? Need we travel through history from Persians and Greeks, to Greeks and Romans, and then to Romans and Carthaginians, and point to the blood which was shed and the sufferings which were endured in the rival nationalities of ancient history? Modern records are but a repetition of similar details; and if we want an illustration, let us see it in the relationship which has existed for seven hundred years between this country and Ireland. An Englishman, until a very recent period, has looked upon an Irishman much in the same way as a savage looked upon his captive—as a fit subject for torture and death: an Irishman has naturally regarded his persecutor as a victim for revenge. No matter what happened, there were few qualms of conscience on either side. Things have been done to an Irishman which done to an American would have sent a thrill of horror through the land, and done no longer since than the days of our grandfathers. If we could only get Englishmen and the people of every country to read attentively, and not as individuals, that parable of the Good Samaritan, nationality would soon become what it should be. Heaven has made nations; the enemy of Heaven uses them, and will continue to use them while we continue to believe that the commandment to love our neighbors simply means that we are to love those of the same religion and the same race, and that all others may be hated, and hunted, and made stepping-stones to what men call glory. When nations are only different that they may display the beauty of union, no Chatham of the future shall rise in the British Commons, talk of the horrors of war with our brethren, and be silent about the sin of slaying those who are not of our race; and no one shall enforce the special duty of keeping peace with those who speak our language without being equally earnest in protecting from destruction those who adopt a different tongue; the world shall be one great nation with God as its ruler, and injustice shall be injustice wherever perpetrated."

EXTRACTS

"The plot and passion in 'Exeter Hall' show an experienced hand in their delineation. We shall be happy to read either a sermon on the failure of Christianity, or any other theological nut that the author wishes to crack, or a pure work of fiction; because 'Exeter Hall' proves that the author has something to say, and knows how to say it." — *From Public Opinion, London, England.*

"After a careful and candid perusal of this work, we are constrained to admit, that it is one of the ablest and most dangerous opponents of the creed of Christendom and the divine inspiration of the Scriptures that has ever been laid on our table. There are, however, we are satisfied, those who will not be inclined to stop here, but who will assert boldly, that, for excellence of conception, strength of argument, harmonious sequences, sound logic, keen analysis, profound research, admirable humor, and, withal, deep pathos, 'Exeter Hall' has no rival in its peculiar field." — *Watson's Art Journal, New York.*

"The author propounds on the title-page the rather comprehensive question, 'What is truth?' He will scarcely expect us to say, that he has satisfactorily and completely answered this query; but we may and do say, that he has introduced much theological, philosophical, sensational, and other information, which we cordially commend to those who may have the time and patience to devote to his great and closely printed work. It is indeed a wonderful book." — *New York Evening Mail.*

"So striking and effective an exposition of the inconsistencies, follies, dogmatism, puerilities, and general mischievousness of theology as this book sets forth must produce a profound impression wherever read, and lead on other readers innumerable to be enlightened and impressed by its first effect. We commend it to the widest popular approval, for the sake of its singular merits." — *Banner of Light, Boston.*

"The liberal public ought to give 'Exeter Hall' a very extensive circulation; for it well deserves that honor. A better devised book to secure the object in view — the development of the practical effects of religious fanaticism, as seen in the family and in society — has not appeared for many years. Nor is it merely theoretical; for its arguments are based upon the iron 'logic of events,' as found recorded in the annals of courts and prisons, and in the actualities of every day life: therefore it is a book whose influence cannot fail to be healthy, because founded in truth." — *Boston Investigator.*

"This novel is one of the most exciting romances of the day in its peculiar line. It deals with some of the most startling phases of religious excitement, and makes curious disclosures of the motives which control the apostles of modern fanaticism." — *Demorest's Magazine, New York.*

"The book is well and powerfully written. Our many friends will find 'Exeter Hall' an interesting book, — a book they will rejoice to see put before the public, and one which will be useful, as something they can purchase and lend their friends, whose orthodoxy we will not guarantee after they shall have digested but half its contents." — *The Liberal, Chicago.*

"We have no hesitation in declaring this a great work, — great in design, great in scope, great in execution. It names things in plain English which have too long been mentioned only in the stiff and formal dialect of the pulpit. It grasps tenets and ideas with a bare and bold hand, which have too long been handled with sectarian gloves. We consider it a book that no one need fear to read.... The interest of the plot holds the attention of the reader to the end." — *The Universe, Chicago.*

"The humane and charitable tendencies of the book must receive the approbation of every friend of humanity; and the enlightened and progressive legislation of the future may not improbably embody some of the author's suggestions in reference to the land monopoly and pauperism, which form two of the most social evils of the mother country." — *Daily Telegraph, Toronto, Canada.*

"In the story, the life-like portrayal of religious character, and the truthful illustration of the mischievous tendency of religion, as well as the beautiful picture of domestic happiness where the teachings of Nature had been substituted for the dogmas of theology, cannot fail to make the work doubly interesting. . . . I wish a copy of 'Exeter Hall' could be put into the hands of every intelligent person in the United States." — *B. F. Underwood, in the Investigator.*

"It treats on matters of which I have had a life-long experience; and the pictures are all of them most truthfully drawn. It is called a romance; but it is the romance of truth. Truth is stranger than fiction. It is a book for the million; and it should have an extensive circulation." — *La Roy Sunderland, in the Liberal.*

"A veritable destroyer is upon them (*the priests*); and no description of opposition or petty manœuvring can stay his course. His thunderbolts are forged on the very same anvil that they use in the moulding of their superstitions; and, in dealing with them, he subjects them to their own racks and thumb-screws. The truth is, 'Exeter Hall' is, in my opinion, the ablest work written from an infidel point of view since the days of Paine; and, as such, it cannot but create intense commotion and alarm among the churches." — *A New York Correspondent in the Boston Investigator.*

"No book has ever appeared of a liberal or progressive character so effective and deadly a foe to old theology as this work, so deep and thorough in its research, so profound in its knowledge of the sects of the day, so biting and keen in its sarcasm, and so beautiful in its tender, delicate, and pathetic appeals. Its plot is developed and wrought up with masterly effect, sufficient to gratify the most sensational appetite; with incidents, founded on facts, which must make the ears of the reverend doctors of divinity tingle when they hear of it. The time has fully come when hard knocks must be laid on, thick and fast, and with vigor, too, even to the destruction of falsehood's most sacred propagandists." — *Boston Correspondent, Investigator.*

www.ingramcontent.com/pod-product-compliance
Lightning Source LLC
Chambersburg PA
CBHW030559040726
47497CB00008B/2797